Inspirational Romance Reader No. 1

A Collection of Four Complete, Unabridged
Inspirational Romances
in One Volume

• Historical Collection No. 1 •

A Torch for Trinity
Colleen L. Reece

Cottonwood Dreams
Norene Morris

Whispers on the Wind
Maryn Langer

A Place to Belong
Tracie J. Peterson

BARBOUR
PUBLISHING, INC.
Uhrichsville, Ohio

Published by Barbour Publishing, Inc., P.O. Box 719, Uhrichsville, Ohio 44683
http://www.barbourbooks.com

Member of the
Evangelical Christian
Publishers Association

A Torch for Trinity

Colleen L. Reece

$Prologue$
Late Summer 1912

She didn't look back. She didn't dare.

Only after the westbound train hurled around a bend and gathered enough momentum that a leap to freedom would mean certain death did fourteen-year-old Trinity Mason unclench her fingers and stare out the window. Her future seemed bleak indeed.

A-way, a-way, taunted the clacking wheels. Trinity's blue eyes darkened to almost black, the same color as the soft waves framing a delicate complexion that even the hottest summers never tanned.

"Why, God? Why did I agree?" The words tumbled out helplessly.

A-gree, a-gree, mocked the churning wheels that were carrying her from Cedar Ridge, a small logging town in northwest Washington State, forty miles west to Bellingham, her new home. Home? Never! When she finished school she would go back to Mama and Dad, her brothers, sisters, and friends.

Trinity resolutely lifted her chin. No one had forced her to start school when she was five. No one had forced her to follow dear Mr. Conroy's suggestion that she take the eighth grade state exams when she finished seventh grade. She had wanted to do it then, never thinking of the inevitable result, never thinking that Cedar Ridge had no accredited school beyond the eighth grade.

If she had known how Mr. Conroy's coaching over the next two years would prepare her so well the tests administered by the high school in Bellingham seemed easy, would she have done her best?

Her chin wavered. God had given her intelligence and expected her to use it, her parents always said.

"Two years," she whispered, shuddering. "I should feel proud. How many not-yet fifteen year olds enter their junior year? Besides, I'll be staying with Grandma Clarissa's friends. The Butterfields' letter said all I had to do was wipe the dishes at night and watch the two little ones when they go out in the evenings." Tears welled in her eyes. No small Butterfields could take the place of baby Albert at home who had howled when she left. Ed and Vi, just younger than Trinity, had looked as if they wanted to join in. Hope and Faith, her older sisters, had looked solemn in their Sunday best. Hope whispered, "Remember, you'll be home at Christmas."

Four months. *Could a ball of misery live that long?* Trinity wondered.

The sudden memory of her over-six-foot tall father towering above her five-foot three-inch mother Mercy quieted the distraught girl. "You can do what you must," Edmund Mason softly said. "And you must finish school and become what God intends you to be."

Trinity sighed and wadded her lace-edged handkerchief into a crumpled knot. Only too well did she know how set her parents were on their children getting an education. A dear cousin with no job training had been widowed and left with several children and another on the way. She was finally offered a job cooking for the wheat harvesters while a sister watched her children. Seeing her struggles had made Mercy and Edmund determined none of their children would have to suffer for lack of a marketable skill.

Trinity mentally turned her back on the past. If only the future weren't so frightening! What if the Bellingham girls laughed at her, or worse, at the clothes Mama had carefully fitted, copying the latest magazine styles? She smoothed a wrinkle from her long, dark blue skirt and straightened her plain white shirtwaist. With her frogged dark blue coat Mama had stitched so carefully she felt like a wren beside peacocks next to the elaborate dresses and coats and beflowered hats of the other passengers. At least her buttoned shoes were new.

A new horror attacked the sensitive girl. Would God punish her if she changed her name to Elizabeth or Sarah or anything but Trinity? Until now she'd laughed with the rest of the family about how she got her name. When she was born, her oldest sister overheard her parents talking about names. She pointed to herself—"Faith." She pointed to her younger sister—"Hope." Then she pointed to the new baby, but her face puckered with thought. Suddenly she jumped up and down. A smile lit her face—"Trinity!"

"Even if she's a little mixed up, it shows she's been listening to your sermons," Mercy teased Edmund. "Trinity our little one will be."

It hadn't mattered in Cedar Ridge, but it did now. Trinity pressed her hot forehead against the cool window. They had left the dark forests with glimpses of snow-capped Mount Baker and shining silver streams. Open valleys lay ahead, with a few farms now and then nestled into wooded hillsides. A large body of water Trinity knew to be Bellingham Bay sparkled in the distance. With a mournful whistle of farewell to all she held dear, the train slowed, chugged past several buildings, and came to a stop.

Trinity gathered her scant possessions, took a deep breath that made her heart ache even more, and stepped into an unfamiliar world, her only security the love of her Heavenly Father and her faith in His Son.

Chapter One
Early Summer 1918

She didn't look back. She didn't dare.

Only after the eastbound train hurled around a bend and gathered enough momentum that a leap to freedom would mean certain death did twenty-year-old Trinity Mason unclench her fingers and stare out the window. Her future seemed bleak indeed.

Ba-ack, ba-ack, taunted the clacking wheels. Trinity's blue eyes darkened to almost black, matching the soft waves that framed her ivory cheeks and were gathered into a loose knot at the nape of her neck. "Why, God? Is there no other way?"

No-way, no-way, mocked the churning wheels carrying her from Bellingham to Cedar Ridge, almost six years after that fateful September day in 1912. A bitter smile marred Trinity's features. How could she ever have cried herself to sleep those long-ago first nights in Bellingham?

Bellingham, that beautiful city by Bellingham Bay, was the home of Bellingham Normal School where she had spent two happy years after high school graduation training to be a teacher. Soon she would be issued a Life Certificate that guaranteed her the right to teach anywhere in the state of Washington.

Trinity sighed. How distant were those days when she lived waiting for her first Christmas vacation at home! In the hard studying that followed, the making of friends at school, and in the little church where the pastor preached the Gospel as her own father did, the homesick girl gradually grew away from Cedar Ridge. *Never from the family*, she quickly thought. Deep loyalties provided a little comfort now that she had been called back into exile. The interurban rides, moonlight beach picnics, Bible study groups, and church activities would now have to become only memories.

Why must Germany wish to conquer the world? A few short years ago the devastating panorama about to unfold on the world would have seemed unthinkable. Indeed the 1914 assassination of Archduke Ferdinand had triggered a bizarre chain of events that brought Trinity Mason to a crossroads in her life.

The past continued to haunt her. Did the young Trinity still exist, hidden deep inside beneath the dark skirt and spotless white middy blouse that faintly resembled her going-away outfit years ago? If not, why was she here?

The plush seats and brass kerosene lamps hanging from the ceiling and around her faded and a multitude of scenes filled her vision. Mama's letter just a few months earlier asking her to come home was still fresh in her mind.

> *We need you....Ed has already enlisted now that America has gone to war. He's at Camp Lewis. Faith is run ragged teaching at the Prairie School. The school is too far out of town for her to live at home and help with the war efforts.*
>
> *While we rejoice over Hope's great opportunity to continue to teach in the Panama Canal Zone, we cannot rely on her help. Besides, her place is with her husband. We're just thankful she met such a wonderful man on her way down last year. We believe it is more than chance that he took the same ship on his way back to his police job there that carried our Hope.*
>
> *This leaves you, Trinity. Vi is a great help and even little Albert at ten just about runs his legs off. We'd never remind you of your promise except in the direst circumstances. But with a new baby on its way at my age and due in December and your father not at all well, there seems to be no choice.*
>
> *Grandma Clarissa hasn't been too well either since Grandpa died and she came to live with us. I know you've made a wonderful record and we're proud of you. Trinity, please come home for the summer. See if the school board will release you midterm so you can be here after the baby comes.*
>
> *Your loving Mother.*

Concern over her family drove some of the resentment from Trinity's heart. Mama was old to be having another baby and at Christmastime Dad hadn't looked well. He carried the sorrow of the community as all good shepherds did. Having her home could lift some of the burdens—but what about her?

"God, am I just being selfish?" she whispered so low not even the man in front of her could hear. "I should be glad, glad, glad to help my family but oh, how I'll miss Bellingham."

Her mind flew to the tiny but immaculate rooms she rented that now lay empty, bare of everything that had made them hers. The Butterfields had added on a little sitting room for her when she finished Normal School and decided to remain with them. It gave her privacy and a place to read, correct papers, and dream. Of course when would-be beaux called, she met them only in the formal downstairs parlor with its horsehair furniture and red plush drapes, worn but still faintly elegant.

What would John think when he received her letter? Her heart fluttered with a strange kind of relief. John Standish, with hair as fair as the blowing wheat on his enormous ranch in Canada, had sought an introduction to Trinity after first seeing her in the Bellingham Bank. Unlike the boys who followed her and vied for the privilege of escorting her from church by bashfully saying, "I'm going your way," John scorned such subterfuge.

"Miss Mason," he said immediately after being introduced one Sunday evening following church, "I have my automobile here and will be happy to take you and your friends home." Letty and Mollie almost melted on the spot but Trinity simply thanked him, gathered her soft white skirt around her, and stepped into the front seat when he held the door open.

John managed effectively to block other beaux until Trinity knew he had begun to care for her.

One part of her remained flattered and thrilled that such a "good catch" singled her out. But Trinity also saw how John's feelings could not be laughed off the way she had fended away any hint of sentimentality from others.

At least her departure would allow time to think. She knew no amount of wealth would tempt her unless she also learned to love John with all her heart. What would he do? Follow her? A delicious chill left her shaken. How would Cedar Ridge appear to someone with his background? Would he meet the inevitable test of Dad's keen searching if things grew serious?

Trinity impatiently shoved aside such musings. She had enough to consider without worrying over something that might never happen.

The little train had slowed to wind up a steep hill. Its *chug-chug-chug* reminded Trinity of the many times she had sat in this same car coming and going between two different worlds. City and hamlet. Mountains and shore. Years as well as miles apart in customs, ideas, and opportunities. "I feel like a wishbone," Trinity admitted. "Pulled and pulled. Will I break?" She thought of the jagged splinters left when a wishbone gave way and chided herself for self-pity. *The Lord loves a cheerful giver,* she reminded herself, and quickly added in her heart, *but You're going to have to give me the strength to be one.*

Thankfulness for her wellspring of strength filled her. Time after time God had provided when she needed power beyond her own to meet situations. A trill of laughter escaped into the quiet car. How could she forget her Father's help the day of her student teaching demonstration?

Only fervent prayer that day had prevented her undoing. The day the supervisors filed into the back of the room to observe her fell on the day she had scheduled the teaching of the letter F. What should she do? She had no time to prepare other lesson plans. Bolstered by her Scottish-Irish stubbornness, she raised her chin, gave thanks her long skirt hid her shaking knees, and began.

"Today we're going to learn the letter F. I want each of you to repeat after me. F." A chorus of Fs from the row of solemn professors sent through her an insane desire to laugh. She bit her lip.

"Now, Johnny." She addressed the most serious of her observers and pretended he was a five year old. "A big dog chased a cat up a tree. When the cat reached safety on a limb, it looked down at the dog. What did it say?"

"*Ffffff*," the good professor replied.

"Right. And that's the sound F makes." Trinity went on with the lesson but unashamedly eavesdropped when the bell released her. Gratitude to God filled her when she overheard the professor she had nicknamed Johnny chuckle and say, "I like that young woman's approach. It's fresh and children are bound to respond to it, and to her. When she's ready, we'll find her a good school."

The professor proved as good as his word. He wrote up a report of her demonstration in such glowing terms Trinity was offered a job teaching third grade in an outlying Bellingham school, one close enough to town that she could ride the interurban and remain with the Butterfields.

"It's a fairy tale," she exulted when she got final word of her acceptance. "Can you believe it? A whole sixty-five dollars every month! I'll take out just what I need and send the rest home. They can certainly use it." A cloud crossed her bright future. "They've sacrificed so much for me to get through school now I can begin to repay them."

For two years—from 1916 to 1918—Trinity taught and won the hearts of her students and their parents. Her eyes shone when her principal called her in at the end of the year and told her because she had shown excellence in service she would receive seventy dollars a month for the next year. With America still at war she rejoiced. Every bit of money helped.

Then Mama's letter came, and Trinity's dreams of spending the summer taking further schooling were dismissed. Before Trinity stopped reeling with disappointment, however, a bolt to rival lightning split her world even wider.

She hummed to herself one late May afternoon in an attempt to banish fear about Ed, the war, and the coming summer at home. The war had surely brought an influx of new songs. Sheet music appeared regularly on the Butterfields' piano, a hint for Trinity and their friends to feel welcome and sing. She knew the strains of "Roses in Picardy," and "Long, Long Trail" brought thoughts to her hosts of their son now fighting overseas.

"We've put our boy in the Lord's keeping," roundfaced Mrs. Butterfield once said, her hands busy with a shapeless mass of dough destined to become the lightest of rolls. One tear fell and she wiped it away, leaving a flour streak on her cheek. "Now He knows what's best and I guess He doesn't want us moping." Her hands stilled, "Time enough for sadness...."

Trinity never forgot the moment and the good woman's faith added another pearl to the girl's string of experiences that brightened the hardest, darkest days.

"Trinity? Someone here to see you," Mrs. Butterfield called up the stairs. Trinity finished patting her dark waves into place and skipped down. Probably John. She hoped he wasn't going to declare himself.

A tall, heavy-set man, the antithesis of John, awaited her. "Miss Trinity, do you remember me?"

"Why—" She searched her memory. "Of course. You're Joe Baldwin. What are you doing here in the big city?"

With the usual Cedar Ridge directness, Joe Baldwin looked straight into her surprised blue eyes. "To get you."

"What?" Fear zigzagged through her body. Her mouth went dry. "Mama, Dad—is everyone all right?"

"Fine, just fine." His hearty tone left no room for doubt.

"Then, why—?"

"Miss Trinity," Joe began, twirling his big hat in gnarled hands, "the way I hear it, you're about the best teacher in western Washington."

Red flags flew in her white cheeks.

"Now, we're building a new one-room school just five miles out of Cedar Ridge. We need the best teacher we can find—and from where I stand, that's you." His gaze never left hers.

"I talked with the head men up at the Normal School. Didn't want to just go on Cedar Ridge hearsay." A grin lightened his weathered face. "When I told them what I had in mind, why, they said they wouldn't stand in your way."

"I'm not sure I understand," Trinity faltered. "A one-room school? I teach third grade."

He dismissed her weak protest. "According to those who know best, you're qualified to teach all eight grades."

"Yes, but—"

"How much are you making a month, if you don't mind saying?"

"It will be seventy dollars next term." Her brain whirled. Did God have anything to do with Mr. Baldwin's offer?

"I'll give you double, 140 dollars a month, if you take the job," Joe stated flatly.

The floor felt strange beneath her feet. She gasped at the unbelievable sum. It would take her years and years to ever build up to such a magnificent salary, even if she earned a raise every single year.

"Mr. Baldwin, I think we'd better sit down." With a silent prayer for guidance, Trinity seated herself and waited until the courteous logger did the same. "Is-is there some catch? Something I need to know about this job?"

He laid his hat on the floor and his frank gaze met hers. "The fact is, we've had a mite of trouble with some of the bigger boys who should be in eighth grade. They've been going to another school an' the teacher let them get the upper hand. Don't worry, Miss Trinity. We've told them this is their last chance. One crack out of the bucket and they're out—for good." He smiled and she relaxed a bit.

"Now, my wife and me will be proud to have you board with us durin' the week and we'll see to it you get home for the weekends, too, any time you want to go. We figure what you eat won't cost much, so if you want to give my missus twenty dollars a month we'll call it square."

Trinity felt her jaw drop. Even the Butterfields charged thirty-five dollars a month and that was rock bottom for board and room. Still she hesitated. "I've already said I'd come back here next year."

"Sho', that's no problem." Joe clapped his hat on and stood. "The Cedarton school building won't be ready until after Christmas. The school board here's so glad you can earn more than what they pay, why, they said if you'll just teach 'til Christmas they'll release you. Is it a deal?" He hesitated, then a warm, slow smile crossed his face. "Don't answer now. I've got an old friend here I've been hankerin' to look up. Why don't you take tonight to think about it? I guess it's kinda a shock, an' all. I'll be back tomorrow."

"Good afternoon, Mr. Baldwin." Trinity held out one trembling hand, still dazed by the rapid succession of events.

"Better make that Joe, Miss Trinity. I allow how you'll be livin' with us." He squeezed her hand until she wanted to yell, bowed, and whistled his way out and down the steps.

What should she do? She thought wildly.

All evening Trinity paced the floor, glad for the Butterfields' absence. The quiet house reached out to her, reminding her of the happy years once she had overcome her early homesickness and learned to love the Butterfields.

Yet how could she refuse this opportunity? The much-needed money could make a crucial difference. So could her presence at home on the weekends. If she did the heavy cleaning, baking, and laundry, then Vi and Albert could manage during the week. Was it right to even think of refusing because the prospect of going back appalled her?

For hours she battled, determined to be objective, yet knowing every tick of the clock brought her closer to the end of her Bellingham era. At last she dropped to her knees and poured out her heart in prayer.

"Oh, Lord, you know me. You know my fears and desires and rebelliousness. I don't want to go back, to try and teach all eight grades in a crowded little school! I want to stay here, to be someone. Please, what shall I do?"

Breathless, hoping for an answer, she waited.

Nothing happened.

She prayed again, more fervently, until she could honestly say, "Not my will, but Thine." Exhausted, and still unclear as to the answer, she rose and prepared for bed. By the time the Butterfields returned that night, no crack of light showed under her doorway. She heard their quiet movements and then silence.

Outside her open window the friendly moon shone anxiously on the troubled young woman. The fragrance of climber roses on the tall trellis just outside spilled into her room. A seagull mourned in the distance.

"Lord, in James 1:5 we're told that if we lack wisdom to ask You and it shall be given. You've directed my paths all of my life. If I ever needed Your guidance, it's now."

Scarcely had the words slipped from her mouth than the room seemed to change to her home just after Trinity's high school graduation. She could see in detail Dad, Mama, and Grandma Clarissa who moved in after Grandpa died, and Faith, Hope, and herself in light muslin dresses. Work caught up for a change, they rested in rockers and chairs and the wide front porch swing. Trinity loved such rare occasions with Vi and Ed off at their own games and baby Albert asleep in his corner of the porch after assuring them he was "too ol' to have a nap."

"I'm glad the children are playing," Grandma began. "I have something to say to you older ones."

Trinity glanced up from the embroidered pillowcase she had almost finished for her hope chest. Faith and Hope did the same. The family resemblance of wholesome attractiveness gave the scene a quiet charm.

"You insisted that I live with you and I am glad." Tiny Grandma, with her wise eyes and wide lap that encouraged children's confidences! "Now I can return something."

A chorus of protest rose. "*Return?* Goodness, Grandma, you're never still. Who mends the piles of stockings and makes cookies when Mama's too busy?"

She laughed and the familiar crinkles creased her faded roseleaf cheeks. A little color touched them and she pulled a letter from inside the little shawl she wore even on warm days.

"What's that, Grandma?" Trinity forgot to be polite.

"It's a torch."

"A *what?*" Hope's mouth dropped open and Trinity craned her neck to get a better look. What could Grandma mean by that?

"Girls, mind your manners," their mother said.

"Yes, Mama." They subsided, buy Trinity couldn't keep her gaze off the letter with spidery writing Grandma took from the envelope.

"It really is a torch," Grandma insisted. A small smile played around her lips. "Remember your father's sermon last week? '*Thy word is a lamp unto my feet, and a light unto my path.*' Psalm 119:105." She smiled at their growing puzzlement then turned serious.

"Girls, you're at a time where you must choose your lives. None of you is old enough to marry except Faith and she hasn't found the right person yet. You know that as far back as we can trace, our ancestors were God-fearing, upright men and women. Our families on both sides have held high the lamp of God's Word, often in terrible darkness. From the time they left Scotland and Ireland years ago and came to America, they have been among the settlers, pioneers, and brave-hearted ones who overcame evil with their lamp in darkness."

In the little pool of silence Trinity thought how in the late 1800s Grandma and Grandpa Mason came to Cedar Ridge, bringing their sturdy Scottish-Irish bodies and minds and hearts to the dark forest. They helped establish the first school, arranged for the first church to be built, and rejoiced when their son Edmund became a minister and returned to Cedar Ridge. If ever the lamp of God's Word had been needed, it was in that rough and tumble outpost that once saw murderous fights every Saturday night and injured men who required the doctor's services by lamplight.

"What does this have to do with us, Grandma?" Trinity asked in spite of her mother's frown and slight shake of head.

Veined hands smoothed the letter in Clarissa's lap. "Every generation must eventually pass the torch to the next. Grandpa's gone now and I'm getting old." She raised her hand to still the girls' involuntary protest. "I plan to be with you for a long time but my feet and hands are slowing." She looked at each of the girls in turn: Faith, so strong and patient; Hope, fiery with life; and Trinity, teetering behind childhood and womanhood.

"A distant cousin I barely knew has left me a small inheritance. Not a lot but enough to give you each a chance for Normal School, if you want to go."

Normal School! Trinity pinched herself. She and her sisters had already discussed attending the two-year college course at Bellingham Normal School that would result in a Life Diploma to teach anywhere in the state of Washington. With Ed and Vi and Albert needing schooling, the older girls had resigned themselves to seeking some honorable work to help out.

"Wouldn't it be better to give it to Mama and Dad for the children?" Unselfish Faith's suggestion sent a pang of disappointment through Trinity. She'd already envisioned herself swishing into her own school and teaching small children.

"No, my dear. We will get by on what we earn. This windfall must go to the work of the Lord and I can think of nothing better than investing in your futures so you can teach little children."

Trinity's spirits leaped. "Really, Grandma?" She left her chair and knelt at her grandmother's knees.

"There is just one thing," said Clarissa hesitating, her face troubled. Faith and Hope knelt beside Trinity. "When you accept the help I can give, it is with the understanding you must pass it on. If the time ever comes and I or your parents call on you to sacrifice for the sake of the others, you must do it." Her keen eyes searched their faces.

"Of course." Faith sounded choked up and she blinked hard.

Hope raised her shoulders in an almost imperceptible shrug and agreed. "Yes, Grandma."

"Trinity?"

Why should a little chill touch her, as if the sun had momentarily hidden behind a cloud? Trinity shook her head impatiently and said, "You know we always do what you ask us to." Her wave included her parents.

"Then it's settled." Grandma gently stoked the girls' hair. Trinity felt blessed when Clarissa added, "Never let the torch go out, girls. It may flicker and get low but God's Holy Spirit will renew you and give you the strength and courage to go on."

The scene faded. Trinity drew in a quivering breath. "Thank You, Father." Tomorrow she would say yes to Joe Baldwin—and only God would know how much that one word cost.

Chapter Two

Crouching shadows sprang to life with the last rays of twilight. An owl hooted in a tall pine that pointed the way to heaven with its ramrod-straight spire. The midsummer moon cautiously raised over a hill, surveyed the valley below, and rose in splendor. It searched for an object worthy of illumination and chose a lone figure silhouetted against the night sky.

The lithe, broad-shouldered young man stood statuelike on the crest of the hill. A curious trick of light and shadow hollowed his face and gave an appearance of added years. Even when Will Thatcher threw his head back and let the light pour over him the illusion remained.

Reassured by the stillness, forest creatures came out. A giant hawk sailed by, searching for food. Rabbits quickly hopped from bright-as-day clearings to the cover of darkness. A porcupine chuckled by, unafraid. The barking of coyotes in the distance enlivened the night.

But Will Thatcher, who had just celebrated his twenty-first birthday, saw or heard little of the beloved symphony. A long night lay ahead, a night of fighting a thousand tempting demons. What better place to contemplate than here where snowcapped Mount Baker dwarfed even the knottiest human problems and stood firm in a world whose very foundations had crumbled?

Protest rose in Will's soul. Must he again sacrifice every dream and every secret desire? Cold sweat filmed his intense blue eyes in spite of the warmth of the night. Bitterness gnawed at his heart. What good had that other sacrifice been—the noble shelving of his future for the sake of others—if he must die on foreign soil? Will's sensitive, curved lips tightened: He would do what he must if called. Until then an eternal round of chores would fill every waking minute.

"What if I had refused?" he challenged the inky blue and silver sky. Only the *whoo, whoo* of a tiny breeze replied. Will flung himself down on a mossy knoll and propped his hands beneath his head. Closing his eyes, in his mind he relived the fateful day five years ago, just days before his sixteenth birthday.......

"Will, I need your help," stalwart Lewis Thatcher announced one sunny morning. He stood from the breakfast table and stretched. " Meet me outside when you're through." He strode away without another word.

Caught by an unusual tone in his father's voice, Will quickly finished the biscuit and ham gravy on his plate, decided not to take time for another helping, and wiped his mouth. Moments later he joined Lewis on the front porch of their old-fashioned white frame home in Hamilton, Washington. "What do you need me for?"

Lewis didn't speak for a long time. When he did, the blue eyes that matched his son's held a mixture of excitement and defeat. "I have a chance to buy eighty acres north of here." A sparkle crept into his face. "It's in a valley so rich we'll grow crops enough to feed all of us and make a profit selling to others."

"But Pa, you're a carpenter!" Will could scarcely believe his ears. He ran his fingers through light brown hair that lay in waves deep enough to be the envy of any girl. "That's why we came out from North Carolina. So you could carpenter."

"I know." Lewis Thatcher's features on his "pioneer face"—as his family called it—became more pronounced. "Times got so hard back home my brother Mark and I and a lot of other Tarheels couldn't make a decent living. Washington offered the chance for a new start. Well, I've made it. Now I've saved up enough for a down payment on land about five miles out of Cedar Ridge."

"You've already decided," Will said, wondering what it meant to his own future. A horrifying thought brought him out of his lounging position. "There won't be a high school there, will there? How can I finish my last two years?"

"You won't," he told his son quietly. "Much of the eighty acres is timbered. We'll need to clear before we can plow and plant. We can use the logs to build a new and bigger house, barns, and corral. You've always wanted a horse. Now there will be a place for one."

Will lost track of the conversation after the crushing acknowledgment of the sacrifice he faced. "You mean—"

"It's our chance to make a good life for the family," Lewis pointed out. "I won't be able to do it alone."

"And I'm the oldest."

"Yes." Shame crept into Lewis's honest blue eyes. "I know what I'm asking, Will. I've thought and prayed and tried to come up with another way. I can't. Daniel and Curtis can help some but neither has yet gained a man's strength. Besides, they need more schooling." Pride warred with the natural reticence Pa had toward his children. "I can depend on you to do a man's work. You've made the most of your ten years of school and studied hard."

"If I help for a year or so, can I be spared? I *have* to get an education," Will pleaded. Should he tell Pa how the sight of every bridge, every steel and concrete structure thrilled him? How someday he would be an engineer, responsible for planning and overseeing great buildings? He longed to share his dreams but the sense of duty instilled since childhood stopped him.

Take care of your little brothers. See they don't get into trouble. Don't let anyone pick on Ellen and Rachel and little Andrew. Be a little man, Will. You're Pa's helper. Admonitions rose and bound him with invisible chains.

He jerked his thoughts back to the present when he heard Pa's voice.

"I don't know. Everything will depend on how the crops do and on how much we can put aside. If things go well, perhaps in a year or two something can be worked out. By then Daniel and Curtis will be of more help." Pa suddenly stuck out his hand. "Are you with me, Will?"

"Yes, Pa." His firm young grip tightened but Will ducked his head to hide the rush of regret already attacking him.

All during the selling of the house in Hamilton and the flurry of moving Will stubbornly clung to his dreams. Someday it would be his turn. Someday he would turn over his position to Daniel and be free to pursue his own career. Even if Pa couldn't help, Will would work his way through college and be someone, someday.

His first chance for real independence came when Pa took him to one side the week before they moved to the Cedar Ridge spread. "Think you can drive Old Bossy and our six new cows up by yourself or do you need help?" Pa frowned. "If you can do it, I need Daniel and Curtis with me." He sighed. "I wish I could have managed a horse but that will have to come later. It's a good twenty-five miles. Can you do it?"

Will felt his measure was being taken. He drew himself up to his full six feet and nodded. "Just a nice little stroll, Pa." His twinkly blue eyes matched the sparkle in his father's gaze.

"Twenty-five miles of bawling cows won't be a picnic," Lewis warned but relief showed in his joshing.

"I don't expect it to be." Will set his jaw in the way he had learned since his future changed so drastically.

"There are a few cabins and small places along the way. Any of them will be glad to take you in," Pa advised. "Walk slow but don't loiter, even when you get close to Cedar Ridge and start fording the pretty little trout streams. Time enough for fishing later." A smile softened his stern features.

If Will lived to be older than Methuselah, he'd never forget his first experience herding cows. Old Bossy behaved. The six new cows did not. As Will told Pa later, "What with chasing those critters, I bet I walked closer to fifty miles than twenty-five!" When he finally drove his charges into a rudely constructed corral thrown up to house the cows until Uncle Mark and neighboring men came for a barn-raising, Will didn't care if he ever saw another cow again.... except sizzling on a steak platter in front of him.

Weeks flew into months. Season followed season. Determined to be ready when his time came, Will spent what little free time he had with his nose in a book. Before leaving Hamilton the persistent young man had arranged with his favorite high school teacher to send him mathematics, literature, history, and geography books. The kindly teacher parted with this admonition:

"Remember, some of our country's greatest—including Abraham

Lincoln—were self-educated men. Lack of formal schooling is no excuse for ignorance."

So Will muttered equations while he plowed and quoted famous authors while he milked. At the end of the first year Pa said, "If things continue as they have, next year we'll talk about sparing you."

That hope sustained Will when his younger brothers and sisters set off for school in their second Cedar Ridge year. But a long and costly illness that almost took little Andrew followed by a skimpy crop the next year shattered Will's expectations. Instead of freedom to study and forge ahead, spring 1915 found seventeen-year-old Will working in the woods to bring in badly needed cash for the family. The whine of saws, the ring of axes, and the ever-threatening cry of "Timberrrr!" when a forest monarch toppled slowly drowned out his belief life held more for him than loyalty to his family.

Pa never mentioned his eldest son's sacrifice. Yet now and then when Will unexpectedly raised his head, he read in Lewis's blue eyes a poignant appreciation and an apology. His bitterness was held in check until spring 1918 when America entered World War I.

Will Thatcher shifted position, noting how low the moon had fallen. Blanking out his mind he watched it set and in the dark hour preceding dawn he faced Gethsemane and knew a little of what Jesus experienced centuries before. *Had God forsaken Will?*

Never before had Will felt so entirely alone, so cut off from other human beings. Did each man at some time in his life come to this aloneness? Behind lay disappointment; ahead lay duty, perhaps death. A terrifying moment, this facing of self and God.

With a low cry Will sprang to his feet. Straight from the heart in a voice that began as a whisper and rose to a shout, Will challenged the forces of evil, war, and weakness with the words of poet James Russell Lowell:

> Once to every man and nation comes the moment to decide;
> In the strife of Truth with Falsehood, for the good or evil side;
> Some great cause, God's new Messiah, offering each the bloom or blight;
> Parts the goats upon the left hand and the sheep upon the right,
> And the choice goes by forever 'twixt that darkness and that light.

Exaltation filled him. He mentally reviewed more verses, discarded them, then filled with the Holy Spirit his strong voice rang out in affirmation.

> By the light of burning heretics Christ's bleeding feet I track,
> Toiling up new Calvaries ever with the cross that turns not back,

And these mounts of anguish number how each generation learned
One new word of that grand *Credo* which in prophet-hearts has burned
Since the first man stood God-conquered with his face to heaven upturned.*

For the first time since that day of decision Will felt free. "God-conquered with my face to heaven upturned," he paraphrased. His head thrown back and his face wet with tears, Will knew nothing on earth mattered except his commitment to whatever cross God gave him.

Hours later Will met Pa at the barn. He had done the morning milking, cleaned out the stalls, and fed and watered the animals.

Lewis gazed into his son's face and recoiled. "Son, *where have you been?*"

"To the mountaintop." Keen understanding flashed between them.

"You will never be the same." Lewis swallowed hard.

"No." Will bent to pick up the brimming milk pails.

"William."

Pa's voice stopped him. Only in moments of deepest stress did Pa use his son's full name. "Yes?"

"After the mountaintop comes the valley." A shroud of sadness underscored the warning.

"I know, Pa." Will listened to a rooster crow and faced the morning light that flooded through the barn windows. "Last night—this morning—I know it's to prepare me for something."

"You are a son to be proud of." Lewis made no effort to hide the sparkling dew in his eyes, but before Will could answer he added, "Better get the milk in the house. Your ride to the woods comes early."

Will watched his father march out the open barn door and across to the house. Strange, the shoulders so often bowed with care these days sat square and sturdy and Pa looked as if he kept time to martial music even in his worn barn boots.

For the next few weeks Will held and treasured his mountaintop experience against all adversity, even when his younger brothers and sisters talked about the upcoming school year. But when Daniel insisted he'd had enough learning and had been given a logging job with the same company that employed Will, Will's reverie ended.

"Don't be foolish and throw away your chances," Will ordered. "Don't you want to be someone?"

"I reckon Pa's the best someone I ever knew and he's a logger-farmer," good-natured Daniel retorted. The few freckles on his sunburned elfin nose looked like copper specks. "'Sides, if I can bring in money maybe you can go be whatever you want to be."

---

* From "The Present Crisis" by James Russell Lowell (1819-1891)

Hope flared inside Will then died. "I'll get called into the army before then, I imagine."

"I may, too," Daniel admitted. "But until I do there's no sense going on to school when all I want to do is work."

Despite Will's raging, his formerly tractable brother dug in his heels and absolutely refused to listen. Even his first few days in the woods that left him exhausted did not discourage him. Gradually Will came to enjoy having Daniel beside him. Always a loner, he found himself accepting Daniel as an equal instead of a younger brother. Most dinner breaks found them a little apart from their fellow loggers sharing in a way they never had been able to before. One day Will opened up and told Daniel of the midsummer night when he faced his God.

Daniel listened quietly, but the look in his eyes was far from placid. "I'm glad you told me. I've always wondered how much stock you took in what Pa and Ma taught us about God."

Will caught a yearning wistfulness and instantly replied, "I know now life isn't worth living without that faith."

"Then it's all right," said Daniel smiling. "I decided that when I knew we might get called to fight." He idly picked at a blade of grass. "News is the war might be over soon. I hope so. Not that I'm afraid to go. It's just that so far I haven't really given much to the world. I'd like to make some kind of mark before my number comes up." He leaped to his feet. "Better get back to work."

Their talk sank deep into Will's consciousness. How well he knew the futile longing to make a mark! Would he? With his new commitment to God and His Son somehow it seemed more possible than a few weeks earlier. He whistled while he sawed and chopped and managed to recapture some of that life-changing experience, sharing deeply with Daniel whenever they had time.

From mountaintop to valley, as Pa said, came without warning. A half-hour before quitting time on a drizzly late-September afternoon Will and Daniel finished sawing through an enormous fir tree. They'd made their undercut on the other side and gauged the path of the tree's fall. In a bizarre twist, when the fir fell it changed direction, straight toward a widowmaker.*

"Run!" Will screamed, and he tore toward Daniel who stood directly in the big tree's path.

Daniel leaped for safety, but it was too late.

The falling tree continued its ponderous drop, tearing limbs from other trees as it crashed to the ground. To Will's utter horror Daniel fell. A heartbeat later the tree toppled onto his prone body.

Will screamed for help and then with superhuman strength attacked the

---

* A dead tree, a snag.

enemy tree with his bare hands. Arriving loggers pulled him off and chopped as rapidly as they could. Daniel's inert form lay covered with bright stains when they finally freed him.

"Oh, God, no!" Will lifted his brother's broken body and cradled it in his arms. "Daniel, Daniel."

The loggers bared their heads and stood silent, too wise to hope in the face of the evidence before them. A ragged gasp ran through the circle of rough, caring men when Daniel opened pain-dazed eyes.

"Will?"

"I'm here." Tears splashed on the twisted face.

"I'm—glad. Tell Pa, and Ma—guess I won't make mark—" His eyes cleared and he looked beyond Will, up, past the waving treetops. A glorious smile erased the pain in his face and brightened it until his freckles shone. "It doesn't matter—now."

Daniel's eyes closed but the light stayed in his face even when he went slack in Will's arms. The others slowly withdrew, leaving a heartbroken man holding the brother he had learned to love more than life itself.

After a long time he stood. It was long past time to go home.

Chapter Three

Will felt propelled by a silent screaming inside all the way down the steep mountainside to the jitney* that carried the logging crew to and from the woods.

Take care of your little brothers. See they don't get into trouble.

Only when his arms threatened to give out did he surrender his place among the four men carrying the stretcher bearing Daniel's body. How he made it remained dim in his mind forever. The awful feeling he should have been able to save Daniel joined with dread. *What would Pa and Ma do? Oh, dear God, if this were only a nightmare from which he could awaken!*

Much later Will roused to the touch of his head logger's rough hand on his shoulder.

"Better go prepare the folks, son." Kindness showed in every seam of the weathered face.

Will staggered out of the jitney. *Too late*! Pa and Ma must have seen the jitney pull to the side of the dusty road and stop instead of merely halting to let off Will and Daniel. They ran down the lane leading from the big log house the Thatchers had built the first summer after they reached Cedar Ridge. Young Curtis, Ellen, Rachel, and even Andrew followed.

"Will? Daniel?" Pa managed to gasp between heavy breathing.

Will shook his head. "Pa, he's—"

Ma's glazed eyes staring behind Will whipped him around. Four earth-stained loggers carried a blanket-shrouded figure that told the story.

"Not Daniel! Oh, God, not Daniel!" Ma screamed.

Something in Will snapped. *Why would Ma say such a thing? Did she wish it had been Will instead?* He brokenly tried to reach out to her but Ruth Thatcher had flown to the stretcher and buried her face in the folds of the faded blanket.

"Where were you, Will?" Did he imagine it or had doubt and accusation crept into Pa's eyes? A red-hot poker of pain seared Will's heart and he could only shake his head.

"Not a thing anyone could do," the head logger said soberly. "First thing we knew, Will was yelling for help an' diving toward Daniel." He mopped his sweaty forehead. "It's a miracle you didn't lose two sons instead of one."

"Thank God!" Pa's fervent prayer started Will's heart beating again.

Later Will sought him out for a private moment. "If only he'd listened and stayed in school. Why didn't I make him?" Pa seized his eldest son in a mighty

---

* A buslike vehicle.

grip and shook him as a cat shakes a mouse. His blue eyes blazed. "William, much as we want to, we can't decide for anyone on this earth except ourselves." Pain laced his denunciation. "You think I don't want to step in and make choices for my family? I do and once—when I asked you to help me—I did."

His face changed. "I've regretted it ever since. At the time I felt we had no choice. But son, it makes no more sense for you to feel this is your fault than for me to believe if we'd stayed in Hamilton this wouldn't have happened." The hands that bit deep into Will's arms loosened. "Looking back does no good." For the first time, Pa looked old and almost beaten.

The next moment he raised his strong head and gazed into the achingly blue sky. "I reckon if I could know Daniel had got right with God and accepted Jesus into his heart—"

"He had, Pa." Some of Will's agony faded. "Just a few days ago we talked." In stumbling words Will told what Daniel said.

Pa's fingers tightened again until sturdy as he was Will wanted to cry out. "Tell Ma, right away. It'll bring what comfort there is." But it wasn't until the sorrowful little family gathered for family worship after a long-delayed evening meal that Will had a chance. When he did, Ma's somber dark eyes didn't lighten but a perceptible relaxing of the muscles in her closed face showed Will Pa had been right.

Out of tragedy came a few rays of light. Will had never felt the love and support of neighbors the way he did now. They came with cooked food. They stopped by and helped with chores. And always they left the warmth of their caring and prayers. Will also drew closer to Pa. That first talk led to others, but one stood out. Will had thought about Pa's admonition on trying to direct others' lives. Encouraged, Pa added more from the deep store of wisdom gained while uprooting and cleaning enormous stumps and following the plow in the straightest furrows to be found.

"Don't you ever wish God would just make folks do what they ought to?" Will asked the morning of Daniel's funeral.

"Amen! It's a good thing I'm not God." Pa's lips set in a grim line. "Sometimes I even go so far as to tell Him so."

"Really, Pa?" Will had never suspected such a thing. "Then what?"

Pa slowly said, "He kind of reminds me in my heart that if God Himself has enough faith in folks not to interfere with their choices—even when He may hate and despise those choices—why, I have to do the same." His farseeing eyes looked across the fields dotted with autumn's orange and gold dying leaves. "It's hard, though."

Will couldn't speak then or later when well-meaning friends offered rude comfort.

"It ain't like he wasn't ready," one good woman said. "Or like he was your

Pa and Ma's only boy."

What difference does that make? Will wanted to shout. As he spun on his heels and rushed away, he heard the woman exclaim, "Land sakes, he's taking it hard."

Will walked for hours in the moist fall night. His faith in God remained intact but the need for companionship grew. The loss of Daniel had created a void in himself. Never one to surround himself with comrades, Will preferred his own company or that of a choice few. Daniel had slipped into his life after they began working together and he had provided the missing part.

Gradually life took up its usual pace. Will had little time for solitude except at night and logging and chores left him too tired to appreciate those hours. He had a new logging partner now. Donald McKenna, one of Daniel's best friends, had begged the head logger to let him work with Will and assign whatever new man they hired to Donald's former partner. The head logger had consented kindly on behalf of Will.

Red-headed Donald didn't attempt to avoid discussing Daniel. Once he said with misty auburn eyes, "If we never talk about him it's like he never lived."

The more Will thought of it, the more sense it made. Ma seldom mentioned Daniel and Will knew the hurt she carried made it worse. He began to pray for her, pleading with God to somehow help them—and Ma—through this.

A few days later he tore into the quiet kitchen. "Ma! Come see the gorgeous rainbow." He raced upstairs. "Ma! Where are you?" His racing feet stilled in the open doorway of his parents' bedroom. "What—"

His question died on his lips. The most beautiful music he had ever heard swelled and shimmered in the quiet room. Ma stood transfixed with one hand on an open bureau drawer. Soft light filtered through handmade lace curtains and shifted and changed. So did the music. It seemed to come from that open drawer, but how could it? Rising and falling, the notes of liquid clearness like a thrush at prayer crept into Will's heart. He saw Ma's face brighten and her eyes fill for the first time since Daniel's death.

For a minute, an hour, an eternity—Will didn't know which—the birdsong symphony could be heard. Then with a glorious finale it ceased.

Like one awakening from a dream, Ma moved. Her gaze sought Will. "My son, my splendid son!" She tottered toward him and wept in his arms, washing away the last lingering hurt and doubt of her love for him.

"How did it happen?" he asked when they at last sat down on the bed.

"I had to know he was with God. I had to be sure, in spite of what he told you. I've prayed and prayed. I finally just told God I didn't see how I could go on without some kind of sign." Her eyes filled again. "I know it's probably being weak in the faith but God heard my pitiful cry and had mercy on me." Some of the glory Will had seen in her face returned. "No matter what anyone says, ever, I know my son's with His Son and someday I'll see them both." The last word dropped to a whisper.

Will put his hot face into her aproned lap, something he hadn't done since he was a small child. There had been too many others coming after him who needed that lap for childish hurts. Every trace of guilt that had lingered now vanished.

"I wonder why just you and I heard the music," he finally said.

Ma's hand lay light on the crisp waves of bright brown hair now tousled in her lap. "Perhaps we needed it most. God has comforted Pa and the others in different ways."

Great rejoicing followed the late afternoon experience. Ellen and Rachel wished out loud they could have heard the music, too. "God's ways aren't our ways," Pa said sternly. "He sends what we need when we need it most."

He smiled and added, "Just stay close to our Lord and trust Him. Never envy others' experiences but seek and find your own." Peace seemed to fill the family circle.

A few days later Pa called Will apart from the others. "We're pretty caught up on the chores. Why don't you whistle up Tige and take Saturday off? Maybe you can bring home a deer. I've a hankering for venison steaks."

"Will you come with me?" Will was already planning what he'd need to pack if he left Friday night.

"No, I promised Curtis I'd take him pheasant hunting. He needs some extra rifle practice before I let him out alone." Pa thought for a minute. "Why don't you ask Donald? Or Jimmy Crowfoot? He and his tribe will be here tomorrow to winter in the big meadow back of the south forty."

Will thought of his Indian friend his own age who had been coming every fall for years. "Good idea. He and Donald get along and both are good company."

On Friday night the three lounged around a fire built with an enormous stump as a backlog. October had heralded and brought frosty evenings and the fire felt good. Will finished the last of the cookies Ruth Thatcher sent and grinned, satisfied. "Good thing we're only going to be here one night, the way you two eat."

Indignant, Donald said, "Don't think Jimmy and I didn't notice you ate four helpings of fried potatoes, not counting all the beans and meat and most of those cookies!" Tige, the black Labrador, growled in agreement.

Jimmy just smiled, his dark face expressing wordless enjoyment. Not many white men earned a smile from him but Thatcher's and McKenna's honest dealing and frank friendship had long ago welded bonds of brotherhood. The Thatcher boys and Donald were among the select few with whom Indian loggers would consent to work.

Little by little the bantering changed. Great stars blazed down through sentinel trees and cast an unearthly light on the already frost-covered world. Every blade of grass glistened under its coating of rime.

Will hunkered down farther under his heavy wool blanket. "Well, boys, I guess this will be our last hunting trip for a while."

"How come?" Donald's half-closed eyes opened wide and Jimmy Crowfoot grunted in surprise.

"My papers came today. I'll be reporting to Camp Lewis soon." His long arm reached for a stout stick and stirred the glowing embers into flames, exposing their faces.

"Then I'll enlist and go with you." Donald leaped up, stamped his feet, and blew out a gust of air that quivered in the cold night.

"You'd do that for me?" Will's eyes stung.

Donald shrugged. "Why not? How about it, Jimmy? Want to come? We can be like those three guys in that book—— you know, one for all, all for one. Who were they, anyway, Prof?" He turned to Will.

"The Three Musketeers. Dumas wrote it." But Will's gaze switched to Jimmy Crowfoot. Why did Donald blurt out such a thing? Why should Jimmy fight for a country that had mistreated his people so decisively? Will wanted to kick Donald when he continued to prod Jimmy.

"Well?"

Jimmy uncoiled from his position on his tarp. His blanket dropped unheeded to the ground and revealed the lithe, deerskin-clad figure. His coal-black eyes never wavered. "I'll go with you." Before either could speak, Jimmy slipped inexplicably from the firelit circle into the night. He reappeared just before Will and Donald fell asleep, sliding into his blankets and pulling the tarp up around him to keep off the heavy dew that came with morning.

"Don't tell my folks," Will said at breakfast. "I don't want them to know. I'll just leave a note when I have to go so they won't start worrying right away." He quickly changed the subject to the day ahead before either of his comrades could respond.

Alone on a deer trail after having agreed to separate and cover more territory, Will had a chance to reflect. He had spoken truly the night before. This could be his last hunt, his last trip up the timbered slopes past brush thickets he knew and loved. Perhaps a slight melancholy colored his feelings and sharpened his vision but never had the forests and mountains seemed more beautiful. Drifting, swirling leaves of red, orange, gold, and rust contrasted sharply with the white-frosted peaks and bluer-than-sapphire skies. Shades of green offered relief from the blazing vine maples and cottonwoods. He dropped his hand to Tige's sleek back.

Although he knew a single shot would bring Jimmy and Donald, Will felt the same loneliness creep into his heart that had been haunting him ever since he received his marching orders. Faces of friends rose, young men, girls Will knew would gladly accept him as a beau . . . He shrugged. He'd never yet seen a girl who interested him enough to offer more than friendship. Pa said God had led him to Ma, or her to him. Will grinned, thinking of Pa as a young man in North Carolina teaching school and falling in love with Ruth, one of his pupils!

They'd had a good marriage. Not ones to express their feelings in front of their children, their quiet exchange of glances across the dinner table spoke volumes to Will. He determined never to marry until he felt what he saw in his folks' eyes.

No danger of his being forgotten while gone, Will thought ruefully. He'd had to dodge some well-set snares from a few of the Cedar Ridge girls who didn't have the sense to know if he wanted them around, *he'd* make the first move. He'd grown adept at simply not being around when those he considered too silly for words stalked him by playing up to Ellen and Rachel.

"The only girl close by that I like to be around is Faith Mason," he told an inquisitive woodpecker who tapped back an answer against a tree trunk. He thought to himself about Faith. She's modest and nice, and she's enough older that I don't have to worry about being chased. He laughed aloud. Faith was doing a fine job teaching the young ones and Will knew his father was going to ask her to live with the Thatchers now that the Browns were moving. She would be good company for Ma and the kids. In fact, Donald had been taking a shine to Faith lately. Will thought they'd make a good pair—if he comes back.

With a thud Will fell from pleasant musing to reality. None of them might come back or, if they did, what shape would they be in? He'd rather die and lie in a lonely, unmarked grave somewhere in France than come home gassed or broken, to be a burden on someone. Uncertainty filled him. Nothing would stop him from going but shouldn't he try and discourage Donald and Jimmy?

A shot. A second. Will bounded to his feet and waited. A faint yell in the distance reached him, then the crashing of brush to his left. He snapped his rifle to his shoulder, threw a shell into the chamber, and waited. Within seconds a buck deer leaped into view. Tige bayed and dashed in pursuit.

Spang.

The buck fell, a beauty. Pa's hankering for venison steaks meant skinning, cutting, and packing out.

"Got him, I see." Donald burst into the small clearing closely followed by Jimmy, whose wide grin bore little resemblance to his usual placid face.

"Jimmy killed his buck, but I shot at this one and missed." Donald looked disgusted. "I was too hurried when I should have taken better aim. When we get to fighting, it will be different."

"Why don't you and Jimmy wait?" Will casually asked. "There's no guarantee we'd be together if you enlist."

Donald scratched his red head. "Jimmy, what do you say? Hey, we'll just wait until you know where you'll be then tell the army if we can't be together, we ain't going."

Jimmy just grinned and took out his hunting knife, hint enough for Will and Donald to attend to the present and let the future alone for now.

For a week Will kept secret the news he had been called up. During that time he visited all his favorite places close to the farm and dropped in on friends to bid an unspoken farewell. Last of all, he returned to the crest of the hill just before dark on his final Saturday night at home.

If the Thatchers hadn't been so busy welcoming Faith Mason into their family circle, he might not have succeeded in his self-imposed silence. As Will returned from the mountain, he was greeted by yellow lamplight spilling from the windows of the log home, merry laughter, and whistles echoing into the night. His dog Tige crouched against his foot and a horse whinnied in the pasture. Only the strength he had received from his tryst with God lent Will enough courage to go inside, pretend all was normal, then excuse himself early and go up to his room.

But before he could throw off the open-necked shirt and jeans, the sound of doors opening and a babble of voices reached him. Will considered climbing into bed the way he was then felt ashamed. His neighbors deserved better. Besides, he heard Ma calling from the foot of the stairs. "Will? Come down, please."

Carefully brushing his hair, he lightly ran downstairs into the living room and looked straight into the most beautiful blue eyes he had ever seen.

Chapter Four
Autumn 1918

Trinity hurried up the threadbare strip of carpet that graced the center aisle of the little church. Embarrassment and nervousness together sent color to her face. How could she let herself be late to the first fall meeting of the Epworth League,* especially when she had been elected president? All her protests that she'd be leaving after Christmas changed nothing. As long as she remained in Bellingham, her friends wanted her to serve.

In the front row Mollie Perkins fretfully picked at the fine lace trim on her gown and scowled. "I don't see how she does it," she muttered half under her breath into her sister Letty's ear. "*We* dress up and *she* wears a middy and plain gored skirt that barely hides her shabby shoes. Guess who gets all the attention?" Mollie sighed, her gaze glued on the trim girl in navy blue on the raised platform. "I declare, if I didn't love her so much I'd be pea green with envy."

Letty's big brown eyes turned to her pretty blond sister, so unlike her own dark subdued self. "That's it, you know. No one can help loving Trinity, and I'm glad," she added in a burst of honesty. "She has so few clothes, just this outfit and a white one, a couple of wash dresses, and a dark suit and two blouses for teaching, and, oh yes, her mother made her a summer lawn while she was home. Anyway, it's not what she wears, Mollie. It's what she is."

"I know." Mollie squeezed Letty's hand. "But why didn't *we* think to tuck a late yellow rose in our hair? Maybe then John Standish would look our way. As much as I love Trinity I'd sure beat her time with him if I could!"

"Shhh, we're ready to start," Letty warned. Yet she let her gaze follow Mollie's. Would anyone ever look at her or single her out as John did Trinity? Letty blushed and clasped her hands in her lap, then dared peep across the aisle in the other direction.

From her vantage point in front Trinity saw and correctly interpreted the look. Although her mind was filled with the upcoming meeting, she silently wished Blakely Butterfield, so handsome in his sailor uniform, would see and appreciate Letty's worth. Instead of sending languishing glances toward the new Epworth League president! Letty would make a faithful, adoring wife to Blakely. While Mollie had more outward beauty, Letty Perkins in her soft blue gown loved the Lord and shyly reflected that love in her brown eyes.

Good heavens, Trinity thought. The last thing I have time for is matchmaking. The idea brought a smile to her lips and she hastily rose. "Let us turn to

---

* A young people's group.

page 261 and sing 'Day is Dying in the West'," she announced. The natural blending of many voices sent the lovely words soaring from church windows open to the soft September evening.

Only with a mighty effort could Trinity go on singing. Last spring their songs had held a deeper bass quality; the ranks of young men and boys had thinned since then and Blakely and the few others in uniform could not compensate.

"Pastor Sullivan and I have discussed at length some ideas to help our group grow," Trinity said simply after prayer. "As you know, if ever young people need to know about God's love and His plan of salvation it's now." She raised her chin proudly but her blue eyes darkened. "We all must do everything we can to spread the news of that plan. One way is by increasing attendance at our meetings."

She smiled at their gray-haired, youthful-faced minister. "We propose that our group will be split into two teams. Every Sunday night at our meeting we will tally up points." She ticked them off on her fingers.

"One point is for attendance and an extra point for every new person you bring with you. Another point for each person who memorizes Scripture to quote at the beginning of our service. We'll go right through the alphabet. Next week learn verses that begin with the letter A."

She paused and Blakely Butterfield called out, "Too bad we can't start with J. We already all know 'Jesus wept.'" Everyone laughed.

Trinity's heart thrilled at the eager agreement in their faces. "Now, once a month Pastor Sullivan will total all the points from the month before. And——" She dramatically lowered her voice, then loudly said, "The team that has the least points must host a social activity for the winners for that month! A party or special event——"

Cheers drowned her out and conversation quieted only when Trinity raised her hand. "Remember, although the socials will be fun, our real purpose is to honor our Lord. We won't give points for those who stay for evening service after our meeting but I hope all of you will make it a regular part of your week."

Her wistful voice and earnest face effectively led into the Bible study two of the boys had prepared, the preselected hymns, and the closing prayer. *And every person stayed*—although a couple of newcomers looked a bit uncomfortable and slid into the back seats. Trinity made a point of following them and making sure they knew the place for the Bible reading and hymns. She felt John's scowl from across the aisle but ignored it. More and more she felt tangled in a web of feelings and his unspoken questions.

She sighed and missed part of the sermon. How long could she keep him from declaring the love she saw in his eyes? Her little ruses to avoid being alone with him had long since worn thin. Why did she feel so mixed up inside? She liked John a great deal. Her heartbeat raced when he singled her out, but the few times he'd attempted an embrace or to take her hand, other than to help her in or out of his car, she had shrunk from him.

Oh, brother, she thought. *Why can't young men be content with just being friends? Why must they get all sentimental and spoil everything?*

A tiny voice inside spoke up. *If you really loved John—or anyone—you wouldn't feel that way.* Trinity had to admit it was true. What she saw in Letty's quickly hidden gaze contrasted sharply with her own confusion. Shy as she was, if Blakely Butterfield crooked his finger, Letty would follow.

I don't want to think about love until this horrible war is over, Trinity decided. *I only have a few short months to get the Epworth League growing so it can carry on when I go to Cedar Ridge.* A pang went through her but she firmly refused to let it stay.

As soon as church ended, Trinity saw Blakely and John both start her way. She met them in the center aisle, turned, and drew Mollie and Letty into the little circle. "What a fine sermon! Pastor Sullivan certainly has a shepherd's heart, doesn't he?" She managed to chatter until they got into their wraps and stepped outside. "We're all going the same way, aren't we? It's such a nice night. Suppose that we walk."

"I have my car here," John said eagerly. "We can walk another time."

"Oh, all right." Trinity stepped in after Mollie, Letty, and Blakely climbed in the back, glad for Blakely's presence after they delivered the Perkins sisters home. As Blakely held the door open for her, John announced, "I will pick you up after school tomorrow, Miss Mason. I have something especially important to tell you." A few moments later his car purred away into the night.

Trinity and Blakely sauntered up the walk. "I am so glad your parents told the young couple who rented this summer they could only have the rooms until September," Trinity said. She tilted back her head and affectionately looked at the old house that had been home for so long.

"I'm just sorry I went off to school before you came," Blakely said. He winced and rubbed his leg.

"Is your wound bothering you again?" she anxiously asked.

"Yes, a bit. If it doesn't heal properly, I can't go back to finish my job." He wasn't to be sidetracked. "Trinity, I know it's brash for me to ask, but do you care for me—even a little?"

"I care for you a great deal, Blakely," she told him quietly, determined to forestall him before he grew serious. "But I don't care for you in the way God wants people to care when they join their lives."

"Could you—sometime?"

"No, Blakely. Although you're older, I sometimes feel you are more my brother Ed's age."

"That's shooting straight!"

To her relief he looked more rueful than heartbroken. On impulse she said, "I know someone very special who isn't that far away but who admires you with her whole heart." She mischievously smiled up at him in the dim streetlight.

"Really?" Blakely looked flattered. The next instant he laughed. "Guess I just wanted to be sure you couldn't be interested. Say, who is this girl with such exquisite taste?"

"I'll leave you to find that out for yourself." Trinity's saucy reply made him chuckle again.

"Won't you even give me a hint? After all, it's hard to believe any girl would admire a guy with a bad leg." He glanced down and frowned.

Trinity thought fast. She didn't dare give Letty away, yet would it hurt to plant a clue? "Blakely, look for the sweetest, most sincere Christian girl at church and you'll have no trouble figuring it out." Her eyes glowed. "She wouldn't care if you had no legs. She's that good."

Blakely's shoulders squared. "Then I have to discover who this paragon is. Uh, Trinity, you're not angry about what I said, are you?"

"Of course not, dear boy." She patted his hand the way she used to pat little Albert's.

He burst out laughing. "You're right, you know. In some ways you're a hundred years older than I am. I can hardly wait to see what kind of man it takes to capture you!"

"I can wait." She pretended haughtiness.

"Now it's my turn to talk to you like a Dutch uncle," he told her, his eyes gleaming with devilment. "If you don't watch out, you're going to be Trinity Standish before you know it." He ducked her outraged blow and limped up the steps. "'Night-night, poor old lady."

Better for him to laugh than be hurt, Trinity told herself after prayers. "Dear God, he and Letty would be so happy. She would curb his high spirits and he'd add color to her rather drab life in Mollie's shadow. But they're in Your hands." She turned and slept, but not until she muttered, "One down, one to go," thinking of tomorrow's interview with John.

True to his word, John's car panted at the schoolhouse door when Trinity finished her work the next afternoon. Without asking her preference as usual, he swung into a road that led out above Chuckanut Bay. Trinity's heart prayed for help. John Standish was no boyish Blakely Butterfield to be nipped in the bud. Used to having what he wanted when he wanted it, even though she had no reason to doubt his Christian commitment, she could easily lose a good friend unless God sent wisdom in dealing with John.

When he had stopped the car above the shining bay framed in soft hills and blue sky he said, "I'm leaving for Canada tomorrow."

"*So soon?*" Surprise gripped Trinity and her heart pounded. Perhaps she cared more than she realized.

"Father and the ranch need me. Now that I've finished my special studies here in the States, I must go back. Miss Mason—Trinity—if you loved a fellow would you give up your American citizenship and follow him to his country as Ruth followed Naomi?"

Trinity didn't answer for a long time. Suddenly she felt as old as Blakely had called her teasingly the night before. She liked him tremendously. If she consented to be his wife she knew he'd generously allow her to make things easier for those at home. She'd never have to teach again. Her eyes widened at the thought. *Never teach?* Never again know the joy of sticky fingers on her arm, or the eagerness of trusting faces? Why, it would be like dousing the torch Grandma Clarissa once handed her into icy water!

John suddenly said, "I can answer my own question. If you really loved someone you would be a Ruth, wouldn't you?" His wheatened hair glistened in the late afternoon sunlight and he took her hand. "Can I ever be that man, Trinity?"

Compelled to painful honesty, she looked straight into his hopeful eyes. "I don't know."

Something leaped into life, a triumphant but hesitant look. "Haven't you had enough time? You asked for time when you went back to Cedar Ridge for the summer." Anger flushed his fair skin. "You aren't just keeping me dangling, are you?"

"Certainly not!" She tugged her hand free, furious at the absurd idea.

"I'm sorry. It's just that I care so much for you."

"John," Trinity said as she straightened her shoulders and took a deep breath, "Until this war ends I can't even consider falling in love or becoming betrothed. I've told you I like being with you and see wonderful qualities in you. But that's all. If I have to give an answer, it's no."

The color left his face. "I don't want that kind of answer and I regret my impatience. I know that even if you cared the way I hope you will one day you're committed to teach the rest of the year in Cedar Ridge." A tiny smile lightened his features.

Did he think she was bound to contrast the unlearned and rugged men in her hometown with his polish? She glanced down to hide her annoyance at such an idea. Rugged they might be, but no men or boys on earth were finer than those who tilled the land and took their living from the forests. She hadn't known until that moment how strongly she believed it.

"Can't we just be good friends, John?" she asked.

"Not forever." He started the engine but managed a smile. "You'll write, won't you?"

Reprieved, she quickly answered, "Of course," and led the conversation back to lighter topics for the ride home.

To Trinity's amusement, Blakely began a serious search for his secret admirer immediately. At Thursday night prayer meeting he scanned every face until everyone knelt for prayer. Afterward he continued his spy activities and chortled when he and Trinity arrived home. "I don't know who it is but I know some girls it isn't."

"Really?" Trinity's brows raised at his assurance. "Who and how?"

"Well, it isn't Mollie—she's too busy thinking about how she looks and if her frills are straight. It isn't Fan or Beth; they whispered all through the prayers and you said my girl is sincere and Christian all the way through. I overheard Sally making a cutting remark about the way Tim prayed so it can't be her."

"Excellent, dear sleuth." But Trinity gave no more hints.

She didn't have to. When Letty recited her Scripture verse by heart on Sunday night, her brown eyes glowing with excitement, Blakely cocked his head to one side, searched out Trinity's laughing gaze, and slowly nodded. He crossed his arms and a satisfied smile—not unlike that of the infamous Cheshire Cat—spread from ear to ear.

"Am I right?" he demanded in an undertone between Epworth League and the Sunday night service.

"I can't say." Trinity pressed her lips together to keep from laughing.

"You don't have to." He turned. "Miss Perkins, may I see you home tonight?"

To both his and Trinity's dismay, Mollie eagerly cried, "Why, of course, Mr. Butterfield."

"Get me out of this," Blakely pleaded the moment church ended and he could sidle next to Trinity. "I want *my* girl, not Mollie."

"And since when has Letty been *your* girl?" Trinity teased.

Color rose from the sailor collar to Blakely's hairline. "I—I think she has been for a long time but I just didn't know it."

With her usual tact, Trinity gathered a group who all lived close and saw to it that she took Mollie aside for a private word on the way home. "Isn't it splendid that Blakely has finally discovered Letty?" She slipped her arm through her friend's and kept her voice low. "Thank goodness you spoke right up for her tonight! She's so modest I don't know if Letty could bring herself to accept even though it's obvious how much Blakely admires her." She felt Mollie's involuntary jerk then Mollie's quick wits took over.

"You are *so* right. That sister of mine is sweet but she's never had what you call a special beau." Mollie gained assurance as she spoke. "You really think Blakely's serious?"

"Just between us, I don't see how he could be more serious," Trinity said honestly. "By the way, when Tad Thorson asked tonight for us to write him—you know, he leaves soon—did you notice how he looked right at you?"

Mollie's face shone in the moonlight. "Why, no, I didn't." She laughed a little self-consciously and played with a blond curl that had escaped her close-fitting hat. "He's new and I don't know him very well yet."

Trinity turned her head to keep from laughing at the word *yet*. Trust the lovable but featherheaded Mollie to add that.

Two hours later she lay in bed, well pleased at the results of her Machiavellian schemes. Great happiness lay ahead for Blakely and Letty in spite of the war, and Mollie had been successfully sidetracked from possible interference by a pursuit of her own. Now she could concentrate on her own problems! She had missed John greatly even in the few days he'd been gone. Did missing him signal a deeper affection than she'd suspected?

Trinity tossed and turned, reducing her pillow to a lumpy mass before deliberately shutting her mind to wheat ranches, social position, Canadian citizenship, and John Standish. Only God knew her heart and, at least for now, He wasn't telling her what might be buried there.

Chapter Five

Now that John had gone back to Canada—and Trinity wore no ring on her engagement finger—other young men hastened to fill the spot by her side. She treated them all alike, to Blakely Butterfield's enjoyment. Secure in his growing courtship of Letty, he became a self-styled expert in matters of the heart and never missed a chance to give Trinity the benefit of his newfound wisdom.

"I always say," he began ponderously one evening when they arrived home from church, "girls should keep men guessing." He dropped to a chair and grinned up at Trinity who stood by the door.

"Letty will be eager to hear that, I'm sure," she retorted.

"Hey, wait a minute! Not Letty." He scrambled up and had the grace to laugh. "She doesn't need to keep me guessing and she won't after Thursday's prayer meeting."

Trinity abandoned her teasing. "Why not?"

"This is why." Blakely slowly took a tiny box from his pocket. "I wanted to give it to her tonight but I couldn't get her away from the others." He pressed a spring. "Think she'll like it?"

How boyish he continued to be, in spite of the horrors of fighting that sometimes lurked in his eyes. How eager he seemed that the sweet girl he'd overlooked and now worshiped only next to his Lord would like his gift.

"She said once she didn't like diamonds so I thought she'd like my great-grandma's ring. It's a forget-me-not, see?"

Trinity's throat felt tight when she held the simple worn golden band with an enamel forget-me-not surrounding a small but perfect sapphire on top. "It's beautiful."

"I haven't forgotten who helped open my eyes to what was there all the time." He squeezed Trinity's hand in a comradely fashion. "Someday I hope you'll find someone as special as Letty." As he released her hand he managed a little laugh. "No doubt of that. I'll bet somewhere right now a certain someone is wondering who God has in mind for him, never knowing or even suspecting it will be Trinity Mason."

Tears blurred the girl's eyes. "Thank you, Blakely." She turned and fled. Why should a hazy image form in her mind, not of John Standish, but a stranger whose face she could not see? Yet, how could such a person find her once she moved back to Cedar Ridge? All things were possible with God, but no one in the little mountain hamlet fit her ideas of a lifetime mate!

Under Trinity's leadership, the Epworth League thrived. Within weeks, eager members had brought in friends by ones, two, and half-dozens, determined to be on the winning team and be honored at the monthly socials. The newcomers came, returned, learned Bible verses, and brought others. When time came to tally the scores, to everyone's amazement the winning team had only one point more than their good-natured competitors!

Trinity's eyes sparkled when she made her announcement. "If the weather holds, next Saturday will be an all-day outing. Our host team has arranged for launches to take us across Lummi Bay to Lummi Island. This may well be our last outdoor picnic for a while so make sure everyone's invited."

Saturday came cool and overcast but warm enough for the eager group. Laughing and joking—"If we stayed home every time it clouded up in Washington we'd become housebound!"—but above all, eating, the day sped by. Trinity observed the results of her faithful friends' efforts with a bittersweet ache in her heart. Although so many new faces surrounded her, the empty spaces that should have been filled with men now overseas were obvious. She thought of Ed, still at Camp Lewis baking hundreds of loaves of bread in the monstrous ovens. Thankfulness went through her but shame quickly replaced it. How could she rejoice that her brother remained safe when many here had brothers and sisters even now in grave danger?

By midafternoon the leaden sky began to leak. Big, single drops were followed by an absolute deluge.

"Into the launches," Pastor Sullivan ordered with an anxious look at the scowling skies. Trinity and the others quickly gathered blankets, picnic baskets, and sweaters. Long before the last nose count to make sure everyone was present, the launches tossed wildly at their moorings.

"I—I'm afraid," Letty whispered to Mollie and Trinity. "So am I!" Mollie clung to her sister.

"It's all right," Trinity forced out between clenched teeth. The friendly waters that had offered salty coolness just hours before when the girls trailed their fingers over the side of the boat had changed to an angry enemy. Greedy, sucking waves made hard going and even the best prepared were soaked.

Miserable, frightened, and thoroughly upset, the band of pleasure seekers crouched low in the launches until Blakely took things in his own hands and yelled above the storm's roar. "Well, if you losers are such poor sports you didn't want to give us a party, why didn't you just say so?" He waved at their grim surroundings. "I mean, this is really going to pretty drastic lengths, isn't it?"

A moment of startled silence then laughter followed.

"Come on, friends, let's sing," Trinity called.

"What?" shouted those in the other boats.

Undaunted by a wave that dumped icy water over them, Blakely cupped his hands around his mouth and bellowed, "What else? 'Jesus, Savior, Pilot Me!'"

Trinity clung to Letty and laughed until she cried but Mollie's clear voice rang out, soon followed by others. Amid the cresting waves and beating rain, their singing rose.

In the semidarkness of the storm, the launches at last reached the mainland. Pastor Sullivan hurried the drenched but happy crew into waiting cars and raised his hand in blessing. "Thank God for His goodness and care."

A chorus of "amens" echoed in the lowering fog but Blakely had the last word. "See you all in church," he cried, and slid in beside Letty, who now proudly wore his forget-me-not ring.

"I n-never saw anything that looked so g-good as the l-lights on the shore," Mollie chattered and scooted a little closer to Tad, their driver.

"You never appreciate light until you are in darkness," Tad told her. "We just take it for granted until it's gone. Or maybe we don't think about it at all."

Trinity caught something in his voice that made her heart quicken. She quietly said, "That's why it's so important to let Jesus be our light." Before Tad might feel uncomfortable she added, "Speaking of lights, what I want right now is my own well-lighted room and a hot bath, if I can beat Blakely to the bathroom!"

"Don't I always let ladies go first, even when it means bathing in a flower-scented room?" he demanded.

"Usually, except when it's time to pick up Letty," she retorted, but their arrival at the Perkins home ended the argument.

Later, ensconced in her bed, Trinity reflected on the day. What had been said about light and darkness fit in so well with Grandma Clarissa's little sermon all those years before. Mingled with her reluctance to leave Bellingham, she found a tiny spark glowing, a curious, eager wondering at what life in Cedar Ridge would bring. All eight grades in a one-room school? How many classes was that in all? She drowsily ran over them: reading, writing, arithmetic, history, geography, spelling, and science and nature. Seven subjects times eight grades....

She sat bolt upright in bed. *"Fifty-six classes? Impossible!"* Trinity fell back against her pillows and pulled warm blankets high under her chin. "Dear God, if You want me to hold a torch for You in that one-room school...." She drifted of to sleep before finishing.

One Thursday morning in late October Trinity came home from school rejoicing. She had the next day off due to a fault in the heating system that must be fixed. "I'm going home for the weekend," she told a surprised Mrs. Butterfield, and quickly sorted out what few clothes she'd need. No use bothering with house dresses; she still had old dresses in her closet at home. The suit she traveled in and a middy outfit would do. By the time Blakely brought the family car around to take her to the train station, she was ready.

Although the Butterfields had invited her to spend Thanksgiving with them, Trinity's farewell to Blakely seemed somehow final.

Blakely covered her hand with one of his. "You know we don't want to lose you but just think of the opportunity you have in Cedar Ridge. I remember you saying the church there doesn't have much for the young people yet. Maybe God knows they need you even more than we do."

Trinity gathered her skirts and stepped from the car. But on the long journey she considered his words as she gazed out the window. How many of the glorious colored leaves held on to their secure position on branches, she thought. Only when a strong breeze came along did the leaves swirl and float down. *They're a lot like me,* she mused, *they cling to the familiar.*

All day Friday and Saturday Trinity helped at home. Mama had grown rounder and rounder; the new baby would probably come before Christmas. Late Saturday afternoon Faith burst into Trinity's room. "Come on, it's a long walk to the party."

Trinity smoothed her navy skirt and middy blouse and adjusted a white tie she'd added. "I don't know why I'm going. I don't even know the Thatchers. They moved in after I went away to school."

"I know you'll love them." Faith's bright face encouraged her sister. "I'm so glad I get to board with them during the week now and come home weekends. I adore my school——but it's a real challenge."

"That's what I'm afraid of," Trinity sighed, but obediently got into a warm coat for the long walk. Unwilling to dwell on the future she asked, "What's the party for?"

"It's a surprise going-away party for the oldest son Will. His draft papers are due any minute. The old ranchhouse will ring tonight." Joy left her face. "I wish this war would end. Every time mail comes I dread hearing for fear some of our boys will be listed killed or missing."

A tiny bell rang in Trinity's mind. "Faith, is there someone special—for you, I mean?"

Faith turned toward her sister and beamed shyly. "A good friend of the Thatchers, Donald McKenna." She laughed shakily. "Oh, I'm a couple of years older than he and I don't know if he would ever look at me but I can't bear to think he may be called." Desolation filled her voice and she wiped her eyes with the back of her hand.

"It's selfish to think of my feelings when others have so much more to face. Just a few weeks ago the Thatchers' second son Daniel was killed in a logging accident." She quickly sketched in the details for Trinity's soft heart. "How could he stand it?"

"Through the faith in God and His Son that has been the foundation of generations of Thatchers." Respect shone in Faith's eyes. "I've never seen such a family outside of ours that relied on the Lord for absolutely everything. Why, even if the hay isn't all in on Saturday night and a heavy rainstorm is predicted, no Thatcher works in the fields on Sunday."

Trinity's eyes opened wide. "Really? What do they do about we hay? It molds, doesn't it?"

"Believe it or not, the Thatcher hay never gets wet on Sundays." Faith's eyes twinkled at the look in Trinity's face. "It rains all around their place but not on their hay."

"I've never heard such a thing," Trinity gasped and almost stumbled over a rock in the road.

"It's true." A worried frown marred Faith's pretty face. "I am concerned over Will, though. He wanted to go to college and become an engineer but because he's the oldest son, he could only finish tenth grade."

"Sounds like quite the paragon." Trinity wondered at her flip reply. *Didn't she know how it felt to be bound one place and long to be another?*

"He's a fine young man. Sensitive, handsome, a real gentleman."

Trinity's lip curled. "A gentleman logger? My college professors would have trouble believing that."

"Not if they met Will Thatcher," Faith sturdily insisted.

"How can you be interested in this Donald McKenna with your Will Thatcher around?"

Faith threw back her head and laughed. "Not *my* Will Thatcher, worse luck. Even if I hadn't picked Donald I wouldn't get any ideas about Will. Practically every girl up and down the Skagit Valley and around Cedar Ridge has set her cap for him. He is absolutely *the* catch in these parts."

"How does he feel about the girls, the ones who chase him?"

Faith shrugged. "According to Ellen and Rachel, his sisters, he likes them all. Takes one to one party, a different one to the next. He's a real loner, though. Never lets anyone get too close. After Daniel died, he had it really rough. It took time for even Donald with all his charm to get through and become Will's close friend." Faith paused a minute. "Any time a girl tries to drop a halter on Will, he gracefully slides away."

"So what is it that intrigues all the girls? His remoteness? Or is he some kind of modern Pied Piper, conceited and unbearable?" Trinity's curiosity was piqued.

Faith's eyes flashed fire. "Absolutely not! I've never known a more unspoiled young man."

She sounded hypnotized by Will Thatcher! It wasn't like Faith to rave about young men. Well, bring on Mr. Ideal. Trinity tossed her proud head. At least one girl wouldn't follow after him like a pathetic lamb. Yet she couldn't help feeling a little pain at the thought of the young man who held his dying brother, powerless to do anything.

In an effort to overcome her mixed feelings, Trinity begged, "Tell me more about your school. How *do* you handle all those classes?"

"It isn't as hard as you'd expect. The older ones hear the little ones reading lessons while I work with another group." Faith's whole face came alive. "I have twenty pupils this year so I have just a few in each grade. These children really learn. When the older ones hear the younger pupils' lessons, they benefit; likewise the young ones benefit from the discussions among the older pupils." All the rest of the way to the Thatcher farm Trinity questioned and Faith answered.

When they reached the well-lighted ranchhouse, people of all ages spilled from the doorways. The light from freshly polished kerosene lamps and the roaring fire in the fireplace was complemented by the good smells of country cooking.

The Thatchers themselves were warm and welcoming. Trinity would never forget her first encounters with: Mr. Thatcher and his drooping mustache and bright blue eyes; busy Mrs. Thatcher among her pots and pans; Curtis and young Andrew, Ellen, and Rachel all mingled into a happy, laughing crowd.

"Where's Will?" Faith asked and craned her neck to scan the group.

"Out riding, as usual," Rachel piped up. "Ma says he'll be back soon."

With the arrival of more guests by horse-drawn wagons, on foot, and in a few well-loaded cars, came a few uniformed men. To Trinity's surprise, a sailor and a soldier she had briefly met the summer before soon sought her out.

"Why, Miss Mason!" Delight showed on their wellscrubbed faces. "What a nice surprise." The soldier sat down on her right and beamed. "May I show you the family album?" He reached for the inevitable pictured record on the small table next to the couch.

Not to be outdone, the sailor who had immediately grabbed the vacant spot on her left asked, "May I get you a cup of punch, Miss Mason?"

"Thank you. It's a thirsty walk out from Cedar Ridge, isn't it?" Trinity smiled, all thought of the missing guest of honor driven away by the unexpected meeting.

Head bent over the album, Trinity idly flipped pages wondering who the people in the pictures might be. Then a little ripple ran through the crowd. She raised her head and glanced at the staircase off to one side of the room. A young man appeared at the top and came down two steps at a time. This was no suit-clad man, but neither did he wear a uniform. His dark blue flannel shirt, open at the neck, exposed a tanned throat. Jeans covered a slim waist and lean legs. Over six feet tall, not an ounce of fat marred his strong body.

Trinity looked into his face. Golden brown hair lay in ripples and his wide mouth stretched in a laugh that sent sparkles into eyes as blue as her own.

Something happened inside Trinity. A strange sense of familiarity for the stranger left her unable to look away from the penetrating blue eyes that held surprise and something else she couldn't define. A swarm of friends surged between them and she tore free her gaze.

"Who is *that*?" she demanded of her self-appointed escorts, knowing the answer before it came yet unwilling to admit it. "I must be the only person here who doesn't know him."

"Oh, haven't you met Will Thatcher?" The soldier flipped album pages. "I thought everyone knew Will. Nice chap."

Trinity recalled Faith's earlier words of praise for the young man who had looked at her so intently yet with respect and almost reverence.

Don't be a fool, she ordered herself. *What are you to him or he to you? You are a grown woman who will soon be responsible for an entire school, not a schoolgirl meeting the new boy in class!*

Yet when someone slid into the empty place at her left and she observed through downcast lashes dark blue jeans instead of sailor trousers, Trinity experienced a moment of total panic unlike any emotion she'd ever known.

Chapter Six

Her mind gone blank, Trinity stubbornly stared at the floor until the tips of two highly polished shoes stepped into her line of vision. A voice barely suppressing outrage said, "Here's your punch, Miss Mason."

She forced a smile and looked up. "Why, thank you," she said, when she wanted to laugh out loud. Never had she seen such a frustrated young man as the sailor whose place by her side had been claimed in the few minutes he'd been gone. This was a trick worthy of John Standish.

Trinity sipped the ice-cold punch, glad for its coolness in the suddenly too-warm room. The soldier on her right made a noble effort to regain her attention by turning more album pages when an amused voice cut in.

"It would be easier for me to explain the photographs to Miss Mason since it's our family album." Will Thatcher's smile took any possible sting from the words and he held out his hand for the album. The soldier's glare matched the sailor's but he had no choice but to hand over the heavy album.

Trinity's heart beat faster. So this was Will Thatcher, and he was everything Faith described—and more. Faith hadn't told of the innocent mischief that sent twinkles in the blue eyes and made Trinity part of the little ploy. Neither had she predicted how his smile took away a girl's breath and made her stomach turn upside down. Trinity had never believed in love at first sight and yet...

"Will, Will!" A nightgowned urchin dashed into the room and hurled himself into open, welcoming arms.

"What are you doing out of bed, Bruce?" Will held the small boy up in both strong hands.

Trinity noticed how much little Bruce resembled Will from the lake-blue eyes and soft golden ringlets to the totally enchanting smile. "He's adorable! Who is he?"

"Miss Mason, may I present Bruce Thatcher, my cousin Jamie's boy? Here comes his mother now." He nodded to a charming brown-haired, brown-eyed young woman who had stopped to chat with Ellen and Rachel. "Bruce, this is Miss Mason. She's Miss Faith's sister."

"Ooh, you're pretty!" He stuck one finger in his mouth and beamed up at her.

"And you're handsome," Trinity told him gravely. Bruce giggled and showed small, pearly teeth.

"You're a scamp," Sarah Thatcher announced, and reached for her son. Her merry eyes denied annoyance at Bruce's antics.

Trinity shared a look with Sarah that won her over completely. Of all the girls and women she'd met, only Letty and Mollie had earned her deepest friendship.

Yet she knew a bond existed between Sarah and her from their first exchange of glances.

"May I go up with you to put him down?" she impulsively asked. "It's been a long time since we had one that age at home—although we will again soon."

"Please do." Sarah smiled at Will. "I'll bring her back."

Will just grinned but Trinity turned as pink as a peony and held her head high when she followed Sarah.

"He's a perfect cherub," she whispered, after Bruce lay tucked in blankets up to his chin, desperately trying to keep his eyes open. "How old is he?"

"Me's fwee," came a high-pitched voice as absurdly long lashes drooped against tender flushed cheeks and sleep came.

"I should have known he'd never go to sleep until he saw Will," Sarah confessed. They tiptoed out into the hall. "He's crazy about Will, has been ever since he could recognize people. It's not surprising, though. Everyone loves Will." Her smile was gentle and quick. "I'm so glad you came. Will needs someone—"

Before she could finish her sentence that had already sent warm blood pumping through Trinity's veins, someone called, "Come on, you two! We need you," and the evening's simple games and fun claimed them.

Was it coincidence that in every game Will just happened to be her partner? Trinity wondered. Near the end of the evening the Thatchers brought out musical instruments and the party ended with singing. Faith at the piano, Will strumming his guitar, and Thatcher cousins with fiddles and a mandolin made the rafters ring. Trinity closed her eyes. She was almost back with the Bellingham group! They closed their parties the same way. Her eyes opened wide. Strange, the permanent ache over having to leave her city friends had disappeared in the gaiety and genuine welcome of these Cedar Ridge folks. With Will on one side and Sarah and her Jamie on the other, nostalgia had no place.

Then a terrible thought intruded. *"I've just met him but this is his farewell party. He's going away to fight. I may never see him again.* Trinity felt shaken and confused. Why should the idea upset her so? She wanted to cry out against this war that demanded the sacrifice of America's brightest and best. When the time came to stand and sing the beautiful farewell blessing, "God be with you till we meet again," not one word could get through Trinity's constricted throat. Upstairs little Bruce lay sleeping secure in his family's love. Downstairs his beloved Will prepared to answer the call of his country. It took every bit of control Trinity had to hold back tears with the last note of the song. Around her she saw tightened lips and misty eyes of the others who shared her feelings.

Will broke the emotion-charged moment. "Thanks, folks. If I'd known you were coming I'd have put on a suit and high collar." He ran tanned fingers around the open neck of his flannel shirt. "Have to admit, this is a lot more comfortable."

"You can say that again," said Donald McKenna, crossing his eyes, his tongue hanging out. "Being polite sure is painful." The burst of laughter eased the tension.

Those with small children left first. Bruce opened one sleepy eye and said, "'Bye, Will. 'Bye pretty lady. I like you."

Trinity hugged Bruce as well as she could with his all bundled up in Jamie's arms. "I like you, too, a whole bunch," she whispered into his sleep-creased neck and felt rewarded when he bestowed another smile on her.

A few minutes later the determined soldier who had kept near her all evening said with a glint in his eyes, "I'll see you home, Miss Mason."

At the same moment the equally stubborn sailor appeared in the doorway with her coat. "I have your coat, Miss Mason. Shall we go?"

Now what? Trinity stifled a nervous giggle and didn't dare look at Will who stood just behind her. She needn't have worried.

"Thank you both, men, but that won't be necessary. Miss Mason and her sister are spending the night here." Will's bland smile and courteous air drew glares from the would-be beaux but Trinity's heart leaped. *When had that been decided?* Surely not before they arrived or Faith would have told her.

She couldn't help pitying the servicemen, both fine young men. "Thank you," she told them. "I appreciate your kindness." She gave each a warm smile and some of the frost in their manner melted.

"We'll see you in church tomorrow morning?" one asked.

"Of course." Will again took charge. "An early morning walk is just what we need after tonight's good food." He showed them out but not before Trinity discovered the little look of triumph in his eyes.

"Well, what do you think of him?" Faith demanded when the girls huddled close in her room.

Trinity snuggled deeper into the warm gown Faith had offered. "Who?" She yawned and pretended innocence when inside she burned to learn more of the fascinating Will Thatcher.

"You know who I mean."

"Oh, Donald. I think he's a grand person and very much attracted if not downright in love with you."

Her diversionary tactics worked. Faith sat up in bed and clutched the blankets to her. "Do you really think so?"

Trinity smiled in the darkness and honestly added, "I do. And if it weren't for this awful war I think he'd have told you long ago. His gaze follows you the way a child follows its mother." She reached over and squeezed her sister's hand. "I'm so happy for you, Faith. You deserve the best."

"So do you." But Faith's voice sounded muffled, as if tears of joy flowed into her feather pillow.

It snowed lightly during the night and then cleared. Early Sunday morning well stocked with a breakfast of ham, biscuits, and gravy, far more than Trinity usually ate, Donald and Faith and Will and Trinity set off for Cedar Ridge.

"It's going to be a long, cold walk for you both ways," Trinity told the others doubtfully.

"It's so beautiful, who cares?" Usually quiet Faith had blossomed overnight. A new softness shone in her eyes and Trinity knew it came from knowing she was loved. A burning blush rose from the fur collar of her warm forest green coat. What if someday Will Thatcher learned to care for her the way Donald cared for Faith? Only by reminding herself Will shied away from girls who chased him could she hang onto her rapidly fleeing dignity.

Never had miles passed so quickly. When Donald and Faith gradually lagged behind, a new worry nagged at Trinity. Would Will try to hold her hand? She hated boys who got spoony yet it would show he liked her.

Will took no liberties but kept up the conversation with a dozen funny stories. Often he pointed out special sights and sounds and smells. "Look," he said over and over. Trinity quickly followed his pointing finger and discovered frisking squirrels, bluejays, and snowbirds, and once a red fox bounded into view, surveyed them, then continued on his way.

Trinity threw her head back and gazed into the inverted blue bowl of sky above them.

"But how can you see things so quickly, Mr. Thatcher? I didn't know there was a fox within a hundred miles and then here one came."

"I saw the tip of his ear behind the stump before he came out into the open."

Trinity looked at him suspiciously. He must be joking but his matter-of-fact tone supported his statement.

The farther they walked, the more Trinity wondered about her unusual escort. A spirit of perversity seized her. She'd see how far he'd carry his courtesy. "My hands are cold." Now Will would reach for them, she thought.

"Would you like to put them in my pocket?" He held out the wide, deep pocket of his coat.

"Yes, I would." She slid her left hand in and hid her right hand in her own pocket, not nearly so warm, and waited for Will's hand to clasp her own.

It didn't. Her hand lay in his pocket untouched.

It piqued her curiosity more than ever. Any other man she knew would have taken her hand—and she would have drawn it away!

Donald and Faith caught up with them just before they arrived in Cedar Ridge. Will and Donald were invited in for hot chocolate then all four went to church. Trinity couldn't help but see the envious looks they received, especially from Mamie Arman, one of Faith's girlfriends who prided herself on capturing every good-looking man around. Small and charming, she possessed a grasping nature that demanded attention and soft blond curls that peeped from under her hat. The minute church ended, she attached herself to their little party.

"Well, Donald and Will, how nice to see you! How can that little church out near your place get along without you for a Sunday?"

The boys grinned and Mamie rushed on. "You must come again." Her music-box laugh tinkled. "And Trinity, we simply cannot wait until you get home." She floated away in response to an urgent call with a gorgeous smile. "Remember, we'll be looking for you."

"Pretty little bit of fluff," Donald's eyes danced.

"If you like fluff." Will's drawl indicated he did not—and his one raised eyebrow did something to Trinity's heart.

"Can you stay for dinner?" Faith asked but Will shook his head.

"No, thank you. Ma already had invited some of the family. I have to get back. Donald, why don't you and Miss Faith stay and come back later? There's no need for you to rush." He lifted his hat to Trinity. "You're going back this afternoon?"

"Yes, I have to teach tomorrow. It's been nice meeting you." She held out her hand.

"And you're coming home at Christmas, for good." A poignant light deepened the blue of Will's eyes. "I'll be gone but have a happy Christmas, Miss Mason. Goodbye." He swung away in his ground-covering stride, leaving Trinity staring after him. She knew then she had lost something precious.

"Oh, God," she prayed that night in the privacy of her room, kneeling by her bed. "Keep him safe. Please, don't let anything happen to Will. Or Donald or Ed," she quickly added.

Later that day Donald kept vigil with his friend. Only he knew that tomorrow Will would go into town and take the train for Camp Lewis, leaving him behind to explain to Will's family.

By the dim light of a dying fire they talked. Donald confessed his hope that Faith did care. "If I go and make it back, I'll tell her. It isn't fair to tie her down for who knows how long." His boyish lips set into manhood. "Say, her sister's quite a girl, isn't she?"

"Yes."

Something in the quiet voice compelled Donald to continue. "Don't get any ideas about her. From what I hear she's the belle of wherever she goes. Besides, schoolteachers are usually a little high-toned, too good for the likes of us."

"Oh?"

Donald blundered on, hating what he felt he must say. "Talk has it every man over eighteen wants to marry her. Faith says she knows of two who are on the verge of proposing in spite of the fact her sister doesn't say much."

"It figures." Will stood from his chair, stretched, and walked to the window. A million stars hovered above the earth as the same number of thought crossed his mind. *Will they look the same when I'm overseas fighting?*

At least I met her. Trinity—what an unusual name for an unusual person. He yawned again. Pursued, sought after, and loved she might be, but nothing could take from his heart and mind the look of her vivid face. Beside it every other woman paled into insignificance. The pure blue eyes framed by dark, curling lashes, the white skin that flew bright banners of color when she laughed, and the incredible look when she hugged little Bruce all belonged to Will, to warm the long, cold times ahead.

Did he dare write to her? He set his jaw. *Why not?* Even young Ellen and Rachel sent letters overseas to homesick men, notes of cheer and a taste of home. The little flicker his keen eyes caught in her face when he told her good-bye brought a smile to his carved lips. He just bet she'd answer.

"Dear God, I know You're in charge. You know all about me. Now I ask You to walk with me and help me do what I have to, for the sake of those who are depending on us." He wheeled from the window. "Donald, if you don't come over for a while, look after things, will you?"

Donald poked at the last embers until they briefly flared. "I can't take your place but if ever your family or friends—" he paused. "I'll do all I can." The blaze died, leaving ashes gray as the coming dawn.

The next afternoon Will rode back from town into the yard and leaped from the saddle.

"Why, what—?" The family burst from the house.

"Whoooooeeeee!" Will threw his hat into the air and jumped to catch it. "Guess you'll have to put up with me for a while longer."

A babble of questions finally stilled. "There's influenza at Camp Lewis and they aren't taking any more men until they can get it under control. But that isn't all. News is that we've got the enemy on the run and by the time this flu's under control, the war may be over."

"Thank God!" Lewis Thatcher's face brightened. "Too many of our men have already been lost or crippled or gassed." A shadow crept over his face. "May God comfort all those who have lost loved ones."

For once the rumors proved true. Peace was realized November 11, 1918, with the signing of the Armistice and in towns and hamlets and cities across the nation the celebration was unequivocal. Even in Bellingham a dark-haired schoolteacher dismissed her class and paraded in the streets with her students in tribute to God and country.

Chapter Seven

From the exact instant Trinity Mason knew Will Thatcher would not be going away to war, her dread of leaving Bellingham faded. Although she knew she would miss the Butterfields, Letty, Mollie, and the others, she made them promise to come visit Cedar Ridge during holidays and in the summer. Now each day came in a splendor of glory that transcended the rainy November weather and brightened Trinity's smile.

Even when one of her third grade pupils tugged at her skirt and anxiously asked, "Miss Mason, will our new teacher be nice as you?" she only felt a twinge at leaving.

"Of course. She's one of my good friends and her name is Miss Perkins." How fortunate that Mollie finished midterm, she thought.

"But will she love us?" the little inquirer continued.

Trinity dropped to her knees, heedless of crushing her skirt. "How can she help it? I know you and the rest of my class will be as good for her as you are for me."

The early December days passed, marred by the growing specter of the influenza epidemic that had ravaged the world. One of Trinity's schoolchildren fell sick and within days news came she had died. Children lost mothers and fathers and even strong men died. No one knew why some made it and others did not. Trinity dreaded going to school for fear another of the children she loved would fall victim.

A week before the holidays the school board closed the school until January, freeing Trinity earlier than expected. Bidding a quick and tearful farewell to the Butterfields and promising to write, she caught the train home. With Mama due any minute and a houseful of people who might grow ill, her help was needed desperately.

Would she see Will right away? She fumbled in her dress and took out a crumpled single page. Faith's scrawl showed how hurriedly she had written it. So far Mama and all were well. Jamie Thatcher and Sarah had been sick but Will took charge, sent Bruce to his parents, and nursed his cousin and wife back to health. The doctor seemed a bit dubious about Sarah, who was slow to regain her strength.

Faith finished with, "Everyone helps one another. We haven't lost any but Cedar Ridge hasn't been that hard hit yet. Oh, Will and Vi have become good pals. He stops by when he can."

Vi with her sparkling black eyes and curls might be years younger than Trinity but she was still a beautiful girl. Had Will discovered in his fun-loving "pal" the girl he'd like to court?

Trinity's eyes blazed. If so, no one would hear her whimper. Who was Will Thatcher, anyway? Just a logger, a man who caught her fancy for a fleeting time and had no business taking her attention in quiet moments of remembering. If he cared for Vi, so be it.

Every well member of Epworth League, school friends, members of her class, and many other gathered at the train station to send off Trinity to her new life in Cedar Ridge. Boxes of candy, a few flowers from a hothouse, magazines, and tears mingled in a grand rush of goodbyes. Letty and Blakely and Mollie held back until the others made way for them.

"Don't forget that you're coming to see me," Trinity told them, her eyes shining.

"Don't *you* forget you're going to be Letty's bridesmaid in April," Blakely reminded, and smiled at his girl until Letty's blush rivaled the few red leaves still hanging on a nearby bush.

"I'll take good care of your class," Mollie promised. Trinity's quick eyes saw the sidelong glance she gave Tad, who stood just a step behind her. She wondered just how long Mollie's teaching career would last! The new softness in her face betrayed far more than the desire to beat someone's time with a good-looking man.

Every inch of railroad track widened the gap between the old and the new. Trinity dreamed her way back to Cedar Ridge. All thoughts, not so remarkably, came to dwell on the only young man she knew who had never tried to hold her hand when he walked with her. Had Will really learned to care for Vi in the short time since the farewell party? Yet when she swung down to the little station platform in Cedar Ridge, her gaze eagerly sought for the laughing man who so quickly had found lodging in her heart.

Will wasn't there.

Keen disappointment shot through Trinity but she managed to hide it amid the attention of her family. Faith hugged her and whispered, "Mama says the new baby will be here soon—maybe tonight or tomorrow!"

Forgetting their schoolteacher status the two raced like young girls down the streets toward the Masons' sprawling, white frame house. The light from a dozen lamps spilled out into the darkening day that heralded snow before morning. In a rush of excitement Trinity almost fell into her mother's welcoming arms and then turned to her smiling father.

Faith chattered far more than usual while the girls prepared supper. Never had Trinity seen her sister so pretty. "Has Donald spoken?" she demanded.

Faith's blushed deepened. "Yes, and Dad and Mama approve." The quaint wording fitted Faith perfectly.

"I couldn't be happier! Donald McKenna's so in love with you." In high spirits Trinity twitched the bow on her sister's enveloping apron. Then she sobered, "Faith, do—how is Will?" *And Vi*, she burned to add.

Some of Faith's happiness fled and she dropped to the rocking chair that had stood in their big kitchen ever since Trinity could remember. "We haven't seen much of him lately. Jamie came through the flu all right but Sarah's heart was weakened." She frowned. "Dr. Ryan told Mama he wished Sarah would see a specialist but she isn't strong enough yet to make the trip to Seattle."

"I hope she will be all right." Trinity's busy hands stilled among the mound of vegetable parings before her. Sarah's warm, laughing face rose and Trinity recalled their immediate kinship. "It would be terrible if anything happened to her. Bruce didn't get sick, did he?"

"No, the Thatchers still have him. It makes a real burden on Mrs. Thatcher, though. She has so much to do with her own family and neighbors call on her for everything!" Pity sparkled in Faith's eyes. "Mercy, there isn't a family with a sick one or trouble who doesn't eventually wind up asking Ruth Thatcher for help, the same way they did Mama until a few weeks ago when Doc Ryan roared a mighty, 'No more!' He ordered Mama to stay home until after the baby's born."

The arrival of Ed, who had been honorably discharged from the service, sparkly-eyed Vi, and young Albert, who had been out scouting for *the* special tree to cut, postponed the sisters' confidences. The family was still at the table when Mamie Arman rushed in.

"Hey, everyone, Mama says we can have a little party tonight and you're all invited. Just those who haven't shown any sign of getting this awful flue, that is," she hastily added. A sprinkling of snow on her fetching blue hat made her blond curls prettier than ever. No wonder all the boys admired her, Trinity thought, as she noticed Ed's gaze fixed on their visitor.

Mamie hurried on with her news. "I just happened to see Will Thatcher in town and asked him to come and bring Curtis—and Donald." She sent a roguish glance toward Faith then another at Vi and Trinity. "Hmmm, wonder which Mason girl will be escorted tonight?"

Vi bit her lip and Trinity didn't miss her quick look. Recovering, Vi said practically, "If the boys stop by we'll all go together, as usual." But a pretty rose color crept into her face and her black eyes shone.

Trinity's spirits fell. *So Vi did like Will.*

"I'll just stay over here and walk with you," Mamie announced. She made a show of helping with the dishes and kept up a steady stream of gossip. Trinity said little. Should she plead a headache and excuse herself from the party? No, as a child of God, she had no right to lie just to get out of an uncomfortable situation.

Yet when it came time to get ready she loitered on purpose. Truthfully she told the other girls, "I'm not quite through. You go ahead."

A buzz of laughter downstairs made her feel strangely lonely and left out. How could she spend an evening seeing Will and her charming younger sister together? The very idea made her ache inside. She halfheartedly completed her toilette then crept unobserved to the head of the stairs.

"Come on, Donald, Vi, everyone." Mamie's light commanding vice drifted up to Trinity.

"Where's Miss Mason, I mean, Trinity?" a deep voice inquired.

Trinity opened her mouth to cry gladly, "Here!" Will hadn't forgotten her after all. Perhaps he and Vi *were* just pals.

The word never came out. Then Mamie drawled, "Oh, she had to go on ahead and help with some arrangements. Come on, or we'll be late."

Why didn't Faith deny it? From her vantage point Trinity suddenly realized Donald and Faith had already stepped outside, out of earshot. So had Curtis and Ed and the others. Even Vi, struggling into a heavy coat, couldn't have overheard. Only Will and Mamie, out of sight but not out of hearing distance, remained in the hall below.

Trinity shrank back for fear she'd be discovered. A door banged and stillness filled the hall. Mamie with her sneaky tricks! Trinity's blue eyes shot angry sparks. Well, she wouldn't give anyone the satisfaction of knowing she cared one little bit. She noiselessly slipped back to her room. Let them go on without her. Who cared? In a minute she'd go downstairs. If anyone asked afterward what happened, she'd say she decided to spend the evening with Dad and Mama and Grandma Clarissa.

Her face aflame but her heart at peace, after a quick prayer, Trinity swept downstairs, her long skirts trailing behind her. At the bottom she hesitated. A slight movement showed the heavy front door had been left ajar.

Curious to see if everyone *had* left her behind, she opened it and peered out. The scrunch of boots on light snow arrested her.

"Will?" Her throat burned. It couldn't be.

"I'm here, Miss Mason. If you'll get your coat we can go," said a voice in the darkness.

Ten minutes later a thrilled and ecstatic Trinity proudly walked into Mamie's party on Will's arm. Although Mamie said nothing of her attempt to steal another girl's beau, Trinity only remembered Will's quiet words.

"Mamie said you'd already gone but I knew better."

"How?" Trinity inquired and held her breath in the snowy night air.

"I know Mamie." A hint of laughter quieted Trinity's doubts and she quickly changed the subject to firmer ground. Further reassurance came when Will casually added, "Your sister Vi's a good little pal, isn't she? Just about the same age as Curtis and pretty as a spotted pony. You know about Donald and

Faith, of course?"

"Oh, yes, and we're all happy. He seems to be a fine man." Trinity couldn't keep the lilt from her voice.

"We wondered if she'd ever consider him, her being a schoolteacher and all."

Was there a deeper meaning in Will's statement? Trinity immediately said, "What difference does that make? Schoolteachers don't have to be snobs."

Will's heartfelt, "Glad to hear it," sent shivers through her and she actually welcomed the sight of Mamie's well-lighted porch.

Will never left Trinity's side throughout the party. He claimed her for the walk home and the next evening rode his horse into town, along with Donald and Curtis. A few days later after Dr. Ryan delivered a lusty son and Mama named him Robert William, Will paid another visit, bringing a basket of fresh oranges he had sent in on the train.

"Mighty fine name," he told Mama.

Her eyes twinkled back. "Vi got hold of a book of names and we found out Robert meant 'bright fame' and William meant 'determined guardian' so we figured our son couldn't go wrong with those names."

Trinity caught Will's look before he lifted his eyebrows in a droll way. "Determined guardian. A girl might like that, don't you think?"

Mama innocently replied, "A girl might," as Trinity made an excuse to leave the room to hide her burning face. Will found her busy in the kitchen when he had to leave and contented himself with merely saying, "You have a fine new brother." But his eyes held a poignancy that remained in Trinity's heart and mind long after he had gone. She walked around in a glow until the next day when Albert came back from the general store that also served as a post office.

"Letter for you." He danced around his big sister's chair and tantalizingly held it just out of reach.

"Give your sister her letter," Grandma Clarissa quietly said, and Albert tossed it in Trinity's lap.

She picked it up and quickly stood. "I'll read it upstairs."

"Why?" Albert tormented in typical fashion for his age. "What's Will gonna say when he learns you get letters from *Canada*?"

"I can't see why he should even know unless certain people can't keep still about things that don't concern them."

"Aw, Trinity, I didn't mean to make you mad. You know I don't tattle."

She relented enough to give him a friendly grin then ran upstairs and with trembling fingers opened the letter. She read it and then read it again.

> *Dear Miss Mason or Trinity as I think of you,*
> *It seems years rather than months since we said goodbye and I came back to my wheat ranch. My kingdom seems to stretch as far as I can see*

*in all directions. I have all the money I will need for a lifetime and
enough to leave my sons and daughters for their lifetimes.*

> *My darling girl, my kingdom lacks only one thing: a queen to rule
my heart and reign over it. I plan to come to Cedar Ridge very soon. I
am bringing a ring for you and hopefully one day in the near future my
empire will be complete.*
> > *Devotedly,*
> > *John Standish*

"Oh, no!" Trinity let out a cry of pure horror. Visions of the scorn and fury
Will's expressive eyes would surely hold if he knew about this letter rose and
accused her. A wave of anger followed. *What right did John have to send such
a letter?* She had made no promises to him. She owed him nothing.

Before her fury could recede, she snatched pen and paper to write back in no
uncertain terms what she thought of him.

Yet the ink dried on the pen point and the right words eluded her. She had
liked John and he couldn't have helped knowing it. Any coy reply of less than
direct answer would simply whet her determination to a cutting edge. She must
stop him from coming to Cedar Ridge at all costs. The tendrils of friendship
and something more had only begun to entwine her and Will. John's arrival
could tear down those fragile strands.

At last a mischievous smile crossed her face. She hurriedly began to write:

> *Dear John Standish,*
> *While I am flattered by your offer and appreciate the great honor you
have paid me, I am afraid that a visit from you would be inappropriate.*
> *You see, I am to be married, so your coming here is sure to prove
awkward.*
> *Again, let me thank you for your respect and affection.*
> > *Your sincere friend,*
> > *Trinity Mason*

She hastily addressed an envelope and stuffed in the letter. Before she could
seal it, Faith came in.

"Albert said you got a letter from Canada." The statement sounded more like
a question and Faith's raised eyebrows showed her disapproval.

"Did I!" Trinity groaned and handed John's letter to her sister.

"My stars," Faith exploded when she finished it, "How could you lead him
on?"

"I didn't," Trinity protested. "He escorted me to church activities but I never,
ever, let him think I cared for him more than as a friend. Why, when he asked
me to think about it months ago and wanted to know if I ever could care, I told

him I didn't know."

"And you know now?"

Her intelligent eyes brought color to Trinity's delicate complexion. "I know I—I don't care for John the way you care for Donald."

"Then you did exactly right except how could you tell him such an untruth and say you are to be married?" Disappointment turned the corner of Faith's lips down. "Dad and Mama have always taught us never to tell anything but the truth."

"It is the truth," Trinity mumbled. "I *will* be married, sometime." She ignored the storm clouds in Faith's face and added, "I can't have him coming here, can I?"

"Well, no." Faith shook her head. "If you're going to mail that, you better do it right away. I'm sure Albert will be glad to run back to the store, especially if you let him know we won't be having a visitor. He's crazy about Will." She ducked a pillow Trinity impulsively tossed at her and fled with a parting shot.

"So is someone else around here if I know people — and I do!"

Trinity devoutly hoped her letter would end John's pursuit. But she wasn't prepared for a second letter that accused her of making a fool of him. She wrote a cold note denying any such accusations and received a broken, apologetic letter saying he had cared too much. This time Trinity didn't reply. Further communication could only result in greater hurt.

Chapter Eight

A few days before Christmas, Will, Donald, and Curtis arrived bearing gifts. The enormous boxes of chocolates, French creams, and bonbons filled Mama's biggest washtub! The generous trio also managed to get fresh flowers sent, but one bouquet nearly ended in disaster.

Now that the young men came so often to the Mason home, Mamie had practically become a permanent guest. She had obviously set her cap for Will after failing to impress Donald. Even young Curtis and lanky Ed came in for their share of smiles from the fickle and flirtatious young woman.

If she could make a girl miserable, she did. The day Donald arrived with a specially ordered nosegay surrounded by a paper frill Mamie met him in the lower hall. Trinity heard everything from her vantage point in the upstairs hall, scrubbing floors.

"Oh, Donald, the flowers are so beautiful!" Mamie's upturned face showed nothing but innocence and delight. "I know they're for Faith, but there are so many. Could I have just one posy? You don't mind, do you?" She didn't wait for an answer but helped herself to a flower, stuck it in her blond curls, and preened before a mirror. "Oh, thank you so much. I'll tell Faith you're here." She rewarded Donald with a dazzling smile and scurried upstairs. Ignoring Trinity, who was silently counting to ten before calling Mamie something unChristian, the vain girl lightly ran into Faith's room.

"Donald's here, Faith. He brought you a bouquet." She twirled and pointed to her hair. From the doorway Trinity longed to snatch down those curls and fling the flower into the ashcan. "Of course, he gave me the first pick." Leaving two speechless girls she bounced back out again.

"Of all the—" Trinity flared.

"Don't mind her," said Faith shrugging, yet a little hurt look crept into her eyes that made Trinity want to cry. Faith's shining love for Donald shouldn't have to be marred by a flirt like Mamie.

"He didn't give her first pick or *any* pick," Trinity raged. "I heard the whole thing and she asked in a way no one could refuse even if she'd given him opportunity. She just reached out and took."

"That's Mamie." Relief erased the doubt in Faith's face. "Reach out and take is her motto."

Two evenings later a similar scene transpired. Trinity had eagerly finished dressing and stood unseen on the top step while Mamie practiced her could-I-have-just one-posy routine on Will. He carried a sheaf of gorgeous hothouse red roses. This time when she confidently reached out to get a flower Mamie more than met her match. Will held the bouquet out of reach over his head and laughed.

"Sorry, Mamie, these flowers are for Trinity." All Mamie's teasing and fluttering proved useless and Trinity's cheeks rivaled the roses when Will met her halfway up the staircase and presented them to her. Her heart swelled at the way he looked when she buried her nose in their fragrant depths and held them close to her simple white gown.

Mamie pouted and turned her back to them, but Trinity's keen ears heard her fiercely whisper, "Mean old thing, stingy too." The next instant the tiny beribboned girl vanished toward the parlor calling, "Ed? Are you in here? I declare, it's been so long since we've talked."

Yet all through the happiness of Will's courtship ran the darker strain of trouble. Flu that Cedar Ridge hoped would pass it by descended like the inevitable winter snow. Doc Ryan was run off his feet and often found asleep behind the patient horse that pulled his buggy when some kind of road was available to get him where he needed to be. The rest of the time he rode horseback or walked. One night he rode sixteen miles into the forest to attend one of Jimmy Crowfoot's tribe and found many of the Indian people sick. He did what he could and rode back to Cedar Ridge, gulped a few bites of breakfast, and headed out again.

Fresh mounds that indicated newly dug graves increased. With the logging camps shut down for the winter, Will, Donald, Jimmy, and others spent their time helping where they could. Some farms had every member of the family sick. The young men milked and fed stock while the women prepared and delivered broth and took in children when the parents lay too ill to care for them.

After the Christmas holidays Trinity was faced with parting again from the big, happy Mason household. She would still come home weekends but now she faced the task of teaching all eight grades in the new Cedarton one-room school. Joe Baldwin and his family welcomed her openly and she discovered he'd equipped her new school with everything she needed. The only problem was not seeing Will. His home lay five miles out of Cedar Ridge one way; the Cedarton school was an equal distance a different way. Besides, with the mountains of homework she had to tackle every night Trinity had little time to visit.

However her schedule didn't stop the young bucks on *that* side of the river. Night after night one, two, or more would be beaux appeared on the Baldwin doorstep. Trinity had to excuse herself and seek refuge with her homework in her own little room. Her flight didn't stop jealous neighbor girls from spreading how much attention she had and how many men were after her. The tormented girl silently rebelled, but what could she do? She couldn't order the Baldwins' neighbors out. She just hoped the troublemakers wouldn't run with their gossip to the Thatchers.

To her own amazement, she adored her new job. The hulking eighth graders who had run out former teachers respected her and worked hard to show how well they could learn and behave. There was little chance that any of them would fail the tough eighth grade state exams.

As Faith predicted, the younger pupils and older ones worked and learned and played together. A quiet word from Trinity quelled any rising rebellion before it burst into a problem. When the young teacher went back to Bellingham in April to serve as Letty's bridesmaid, her last doubts fled.

"I really feel the true meaning of what my grandmother said so long ago. The children look to me not only for what some of them still call 'book-larnin' but for an example too. We read from the Bible every morning and I make sure to choose verses that will teach how Jesus is with us all the time."

"Have you found your Price Charming?" Mollie asked as she proudly displayed a diamond ring from Tad. They would be married as soon as her spring school term ended.

"Perhaps." But Trinity would say no more. To admit the growing love in her heart and soul for one who had not yet spoken might bring her pain if it turned out that Will really didn't care.

How much Will cared became evident a week after Trinity came back from Bellingham. Gap-toothed Joey Baldwin set the scene.

"Mith Mathon, Mith Mathon, there'th gonna be a box thothial."

She hid a grin and translated "box social." She smiled at the excited child and the others who gathered around her. "That will be fun. Who is it for?"

"Everyone." Big Joe stomped in just in time to hear his son's bulletin. "We'd like to get s'more things for our school so we're asking everyone for miles around." He grinned. "I reckon we can get a good price for *your* basket, Miss Trinity."

A few days before the box social Will unexpectedly showed up just after Trinity dismissed her school.

"Why, Will!" She couldn't keep her pleasure from bursting out.

"Thought I'd ride over and get some information," he teased. "I've got fifty dollars saved up and Donald has the same or a little more. We plan to get our girls' baskets at the box social."

Torn between his comment "our girls" and what else he said, Trinity could only stare. "You aren't planning to spend that kind of money just to eat one dinner with us, are you?"

Will looked shocked. "Of course. That's why we have box socials, so folks can buy the dinners the girls and women put up in fancy trimmings and eat with someone they like."

Trinity shook her head. "I'm sorry, Will. I'd love for you to buy my box but you need that money."

"You mean you won't tell me what your box will be like?"

"I can't." She twisted her handkerchief. "You'll still come, won't you?"

"I don't know." He sounded doubtful. "The way I hear it, a bunch of men around here are betting on which one will get your basket. It's too bad, too. They'll spend all their money trying to get yours and a few others and then maybe just offer two bits or so for some of the less popular girls."

She sighed. "Maybe I shouldn't go."

A little smile grew on Will's face. "I have a better idea. You come, but don't tell anyone, especially that talky Joe Baldwin or his wife, what your basket is like." Will touched his horse's flanks lightly with his heels. "See you Saturday night!" He lifted his hat and rode off, his back ramrod straight.

Trinity did exactly what Will said. She locked her door on Saturday afternoon and turned a shoebox filled with fired chicken, potato salad, chocolate cake, and other good eats into a replica of the American flag. Then she wrapped it in brown paper, tied it with string, and smuggled it onto the table with the other gaily decorated boxes and baskets.

Some girls had dressed to match their baskets, including Mamie. Her blue and white checked basket with lacy frills was an easy match with her dress. She crowed when her basket brought ten dollars. One by one the baskets were auctioned off. The modest brown paper one sold for a dollar to one of Trinity's eighth grade boys. A roar of disappointment went up when he took off the disguise, held up the cleverly designed flag box, and yelled, "Miss Trinity Mason!"

Will caught her gaze and raised both hands above his head in a prizefighter's winning clasp. Some of the jealous young men offered the buyer a lot more money to sell "teacher's basket" but he just grinned and proudly led Trinity to a nearby table.

Meanwhile, Will and Donald squelched the plans of some to not spend more than fifty cents for a basket. Every time the bidding stayed low one of them ran it up to at least a couple of dollars. When the auction ended, the boys gathered all the girls and women whose baskets they'd bought, plus some of the boys and men who simply didn't have enough money, and formed a noisy potluck-style group.

"Would you like to join them?" Trinity's escort whispered, his gaze on a pretty seventh-grade girl who kept looking their way.

"If you would."

As he escorted her to the larger group, he won Trinity's devotion. "You're the best teacher we ever had. You make things interesting. I never cared about going to high school before but I do now. Pa and Ma say it's fine."

Spring came in green skirts. Winter snow melted overnight and the land lay soft and new. Gradually the influenza passed, yet new lines lay in the faces of those who lost friends and loved ones. Jimmy Crowfoot's tribe had been cut in half while Sarah Thatcher continued to fight desperately.

Trinity had long since recognized Will's place in her life. Not once since she looked into his blue eyes had she been interested in anyone else and she never would. Likewise, Will no longer visited any girl but Trinity. Sometimes she wondered why he didn't confess the feelings she saw mirrored in the depths of his soul. Perhaps he felt it was too soon. He still carried a lot of responsibility toward his family, as did she.

Even if they became engaged, how could they ever marry when both families needed them so much? Faith also hesitated. Did she have a right to seize happiness of her own when her brothers and sisters needed so much?

One tender moonlit night Will rode up and asked Trinity to go for a walk. He led her to a rustic bridge spanning a small stream silvered by the moon and happily bubbling secrets to its banks. He placed both hands on her shoulders. "Trinity, I have to know. Someday, when things change, will you be my wife? I love you more than life itself and I've never felt this way before."

She had always wondered how the moment of proposal would be, the opening of a heart she realized had been hers since the farewell party. "I will be honored. I've never loved any man but you."

His hands tightened. His gentle kiss held respect, love and appreciation. There in the moonlight he slipped a diamond ring on her left hand and they knelt together and thanked God. "It may be a long time," he warned. "We both have obligations."

"I know." She ached inside. Now that they were promised, she wanted time to fly. Feelings of resentment filled her, not against their families but against the circumstances that kept them apart. Yet they must not spoil this precious moment by thoughts of the future.

Joey Baldwin was the first to spot the ring she wore to breakfast the next day. "Hey, look at that!" He pointed.

Trinity blushed but held her hand out for inspection. The perfect stone that she knew must have cost far more than Will should have paid caught every glint of morning sunlight. All day her pupils exclaimed over the ring. It made it all seem real, not just a wonderful dream to be interrupted by Joe's lusty yell, "Roll out, everyone."

The Masons and Thatchers exchanged satisfied glances that silently shouted they'd suspected all along. Little by little they considered ways so the young couple wouldn't have to put off their wedding. One Saturday Will burst in and carried Trinity off on horseback to his home. He didn't stop at the house, however, but rode about a mile on down the valley between the mountains to a gentle slope. There a picturesque cabin stood facing the white-capped mountains and overlooking the whole Thatcher spread.

"Old Man Thomas says we can have that cabin if we give him half of what we raise," he told her. "It isn't much but we can fix it up any way we like. I'm a good house painter."

"And I can make curtains," Trinity eagerly said. They stepped inside. "How cozy!" She eyed the shabby room seeing it with the floorboards scrubbed, table and chairs painted a bright color with curtain tiebacks to match, and flowers in the window. She peered into the second room. "Oh, big enough for a large bed, a bureau, and—"

"Pa will build cupboards for us," Will promised. "Closets, too. Think you can be happy here?"

"Supremely." She whirled and threw her arms around his neck. "When can we move in?" Her arms fell. "Will? What about our folks?"

"Donald and Faith and you and I will still give something to help them. Your dad says you girls have already done too much, and with the good wages from the Cedarton School they think they can get by. If you don't mind teaching for a little longer, we'll make it."

"Of course I don't mind, but is there a school nearby that needs a teacher?" I know Faith's going back to hers."

"The White Rock School does need a new teacher, come to think of it. Joe Baldwin's a good sport, so when he knows what we have planned he will fret and fume but he'll give us his blessing." He drew her close. "Trinity, can you be ready by August?"

Trinity thought of her hope chest already filled with handmade sheets, towels, dish cloths, pillowcases, and the like. "I don't have many clothes so if you don't mind a beggar maid coming to you—"

"Sweetheart, someday I'll dress you in silks and satins," he promised grandly.

"I'll settle for gingham and muslin and dimity with some warm woolens for winter," she teased then kissed him. "August it is." She sighed. "Now that it's settled it's going to be hard to wait."

Overnight everything changed. The sound of hooves on an early May morning awoke the Mason household. Trinity recognized Will's voice mingled with a pounding on the door. She tossed on a dressing gown and hurried down the stairs as her father opened the door.

"Trinity," Will gasped, his blue eyes nearly black with urgency. "It's Sarah—she's bad and she wants you. Dress and I'll be back as soon as I get Doc Ryan. We need you, too, sir," he told Edmund.

"Sarah?" Trinity's confused thoughts halted. "How—what—?"

Will had already raced away.

"Go upstairs and get ready, child," her father's quiet voice ordered. "And pray. I doubt if Sarah would be asking for me unless she knows . . . ." His voice trailed off and he disappeared toward his room, leaving Trinity to stumble upstairs and into riding clothing while her heart slowly froze.

Chapter Nine

The long ride with her father, Doc Ryan, and Will from Cedar Ridge to Jamie and Sarah Thatcher's place remained a blur in Trinity's mind. The tall firs and hemlocks at times reached and joined above the hard-packed dirt road until it appeared they rode in a green tunnel. Trinity tried to pray but found it impossible to get words past the lump of fear in her throat. Yet her rapidly beating heart kept cadence with the drumming hooves. *Help her, help her.*

After they arrived and threw off their coats, Trinity's pitying eyes noticed the kitchen and sitting room. Such disorder spoke eloquently of just how sick Sarah was. Never had such untidiness reigned in Sarah Thatcher's home, although Jamie's rude efforts to brush up were evident. Little Bruce lay disconsolately on his mother's bed, his face tear streaked, seeming to sense his mother's weakness and danger. When the little group came in he sat up and crowed, "Will!" then smiled his enchanting smile as his hero raised him to a strong shoulder and held him perched there.

"Now, now, what's this all about?" Doc blustered.

Sarah had gone downhill rapidly in the few weeks since Trinity had seen her. Thin, pale, and wasted, only her big brown eyes looked the same.

"Everyone out while I examine her," Doc ordered.

"Let Trinity stay." Even the whisper cost Sarah and she took in a deep breath and held it before slowly exhaling.

Jamie's red-rimmed eyes bespoke his anguish as he gently held his wife's hand. So would Will look if it were his wife. He turned at the persuasion of Edmund Mason's hand on his shoulder and together they ambled out the door, closing it behind them.

Doc Ryan placed his stethoscope on Sarah's chest, frowned, and attempted to cover his findings by shrugging. "Now too much change." He busied himself with his worn black bag.

"I want the truth, Doctor Ryan. How long?" Sarah whispered.

He wheeled and squared his shoulders. His gnarled hand lay on Sarah's grown hair in a blessing. "Child, only our good Lord knows that, but . . . ." He pulled a large white handkerchief from his pocket and noisily blew his nose.

"Tell Jamie and the others, but send Bruce to me first."

Trinity gasped. Where had Sarah's strength come from? As she struggled to lean up against her pillows in a sitting position, twin spots of color rose in her cheeks.

"You need to rest now." But little remained of Doc's bark.

"I will, later. Give me five minutes with Trinity then send Bruce in."

Something regal in her command sent Doc to the door without another word. Before it closed behind him Sarah turned her luminous eyes on Trinity. "Will you take Bruce for me?"

"I will." There was no hesitation, no pondering what her promise would mean or how she could accomplish it. Her heart had reached out to the young woman who had come to mean so much.

"Then it will be all right." Sarah sagged against the pillows but her iron determination to leave the world as right as she could sustained her. "Jamie will want our son with him nights, but I thought if you'd keep him while Jamie works, perhaps you'd give them both their supper." Her brown eyes frankly pleaded. "Trinity, someday when it's right, I want you to tell Jamie something for me. I tried but he wouldn't listen. The Thatchers are one-woman-for-a-life-time men but I don't want my Jamie to live alone for forty of fifty years. Tell him to find another woman, one who will love him and Bruce and perhaps give him more children. We'd planned a houseful." Her lips trembled and Trinity wanted to scream.

"I'll tell him. And Will and I will look after them both, as long as they need us."

"I knew you would. From the first night, I knew your friendship and love could surround me and they have, even when we were apart." A radiant smile highlighted the wan face.

The door opened slowly and little Bruce ran to his mother with outstretched arms. Trinity felt speechless but she mouthed, *Shall I go?* Sarah's almost imperceptible shake of her head sent her to a shadowed corner. She could not intrude on a mother's goodbye. Yet as Sarah talked with her little son, some of the resentment and dread left the trembling young woman.

"Bruce, you've always liked my patchwork quilt. Today I want to tell you a story. Life is kind of like our quilt." She took his chubby fingers and ran them over the many bits and pieces hand-stitched together in tiny but firm stitches.

"Here's a piece of your first little shirt and this is a dress I wore when I first met Daddy."

Trinity marveled at Sarah's steady voice, fascinated at the story.

"Now, son, Mama has to go away. Daddy and Will and Trinity will take good care of you."

Bruce's blue eyes widened and he put one finger in his mouth. "I don't want you to go."

A bright drop fell on a dark patch in the quilt. "I'd like to stay but God wants me to go be with Him and Jesus. Remember your friend Jesus in the picture?" She pointed to an inexpensive but beautiful artistic interpretation of Jesus surrounded by children.

"Always stay close to Jesus and someday you and Daddy and all of us who love Him will be together again." Before Bruce could answer, she rushed on.

"Bruce, look." She crumpled the patchwork quilt and draped it over her head.

"I can't see you, Mama!" Bruce tugged at the quilt. "Are you still there?"

"I'm here, son. My love will always be here. You don't understand everything now but Daddy and Will and Trinity will teach you more as you grow to be a fine boy, then a man like Daddy." She took down the quilt. "When I go away, you won't be able to see me either, but remember this. I will be close to you as long as you live."

Trinity's eyes spilled over but she clenched her hands into fists and regained control. In no way would she spoil these moments for Bruce — or Sarah.

How much did the solemn little boy understand? He looked at the picture of Jesus and said, "Will you have a little boy where you go?"

Thin arms crept around his sturdy body. "I'd like that."

"Will you love him more than me?"

Trinity thought her heart would break with pain at the childish question but her agony turned to triumph when Sarah hugged Bruce.

"I could never love any other little boy, anywhere, even half as much as I love you!" Her face flowed with unearthly beauty and her far-seeing eyes shone.

"And someday I'll come?" Bruce asked anxiously. "Daddy and Will and Trinity too?"

"Yes, Bruce. And Grandma and Grandpa and all the others." Sarah silently signaled Trinity in a wordless glance then said, "Go with Trinity, now. Do you know she's going to be your Auntie Trinity very soon?" She hugged him again. "Now scoot and tell Daddy to come see me. Goodbye, son."

"Bye, Mama." Bruce accepted Trinity's outstretched hand but patted Sarah's with his other. "I love you."

"I love you too," Sarah whispered.

For their sake, Trinity once more fought tears, knowing she wouldn't have traded those last moments for anything. Her own faith felt renewed as she led Bruce into the other room, now filled with anxious family members and Donald and Faith.

"Ho, there, young 'un." Donald reached for Bruce. "How about you and me going for a walk down to the pond? I saw some brand-new baby ducks there yesterday."

With the ability of childhood to leave one situation for another, Bruce contentedly climbed up Donald and his silver laughter echoed in the room when they went out. Jamie vanished into the bedroom. The others simple waited.

Somehow Trinity felt exalted. Years before her grandmother had passed a torch into her keeping. Today, Sarah had passed a new and different torch, her little son. *God, help me to keep my promise,* her soul cried. *Help me to comfort and nurture this beautiful child You have sent to the Thatchers, and now to me.*

A few hours later Jamie returned to them, strangely at peace. Whatever he and Sarah had shared in that time had given him the same radiance that remained in her now-still face when Trinity and the others went back in for a few moments. In death Sarah's lips still curved in a smile and Trinity remembered a conversation they once had.

"Before I got married I heard a woman say that when she lost her husband, she felt sorry that she didn't treat him the way she wished she had. I made up my mind that I would always treat Jamie with all the love in my heart so if I ever lost him, I wouldn't be like that woman." Softness crept into her eyes. "I have too."

"I know," Trinity had replied, little thinking Sarah would be taken first and vowing the same for herself and Will.

Doc and Dad considerately fell back on the ride into Cedar Ridge, giving Trinity and Will time to talk. She shared with him all Sarah said. "Will, let's don't wait and miss out on time together! We're so young, and I promised Sarah. What are we going to do?"

He slowed his horse and hers and guided them to a grassy patch alongside the road. Dismounting, Will helped her from the saddle to a nearby stump. "I've been thinking all day. I suspected what Sarah wanted because she mentioned it to me, but you had to be the one to agree." He dug his boot heel into the soft earth and stroked a fern. "Trinity, Ma can keep Bruce until you finish in a couple of weeks at Cedarton." He breathed deeply and looked into her eyes. "Will you marry me at the end of May? I know everyone will pitch in and help get our house ready." Blue lights danced in his eyes. "Then you'll have all summer with Bruce." He clasped her hand and she curled her fingers into his strong palm, remembering his laughing comment months before when Robert William was born about a girl wanting a determined guardian.

The strength to meet all the uncertain tomorrows flowed between them. God created male and female to be joined in His plan of marriage and to sustain one another.

"Are you really prepared to take on a four year old as well as a husband?" Will asked. "You didn't bargain for this."

Trinity squeezed his hand. " Will Thatcher, I'd take on a whole passel of children if it meant keeping my promise to Sarah. The only thing is, what about when it's time for me to teach at White Rock School next fall?" She frowned and gazed unseeingly at the swaying wildflowers between the tall ferns. "I don't see how we can get by just now if I don't teach." A thought struck her. "Do you suppose that under the unusual circumstances the school board would agree to let me have him with me, at least for part of the day?"

"I don't know, but it would solve the problem." Will considered for a moment while a magnificent eagle swooped past looking for prey from its aerial vantage point.

Trinity explored the idea further. "He's such a darling and I know he would-n't disrupt anything. If I could keep him at school mornings then take him to your mother at the dinner break he'd sleep most of the afternoon and I could pick him up on the way home." The more she thought about it, the more logical it sounded. "Jamie will be coming to us for supper, and—"

"He's already said he won't come unless he can pay." Will told her. "He wants you to figure out what it will cost to feed him and Bruce nights and maybe put up a lunch for him when you do mine. He can manage breakfast for himself but it's too early for Bruce to eat." His brows came together in a straight line. "You'll be up anyway with me, and how much breakfast can a little guy like that eat?"

"We'll work it out," she reassured her tall husband-to-be.

"The only thing that worries Jamie is our not having the privacy newlyweds are entitled to." Will released her hand and slipped his arm around her. Pure mischief replaced his grave manner. "I told him not to worry about that—we'll make sure we spend a lot of time alone. And—" He stopped and held his head back so he could look directly into her eyes. "We don't start keeping Bruce until *after* our honeymoon."

Trinity could feel hot blood flow to her cheeks. "I—I hadn't even thought about that."

"Where do you want to go?" Will waved his hand expansively to include the far horizons.

"With you."

Her simple answer brought an unforgettable look into Will's face, but he teased, "What? No hankering for a trip to Europe or at least Seattle?"

"You know what I'd really like to do?" she grinned.

"What?" He cocked his head and looked a little suspicious.

"Go camping in the mountains. Find mountain meadows and little lakes. Climb and fish and sleep under the stars." The very prospect of such a trip fired Trinity with enthusiasm.

Will leaped to his feet and pulled her up with him. "My dear, that's just what I had in mind, but I didn't dare propose it for fear you'd be disappointed. There's a certain trip I've wanted to make with you ever since we met—but it's only proper for married couples," he added piously.

"Where? Where?" She hugged him then leaned away to look eagerly into his laughing eyes.

"First Pa takes us up past Darrington into the mountains by car. We have Jimmy Crowfoot meet us at the foot of this trail I know with saddles and pack ponies—he will be glad to do it. We ride up and come to what seems like the top of the world but is really Buck Pass. It's as close to heaven as I've been able to get so far." He cleared his throat but his voice stayed husky. "You can see down the east side of the Cascades to Lake Wenatchee." He held her close and kissed her tenderly. "I'm sure glad God sent me a girl who loves what He created the same way I do."

"So am I." She leaned against his strength. "Will, you asked if I minded about Bruce and I really don't but what about you? I have to know. I'm the one who promised but it means a different start than you expected too."

His encircling arms tightened. "*Mind?* That little tyke? Never. I couldn't help thinking all day, what if he were ours and you—" He buried his face in her soft dark brown hair. "Trinity, never go away and leave me, will you?"

What a strange thing for him to say! At that moment Trinity knew what a lonely man Will had been since the death of his brother Daniel. "Never," she whispered and stroked his sleeve. "You're all I ever wanted."

A little later she shared the feeling that came when Sarah entrusted her son's care to her friend.

"If teaching children is carrying a lamp in darkness, then training our own, or in this case, Bruce, is that much more important." A rush of tears threatened but she impatiently brushed them aside. "God gives the greatest responsibility of all when a child is born. Jamie and Sarah have done such a good job. I just hope we can continue what they've started." She swallowed hard. "I know I could never have had the strength to talk with my son the way Sarah did with Bruce, but he will have a memory of his mother to build on. Even if he doesn't remember it exactly—"

"—you'll be right here to impress it in his mind," Will added. "I believe that's why Sarah wanted you to stay in the room, don't you?"

"Yes." Trinity closed her eyes, drained from the day's events yet curiously peaceful.

"Much as I'd like to stay here, we have to get into Cedar Ridge so you can go back to the Baldwins," Will reminded. His bright smile widened. "Things will be different on our honeymoon. Think you can be happy seeing no one but me for two whole weeks, Mrs. Thatcher-to-be?"

Trinity's whole heart confirmed her answer, but she said primly, "I can't think of anything else on earth that would make me happier."

He scooped her up with a shout, placed her in the saddle, then leaped onto his own horse. One shout not enough, he let out a yell that brought the lagging Doc Ryan and Edmund Mason hurrying up the road behind them.

Chapter Ten

Jimmy Crowfoot squinted at the late May morning sky. His dark face and eyes brightened when Will sauntered over to the corral and grinned.

"What do I owe you for the use of your ponies?" Will asked. He slapped the pack pony's rump and sent it dancing across the packed earth. With experienced eyes he noted the pretty little mare's fine points and stroked her silky mane. "Trinity's going to love her. Is she easy on the road?"

"Single-footer." Jimmy's strong hand rested on the top rail of the fence.

"Good. That's like riding a rocking horse."

As if jealous of the attention given the other horses, Will's own bay thundered up and screeched to a halt a few feet away. "It's okay, Bullet, old boy," Will said as he petted his favorite. "How much, Jimmy?"

"No money, please. Ponies gift." A rare smile highlighted Jimmy's high cheekbones and betrayed his love for Will. But the smile faded when Will asked for advice.

"Is it too early for the mountains? I'd thought we'd be married in August, when the snows had gone." He cast an anxious eye at the distant hills.

Jimmy shook his head. "Skookum horses. Skookum man and woman. Early spring makes snows melt. It's okay."

Will heaved a sigh of relief. When Jimmy Crowfoot pronounced something *skookum*—strong and good—Will need not worry. Jimmy had an uncanny way of knowing weather and he had never once been proved wrong in all the time the Thatchers knew him.

"When Will come back, Jimmy get wife." Not a muscle moved to show Jimmy had said anything out of the ordinary but Will shouted with glee.

"Really? Who?"

"Minnie Manyponies make good wife."

Will's hand shot out to grip his friend's. "She's a beautiful girl, Jimmy. I'm happy for you."

"Will come to powwow. Dance with friend."

"Of course." Will successfully hid his surprise at the great honor. To his knowledge, no other white man had ever been asked to dance at an Indian pow-wow. They could attend only if they treated the ceremony for what it was, a reli-gious celebration. Once when some townspeople had gone and poked fun at the rituals, they were summarily ordered out and told never to come back.

Will's eyes danced with mischief. "Minnie is almost as pretty as Trinity Mason," he observed.

Jimmy guffawed and crossed his arms on his massive chest. "Will Thatcher, listen to story. When Great Spirit make man. He put together like dough then bake in hot sun. First time, man too white, paleface. Great Spirit make new man, bake in sun. Too dark, black man."

Jimmy's eyes gleamed. "Great Spirit make man third time, bake in sun, just right. Indian."

"That's a good story," Will told his friend. "But you know Jesus, God's Son, loves everyone, no matter what color they are." If only he could help Jimmy understand God's salvation!

"Someday Jimmy catch Great Spirit's son Jesus, maybe."

"Don't wait," Will urged. "Jesus loves you, Jimmy, the same as He loves me and everybody."

"Will, Great Spirit let tribe die?"

Sickness filled the pit of Will's stomach. "I don't know, Jimmy, no one completely understands why those we love have to die." He thought of Sarah Thatcher and of Jimmy's people wiped out in the flu epidemic. "We just take comfort in knowing that if we follow Jesus someday we will be with them again, forever."

"There!"

Will's gaze traced Jimmy's outflung hand toward the horizon slowly brightening into a glorious day that promised to hold.

"B-r-e-a-k-f-a-s-t!"

The call from the farmhouse porch cut short their conversation and Will and Jimmy headed up to get washed for the ample breakfast Ma and the girls had steaming on the table.

"For what we are about to receive, we give You thanks. For Jesus' sake, Amen." Lewis finished the blessing and passed serving dishes of thick-sliced homecured ham, over-easy eggs, biscuits light as a dandelion puff, rich gravy, and a gigantic bowl of fresh applesauce.

As Will loaded his plate, his brother Curtis lifted one eyebrow and said, "Getting married sure doesn't change your appetite, does it?"

Even Jimmy laughed but Will didn't care. "For the next two weeks you can sit at home, pardon me, stay at home and do my share of the work—and think about how Trinity and I'll be eating fresh trout and fired potatoes and—"

"I give, I give." Curtis threw up his hands in defeat.

"'Course one of these days I may be doing the same for you, that is, when you get old enough and smart enough to make some pretty girl like Vi Mason fall for you." Will calmly reached for another biscuit and the others gleefully pointed to the red creeping up in Curtis's tanned skin.

He got even later. Two mornings from then when Will went to get out his wedding suit Curtis followed, his eyes dancing. "I dare you to wear your clown suit."

"Wha-at?" Will whipped around.

"Your clown suit," Curtis held his sides from laughing. "We're bringing your wedding clothes in the car but you're riding in on Grandy, aren't you? You need something to keep the dust off your riding clothes. Wear the clown suit."

Will's lips twitched. "I will."

"You will? Whoopee!" Curtis yelled and rolled on the floor. But when he finally settled down and his brother stood dressed in the wide-ruffled, spotted clown costume someone had worn for a party, he sobered. "Uh, maybe you shouldn't. What if it makes Trinity mad on your wedding day?"

"It won't." Will adjusted the long sleeves.

"You don't have to. I take back the dare." Curtis looked worried now.

"Too late, little brother. If you're a good sport, though, you'll climb into that old buckskin outfit you wear to hunt in and ride with me."

"Not me!" Curtis pulled back in alarm. "Last time we got smart and each wore one red sock and one green sock Vi turned up her nose."

Will threw back his head and roared. He pounded Curtis on the back and crowed, "I knew it!" then lightly ran downstairs and out to the corral. He vaulted up on Grandy's saddle, leaving the rest of the family spilling out into the yard and calling, "Mercy, Will, what *are* you doing in that rig?"

"Going to get married," he flung back. "See you later!"

If ever Cedar Ridge had seen a perfect day, today was it. Once his burst of excitement dwindled, Will slowed Grandy into a steady, east gait. He savored every foot of his ride to town. How could anyone experience such a morning —one that had started with cleansing dew and and had melted into a cloudless sky with fresh-washed flowers and trees, set against rolling land that gave way to low foothills then towering mountains—and not believe in God?

His untrained but perfectly pitched tenor voice rose in praise.

> The Lord's my shepherd, I'll not want.
> He makes me down to lie
> In pastures green, He leadeth me
> The quiet waters by.

The wonderful words of the old Scottish Psalter* mingled with birdsong until Will poured out heart and soul to his Heavenly Father in the last stanza.

> Goodness and mercy all my life
> Shall surely follow me;
> And in God's house forever more

---

* From Psalm 23, *Scottish Psalter,* 1650.

My dwelling place shall be.
Shall be, echoed back to him.

Will reined in Grandy, slipped from the saddle, and bared his head. Was this how Moses felt when he stood on holy ground? Too filled with the Spirit of God to consider how ridiculous the clown suit was, Will simply stood silent for a long moment. Back in the saddle he then faced forward toward the girl who would be in his keeping from this day on.

Trinity had also awakened early. She had shared a bed last night with Faith due to the influx of visitors, including Blakely and Letty Butterfield, Mollie, Tad, and the elder Butterfields. Slipping from the bed, unwilling to share these moments even with Faith, she saw with relief that her sister lay undisturbed. Suddenly a pang went through her. Faith and Donald's wedding should have come first.

Was anyone on earth so unselfish as Faith? When she heard the change in circumstances due to Sarah's death, she folded her hands and quietly said, "We can wait until you get back from your honeymoon. It's right that we do."

Trinity blinked hard. If only she could be like her adored older sister! She tossed a light dressing gown over her nightgown and crossed to the chair by the window. What a day! With a prayer of thanksgiving, she slipped a letter from the nearby desk and reread it in the softly curtained light.

> *Dear sister Trinity,*
>
> *How happy I am that you have found such a man as Will Thatcher. Mama, Faith, and Vi—even Ed—all have written and confirmed what your letters tell me. I only wish I could be there with you in body as well as spirit to see you join your life with Will's.*
>
> *I won't give any advice. I know you well enough to realize you would never consent to marry anyone you didn't love next only to our Lord, as I do my husband.*
>
> *Be sure to remember every detail so you can write to me later. I wouldn't trade my life for anything but sometimes Panama feels a world away. I do have some exciting news. If all goes well we may get home for a visit later in the summer. Don't tell anyone. If we can't come, we don't want the family disappointed.*
>
> *Trinity, if you ever discover even half the joy I've found in my marriage, you will be blessed. I pray for you and love you,*
> > *Your sister,*
> > *Hope*

Trinity folded the letter in its original creases and hid it in the folds of her gown. Will's face swam in the still morning air, sometimes laughing, often poignant, always filled with love. Humility wrapped her like a soft quilt. What had she ever done to deserve such a lifetime companion? Caught in her memories, her eyes flashed when an incident last night came to mind.

Couldn't Mamie ever say anything nice? Trinity unwillingly remembered the frivolous girl's parting shot before she took her tiresome self home and stopped pestering the bride-to-be half to death. "Well, it's nice you're getting married," Mamie condescended. "Will's a good catch." She shrugged in the maddening way she had. "Of course everyone knows when you get a husband you lose a sweetheart," she smirked. "Not me." Trinity prepared to do battle, indignant at the idea. Fortunately, Grandma Clarissa, who continued to be as spry as ever and thought Will the best man in Cedar Ridge, called from upstairs and Trinity left Mamie in the hall.

"I won't lose a sweetheart," Trinity whispered. "Oh, I know we'll change over the years but I'm sure Will will always be as much in love with me as I am with him." She stirred restlessly in the chair and Faith moved slightly. "Besides," Trinity whispered again, "I know You brought us together, Lord. With You as the head of our home, we can face what the future brings."

She had only a moment longer to cling to the past, blend it into the present, and leave the future in God's hands. When Faith yawned and sat up in a sleepy trance, Trinity's reverie had ended.

"How long have you been awake?" Faith mumbled.

"Not long." Yet Trinity had the sense of having been awake for an eon; she had seen herself grow upward toward the person God longed for her to be.

"Dearly beloved, we are gathered together . . . ."

Clad in a silky white gown, handmade by her mother, Trinity stared through her misty veil.

Bzzzzz. Bzzzzz.

Good heavens! Why had they decided to be married beside an open window with the climbing, blooming roses just outside?

Bzzzzz. Bzzzzz. A bumblebee, drunk with pollen from the sweet pink blossoms, dizzily lurched around Reverend Edmund Mason's head. Not by look or word did he acknowledge its presence.

Trinity glanced down then stole a peek at Will by her side, so fine in his new dark blue suit. A muscle twitched in his cheek and she knew he wanted to laugh as hard as she.

Bzzzzz. Bzzzzz. The bee divebombed once more then flew its tipsy way back out the window and into the roses. Family and friends gave an audible sigh of relief and Trinity could finally concentrate on her wedding service.

"Do you, William, take this woman . . . ?"

"Do you, Trinity, take this man . . . ?"

A gold ring slid onto her finger. Will's familiar brown hands rested lightly on her shoulders as he drew her to him. "Trinity, my wife," he whispered, and then kissed her.

Unlike most weddings where the bride and groom stay to open gifts, Will and Trinity discarded their finery and donned riding clothes less than an hour after the wedding. Many miles lay between them and the place Jimmy would meet them with the horses. Curtis would ride Grandy back to the ranch.

"I wish Jimmy could have been at our wedding," Will said wistfully when he climbed into Pa's old car after ushering Trinity into the middle and leaving the passenger side for Pa.

"It would be hard for Jimmy to be at your wedding and still have those ponies waiting for you." Pa's candid blue eyes twinkled. "Unless he could fly. Besides, I'll be glad for his company on the way back." He suddenly got down to business. "Exactly when do you want us to come meet you?"

"Two weeks from today." Will's delighted grin showed all the anticipation Trinity felt.

"Two weeks it is." Pa yawned. "Now if you folks don't mind, I'll catch me a quick nap. We're going to be late getting home tonight." He pulled his hat over his face and tactfully left the newlyweds to themselves for most of the long drive to the meeting place.

"What if Jimmy isn't there?" Trinity ventured.

"He will be." Will slid one hand from the wheel and took hers. "I've never known Jimmy Crowfoot to fail anyone once he gave his word. Wish I could say the same for others."

Jimmy, Bullet, Cloud the single-footer mare, and the pack pony waited at the beginning of the trail leading into the mountains. Pa and Jimmy wasted no time on long goodbyes but headed back as soon as they unloaded the gear. "Two weeks," Pa reminded. "God bless." He raised one hand and put the car in gear. Its motor died away in the distance and Will and Trinity stood surrounded by the green of towering pines, salmonberry, elderberry, and thimbleberry bushes, devil's club, and nettles Will warned her not to touch.

"Where do we go from here?" Trinity's heart beat fast. What did one say to a brand-new husband, anyway?

She settled down when he assumed his role as wilderness guide. Matter-of-factly he said, "There's a good spot just a few miles up the trail, right near a rushing, white-water stream and level enough to set up camp." He glanced at the sun. "We've just about enough time to make it."

How could she feel strange when Will was the one with whom she had begun a new part of her life? They rode hand in hand and the spot he'd described more than lived up to her expectations. By the time they'd eaten the good supper Ruth Thatcher had so thoughtfully packed, darkness threatened. Yet close in the circle of Will's arms, Trinity felt she could face any darkness. "Determined guardian," she murmured, content just to watch the fire die and the stars peer down through the treetops.

"Who, me?" he teased. "If wild animals come around in the night, I expect my new wife to protect *me*." His laugh rang out in the magic clearing. "Haven't you ever hear the story of Betty and the Bear?"

Trinity raised one sleepy eyelid. "I don't think so."

"Well, then, I'll have to educate our schoolmarm," he drawled. Releasing her, he sprang to his feet. "Now I want you to know this isn't the most classy in my repertoire but you may enjoy it." Dramatically, using exaggerated gestures, he recited "Betty and the Bear"*

> *In a pioneer's cabin out West, so they say,*
> *A great big black grizzly trotted one day*
> *To lap the contents of a two-gallon pan*
> *Of milk and potatoes—an excellent meal—*
> *And then looked about to see what he could steal.*
>> *And the lord on the mansion awoke from his sleep,*
>> *And, hearing a racket, he ventured to peep*
>> *Just out in the kitchen to see what was there.*
>> *And was scared to behold the great grizzly bear.*
> *He screamed in alarm to his slumbering frau,*
> *"There's a bar in the kitchen as big as a cow!"*
> *"A what?" "Why, a bar!" "Well, murder him then."*
> *"Yes, Betty, I will if you'll first venture in."*
>> *So Betty leaped up, the poker she seized*
>> *While her man shut the door and against it he squeezed.*
>> *As Betty laid on the grizzly her blows—*
>> *Now on his forehead and now on his nose—*
>> *Her man through the keyhole kept shouting within,*
>> *"Well done, my brave Betty, now hit him again.*
>> *"Poke with the poker, poke his eyes out."*
>> *So with rapping and poking poor Betty alone*
>> *At last laid Sir Bruin dead as a stone.*
> *Now when the old man saw the bear was no more,*
> *He ventured to poke his nose out of the door.*
> *And there was the grizzly stretched out on the floor.*

---

* Author unknown.

> *Then off to the neighbors he hastened to tell*
> *All the wonderful things that that morning befell;*
> *And he published the marvelous story afar how*
> *"Me and my Betty jist slaughtered a bar.*
> *"Oh yes, come and see, all the neighbors have seed it,*
> *"Come and see what we did,*
> *"Me an' Betty, we did it."*

With a final, stagey pose, Will stood statuelike. Trinity pleaded between peals of laughter, "Oh, Will, stop! I ache." She held her sides and rocked back and forth. "Has any bride ever been quoted to like this before?"

When their shared joy dwindled to occasional spasms, Will knelt by her side and took both her hands.

"I never dreamed I could love anyone the way I love you, Mrs. Thatcher," he whispered. "Someday I'll quote other poems, ones about love." Even the dying light couldn't hide the blueness of his eyes. "Tonight I'll just say I've never known such a good pal as well as a sweetheart. I'm just sorry we can't live as long as people did in Old Testament days so you would be my wife for centuries and not just years."

Trinity nodded and said brokenly, "I can't even tell you how much I care, Will." She leaned against his shoulder and the round, white moon poured light into the little glade.

Chapter Eleven

Trinity sniffed then opened her eyes. Where on earth was she? Gradually she came awake enough to identify her forested surroundings. *Fine thing,* she chided herself. *Sleeping late on your honeymoon.* She scrambled into her warm outdoor clothing wondering where Will might be. Signs of his early rising to provide luxury in the wilderness brought a delighted smile.

A heavy Dutch oven on a bed of coals sent forth the smell of baking biscuits. A string of mouth-watering trout delicately browned above more coals. A coffeepot sang and enticed. Two camp plates, crude cutlery, and tin cups waited on a large stump carefully covered with a cloth. Too tempting to miss, a bowl of wild strawberries almost as large as the ones in the garden at home rested nearby.

"Manna in the wilderness," she exclaimed. If all of married life proved so unexpectedly satisfying, Trinity could ask for no more.

"My goodness! Even a boudoir." She giggled at the pan of hot water, wash dish, new soap, and washcloth and towel on another stump. Glowing from a final splash of ice-cold stream water on her face, she braided her hair into one fat plait that would be out of the way. Will had warned of a long ride ahead.

"Morning, Mrs. Thatcher," Will said eyeing her in approval, his cheeks as scarlet as her own.

"I could have made breakfast." She grinned. "Can't say I'd have provided so lavishly, though. Is it ready?"

"All done but our blessing." He took her hand, bowed his head, and repeated the blessing she'd heard his father give. Then Trinity ate until she was ashamed.

"It's the fresh air," Will excused her, but she caught his delighted grin.

"Of course." She sprang up. "I'll do the dishes while you get the horses ready."

The first morning set the pattern. "I like doing camp cooking," Will insisted. "Once we get home, everything in the kitchen's your department—except for the rocking chair like we have at home. For as long as I can remember, Pa's sat there at the end of the day so he could be with his family before bedtime. He says it irons out the day's wrinkles."

"I like that." Trinity looked up from her dishwashing. She could already picture Will in a rocker in their own kitchen while she set bread or oatmeal for the next day.

"Curtis and Andrew nicknamed our new little home the Doll House," Will told her, busy with bit and bridle.

Trinity clapped her hands. "I can hardly wait to get settled. After our honeymoon, of course," she quickly amended.

Day after satisfying day Will and Trinity climbed higher and higher. Early on the morning after they reached the high country near Buck Pass, the delighted bride awakened to the sound of bells. "What on earth—"

"Sheep," Will told her.

She struggled out of the small tent they sometimes used in the cold, high altitude and brushed sleep from her eyes. "My goodness!"

As far as she could see, flocks of sheep browsed and moved. Gentle *baaas* rose above the tinkling bells. A fine sheep dog, untiring, made her rounds, searching out frisky lambs or strays. "Just like the Good Shepherd," Trinity said, entranced at the wise dog's persistence.

"Ho!" A clear call split the frosty air and a wiry whitehaired shepherd came toward them, smiling and welcoming visitors to his lofty domain. The peace that comes form working with God's creatures filled his blue eyes and tranquil face and the burr of Scotland touched his tongue. "Will ye be havin' the breakfast wi' me?" he eagerly asked.

Will glanced at Trinity and nodded.

What a breakfast it was with crisp bacon, flapjacks, and rich honey. After they bid their unexpected host farewell, the sole keeper except for the dog of over 1500 sheep, Trinity marveled, "He must get lonely."

"I wouldn't, as long as you were here." The special blue light she loved shone in Will's eyes. She blushed and admitted, in those circumstances, neither would she.

"We'll have to write and tell him he gave us a honeymoon breakfast," she observed but Will laughed and busied himself with taking down the tent.

"He's a canny old man. I'll bet he already knows."

Not a slip of foot or drop of rain marred their mountain trip and on the appointed day when they waited for Pa Thatcher and Jimmy to meet them at the foot of the trail, Trinity sighed. "I hate for it to end. Will, let's come back here every year."

"I just hope we can." He gazed longingly back up the winding, forested trail they'd just descended. His sigh matched hers but he quickly brightened. "Remember, we've the Doll House and Bruce."

"I know and I'm just being selfish." She hugged him. "But if other people weren't involved I'd be perfectly happy to have our shepherd friend's job, at least for the summer."

His blinding smile made her heart flutter.

But all too quickly Will and Trinity were jerked back to reality. Two days after they got home they loaded the wedding gifts the Masons had stored for them, the extra linens for the hope chest, and Will's guitar into Pa's side-curtained car and started for the Doll House.

When they arrived at the ferry to cross the river the ferryman told Pa, who was driving, "Go forward a bit."

Trinity nervously noticed the security bar across the front of the ferry was missing. She held her breath in a dreadful premonition.

The old car rolled forward. Pa reached for the brake, missed it, and hit the gas pedal.

A heartbeat later, the car shot off the ferry, into the river, and sank to the bottom.

Almost before Trinity's mind accepted what had happened Pa Thatcher was washed out of the car and swept away. Will lunged through the side curtains, his iron hands grasping Trinity's full skirts. Coughing and sputtering, he yanked her out of the car and onto the top of the now-settled car. He held her tight against the current that should have been swift and dangerous but now slowly eddied around them. "Thank God the early spring already sent the snow water down," Will gasped.

"Will, your father—" Trinity shook as much from fear now the extreme danger had passed as from the icy river water.

"He's an excellent swimmer." Will's far-seeing eyes scanned the river downstream and his arms tightened around Trinity.

"Here comes help." In a few moments the Indian ferryman lifted Trinity into his canoe, gave Will a hand in, and rapidly paddled back to the shack he used while on ferry duty. Hot coffee and warm blankets plus the warm June day took away much of her chill. The rest dissolved when Pa Thatcher lunged in, bedraggled but safe.

"Got washed down around the bend, about a half-mile, to the sand bar," he explained. "Trinity, Will, I'm so sorry." Unashamed tears sprang into his eyes. "You've lost all your goods."

"We could have lost a whole lot more, Pa." Will's quiet acceptance of things that couldn't be changed comforted Trinity.

So did the response of the Thatchers and their neighbors. That night everyone who lived near gathered at the Doll House for a surprise party, alerted to the young couple's loss by Curtis and Andrew who rode to the different farms. Every family that came brought what they could ill afford to spare. Trinity had to fight inside to protest the generosity she knew would in many cases cause hardship to the givers. She had caught how Will shook his head when she first realized the extent of her new neighbors' caring. All she could do was to spread wide her hands, murmur, "Thank you and God bless you all," then join with the other women in setting out the variety of food they'd brought and adding what she could to it.

Near the end of the evening, little Bruce climbed into Trinity's apron-clad lap. "Now I get to come here, don't I?"

She realized Jamie and the older Thatchers must have prepared him for his new schedule. "Every day until I start teaching in September you'll be here while your daddy works. Then you get to go to school with me." A fleeting gratitude to the school board who had agreed to the plan touched her.

"I'll still take naps at Grandma and Grandpa's." Bruce's eyes closed then opened then closed again as he drifted to sleep.

As Trinity glanced up her gaze locked with Will's much as it had that late-fall evening when they first met. Slow color mounted to her forehead. In the days and evenings they'd spent in the high country Will opened his heart to her about his plans for their family.

"I don't care how soon a—a little one comes along. A girl who looks just like her mother—"

"Or a little Will." Her heart thumped.

Now as Trinity held four-year-old Bruce close to her heart she knew how much their own child would mean, and what a wonderful, devoted father Will would be.

Summer continued in earnest. Trinity formed the habit of getting her work done early so she could spend long afternoons tramping the nearby woods down to the river with Bruce. His sturdy, brown legs trotted after her while she baked, sewed, cleaned, and gardened. Wise beyond his years, once she showed him the difference between weeds and vegetables, his little fingers happily pulled out the pests and he crowed with delight every time Trinity let him pull up early carrots or help her wash the leaf lettuce.

Weeks drifted into months. In August Trinity hugged a wonderful secret to her heart, savoring it alone for a few days until the right time came to share it with Will. One warm evening when they sat on the top step of the Doll House porch, her head on his shoulder, Trinity whispered, "How do you feel about having someone come live with us?" She held her breath and waited.

Will's exasperated laugh doused cold water over her. "Has Andrew been pestering you again? All I hear when I see him is how much he likes it over here and why cant' he be here all the time."

The spirit of mischief marriage hadn't dimmed came fully alive in Trinity. "Oh, I'm thinking of someone younger than Andrew. Much, much younger. Even younger than Bruce."

Will held her at arm's length and his blue eyes questioned. "Who—what—why, Trinity, are we going to have a *baby?*

Even in the laugh that followed she treasured the way he had said "we" and not just "you."

"Early, next spring."

"Yaaaaa-hooooo!" Will hugged then released her and did a dance in the yard that even surpassed the one he had done at the Indian powwow a few weeks earlier. Breathless from the wild contortions, he raced back up the steps and held her until she felt the steady beat of his strong heart.

Hours later, after the first ecstatic reaction, Will and Trinity watched the moon rise and planned for the new life God would send into their keeping.

"Trinity, about Bruce—" Will cleared his throat. "Will you feel like keeping him?"

"Why not?" She looked into his shadowed face. "I thought I could teach until the Christmas holidays. After that, I'll be home anyway." She settled her head back in the hollow of Will's shoulder where it fit so well. "I also thought I'd tell him first so he will feel our new baby is special and part his."

"You darling!" Will stroked the dark brown hair back from her forehead and kissed her temple. "I don't know why God has been so good to me in sending you into my life."

"Once I saw you, no one else mattered at all," she said softly.

"No one else really mattered to me even before I saw you," he responded. "I mean, girls or women."

Trinity smiled into the darkness. "And to think I once felt a little envious of Vi!"

"I won't be a bit surprised if Curtis and Vi make a match of it. I had that in mind when I used to drop by—that, and hoping I'd get word of Miss Schoolmarm Trinity Mason and her doings in the big city," he confessed.

"That mean Mamie said when I got married I'd gain a husband but lose a sweetheart," Trinity said, tightening her hold.

"That's what she thinks." As Will swung her up into his lap, her laugh rang over the moonlit valley and into the tall sentinel trees.

The next day Trinity sat down in the same spot on the top step and took Bruce in her lap. "How would you like to hear a special secret that no one except Will and Doc Ryan and I know?"

"Yes, yes." His eyes shone so like Will's a little pang went through Trinity.

"Many months from now, after the snow comes and goes, God is going to send a new baby to the Doll House," she told him. "A little boy or girl that will live here with us all the time so when you go home to Daddy at night Will and I won't be so lonely."

Bruce thought about it for a moment. "Will I play with the baby when it gets big like me?"

"Of course. I'll need your help a lot since you'll be almost five years older. You'll be a cousin but I know the new baby will think you're more like a big brother."

"I never had a brother. Just Daddy and—" He wrinkled his face trying to remember. "And Mommy-who-went-to-be-with-Jesus."

How glad she felt she had told Bruce over and over about the patchwork quilt and the way dear Sarah explained her leaving him. Her arms tightened around him. "Bruce, maybe someday your daddy will find a new mommy for you and you'll have a brother or sister of your own. Will you like that?"

"Can I still be your baby's big brother?" he asked anxiously.

"We can't get along without you doing that," Trinity reassured.

"Then I think a new mommy might be nice, if I could still come here. I love you, Trin'ty."

"And I love you."

"Don't squeeze me so hard," he complained, but gave her a smile that said he really didn't mind at all. He slid down to run toward a rabbit that had curiously hopped out of a nearby bush and sat watching them with round, interested eyes.

Trinity laughed at his surprised look when the bunny disappeared before Bruce could reach him and counted her many blessings. It seemed odd that a little over a year ago she wondered if life in Cedar Ridge would stifle her. She smiled at the rebellious way she had picked up the torch thrust into her hesitant hands. If only she had known!

A wave of sheer joy washed over and through her. By Bellingham standards, she and Will had little. The hard work with few conveniences had provided a tiny home, yet that home had been furnished with *love*. The work itself brought glowing satisfaction when harvest came, but such joy paled in comparison to being cherished by a husband as Will Thatcher.

Why, she wouldn't trade places with the Queen of England with all her jewels and wealth! At this moment, Trinity Mason Thatcher was the richest woman on earth. Soon Will would bound off the crew bus bearing little resemblance to the knight in shining armor she once dreamed about—at least until he could get washed—but eager to find her waiting. He and Jamie, Trinity, and Bruce would feast on simple fare, much of it grown in her garden or from her well-stocked pantry. After Jamie and Bruce left, a late sunset promised to be spectacular and free entertainment for those who watched.

Pity the person who missed out on life as she knew it! A maple leaf drifted down from the big tree in the yard, fluttered, and lay still. Soon leaves would pack up their green for the year and don autumn coats of yellow, red and orange, russet and gold, and brown. A few months of snow and cold lay ahead, a time of white brilliance and a time for the earth to rest. Then—*spring*.

A new life, a tiny light to be fed, nurtured, and led into a steady flame for the Master.

Trinity bowed her head and thanked God.

Chapter Twelve

Life took on new meaning that fall of 1919. With every stroke of ax or saw, every jar of homegrown vegetables and canned fruit labeled and stashed in the root cellar, Will and Trinity sang and laughed and loved.

The Doll House seemed to attract visitors like honeysuckle attracts insects. For those seeking sympathy and guidance, and the determination to go on and learn to prepare for whatever God had in mind for their lives, Trinity and Will were able hosts. Those who had observed the love in the Doll House and wisely broke off with non-Christian sweethearts couldn't be counted.

If at times Will and Trinity felt their idyll interrupted by too many troubled persons seeking advice or just a listening ear, they smiled and made up for it when they could. Their "Doll House Ministry," as Will labeled it, left them humbled and more determined than ever to use their little home in the service of their Heavenly Father.

But storm clouds beckoned on the horizon.

Old Man Thomas, who had so eagerly bargained with Will for his rundown cabin, experienced a change of heart. Pursing his lips like a drawstring, with a greedy glint he eyed the spotless, charming Doll House and well-tended garden. All summer he'd come for his half of the produce. Now in early October his avarice overcame any scruples he might still have buried beneath his miserly grasping.

One gorgeous Saturday he reined in his horse and sidled up to the Thatchers' open front door. "Anyone home?"

"Come in, come in," Will welcomed. "Just in time for breakfast."

The visitor sniffed and his mouth watered but a single remaining shred of decency wouldn't let him break bread with them. "Naw, thanks. I just stopped by to tell you I need the place back. I 'preciate what you folks've done and all but with winter comin' on I can get a good price so I'm gonna sell." He cackled. "Fact is, it's already been sold. You can have 'til the first to get out."

Thunderstruck, Will stared and Trinity burst into tears. "You mean you've *sold* the Doll House? But you said—you promised—"

"There weren't no papers signed," the crafty old man said. "Don't forget. Be out by the first." He dodged back outdoors and down the steps and hauled himself onto his horse as if pursued by devils. A long whinny and the pounding of hooves showed some uncertainty as to what he thought Will Thatcher might do if he prolonged his visit.

"It can't be true, we shook hands on it." Will's bewildered gaze sought out

Trinity's confirmation. "Hardly anyone signs papers. We've always trusted everyone."

"Oh, my dear." Trinity couldn't bear the desolate look on Will's face. She ran to him and managed to smile through tears that overflowed from a breaking heart. "It's just a house." Only compassion for her tall, suffering husband kept her from wailing. All their hard work, the hours scraping and painting and building, and the shared moments alone and with family and friends rose to haunt her. A little white line came around Will's finely modeled lips and she threw her arms around him. "Please, Will, don't look like that."

For once her entreaty went unheeded. Will remained dazed. "Honorable men don't break their word," he muttered.

With sudden insight Trinity realized that all through life Will would expect from others the total honesty and integrity by which he lived. It wouldn't be the last time he'd be disillusioned. Yet she'd rather have him as he was than a skeptic or cynic.

"It doesn't matter," she told him. "We can be thankful for the time we've had the Doll House. The real tragedy would be if we were like Old Man Thomas. Do you think he won't sometime feel guilty? Miserable at what he's done? I do." She looked into Will's face. "Besides, what's the use of worrying? Why, when Jesus comes for us we're going to be living in a mansion."

In a desperate effort to remove the stricken look from his eyes Trinity freed herself, stepped back, and lifted her skirts. As she curtsied then smiled over one shoulder she said, "Oh, yes. Do come in, everyone, and see what our Lord has already prepared."

Still inconsolable, Will turned away and ran outside. The longest hour in Trinity's life crawled by. But when Will came back although his eyes showed the result of struggle, a half-cheery smile and look of peace were evidence of his unconquerable soul. Quietly he took the dishcloth from his wife's hands and seated her in a brightly painted chair by the matching table before sitting down across from her.

"We're going to have to decide what to do." No looking back or screaming against an unkind fate for Will Thatcher.

"I know." Trinity's shoulders slumped but she managed to straighten them.

"First thing, we need to talk with Pa."

How typical! No matter how old the Thatchers got, always the need to talk with Pa remained a vital part of their lives.

The retelling of the story kindled blue fire in Lewis Thatcher's eyes. Ruth Thatcher could not hold her tongue. "That miserable sneak! Not even the decency to warn a body." Her hands punched down bread dough as if she had Thomas pinned to the floury board.

"But where are we going to go?" Will set his lips in a straight line and crossed his arms over his chest.

How alike father and son were, Trinity noticed. One day Will would look as white-haired as Lewis now did . . . and she'd love him even more, if that were possible.

Pa's anger slowly died and a gleam of excitement filled his face. "The good Lord brings good from evil, I reckon." He hooked his thumbs beneath his suspenders. "One of the neighbors asked me just the other day if I wanted to buy his forty acres next to the river. Good bottom land that needs clearing but will raise fine crops. The house is sturdy too."

"I don't know what we'd use to buy it." But Will looked excited. He knew the place well and everything Pa said about it was true.

"We can borrow at the bank. Ma and I'll cosign for you."

Trinity wanted to cry. Leave it to the Thatchers to pour the rain out of the rainbow and make things right.

"How soon could we get in? Old Man Thomas generously gave us until the first to get out of the Doll House." Will's mouth twisted but he managed a reassuring smile for Trinity.

"If necessary you can always move in with us," Ma reminded them, her dark eyes welcoming while her hands formed bread loaves so automatically she didn't have to watch.

"I doubt that you'll need to." Pa rose and stretched. "We'll just go along and see about things now, Will. We can probably sign the papers Monday."

"This time there *will* be papers," Will flared. "Like there should have been before. I was a fool to trust Thomas."

Pa's intense gaze fixed on Will. "The way I figure, son, it's better to trust folks and sometimes have them let you down than to go through this life never trusting anyone."

"He's right." Ma smiled. "And if the milk spills, don't cry over it. Just get a mop and do something about it."

Trinity knew she'd remember Ma's advice when other hard times came. Yet on the last day of the month when she and Will closed the Doll House chapter of their life story, not even Ma's words kept back regret. For Will's sake, she didn't look back, but just tossed her head.

"Well, if you think we made this place pretty, just wait until we get in the bigger house! Your mother's already told me the neighbors ar furious and to expect the biggest house-warming party ever heard of in Cedar Ridge." She linked her arm in his for the walk to their new home by the river.

Hard work lay ahead, not so much in the house but outside. Only a portion of the forty acres had been cleared for crops and Will and Pa spent every spare moment cutting timber to be sold for cash, burning out stumps, and turning the land into rich fields ready for spring planting.

Trinity's schedule proved as busy. Between teaching, cooking, cleaning, and fixing up her house December crept up on her, a time of occasional snow but unseasonably warm. Will rejoiced. The longer a real freeze held off, the easier to till the ground.

"I think you're working too hard," he told Trinity one night. His keen eyes saw the tired droop of her lips when she didn't realize he was watching her.

"I'm all right." Yet pale blue shadows lay under her eyes.

"Are you sure? Maybe you should see Doc Ryan again."

She laughed and a warm flush erased signs of weariness. "He has enough to do without my bothering him." She yawned. "Nothing like fresh air and a good supper to make a person sleepy." She yawned again, and stretched like a lazy cat. "Will, on our honeymoon, you said someday you'd quote some other poetry. Besides 'Betty and the Bear.'"

He left his chair and came to the couch where she'd curled up after supper.

"Good old William Wordsworth said it all." He began softly and tenderly. "'She was a phantom of delight when first she gleamed upon my sight.'" Before Trinity could reply he smiled. "Since we've been married I appreciate some things that come later in the poem. 'A creature no too bright or good for human nature's daily food.'" He took her hand in both of his. "The last lines are the best. 'A perfect woman, nobly planned to warn, to comfort and command; And yet a spirit still, and bright with something of angelic light.'"

Trinity's heart jumped the same way it had when she first saw Will coming down the stairs more than a year before. How wrong Mamie had been! Will remained her sweetheart as well as her husband. A little prayer winged upward from her overflowing heart.

Although she loved teaching at the White Rock School, Trinity rejoiced when the Christmas holidays came. Will had not been the first to notice she looked tired; she had felt that way for some time. Maybe Will was right: The next time they went into town she *would* go see Doc. Probably all she needed was a tonic.

That same night snow came like fleece. All night it silently covered the countryside, softening the naked fields exposed by Will's clearing, and adding jaunty caps to the fenceposts. When the moon finally peeked out to illumine the transformed mountains and valley, more than a foot of fluff clung to the ground.

"How beautiful!" Trinity flung open the front door, heedless of the cold air rushing in. Red spots of excitement colored her cheeks and her eyes danced. When Will protested and closed the door, she washed his face with the handful of white she'd snatched from outside the door.

"Just for that you have to make biscuits for breakfast," he ordered in his best lord-of-the-manor voice then followed her to the kitchen, cut bacon from a big slab, then brought in an enormous pile of wood. "Looks like it may snow again. We might as well be prepared." He grinned and stamped out. "I'll milk the cow and see if there are any eggs."

Trinity sang while she worked. Being snowed in could be fun and give her time to talk with Will. So often they were both tired by the time evening came. Today would be different. She busily planned meals in her mind, simple ones that would cook themselves and leave her free.

For three days it snowed most of the time, sometimes twenty-four inches in twenty-four hours. Will quoted John Greenleaf Whittier's "Snowbound" in his most dramatic style and Trinity marveled again at how a young boy's determination to learn had committed to memory far more than many college professors she knew!

"I'll never forget these three days," Trinity confessed on Christmas Eve afternoon. "I love having our families come—and Bruce—but for once it's nice just to have you." She patted her hair smooth and reached for a warm cap. Although the snow had ceased and the benevolent moon turned the valley to silver, a cold snap crisped the air.

"Will you be warm enough?" Will asked. A little frown crossed his forehead. "I should have gone over earlier and borrowed Pa's car so we wouldn't have to walk. The snow's crusty enough to hold us but it won't hold the horses." He frowned again. "It isn't too late and I know Pa's broken out the lane to the main road."

"For that little way?" Trinity teased. "I'm neither sugar nor salt. Then again, I'm so bundled up I just might melt from all the layers of clothes!" She pulled the bright stocking cap over her hair and buttoned her warm coat clear to her chin.

Ten minutes later as she stood in the crystal night she whispered, "I wouldn't have missed this for anything." She clutched Will's mittened hand with her own and gazing skyward drew in a deep breath. "Can even heaven be more beautiful?"

Will silently shook his head. White-clad trees dripped long, gleaming icicles. Diamond dust sparkled in the moonlight. The howl of a distant wolf and the cry of a lone eagle drifted in the pure air, a psalm of praise to their Creator.

They stood until Trinity shivered in spite of her warm clothing as much from the night splendor as the cold. Will wrapped his arms around her and held his cold cheek next to hers. In a husky voice he said, "We'd better go, you mustn't get chilled."

She turned a reluctant glance at the shimmering night and trotted with him down the cleared lane to the big, noisy house that spilled over with lamplight and laughter.

All evening in the midst of the gaiety Trinity thought of the rare beauty they had been privileged to see. She laughed and ate and exclaimed over the many gifts from the family, secretly proud of the hours she'd spent embroidering pillow cases and making rag dolls and toys for the others. *Here she belonged.*

Later as Trinity and Will walked home neither cold have foreseen the dangers of such an exquisite winter night. As they walked close to the river, the mischievous spirit Trinity had never lost made her break free of Will's protective arm and whirl in a circle in front of him. "Isn't this wonderful?"

"Trinity, be careful!"

His warning cry came too late.

Trinity's right foot slipped on an icy patch. A pulse beat later she fell hard and skidded toward the sluggish water.

"Trinity!" Will leaped for her with incredible speed. He grabbed her coat sleeve and yanked, but not before she'd broken the thin ice and plunged waist-deep into the freezing water.

Will snatched off his heavy coat and bundled it around her legs, caught her in his arms, and staggered toward home in one swift motion. By the time he got her inside their own warm home, Trinity's teeth chattered like hail on a milk can.

"I-I-I'm all r-r-right," she tried to tell him but she couldn't stop shaking. Even a rubdown in front of the glowing fire, her warmest robe, and a steaming mug of hot chocolate did little to melt the cold core inside her.

"It's to bed with you." Will scooped her up and tucked her in. For hours she lay close to him, firmly putting from her mind the terrible fear that attacked when she felt herself sliding into the river. Gradually the shivers stopped and she slept, only to awaken burning hot. "Hot, so hot." Why couldn't she speak clearly? Her tongue felt thick and fuzzy. She flung off the quilts and half sat up.

In an instant Will had her in his arms. "What is it?"

"I'm so hot." She raised one hand to her forehead and licked parched lips.

"You're burning up." Will gently pushed her back on the pillow, then went to the kitchen for a tall glass of ice-cold water.

Trinity eagerly snatched the glass and drained it. "More."

He refilled her glass then brought a basin and soft cloth. He washed her face and hands. "Feel better?"

"Yes." Then why did she feel so dizzy the room whirled? "Will, I think I'm sick."

"Are you in any pain?" His sharp question cut through her semiconscious state.

"No, just tired." She closed her eyes.

"Trinity, I'm going for Ma. I won't be long. Don't get out of bed."

She camouflaged a sob with a croaky laugh. A door opened then closed. She didn't care. Had the house caught fire? She fought the quilts and gave up, too tired to push them away. "God, are You here? I'm so hot. The baby . . .

Jumbled sights and sounds haunted her. Will's voice saying something about a river. Periods of shivering followed by burning up. Something pressing on her chest. Why, where did Doc Ryan come from? Was someone sick?

"Pneumonia." She caught the word then whirled down into a void broken at last by excruciating pain. "Will, help me! God, are You here?"

Something stung her arm. A pungent, smothering cloth fell over her nose . . . then, nothing.

Chapter Thirteen

The strands of sleep that had clouded Trinity's mind one by one drifted away. At last she opened her eyes. She must be late. Why hadn't Will called her? She'd never arrived late to school, even when she was a child. She struggled up and tried to swing her feet out of bed.

"No, Trinity." Will came in from the kitchen, haggard and thinner than she'd ever seen him. He quickly covered her again and sat on the edge of their bed.

"Don't talk," he told her. "You've been very sick but now you're better. Rest, and I'll bring you some broth a little later."

It was enough—for then.

When Trinity woke a few hours later with a clearer mind she lay still, trying to piece together what had happened. Never before had she felt so weak, so like a newborn calf trying to stand on wobbly legs.

Newborn. Panic gripped her. She laid one hand on her flat stomach. Please, God, let me find this is a nightmare, she pleaded and blinked hard.

"Will!" She screamed, and sat up, ignoring the weakness that threatened to claim her again with greedy fingers.

"I'm here." He came to the bed in long strides and took her in his arms.

"The baby, little Will, I—"

"Trinity." His steady grasp on her shoulders kept her from falling. "You've had pneumonia. We all thought we'd lose you." Unchecked tears flowed in furrows down his gaunt face.

"But little Will," she protested, knowing in her heart what she had to hear but unwilling and unable to believe it.

Will's grip tightened. Trinity could see her disheveled self reflected in his eyes. He took a long, unsteady breath.

"He didn't make it, my darling."

She sagged against him. How could life be so punishing? Didn't God love her anymore? What had she done to deserve this? Through her churning thoughts came the invading, terrible truth. "It's my fault." She tore free of Will's arms. "In the woods. I shouldn't have—"

"Listen to me, Trinity Thatcher!" Something in Will's face and his fierce voice stilled her torment. "Have I ever lied to you?"

Surprise jerked her head into a shake.

"Do you believe I ever will?"

"N-no." Why didn't he just go and leave her alone?

Will's eyes blazed and he forced her chin up until she had to look into his face. "Little Will couldn't have lived anyway." The muscles of his strong throat contracted. "Doc Ryan discovered first off when he examined you that the little guy's heart had something wrong with it. Even if he had made it the full time, Doc says he wasn't strong enough to live. Nothing you did changed things except we thought we'd lose both of you."

"Wh-where is he?" The words almost stuck in her throat.

Will's face grayed and he nodded toward the window. To Trinity's amazement the snow had gone. "Out there, beneath the cottonwood."

"Why, how long have I been sick?" Trinity demanded. "I want to hold my baby." She slumped and Will let her down.

"We couldn't wait. We buried him a week ago. You were too sick to—" Will's lips set then he forced a smile. "We gave little Will back to God on Christmas, the same day He sent His Son. It's a new year now, Trinity. God willing, a better one."

Long after he slipped out to do a few chores Trinity lay still. Her empty arms ached for the too-small baby Will had told her about. Dry-eyed, she wondered how she could live. A passionate wave of protest born of sickness and nurtured by loss welled up inside her. "Oh, God, how could You let this happen?" Did she shout or whisper? What difference did it make? Where had God been when she needed Him so much? Why had He forsaken her?

She closed her eyes, willing away the agony. For her husband's sake she must be strong. Could even God help her do this?

Will quietly opened the back door and crossed to the bedroom. "Trinity?"

"Shh." She raised her thin, white hand. "Listen!"

Like a melody from the past, glorious strains of music reached Will's ears. Months vanished. Once again he stood in Ma's doorway, transfixed by an indescribable song. Now it sounded familiar. Swelling, dying, rising again to triumph, it brought healing, even as it had done when Daniel died.

When the last note faded Trinity held out her hands to him. "We can go on." Every trace of bitterness had fled with the music.

"It's what Ma and I heard after we lost Daniel," Will said. He stumbled to the bedside and buried his face in Trinity's lap. Great sobs shook him. All she could do was stroke the thick, waving, golden-brown hair until he stilled. It might be weeks, months, or even years before they could talk about this moment but another strong link in the chains that bound them had been forged by their loss.

Within a few weeks Trinity had regained much of her strength. Yet a little dread filled her. In spite of the comfort received through God's loving mercy, she didn't know how she could face Bruce when he came back to her.

The first time, she couldn't speak. She opened her arms wide and he climbed into them. They rocked silently for a long while before the little boy said, "Daddy told me little Will went to live with Mama and Jesus."

Trinity's arms tightened. "Yes." Warm tears splashed onto Bruce's hand.

"Daddy said heaven's better than here." Bruce wiggled until he could look directly into her eyes. The same blueness that characterized his father and Will demanded her full attention. "He said little Will wasn't strong like me and if he got borned I couldn't play with him when he got big." He hesitated.

"Trin'ty, is Daddy right? Is little Will all better now and does he love Mommy like I love you? Is he happy? Is Jesus glad Mommy and little Will's with Him and God?"

"Of course." Just saying it brought back all Trinity's hope for eternal life.

Bruce wiped away her tears with a grubby little hand. "Then why are you crying?" He anxiously peered into her face, seeking reassurance.

This time the rush of tears healed instead of hurt. Trinity hugged the perceptive little boy who in his own childish way had gone straight to the heart of what life was about. "Sometimes people cry when they're happy and sometimes when they're sad, Bruce. I miss little Will and so does his father, but I'm glad he's well and happy." She took a long, unsteady breath.

"So am I," a voice said.

How long had Will stood in the doorway listening? Trinity wondered.

Bruce slid from her lap and ran to his beloved Will. "Do you cry 'cause you miss little Will?" he demanded.

The tall man caught the little boy up in his strong arms. "Sometimes." Trinity swallowed hard but Bruce hadn't finished. From the shelter of the welcoming hug he looked at Trinity, then back at Will. He patted Will's face and said, "Don't cry, Will. You've still got me. And Trin'ty."

Will pulled him close and his gaze met Trinity's across the loving child's shoulder. "Yes, I do, Bruce, and I thank God."

So did Trinity.

A few weeks later Pa Thatcher crossed the January fields to Will and Trinity's home. "Well, that's good," he said after shrugging out of his coat and seeing the roaring fire in the fireplace. He held his workworn hands to the welcome blaze. "'Pears to me you folks've made this place every bit as cozy as the Doll House."

Trinity looked around in satisfaction. The perky red tiebacks she'd finished just this morning and fastened around the white curtains matched the bright red of their table and chairs. She laughed. "Every time we want to change colors we just paint our chairs and table and find matching strips to tie back the curtains."

"Yellow first, now red. We still have blue and green and orange and purple—"

"Purple!" Trinity swung toward Will in protest. "No purple chairs and table for us. They'd give us indigestion."

"I reckon they might at that," Pa agreed, and his eyes twinkled.

"I don't suppose you walked over tonight just to admire our red table and chairs, now did you, Pa?" Will lounged back in his chair and grinned.

"Well, no." Pa's twinkle faded and he cleared his throat. "I—we—the School Board—" He shot a quick glance at Trinity. "The teacher we got to take your place since you were sick and all isn't working out. Come to find out, the city slicker's letting the big boys get away with all kinds of mischief when they should be learning their lessons. T'other day I drove past and you know what I saw?"

His face turned red with indignation. "There was the teacher chasing around and around White Rock School after one of the boys, and the rest of the school, even the little ones, chased around right behind her like the tail of a kite! I called a special board meeting right away and—" His eyes gleamed. "Let's just say that by mutual agreement we now need a teacher."

Trinity's fingers tightened in her lap. "You need *me*?"

"We sure do." Pa's hearty endorsement ended with a frown. "Now if you feel you can't, we'll understand, but meanwhile our young folks aren't being taught."

"You don't have to go back if you don't want to, Trinity."

She caught Will's anxious glance and thought for a moment. Just this afternoon when she put the last stitches in the tiebacks she'd wondered what to do next. Once her energy returned after her sickness and the loss of little Will, she found herself filling the hours with hard, healing work. Until spring came and she could get out in the garden the barren hours could only bring back the lurking sadness.

"I can start Monday morning," she told Pa and his big smile showed pride in her as well as relief. "I'm sorry my pupils have changed so much in such a short time but I won't take sauciness."

"You don't have to. The troublemakers have been warned that one complaint and they're out."

Trinity felt troubled. "I hope that never happens." In the remaining days she went over her meager wardrobe and prayed for wisdom—and strength—in the new situation.

The new schoolmarm, as Will persisted in calling her, found the boys who had come since Christmas gave her no trouble. Will's own brother Andrew was one of the eighth graders she'd be expected to prepare well enough to put through the state exams. Would the fun-loving boy take advantage of how well he knew her and the hours they'd enjoyed together at the Doll House? She couldn't help asking Will about it.

"Ha! Pa told Andrew he'd be in real trouble if he got out of line. Besides, he thinks too much of you to be a nuisance."

Will's prophecy came true. Not only did Andrew call her Mrs. Thatcher as respectfully as if she hadn't been Trinity to him for months, he excelled in his studies, especially in mathematics. A few weeks after Trinity began teaching the White Rock pupils, a group of neighbors came to school one morning with a problem

"We have a piece of land that needs splitting up," one of them said scratching his head. "Now it has a creek and trees and—" He went on to explain all the factors. "We just can't figger how to cut it in pieces and be fair to everyone." He smiled at Trinity. "Most of us didn't have the chance to get past third or fourth grade. D'you s'pose some of your class can help us out? We're offering a brand-new twenty-dollar bill to whoever solves the problem." His grin broadened. "Mayhap it'll have to be you, teacher."

"Oh, I'd like our class to try first," she told him. The older pupils' eyes shone at the mention of twenty dollars. What couldn't they buy with it!

"Now what we need's a dee-tailed written-out way to split up the parcel of land," the spokesman said. "This is what we've got." He took a piece of chalk and drew a rude sketch outlining the land and its features on the blackboard behind Trinity's desk. "Remember, it has to be fair to all four of us." He dusted his hands off on his overalls. "When can we get an answer?"

"Today's Monday. Give us until Friday." Trinity shook hands with each of the visitors and then turned to her class. "How exciting! I hope many of you will try to earn the prize. Copy the picture to take home and good luck."

Tuesday morning Andrew Thatcher burst into the one-room school waving a piece of paper. "I've got it, Mrs. Thatcher, I mean, I have it," he quickly corrected himself. His dark eyes inherited from his mother sparkled and his white teeth shone.

"So soon? Oh, Andrew, I'm afraid you worked too fast."

He shook his head emphatically. "Look, each of the families should have some trees and access to the creek and a field. See how I did it?

Trinity gasped. With painstaking care, the tall boy had accurately pinpointed the only way the property could be divided without sacrificing one thing in favor of another. "Good for you," she burst out. "I believe that twenty-dollar bill is already yours."

"I hate to wait 'til Friday," Andrew admitted, and sat down behind his desk to wait for the rest of the pupils to arrive.

"So do I." Trinity laughed with her star mathematics student.

She had barely rung the bell on Friday morning before the four men returned. "I hear tell by the grapevine we've got ourselves a winner," their leader announced. He and the other men gathered around Trinity's desk and looked over the many suggestions given, sometimes nodding but always going on.

Andrew's solution, written clearly and in simple, explanatory language, came last. The minute the men saw it a grunt of approval told the waiting class the verdict.

"Now why didn't *we* think of that?" One strong farmer shook his head.

"'Cause we ain't eddicated," another said.

Trinity caught the wistfulness in his voice. "There are many kinds of education, gentlemen. You know crops and weather and the land better than most who have heads stuffed with book knowledge." She noticed the involuntary straightening of shoulders bent with honest toil. She continued, "You also understand God's creation and His loving care. You've taught your children the really important things in life. I just give them new ways to help solve old problems."

"And we're thankful for that," the spokesman said.

Trinity felt choked up and the wave of applause from her students only ended when the farmer raised one hand.

"Andy Thatcher, we're beholden to you." He carefully folded the paper and tucked it in his pocket. With his other hand he took out the promised twenty-dollar bill and gave it to the excited boy. "You keep right on listenin' to your teacher and your ma and pa and you'll be all right."

Each of the grateful men shook hands first with Andrew, then with Trinity, and left. While the class settled down Trinity asked, "What are you going to do with your money, Andrew?"

His whole face lit up. "Pa needs a new plow but he says he won't take my money, so I'm going to get a horse. Curtis promised if I won the prize he'd give me enough more to get a first-rate horse. It won't be as good as Will's Bullet but it will be all mine. I may even get a colt or a filly and raise it myself."

Trinity congratulated him again and got busy with her lessons. In a considerate gesture, she didn't call Andrew to attention when she caught him gazing out the window. Her spirit empathized with his—already free and racing with the wind, hair flying along with his horse's mane and tail. A surge of longing for spring left her shaken.

But February continued to bring more snowstorms and Will even had to break trail for Trinity to get to school. One night she awakened to a strange whining sound and an unusual smell in the air. She reached out for Will, but the place beside her was empty.

"Will?"

"Here, Trinity," he called from the window.

"What is it?"

"The Chinook wind. Tomorrow the snow will be gone. Feel how warm it is?"

Barefoot, she padded to his side and looked out. Branches swayed against the side of the house and warm, moist air billowed the curtains at the open window. She breathed deeply. How could she have forgotten the Chinook wind, a true harbinger of spring in the Northwest?

All night the Chinook continued and when morning came only stray patches of snow remained, mostly under the shelter of tall trees.

Now a new roaring had replaced the gentle whine. While Trinity dressed and started making breakfast, the sound filled her ears.

"Trinity, come see." Will dashed into the house, full milk pails in each hand. He set them on the counter, grabbed her arm, and hurried her outdoors across the plowed garden spot toward the increasing roar.

They stepped out from trees that hid the view and Trinity stopped short. "My word!"

Where had the friendly river gone, the stream in which she'd often waded? Worse, where had this greedy, sucking brown monster come from, roiling, tossing, bearing mighty downed logs as if they were chips? Jolted by the terrible but compelling sight, she could do nothing but stand and gaze. She had seen what happened when a Chinook wind brought the snow from the encircling hills too fast. Humans in all their wisdom could not control the elements and Trinity shivered and stared at the face of flood.

"I just hope it doesn't get much higher," Will said in her ear.

"Why? You don't mean . . . ." Her voice failed her.

Will's far-seeing eyes and pointing finger stopped her heart. "It's already crept up a foot since we got here. Most of the big log jam is gone." Worry filled his stern face.

Trinity clutched his arm for support and riveted her gaze at the encroaching danger. "It won't take our place. It can't, can it?" she pleaded.

"I pray to God it won't but I've never seen the Cedar so high," he admitted between tightened lips. "We'd better get back and be prepared, just in case."

With a final look at the menacing waters, Trinity stumbled after him back toward their home, too stunned even to pray for deliverance.

Chapter Fourteen

Will checked the rising water every hour, yet every time he came in he had to report it was higher. By noon he no longer needed to tell her: The river had cut to the edge of their garden-to-be and Trinity could see its gleam from their window.

Trinity frantically gathered clothing and dishes, anything she could quickly pack in case they were forced to flee. She prayed as she worked. "God, please make the water recede. We've worked so hard after losing the Doll House — and little Will." Her lips trembled and she refused to look out again, even though the *lap, lap* sound came from the sheet of water that had already reached the barn. She knew the cow was safe, and Will's horse. He'd taken them earlier to the far end of the forty acres. No flood except the one in the time of Noah could reach them there.

Her will power caved in when she heard a crash. She flew to the door and looked out. Empty wooden boxes they'd stacked behind the barn floated like miniature arks. A gray squirrel scolded, rode one until it beached against a fir, and scurried to safety in the top branches.

Will looked ten years older when he splashed back to the porch. Trinity saw how he measured the scant ten feet between the creeping waters and where they stood.

"If it comes five feet closer, we leave. Have you got things ready? Pa's on his way with the car."

"Yes, all I could. I stacked the chairs on top of the table in case water and mud come in the house and took up the rugs in the bedroom." She tried to smile and knew how weak it must look. "If it isn't Old Man Thomas, it's something else."

"We still have each other—and God, no matter what happens."

"I know." She put her arms around him, feeling ashamed. For a moment she closed her eyes against the relentless flood. When she opened them, she blinked twice. "Will, I think it's receding!"

He tore free of her grasp and whirled. Joy lit up his face. "You're right, thank God!" Arms around each other they watched the Cedar River move back inch by inch, as if angry at being cheated of its prey. Although the ground remained sodden, by night Trinity could no longer see the water. She thanked God again.

March stormed its way in and out; April bloomed and so did Trinity. If what she suspected were true, soon she'd have wonderful news for Will but she must wait a few weeks to make sure.

Doc Ryan confirmed her suspicions and in late May Trinity cooked a special supper on a Saturday night. Jamie and Bruce still ate with them Mondays through Fridays and, dear as they were, her news must first be shared with Will.

"Do you know you get prettier all the time?" Will asked when after supper they walked the greening fields, already showing signs of early garden produce planted after the flood.

"Do I? I'm glad you think so." Trinity breathed in the fresh April air and led him to a downed tree stump. "Will, something good has come from all our sadness. We're going to have a child."

Will looked at her and then did an Irish jig in the clearing. A passing night hawk paused in flight, and seemed to cry out congratulations.

"When?"

"Probably early January." Will lifted and whirled her and then held her a little way off from him. "God is good." His tender smile curled into her heart and warmed it.

A little later she tremulously asked, "Do you want a boy?" She saw the quick flash of pain before he whispered, "I don't care. Just as long as our baby's healthy."

Time seemed to fly after Trinity finished out the school term, and spent a happy, dreaming summer working with Will as much as he allowed and sewing garments for the new spark growing within her. She often thought of the tiny soul that had come and gone without her ever seeing him, but she rejoiced knowing that, through God's love, someday they would be reunited. Now a new child must claim her attention.

"Will, I'd like to name our baby Candace if it's a girl," she said one day in early fall. "I looked it up in that old book Vi still has and Candace means 'glittering' or 'flowing white.'" She bent her head. "But I want to call her Candleshine, just in the family."

"Suits me." Will looked puzzled, however, and Trinity tried to explain.

"I keep feeling God and my ancestors who served Him expect me to hold high the torch they've passed to me." She let her hands rest in her lap. "Sometimes my torch isn't very bright and I wonder if it's gone out. Then, like the flame of the smallest candle, it keeps burning but it needs to be carefully tended. Today while I was reading my Bible I found a verse I'd never seen before, or at least I don't remember it."

Trinity reached into the modest V-neck of her printed gown and withdrew a small paper tucked just above her heart.

"'*For thou wilt light my candle; the Lord my God will enlighten my darkness.*'" She refolded the paper and replaced it in her dress. "It's Psalm 18:28 and it's almost like David wrote it for me." Her long lashes sparkled in the firelight. "I know without God I—we could never have made it through the last year."

"Candleshine she shall be. If it's a boy, how about Daniel Edmund?"

"Doesn't Pa want us to use his name?" Trinity asked.

Will shook her head. "I already mentioned it but Pa said he'd rather we used Daniel. What does that mean, anyway?"

Wrinkling her forehead to remember, Trinity finally said, "It means 'God is my judge.'"

"Good enough." Will stretched and yawned. "Well, Mrs. Thatcher, five o'clock comes mighty early. Let's go to bed."

Thanksgiving came and went, a time of harvest and praising God. Christmas neared, not white and frozen like the year before but rainy and gray. Yet no gray existed in Will and Trinity's world. Doc Ryan pronounced her in excellent health and the baby's heartbeat sound and strong.

Before Christmas Trinity awakened in the night and for a moment she felt the past year had been a dream. Pain clutched at her as it had then.

"Will, I'm really sick."

"The baby? It's too early, isn't it?"

"Yes, you know I'm not due until January." A spasm caught her and she gripped his strong arm. "Go get your mother. I don't think I can hold off until Doc comes."

Will leaped into his clothes and tore out the door. Again Trinity heard the sound of racing hooves. She fought fear that attacked even sooner than the premature pains. "God, don't let it be like before!"

Incredibly, Ruth Thatcher appeared by the bed, her clothing askew but the certainty of her own skill plain on her face. In quiet tones she told Will what to do and encouraged Trinity. "So what if the baby's early? Maybe you didn't figure right. Or perhaps the little one's tired of doing nothing but sleeping." Her soothing flow relaxed the struggling girl and in less than an hour a lusty yell told Trinity everything was all right.

"A girl! Candace or Candleshine," Will whispered. Ma quickly cleaned and wrapped the baby while Will mopped Trinity's hot face. Bathed, powdered, and in a clean gown and freshly made bed, Trinity held her tiny, perfect girl. A final wail broke off sharply and, minutes later, the newest Thatcher fell asleep, filled and content.

Doc Ryan arrived a few hours later and his beaming face resembled nothing more than the rising sun. "Don't know why you called me," he grumbled in mock disgust. "Ruth Thatcher's as good as a doctor any day. Sorry your own ma couldn't be here, though. She's another dandy when it comes to bringing babies."

Trinity smiled at Mama who had ridden out with the doctor. "She's staying for a few days until I can care for our baby."

Mama's slow smile showed the new bond between them. More than mother and daughter, the two women now shared an interest in the blanketed bundle at Trinity's breast.

A few days later when Will had gone to work and Candace lay asleep in the handmade cradle Pa had once fashioned for little Will, Mercy Mason was alone with Trinity. "Trinity, there's something I have to say to you."

It had been years since she used that no-nonsense tone of voice to her grown daughter. Trinity couldn't imagine what Mama had in mind.

"It's about Candleshine." Already the family had begun to use the nickname instead of the more formal Candace. "Now, I know how hard it is to lose a baby." Her face shadowed and Trinity remembered the little one that came after Albert and before Robert William. "The hardest thing I've found in raising Rob is in not trying to smother him."

A rush of understanding came to Trinity. "You mean, once you've lost one, it's natural to be too protective?"

"Yes," Mama sighed, "It isn't good for mother or child to have so much concern neither one can grow." Her smile brightened the whole room. "Enough said. Now, what did you want me to get ready for supper?"

Long after Mama went back to tend her own happy, noisy family, Trinity thought about what she'd said. It made sense. But had the warning come in time? Already Trinity had held her breath and checked on Candleshine again and again just to make sure she was all right. Will laughingly threatened to kidnap Candleshine and bundle her off to his parents so his wife could get some rest.

"Lord," she suddenly prayed. "This is Your child, the candle You lit and sent to shine in our lives. Forgive me for my fears. Help me trust You. I give this child's life to You. In Jesus' name, Amen."

Trinity never forgot either the prayer or the promise she made on that winter day. Every time Candace coughed or cried, the young mother reminded herself that God controlled the beautiful child. In time, it became such a habit that even when real danger threatened, she could rely on the ingrained faith won by persistence and prayer.

The baby grew like rushes in a swamp. At a year old, she toddled after six-year-old Bruce the way a caboose chases a long train. "Big Brother Bruce" loved his tiny cousin even more than he loved going to school. From his first glimpse to make sure the new baby really *was* all right, he hung on the crib, talked to the child, and adored her. Even when his father Jamie married a kind-hearted neighbor woman whose heart proved big enough to accept both Jamie and his son without question, Bruce spent as much time with Trinity and Candleshine as possible. His new stepmother Charity didn't have an envious bone in her body and openly rejoiced at the unusual bond that existed between Bruce and the other Thatchers.

Sometimes when no one could hear, Trinity sighed. No more babies had come and Doc Ryan said he suspected none would. *If only she could have given*

Will a son! Yet he worshiped his daughter next to God and his wife. Jamie graciously consented to Bruce tagging Will, and the tall man, stripling boy, and tiny girl became a familiar sight. Often Trinity accompanied them on tramps, but even when she had inside chores, pride lifted the corners of her mouth.

One late afternoon she dropped to a chair on the porch and took stock. She thought of gentle Faith, now happily married and living within riding distance. Donald McKenna had proved to be the fine man Trinity recognized so long ago and a baby would be arriving soon to complete their household.

Hope and her John remained in Panama. The trip Hope promised long ago had been delayed by the birth of a daughter—also named Hope—but the past summer the three had finally come home. What a glorious reunion!

Edmund found a special Christian girl and had recently purchased a small home in Cedar Ridge.

Albert liked school, the outdoors, and trains, hoping someday to "drive a ying-yanger." When he wasn't busy with studies and chores and playing ball, he spent every free minute with the engineers and firemen asking all sorts of questions.

Rob continued healthy, but Grandma Clarissa did not. Every time she saw her little grandmother Trinity felt happy and sad at the same time. Grandma Clarissa had prepared to meet her God. The radiance of her thin face and wrinkled cheeks showed more clearly than words her longing to answer God's call when it came time to be with her husband.

Once Trinity found Grandma Clarissa alone in the twilight. She took the worn hand and impulsively asked, "Grandma, if you could live life all over again, what would you want changed or do differently?"

A final ray of sun gleamed in the soft, white hair, lingered on the wise eyes, and highlighted a face at peace.

For a long moment Grandma didn't answer. Then she patted Trinity's hand with her free one. "Why, child, how could I ask for things to be different when our Heavenly Father has walked with me every day of my life?"

She leaned her head back on the crocheted chair cover and gazed into the sky. "Many times I cried out for answers when trouble came. Sometimes I forgot to thank our Lord for His mercy. Yes, I would have changed things to suit myself, especially when your grandfather died." Her lips trembled and Trinity thought she looked like a young girl.

"You still miss him, don't you?"

Clarissa squeezed her granddaughter's hand. "Every day since he went ahead the way he used to do when we walked brushy trails and he cleared the path for me to follow." Her unsteady voice told its own story.

"Child, it's the hard times that bring you together—and the little things. You told me once that one of the greatest gifts Will ever gave you was when he built a sleeping porch on your home." She smiled at Trinity again. "You've learned the secret of real happiness. It's in sharing whatever life offers and going on when you aren't sure you can."

"Ma Thatcher says instead of crying over spilled milk we have to get a mop and do something about it," Trinity said.

"She's right." The frail little woman sat up straight and strength seemed to flow from her to Trinity. "A body who sits around and moans too long about things that can't be changed is a disgrace to God."

"Grandma!" Trinity had never heard such a statement from her gentle grandmother.

"It's true. We're supposed to have faith. How do you think God feels when we snivel and complain instead of hanging onto His coattails for dear life until He makes things better?"

Trinity tucked away the startling piece of advice in her workbox of memories. When needed, she would examine and test it for herself. "Grandma, will I ever be as good as you?"

"Land sakes, Trinity, if you don't make a heap better job of living than I've done, what will happen to that torch I passed down? It's up to every generation to raise truth higher and brighter . . . for the times ahead will be dark, as dark as that."

She pointed into the blackness that had fallen and Trinity shivered at the certainty in her grandmother's voice.

Chapter Fifteen

The first of Grandma Clarissa's "black times" arrived late in 1929. Caught up in the changing seasons, and watching Bruce and baby Candleshine grow the Thatchers and Masons paid little head to the larger world except to shake their heads at the painted flappers and news of gangsters, bootleg whiskey, and speakeasies. More interest lay with the wave of revival meetings sweeping the country. Billy Sunday, a baseball player turned evangelist, became the most popular religious leader of the time. Some said during his ministry he preached to over 100 million and saw over a million converted to Christ!

Grandma Clarissa died when Candleshine was still small, but her excitement over going on lessened the sadness of those left behind. Her passing seemed to increase their determination to live for Jesus and join her someday.

Fourteen-year-old Bruce and nine-year-old Candleshine surprisingly kept their special friendship. Trinity sometimes despaired of her daughter ever being anything but a tomboy. Time after time she answered a cheerfull call and found Candleshine nonchalantly hanging upside down from a sturdy tree branch, or with Bruce playing marbles. After a battle royal before Candleshine entered first grade, already reading and eager to learn more, Trinity accepted the inevitable. Later she would laugh about it, but the day Candleshine made her own little declaration of independence was *not* funny.

Grandma Mercy loved the flaxen-haired little girl and was loved in return, but not enough for Candleshine to suffer the indignity of having her hair fixed in long curls for school.

"I don't like curls," she told her grandmother and shook her head. "They get in the way when I play."

"You look lovely," said Grandma finishing her handiwork with a huge blue bow.

A half-hour later when the house felt too quiet Trinity looked around for Candleshine. She finally found her—huddled in the warm triangle made by the kitchen wood range, scissors in hand. A pile of shining curls lay scattered over her lap and the floor.

"Candleshine, what a naughty thing to do!" Trinity exclaimed.

Unrepentant, her five-year-old muttered, "I don't like curls."

The next morning all Trinity could do with the jagged hair was pull it back into two skimpy pigtails so tight Candleshine felt her eyes slant. Never again did her mother or grandmother put curls in the fair hair.

When Wall Street crashed and the world panicked, Will and Trinity wondered how it would affect them and those they loved. Before long, they found out.

Many of their friends and neighbors who depended on now-closed banks lost everything, took what they could get, and moved away in search of nonexistent work. Trinity's heart ached and the dread she'd felt years before when her grandmother predicted hard and dark times almost overwhelmed her. Only her faith in God and love for her family kept her going.

Months passed. Will took on every job he could find but times got even worse. Now Trinity's early training served her well. Will's worn coats and pants became treasures to cut down and sew into clothing for Candleshine. Along with floursacks bleached for underclothes and knitted mittens, Trinity's knack with fancy stitches added flair to the garments. Yet even her talents couldn't stop the juggernaut of poverty rolling over the land. Trinity shared her distress in a letter to Hope.

> *Although I have time, I can't mail this letter right away. Frankly, my dear sister, I have neither a postage stamp not the money to buy one. At least we have plenty to eat from our garden. Our cows and chickens supply us well and Will killed a deer not long ago. He brings in fish once in awhile when he has time.*
>
> *Yet we are wondrously happy. Candleshine is long-legged, knobby-kneed, and sweet-tempered. I just pray for all those who have so much less, the ones who fight over garbage in the cities.*
>
> *We try to help where we can. Will has told many of the townspeople who are down and out they can come help themselves to our garden surplus. But Hope, can you believe only one family came? The others complained and asked why Will couldn't load up the produce and deliver it to their doors!*
>
> *He replied that he's working day and night for his own family and if they're too blasted lazy to walk or ride out and get food they'll just have to do without. I don't blame him.*

There was more, but Trinity had to hold her letter for over a week until Will brought home a little cash earned by hauling wood.

Trinity scrupulously kept track of every penny he earned. Ironically, now when they needed money so badly, the teaching doors had closed for her. School boards told her pointblank they regretted it but jobs must go to men who had families to feed. She could understand, even while wondering what would become of them. During the worst year of all, Trinity discovered on the last day of December Will's earnings for twelve-hour days, not counting the farm chores she and Candleshine couldn't handle, amounted to only fifty dollars. Fifty dollars—to stretch for things they couldn't raise or do without! To make matters worse, Edmund Mason fell ill and died. Mercy Mason had barely enough money to keep herself and Rob, the only child left at home. Will insisted on helping all they could.

Trinity never forgot her mother's tear-stained face, surrounded by a wreath of white hair, when she poured out her heart. "It's so terrible. Every month a rude, demanding letter comes from the undertaker. He knows I'm paying everything I can! I've even dreamed that Edmund returned and confronted the man, demanding that he stop persecuting us."

Yet somehow they lived through it all. If Trinity's torch of hope flickered and almost went out, knowledge it had been lit and placed in her hands by God kept her from total despair. Even when they could no longer make payments on their home and forty acres now under cultivation, the belief that God would never forsake them upheld her—and Will.

"I'll go see Pa," Will said when he told her the bad news.

Her mind flicked back. The very predictableness of Will's response offered security.

A month later, Will and his family moved their remaining possessions into their new home, the White Rock School in which Trinity had once taught! Situated on land donated by Pa Thatcher years before, the building belonged to him as well. When the schools consolidated and forced all students to attend school in Cedar Ridge, the building had reverted back to the Thatchers. Pa remodeled the one-room school into a huge kitchen and dining room. The old cloak room became a bedroom and he built on a living room and two more bedrooms, plus a wide front and small back porch. The two acres had sandy soil, stumps, and rocks. Subject to vandalism from standing empty it also had broken glass. Trinity raked and Will hauled away loads of debris to make the new place safe. Candleshine pulled weeds and rejoiced. This home was much closer to Jamie, Charity, Bruce, and his stepbrother and stepsister who had completed their family.

One evening when Trinity felt even her bones would protest if she took one more step, Will found her curled in an old chair on the porch. The sounds of Bruce and Candleshine's voices drifted out from a game they played at the kitchen table.

Will silently dropped to another chair and let himself relax. Nightbirds cried mournfully as the first star came out, then another. "Well, one thing about it. When things hit bedrock, the only place they can go is up."

Trinity looked into the now-spangled sky and reached for his hand. "I know. One of these days something wonderful will happen. I've been feeling it for a long time." She tightened her hold, feeling the calluses formed by the many garden hours she had spent to save Will from the extra work.

"I hope so." Will closed his eyes. A few minutes later his hand fell from Trinity's and she realized he had fallen asleep. With a tender smile she slipped into the house for a worn blanket and covered him then returned to her chair to keep vigil in the soft night air.

Threads of silver glinted in Will's tossed hair, Trinity observed, as once again her heart swelled with gratitude for his relentless devotion. Once in a long time she thought of John Standish and his proposal that seemed a century ago. Most likely his wheat kingdom had survived. Still, the kingdom he'd offered could not compare with her own humble domain.

A few weeks later, Will burst in looking younger than he had in years. "I've got a job. A real, pay-for-sure job!" He caught his wife and did his own version of the Highland fling.

Breathless and laughing, Trinity demanded, "Where? How?"

"The WPA* Works Progress started by President Roosevelt is going to build a new high school in Cedar Ridge. I've been hired as a laborer to haul concrete. A regular paycheck instead of a few dollars here and there! Why, you can buy silk dresses and plan a trip to Europe and—"

"Don't be silly, Daddy." Candleshine appeared in the doorway. "We'll just be glad for you to have a good job." Her lake-blue eyes shone.

But a week later Will trudged in with steps heavier than concrete. He washed up and ate supper in silence. When Trinity began to clean up, he spoke in a low, soft voice. "I may lose my job."

Trinity's hands stilled in her soapy dishwater. "Why?" His look of despair sent a shaft of pain to her heart.

"The foreman ordered me today to water down the concrete."

"I don't understand." She dried her hands and knelt in front of the same kitchen rocking chair that once graced the Doll House.

"Strong concrete calls for a certain percentage of cement which is the fine, gray powder that mixes with water into a bonding material when added to sand and crushed gravel." His troubled eyes looked straight into hers. "If you don't mix it properly, the final product won't wear right. I overheard the foreman talking with one of the men. Seems the more he can keep the cost down, the better job he will be given later."

"But you can't mix concrete that won't hold up," she protested. "Why, it could be unsafe! What if an earthquake came?"

"I need the job, God knows how much." He stood. "Trinity, you'll back me in what I have to do?" He lifted her to her feet.

She bit her lip. In a way it wasn't *his* responsibility. He had to follow orders. But on the other hand . . . .

"I don't think I need any job badly enough to compromise what I believe."

The same integrity she'd seen in the bewildered young married man who

---

* Works Progress (later, Work Projects) Administration.

expected others to live by his inflexible honor reflected in his eyes. "You must do what is right, no matter what happens."

"Thanks, dear one." He kissed her and walked to the door. "Don't wait up if I'm late. I need to think." Yet the sound of his footsteps going out the door and across the porch little resembled the plodding ones when he came home from work.

Will walked across stump-dotted fields, past Trinity's garden, and through neighboring land toward the river bottoms. Cottonwoods swished and willows whispered. Tall grass bent beneath his light steps. When he reached a cherished spot that gave him a view of the river, the valley, and the protecting mountains, he leaned against a tree.

"Well, God, the way I see it I don't have a choice. You know how happy I was to get the job, but I can't go along with cheap work. Maybe You let me have the job so I could stop something bad from happening by speaking up." He raised his stern face to the cloud-clotted sky and hunched hills. "It isn't just Trinity who's supposed to carry Your torch. Now it's my turn." Hours later he returned, quietly undressed, and slipped into bed.

A soft voice said, "There was never any doubt, was there?"

Glad that she'd stayed awake, he whispered, "No," and knew how truly he spoke. "I'll talk to the head man tomorrow—and look for another job the day after."

Trinity giggled. "Don't forget, when we serve God we're never out of work!"

He grinned in the darkness and agreed.

Trinity expected Will home shortly after he reached Cedar Ridge the next day. But the kitchen clock slowly ticked off minutes then hours. Maybe the head man hadn't been on the job. Maybe Will couldn't get him aside and report what was happening. Or—Trinity flinched. Would the foreman retaliate? She finally decided Will had simply given his report and gone out to hunt a new job so she prepared the best supper she could. He'd make sure to be home at the usual time.

Promptly at five-thirty Will marched in the door, grabbed a pan, and poured in hot water to wash. He kept his head down while he muttered, "Well, I'm no longer a laborer."

She had expected it but Trinity still caught back a sigh. "What happened?"

Will soaped and splashed his face then buried it in the folds of a towel. "First thing this morning I told the foreman I couldn't accept his orders. He fired me on the spot." He toweled briskly. "I grabbed my jacket and started to walk away after I told him if he didn't tell the supervisor about making inferior concrete I would. He started yelling and swearing it was none of my business."

Trinity held her breath.

Will's cheeks were pink. "I told him it was every man's business to protect young people's lives. About then the supervisor came tearing up."

"'What the blue blazes is going on here?' he yelled."

"'Thatcher refuses to take orders,' the foreman yelled back."

"'How come? What orders? He's been here all week and knows what to do. Why does he need new orders?'"

Will's eyes started to shine. "The supervisor turned to me. 'What's he talking about?'

"'Ask him,' I said, and the supervisor's gaze bored into the foreman.

"'Beggin' your pardon, Boss, but he's tryin' to get Thatcher to water down the concrete,' one of the builders called.

"'*What?*' I never heard such cussing as I heard from the supervisor." Will couldn't contain his glee. "The foreman couldn't get in one word in his own defense." He threw down the towel and doubled over laughing.

"I don't understand," Trinity told him when he stopped laughing enough to hear. "You said this happened early this morning. Where have you been all day?"

"Working."

"*Working!* Will, you told me you were no longer a laborer." How could he joke, or had he really found another job so soon? God could certainly make a door and open it when needed.

"I'm not a laborer, I'm a *foreman*," Will declared proudly.

Trinity's knees gave way. She dropped into the kitchen rocker and wordlessly demanded an explanation of his crazy behavior.

"Trinity, darling girl, the supervisor had a lot to say about expecting honest work and needing men who weren't afraid to do it. He said he wanted people he could trust when he couldn't be around to check everything out. Then he said, polite as can be, 'Mr. Thatcher, I'd be proud to hire you as foreman for this job. The pay's ten dollars a month more.'

"So I said, just as politely, 'Thanks, Boss. Shall I start now?'" Suddenly the boisterous gladness faded. "I knew God would take care of us but I didn't know how quick He'd do it!"

For the rest of the 1930s Will had work from jobs offered on the strong recommendation of the WPA supervisor.

On a cloudless late spring day in 1938 a little group of Cedar Ridge men visited Trinity while Will was at work. The spokesman of the group went right to the point.

"Mrs. Thatcher, we desperately need you. Now that things are a mite better, folks are pouring into Cedar Ridge bringing their kids. The fact is, we don't have enough teachers and can't get enough good ones. Will you teach in Cedar Ridge next fall? Now that your gal's grown, isn't it time you considered going back to teaching?"

Trinity's brain whirled. She hadn't thought of teaching for a long time. Home and family had kept her busy but what he said was true. Bruce had long since left her care and was in Seattle studying medicine. Candleshine, faithful as ever, declared if he meant to be a doctor, then she'd be a nurse. When Trinity gently tried to persuade her to go into teaching, and shared how Grandma Clarissa had passed on the torch of responsibility to others, Candleshine's eyes glowed.

"Mother, I'll carry the torch! Think of Florence Nightingale, the lady of the lamp. Why, the beams from her light have spread into some of the darkest corners. I can hardly wait to get started."

"She's right," Will chimed in, and Trinity found her eyes wet. She put her hands on Candleshine's shoulders and looked deep into the beautiful, earnest eyes. "Then be the best nurse anywhere," she whispered.

"Well, Mrs. Thatcher, will you at least talk it over with your husband?"

Her visitor's voice brought Trinity back to the present. "Of course." But she still felt dazed when they left, wondering why she hadn't simply said no.

That night after supper she and Will walked down to the river. Trinity stopped to touch a wildflower. "Will, the Cedar Ridge school board visited me today. They want me to teach for them starting in the fall."

He solemnly stared at her, his eyes thoughtful. "Aren't we getting along all right without you having to work?"

She smiled at his initial reaction.

"Aren't you happy at home?'

"No one could be happier." Her lips trembled. "But Will, with Candleshine going away for nurses' training soon, I honestly don't know if I have enough to do to keep me busy now that it will be just the two of us."

Will understood at once. "And even worse, with me gone all day, it's going to be pretty lonesome—not like knowing Candleshine will be home from school in the middle of the afternoon. If you'll be happier, it's fine with me."

"Thank you," Trinity whispered, and leaned against his strength, passionately wishing to hold this moment forever. A combination of expectancy and fear clutched her. It had been years since she'd taught and now instead of all eight grades in a one-room school, she'd teach a combination room of top sixth and seventh graders. She'd need to catch up on changes in education, perhaps take summer school courses in Bellingham. Yet the school board had said not to let modern methods change her own skilled teaching of reading, writing, and arithmetic.

Trinity closed her eyes. This time when she boarded the train for Bellingham, even if only for a month's summer school, would she be better prepared to leave her family than she had been in 1912? What if something happened to Will? Could she stand not being there when he came home from work every night, his blue eyes telling her how much more he loved her?

The unfamiliar verse she had found long ago and made her own whispered in her ears. *For thou wilt light my candle: the Lord my God will enlighten my darkness.* (Psalm 18:28).

If ever the world needed more light it was now. She and Will had studied the rise of the godless dictator, Adolf Hitler. His ruthless motto, "Close your eyes to pity! Act brutally," even now prepared young men for the destruction that must inevitably follow. How could Trinity sit in her cozy home when American young people desperately needed to be taught the values on which their country must stand?

Yes, she must again lift high her torch. Trinity squared her shoulders, breathed a prayer, and surrendered to the future, upheld by Will's love and God's beckoning, cradling hand.

Cottonwood Dreams

Norene Morris

*To my dear husband Paul
who made all my dreams come true.*

Chapter One

Mary Lou Mackey hung her dish towel on its hook and retied the ribbon that bound her long, brown hair at the nape of her neck. Her head turned toward the sound of hoofbeats—Missy coming in at full gallop.

Jenny Wimbley flapped Missy's reins over the rail and ran for the cabin. "Tom wants you to meet him in the cottonwood grove right away. Says it's real important," she announced.

"I can't." Mary Lou's heart sank. "I can't leave Mama alone. She was sick last night. Pa had to get Doc Gray."

The two girls crossed to the bedroom. Ellen Mackey lay asleep, a tiny doll almost lost in the feather tick. Chestnut hair framed her pale, porcelain face. A hint of a smile curved her lips.

Jenny pushed Mary Lou toward the door. "She's sleeping. Go on. I'll stay with your mama."

Jenny sat down in the rocking chair and poked into the large basket on the floor beside it. "I'll just sit here and knit," she whispered. "T'will keep my hands busy. Take Missy and you won't have to saddle Dulcie."

Mary Lou lingered over Mama. She had been sleeping quietly for the past couple hours. Jenny would be here. "I won't be long," she promised.

Mary Lou dug her heels into Missy's side to spur her on. The Kansas wind tore free her ribbon and released her hair to trail out behind like a young colt's tail.

When she neared Point Lane, Mary Lou's heart beat in time with the steady pounding of Missy's hooves. The harvest dance was a week away and Tom had asked her to go with him. She smiled thinking of Tom's long legs and big feet on the dance floor. Could he possibly keep them untangled? Things felt so different when she was with Tom. She would have to ask Mama if these feelings were real love. Mama would know—she loved Pa.

She rounded the bend on Point Lane. Tom and Tinder waited in the shade of the cottonwoods. Mary Lou pulled Missy to a halt and dismounted in a cloud of dust swirls. Tom quickly erased the distance between them and took her into his arms.

His kiss lingered long and sweet. Mary Lou clung to him, relishing the strength of his embrace and the smell of scrub soap, horse, and leather. She tightened her arms around his neck and he swung her around and around. It felt exhilarating. Their gaze clung and they laughed. This had to be real love. Mary Lou could picture herself as Tom's wife, raising his children. Her thoughts shocked her. She blushed and hid her face in his neck. Tom had not told her he loved her. But he had never acted this way either, like she was his. Maybe today.

Tom set Mary Lou on her feet. He raised her hands to his lips and kissed them. His laughter faded. The blue eyes riveted on hers looked serious. "Mary Lou," he spoke her name softly, almost reverently, then shifted his gaze to Tinder, saddled and loaded. "I have to leave this afternoon. To go back to Texas."

Right on cue, the sun sneaked behind a cloud.

"I don't understand. I thought we'd planned to go to the harvest dance. Why?"

Tom stopped her words with a kiss and led her to the fallen log where they had sat two days before and talked about the dance. Facing him, Mary Lou read deep sadness in his eyes. Something must be wrong.

"It's sooner than I hoped. The cattle are railed and I have to report back with the money." He labored over each word.

We haven't made any plans, her heart protested. *We need time to know each other*. Mary Lou opened her mouth, but her dry, tight throat stopped her voice. Tom leaving? Uneasy, she waited for him to say the words she longed to hear.

Tom did not speak. His gaze roamed her face. He smoothed his hands over her loose hair and kissed her lips as if planting them firmly in his mind.

Mary Lou's stubborn heart refused to accept that she would not see him tomorrow, or the day after, or maybe for several months. How she would miss his curly red hair, the tanned smoothness of his fresh shaven cheeks, and the eyes that drew her into their shimmering blue depths. Just knowing he was near made everything come alive.

"It's just. . ." Tom paused and looked beyond her, "the drive is over. A cowboy moves with the cattle."

What did that mean?

"I'll write you," Tom added and laughed stiffly. "Being postmistress, you'll get my letters special delivery."

He had to be keeping something from her. Had she done something to offend him? Worse, had she misinterpreted his intentions? Today he had been bold, yet the next minute far away.

Mary Lou cleared her throat and smiled. "I'll write you, too. I memorized your address from the letters you mailed your mother." She laughed half-heartedly and shook her finger at him like a schoolmarm. "That's what you get for courting the postmistress."

Tom did not laugh. He brushed her forehead with his lips and moved in search of her mouth. She raised her face and he captured her lips, sending a rush of bewildering, frightening feelings surging through her. Suddenly, he picked her up in his arms, carried her to Missy, and swung her into the saddle.

"I . . ." he began, but did not finish. His long legs swallowed the space between him and Tinder. He mounted, waved, and rode off in a dead run.

Mary Lou watched the cloud of dust blur the image of the man she loved. Suddenly, Mama and Jenny invaded her thoughts. She reluctantly swung Missy in the direction of home and nudged her into a gallop.

When Missy slowed to take the turn in the lane to the cabin, Mary Lou spotted Doc Grey's buggy. A knot tightened her stomach. Mama? Mary Lou slid to the ground and ran. She rushed through the open door and collided with her father.

"Where have you been?" He added a rough oath.

Pa cursing? She had never heard him swear. Mama did not allow it. The fury in Pa's face paralyzed Mary Lou. He grabbed her by the shoulders and shook her. His fingers bit in, stabbing with pain.

"You met that cowboy, did not you?" he accused. "You left your mama to die alone. You're no daughter of mine."

"Buck! Stop it!" Doc Gray jumped at the man and pried his hands from Mary Lou's shoulders. "Let go of her! Let go!"

Mary Lou dropped to the floor, too stunned to cry out.

The two men scuffled, and Buck shoved Doc toward the fireplace. By the time Doc got his balance, Buck had limped into the bedroom with Ellen and slammed the door.

Suddenly, words came out of the air and hit Mary Lou. "You left your mama alone to die."

"Mama?" She staggered to the bedroom door and opened it part way, then felt it slammed shut against her.

"Stay out of here!" Buck hollered. "You had to see your cowboy. Now your mama is dead."

A cumbersome wagon rumbled noisily into the yard carrying Tibby Bradford and Henrietta Wimbley. Mary Lou ran into Aunt Tibby's arms.

Tibby looked from one person to another. "Is it true?"

"Mama's dead, Aunt Tibby," Mary Lou sobbed. "I did not know, I did not know. . . ." Mary Lou clung to her aunt.

Tibby held Mary Lou close and kissed her wet cheeks. "Where's your Pa?" she asked softly.

"In the bedroom with Ellen," Doc said. "He won't let anyone else in."

Tibby transferred Mary Lou into Henrietta's arms and knocked on the bedroom door. "Buck? It's Tibby. I want to see my sister."

"Keep out, I told you. Everybody keep out," Buck's gruff voice replied.

Doc Gray left to get Henrietta's husband, Big Jon Wimbley. If it became necessary to bodily remove Buck, Big Jon was the man to do it. His six feet six inches, broad shoulders, and vise-like grip had steadied the thinking of many men in Venture.

Tibby knocked on the door again, harder. "Let me in, Buck. I have to see

Ellen." She wiggled the latch.

The door slowly opened. Buck's hoarse voice warned, "Just you, Tibby."

Tibby slipped through the opening and the door closed. Mary Lou ran sobbing to the door and pounded on it with her fists. "Pa, let me see Mama. Please. I've got to see Mama."

She turned in agony to Jenny. "I shouldn't have gone. What happened after I left?"

"There was no hurt. Your mama just went to sleep and never woke up," Jenny answered. "I was right there beside her knittin'. I heard her take a deep breath, then give a big sigh. That must have been when she went home to Jesus. She died peaceful, Mary Lou. That's God's blessin'."

Two voices rose and fell in the bedroom. Everyone strained to hear. When Big Jon stomped across the porch, the voices stilled. Big Jon spoke with his wife and daughter first, then crossed to the door and walked in. Three voices raised, lowered, then quieted. The door opened. Without a word, Buck hobbled outside, climbed into his buggy, and rattled off.

Aunt Tibby came out to Mary Lou, put an arm around her, and took her in to see her mother. The distraught girl moved mechanically to Ellen's bedside and stared down at her. She lay peacefully sleeping just as Mary Lou had left her.

"No." The word rose up in disbelief. "No," she repeated. "Mama. Oh Mama, don't leave me." She dropped across her mother's body. Its stiffness shocked her. "I'm sorry, Mama. I should have been here. Forgive me, Mama."

Tibby lifted Mary Lou from the body. They sat on either side of the bed, holding Ellen's hands, mourning their loss. Henrietta finally came in and insisted they leave. She guided them to the rocking chairs beside the fireplace and placed steaming cups of coffee in their hands.

Mary Lou sipped and stared. Nothing felt real. Mama dead? Impossible! She got up and started for the bedroom. Henrietta intercepted her.

"It's good to cry, child. God gave us tears to wash away the hurt."

In the comfort of Henrietta's arms, Mary Lou clung, dry-eyed and numb. Tom was gone. Mama lay dead. Pa had disowned her. *Dear Lord, what reason can you give me to go on living? Help me God, help me!*

Chapter Two

Mary Lou clutched her mother's shawl close in a vain attempt to protect her shivering body from the September rain. Her bonnet drooped and a small waterfall cascaded from its brim.

Pastor Miles fingered the worn edge of Ellen Mackey's Bible and opened to a ribboned page. Big Jon stood behind him with an umbrella to protect both Pastor and Bible.

It had poured steadily from early morning. Tall prairie grass squished underfoot as friends crowded around the open grave. The women embraced themselves in large shawls, big enough to cover a wide-eyed child or two huddling in their skirts. Men stood hunched with necks shoved into their shoulders to keep the water from running down their necks.

Pastor lifted the Bible higher out of the rain. His rich voice spoke familiar comfort.

"'Let not your heart be troubled: Ye believe in God, believe also in Me. In My Father's house are many mansions: If it were not so, I would have told you' " (John 14:1, 2).

Mary Lou drank the words into her parched heart. Her mother had read them to her often.

Pastor continued, " 'I go to prepare a place for you. And if I go and prepare a place for you, I will come again, and receive you unto Myself; that where I am, there ye may be also' " (John 14:2, 3).

Oh Mama, Mary Lou cried inside. *Don't leave me.*

"Father, into Thy hands we commit the spirit of Ellen Lisbeth Mackey. Have mercy upon her soul."

Shovels dug into dirt piled high at the back of the grave. Soaked clods drummed the handmade coffin. One by one, the neighbors filed past the Mackeys to express sympathy and support, then hastened to the lineup of buggies where dripping horses waited.

Tibby, held in her husband's arms, stared into the open grave, eyes flooded with the loss of her sister and best friend. Buck and Mary Lou stood rooted, watching rivulets of water spill into the grave. Pastor Miles gently took Ellen's Bible from under his coat and placed it in Buck's hands. "If you need me . . ." he said. Buck nodded and stuffed the Bible inside his coat.

Mary Lou watched her father. His jaw flexed repeatedly. One tear squeezed out the corner of his eye. Abruptly, he stared at Mary Lou. She saw his eyes fill with hate. *He blames me for Mama's death!* Mary Lou shivered more from her father's coldness than the chilling rain. She raised her arm to touch him. "Pa?"

He jerked away, grabbed his shovel, and joined the men at the grave. Mary Lou watched dirt fill the hole, each thundering shovelful building a wall between her and Mama. Finally, silence.

Mary Lou's father hung on his shovel over the grave for a long moment. Then he lumbered to his buggy, using the shovel as a staff. Mary Lou watched him haul himself into the seat, give a slap of the reins to Morgan, and slowly move away. She covered her face with her hands.

The wide expanse of Kansas sky hung its swollen clouds low and wept. Mary Lou dropped to her knees beside her mother's grave, mindless of the mud. "Mama, he hasn't spoken to me yet. Pa's mad at me 'cause I went to see Tom. But you were asleep, Mama . . . just asleep."

She felt a pair of familiar arms and looked up into Jenny's concerned face. "Oh Jenny, what am I going to do?"

Jenny pulled her to her feet. "Mary Lou, honey, it's rainin'. You'll catch your death out here. Your mama isn't here, anyway. She's in heaven with the Lord. Come on. Let's get you home."

"Pa left me." Mary Lou let Jenny pull her along. "Jenny, Mama's dead."

"Why, Mary Lou, you're talkin' like a heathen! If anyone believed in heaven, your mama did and that's where she is. And your mama's still with you in all the sweet memories you have of her."

Big Jon towered like a silent giant watching the scene. Without a word, he gathered Mary Lou into his massive arms. The grief-stricken girl collapsed against his chest, absorbing the tender father-love she needed so desperately. Jenny at his heels, Big Jon carried Mary Lou to the Wimbley wagon that had brought Ellen's body to the cemetery.

In Mary Lou's small bedroom, Jenny peeled off her friend's wet clothes, pulled a flannel nightgown over her shivering body, and tucked her into bed.

"Just settle some. I'm goin' to make hot tea to warm us up." Jenny gathered Mary Lou's wet clothes and left.

Mary Lou lay with open, unseeing eyes. The words hammered in her head. *Mama is dead. Mama is gone.* Tears ran down into her ears. The thought of her beautiful Mama out there in that cold, wet grave, alone. . . . *Not alone, My child, she's with Me.*

Mary Lou sat up. "But I need her, Lord," she cried aloud. "Lord, help me!"

Jenny bounded through the door and threw her arms around Mary Lou. "He is, honey, and we can count on Him. Look at me. When my mama and pa died in that wagon accident, God gave me not only a new mama and papa but ten new brothers and sisters."

The two girls clung to each other and sobbed, longing for their mothers. When their sobs subsided, Jenny pushed Mary Lou down and tucked a second pillow under her head. "The tea'll be ready. I'll be right back."

They were sipping their tea when Buck stuck his head in.

Jenny rose and Mary Lou held her breath. "Pa?"

He stared blankly at the two girls, then withdrew without a word.

"I guess I better be goin'," Jenny said.

"He hasn't said one word to me since she died. Jenny, was it my fault?"

"Of course not! Your mama was a lot sicker than anybody knew. Talk to Doc Gray. He'll tell you." Jenny leaned over, kissed Mary Lou on the cheek, and gathered the cups. "What you need is some sleep. Thank God for givin' you such a good mama, then pray you'll be able to help your pa. He's grievin' now, but your pa loves you. You'll see."

Alone, relaxed by the tea, Mary Lou let herself sink into the softness of the feather tick. The thought of Pa hurting swelled her heart with sadness and fresh love for him. *Lord, how are we ever going to live without Mama?*

Warmth and exhaustion crept in. Mary Lou slept.

When Mary Lou opened her eyes, her father stood at the foot of her bed. Abruptly, he turned and walked out.

Mary Lou flung back the covers and jumped out of bed. *Why had not Mama. . . .* The surge of energy drained, leaving a horrible emptiness. "Mama," she whispered. Hot tears flowed while she dressed. By habit she pulled up the bed covers and hurried out.

Pa sat in his chair by the fireplace staring into the flames. Mary Lou yearned to throw herself into his arms. Maybe together they could ease the void of Mama being gone.

A knock on the door startled Mary Lou. She opened it to four smiling faces. Henrietta, Jenny, Young Jon, and Miriam Wimbley, their hands full of dishes, trailed across the room.

"Brought your supper and enough to tide you over a day," Henrietta explained. "Jenny, Miriam, set the table. It's ready to eat."

Mary Lou sighed in relief.

Henrietta busied everyone with preparation. "Mary Lou, get a big spoon to dish out the chicken and dumplin's. Come to the table, Buck. Big Jon will be along in a minute."

Buck grunted.

Undaunted, Henrietta hustled about, lifting the lid off the tureen and releasing the savory aroma of cooked chicken.

Another knock announced Big Jon. Placing his hand on Buck's shoulder, he said, "Come on, old man. My woman makes the best chicken and dumplin's in these parts."

"I'm not hungry," Buck mumbled.

"Well, you may not be but your body is. Come on."

Buck capitulated and limped to his place at the head of the table. Big Jon sat down beside Henrietta, and the others filled in. Mary Lou hesitated, then slid into her mother's place opposite her father.

Big Jon folded his hands on the edge of the table. All heads bowed. His voice boomed out thanks to God for the food, the land, and company present. Mary Lou's eyes grew hot. Mama had always said grace. Now who would do it?

Big Jon expertly ladled steaming chicken surrounded by potatoes, carrots, and fat dumplings. Henrietta passed the fried cabbage and a large wooden tray of homemade bread followed by a white crock of freshly-churned butter.

Mary Lou swallowed the best she could. She watched Pa clean up his plate and mop gravy with his bread. He was hungry. Was that why he had come to her room—to tell her it was suppertime? Why did not he say so?

Jenny and Miriam served huge pieces of warm apple pie. Between bites, Big Jon told the latest news he had heard at the train station about some women creating a stir axing saloons.

"They're gatherin' women together to form unions of some kind against Demon Rum. I hear Tibby Bradford is recruiting women in Venture."

Big Jon laughed. "Nate better stop her or he'll be surrounded by a bigger storm than usual."

When everyone finished, the women rose, cleared the table, and washed dishes. The men returned to the fireplace and discussed opportunities the Kansas Pacific railroad could bring to Venture.

Henrietta swung her shawl around her shoulders and motioned for the girls to get theirs. They stepped out into the coolness of the back porch. The drizzling rain had stopped.

"Here," Jenny moved Mary Lou to Ellen's rocking chair. Mary Lou slid slowly into it and closed her eyes. Memories of her mother's presence soothed her.

Henrietta began. "Now, my dear, if you need anythin' at all, you know where we are. We've always considered you part of our family.

"Your mama worried about you when she knew she did not have long to live," Henrietta continued. "She made Tibby and me promise we would look after you. It's hard for fathers to care for girls."

Amazed, Mary Lou rose from her chair. "You mean Mama knew she was going to die? Why did not she tell me? Why did not somebody tell me?"

"She would not let us. She kept prayin' she would live long enough to see you married, but it came too soon."

Mary Lou staggered. *Had everyone known but her? Mama, why did not you tell me?*

Henrietta encircled Mary Lou with her arms. "Your mama had such faith. She even hoped to hold her first grandchild. Doc kept tellin' her she had have to get more rest. Of all people, a doctor should know that homesteadin' women don't get time to rest."

Mary Lou looked up into Henrietta's face. Such kind eyes. They twinkled like Mama's. Prairie life was hard, but like Mama, Henrietta never lost her joy and hope. Fresh guilt swamped Mary Lou. She had never suspected Mama was so sick. The salty fountain broke and Henrietta held her close. Jenny and Miriam put their arms around them both and they cried together in their loss.

"Now," Henrietta said and loosed the girls, "We must dry our tears, set a spell, and enjoy the evening as if Ellen were here."

They sat down again. Mary Lou looked around at the simple wooden porch that Mama had made her sanctuary. Every nice evening after dinner, she had settled in her rocking chair with her Bible and read till it was too dark to see. She had called it "God's Time." Not even Pa's berating had moved her. Finally, Pa let her be. This was where Mama and Mary Lou talked of woman things.

Mama had spoken often about the wonder of God's love and read Scripture aloud. Mary Lou loved to hear her. The words came alive in a way they never did when Mary Lou read them herself.

On one of those evenings, Mary Lou had given her heart to Jesus. Ellen had put her arms around Mary Lou and squeezed her breathless. "I am so happy," she had cried. "Now I will never lose you. We belong to Jesus."

Pa had stepped out on the porch at that moment and they had bubbled their new-found joy to him. He had shrugged and walked back into the house, mumbling something about women's foolishness.

Henrietta rose. "It's time we're on our way." She and Big Jon swept their family out, loaded with clean dishes.

When the door closed, Mary Lou turned and looked at her father. "Pa," she began. "I want to talk with you."

Without a word, Buck rose, hobbled out the door, and headed for the barn. Morgan nickered.

Minutes later, Mary Lou stood at the window and watched the horse and buggy emerge, carrying Pa to town. Trembling, she dropped into her father's chair beside the dying fire. Stillness seeped through the cabin walls and enveloped her with fear. She got up, threw herself against the door, and locked it. Fighting panic, she grabbed the lamp and sought the comfort of her own bed. *Dear Lord. . . .*

Chapter Three

Mary Lou rolled over and stared at the beams in the ceiling. A chill shuddered through her body even though warm rays of morning sun rested on her legs. Tired. She was so tired. With great effort, she sat up.

Mama. The ache and longing returned.

She listened to the familiar morning symphony of the prairie: the eerie wail of a coyote giving up the night, the swish of the wind through prairie grass, the distant bark of a prairie dog as he poked his nose out of his hole.

Pa? She rose and opened her bedroom door. His chair was empty. She crossed to her parents' bedroom and knocked. Silence. She opened the door and peeked in. The bed was empty.

Probably in the barn. It would not be the first time her father had come home late, flopped into a hay pile, and slept. Her mother had protested, but Pa had laughed and said as a boy, he had slept more often in a haystack than in a bed.

Mary Lou grabbed her bonnet on her way out the door. The sun was high and hot, but the sweet prairie air was fresh and warm. Both barn doors were wide open and Pa's buggy was gone. Her heart sank. He must have stayed in the back rooms at the store.

Dulcie nickered.

Dulcie. Her poor horse had not been watered or fed. She released Dulcie from the stall and laid her head against the animal's warm, soft hair. "I'm sorry."

Dulcie gave a low whinny of sympathy.

Mary Lou grabbed a bucket and filled it from the well. Dulcie followed like a shadow, then eagerly dipped her nose and drank.

A dust cloud signaled a visitor. Mary Lou shaded her eyes. It looked like one of Uncle Nate's wagons. She threw an armful of hay to Dulcie and ran to meet her aunt.

Tibby expertly pulled the horses to a quick halt, jumped down, and held Mary Lou at arm's length. A backlog of grief welled up, and they clung to each other and cried until Tibby broke away.

"Heavens!" she sniffed. "We'll drown in our own tears." Aunt Tibby, ever efficient, carried a wealth of hankies in her pockets. The two women dried their eyes and faced each other with a smile.

"Ellen's probably frowning at us. Stafford girls are made of strong stuff." Tibby threw her head back and laughed. "We learned that from Mother. Think how courageous your grandmother was to live with Grandfather Stafford for thirty years."

Mary Lou took a deep breath. "I'm sorry."

"Nothing to be sorry for. A time of grieving is a necessary comfort. But life goes on and Ellen is in a better place. She's with Jesus, well and smiling and probably singing in the heavenly choir!" Tibby settled her shoulders with a big sigh. "You should have heard your mama sing in the choir back home."

Lost in their own memories, Mary Lou and her aunt walked arm in arm toward the cabin. It soothed them to work at tasks that spoke of Ellen. Bread dough was soon made, slapped into fat rounds, and covered with warmed flannel to raise quicker.

They packed Ellen's clothes in a trunk. "These will all fit you and are yours now. After a bit you'll wear them proudly." Tibby cupped Mary Lou's face in her hands. "You are as beautiful as your mother, inside as well as out. Ellen taught you well."

Tibby walked to the fireplace and disturbed the burning cow chips. They burst into flame, then settled to a steady hot fire. She peered into an iron kettle, dumped grits into the simmering water, and stirred vigorously. At the coffee mill, she ground roasted beans and poured them into a pot. "What time this morning did your pa leave?"

Mary Lou hung her head. "He left last night."

Tibby gasped. "You mean you were here alone all night? What's the matter with that man?"

"He's grieving, Aunt Tibby. He'll come around." That's what Mama had always said. But she and Mama had waited through ten years for him to come around. Ever since the accident, Pa had been a different man. And now he had disowned her. Did not he need her? With Mama gone, she desperately needed him.

"But he shouldn't leave you alone, especially now." Tibby was incensed. "Maybe your Uncle Nate can straighten out his thinking." As if reading Mary Lou's thoughts, she added, "Disowning you was a result of despair at Ellen's death. He'll get over that. But leaving you out here alone at night isn't manly."

A clatter of hoofbeats pounded to a stop outside.

Jenny Wimbley wafted in with the tantalizing aroma of fresh-baked bread. Her basket held two brown-crusted loaves, fresh butter, and some vegetables. Suddenly Mary Lou was hungry.

Aunt Tibby lifted three cups from the shelf, filled them with coffee, and brought them to the table.

"Let's set a spell." she said. "We've been working long enough." She peeked in the basket and held up a loaf. "Mmmmm. Thank your ma. Our bread isn't ready yet."

Tibby sliced bread while Mary Lou brought a jar of her mother's prairie globe apple jelly and placed it on the table. A stir of the grits revealed they were not cooked.

The three sat at the table and sipped coffee. Normally Jenny would have filled the silence with a stream of chatter. Today, her eyes flicked from Mary Lou to Tibby.

Each was absorbed in her own thoughts, comforted by the covenant that bound prairie women in their need for companionship and survival. Every mother taught her daughter the myriad tasks that would consume her days. Even the very young learned their primary task in this enormous land was to plant a home and sink deep roots for their family.

Jenny offered, "Ma said not to worry about supper. You and your pa can come for supper, or if you want, I could bring it here."

"Thank your ma," Tibby answered, "but Mary Lou is coming to stay with us."

Mary Lou shook her head. "No, I'm staying here. Home has to be here when Pa comes." She was afraid to stay alone, but more afraid of failing Pa if she did not. He needed her. She needed him. Eventually, they would talk.

Tibby drained her coffee cup and carried it to the sink table. "I must be heading home." She placed her hand on Mary Lou's shoulder. "If you change your mind, come." She was gone as quickly as she came.

Mary Lou and Jenny continued the round of chores. Normally when they were together, words tumbled over each other. Today, Mary Lou had a difficult time with casual chitchat. It seemed meaningless.

After Jenny left, Mary Lou milked the cows and lowered the milk cans into the well to keep the milk cool. She fixed herself a light supper of dried beef, some of Henrietta's vegetables, bread, and tea. After eating, she rounded up soiled clothing to launder in the morning. A sudden tiredness enveloped her.

She walked absently around the cabin touching Mama's things. Tears flowed freely down her cheeks. Then Mama's face filled her mind. Smiling. Always smiling. Even the tears she had cried were tears of joy.

Mary Lou's gaze wandered around the room and rested on Mama's Bible on the shelf Pa'd built for Mama's books. She crossed the room, picked it up, and carried it out to the back porch. She ran her hand over her mother's empty chair and sat down. This Bible was hers now. She turned it lovingly in her hands. She noticed something she had never seen before—the faint imprint of Mama's hand around the outside binding. Slowly, Mary Lou shaped her fingers into Mama's handprint. They matched perfectly. She hugged the book to her breast. Silently, Mary Lou prayed, *Help me find the comfort and wisdom Mama breathed from this book.*

She fluttered its pages. The Bible fell open to a well-used, tear-stained page marked with a faded blue ribbon. Verse 5 of Psalm 30 was circled in pencil: "For His anger endureth but a moment; in His favor is life: weeping may endure for a night, but joy cometh in the morning."

Mary Lou looked out over her beloved prairie. A calming peace gently held her, sensitizing her to the beauty she so often took for granted. The sun slowly climbed into bed and drew the sunset over the horizon like a flaming orange comforter.

Uninvited, Tom invaded her thoughts. His abrupt departure had left her disappointed. Yet she clung to the feeling there had been something he had wanted to tell her. Or could not? Did it have to do with Laura? He had mentioned her so casually, but just how did Laura fit into his life?

Mary Lou's anger flared. If Laura meant something to Tom, he was no gentleman to hold Mary Lou in his arms and kiss her! Pa had warned her about cowboys. If anyone knew about them, Pa did. Her mind whirled for an answer. She found none, but her stubborn heart persisted in hoping that when Tom wrote, he would explain.

"Silly thing." She scolded her heart sternly and shut her eyes against the descending nightfall. The minute her eyes closed, Tom's image formed. He stood leaning against Tinder and smiling in that wry way that made Mary Lou feel as if he knew her innermost secrets. She opened her eyes quickly, flushed with the memory that she had made a fool of herself.

Night shadows crept in, hunting a resting place. Her eyes focused sharply as the shadows took ghostly shapes, then changed and reshaped again. Apprehension threw fear around her like a cloak. Chirring crickets sang noisily and crescendoed into a screaming accompaniment to the night howling choir of gray wolves. Mary Lou had heard stories about gray wolves. When food was scarce, they dared to scratch on the doors and windows of the cabins. One time when a neighbor was in town, the wolves had gotten in and torn the cabin apart in their search for food.

She strained to hear Pa's buggy. Her ears sifted through the cacophony of sound, but nothing resembled the clop of a horse or the rattle of a buggy.

With false bravado, she stood abruptly and scolded aloud. "You're a big girl now and have heard and seen this all before." *But not alone!*

Chapter Four

The sun yawned, stretched, and climbed over the eastern horizon. The town of Venture slept except for a few stray dogs scrounging for something to fill their empty stomachs. A rider entered the west end of Center Street and the dogs sprang clear of the horse's hooves.

Mary Lou gave Dulcie her head and the pony quietly made her way to the store for the first time in two weeks. Usually Mary Lou rode in with her father, but since Ellen's death, he had returned to the cabin only once—the day of the funeral. She guessed she would find him in rooms at the back of the store. They were as much home to him as the cabin. Yes, his buggy stood there and Morgan nickered to her from the lean-to.

She dismounted, tied Dulcie, and paused at the back door wondering whether her father would open it if she knocked. Her stomach twisted into knots. As much as she wanted to see Pa and talk with him, she could not face another rejection. She shook her head and continued along the side of the store to the front door.

At the front corner, she paused to look up and down the street. Venture resembled most other towns in northeastern Kansas. Mary Lou stepped up on the warped timber planks nailed together to resemble a sidewalk in front of the store. Old wooden posts and crooked tree limbs at the street edge did their best to stand straight for hitching posts and rails.

Mary Lou thought back. She had lived half her life in Schineberg's Grocery. Ellen had run the post office, so Mary Lou had spent hours looking out the front window. She had watched frame structures rise on both sides of Center Street. It had taken Buck a long time to change the name of his business to Mackey's General Store out of respect to the man who had willed it to him.

Across the street, Glenn Farrell walked out of Mrs. Barton's Boarding House. He waved and grinned. "Good morning, Mary Lou," he called and ran to catch up with her. He unlocked the store door and stepped aside to let her pass. "You planning on staying a while today?"

"Yes, I'll be coming in every day now. I'm sorry I put the whole load on you Glenn, but with Mama. . . ." She welled up with tears. Just when she seemed to have things under control, a mention of Mama swallowed her in grief. But she had to get back to the post office. She could not expect Glenn to do her work, and she needed to be busy—too busy to think.

An early customer came at that moment and approached Glenn. "Thank you, Lord," Mary Lou breathed. She was not in the mood to talk. She even sighed a thanks that the post office was as she expected—in chaos. Piles of unsorted mail lay stacked on shelves, the counter, even on the chair. She checked their mailbox. Nothing from Tom.

Glenn poked his head in and mumbled excuses for not getting the mail sorted. "I'd better check at the stage depot and get this week's bag." He vanished.

"I'll do it," she called after him, but the door banged. Looking out the window at Glenn's retreating back, Mary Lou relived the day Tom Langdon had first sauntered across the street, tall and lean in chaps and clinking spurs. He had opened the door and brought in a burst of energy that filled the room.

"Mornin', ma'am," he had drawled. "How much to mail this letter?"

Mary Lou had looked at the bold handwriting. "Mrs. Zachary Langdon, Harness, Texas," she had read aloud.

"My mother," he had grinned and pointed to the address. His fingers had brushed her hand.

Color had risen on Mary Lou's cheeks. She had moved to the stamp box. "Three cents, please," she had said. *What's the matter?* she had scolded herself. *A handsome cowboy walks in and you fall apart. Ridiculous!*

She also remembered the day the address on his letters changed to "Miss Laura Shepard." Tom had said he was sending them to Laura to be sure his mother got his mail. Now she wondered. *Was Laura why he had left? Was that why he had never said he loved Mary Lou?*

Her gaze caught Glenn returning with the mailbag. Sunlight highlighted his straight blond hair and the wind rumpled it every time he smoothed it.

Glenn bumped through the door and dropped the mailbag on the chair. Mary Lou rescued the pile of old mail before the bag fell. The store bell jangled. Glenn looked apologetic and hurried to a customer.

Mary Lou was grateful for the small alcove that housed the post office at the front corner of the store. Pa had built it there because the window provided better light. Pa, she thought, I must see Pa. She walked out the door and into Ida Hensley.

"Oh, my dear," Ida said, "I'm so sorry about your mama. Anythin' I can do, just let me know. I've been prayin' for you." She patted Mary Lou on the shoulder.

"Thank you, Mrs. Hensley. You're very kind."

"I 'spect your Pa is grievin' terrible. He must miss Ellen."

"Yes, we do. I'm on my way to see Pa now. Thank you, Mrs. Hensley." Mary Lou hurried to the back. She knew their neighbor meant well, but Mary Lou could not talk about Mama's death. It hurt too much.

The two rooms across the back of the store had been the home of Jacob Schineberg and his wife, Naomi, former owners. When Naomi gave birth to their only son, she and the baby both died, leaving Jacob alone.

Then Buck had had his accident. He had been too proud to take charity, so

Jacob had talked Buck into staying with him to help in the store. He had cared for Buck like a son until Buck had got back on his feet. Then he had taught Buck to run the store.

A couple years later, a wagonload of barrels had toppled onto Jacob. Before he died, Jacob had willed the store to Buck in front of a dozen witnesses.

At the door of the back room, Mary Lou stood, her hand poised to knock. They had to resolve this. She could not go on not talking. "Pa?" she called and tapped the door. Silence. She tapped again. "Pa, are you there?" Not a sound.

Her tears ran unchecked. He still had not forgiven her. Her own guilt returned, even though Doc Gray had told her Mama had been sick for years.

"It was only a matter of time," he had said. "She would have died if you'd been at her side. I told her to get more rest. She would not listen."

Sorrowfully, Mary Lou went back to the post office. Sun streamed through the window. She wiped her tears and took a handful of letters out of the bag.

Her heart quickened. Maybe there would be one from Tom. As the piles grew smaller, her heart grew heavy.

"Mr. William Owen Mackey," the envelope read. "From Mrs. Lars Thurston."

Mary Lou ran to the back room and knocked again. "Pa, there's a letter for you from Aunt Nelda."

She heard stirrings. The door opened. The smell of whiskey preceded Pa's head. He appeared unshaven, his eyes bloodshot. He took the letter from Mary Lou's hand and tore it open. After reading it quickly, he handed it back and closed the door.

Mary Lou heaved a sigh and turned away. Like her, Pa felt lost without Mama. He had never treated her like this before. When she was little, he would pick her up and throw her into the air. Mary Lou had not been the least bit afraid. Pa always had caught her in his big arms and tickled her till she begged to be put down. Later, Pa had taught her to love horses, to handle them with respect, and to ride like the wind.

Nothing was the same now. Mama had been the joy of their family, always encouraging them. Oh, Mama, I miss you so much. She walked back to the post office, sat down, and opened the letter.

> *Dear Brother Owen,*
>
> *I was so sorry to learn of your Ellen's death and my heart aches for you. As you know, I lost my Lars last winter and life has been hard. I am staying with a good family who treats me well. I cook, clean, and help with the children. They pay me some so I have a little money. But it's not the same as family.*
>
> *I have not been able to get you out of my mind. I know how much work there is to be done in a home, and you have the store as well. Mary Lou*

is young, and I am sure I could help by keeping house and cooking for you both. I would not expect any pay.

Please let me know before the cold weather sets in.

Your loving sister,
Nelda

Mary Lou put down the letter. "Thank you, Lord, for Aunt Nelda," she said. She took a deep breath and knocked again on the back room door.

"Pa, I read Aunt Nelda's letter and I want to know what to write back." Mary Lou waited, praying the door would open.

Finally, there was scuffling within and the door opened. Mary Lou's father tried to focus his glassy eyes on her.

"Oh, Pa." She swallowed hard. "What shall I tell Aunt Nelda?" She fought the urge to fling herself into his arms. For the moment, it was enough that he looked at her.

"Tell her to come," he said thickly. "She'll be a help to you."

Mary Lou stepped forward. "Pa?"

He closed the door.

Mary Lou's voice lifted in prayer. "He spoke to me! Thank You, Lord, for answering my prayer. Please help him find You. Mama prayed for that. He needs You now more than ever."

Mary Lou went back to the post office with a lighter step. She could feel Mama smiling down at them from heaven. Mary Lou looked up—and smiled back.

Chapter Five

Tom Langdon slowed Tinder to a walk. An hour ago he had crossed out of Oklahoma Indian Territory into the Texas panhandle. He would be home for supper.

It had been a long ride. The first fifty miles he had ridden like a madman to put space between himself and Mary Lou, fighting the desire to turn back and claim the woman he loved. His heart twinged at the sight of every cottonwood.

Approaching a stream, Tom dismounted, tied Tinder to a tree, and banged the dust from himself with his hat. He fell flat on his stomach and slaked his thirst. Then he dunked his whole head in the cool water and rubbed away the trail grime.

"I don't want no cowboy marryin' my daughter. You're a wanderlust bunch. I know. I was one."

Buck had never given Tom a chance to say his intentions were honorable and that he was not just a cowboy. He had refused to listen to anything Tom had to say.

Tom knew Mary Lou loved him. He prayed she could wait until he received his inheritance in the Circle Z. Even then, his brother Doug would fight him all the way. Until things were settled, Tom had nothing to offer but his love. That was not enough for Buck. Mary Lou's confused face hung in Tom's mind. He flinched. How else could he have honored his promise to Buck Mackey? It had to be a flat cut off. He regretted telling Mary Lou he would write. He pictured her sorting the mail for the letter that would not come.

The cowhands jawed Buck to Tom. He had been on his way to becoming a big man in those parts, had bought land and cattle to go into ranching. Buck had worked as head man for Nate Bradford.

One hot, summer night, Buck had been riding the range on his black stallion, Morgan, when a nest of rattlers had spooked the horse. The big black had skittered, reared, and thrown Buck. His left foot had tangled in the stirrup, and Morgan had dragged him, seriously injuring his back and left leg. As a result, he was unable to ride a horse.

Tom felt for Buck. Settling for a buggy after riding the range would be death. Tom could not remember learning to ride. His earliest memory was astride Big Diamond with his father, Zachary Langdon. He missed his dad. Things at the ranch would be different if he were still alive.

Tom loosed Tinder and moved him to the stream. The horse submerged his nose for a long drink, then moved into a shaggy grass patch to stock up. Tom dropped to the ground on his back and flopped his arm over his eyes to shade the sun. He would give Tinder a little more rest.

The moment he closed his eyes, Mary Lou's heart-shaped face filled his mind. In his arms she felt like a little girl. But nineteen was no little girl. She was a woman—the woman he wanted to marry.

Tom wondered what his mother would say. Allena Langdon had her own ideas about who her sons should marry. Except Zachary, his oldest brother. Zack hated ranching and had left for Massachusetts to study law right after their father had died. Allena had given up on Zack but made no secret of her wishes for Doug and Tom. Marlena Kincaid for Doug, and Laura Shepard for Tom. Tom had agreed—until he met Mary Lou.

He wondered what to do when he got home. Doug would strut out, grab the money, and dismiss him like one of the cowhands. There had never been words between them, but Tom knew Doug wanted the ranch.

Tom, like his father, loved every blade of grass on the ranch. Land was not a thing, it was a living entity and would remain after every Langdon returned to dust. As a young boy, Tom dreamed of teaching his sons to ride and of someday, like his father, giving them their heritage.

In five months, according to his father's will, one quarter of Circle Z would be his. For Doug, a day of reckoning.

Tinder whinnied.

Tom got up and grabbed his hat. This time he would fight for what was his and go back to Buck as a rancher. He whistled for Tinder. The horse chomped one last mouthful and pranced to his side. Tom angled his hat, mounted, and headed south.

Tinder tossed his head and sniffed the air when they neared the Circle Z. Tom leaned forward and patted his neck. "You're as glad to get home as I am." The thought of a bath, a hot meal, and a soft bed made him relax the reins and let Tinder go. They went through the Circle Z arch at full gallop.

The cowboys had not arrived yet. They had given him a hard time when he had told them he was traveling alone, but he had needed thinking time.

"Tom. You're home!"

Tom turned toward the shout, slid off Tinder, and ran to Nelson who was hobbling on his crutches as fast as he could. When they met, Nelson flung his crutches and threw himself into Tom's arms. They pounded each other on the back, laughing and talking at once.

Allena Langdon hurried through the ranch door to greet her son. Tom waved and picked up Nelson's crutches. Arm in arm, the two boys walked to meet their mother.

"I'm glad you're back, son." His mother hugged both sons and sighed, "My prayers are answered."

Tom teased, "Aren't you the one who always says 'prayer and worry don't mix'?"

His mother laughed. "I know. But you boys are all I have." She linked her arm around the other side of Nelson and the three walked back to the house.

"Where's Doug?" Tom asked. "I thought he would be waiting at the door for the money."

"Now, Tom. Doug takes his responsibilities seriously. He's in town. The cattle ranchers are having a meeting about the new Kansas law that forbids Texas cattle to be driven across their state to the railroads because of Texas ticks. Everyone's up in arms."

Funny. Tom had not heard a word about that when he was in Kansas. He would write Nate Bradford.

They were just finishing dinner when Doug stormed in. As usual, half the clothes he wore were Tom's. The boots had to be too small, but they did not affect Doug's strut. Tom noticed he was wearing his own pants. His middle had grown. Must have spent too many nights in town.

"What'd you hear about this business of not allowing us to drive cattle across Kansas?" Without taking a breath, Doug put his hand out. "I'll take the money."

"It's still in my saddle bag."

"Still in your saddle bag! That's a pretty careless way to handle money. It's a good thing I'm boss around here."

"I'll get it." Tom ambled to the hall chair where his saddle bag was waiting, Doug at his heels.

Doug snatched the bag out of Tom's hands and pulled out the money bags. "Is it all here?"

"Everything but cowboy pay and my share."

"Your share! I get it all to pay the bills."

"Now you won't have to pay me."

Doug's eyes narrowed. "I pay you like I pay the rest of the hands around here."

"You forget, brother, I'm not a hand. I own part of this ranch."

"Not yet, you don't." Doug glared at Tom and stomped off to the ranch office.

Welcome home. Tom smiled, surprised at his inner calmness. When his father had died, Tom had been seventeen. Zack, twenty-three, should have taken over, but he had said he had waited long enough. Within two months he had packed his books and headed East to study law.

Doug, just turned twenty-one, had taken over the ranch and run it as he pleased. He was heavy handed and they had lost a couple good men, but most stayed. When Doug had treated Tom like one of the hired help, the cowboys had rallied and trained him. Without them, the ranch would have folded. They were good, hard-working men. Tom respected them.

Tom was Doug's only contender to run the ranch. Zack had bowed out and Nelson could not physically handle it. Tom itched to look at the books, but he needed a reason. Doug kept them locked up. Zack! He would contact Zack and find out his legal rights. In the meantime, he would keep his eyes open and be patient.

Tom returned to the dining room, kissed his mother, and rumpled Nelson's hair. "All I need is a bed. Don't be surprised if I sleep for a week. Good night."

His head scarcely touched the pillow when a longing ache filled him. Mary Lou. He closed his eyes and her sad, puzzled face stared at him. Tomorrow he would throw himself into work and try to forget.

The next morning, Tom rose early and saddled the black stallion Victor to give Tinder a rest. As tired as he had felt yesterday, he could not wait to look over the land his father had worked and died for.

The cattle spread as far as he could see. They would be the next drive, and he could not decide whether to ride with them. It all depended on how things turned out with Doug. He would get a letter off to Zack.

Victor snorted and danced. Tom patted his neck. "You're ready for a wild ride, aren't you? All right, boy, let's go."

Man and horse merged with wind and land. Victor stretched his legs to their utmost and Tom clung like a burr. This was life, the life he loved—his heritage he hoped to share with Mary Lou.

The corral came into view. Men and animals stirred from their night's rest. Smitty waved his hat high over his head. Tom slowed and veered Victor in his direction.

"When'd ya get back?" Smitty hollered.

Tom reined Victor and dismounted. "Yesterday, about supper time. When did you boys get in?"

"During the night. After we left Oklahoma Territory, we just kept comin'. Anxious to git home."

"Funny, I did not hear you come in."

"We was quiet. Did not want to stir up nothin'."

Tom walked Victor beside Smitty and caught up on news of the ride home. Tom liked Smitty. He had been around a long time.

Jess, the cook, filled the air with scents of breakfast, and the cowboys emerged unshaven, sleepy, and hungry. Tom would have joined them, but his mother and Nelson would be waiting for him. After some joshing, Tom made his way up to the ranch house.

Allena sat in her place at the dining room table. "I could not believe you went for a ride this morning after your long trip home," she said when Tom came in.

"I just wanted to look the place over," Tom answered.

"How'd you find things?"

"Lookin' good." Tom replied. "Dad would be pleased. Doug still sleeping?"

"No, he went off to town right after you left." His mother passed a plate of fragrant sour dough biscuits.

Tom laughed. "Is there anything that goes on around here you don't know about?"

"No," she answered matter-of-factly.

Nelson fidgeted and blurted, "Tell me about the drive, Tom. You're gonna take me with you sometime, aren't ya?"

"Mother will have to decide if you're strong enough to take it," Tom answered. "It's a grueling ride, Nelson. I don't know if you could stay in the saddle as long as you'd have to."

Nelson, crushed, bent over his steak and eggs.

His mother laid her hand on Nelson's arm. "Son, God does not give the same job to everyone. Look at the beautiful pictures you draw and paint. I don't see anyone else around here doing that."

Nelson disregarded his mother, unconvinced.

"And there's plenty of work you can do on the ranch. Someone has to stay home and watch things," Allena added to comfort her son.

"But Doug does not let me do anything," Nelson protested. "Every time he finds me with the cowboys, he sends me back to the house."

Tom said, "I'll talk to him and see if I can't get him to agree on certain jobs for you."

Nelson brightened and dove into his breakfast.

The ensuing silence hung heavy. Tom had the feeling his mother wanted to discuss something.

Allena cleared her throat. "You're going to be twenty-one soon, Tom, and some legal things need to be settled. I've written Zack and told him that he should come back and take care of everything lawful and proper."

Tom grinned. His mother had shown concern about the way Doug handled things now and then, but she had always kept the peace. He was relieved to know she felt the same uneasiness he was feeling.

"I'm glad you wrote Zack, Mom. I've a hunch we're going to need him."

Footsteps on the porch announced the arrival of a blond-haired wisp of a girl who came in as if she lived there. Tom rose and Laura Shepard ran and threw her arms around him. "It's about time you came back. I thought you'd found yourself a girl up there."

He hoped he had. "It was a big drive and took lots of time." But not enough time to tell Mary Lou he loved her. He sat back down.

Laura took the chair beside him and received the plate of food Allena passed to her. She fell on it like a starved animal.

Tom cast a brief glance at Laura. A Texas beauty, born and bred with a heart for Texas. At one time he had taken for granted Laura would be his wife. But compared with Mary Lou, Laura still had growing up to do.

She turned to Tom and bumped his arm. "You got back in time for the hoedown next Saturday at Schroeder's barn." She hooked his gaze. "Gonna take me?"

"Sure," Tom answered quickly and grinned. "It's time I got some Texas hayseed in my hair."

The conversation turned to the usual ranch and neighbor talk, but it was not the same. For Tom, everything sounded different. Yep. It was biding time.

Chapter Six

The westbound stagecoach lumbered into Center Street, stirring up a thick cloud of dust. People came running from all directions.

Mary Lou stepped out of the store and hurried to meet Aunt Nelda. Jake, one of Nate Bradford's cowboys, waited in a buckboard to transport Nelda's luggage to the cabin.

Mary Lou wondered if her father would come out. She had told him Nelda would arrive that day, but if he had heard, he had not answered. Surely he would welcome his own sister!

Her heart leaped. Pa leaned against one of the roof poles. She curbed the urge to run to him. Instead, she walked over. Their gaze met for a second as they turned to the passengers alighting from the coach.

Aunt Nelda gathered her skirts, grabbed an offered hand to step down, and threw herself into Buck's arms. "I'm sure glad that's over. My back would have snapped had we gone another five miles." She looked for her luggage and watched Jake pile it in the buckboard. Then she turned to Buck and patted his arm.

Mary Lou interpreted a world of feeling in that small gesture. Aunt Nelda was Pa's favorite of two sisters and four brothers. He had not seen any of them for years. But Aunt Nelda kept in touch. Pa had told Mary Lou once that Nelda was the only one of his family who cared a hoot about him.

Nelda swung around and appraised Mary Lou. "And lookee here! Why Mary Lou, you've grown into a pretty young lady." To Buck, she grinned. "I bet these town boys are doing so much buzzing around her you're having heart failure."

Mary Lou blushed. Buck mumbled something she did not catch, hobbled toward his buggy, and climbed in. Before Mary Lou could help Aunt Nelda into the buggy, the energetic woman hoisted herself up. Jake stretched his arm to hand Mary Lou up to the seat beside him on the buckboard.

The two women would share Mary Lou's room. Buck had sent a new bed home from the store. Jake carried in Nelda's luggage and in no time she had her belongings neatly in place. With Mary Lou's help, she perused the kitchen supplies and soon a soup pot bubbled away on the stove.

Pa unhitched Morgan from the buggy, came in, and sat down in his chair by the fireplace. Mary Lou sent a grateful prayer heavenward. Pa was going to stay at the cabin! They would be family again.

Days flew by. Aunt Nelda sang hymns and moved constantly. "Would you mind if I was to change your kitchen around a bit for my convenience?" she asked Mary Lou one day.

"Of course not, Aunt Nelda. You do most of the cooking. Make it easy for you." Mary Lou felt comforted by Nelda's thoughtfulness.

A harmonious warmth filled the cabin. Buck came home every evening, and after Mary Lou went to bed, she heard her father and aunt talk for hours. Mornings, he and Mary Lou rode to town together except when she did not stay all day. Then she rode Dulcie. Although they did not talk the way they used to, the tension had eased.

December blew in with a mild snowstorm that heightened enthusiasm for Christmas. The Kansas Pacific kept bringing more people and merchandise from the East. It was a prosperous time and the busyness eased the pain of Ellen's absence at Christmas.

Everything changed. Aunt Nelda baked her brother's favorites. He ate heartily, lost his haggard look, and stopped drinking. Mary Lou thanked God for Aunt Nelda.

Christmas. Two weeks away. The store had buzzed all morning with customers buying and trading. Women brought eggs, vegetables, prairie chickens, anything they could trade. Most families kept a small flock of sheep and some traded their carded wool and items they had woven on their looms to buy shoes, boots, coats, and Christmas gifts for their families.

By noon, the customers had thinned out. Glenn joined Mary Lou folding and straightening bolts of colorful calico. "Too bad we can't have Christmas every week. It sure helps business."

Mary Lou laughed. "Then I'd never get the mail sorted."

"I like having you work in the store here—with me," Glenn said quietly.

Mary Lou's stomach tightened. She had never thought of Glenn as a suitor. She seldom thought of Glenn at all. Pa had hired him to run the store and he did a good job. Mama, Pa, and Tom consumed her thoughts. Two months had crawled by. Still no letter from Tom. A gnawing thought tried to invade her mind. She had dismissed it before. Now it broke through. *Tom does not love you.* The blue of the calico in her hands grew misty. *If he loved you, he would have written. Perhaps I should write to him. Maybe something has happened.*

"No." she said aloud and glanced quickly to see if Glenn had heard.

Glenn peered over a bolt halfway to the shelf. "What did you say?"

"Uh . . . nothing." She sent him a half smile and smoothed the cloth with shaking fingers. She glanced again. Handsome, tall, always neatly dressed, Glenn was a gentleman in every sense.

He patted the last bolt and moved decisively along the counter to Mary Lou. He searched her face. "I wondered if you would go with me to the church service and party afterward on Christmas Eve."

Taken by surprise, Mary Lou said quickly, "Oh, no. I don't think it would be seemly—it's too soon after Mama's . . ." She could not say it.

Glenn did not move. He cleared his throat. "If you'll pardon my saying so, Mary Lou, I don't see why it would not be proper. We could go to the service and stay at the party a little while. We'd only be sitting and eating and watching the children when Santa Claus comes."

Glenn's eyes disarmed her. She had never given a thought to the Christmas party and she had never missed one. Uneasy, she moved to the end of the counter, picked up the scissors, and hung them on a hook.

Glenn followed her. "I remember your mama always enjoyed those church parties. I don't think it would show any disrespect for you to go—with me," he added.

She glanced into Glenn's pleading face. The intensity of his eyes unnerved her. "I'll speak to Aunt Nelda about it."

Mary Lou escaped to the post office. She dug into the half-sorted mailbag for a fistful of letters and forced her mind to concentrate as she stuffed them into their boxes. She ran her hand around the bottom of the bag for the last few letters.

"Mrs. Henrietta Wimbley," she read and put it in the Wimbley box. Henrietta's mother wrote regularly.

"Mr. Nate Bradford." Her heart flipped. She read it again, slowly. "Mr. Nate Bradford." That was Tom's handwriting! She flipped the letter to the back. To the front. Nothing. *Why is it addressed to Uncle Nate? Why not me?* She peered into the bag to see if she had missed hers. Empty.

Mary Lou slumped into the chair and stared at the letter. Hot tears returned. Tom was toying with her just as he had done last summer, making her think he loved her.

Anger flamed and she shot to her feet. Not anger at Tom. At herself. How he must have laughed as he rode away. And she had let him hold her in his arms and kiss her. Worse, she had liked it, even thought of having his children! She shuddered with shame. She had never allowed any boy in Venture to be so bold.

The letter burned in her hand. She threw it on the counter and a whirlwind could not have blown the post office into order any quicker. She locked the stamp box and took it to the safe. Without a break in her step, she grabbed the letter, fled to the back room, changed into riding clothes, and marched out the door to saddle Dulcie.

Glenn ran after her. "Are you going home?"

"Got a special letter to deliver to Uncle Nate. See you tomorrow."

Crestfallen, Glenn watched her saddle Dulcie. "Don't forget about the Christmas party."

"I won't." She mounted Dulcie and urged her into a gallop. Hoofbeats almost closed out his "Could you tell me tomorrow?" She did not answer.

Normally, the pristine snow would have conveyed God's beauty to Mary

Lou's soul. She rode blind. Her eyes stung, her heart pounded, and she felt angry enough to explode.

Dulcie's frosty breath curled from her nostrils as she worked hard through the snow. She reached the Bradford ranch. One of the cowboys came running and took Dulcie. Mary Lou slid off and raced to the cabin door.

A smiling Aunt Tibby pulled her to the fireplace and rubbed warmth into her hands. The kitchen smelled of fresh bread and roasting meat. Mary Lou could use the peace of this friendly kitchen.

"Gracious, Mary Lou, it's too cold to be out riding. You should ride with your Pa with hot stones at your feet."

"Is Uncle Nate here?"

"He's out in the barn inspecting our new colt. He'll be in shortly."

"A letter came for him and I thought it might be something important." Mary Lou gave the letter to Aunt Tibby.

Tibby laid it casually on the table. "I'm glad you came. I've been wanting to talk to you about the W.C.T.U.."

Mary Lou frowned. "W-C-T-U? What's that?"

"It's the Women's Christian Temperance Union. I'd like you to come to a meeting next Tuesday. The women of Venture are going to have their say, or Mac Ludden and his saloon are going to lead this town straight to hell."

"Have you heard Pa stopped drinking?"

Tibby nodded. "I'm glad. Buck's not a drinking man. I like Nelda. She has backbone and I bet Buck jumped to her tune when he was a young boy. Ellen would be pleased." She leaned forward. "I've been worried about you."

"About me? What for?" Mary Lou gazed into the flames fearing her eyes would betray her. Aunt Tibby, like her mother, could usually guess what she was thinking. "It's much better since Aunt Nelda came."

"That's not what I mean. I'm talking about that young cowboy you swooned over last September."

Mary Lou's eyes blazed. "What do you mean swooned?" Words stuck in her throat.

Tibby patted her hand. "Honey, any woman can tell when another woman's in love. You sparkled like a firefly every time he came into view."

Mary Lou stood defenseless. She stared into the fire fumbling to contain herself.

"Have you heard from him since he left?"

"No." It barely came out.

"Do you wish you had?"

The thought of Tom's brazen arms around her and his stolen kisses stiffened her resolve. "It was just a summer friendship. Like Pa says, cowboys are a wanderlust bunch and not for marrying."

"Your mama married one. And he's a good man. You did not know your pa before his accident. He was magnificent. He knew horseflesh like no other man in these parts. I did not blame Ellen for falling in love with him. And Uncle Nate was a cowboy. Honey, most cowboys are just young men doing a tough job. A lot of them end up good, strong men—and make marvelous husbands."

"Well." Mary Lou swallowed hard. "Tom did his job and went home." She lifted her chin and smiled. "And that is that."

Stomping feet ended the conversation. The door opened and Nate blew in looking like a snowman. "It's gonna blow up a good one if this keeps up." A wide grin brightened his face. "That colt is the prettiest little filly you ever saw. She's got a diamond shape right in the middle of her forehead." He hung up his coat and huddled in front of the fire.

Mary Lou could stand it no longer. She picked up the letter and handed it to Nate. "This came today. Thought it might be something important."

Nate ripped it open. "Why it's from Tom Langdon, that young cowboy you were sweet on last summer."

Did everybody know? Mary Lou bit her lip to keep her mouth shut.

"He says the Texas ranchers are up in arms about the quarantine forbidding Texas Longhorns to cross the Kansas borders during the warm months." Nate looked up from the letter. "I'm not surprised. But those Texans aren't considering how many of our cattle die from Texas fever. Their longhorns are immune but drop those ticks on the ground and infect our cattle. Joe Edel said he lost almost a third of his animals last year and he's not the only one. We Kansans can't sit back and lose our stock. Nope, the legislature did the right thing whether Texas likes it or not."

Mary Lou blurted, "Does he say anything else?"

"Nope. Just says he would like an answer as soon as possible." He flipped the letter over and shook his head. "That's all."

Mary Lou's last hope drained. If he had only added one line in the letter to tell her . . . what? That he did not love her and their wonderful times together meant nothing? She felt betrayed.

"Aunt Tibby," she asked. "Do you think it would be improper for me to go to the Christmas church service and party with Glenn Farrell? It's so soon after Mama died, I did not know—"

"I certainly do not and your mother would be the first one to say 'Go.' Ellen would not have missed it. You know how she enjoyed being with God's people every time she could. I agree with her. You don't honor the dead with your denial of living."

Mary Lou smiled. She would ask Aunt Nelda and Pa, and then give Glenn his answer.

Chapter Seven

Christmas Eve was perfect. Snowflakes floated from a windless blue-black sky and settled into soft mounds. Church windows beckoned sleighs and buggies from east and west. The air reverberated with laughter and greetings of parishioners. Bundled in his coat and hat, Pastor Miles stood at the door and welcomed everyone.

Big Jon, Henrietta, and their twelve children filed past, each carrying a log they neatly piled in the corner. Big Jon stuffed his into the stove and poked at the fire until it flared and spread warmth into the room.

In a rented buggy, Glenn and Mary Lou rolled to the side of the church. Glenn tied the reins and hopped out, pleasure reflected in every movement. His hands encircled Mary Lou's tiny waist and he lifted her down into the ankle-deep snow.

Nate, Tibby, and Nelda drove in and pulled their buggy alongside. "Wait!" Tibby called. "Help us carry some of this food in." They trooped to the door, fumbled for a free hand to greet Pastor, then deposited their baskets on the wall of food tables.

Chairs filled quickly. The room murmured with congenial conversation. Finally, Pastor Miles stepped to the platform. The hum of voices quieted.

"Welcome, friends and neighbors." His face beamed from behind the pulpit. "We gather on this night to celebrate the birth of our Lord Jesus Christ, God incarnate, Who came to earth to rescue His people from sin. Let's open our service with prayerful hearts and receive God's great gift by reciting John 3:16 and 17." He raised his arms.

Everyone stood and spoke words most had learned as a child.

"For God so loved the world, that He gave His only begotten Son, that whosoever believeth in Him should not perish, but have everlasting life. For God sent not His Son into the world to condemn the world; but that the world through Him might be saved."

The congregation sat down.

Pastor fluttered the pages of his Bible to the Gospel of Luke and read from chapter 2: "And Joseph also went up from Galilee . . ."

Young Jon Wimbley and Clarissa Jordan, dressed as Joseph and Mary, walked slowly down the aisle carrying Alexander Walford as the Baby Jesus. Other children clothed as angels and shepherds followed. At the front, they turned, wearing shy smiles.

"And she brought forth her firstborn son—"

A baby cried out.

"And all they that heard it wondered at those things which were told them by the shepherds." Pastor folded his hands and bowed his head.

Someone started to sing, "Away in a manger no crib for a bed," soon joined by others. The singing flowed reverently into *"Silent Night, Holy Night."*

Joseph, Mary carrying Baby Jesus, the angels, and shepherds returned up the aisle. The singing voices faded.

Pastor Miles said, "Let us pray." Thankfulness lifted heavenward and settled a benediction of peace upon everyone.

At the "Amen," someone moved a chair. The room sprang into activity. Men and boys moved tables and placed chairs. Women uncovered dried fruit, cakes, cookies, pies, and candy. Each family brought their own place settings and tables were soon set. Pastor Miles had filled the huge coffeepot on top of the pot-belly stove with water before the service. When Sarah George had arrived, she had added coffee. The aroma whet healthy appetites. Families quickly settled into places.

Although Mary Lou missed Mama, she relaxed. She loved these people. Mama had said they were the best. Sudden peace flooded her.

"Mary Lou, can I get you something?" Glenn asked for the third time.

"No, thank you." She smiled and patted the chair beside her. He perched on the edge and talked incessantly.

"Listen!" Clarissa shouted. Everyone quieted. Bells could be heard in the distance. They grew louder. Children squealed and jumped up and down.

Suddenly, the door burst open. With a shout, a snowy Santa Claus stomped in. He set his lumpy bag in the middle of the room. The children quieted immediately, stared with wide eyes, and waited. When Santa called their names, they came forward timidly to receive packages wrapped in newspaper or brown paper—carved wooden horses for the boys, rag dolls for the girls, and a new pair of mittens for every child.

Mary Lou laughed with the children. She remembered her own young excitement waiting for her name to be called. She watched each eager face and a new awareness of passing the simple joys of tradition to children hung in her mind.

As suddenly as he appeared, Santa Claus vanished for another year and the party ended. Glenn helped Mary Lou into the buggy, draped the blanket over her knees, and placed warm stones at her feet. He talked as he drove, but Mary Lou did not hear. Her thoughts were on other nights when she, Pa, and Mama had snuggled under a blanket in Pa's buggy, ridden home, and trimmed a little tree with strings of popcorn, cranberries, and colored ribbons.

"Mary Lou?" Glenn's voice pulled her to the present.

"Forgive me, Glenn. I was thinking about Christmas when Mama was here."

Glenn ducked his head, embarrassed. "I guess I've been talking too much." After a long silence he said quietly, "There are lots of things I'd like to say to you."

A fleeting thought of Tom passed through Mary Lou's mind. *If he had only said he loved her, she could hang on. But. . . .* She turned her full attention to Glenn. His eyes filled with hope.

It had stopped snowing. Glenn slowed the horse to a walk. "I don't want to rush you, Mary Lou, but I'd like to be . . . your . . . uh . . . beau."

Mary Lou's heart twinged. She shushed it. "Thank you, Glenn. Perhaps, but right now . . ."

Glenn's face lit with surprise. He smiled broadly, sat up straighter. "I understand. It's too soon after your mama's —" He did not say it. His thoughtfulness touched her.

The cabin came into view curtained by a fine sifting snow. Nelda and Pa were waiting to trim the tree, so Mary Lou hurried inside.

Later, lying in bed, Mary Lou pushed Tom out of her thoughts and tried to replace him with Glenn. Her heart objected. She tried to envision Glenn's warm, eager face. Nothing. Regardless, the next time Glenn asked, she would accept. She had be twenty next month. She drifted off to sleep walking beside Tom in the cottonwood grove.

Trade slowed in January, a relief because the store was jumbled from Christmas. Mary Lou and Glenn checked stock, cleaned shelves, and scrubbed everywhere. By the middle of February, the store was clean, neat, and well-stocked.

That morning, they had put away a new shipment from the East. Glenn had hung shiny lanterns on spikes pounded in the wooden beam that stretched the length of the store. He looked around, obviously pleased at the result. Mary Lou climbed up and down a ladder carrying lamp chimneys to the top shelf where they would be safe. Glenn hurried to help her down. When she reached bottom, he grabbed her other hand and pulled her to face him. "Mary Lou?"

She knew what was coming.

"This may not be the right time to ask, but . . ." he swallowed hard. "Would you . . . could you accept me as your steady beau?"

Her heart did not give the least recognition of this life-changing moment. Was not a girl supposed to be elated, ecstatic, or something?

Glenn's gaze never left her face.

She plunged. "Yes, Glenn." She had dreamed of this moment all her life, wondering what it would be like to be courted by a handsome young man. Her heart remained silent.

Glenn reached out as if to take her in his arms, hesitated, then took her hand and raised it to his lips. "Thank you, Mary Lou," he said humbly. "Would you go to supper with me at Mrs. Barton's tomorrow night? She cooks a special supper for anyone who has a birthday."

Mary Lou warmed. "Is tomorrow your birthday?"

Glenn nodded. "Twenty-six. Time I was getting—"

"I'd be delighted to go," she answered quickly.

"Supper is promptly at five. We could go from here." Glenn dipped his head. "If you don't mind, I'll be talking to your father about us. I'll also ask if we can leave an hour early tomorrow."

Us. We. Glenn and me. That is how it would be. Mary Lou's heart finally responded. It beat on its chamber walls like a butterfly she had once caught and put in a jar. It had hammered its wings incessantly against the glass. She had felt so sorry for it, she had let it go.

Mary Lou nodded and headed for the post office. She was sorting the mail when a buggy rattled to a halt at the hitching post. Aunt Tibby climbed out and hurried in.

"You're just the one I want to see. We're having a meeting tomorrow at the church to form a W.C.T.U. I'd like you and Jenny to round up as many young women as you can. It's at two o'clock."

"Will we be through by four? I have a supper invitation at five."

Tibby's eyebrows went up. "With whom?"

"Glenn. It's his birthday. Mrs. Barton cooks a special supper and lets the boarder have a guest. Glenn asked me."

"That's nice." Tibby searched Mary Lou's face. "It is nice, isn't it?"

Mary Lou reached for more letters. "My life is here, and Glenn is just about the best catch in Venture."

Tibby nodded. "Glenn is a nice boy."

"Boy? Twenty-six is a bit more than a boy."

Tibby turned to go into the store. "I need some quilting thread. Did any come in the new shipment?"

Tibby bought her thread, then peered around for Glenn. She took Mary Lou's hand and pulled her out to her buggy. "If you want to," she whispered, "we could have a surprise birthday party. Have Glenn bring you to the ranch after dinner. Tell Jenny to round up everyone."

Mary Lou smiled. Leave it to Aunt Tibby to jump in. It would be fun to surprise Glenn. He had no family here, nor had she ever heard him mention one.

Tibby climbed into her buggy. "I'm going to the church. We're quilting this afternoon." She slapped the reins. The horses gave a tug and the wagon rolled. "Don't forget," she called over her shoulder. "Mention the meeting to all the women you see. Got to get prepared for the fall cattle drives. When it's not safe for a woman to walk the streets of her own town, something had better be done."

Mary Lou watched the buggy bounce up Center Street. Aunt Tibby and her mother were so different, yet so alike. Mary Lou went back into the store and put the mail away. Enough for today. If she went home now, she would have time to wash her hair. What dress should she wear? The blue one? It was the last dress Mama had made—and Tom's favorite. He had said it matched her eyes. She shook her head. Forget Tom. The mail box had been empty again today. No, she would wear her gray dress with the white lace collar. It made her look older. She would save the blue.

Pa came through the back door. "Mary Lou, are you ready to go home?"

"Yes, Pa. I'm ready."

Chapter Eight

Mary Lou tossed the last letter into its box and sighed. No message from Tom. She told herself it was a futile hope, but her heart paid no attention and she eagerly searched each mail bag.

The window framed a green haze of burgeoning prairie grass persistently edging the ruts on Center Street. Balmy air swept in the open door and shooed out the musty odors of winter. A familiar horse came on a fast trot. Jenny Wimbley dismounted and tied Missy to the rail. Mary Lou glanced at the clock. One-thirty! Where had the morning gone?

Jenny hustled into the post office out of breath. "I did not know whether we'd get here or not. We washed all mornin'."

"Your ma coming to the meeting?"

"Yep, would not miss it. Says it's high time somebody did something to get decent laws in Venture. Pa laughed and told her not to forget her knittin'. "

Mary Lou smoothed her dress. "Uncle Nate says it's foolishness, but he knows Aunt Tibby. Once a bee starts buzzing in her bonnet, look out!"

Their laugh subsided into a rare awkward silence.

Jenny blurted, "Mary Lou, are you serious about accepting Glenn as a suitor?"

"Yes, Jenny, but it won't make any difference between us."

"It always makes a difference. My sister Sybil changed when she and Charlie became betrothed."

"I'm not betrothed, Jenny." She inwardly shuddered.

"You will be. Everybody knows Glenn is smitten with you."

"He hasn't told me yet."

"He will. What am I going to do when you get married?"

Mary Lou threw her arms around her friend. "If Glenn and I marry, it won't change a thing between you and me. Look at your ma and Mama. They were best friends in good and bad times. It'll be the same with us." Mary Lou reached for her shawl. "Come on, we'd better get to the church."

From east and west the ladies of Venture headed toward the church yard. Mary Lou and Jenny joined the flow entering the building, spotted two chairs in the second row, and slid into them. Amiable chatter drifted out the church door and windows. Several men cast curious glances and moved on about their business.

Aunt Tibby and Henrietta sat at a table in front, engrossed in conversation with a woman Mary Lou had never seen. At the small organ, Mary Wescott pumped out one hymn after another.

Suddenly, Tibby rapped her knuckles on the table, stood up, and cleared her throat.

The room quieted.

"Good afternoon, ladies. Let's all stand and pray."

The ladies stood, their heads bowed. Tibby tilted her face toward heaven. "Our Father," she began, "we know You have seen the wickedness in our town, and we are ashamed to have waited so long to ask for Thy help to drive this evil from our midst. Now it's tearing at the fabric of our families. Alcoholic spirits are brewed in the cauldrons of hell. They take the minds of men, women, even our children. God, bless our gathering and help us find a way to drive this plague from us. In Jesus' name we pray. Amen."

Mary Wescott played an introduction and the women sang *"Yield Not to Temptation."* Then they sat down and gave Tibby their full attention.

"All of you know why we're here. It's time decent people took hold of this town instead of letting men like Mac Ludden dictate the law. As women and mothers, it's our duty to demand Venture be cleaned up. We must demand the men make this town a safe place."

Effie Jackson shot her arm up. "We know all that, Tibby, but what can we do about it? It's up to the men."

Sarah George rose and shook her head in dismay. "But the men aren't doing anything about it."

Libby nodded. "Ladies, that's why we're here. There is something we can do. Sitting beside me is Amanda Way. She is a Methodist and Quaker preacher."

The ladies applauded.

Tibby continued. "She recently moved to Kansas from Indiana where she organized their first women's suffrage movement in the 1850s. She is continuing her fight for temperance and suffrage and organized the National Women's Christian Temperance Union of Kansas. She travels to encourage women to unite and fight for prohibition. That's why she's here today—to help us form that union. Ladies, please welcome Amanda Way."

Amanda stood to speak. The ladies applauded and gave her their full attention.

"Christian sisters, your presence is a testimony that you recognize women should have a say in what goes on in your town. Women are one-half the population of America, but we have no opportunity to determine the laws we live under. The best place to begin is to fight for temperance. The evils of alcohol ruin more people's lives than all the wars this country has fought."

The women nodded agreement.

Amanda pointed to Sarah George. "Like Sarah said, 'The men aren't doing anything about it.' Why should they? Things are going the way they want them. Saloons and gambling flourish because men get rich. The only way to stop them is to make it against the law to manufacture or sell intoxicants. Unfortunately we have no vote. But we are not powerless. We can join together and rally 'round those men who see the need not only for prohibition, but also for another vital issue. My dear ladies, that issue is the voting privilege for women."

There was a noticeable intake of breath. Some women nodded. Others shook their heads.

"Ladies, please don't shake your heads. We have the right to be more than chattels. We need the right to acquire and possess property and have equal rights to the custody of our children. Our men often get shot out from under us. Where are we then? Cast back upon our sons or charity. Today we are asking you to join together to fight for prohibition."

"What could we do?" called a voice from the back of the room.

"We can be at the next election to hand out literature to voters who haven't made up their minds. We can influence how people vote for prohibition. When the law passes, we can demand our town officials follow the law."

The women sat transfixed by the audacity of what they heard.

"First we pledge ourselves to our task. Then, for the sake of our children, we fight against the evils we abhor. Maybe not today, but God helping us—we will win!"

As one body, the group rose, banging hands together in very unladylike fashion. A buzz of general agreement washed over the room.

Tibby rapped her knuckles on the table several times before the women settled into their seats. "Thank you, Amanda. Ladies, here on the table is a paper for us to sign, pledging ourselves to this task until it's accomplished. Next week, we'll meet to make solid plans to attack the evils of Venture."

Mary Wescott pumped up the organ, and the strains of *"Onward Christian Soldiers"* poured forth. The women rose and sang with fervor. Tibby closed with prayer and the women swarmed to the table. All but a timid few placed their signatures on the paper with W.C.T.U. in large letters across the top. The Women's Christian Temperance Union of Venture, Kansas, was born.

Women gathered in groups talking to Amanda, Tibby, and Henrietta. Mary Lou and Jenny listened, then slowly walked back to the store discussing the meeting. Mary Lou remembered Mama had detested alcoholic spirits and had refused them from the doctor when she fell ill. "To use God's grain and precious food for such brew," she said, "is a slap on the face of God."

After Jenny left, Mary Lou went to the back room to find Pa. He had gone home. Glenn came to meet her. "What was your meeting all about?"

"We've formed a Women's Christian Temperance Union to stop the drinking and shooting in Venture."

Glenn looked puzzled, but smiled and reached out to stop her. "I have something important to ask you."

"Oh?" From his attentiveness lately, Mary Lou suspected what lay ahead. The bigger question was: Am I ready for it? They had gone to church together every Sunday since Christmas. He frequently visited their home and chatted with Aunt Nelda and Pa. Nelda considered him a very nice young man. But—

"We've been keeping company for three months, Mary Lou. I've been wondering what your answer would be if I . . ." He cleared his throat. "If I asked you to marry me."

Mary Lou searched for the answer in her heart. Glenn—her husband?

Glenn's gaze held her, pleading for an answer.

Suddenly Tom took shape, his eyes filled with love. Mary Lou shook herself mentally. The time for daydreaming was over. Mama had always said, "A bird in the hand is worth two in the bush." Did that fit here?

Glenn cupped her face tenderly in his hands. "Mary Lou, I love you. I want you to be my wife."

Those were the words she had longed to hear. The voice was different, but Glenn honored her with living truth. Had Tom been truthful, he would never have told her he would write when he had not intended to.

Mary Lou looked into Glenn's eyes. They radiated love, patience, and respect. Glenn was different from the coarse men who came into the store. Mama had called him a gentleman. Glenn loved her. What more could she ask?

"Mary Lou? Did you hear me?"

"Yes."

"Do you have any love at all for me?"

Desperately Mary Lou searched her heart. Did she love him? She liked and admired him. Enough to marry him? "Yes I do, Glenn. I'll be happy to be your wife." She waited for the earth to shake or her heart to pound. Nothing.

Glenn grabbed both her hands. "Then I may ask your pa for permission?"

"Yes."

Delighted surprise covered Glenn's face. Very slowly he put his arms around her and pulled her close. Mary Lou lifted her face. His soft lips caressed her trembling ones. It was a sweet, loving kiss, nothing like Tom's. Tom's sweet kisses held a fierce urgency.

Glenn released her and smiled. "I've been dreaming of this moment for months, long before Christmas. You've made me the happiest man in Venture." He threw his arms out wide. "In the whole world!" His arms encircled her waist. "I love you, Mary Lou. I'll love you forever."

Without even thinking, she said, "I love you, too, Glenn."

"Your father went home about an hour ago. I'll get a horse from the livery and ride home with you. I want to ask your father formally for your hand in marriage. I talked after Christmas about it, but he was not too . . ." he sought for a proper word, "too talkative."

Mary Lou felt warmed by his words. Of all things, Glenn's patient consideration endeared him to her. "He's much better since Aunt Nelda came. It was hard for him when Mama died."

"Yes." He stood looking at her, then said, "I'll saddle Dulcie."

Mary Lou turned Dulcie into the lane. Glenn followed and they dismounted at the barn. They walked toward the cabin, Glenn's warm hand holding Mary Lou's.

After supper, Glenn accompanied Pa to do chores. Dishes finished, Nelda dug into her mending basket. Mary Lou sat staring into the fire.

"He asked you, did not he?"

Mary Lou smiled. How on earth Aunt Nelda knew so many things, she could not fathom. "Yes."

After a long pause, Nelda looked up from her garment. "Well, aren't you going to tell me what you said?"

"I said yes."

"That's what you want?"

"Of course that's what I want."

Nelda resumed sewing. "What about Tom?"

Mary Lou stiffened. "What about Tom? Aunt Nelda, when a man does not love you, the best thing to do is forget him. In all this time, he hasn't written. He's shown beyond a doubt that I mean nothing to him." She stared into the fire.

"Glenn is loving and kind and treats me like a man treats a woman he loves. He'll make a good husband and. . . ." She was going to say the father of their children but stopped, remembering that moment in Tom's arms.

Nelda looked up. "And?"

"And I love him."

"That's what I wanted to hear. Marriage is serious business. Children are a big responsibility. None of it should be entered into lightly. Besides, he knows the Lord Jesus. Does Tom?"

She did not know! *Oh, Lord, forgive me. I never even thought about Tom knowing You.* How foolish she had been. To marry a non-Christian would have broken Mama's heart. Mary Lou relaxed with a sense of peace.

Nelda laid aside her sewing and kissed her. "My dear child, I feel the same as if you were my own daughter, the daughter I never had. I'm happy if you're happy."

Mary Lou clung to her aunt. "Thank you, Aunt Nelda. The Lord sent the best substitute for Mama He could find when He sent you to us. I feel like your daughter." Even saying that, she could almost sense Mama's blessing in the room. True to His Word, God had provided for her and then restored Pa. Her heart swelled with thankfulness.

Pa and Glenn stomped their feet outside the door. When they came in, Glenn immediately walked to Mary Lou's side. "Your father has accepted me as his future son-in-law. I'm proud to be in the family." He reached into his pocket for a small case and took out a sparkling gold locket. He hung it around Mary Lou's neck and kissed her. His arm around her, he grinned and nodded. "Now, it's official."

Mary Lou felt her cheeks flush.

Glenn took her hand and pulled her outside. The sky, studded with stars, stretched from one dark blue horizon to the other. He kissed her again. "I'll see you tomorrow. I love you," he said. Riding off, Glenn waved back and blew her a kiss.

Mary Lou went in with the brilliance of the stars in her eyes. Nelda glanced up from her sewing and smiled.

For the first time since Mama died, Mary Lou felt happy. She kissed Aunt Nelda's cheek and went to her bedroom to think and pray. It had been a momentous day.

Chapter Nine

It had been a mild winter. Smitty, Tom, and the boys had used it to mend and build new fences for the corrals. Even the ranch house boasted a new fence.

About the middle of January, snow began to fall in earnest. An icy wind blew down from the north and turned feathery flakes into a stinging blizzard. Outside, animals huddled to share their warmth. Inside, fireplaces in the ranch and the bunkhouse stove consumed cow chips and wood almost faster than they could be supplied.

Riding the range, Tom, Smitty, and the cowboys located herds of half frozen cattle that looked like snow mounds on stilts. Texas cattle were not accustomed to such weather. If they lay down, their legs froze.

Tom called to Smitty, "I don't think we'll fare too bad if it quits by tomorrow. Let's go home." Tom swung Tinder, who needed little encouragement to pick up speed when he sensed he was going toward home.

"Animals are pretty tough," Smitty hollered. "After all, they was here long 'fore we came and there's still more of them than there are of us. But my old joints sure could stand a hot cup of coffee and some of Jess's pot-luck stew."

Tom hunched his shoulders and wondered if Mary Lou was warm. The storm probably had crossed Kansas as it traveled south. The thought of her created a lonesome ache. Their parting haunted him. He had handled it badly. But his senses remembered everything: the softness of her lithe body as he swung her around in his arms; her warm response to his kisses; her long, soft hair; her trust . . . That is what worried him most—that he had lost her trust. Regardless, he refused to give up. He loved her.

Back in the ranch house, Allena stood at the kitchen window watching the falling snow. Earlier, a snow curtain had obliterated the bunkhouse. Now she could see a clear outline of it. Movement caught her eye. A horse and rider approached the house and came to a halt outside the door. The animal paused. The rider slid off and tumbled into a heap. The horse shook itself and lumbered to the barn.

Allena and her housekeeper, Hattie, grabbed their shawls and tied them over their heads. A blast of icy air hit them as they opened the door. They half lifted, half dragged the man through the door, laid him on the floor, and removed the scarf tied around his face. The man's eyes were glued shut by frosty lashes.

"Doug!" Allena gasped. His hat was frozen to his head, and his ears resembled frosted white shells. Hattie hurriedly filled a wash basin with snow, and Allena gently held the snow against Doug's ears to encourage slow defrosting. Hattie ran for blankets.

Doug groaned and tried to open his eyes. Allena wiped away the melting frost and was finally able to remove his hat. Slowly, Doug's eyes opened, stared blankly, and then closed.

Hattie poured a cup of coffee from one of the large pots hugging the fireplace and set it aside to cool before they gave it to Doug.

"I hope Jess has plenty of hot coffee ready for the men when they come in," Allena said.

Hattie nodded. "Knowin' him, he will."

The women draped warmed blankets over Doug. He groaned and settled down.

Allena peered out the window. Again snow obliterated the bunkhouse, corrals, and barn. She squinted in an attempt to see through it. Was she mistaken or was there movement around the barn? The men were back! She breathed a sigh of relief.

At the kitchen door, Tom slapped the snow from his hat and jacket and stomped his feet before entering. He swung the door open. His mother was on her knees bending over someone lying on the floor.

At the sight of Tom, Allena sighed in relief. "I'm glad you're home. It's Doug—half frozen."

Tom bent over his brother and rubbed him to encourage stimulation. His hand moved over a lump in Doug's vest pocket. He reached in and withdrew a set of keys. The office keys? How many times he had tried to find them. He slipped them into his shirt pocket and looked at Doug, who would probably be asleep for awhile. Tom seized the moment and headed for the ranch office.

He opened the door to a mess—papers piled everywhere under a thick layer of dust. If Doug's bookkeeping was as slovenly as his office, no wonder the ranch had not shown the profits he thought there should be.

Quickly, Tom flipped through papers piled high on each side of the desk. He tried not to disturb them too much. It would be better if Doug did not know he had gained access.

Tom found an entry ledger in the first desk drawer he opened. He flipped its pages slowly, noting sporadic records of the past year. He recognized money he had given Doug from the cattle drive. He laid the ledger on the chair and tried several keys in the safe lock. The fourth key slid in easily and Tom swung the door open wide.

Ledgers and folded legal papers were shoved here, there, anywhere. Tom glanced through paper after paper. There was a fair amount of money in a green metal box. Tom thought it better to leave it untouched. Doug had an uncanny memory when it came to money. Any missing would be a dead give-away. It was to Tom's advantage to keep his search a secret until the right time.

Not wanting to push his luck, Tom did not look through everything and tried to leave things as he found them. He was sure Doug would not be able to tell if things had been moved. About to swing the safe door shut, he spied something shiny on the bottom of the safe. Keys. He brought them up beside the set in his hand, and compared them. A duplicate set! Tom smiled at his good fortune and tucked the extra keys in his pocket.

Before he left the office, Tom glanced around to see that it looked the same as when he came in. The small changes in the piles of papers would not show, but something nagged him. He grinned. The piles were too neat! He messed them up. After picking up the ledger, he locked the door and left. On the way to the kitchen, Tom slipped the ledger behind a chair in the main room.

In the kitchen, Doug showed signs of returning consciousness. Tom adjusted the blankets covering his brother, and in one smooth movement slid the keys into the vest pocket where he had found them. He turned to his mother. "I'm starved," he said.

Hattie hustled and in minutes placed a steaming dish of stew with dumplings under Tom's nose. He dove in and ate heartily. The hot food conquered the cold that had gripped his bones all day.

Doug stirred and Allena moved immediately to his side. Dazed and shivering, he opened his eyes and struggled to a sitting position.

Hattie wrapped his hands around the warm coffee cup she had poured earlier. He sipped and sipped, finally stopped shaking, and then described his ride home from Harness.

"Why on earth did you start home in this blizzard in the first place?" Allena asked.

"Most everyone else had gone. No reason to stay. I did not think it was bad until I was more than halfway home, so I just kept on coming. I should have stayed in town."

"I'm glad you did not. Families need to be together when storms of any kind come," his mother said quietly.

If Doug heard what his mother said, he gave no response. He ate a half bowl of Hattie's stew, then with Tom's help, staggered to his room.

Tom returned to the kitchen and kissed his mother on her cheek. "If you don't mind, Mother, I think I'll hit the hay. It's been a long, cold day."

"I don't blame you. Hattie put a couple extra quilts on your bed."

"Thanks, Hattie," Tom called as he left. He picked up the ledger he had hidden in the main room and carried it to his room. Later, propped up in bed, he turned its pages not knowing quite what to look for. When his father was alive, family financial discussions had not interested him. But next month he would become a quarter owner of the Circle Z.

His next thought was of Mary Lou. Hopefully by next year at this time, Mary Lou would be his wife. He imagined her here, in this room for him to hold and love. He closed the ledger, slid it under his pillow, and sank into a deep sleep.

Dazzling sun woke Tom. Dazed, he sat up and looked out the window. It had stopped snowing! He hurriedly dressed, started for the door, and stopped. The ledger! He tucked it into his shirt and opened the door. The hall was empty. If Doug were awake, his booming voice would be audible. At the office door, Tom slipped the key in the door and locked it behind him. He had his hand on the desk drawer when he heard Doug's heavy tread in the hall.

Was he coming to the office? In desperation, Tom looked for a place to hide. His father's big leather chair! He squeezed tightly into the corner behind it.

The key turned in the lock and Doug banged in.

Tom did not dare look. If Doug saw him, he would play a game of cat and mouse. For some reason, Doug relished making people squirm. Doug pulled out a drawer, slammed it shut, and left, locking the door behind him.

Afraid to move, Tom waited a few moments before he peeked out. The office was empty. He climbed from behind the chair, put the ledger in the drawer where he had found it, and quietly unlocked the door. Opening it slowly, he slipped into the hall and locked the door. He went back to his bedroom to calm down, then came out as if he were just getting up.

Tom's mother and Hattie had set the kitchen table. They did not want to waste wood firing the dining room fireplace. Allena smiled at her handsome, red-headed son. "Good morning. And it is. It's quit snowing." She glanced out the window. "I'm not fond of snow, but I have to admit it's beautiful. God transforms everything into a display of His beauty."

"Sermon over, Mother." Doug strode across the kitchen and sat down at the table. His ears, cheeks, and nose were fiery red. So was his spirit. He did not try to conceal the anger that twisted his face. "You need to work on goodie boy here," he thumbed at Tom. "He's an outright thief."

Dumbfounded, Allena stared from one son to the other. The obvious hatred on Doug's face resurfaced a fear she had carried since they were small boys. Doug, constantly angry, had fought anything and anyone, especially Tom.

Doug sneered. "Did you hear me? Your perfect son is a thief. He stole the office keys out of my vest pocket last night and stole a ledger from my desk."

Allena looked askance from one son to the other.

Tom recognized the spot he was in, but he told the truth. "Yes, I found the keys in your pocket. You won't give them to me, so I took them to find out for myself what's going on at this ranch. I'm twenty-one in ten days and quarter owner of this ranch. I have a right to know."

Doug leaped to his feet and stumbled halfway across the room, his fists clenched.

Allena ran and stood in front of Tom. "No! Douglas Langdon, I forbid you to fight. Your father, here in spirit, forbids you to fight. The time for little-boy squabbles is over—"

Doug glared at his mother. "This is no little-boy squabble. I'm talking about your son entering my office and stealing the entry ledger. Ask him about that!"

Allena turned to Tom, eyebrows raised.

Tom hated the pain he saw in his mother's eyes. "Yes, I did take the keys from his pocket. I went into the office and looked around, but I do not have the ledger, and that's the truth."

Doug laughed. He started for the office, punching in his vest pocket for the keys.

Allena and Tom followed.

A smirk on his face, Doug swung the door open and stepped back to let his mother enter. Allena's eyes grew wide. "Douglas! This place is a mess. How would you know anything was missing?"

Doug ignored her, marched to the desk, and paused, a triumphant look on his face. He yanked a drawer open. "Look for yourself."

The ledger lay at a crooked angle. Allena and Tom stared at the book, then gazed at Doug. Allena stepped forward and lifted it from the drawer. "Is this what you're looking for, Doug?"

He grabbed it and flicked through pages. Suspicion clouded his face. "Yes, but I came to work on it this morning and it was not here."

Tom smiled. "Are you sure you looked in the right drawer?"

Doug stared knives at Tom.

I have thrown him off balance, Tom thought. *Now if I can just keep it that way.* He shrugged his shoulders and walked out of the office. "I'm hungry."

"Yes, the food will be getting cold. Hattie will have our ears." Allena preceded her sons to the kitchen. Doug, confused, closed in behind Tom and growled, "That ledger was not in the drawer when I went in this morning. I know you were in there."

His voice rose. "But don't think this gives you any hold on the ranch. Mark my words—this whole ranch will be mine!" He marched down the hall to his room.

"Douglas!" Allena started after him.

Tom grabbed her arm. "Mother, let him cool off." He pulled her to face him. "This is a man's fight, not two little boys." His mother's stunned stare betrayed how vulnerable she was. He put his arms around her and pulled her to him. She was trembling.

Tom had won for the moment. Now he would have to be doubly alert. Doug would seize any opportunity to best him. Tom's stomach growled. He turned his mother toward the kitchen. The smell of bacon, ham, home-baked bread, and flapjacks whet his appetite and spurred his feet. "I'm starving."

Hattie had set the table for three. Tom and Allena sat down. Allena patted the third chair. "Join us, Hattie. I hate empty chairs." She smiled and bowed her head. "Tom, say grace, please."

Tom thanked God for His care, for their family, home, and land. Within, he prayed, *Thank You, Father. That was a narrow escape. You know I'm going to need all the help I can get. Thy will be done.*

Chapter Ten

The early morning air blew clean and clear. A red glow in the east promised a warm spring day. Circle Z buzzed with activity.

Tom, astride Tinder, tied Victor to the back of Allena's buggy. He touched his hat to Nelson, whose face radiated his excitement at driving his mother to the stage station.

On the buckboard, Smitty sat with his elbows resting on his knees, the reins hanging limp in his hands. He squinted up at the sun and resettled his hat on top of his eyebrows.

Allena emerged from the ranch door issuing orders to Hattie. She hurried to her buggy and climbed in beside Nelson. The horses moved and she settled back to read aloud from her Bible after they got rolling.

It took two hours to get to the stage station. Tom spotted a dustball way ahead—probably the stage. He reckoned they would just about meet coming into the station.

Tom leaned to Nelson and hollered. "Let's pick it up and beat that stage in."

Nelson grinned, slapped the reins, and took off. He pulled to a stop in the station yard with the westbound stagecoach still a mile up the road. He scooted out of the buggy onto his feet and crutches and stared admiringly as the stage driver handled the team of six snorting horses.

The first four passengers out of the stagecoach went into the station for something to eat. A tall, broad man in a stylish eastern suit stepped out and assisted an elegantly dressed young lady from the coach. She looked up and immediately opened her parasol.

Allena was out of the buggy. "Zack!" she cried and flung her arms around her eldest son. Everyone talked at once. After the boisterous greeting, Zack turned to the beautiful woman who stood slightly behind him and pulled her to his side. "Mom, Tom, Nelson, I'd like you to meet my wife, Darcy."

After an awkward pause, Allena gently embraced her first daughter-in-law. "Well! This is quite a surprise, a delightful one." She held Darcy at arm's length. "My dear, you are lovely."

Darcy smiled and stood with her head high.

Tom came forward, took her hands in his, and bowed. "How did Zack keep you a secret?" He turned to his brother. "I thought you went East to become a lawyer."

Darcy sent an adoring glance to Zack. "He did, and he's a good one. My father wanted to take him into his law firm, but Zack wants to set up his own firm in Texas." Darcy tossed her head and laughed. "I'm going to try and talk him out of it."

Three mouths dropped open in surprise. Zack? The brother who never wanted any part of Texas?

Zack shrugged. "I know what you're thinking. When I left, I never wanted to return except to visit. But it's mighty crowded in the East. You probably won't believe it, but I hankered after these wide, open spaces." He laughed and looked around. "Where's Doug?"

"He had some business to attend to in town and said he had see you at the ranch." Allena sounded apologetic.

Tom waved to Smitty, who came over to give Zack a handshake. "You sure have growed up to be a big man. One look at you, I thought you was your father standin' there."

Zackary Langdon's namesake grinned and said, "I know. Every time I look in the mirror it's a shock to see Father looking back."

"Then your father must have been a handsome, magnificent man." Darcy slipped her arm through her husband's.

"He was," Nelson shifted himself to the other side of Zack.

Darcy leaned across and touched Nelson's cheek, smiled sweetly, then surveyed the rest of the family with cool eyes.

Tom asked, "Would you like a drink of water before we start back? It'll be a long, warm ride."

Darcy surveyed the scene with disgust. "Oh, no thank you. I'll wait until we get . . . home?"

Tom swung onto Tinder's saddle and led Victor to Zack. "Come on, mount up. Let's go home."

Zack inspected Victor. "Not Diamond?"

"No, but next thing to it. He's Diamond's son. Remember the colt with a mind of his own who tossed you?" Tom grinned.

"Diamond's colt! He's as regal as his father." Zack helped his mother and Darcy into the buggy, mounted, and swung Nelson up behind him. Victor danced around under double weight, then tossed his head ready to go.

Allena gave the horse's back a slap and turned the buggy westward. Darcy sat rod-straight, her gloved hands clenched in her lap, her chin in the air. When they faced west, she grabbed her parasol and struggled to find a way to shield herself from the sun.

The men on horseback fell in behind to keep the dust off the ladies. Smitty, luggage loaded in the buckboard, moved into last place, a knowing grin on his face.

When the caravan passed under the Circle Z arch, Hattie stood on the porch peering. Allena waved and Hattie scurried indoors. The buggy pulled to a stop in front of the low, rambling, adobe ranch. Allena tied the reins and got out.

Darcy stared, unbelieving. "This is home?"

"Yes, my dear, and a good one. Won't you come in? Hattie has lunch prepared. I'm sure you must be as ready for it as we are." Allena stepped to the porch without a backward glance and Hattie met her at the door.

Zack assisted his wife into the house, came back out, and joined Tom riding toward the barn. Several cowboys came around the barn and spotted Zack. They pumped his hand, talked a bit, and finally took the horses to unsaddle.

Zack slapped Victor's flank when he handed him over. "This is what I've missed. Any fancy horse back East would be hard put to match that stallion."

The brothers walked toward the ranch. "Good to have you home, Zack, but Darcy sure surprised us. How come you did not tell us you were married?"

Zack grinned. "I thought of it, but knowing Ma, this was the easiest way. Darcy's a city girl. Ma thinks the only wives for Texas men are Texas girls."

"How long you been married?"

"About two months. When I got Ma's letter, I knew I had to come home. Figured Doug might try and pull something. There's a hate in Doug I never understood. Father saw it too and it worried him."

"Did I hear Darcy right? You plan to set up practice here?"

Zack sighed. "Yes. Boston is exciting but it's mighty crowded." He laughed. "When I left, Ma said, 'Once a Texas boy, always a Texas boy.' I did not believe her. But when Darcy's father asked me to join his firm, I got to thinking. There are lots of lawyers in the East. I'd just be one of them. Out this way, there are few. That's what made up my mind. I hope to set up a law firm of my own in Harness.

"Darcy isn't happy about it. At first, she did not understand how I could refuse her father. We'd be set for life! I thought she was going to break our betrothal. Finally, after she knew I was serious, she insisted we be married right away so she could come with me. We had our fancy wedding, went to the Carolinas to visit her sister for a month's honeymoon, then started west."

Tom thought of mentioning Mary Lou but decided to wait. They had reached the porch. Zack and Tom washed and hurried to the dining room. Allena was in her place, but Darcy was not there.

"She was tired and ordered Smitty to take her things to your room. She demanded a bath immediately to get the filth off her." Allena raised her eyebrows. "Did she bring a personal maid?"

Tom, surprised at his mother's tone, suppressed a smile. The shock must have been more than she let on. Zack departed immediately to his room.

Hattie popped her head in and out waiting for Allena's signal to serve. Finally Allena motioned. "Hattie, please go to Zack's room and tell him dinner needs to be served."

Hattie hurried out.

Nelson broke the silence. "Zack and I talked. Says he aims to be a big lawyer in Texas." He bobbed his head decisively. "He will, too." Nelson beamed with a confidence Tom had not seen in a long time. For Nelson, Father had been the world's greatest man. He had been eleven when Father died. When Zack left, he had lost his second father.

Zack returned to the dining room alone, Hattie right behind him. "Mother, would it be too much trouble to have Hattie take Darcy's dinner up to our room? The trip has been long and she's very tired."

"Of course," Allena said. "Hattie, bring our food to the table, then put Darcy's dinner on a tray and take it up to her."

"Yessum." Hattie disappeared.

Zack took his seat. Unless they had had company, it had remained empty during his absence. His father's place opposite Allena was always empty. "Now it's the Lord's place." she said. A framed picture, embroidered by Allena's mother, hung on the wall between the windows: "Jesus, Ever Present Guest in Our Home."

"Zack, would you say the blessing, please?" Allena asked.

He said a short prayer he had learned as a boy. Tom listened and wondered. Zack had given his life to Jesus Christ. So had Doug. Was Darcy a Christian? She acted spoiled. Tom asked forgiveness for the thought. She is Zack's wife and it is obvious Zack loves her. Everything must be new and strange. A sudden longing filled him. It would be the same with Mary Lou. Texas was a world apart from Boston or Venture.

"Tom?"

He roused to the dish of potatoes held out to him. "I'm sorry. I was daydreaming." He served himself and passed them to Zack.

Hattie came in and whispered to Allena.

"Zack, Hattie says Darcy wants to see you."

Noticeably embarrassed, Zack excused himself.

A horse thundered into the yard and a dusty Doug strutted into the dining room. His mother's eyes sent him to the wash basin in the back kitchen.

"Zack here?" he asked as he sat down.

"He's up with his new wife," Allena explained.

"New wife! Zack married? Well, that old book boy is spicier than he looks." Doug did not notice his mother's frown as she passed the steak plate. "Well, wha-d-ya know." His face creased with a secret grin.

All ate in silence until Nelson blurted, "Zack's going to stay and be a lawyer here."

Doug looked up from his plate, his mouth full.

Did Tom imagine it, or did a look of fear flash in Doug's face?

Doug gulped and sneered. "Small town boy makes good and comes home to swagger. Does not Zack know lawyers don't get paid much in Texas?"

"Texas needs good lawyers. Maybe with a good one," Tom emphasized, "we could scare out the land speculators." He looked for Doug's reaction. Doug just ate ravenously.

Zack came in, greeted Doug, and sat down.

"Everything all right?" Allena asked. "I can appreciate how grueling the long ride across Texas can be. I'm surprised you did not come as far as you could by train, then take the stage."

Doug looked up from his dinner. "So our big brother has himself a wife. Congratulations. I'm anxious to see who'd have you. Where's she from?"

"Boston."

"And she married a Texas rancher?"

"No, she married a Boston lawyer."

Tom sensed the rising tension. He did not blame Zack. Doug's sarcasm was hard to handle. Allena broke the ensuing silence with a question about Zack's years in law school. Finally she pushed back her chair and rose. The men stood.

"I agree with Darcy. It's been a long day. Good night, my sons. It's good to have you home again. Don't forget your prayers," she reminded as she left the room.

Tom and Zack smiled. Their mother had reminded them to say their prayers every night as long as they could remember.

"How come you did not accept the offer Darcy's father made?" Tom asked. "You'd have probably become rich."

"I did not feel at home there. While I was getting my law degree, it was fine, but I knew where I belonged." He sipped his cup of coffee. "Fill me in with what's going on here at the ranch."

Doug bristled. "You think you're gonna come back after four years of shoving the work over on me and take over? Think again, brother. You walked away when you had the opportunity. Now this ranch is mine."

Zack's jaw tightened. Tom could not see Zack's eyes, but he knew they contained the steel determination of their father's.

"Then you need help," Zack said. "The payments I received dropped considerably in the last two years. This is the best ranch in these parts and with the demand for beef, you should be thriving."

Doug rose abruptly. His chair clattered to the floor. "This ranch is as good now as it ever was."

Zack never moved. "I agree. But the money is sifting away somewhere. This isn't the same place I left. The barn and corral are in need of repair."

Doug leaped at Zack, eyes blazing. "Who are you to walk in here and criticize me? I've spent these past four years working harder than you ever worked. You're not going to stroll in here and take over." He swung toward Tom. "Nor is your birthday going to change things. This ranch is mine!" Doug stomped out.

Tom and Zack sat silent.

"Something's wrong," Zack said. "I'm used to his anger, but he's like a snorting longhorn under attack. We've got to watch those horns. They're dangerous."

Tom nodded. "I've a hunch it has to do with land speculators. I've been wondering if Doug has been selling off some of the land. We could ask the cowboys if they've seen anything."

"I've seen some men come with Doug and ride out to the range," Nelson offered.

"Did you recognize any of them?" Zack asked.

"No, but they wore eastern clothes."

Zack sighed. "Well we can't do anything tonight. I need to see the books. Have you seen them?" he asked Tom.

"No. Doug keeps the office door locked. As far as he's concerned, I'm just one of the hands."

"Figures. We'll start tomorrow. I'll go into town to the land office and see what activity I can find." He pushed back his chair. "Right now, I'm tired and I have a wife waiting for me so I'll see you in the morning."

Hattie peeked into the dining room.

Tom waved her in. "Come on, Hattie, you can clear. We're leaving." He went to bed and slept sounder than he had in months. Zack was back.

Tom and Zack left early. Long after the sun rose, Allena rapped on Zack's bedroom door. The door opened a crack. A tousled Darcy peered through. She had been crying.

"Did you rest well, my dear?"

Darcy's child-like eyes hardened. "Yes."

"The men will be in for breakfast in half-an-hour. I thought you'd like to join us."

"How do I wash?"

"Hattie will bring you warm water for the basin on the stand."

"Thank you," Darcy said and closed the door.

An hour later deep voices announced Tom and Zack were back. Everyone was seated at the breakfast table when Darcy entered, her nut-brown hair fashionably pinned on top her head. Her simple blue dress had a white lace collar. The men stood as she swished into her seat beside Zack.

All but Doug sat down. He walked around the table with a big smile on his face and kissed Darcy's hand. "So you're the beauty I've been hearing about." He turned to Zack. "I have to admit, you sure can pick 'em."

Zack stood. "Darcy, this is my younger brother, Doug."

"Welcome to the Circle Z." Doug made a magnanimous sweep of his hand. "I'll be glad to show you around while Zack's busy at his law office."

"Zack, Doug, sit down, please. The food is getting cold. Tom, would you say the blessing?" Allena bowed her head.

"Dear Father," Tom prayed. "We thank You that our whole family is gathered at this table and for Darcy, our new member. We thank You for this day and ask Your help in our work. We ask Your blessing on this food so bountifully given. In Jesus' name. . . ."

Everyone except Darcy said "Amen."

After the food was passed and everyone was eating, Allena said, "Zack, I think it would be nice if you gave Darcy a tour of some of the ranch to get her better acquainted." She turned to Darcy. "You do ride?"

"Of course." Darcy sat up straighter. "My father had some of the finest animals in Boston. I've ridden since I was a little girl."

"Good." Allena looked at Zack.

Tom smiled. His mother gave directions without people realizing they were being ordered about. He glanced at Darcy. She looked different this morning. Simple and sweet. No wonder his brother loved her.

He turned to Zack. "We'll be heading out tomorrow on the roundup. You want to try riding with us?" Tom grinned. "After four years of being a city slicker, figured you might not be up to—"

"Hold it, little brother. Once a Texas boy, always a Texas boy. Remember?"

"Then eat hearty. Jess' grub isn't half as good as Hattie's."

No one noticed Darcy stiffen. "Zack! I thought you were going to show me the ranch!"

"Nelson and I will do that," Allena said.

Darcy gave Allena an injured look. "I want Zack to show me. And I want to go to the roundup. Do they dance the Virginia Reel?"

Every face went blank, trying hard to suppress smiles.

Zack turned to Darcy. "A roundup isn't a dance. It's gathering the cattle that have roamed all winter and finding the new calves. We could be gone eight or ten days."

Darcy pushed back her chair, rose, and spit out, "Excuse me!" She flounced out, Zack at her heels.

Everyone else thought, "Poor Zack," but Tom envied him, married to the girl he loved. The next day Tom would come into his quarter of the ranch. His hopes were pinned on the fall cattle drive. He would stop at Venture and hopefully bring his bride back home with him.

Chapter Eleven

The post office door banged open. Mary Lou looked up from sorting mail. Jenny plunged through, breathless.

"He's here! He's come back."

Smiling, Mary Lou asked, "Who's 'he'?"

"Tom Langdon." Jenny's eyes shone.

The letter on its way to the top pigeonhole stopped midair. Mary Lou's mind rushed to the last time she had seen Tom—under the cottonwoods. Without closing her eyes, she felt the press of his hands on her shoulders, the sensation of being drawn into his arms. Other than being with Mama, it was the only place she had ever felt at home.

Jenny slapped the counter. "Well, aren't you gonna say somethin'? You just gonna stand there and poke mail? He's over at the livery."

Mary Lou completed the first letter's journey and started another on its way. She needed to gather her scattered reserves. "It's nice to hear he's back," she said, surprised at the calmness in her voice.

"Mary Lou Mackey, are you pretendin' to me he don't mean nothin' to you? I know you better. You've been moonin' around here since he left."

Evidently she had not concealed her feelings as well as she thought. So many times Mary Lou had smothered the longing for one look at that lanky, red-headed cowboy.

"Cowboy's rarely settle," had been Pa's comment. But that was not true. Pa had settled with Mama. Uncle Nate had married Aunt Tibby. Mary Lou's dream was to be a rancher's wife and own a big spread like Aunt Tibby and Uncle Nate.

"Mary Lou, I declare, you are exasperatin'. I bring you the best news in the world and you just stand there."

"For heaven's sake, Jenny, what do you expect me to do—run out and throw myself into the arms of a man who does not love me?"

"Well! I thought you'd be so glad to see him nothin' could get in your way." Jenny stopped Mary Lou's arm and peeked over it. "You can't fool me. I know you love him."

Mary Lou spun around. "Jenny! Watch what you're saying. I'm betrothed to Glenn and he might hear you." Her disobedient heart struggled to wiggle from her tight control.

"Glenn. Oh pooh. You may be betrothed, but you don't love him." Jenny faced Mary Lou. "This is Jenny, honey. You might fool everybody else, but you don't fool me."

Mary Lou did not dare look at Jenny. She was too angry at herself for the longing that invaded her.

Relentless, Jenny pressed on. "You'll never be happy. I won't be able to stand by and take that and neither will you!"

Dear Jenny who knew her too well. From that first day when the Wimbley family wagon rolled into the old Martindale homestead, they had been inseparable. Jenny was three and Mary Lou four. They had grown closer than sisters. Mary Lou should have known better than to try to disguise her feelings from her dearest friend.

Jenny's eyes pinned her. "Well?"

"There's nothing I can do about it. Tom does not love me and I like Glenn—"

"Like is not good enough," Jenny snapped. "Not for marriage." Jenny grabbed Mary Lou's shoulders and forced her to regard the determination in her eyes. "I'm serious. If you try to marry Glenn, when the preacher asks if there's anyone who knows why these two should not be wed, I'll tell. So help me, I will."

Jenny shook Mary Lou and everything fell apart. The mail in her hands spilled to the floor. Until that moment, Mary Lou had willed herself to accept the neat little package her life was tied in. She and Glenn would be married in two weeks and inherit the store, Pa's wedding gift. Even the townspeople had nodded approval. They all awaited the happy event.

Mary Lou stooped to picked up the mail. Jenny bent to help.

Tom. Here. She had to see him. She shook her head. It would not be right. She was betrothed. Anyway, he had not sent one letter. Where was her pride? Tom was here! A fresh lasso tightened around her heart and her body came alive.

"Mary Lou? You all right?"

Mary Lou glanced up into Jenny's concerned face. She threw her arms around Jenny. "Thank you, dear heart. What would I ever do without you?"

The door opened again and Glenn came in, his blond hair disheveled, a strange look on his face. He breathed like he had been running.

"Miss Jenny, if you please?" Glenn held the door open and waved his arm toward the opening. "I would like to talk to my intended about something personal. If you wish, I'll escort you—"

"I'll go myself, thank you." Jenny swung around to Mary Lou. "Intended," she mimicked and made a face, "I'll see you later." She snapped her skirt around the counter and slammed the door behind her.

Glenn shifted from one foot to the other. "I suppose Jenny told you."

"Told me what?" Mary Lou turned to stuff the last few envelopes into their boxes. She willed her hands to be steady, thankful for the task. It kept her back to Glenn.

"Now, Mary Lou, I saw her turn and come running over here as soon as she saw him."

"Are you referring to Tom Langdon?"

"Yes." Curt, clipped, unlike Glenn.

"Jenny told me." She tried to sound disinterested but did not dare look at him.

"I thought when he left he was never coming back."

"This is a free country." She shrugged. "He's a cowboy and they drive cattle to the railroad. That's his job." She finished the mail and turned to him. He looked troubled, defiant—an expression she had never seen before. "Did the new railroad shipment come?" she asked to change the subject.

Glenn shifted uneasily, then softened. "Yes, the men are unloading the wagon. You staying today?"

"No." Mary Lou busied herself putting away postal supplies. "There's a W.C.T.U. meeting at the church this afternoon."

"What do you ladies do at your meeting?" Glenn took a deep breath and relaxed.

"We're trying to find a way to close Ludden's saloon. It's not safe at night for the people who live in town. I don't know how they put up with all the noise and shooting that goes on."

Glenn smirked. "You just said this was a free country. Those men mean no harm to the ladies of our town."

"Maybe that's true when they're sober, but they become unpredictable when they're liquored up."

Glenn laughed. "You ladies have your little meeting. But I doubt you'll have much effect on Mac Ludden. He's a rich man and does a lot for this town."

"That's another thing. Mac Ludden is taking money families need. The good Lord knows there's never enough of it."

"Come on, Mary Lou, the men come on their own. Mac Ludden has nothing to do with it."

"Nothing to do with it!" She glared, glad for an excuse to challenge him. "Venture is a different town when the cattle drive arrives. Gamblers, speculators, outlaws, barmaids, and those . . . women invade this town like grasshoppers."

Glenn raised his eyebrows. "We all make money during the cattle drive, including your father's store."

"The cattle drives also bring trouble." Her anger mounted. "I'm glad I don't live in town when all that shooting starts. Some of them don't even aim. When they're drunk they just shoot for the fun of it." Mary Lou grabbed her shawl and hurried out to the stalls.

Glenn followed. "You better watch that you ladies don't get into more than you can handle."

She could not suppress her fury. "Then why don't you men do something about it? Would you like your son going to school drunk?" She felt her face crimson. "If it were just the men it would be different, but this affects the women and children." She concentrated on saddling Dulcie.

Glenn leaned against the stall. "It's just I don't want you ladies to get hurt."

She swung and faced him. "That's exactly what I'm saying! The whole town gives in to Mac Ludden's clientele and the cattle drives. Seems to me it should be the other way around. They should give in to our town's law and order."

"Just what do you women plan to do?"

"We don't know yet, but the best thing for Venture would be to get that saloon out of town." She felt the back of her neck prickle. That was it! Get the saloon out of town!

"Goodbye, Glenn, see you tomorrow." She rode off on Dulcie and did not look back.

At the church, Mary Lou tied Dulcie beside Missy. Jenny waved from up front. Mary Lou talked to Aunt Tibby, then joined Jenny and the younger women in the first two rows.

Tibby rapped the table and stood. "Ladies, may I have your attention please?"

Conversation stopped, all eyes on Tibby.

Tibby opened the meeting with prayer. The women sang "*O God Our Help in Ages Past*" and sat down.

Tibby's face reflected good news. "Today one of our young ladies proposed an idea. She suggested that we get the saloon out of town."

"How you goin' to manage that?" a skeptical voice called out. "Problem is, we're too close to Abilene. It might be easier to move the town."

The ladies laughed.

Sarah George stood. "We certainly need law and order in town. It's gotten so we have to get to the town pump before supper time. With the saloon in the center and the town pump at the east end, I have to walk right through it all."

Tibby rapped for order. "Ladies. We all know why it should be done. Let's concentrate on how to do it. Any suggestions?"

There was a momentary lull.

"Let's ask Mr. Ludden to move the saloon," came the young, timid voice of Miriam Wimbley.

The ladies laughed.

"Don't laugh." Henrietta stood, eyes shooting sparks. "Some of the men agree with us. Big Jon has said many times he wished the saloon stood someplace else. Trying to raise seven curious sons with temptation in the center of town is impossible. Other fathers must feel the same. Why can't the saloon be made to conduct its business outside the town limit? That would free the town and keep the ruckus in one area." Henrietta sat down.

The room was quiet.

From the sea of puzzled faces, Bertha Leggett hesitantly rose. "I know we're new homesteaders in Venture, but we have four, fine Christian sons and want to keep them that way. Psalm 101:3 says, "I will set no wicked thing before mine eyes." We need to remove as much temptation as possible from our children. My husband feels like Big Jon. I think we should find out how many men are on our side. It's a difficult task for us alone."

The room hummed with a murmur of agreement.

Tibby tapped again. "All right, there's our task this week. We'll meet next week after we talk to our men. Thank you for coming, ladies. Remember, together we can do more than we think. Let us adjourn with prayer."

The ladies bowed, then hurried out with fear, courage, and determination in their eyes.

At the supper table, Nelda and Mary Lou told Buck about the meeting and asked his opinion.

"I think you women are in over your heads. Mac will never voluntarily move that saloon. It would mean building a new place." Buck shook his head. "You'd better look for another way."

Neither Nelda nor Mary Lou missed Buck's tolerant half smile.

I bet this is the way all the men will react, Mary Lou thought. *Lord, what can we do to make these men recognize the evil right before their eyes?*

Next morning when Mary Lou arrived at the store, she found Glenn arranging barrels of New Orleans molasses, vinegar, flour, salt pork, and white and brown sugar. He came to meet her.

"Good morning." He held Mary Lou in his arms. She accepted his embrace, but her heart hurt. She steeled herself to keep from pushing him away.

"We finally got the white dishes and those steel knives and pewter forks and spoons. I thought they might look good over there." He pointed to a shelf under the lamp chimneys. "And the new dress goods came in."

Halfway through the morning Mary Lou asked, "Can you think of a way we could get the saloon moved out of town?"

Glenn looked up startled, then grinned. "You ladies thinking of moving the saloon? That I must see."

Rankled, Mary Lou snapped, "I did not ask your opinion. I asked if you could think of a way we could do it."

Glenn laughed. "Whoever thought up that wild idea?"

Mary Lou lifted her chin. "I did."

Glenn gulped. "You did!" He shook his head. "There's no way. Mac'll veto that."

Mary Lou bristled. "Well, it won't do any harm to ask him."

"I don't want you mixed up with Mac Ludden."

"You don't want me mixed up! Then you better do something. Either you men do something, or we women will."

Glenn softened. "Mac's in business same as we are. How would you like Mac to tell us to move out of town? You ladies don't know how business works. You compete where you can, but you don't order another man out."

"Not even if he's in the devil's business?" Mary Lou demanded.

Glenn laughed. "Come on, Mary Lou, you're out of place."

"Out of place! And just where is my place?" Her temper rose. "You're just like all the other men."

"Now, Mary Lou—"

She did not stay to hear more. Men never took women seriously. Well, the women of Venture would show them—and soon!

Chapter Twelve

Dulcie picked her way home through the rippling prairie grass, her reins slack. Mary Lou rode oblivious to her surroundings. Her heart was engaged in a battle. She fought the urge to see Tom. If he loved her, he would have written. Too late, anyway. Betrothed to Glenn, the door had closed.

"God does not close doors. He opens them. God is our Father and wants us to have every good and perfect gift." How often Mama's wise words rang in her mind. *Oh Mama, I wish you were here.*

A dust cloud revealed a rider up ahead.

Mary Lou nudged Dulcie into a trot. Daydreaming would not help Aunt Nelda sew white lace on her wedding dress.

The rider slowed, then turned. Her heart recognized Tom before her mind allowed it. The gap closed. Her hungry eyes feasted on the tall, slim cowboy she had longed for since he rode away. She stopped.

Tinder trotted toward her until the two horses were nose to nose. Tom removed his hat. Red hair, curled tight from the dampness under his hat, glistened bronze in the sun. "Hello, Mary Lou. I've been wanting to see you."

His voice sounded more beautiful than any of the songbirds Mary Lou had heard that spring. "Hello, Tom. How's Texas?" She could not think of anything else to say.

"Fine." Tom's gaze clung to her face. "But my heart's been in Venture."

Mary Lou stiffened. "I'd never have known it."

"I'm sorry, Mary Lou. I wanted to write, but under the circumstances, I did not dare."

All her hurt spilled out. "Did not dare write? You wrote to Uncle Nate."

"There are a lot of things I could not say before, but now I can, like I love you, Mary Lou."

Why had he not said it before—or written it and erased the ache of the past year?

"I do love you, Mary Lou, but I did not have the right to tell you before."

"What gives you the right to say it now? I'm betrothed to Glenn."

Tom ran his hands around the brim of his hat. "I know. But now I have something to offer and can ask your father. Your Pa thought I was just a cowboy last fall. At that time, I could not tell him any different."

"What are you now that makes the difference?" Her curiosity and Tom's presence held her like a magnet.

"When I asked your Pa if I could marry you—"

"You asked Pa if you could marry me? You never told me you loved me. You never asked me if I loved you. Yet you asked Pa if you could marry me?" She swung Dulcie's head and jabbed her sides hard. Dulcie took off like a shot.

"Mary Lou! Wait!"

The audacity of the man! She loosed the reins and let Dulcie gallop home. Hurt and disappointment spilled with her tears. When the cabin came in sight, she eased up and slowed Dulcie. She could not go into the cabin in this condition. She would have too much explaining to do. But when she reached the cabin and slid off Dulcie, she barged through the door in tears.

Nelda turned from her pie dough and caught the distraught girl in her arms. When sobs subsided, she pushed Mary Lou into a chair and pulled up her rocker. "I take it you've seen Tom."

Mary Lou sniffed. "He—he told me he loved me!"

Nelda smiled and patted Mary Lou's hands. "Well, now, isn't that the very thing you've wanted to know?"

"No."

"No?" Nelda sat back and shook her head.

"He asked Pa to marry me without even telling me he loved me."

Nelda smiled. "Is that all? I thought it was something serious."

Mary Lou raised a shocked face. "What do you mean? He should have told me first. Am I a horse to be auctioned off?"

"Mary Lou, you're being ridiculous. Did you let Tom explain why he did not ask you first?"

Mary Lou stared in disbelief.

"Did you give him time to tell you that when he asked your father, Buck said a cowboy was the last man he wanted his daughter to marry. Now, evidently he has something to offer and has come to ask your Pa's permission."

"I don't know what you're talking about," Mary Lou wailed.

"That's obvious. You did not give Tom a chance. What must the poor man think?"

Was Aunt Nelda on Tom's side? "Have you talked with Tom?"

"Yes. He came here to see you. He did not think it would be proper to go to the store. I think Tom was very considerate of Glenn. Tom's a gentleman."

"He's a cowboy."

"Cowboys can't be gentlemen?"

"I thought—"

"That's the trouble, Mary Lou, you did not think. At least not with your heart. Can you imagine how Tom feels? He comes back to see you and you verbally smack his face and run. Is that the response of a lady?" Nelda went back to her pie dough.

Mary Lou sank into a chair. She had acted abominably, so taken with her own feelings she never thought of Tom's. "What am I going to do, Aunt Nelda?"

"You're going to be what every Christian should be—completely honest." Nelda crimped the pie crust with her fingers. "There's one important question: Are you in love with Tom or Glenn? Decide that and you'll know what to do."

Mary Lou thought of Glenn. He loved her and would be a good husband. To break their betrothal would hurt him terribly. She really did not know much about Tom. *How could she make an honest decision?*

Nelda slipped a pie in the baker and placed hot coals in the recessed well of the iron lid. "Perhaps we'd better wait to put lace on your wedding dress—at least until you make up your mind."

The rumbling of Buck's buggy announced his arrival. Mary Lou went to the window and watched her father hobble toward the cabin. He looked tired. Life's spark in Pa died with Mama. His love and respect for Mary Lou seemed to have died, also. She and Pa talked, but never about Mama. Would he ever forgive her?

Buck dropped into his place and vacantly watched Mary Lou and Nelda put supper on the table. "Barney Alden's pretty mad," he said. "Last night a shot went through the front window of the land office."

"Don't blame him," Nelda said. "It'll take a month or more to get new glass. The one who shot it should have to pay for it."

Buck shrugged. "Nobody knows who did it."

Nelda brought plates of steaming prairie chicken and corn pudding to the table. Mary Lou sliced bread, opened a jar of prairie globe apple jelly, and sat down.

They bowed while Nelda said grace.

Mary Lou spread a piece of bread with jelly. "Aunt Tibby went to Mac Ludden today and told him the W.C.T.U. ladies felt he should move the saloon out of town."

Buck gulped. "Tibby's crazy. She's going to get her nose pinched if she keeps it where it does not belong."

"Good for Tibby," Nelda said.

"You women better pull in your horns. Somebody's going to get hurt."

A horse galloped into the yard. Matthew Wimbley slid off and dashed breathlessly through the door. "Mr. Mackey, Pa wants you to come right away. Georgie's been shot." Tears ran down his dusty face.

Buck swung in his chair. "Come here, son. Tell me what happened."

Matthew pulled a bandanna from his pocket, wiped his face, and blew his nose. "Georgie and Sam were goin' rabbit huntin' tomorrow and needed some shot, so they rode in to your store. Just as they mounted their ponies to come home, some shootin' started in the street and Georgie got shot in the back."

Buck grabbed his cane. "Where's your pa?"

"At Doc Gray's with Georgie."

"Come help me hitch up. Then go home and tell your ma not to worry." Buck,

Morgan, and the buggy soon thundered out of the barn toward town. Mary Lou and Nelda saddled Dulcie and Jewel, and followed Matthew to the Wimbley farm.

Henrietta, dry eyed, sat outside the door watching the road, her bewildered children gathered round. Nelda dismounted and pulled Henrietta into her arms. Mary Lou hugged Jenny and the other children, too numb and wide-eyed for words.

Two hours later, Big Jon carried his son into the cabin and laid him gently on a bed. Henrietta leaned over Georgie, smoothed her hands over his quiet face, and kissed him. Brothers and sisters crowded around, their faces filled with fear and disbelief.

Big Jon stood at the side of the bed, taking deep breaths to assuage the agony mirrored in his face.

Four-year-old Caroline looked up at the faces above her. "Is Georgie dead?"

Big Jon picked her up. "Yes, child, he's gone home to be with Jesus."

The younger children edged closer to their mother and father and stared.

Sam pinched his lips together and said with hateful determination, "I'm gonna shoot whoever shot Georgie."

Young Jon turned. "If you don't, I will."

"You'll do nothing of the kind," Big Jon ordered. "Remember Romans 12:19: 'Vengeance is mine, I will repay, saith the Lord.' "

One by one the children went timidly to look at Georgie. Caroline touched him. "He still feels like Georgie. But he needs a blanket. He's cold."

Henrietta knelt beside her son and began unbuttoning his shirt. Nelda joined her, unbuttoned Georgie's shoes, and slipped them off.

Big Jon took Caroline and Sam by the hand and moved the other children outside ahead of him.

Mary Lou and Jenny watched the two older women undress Georgie. They left the bandage Doc Gray had placed over the wound and washed and redressed him in his Sunday suit. When they were done, Henrietta rocked him and wept. Then she laid him down tenderly, kissed him, and knelt beside the bed. She stroked his face and her tears ran free. Jenny slipped to her knees beside her mother and stared at Georgie, her cheeks wet.

Mary Lou lifted a cup from the shelf, filled it with steaming coffee, and offered it to Henrietta. She shook her head. Mary Lou took it outside to Big Jon.

The children were full of questions. Mary Lou marveled at this giant of a man whose son had just been shot. He sat answering questions from his ten children, trying to assure them of God's goodness.

"Papa, Georgie never got to grow up." Caroline said.

"I don't know how God will use this for good, but as Christians, we believe that God loves us. Even when we don't understand, we have faith that God will make it right." Big Jon soothed each child with his hand and smiled. "And Georgie is the first one of us to see Jesus."

Mary Lou had a hard time accepting those answers. The same agony she felt at her mother's death crowded her chest. She felt the family's loss. Mama had called God "the God of all comfort" and explained that the comfort we received was given so we could comfort others in trouble. Now Mary Lou knew what that verse meant. And how Henrietta and Big Jon and their children felt. "Help me, Lord, to give the comfort Mama would give if she were here," she whispered.

A tear-stained Jenny came out from the cabin. Mary Lou slipped to her side and hugged her. "Oh God," she prayed, "ease the pain of my dear friend and her family."

A buggy and wagon rattled into the yard. Mary Lou recognized Uncle Nate and Aunt Tibby and Sarah George with baskets and pans of food. Pastor Miles talked a lot about being a Christian family. That is what they were. One big family. God's family. Mary Lou's heart swelled with love. Thank you, Father.

She noticed Pa sitting in his buggy down the road, hunched over. Did Georgie's death bring back the hurt of Mama's death to him? Mary Lou walked out. His pained eyes locked with hers for a second. "Pa, come and eat," she urged.

He shook his head. "I'll eat at home. Tell Big Jon I'll see him later." He swung the buggy around and trotted off.

He is thinking of Mama. Mary Lou ached afresh.

It was dark by the time they finished the meal and cleaned up. Sarah George and Nelda planned to stay the night and sleep in Sarah's wagon. Tibby and Nate took their leave. Mary Lou rode Dulcie alongside.

"I want you to round up as many W.C.T.U. women as you can and we'll meet at the church tomorrow morning after the funeral," Aunt Tibby said. "If any husbands want to come, they're welcome. We've got to do something." They rode silently until Mary Lou turned in the lane to her home and waved good night.

One lantern burning low on the table welcomed Mary Lou. The cabin was quiet, the door to Buck's bedroom closed. Mary Lou went into her room and closed the door.

God does not close doors, he opens them. . . .

"Oh God, open the door between Pa and me so I can talk with him about Tom and Glenn. I don't know what to do. I need his help." Mary Lou sobbed into her pillow. *Did life ever turn out the way you wanted it?* She cried for Mama, for Pa, for her disappointment in Tom, for little Georgie, for. . . . Eons later, sleep finally came.

Chapter Thirteen

Townspeople and homesteaders attended the funeral of young Georgie the next morning and came away thoughtful. A long procession wended its way to the meeting called by Nate and Tibby Bradford. Chairs filled quickly. Latecomers leaned against the walls. Men gave their seats to the ladies.

Nate Bradford faced his neighbors. "Folks, we know why we're here. The death of young Georgie has made us realize something must be done to stop senseless shooting and killing. We've been without a sheriff since Duke Williams got shot last year. We need to find a new sheriff."

Murmurs of assent swept the room.

"There's only one man in this town who qualifies for the job, 'n that's Big Jon," Jeremy Halderan called from the back.

Big Jon shook his head.

The same homesteader shoved his way to Big Jon's side and slapped him on the shoulder. "Here's our man to create law and order in this town."

A number of men rose in agreement. "Big Jon for Sheriff," one shouted.

Big Jon slowly rose. The room quieted. The men sat down.

After a significant pause, Big Jon faced the people. "I'm not your man. I won't carry a gun. I'm a homesteader and a father. I'm as eager as you are—more so—for better law and order in Venture. But I'm a Christian. I can't kill a man, even if he is my enemy. If there is to be a sheriff in this town, I feel the good Lord will make one available. But I'm not that man." He sat down beside Henrietta. She reached for his hand.

Nate stepped into the silence. "A campaign for sheriff is not why we're here. We're here to take immediate action about the saloon. First we need to talk with Mac. I want several men to go with me—immediately."

Big Jon raised his hand. So did Buck; Henry George, who lived in town; and Martin Clay, a farmer south of Venture.

Nate nodded. "Thank you. Let's go." They followed Nate out the church to the saloon.

Half-an-hour passed. An impatient hum reflected the people's restlessness. They had crops to hoe, animals to tend, tasks waiting at home. A few men got up and left.

"They're comin'," a man called from outside.

Mac Ludden walked briskly with the men, talking and nodding. When they approached the church, everyone scurried inside.

Mac strode down the aisle of the church and greeted Pastor Miles. "May I speak to my neighbors?" he asked and turned without waiting for an answer. His fancy vest spread tightly across his ample middle. "I am indeed sorrowed at the accident that killed little Georgie. There was an argument and two men met in the street." He smiled. "I'm sorry one of them had such poor aim."

Henrietta stood abruptly. "If men are so irresponsible with their guns, they shouldn't wear them."

"Madam, I agree with you. I've arranged to have the men who come into my place of business check their guns at the door. If they want to fight, it'll have to be with their fists. At least, it won't hurt anyone but the fellow who gets a bloody nose." His broad smile faded before sullen faces.

"We've heard your agreement in the company of these people, Mac, and it'll be considered binding," Nate said. "Is it agreeable to everyone present?" Affirmative murmurs rippled the room.

"Then it's settled. We'll have no more drunken shootings in the streets of Venture," Nate turned to Mac. "Agreed?"

"Agreed," Mac said soundly. "Venture is my town, too. Whatever's good for the town is good for me and my business." He pushed his way out through the people, handing jovial greetings as he went.

The crowd dispersed in all directions. The nights quieted. Guns remained silent.

A week later, Mary Lou carried the mail bag to the stage station and stacked it with other parcels in the corner.

Two shots rang out.

The station agent and Mary Lou ducked to the floor, then cautiously rose and peeked out the window. Two of Mac's boys were hustling a couple of men back into the saloon. Townspeople who had flattened against a wall or dropped to the ground scurried indoors.

On her way home, Mary Lou stopped at the Bradford Ranch to tell Tibby.

"I knew it!" she exclaimed. "I don't trust that Mac Ludden any farther than I can throw a buffalo. That's it!" She grabbed Mary Lou's shoulder and guided her toward the door. "You and Jenny round up as many women as you can. Spread the word that the W.C.T.U. will meet at the church this afternoon. The men have had their chance. Now it's our turn!"

Shortly after noon, the church filled with questioning women. Tibby marched in, followed by Henrietta, Sarah George, and even Maggie Bartlett, who ran the boarding house. Everyone sat down but Tibby.

"Ladies, we're here to put an end to needless shooting in this town. Any agreement made with Mac Ludden is not worth the breath to speak it. The men tried, but Mac needs something stronger than a gentleman's agreement. Now it's our turn."

"My Barney did not want me to come," Hallie Crompton began. "He said the men will speak to Mac again. But I came anyway."

Tibby smiled. "Glad to see everyone here. Before doing anything, we must decide where we're aiming."

"If the saloon suddenly burned down, could not we keep them from building a new one in town?" The voice came from a tall stocky woman who, with two daughters, farmed her own land. Her husband and son had been killed in a Center Street shootout.

Maggie Bartlett jumped up. "You can't do that! You'd jeopardize my boarding house next door. I've heard some W.C.T.U. women go into saloons to pray and talk to those poor, deluded customers."

"Deluded customers? People are where they want to be most times," said buxom Petula Hilary in the back row. Her husband appeared and disappeared periodically. "The only way to change things is to get rid of the saloon." Petula propped her fists on her hips.

"I heard a train passenger talking about a group of W.C.T.U. women who smashed a saloon with axes and hatchets." The tall woman swung a good wallop into the air with a pretend hatchet and sat down. The women laughed and tension eased.

Tibby called for order. "These are all good suggestions. Do we agree that our number one aim is to get the saloon out of town?"

The women agreed fervently.

"How do you move a saloon?" a small woman asked.

"Well!" Petula responded. "If we can't move it, can't we smash everything so they can't use it?"

Sarah George applauded. "That's a good idea."

The ladies buzzed their assent and dissent.

The small woman raised her hand. "I think we ought to talk to our men once more." Her timid eyes darted to the women on either side.

"I agree. But if mine does not do something, I won't talk to him for a month. I've dodged bullets on my way to the town pump once too often." Bessie Campbell announced.

Town women nodded with understanding. The room lulled.

"I won't talk to mine either." Petula giggled. "He'll probably enjoy the peace and quiet." Everyone laughed.

Tibby clapped for attention. "Is it agreed that we talk to our husbands tonight? If they put us off, tomorrow we go into the saloon with axes and hatchets. I'm sure Buck has lots of them in the store. We'll borrow and return them after we're done. Tonight, talk to your men, but don't tell them what we plan to do."

"And if they refuse to act, we won't talk to them until they get that saloon out of town." All heads turned toward Sarah George.

"That's not a bad idea," chimed in Bessie. "We've got to do something drastic."

"Not talking! That's drastic, all right."

"I don't think I could do it," the small woman responded.

"Ladies," Tibby interrupted. "It's time for us to get on home. Before we leave, let's pray for guidance. Pray about it at home. Remember, we are the Women's Christian Temperance Union. We'll meet same time tomorrow, hopefully with the Lord's blessing and a plan of what to do—or not to do. Let's pray.

"Father," Tibby began, "we know that doing the right thing is important in our witness of Thee. Search our hearts, Lord, bring us into unity with Thy will, and let us be brave and courageous to carry it out, whatever the cost. Amen."

After a momentary silence, the women dispersed.

Early the next afternoon, a determined group of eighteen women faced Tibby. Tibby prayed. A hush followed. "Well, ladies, what comments did you get from your men?"

"Big Jon is concerned for our safety."

"My Barney says there is nothing we women can do."

Hallie glanced around. "My husband said our twin boys learn to be strong when they face challenging situations. He feels we women are hollerin' down a rain barrel."

Mary Lou watched faces clench and backs stiffen.

"Hollerin' down a rain barrel, are we?" Sarah replied. "I'd say we've taken our heads out of the sand. Tibby, what did Nate say?"

"Nate talked to Mac about the shots. Mac said a couple fellows grabbed their guns out of the holsters on the wall and ran into the street to settle their differences. His boys took care of them. Now Mac's put his barkeep, Wade Parker, in charge when he's gone so it won't happen again."

Petula spoke with disgust. "Any barkeep I ever knew was too busy dishin' out booze to be a gatekeeper at the same time. That's just another of Mac's empty promises."

The room lay quiet as a mill pond. The seriousness of what they were considering quivered in the room.

"I say we get our axes and hatchets," Hallie said finally.

Tibby searched their faces. "Are we agreed that we smash the saloon and put Mac out of business?"

"Yes," the women responded.

"Once we start, there's no turning back," Henrietta cautioned.

"It's time to quit talkin' and do it." Petula looked around at the women. "Or are we just goin' to talk and do nothin' like the men? If so, I should've brought my mendin'."

"Then it's agreed. First we proceed to Buck's store and borrow the axes and hatchets." Tibby looked at Mary Lou. "Is that all right with you?"

Mary Lou nodded. She had been fighting anger all morning. When she had tried to discuss the saloon with Pa, he had sneered, "That's no job for women. We men'll talk to Mac again." Mary Lou stuck her chin in the air. "The axes are in a barrel by the overalls, and the hatchets are a little to the left in a wood crate."

Tibby rose. "All right. We'll get our tools, go directly to the saloon, and break everything we meet. Don't stop for anythin'! If a man interferes, holler and we'll come at him with our weapons. When we're finished, take the axes and hatchets back to the store, put them where you found them, and meet back here at the church."

"Nope!" Hallie shook her head. "Mac's just goin' to fix the place up again and be back in business in a week. All we're goin' to have is trouble with our husbands. What'll we have gained?"

"Then let's not talk to our men. You can't have a fight when one person does not talk." Bessie pointed out. "Let them holler, threaten, whatever, but we won't talk to them until the saloon is out of town."

"Bessie, can you keep from talking to your husband day and night?" one woman asked.

"I can do anythin' I have to. So can you. If you could not, you would not be tryin' to make a sod house a home with snakes falling from the ceiling into the middle of the supper table. How many times have you spent blisterin' days under a hot sun nursin' a crop out of dry cracked ground until the rains came? We can do anything it takes to make this land ours. One man and his saloon will be easier than any normal day's livin'."

"She's right. I can do it," called Petula.

"Me, too." "Me, too."

Bessie began singing "*Onward Christian Soldiers.*" The women joined hands, swung their arms in rhythm, and sang with vigor. Then they stood silent, eyes on Tibby.

Tibby straightened her shoulders and spoke. "After we smash the saloon, we won't speak to the men until the saloon is moved to the outskirts of town. Agreed?"

In unison, the women answered, "Agreed."

Tibby started for the door and raised her eyes heavenward. "May God go with us."

As one body, the eighteen women marched into Mackey's Mercantile. Without a word, each lady grabbed an ax or hatchet. Aghast, customers watched them storm down the street into Ludden's saloon.

"Mary Lou!" Glenn called and followed her into the street. He stood transfixed when she lifted her hatchet and crashed it through the glass window of the saloon.

The sound of tearing wood and shattering glass echoed into Center Street.

Astonished men poured into the street, cursing and yelling.

Inside, flying hatchets whacked chairs. Several women attacked the bar's polished walnut surface. It splintered under the onslaught of their wild, swinging axes.

Henrietta picked up a mug and sailed it into the huge mirror behind the bar, which shattered glass everywhere. She chopped the table it had been sitting on until it collapsed into a pile of splinters.

The women, surprisingly silent, thundered their energy through swinging arms. Their fury echoed and re-echoed into Center Street. One smirky fellow waltzed into the saloon and came flying back out, chased by Petula's swinging ax.

Town people stuck their heads out their doors and cheered. Next door, Bartlett's boarders peered out windows and doors but stayed inside.

One of the men from the livery shouted to the station agent, "Why does not somebody stop those crazy women?"

"But they are ladies." he called back.

"Ladies?" the man shouted. "They sure ain't actin' it."

Like a swarm of marauding bees, the women devastated the saloon. Then heads high, they returned to the store, replaced their weapons, and retreated to the church.

A triumphant, breathless Tibby faced the women. "Well done!" she shouted. "Now our job is to get as many women as we can to join in the silence. I know some were afraid to come today or could not get here, but they agree with what we're doing. I'm sure they'll join us in the silence."

"Those who don't, we won't speak to them," Bessie stated emphatically.

Henrietta shook her head. "No, that would not be Christian. And it would divide us. We must stick together no matter what. We need their support even if they could not in good conscience join us today."

Petula gave a decisive nod. "That's right. We gotta stick together."

"Then pass the word," Tibby cried. "Silence until the saloon is moved outside the town limits. And pray a lot!" she added. The women bowed and Henrietta closed in prayer.

Chapter Fourteen

The news of the W.C.T.U axing the saloon spread like prairie fire, but when the women closed their mouths, a tornado struck. Homes became battlegrounds. Energetic, docile wives became fortresses of maddening silence.

At first the men laughed. What woman could keep her mouth shut? Flabbergasted when a week dragged by, the men turned into mad prairie dogs, barking at everyone.

Mary Lou left a written notice to Glenn in the cash drawer of the store: "Under the circumstances, our wedding will be postponed until the matter of the saloon is settled."

Usually a model of gentlemanly deportment, Glenn stormed through the store shouting, "Mary Lou, our wedding is certainly more important than some silly whim you women have about that saloon."

Mary Lou busied herself sorting mail. She was afraid in a moment of anger she might discredit her vow of silence.

Glenn faced her indignantly. "Don't you think our wedding is more important?"

She smiled sweetly and clenched her jaws.

Glenn fumed back into the store.

Movement outside the window caught her eye. Tom. Her heart came alive. He tied Tinder to the rail and moved out of sight. What did he want? She reminded herself that she was betrothed and had dismissed Tom from her life. The store bell jangled his entry and her capricious heart jumped for joy.

Tom stepped into the post office, removed his Stetson, and stood watching her poke letters into the pigeonholes.

Mary Lou's neck prickled. Her stomach churned. Why had she not stayed home?

Tom's spurs clinked as he moved to the counter. "Has any mail come in for me or my men?"

Head high, Mary Lou whisked his mail from one of the extra boxes in the bottom corner. There were several letters, one addressed in a distinguished handwriting. She put it on top and handed the letters to him.

"Good," Tom exclaimed. "One from my brother Zack." He shuffled through the rest, looked up quickly, and captured her gaze.

Mary Lou sank into those clear pools of blue.

"Does this silence ban apply to me too? I'm just an innocent bystander from Texas." His mouth spread into a grin.

He seemed taller than she had remembered, his shoulders broader. The magnetism she had felt the first day he walked into the post office danced up her spine.

Glenn came in and stood beside Tom. "The ladies aren't talking to the men after their silly episode last week," he said to Tom. Glenn frowned at Mary Lou, "I could not believe that Mary Lou would be a part of such unladylike behavior."

How dare he! Mary Lou squashed a cap on a retort that rumbled like a powerful geyser ready to explode. Men! Did they ever understand how a woman thinks or feels? Why did not they both go away and leave her alone?

Tom and Glenn blocked the doorway and stared at her. She grabbed another handful of mail and turned her back on them.

Glenn looked indignantly at Tom. "If I had not seen it myself, I'd never have believed our Venture women would act so. Mac is furious."

Mac! Glenn was concerned for Mac? She had had enough. Mary Lou stuck all the mail in one of the boxes, reached for her bonnet, and walked to the door. Would the gentlemen step aside and let a lady pass?

Tom moved first. "I'd best get along." He touched his fingers in a salute to Glenn. His gaze brushed hers. "Bye, Mary Lou."

The door jangled and she heard him ride off. Her heart floundered.

"Mary Lou, I beg you to stop this foolishness," Glenn pleaded.

Foolishness! When women did something it was foolishness. Why could men shoot at each other's feet and roar with laughter while a victim dodged bullets? Or on the slightest provocation march into the street and kill each other—or a sweet, innocent young boy. Tears welled. Mary Lou stretched to her full height but lowered her eyelids lest they betray her intense anger. She would be as stubborn as he.

Glenn did not move.

Did he plan to physically detain her? Fresh resolve shot up her spine and squelched a desire to defend herself. Her Christian sisters must be finding it equally hard—more so for those who dealt with a husband. Glenn was not her husband yet, but lately he had issued orders as if he owned her.

Ye have not because ye ask not. The verse Mama had often quoted steadied her. *Lord, give us strength to do what we must.* The prayer subsided her inner churning. She faced Glenn and gazed at him with steeled determination. Under no circumstances would she allow him to make her break silence.

"I can see we aren't getting anywhere." Glenn's voice betrayed an undercurrent of anger. Shoulders back, head erect, he strode into the store.

Mary Lou seized the moment and escaped. Outside town, she slowed Dulcie to a walk. She needed thinking time and found her animal friend comforting.

Rapid hoofbeats from behind overtook her and Tom galloped up.

Mary Lou's first thought was to jab Dulcie in the flanks, but her feet would not move. Instead, her disloyal heart hammered in joyous surprise. She took a quick breath to steady herself. A glance at Tom recalled the handsome angle of his jaw, his broad muscular shoulders, his ease in the saddle.

Tom slowed Tinder's pace to Dulcie's and the two mounts fell in step as if they were hitched.

"Please don't run away this time, Mary Lou," Tom pleaded. "I must talk with you."

Aunt Nelda's scathing words about her inconsiderate behavior to Tom shamed Mary Lou into polite composure. The clip-clop of the horses' hooves calmed her fluttering breast. They had ridden together like this last summer.

"When I left you in the cottonwoods. . . ." He paused. "With all my heart, Mary Lou, I wanted to tell you I loved you. Your pa gave me no right to say it. I tried to tell him about my inheritance. He would not listen. I asked his permission to ask you to marry me. That made him angry. He said no daughter of his would ever marry a cowboy. That's all I was then. Last month I inherited my quarter of our family ranch in Texas."

A Texas rancher! Her spirit soared and reached for her dream—to be a rancher's wife like Aunt Tibby. She thanked God for the vow of silence that forced her to be quiet and listen. In all honesty, Tom was still a stranger. Last year there had seemed no need to know. Now she had much to learn.

"I have three brothers and we own the ranch together," Tom continued. "My father died five years ago. My oldest brother, Zack, should have taken charge, but he was determined to be a lawyer, so he went East to study law. Doug, second in line, took over. I have a younger brother, Nelson, whose legs never grew strong enough to hold him. But he's a wonderful boy, you'll like him."

Three brothers? She had always longed for an older brother. Mary Lou glued her gaze on her reins. She dared not look up.

"I'd have told you all this last year, but your pa forbade me to see you. Trouble was, I could not leave without saying goodbye. Jenny offered to take a message to you." He leaned toward her. "Please understand, Mary Lou, riding away from you was the hardest thing I ever did."

It'd been as hard for Tom to leave me as for me to let him go, Mary Lou thought. What manly fortitude Tom had displayed. As a gentleman, he had honored her father's wishes. She had never guessed that at the moment of their parting, he had risked losing the woman he loved.

A whirl of joy danced in her head. *I'm the woman Tom loves.* What beautiful words! They healed the hurt of confusion, abrupt departure, no letters. Mary Lou gazed squarely into Tom's eyes. They mirrored the pain in his voice. She opened her mouth—the vow! She could not betray the silence. Like magnets, their eyes clung. Could hers speak for her? Would they say what her lips could not?

Tom held her gaze tenderly, as a gift. Finally, he lowered his head and splintered the fragile connection.

Mary Lou felt bereft. The vow towered between them, a wall she could not scale. It was not the only wall. Another, even more formidable stood higher and wider—Glenn.

As if he read her thoughts, Tom said, "I know you're betrothed to Glenn and I have no right to say some of the things I'm saying. But I had to make you understand I was not dishonest with you. A vow to your father sealed my lips. I could hardly live until this fall's cattle drive and prayed you'd wait. I'd hoped— to marry you and. . . ." Tom reached for her hand. His gaze held her face, memorizing, then he lifted her hand to his lips.

The touch of his lips on her fingers sent a thousand shivers through her body, dissolving the last vestige of anger. The gate swung open. Fresh love rushed in and answered her question! *She loved Tom.*

Suddenly, her soul washed with guilt. Glenn! Her betrothed, her constant comfort when Mama died and Pa had been too deep in his grief and anger to care. In hard moments, Glenn had been at her side. He had kept her from drowning in the loneliness of Mama's absence and Pa's rejection. How could she brush him aside?

She liked Glenn—no, she loved him, but with a different kind of love than what she felt for Tom. Her mind tried to slam the door on the dreams she and Tom might have shared. Her fickle heart strained to keep the door open. Something in her throbbing chest bowed its head and died. It was not the way she wanted it, but Mama had taught her as a little girl that nobody gets everything they want.

They rode slowly together, Tom and Tinder, Mary Lou and Dulcie. It seemed so right. *Oh, Lord*, her spirit cried out, *help me to know Your will in this matter. Either way, someone gets hurt.*

Tom's voice broke into her thoughts. "If anything should change—" He stopped the horses and looked at her.

Oh, God, what do I do? Tom has nothing to do with all this. But I cannot break silence. I cannot!

After a charged pause, Tom said, "I'll be here for another week—" His words hung in the air. He smiled and patted her hand. "I admire you, Mary Lou, for sticking to your guns." He nudged Tinder. Mary Lou and Tom's fingers clung until Tinder pulled them apart and moved into a slow canter.

Again Mary Lou watched a cloud of dust blur the image of the man she loved. Her mind strayed to the cottonwood grove. She remembered Tom's last tender kiss, the strength of his arms when he had gathered her up and swung her onto Missy. His face had been tense, his eyes clouded. He had said only one word, "I."

Her heart took a giant leap. He had tried to tell her—but his lips were sealed then as hers were now! She watched the bobbing figures move farther and farther away. *Oh, Tom, forgive me.*

Dulcie stamped one foot and tossed her mane. Impervious to her prompting, Mary Lou remained adrift in a sea of rippling prairie grass that waved farewell to her dreams. Unconsciously her heels pressed into Dulcie's flanks and the horse moved into a trot for home. "I wish I could talk with Pa," Mary Lou said aloud. The vow! Mary Lou pressed Dulcie's sides harder and the animal eagerly galloped home.

Nelda and Aunt Tibby sat at the table sipping cups of tea when Mary Lou entered the cabin. "I'm glad you're both here. I have to talk with somebody. I did not know it would be so hard not to talk to the men."

"Be thankful you don't have a husband or a brother. Nate and Buck haven't been gentlemen of valor lately," Tibby commented.

Mary Lou poured herself a cup of tea and told them of her morning with Glenn and Tom. "Tom caught up with me on the way home and—"

"You mean you stood still long enough to let the poor boy explain a few things?" Nelda grinned.

I deserve that, Mary Lou thought. "Yes. Pa told him he did not want his daughter marrying a cowboy. I don't understand. Pa was a cowboy." She shook her head. "He still blames me for Mama's death. Is he going to hold it against me all my life?" Fight as she might, tears came.

Aunt Nelda pressed a handkerchief into Mary Lou's hand, and Aunt Tibby put her arm around her.

"Your pa knows there are cowboys and there are cowboys," Aunt Tibby said. "What else did Tom say?"

Mary Lou's voice quavered. "He said he had planned to take me back as his wife this time." Suppressed sobs broke and Mary Lou covered her face with her hands.

"For someone who's betrothed to another man, you sure are weepy," Aunt Nelda said quietly.

Mary Lou nodded. "Mama always said God gave us tears to wash away the hurt."

"What else did Tom say?" Tibby asked.

Mary Lou mopped her tears. "That he's twenty-one, has inherited a quarter of the family ranch, has three brothers. . . . The problem was, now he could talk, but I could not."

"You did not break silence?"

Mary Lou shot a disappointed glance at Aunt Tibby. "Of course not!"

"Good girl." Tibby smiled.

"But what am I going to do?"

Nelda placed her cup on the table and leaned forward. "Who do you love? Tom or Glenn?"

Mary Lou shook her head. "Glenn has been so wonderful to me. I know he loves me. I don't want to hurt him or. . . ." Her voice trailed off.

The two older women eyed each other knowingly.

"The question is: Which one do you love?" Tibby countered.

"I love both of them." Mary Lou felt silly saying it.

"That may be," Nelda said. "But you're only allowed one husband. Until you decide, there isn't much anyone can do for you."

Aunt Nelda was right. So was Jenny: "Like is not enough."

Tibby said suddenly, "Your uncle Nate said the men had a meeting with Mac. He agreed to move the saloon out of town if the townspeople help build it."

Nelda sniffed. "That seems wrong to me. If we're against it, we're against it. Building a saloon is a travesty. What are people going to think of the W.C.T.U. if we allow that?"

Tibby shrugged her shoulders. "Who cares? There's always someone to complain if he gets his toes stepped on. Venture's problem right now is to get rid of the saloon's disruption to the townspeople and town business. Amanda says our main thrust is for prohibition and the passing of a law that prohibits the making and selling of alcohol. Cutting off the source of supply will eliminate the saloons."

"But to build a new saloon? Even help supply some of the lumber?" Nelda shook her head. "Seems like condoning."

"I think it's just the first step for the town to get some control. Nate said they'll fence the east end of the town-limit line and put a curfew on crossing it. That'll free the townspeople from all the noise and shenanigans underfoot. They can walk to the town pump or come to Buck's Mercantile and post office in peace." Tibby rose and gathered the cups. "I gotta scoot to get supper ready."

"How long will it take to build it?" Mary Lou asked.

"Taking the usable wood from the old saloon and everyone adding some, they could have sides and roof on in a couple weeks. Big Jon says that if Mac wants a fancy place, he's responsible for the fancyin'."

Two weeks? Tom would be gone by then. The bloom of the day withered.

Chapter Fifteen

Mary Lou watched a steady train of wagons pass the post office window. For two days, buckboards and wagons loaded with logs had rattled through Center Street toward the town line. Buck had donated kegs of nails, and Mary Lou could hear axes splitting logs and shakes.

But the women were absent. Mac kept several large pots of coffee brewing. Maggie and women boarders at Bartlett's Boarding House made and sent over pies. At noon, the W.C.T.U. ladies brought dinner and served it silently in the church yard to anyone who came to eat. Promptly at one, they cleaned up and went home.

Glenn avoided Mary Lou. He had only been out to visit once since the saloon episode, then said it was of no use if she would not talk to him. She had not seen Tom either. Someone mentioned the cowboys were driving the herd on to Abilene.

By the end of the first week, the new saloon stood solid on its feet, the roof shakes in place. The battered bar was repaired and polished, but even the best kerosene rubbing could not hide its wounds. The women had done a thorough job on the chairs and tables. The salvageable few were nailed, wired together, and pressed into service until new furniture arrived from the East. Mac bellowed like a wild bull till the men threatened to stop work if he did not tone down. They pounded at fever pitch toward the day they would finish—not for Mac, but to end the vexing silence of their women.

Sixteen days after the smashing, a makeshift saloon opened for business in a brand new building, and the men went home.

"I wonder whether it's been worth it all?" Nelda said to Mary Lou as they gathered cow and buffalo chips. "Kind of makes our work of no effect."

"Aunt Tibby said we accomplished what we set out to do. She talked to Amanda who says now we'll work on the deeper issues of prohibition and women's suffrage and hope to get John P. St. John elected governor. He promises to push the legislature to pass an amendment to stop the manufacture of intoxicants."

Nelda laughed. "That should knock some of the strut out of Mac Ludden."

They pushed the loaded wheelbarrow to the lean-to at the side of the barn.

Buck eyed the two of them when they hurried in. "Well, ladies." He grinned. "You won. The saloon is finished. Now I expect some talking." He looked from one to the other, awaiting any word from either one.

Nelda and Mary Lou nodded to one another. Neither spoke. Mary Lou left for the barn, saddled Dulcie, and rode off. Nelda, Mary Lou, and Henrietta had agreed to check with each other before they said a word. Jake Benson came home on the fifth day and told his wife they had finished with the building. She believed him and talked, much to her chagrin. After that, women made arrangements to contact each other and verify the saloon was built before they opened their mouths.

Dulcie's hooves pounded the dry ground. Jenny waved from the door until Mary Lou got close then ran to meet her.

"Pa came home and said the saloon is finished. Did your Pa say the same?" Mary Lou called.

"Pa ain't here yet," Jenny said.

Henrietta stood in the door and shaded her eyes to look across the fields. If Big Jon were two miles away, a dust cloud would announce his coming.

"When did Buck come home?" Henrietta asked.

"Just now. He said the saloon is finished, so now it's time to talk. I'm checking to see if it's true."

"I'm sure Big Jon would not pull any tricks and I feel guilty doubting him. But the men haven't been themselves since this all started." Henrietta laughed. "Neither have we. I know he'll be as glad as I am it's over." She scanned the horizon again.

Jenny grabbed Mary Lou and pulled her to the shady side of the house. "Now what? Will you and Glenn get married right away or have you decided to marry Tom?"

Mary Lou panicked.

"Come on, Mary Lou," Jenny coaxed. "You're gonna tell me, aren't you?"

Mary Lou shook her head. She was ashamed to admit that she could not make up her mind. Was it possible for a girl to love two men at the same time?

"Don't tell me you still don't know!" Jenny threw her hands up in the air. "That's not bein' fair. It has to be one or the other."

"I think the decision's been made for me." Mary Lou's heart bowed. "Tom's gone back to Texas."

"He went to Abilene with the cattle. He'll be back." Jenny nodded reassuringly.

"But he said he would only be here a week. It's been two weeks, Jenny. I could not talk. What must he think?" She tried to hide her disappointment. "I don't think Tom will be back. It must be the Lord's will I marry Glenn."

Jenny put her arm around her and they walked toward the well. "Which one do you love?"

She had to share her dilemma with Jenny. "I love them both."

Jenny's mouth dropped open. "Can't be, Mary Lou. Like my ma says, God has a husband in mind for each of us. I asked her once how I'd know the man for me. She said if I loved him, I would know without a doubt and be eager to follow God's will. So Mary Lou, choose you this day who you want for your husband."

They laughed together—like old times. Jenny had been right. Her engagement to Glenn had changed things. They did not see each other as often, or go off to the cottonwood grove for little picnics like they used to.

"Besides that," Jenny continued with her hands on her hips, "it ain't fair for you to have two when the rest of us have a hard time findin' one." Jenny chuckled, then her chocolate eyes darkened. She leaned forward, suddenly serious. "Mary Lou, are you marryin' Glenn thinkin' it'll mend fences between you and your pa?"

"Oh, no, Jenny," the answer popped out. But was she?

Big Jon galloped into the yard on his chestnut stallion followed by a dust cloud that enveloped them all. He leaped from the saddle and hollered, "Henrietta, the building's finished. Come here woman, I want to hear your voice tell me you love me!"

Henrietta flew across the yard and landed in his arms. They looked into each other's faces and talked intimately, then strolled arm in arm toward their children pouring out of the cabin.

Henrietta looked up at Big Jon with an impish grin. "Do you have any idea how hard it was for me not to talk to you? I almost burst."

Big Jon guffawed then leaned and kissed her right in front of the children and Mary Lou. When released, Henrietta laughed and called, "Come on children, supper's ready. Mary Lou, you goin' to join us?"

"No thank you, Mrs. Wimbley. Aunt Nelda has supper ready and isn't talking till I get back. I came to check and see if the building was really finished." She mounted Dulcie and trotted off.

Almost home, Mary Lou spotted an exuberant Glenn galloping to meet her. All smiles, he swung his horse to trot beside her. "The silence is over, Mary Lou. The saloon's finished. Mac opened today and served everybody free of charge—as a thank you, he said. Now we can talk and get married."

The silence that had been such a nuisance now seemed golden. Mary Lou cleared her throat. "Glenn," she began, "I still have things to do, put the lace on my dress, and—"

"How long's that going to take?" Glenn grabbed her saddle horn and stopped Dulcie. "Mary Lou, look at me."

Mary Lou steeled her gaze to be as noncommittal as possible.

"Mary Lou, I love you and want to marry you. I seem to have the feeling you aren't of the same mind."

His forthright abruptness tied her tongue. What could she say? "Glenn, I think we should postpone it for a bit—"

"Postpone it! What for?"

"I'm just not ready yet. Everything has been so upsetting and—"

Glenn laughed. "Oh, darling, I'm sorry. This whole business has been an awful ordeal for you, too, hasn't it? I haven't been very pleasant. But it's over and you're just having those nervous symptoms every bride has. I admit, this is new for me, too. . . ."

Amid a constant stream of Glenn's plans, they rode to the barn and tied their horses. As Mary Lou slid from Dulcie's back, Glenn caught her and kissed her.

Walking to the cabin, Glenn chattered about wedding arrangements he had already made. "I figure all could be ready in two days."

Two days? Mary Lou felt numb. Try as she might to avoid the facts, her choice was closing in on her. The cowboys and Tom had gone to Abilene, Jenny had said. But that was over two weeks ago. Tom said he would be here only a week. What was it Mama had often said? "A bird in the hand. . . ."

Aunt Nelda invited Glenn to supper and he eagerly accepted.

Two days. Mary Lou felt leaden.

Glenn would find Pastor Miles and tell him to come . . . she and Aunt Nelda would put the lace collar on the blue dress . . . they would pick bouquets of prairie flowers to decorate the Bradford parlor and for Mary Lou to carry . . . Aunt Tibby would renew preparations for a big wedding party at the Bar-B ranch . . . a sign on the store door would say they were closed for the wedding . . . they would invite everybody. . . .

Mary Lou thought of yesterday. She and Aunt Nelda had spent the day in town cleaning the back rooms of the store so she could set up housekeeping until Glenn arranged for their house to be built—a town house rather than a cabin on the outskirts as Mary Lou had hoped. She loved the openness of the prairie, the quiet, the wind that blew through her hair and gave her a sense of life. But Glenn said a house in town would be more convenient, and he did not have time or money to keep up a cabin and a house.

Just before Glenn left, he told Mary Lou he had a house already picked out. Mary Lou curdled when he told her he could buy the old saloon cheap.

"It's a good, strong building with an upstairs." He had already checked on some men to help him change it into their home.

Aunt Nelda sat in her rocker, listened, and searched Mary Lou with penetrating eyes.

When Glenn finally left, Mary Lou went to her room, dry eyed and wide awake. She slid into the little wooden rocker Pa had made for her when she was eight. *Was God telling her that her dream of being a rancher's wife was not His will?* Pa acted pleased. He had approved of Glenn from the beginning. She heaved a resigned sigh. Maybe her marriage to Glenn would clear the gulf between them.

Her tiny room suddenly became very dear. So much of Mama remained. Mary

Lou's gaze lifted to the print feed-bag curtains. She had helped Mama make them—the first real sewing she had ever done. Mama had said every girl should know how to make a running stitch, a back stitch, and an overcast stitch. She had learned all three when they had made the curtains.

Mary Lou ran her hand over the oak chest. It had been in Mama's bedroom in Toledo, Ohio, when she was a young girl. Grandmother Stafford brought it when she visited Aunt Tibby and Mama after Grandfather Stafford died. Mama and Grandma looked alike, both small, dainty women with pretty faces and an abundance of curly chestnut hair. But Mama laughed a lot and her eyes looked happy. Grandmother's were always sad.

They had tried to make Grandmother live with Aunt Tibby, but she got so homesick, she finally returned home. Not long after, she died.

Mary Lou undressed, climbed into bed, and closed her eyes, hoping to sleep. She could not. She returned to her rocking chair and picked up the sock she was knitting, but her hands finally dropped into her lap and she rested. Her head against the back of the chair, she dozed off and dreamed she saw Tom on Tinder riding toward her but never getting any nearer.

The endless night tried to outreach the faint glimmers of dawn creeping into the corners of the room. Mary Lou finally climbed into bed and cried for what might have been. In an agonized whisper she said, "Goodbye, Tom."

That morning, Mary Lou dragged from bed an hour later than usual. Aunt Nelda had water heating to wash clothes. Mary Lou dressed quickly and hurried out. If Aunt Nelda noticed the deep hollows under her eyes, she did not let on, but Mary Lou was disturbingly aware of her scrutiny.

She picked up the basket of sheets and draped one over the line. A rider pounded toward her. She squinted through the morning haze. It was Jenny! Was something wrong at Wimbleys?

Jenny slid off Missy and marched angrily to Mary Lou. "I thought as your best friend and bridesmaid you'd tell me."

Confused, Mary Lou asked, "Tell you what?"

"That you're marrying Glenn tomorrow at ten-thirty!"

Mary Lou gasped. "But I just made up my mind last night. I haven't even told Glenn. How did you know?"

"Glenn is telling it all over town—and inviting everybody."

Chapter Sixteen

A shudder spiraled up Mary Lou's spine. Tomorrow? 10:30 A.M.? Without conferring with her?

Jenny faced her, eyes smoldering under pinched brows. She spun and marched away.

"Jenny! Wait." Mary Lou caught the back of Jenny's calico dress and hung on. "I did not know, honest. It's as much a surprise to me as you. Ten-thirty? What a horrible hour."

Jenny swung around, her expression disbelieving.

"It's true, Jenny," Mary Lou pleaded. "He said we could be married in two days, but believe me, Glenn's gone ahead and chosen the day without consulting me."

"Well, you'd better do some consulting about something or you're going to be a married woman in twenty-four hours."

How could Glenn do such a thing?

A familiar arm crept around her shoulders. "Mary Lou, I'm sorry. I was so hurt. I'd thought you'd chosen someone else. What're you goin' to do?"

Mary Lou's confused mind reeled. Then rising fury began its course until she felt so angry she took deep, quivering breaths to calm herself. She straightened her shoulders and headed for the barn to saddle Dulcie, Jenny close behind. Her fingers trembled as she saddled and mounted. Mary Lou looked down at Jenny. "I'm going to see Glenn and demand an explanation."

"You'd better put a muzzle on him first or you're goin' to have most of the town in church tomorrow waitin' for a weddin'."

Mary Lou pressed Dulcie into a fast gallop. By the time they reached town, Mary Lou was breathless and the stalwart animal had worked herself into a lather. Mary Lou slid the saddle off Dulcie's back, rubbed her down, threw a blanket over her, and hurried into the back room. Voices of customers halted her. She did not want to make a scene, but if necessary, she would. One customer could relay news faster than wildfire.

The store quieted and she peeked in. Old Mr. Kennard stood leaning on his cane, leisurely talking with Glenn. Resolutely, Mary Lou stepped up the two steps into the store.

Glenn's face brightened at the sight of her. Mr. Kennard grinned and pointed his cane.

"Lookee who's here! Ain't this here the bride?" He chortled good naturedly and nodded his head. "Be seein' ya at yer weddin' tomorree." He straightened. "I'd best be leavin' you two lovebirds." He knowingly patted Glenn on the shoulder, thumped across the floor, and went out the door chuckling.

The minute he disappeared, Glenn crossed the floor to take Mary Lou in his arms. Mary Lou refused his embrace, turned her back, and retraced the two steps into the back room.

Glenn followed. "I was not expecting you, dear. I planned on coming out to see you. I did not think you believed the old superstition that it's bad luck for the groom to see the bride before the wedding."

Mary Lou spun, fanning smoldering coals of anger. "Glenn, I can't believe what I hear. This morning Jenny came all upset, angry because she thought I'd changed bridesmaids. She heard you telling everyone the wedding is going to be tomorrow at ten-thirty and I had not informed her."

Glenn nodded. His cheeks dented with a grin. "That's right."

If she had not been bred a lady, she would have wiped that silly smile off his face with a resounding slap. She steadied her voice. "I'd like to know when we planned the day or time? Or when you asked me if the choice would be suitable?" Her nails dug into the palms of her hands. "How could you make all the arrangements without considering me?"

"Why, I've been telling you what I was going to do." He shook his head, amazed at her outburst.

"I never heard any plans for tomorrow at ten-thirty. Ten-thirty! What kind of a time is that to be married?" She barely controlled the rage rolling through her.

"Well, it was the best day—"

"For whom? I thought the bride had some say. I told you I wanted to postpone things a bit, that I could not be ready. Now, I won't be ready. Have your wedding tomorrow, but I won't be there!" Mary Lou ran into the lean-to and began to re-saddle Dulcie.

Glenn stepped behind her. "Now, Mary Lou. . . ." His voice was tempered as if cajoling a child. "I was coming out as soon as I could leave the store to tell you the plans."

Mary Lou stopped abruptly and faced him. Her eyes snapped defiance. "How kind of you to visit me the afternoon before my wedding and inform me I'm to be married tomorrow. Did it occur to you it might not be suitable for me?" She put her foot in the stirrup.

Glenn grabbed her waist and held her. "I'm sorry. I just found out this morning it's the only time Pastor Miles could be in Venture until he comes for church week. It's ten-thirty because he has a burial in the afternoon and needs time to get there."

Mary Lou opened her mouth in shock, closed it in frustration, shoved Glenn's arms away, and walked Dulcie through the door. Outside, she turned, eyes blazing. "As of this minute, Mr. Farrell, I'm postponing the wedding indefinitely." She mounted and rode off without a backward look. She did not care if she ever married anyone.

Mary Lou trotted Dulcie up Center Street, ignoring the pleased glances and waves. Unconsciously, she guided Dulcie to the cottonwood grove at Point Lane. In the flickering shade, she slid to the ground and paced, hugging herself to keep from falling apart. "Oh, Mama," she cried aloud. "Loving Tom was painful but loving Glenn is exasperating! Isn't it better not to love at all?"

She shook her head. How could she believe that after knowing Mama? On the wall over Mama's rocking chair hung a picture she had embroidered when she was a little girl in Ohio. "God is love," it proclaimed. Mama had said love was the most important thing in heaven and on earth. Mama had given hers unconditionally to everyone. That is what I need to learn, Mary Lou realized.

Far above a hawk hung suspended, then dived to the ground and snatched up a wiggly, brown prairie mouse with his mighty talons. Mary Lou gasped in sympathy for the tiny, helpless thing. She sank on the old log, cradled her head in her arms and sobbed. "Mama." She felt numbed by the day's assault. Waves of anger, shame, frustration, and futility washed over her.

Dulcie whinnied.

"Oh, God," Mary Lou cried, "I don't know what to do. I put myself completely into Your hands. I can't do it alone anymore."

Slowly, beginning at her shoulders, the heavy weight she had carried since Mama's death slid down her body and puddled on the ground at her feet. The warm Kansas breeze floated by and caressed her face. A permeating sense of peace birthed a depth of love she had never felt before.

Mary Lou's thoughts leaped to joyous memories of Mama's picnic lunches under the cottonwoods—simple bread and jelly sandwiches and apple hand pies. How carefree she had been in those days. On this very log, she had discovered a different kind of love with Tom—and lost it. Or had she?

Mama's laughter whispered through the trees. "No matter what happens to His children," she had always said, "God takes it and weaves it into strength, courage, wisdom, and freedom to do His will. Remember James 1:2,3: 'Count it all joy when ye fall into divers temptations; knowing this, that the trying of your faith worketh patience'. "

Faith and patience. Mary Lou needed large doses of both. Her trust in men stood at low ebb, yet loving Pa could not have been easy for Mama. Bitter and frustrated over his accident, sometimes Pa withdrew. Still Mama loved and encouraged him until the mood passed.

Mary Lou stretched her arms toward heaven. "Oh, Father," she cried aloud. "Forgive me for forgetting what Mama taught me, for being so hateful to Glenn, for insulting Tom because I thought he had insulted me. Help me to grow up into a godly woman like Mama." She took a deep breath and relaxed as it released. She had a lot of fences to mend.

Mary Lou walked to Dulcie and circled her arms around her horse's neck. "Come on, dear friend, let's go home," she whispered and mounted her horse.

Aunt Nelda peered from the doorway when Dulcie trotted in. She walked to the barn as Mary Lou dismounted. "I've been worried about you," she said. "What did you find out?"

"That everything was exactly as Jenny said. I've called the whole thing off."

Aunt Nelda's face showed shock, then amusement. "It does not hurt to put these men in their place once in a while." They linked arms and walked silently to the cabin.

Nelda brought out two plates of sandwiches, said grace, and leaned forward. "Tell me what happened."

Mary Lou related the unnerving details of the morning but omitted what had happened at Point Lane. That belonged to her and Jesus. She gazed at her aunt who spoke lovingly of "my Lars." Like Mama, Aunt Nelda loved freely and unconditionally. Mary Lou's world steadied itself.

That afternoon Glenn apologetically arrived to discuss the wedding. Mary Lou's new heart regarded Glenn with forgiveness. Before he left, they planned their wedding to be held at the Bar-B Ranch in one week at two o'clock in the afternoon.

Aunt Tibby and Nate promised a big wedding celebration after the ceremony. This also gave time for Nelda and Mary Lou to finish preparing the back rooms at the store and sew the lace on Mary Lou's dress.

The next day, Henrietta, Jenny, and Caroline stopped for a visit on their way back from town. Mary Lou and Jenny escaped and walked to the small stream not far from the cabin.

"How come you changed your mind so quick?" Jenny asked. "I thought you'd were so mad at Glenn you'd never marry him."

"I was." Mary Lou did not know whether to tell Jenny about her enlightening time at Point Lane. "I guess the good Lord drove the anger out of my heart and put in love."

Jenny wrinkled her brows but did not pursue it. "One of these days, I'm goin' to find some fella who'll marry me," Jenny said solemnly, then laughed. "But it better be soon or I'll be an old maid. There are only two men in Venture I even considered. You got one of them."

Surprised, Mary Lou asked, "Glenn?"

"Yep. At one time I considered him a pretty good catch. But when he chose you, I picked out Wilbur George."

Mary Lou pictured tall, dark-haired young Will who worked part-time in the store and laughed. "I guess I can't think of you ever being serious—even about marriage."

Jenny giggled and made a face. "Aren't most girls? My real hope was to find someone like Big Jon. Even though he's not my real father, Papa Jon became my ideal the day he found Matthew and me."

Jenny did not often talk about the wagon accident that had killed her parents. Mary Lou encouraged her. "Do you ever wonder what your real papa and mama were like?"

"I remember Mama had long hair like mine. She used to let me brush it. Usually it was braided and wrapped around her head. Papa called her Angel, but her real name was Angela. Papa was tall like Big Jon, but skinny."

She lowered her head, then looked up with misty eyes. "The day Big Jon and Henrietta found us, I was so scared. Matthew cried and cried. I did not know what to do to make him stop. Henrietta just took him to their wagon, nursed him, and he quit crying. Samuel was six months old, too. Henrietta said it was like having twins."

Mary Lou seldom saw Jenny so pensive.

"My pa was a soldier—from Virginia, I think. I sort of remember our house 'cause it had an upstairs with a bannister and Pa used to hold me as I slid down. Matthew was born there."

What would it have been like to grow up without Mama and Pa? Mary Lou sensed a blessing she had taken for granted.

The dinner bell rang, and Jenny and Mary Lou wandered back to the cabin.

Alone at night in her bed, Mary Lou could not escape thoughts of Tom. I wonder what it would have been like to be Tom's wife. Even though he had confessed his love, his absence and silence said volumes. His tender kisses on her fingers tugged at her heart. She shook her head. What kind of thinking is this for a woman to be married shortly? Where was he? She could not silence the question.

"I love Glenn. He loves me. My girlish days of dreaming about handsome cowboys are over. It's time I grew up," she reminded herself and deliberately placed a period on her past.

"Father, I accept Your will for my life. Thank You for the family and friends You've given me. Now, bless Pa, Aunt Nelda, Aunt Tibby, Uncle Nate, Jenny, the Wimbleys, Tom. . . ." Mary Lou sank into dreamless sleep.

Chapter Seventeen

Tom halted on Tinder and looked back at the fifteen hundred Texas longhorns that stretched north on the Chisholm Trail. Smitty, the trail boss, scouted forward for water and pasture. Jess had driven the chuck wagon ahead to start the noon meal.

They were on the last leg of the journey to Abilene. There the cattle would be loaded and shipped to Chicago, headquarters of the beef industry.

The sky promised rain, but the hot, muggy day dragged on interminably. Tom pulled his neck wipe, used it to mop his face, and retied it around his neck. The usually exciting trail drive had grown tiresome. The Chisholm Trail, two hundred miles wide and six hundred miles long, seemed twice that length.

He had been restless to get to Venture to see Mary Lou. When they had met on the prairie, her loveliness had locked her in his heart forever. He had feasted his eyes on her sweet, expressive face and those wisps of chestnut hair that defied confinement and curled at her small ears. Try as he might, he could not dislodge her from his mind. Had he let her slip away? Had she lost what Tom thought was love for him because he never wrote? That crazy vow of silence had denied him answers. Yet he could not shake a nagging urge to go back to Venture right after the cattle were railed.

Smitty galloped up. "Chuck wagon up ahead. Better get these cows milled so's we can eat."

Tom nodded and rode the line to pass the word to the boys. It did not take long to work the cows into a circle, and the herd mingled quietly while the hands ate their beans, cornbread, steak, and scalding coffee in shifts.

Riding back to his watch, Tom's mind again filled with Mary Lou. She rode well, knew animals . . . would make a perfect rancher's wife. Whoa! Plain foolish to harbor such thoughts of a girl betrothed to another man. But how could he stop loving her? He took off his hat, wiped the sweat off the inner band, and shoved it back on.

What else could he have done? When they last met, had he read love in her eyes? Or had he imagined what he wanted to see when he kissed her fingers. . . .

The day he and Jess had gone to Mackey's for supplies before heading north to Abilene had been a disappointment. On the outskirts of town, they had passed a crew of Venture men industriously building the new saloon. When they had entered the store, Tom had gone directly to the post office to mail letters to Zack and his mother. Behind the counter had stood a tall, dark-haired young man who had stamped his letters and handed him a letter from Zack. He had tucked it into his pocket for later. Tom's desperate need to see Mary Lou again had been denied.

Glenn had come into the post office and eyed Tom suspiciously. All business, he had said, "Did Will get your mail for you?"

Tom had nodded, patted the letter in his pocket, and joined Jess in the store. Glenn had tailed them, wrapping and stacking as Tom and Jess had picked out supplies.

Back in the saddle, Tom figured it would take a few days to close the deal. He would pay the cowboys, then head back to Venture while they let off steam. He had mentioned that in his letter to Zack. Tom and Zack had discussed the trail drive the night before Tom had left Texas. Tom had also told Zack about Mary Lou.

"Marry the girl you love," Zack had advised. "I did, and even though others find her difficult, I know how sweet she can be. Don't be surprised if you have to fight to get the woman you love."

Those words had strengthened Tom's resolve to straighten things out. With Zack home, he had been content to leave his mother and Nelson.

That last night, Zack had also explained how the use of guns in the West alarmed Darcy. The western lack of refinement whirled her in a critical storm most of the time, much to his mother's distress.

"What Darcy needs is the Lord's direction. Until she recognizes someone else is more important than herself and her eastern ways, she'll be unhappy," Allena had proclaimed. "Evidently Darcy was not brought up to put God first. Our duty is to love her because she's Zack's wife; he loves her and God has placed her in our family. When some of that eastern veneer rubs off, we'll find a fine, spirited young woman. Maybe then, she'll see her need for a Savior."

Tom's mother was usually right.

An orange belt settled on the hips of the horizon. Facing it, Smitty squatted beside Tom and sipped a cup of coffee before supper. "Tomorrow, we'll make it into Abilene. I reckon there's some plans runnin' in your head. Care to tell me what?"

Tom grinned. Smitty substituted as a clucking mother hen to all the cowboys, as adept at reading men as animals. They were out of earshot of the other cowboys, so Tom answered, "Yeah, I have a few. One might surprise you."

"I doubt it, if it concerns a young woman in Venture."

Tom laughed. "I should've known I could not get anything past you. Trouble is, she got herself betrothed to someone else last winter. I saw her when we stopped in Venture, but it was when the women were not talking to the men over that saloon episode, so nothing got settled. I think she still loves me, but," Tom shook his head, "I'm not sure."

"Aw, any man can tell if a woman loves him. All he has to do is kiss her."

Tom raised his eyebrows and punched Smitty's arm. "You old coot! What makes you so smart about women?" .

Smitty grinned. "Since we're tellin' secrets, I was married once. 'Twas before I started workin' fer your pa. She died birthin' our son too early. Poor little fella did not have enough strength to breathe proper and died a day after his ma." Smitty hastily swallowed some coffee.

"I'm sorry, Smitty. You'd have made a great father. Now I understand why you treat the cowhands like a bunch of your kids."

Smitty recovered and looked up grinning. "They are a bunch of kids—you included." He slapped Tom on the shoulder.

Jess banged a spoon on the bottom of a frying pan. "Come and git it or I'll throw it in the creek. A good meal waitin' ain't fit to eat," he hollered.

Half the cowboys gathered, more than ready for supper. One by one, they left to relieve the other half of the crew so they could come into camp. After the usual joshing, singing, and spouting cowboy ballads, those not on duty crawled into their bedrolls to get some sleep before the next watch.

Tom slipped out of his tarp at two o'clock in the morning and rode out to relieve Cooney. An endless expanse of blue-black sky peacefully blanketed the herd and bedded down Tom's turmoil. How long would it take the men to build the saloon? Tom smiled as he thought of those determined women. The men probably gave them a rough time at home. Glenn made it obvious he was not pleased with Mary Lou. Tom admired her. She had Texas spirit.

That is why he had to know who Mary Lou loved. If she still wanted to marry Glenn, Tom would ride out.

The next day, Tom and Smitty watched their Texas longhorns prodded into railroad cattle cars. Their ears rang with shouts and bawling cattle.

Tom stuffed the money inside his shirt. They had made a good profit. He jotted figures down on a piece of paper and stuffed it in beside the money. In his letter, Zack had written that the ranch books looked all right. But that was no proof. Zack and Tom had agreed to make up their own set of books. There was a leak somewhere. Eventually, Zack said, he would find it. When he did, they would face Doug, settle their differences, and hopefully run the Circle-Z together. For their mother's sake, Tom hoped they would be able to solve the problem peacefully.

The day after they railed the cows, Tom rode to Venture. He decided to see Mary Lou's Aunt Nelda first. Maybe it was unfair to involve her, but he had talked to her before and found her understanding. She reminded him of his mother, a faith-filled Christian woman with wisdom to see through surface nonsense.

Tom turned down the lane to Buck's cabin. Would Mary Lou be there? He hoped not, even though he ached to see her. The cabin looked deserted. He dismounted and discovered Nelda grinning in the doorway. "You did not come a hair too soon," she called and turned back into the cabin.

Tom followed her.

"Sit down, Tom," Nelda said. "Mary Lou isn't here. She's at Tibby's. They're getting ready for the wedding tomorrow."

Tom's heart plunged.

"I'm glad you came back. Everything's beginning to get out of hand. First, I want to know just what your intentions are."

Nelda had an abrupt way of catching a fellow off guard, Tom thought. "I love Mary Lou and would like to marry her. Unfortunately, it looks as if I've lost my case."

"Nothing is too late till after it's done." Nelda poured Tom a cup of coffee. "Now, what are you going to do about it?"

Tom frowned and shook his head. "What can I do about it? Glenn was Mary Lou's choice."

"Was he?"

"Well, she's betrothed to him."

After a long silence, Nelda said quietly, "Do you love Mary Lou?"

Tom smiled. Nelda never minced words. He looked her straight in the eye. "Yes, I do."

"Enough to marry her?"

Tom nodded. "Yes." What was Nelda driving at?

"Are you ready to fight for the girl you love?"

Zack's words! Tom hedged. "It's just that I don't want to interfere—"

"Don't want to interfere! What kind of a weak-spined answer is that?"

This woman could punch! "Before I do anything, I have to ask Mary Lou if she loves me."

"She does, but she hasn't admitted it yet."

Hope leaped in his chest. Bless this interfering old lady's heart. "That's why I'm back. I could not get her answer when you women were silent."

"Then we'll go to Tibby's and you'll get your answer. If you'll help me saddle Jewel, we'll get things settled now."

Tom loved this woman. Invincible—ready for any challenge. Thank God for strong women like her. Tom suddenly remembered something his father had said one night. "Women are nesters—this wild country's only stability. Without women, the West would remain a sprawling, brawling, uncivilized land of men." Tom rose from his chair and followed Nelda to the barn.

Tibby's housekeeper met them at the door. "They's gone ta town. We needs more supplies," she said, wiping her hands on her apron.

Tom's heart fell into his boots. Every hope seemed to get trampled.

Nelda walked in and sat down. "We'll wait. Sit down, Tom, and tell me something about your family and Texas."

As he talked, Nelda nodded and smiled.

A single set of hoofbeats came to the front porch, then Tibby kicked the door with her foot. Tom jumped to open it. She came in with her arms full, emptied them on the table, and stared at him. "Oh, you're the other horse," she said. "I recognized Jewel."

Tom stood, not quite sure of her meaning. "I came to see Mary Lou."

Tibby darted a glance at Nelda. "You must be Tom. Well, I'm glad to finally get a look at you. You've made my niece a very unhappy girl."

Tom did not know whether to leave or stay. He shifted uneasily.

"Young man, why did not you include a note to Mary Lou in the letter you wrote to my husband? That girl was heartbroken. I was glad when Glenn paid attention to her. After her mother's death and your neglect, he was just what she needed."

Tom feared to open his mouth.

Then Tibby smiled. "I had to get that out of my system. You being here, I'm assuming you have some honorable intentions."

Tom grinned broadly. "Yes, ma'am!" With these two women on his side, how could he help but win?

Chapter Eighteen

Dulcie padded her way into town, reflecting her rider's reluctance. Mary Lou's insides gnawed with increasing apprehension. Something was wrong.

Her feelings toward Glenn bothered her most. Were all brides as timid as she felt? She remembered Lucy Thompson who ran away the day before her wedding and hid in an empty soddy for over a week until her father found her. Now Mary Lou understood why.

Tom bounced in and out of her thoughts. The memory of their last meeting reached into her soul and evoked longings she thought she had put away. But he was gone. Her only regret was they had not been able to talk.

Mary Lou scolded herself for letting such thoughts pervade her mind. Once married, they would disappear. She closed her eyes and lifted her face to the warm sun. Mama had told her to pray when things did not seem right and God would give her peace. *Father*, she prayed, *I want to do the right thing. Getting married is a big step. Help me.* Her heart warmed and she relaxed.

At the edge of town she noticed a changed Venture. The absence of the saloon brought peaceful days as well as nights. Residents walked about town with a new sense of freedom and order. Sarah George, out early, waved from the town well.

Mary Lou waved back and turned into the small alley at the side of the store. Entering the housekeeping rooms, she bristled. To think that Glenn would consider the saloon building for their new home! Given a choice, she would have taken any small cabin in the fresh openness of the prairie. Some days even the post office and store gave her claustrophobia.

Glenn habitually allowed customers in before the store opened. "Every sale counts," he said. Three browsed this morning. Mary Lou hurried through with a breezy "Good morning" and sought the solitude of the post office. Two mailbags leaned against the counter. She softened. Glenn, always thoughtful, made sure she never carried the bags to or from the station.

Glenn stuck his head in the door. "Good morning, dear. One more day and you'll be Mrs. Glenn Farrell." His knowing smile sent crimson to her cheeks.

She pushed down panic and smiled. "Good morning."

Glenn disappeared to continue his jovial chatter with the customers. Mary Lou immediately dug into the mail bags, sorting letters and stuffing them into their respective boxes. Out of habit, she read the sender's name just before she tucked it into the box.

Mr. Thomas Langdon from Laura Shepard. Her heart stopped. The sudden stab of jealousy surprised her. That name dragged old memories of Tom using

Laura's address last year to send letters to his mother. She stuffed the letter quickly into Tom's box. Dissatisfied, she removed it and studied the handwriting. Sprawly, definitely feminine. What was Laura like? Pretty? Tom never mentioned her other than his explanation that he wanted to make sure his mother got his letters. But did he love her?

All morning Mary Lou plodded, her mind busy with speculations about Laura, wonder about Tom, and interruptions by Glenn. At noon, she gathered her belongings and headed for the back rooms.

"Leaving already?" Glenn followed her and put his arms around her. The tenderness of his touch and the love pouring from his eyes soothed her fears. When he kissed her, she could not help compare it with Tom's kiss. Ashamed of her fickle thoughts, she pecked him on the cheek, patted his face, and left.

Perky, blue cornflowers parted as she rode through the prairie. This was where she felt at home. She dismounted and gathered flowers for Aunt Nelda while Dulcie nibbled on clumps of grass.

When she approached the cabin, she noticed a horse tied to the hitching rail. Tinder? She stayed herself from leaping off her horse and running to the cabin by trotting Dulcie leisurely to the barn. Then, fingers shaking, she slipped off Dulcie's saddle, commanding herself to be calm.

A beaming Aunt Nelda met her at the door with a big hug for the cornflowers. "Somebody to see you," she whispered, leading her to Tom. "Look who's here."

Mary Lou wavered between wanting to run and aching to stay. She stretched out her hand toward Tom. "Glad to see you again before you go back to Texas." Her heart trembled at his touch.

Tom cupped her hand in both his big ones. "Hello, Mary Lou. I had to see you again." He grinned and added, "to hear your voice."

Her crazy heart responded to a rising surge of emotion. Why did not she feel like this around Glenn? Did she imagine it, or did Tom release her hand reluctantly as she pulled away?

"I've got dinner ready so wash up to eat. I invited Tom to stay. We won't wait for Owen. He just left for town."

Mary Lou noticed Tom's quizzical frown. "Owen Mackey is Pa's full name. Aunt Nelda is the only one who uses it."

In no time, dinner spread invitingly on the table.

"Tom, would you say grace?" Aunt Nelda asked.

"Yes ma'm." He bowed his head.

No one seemed to notice Mary Lou's surprised intake of breath.

"Our Father, we give thanks for the blessing of this home, its welcome for me. We're thankful not only for the food on the table but also for Your provision of eternal life. Teach us to number our days and serve You well. In Jesus' name, Amen."

Listening to Tom pray, Mary Lou held her breath. *He's a Christian!* Her whole being responded with a joy she had trouble concealing. She ate little, her gaze fixed on Tom's animated face. He talked of home, his mother, three brothers, and the ranch. Hearing the drawl of his voice made her come alive. He never mentioned Laura.

All too soon, he rose to leave. "Have to get back," he said. "Smitty and the crew are camped outside Venture."

Nelda suddenly busied herself cleaning up the table, noisily rattling dishes and pans.

Mary Lou walked outside with Tom. They took Tinder to the water trough for a drink. Tom surveyed the sky, the barn, the grove of walnut trees.

"Nelson would have a great time painting this. He says he gets tired of painting sagebrush, cactus, and tumbleweeds. He's quite good at it. Mother says it's God's special gift to him since his legs never grew strong."

Tom's mother sounded like Mama. Concerned, Mary Lou asked, "How crippled is he?" The word was out without thinking.

Tom grinned. "He gets around pretty good. He can ride a horse, drive Mother's buggy, and moves mighty fast on his crutches. He's a great boy."

Without warning, Tom turned Mary Lou so she faced him. Mary Lou fought a desire to feel his arms around her.

After an awkward pause, Tom said softly, "Before I go, I have to find out one thing." His eyes searched her face. "Mary Lou, do you have any love for me?"

Her heart hammered against her chest demanding to be recognized. "Why yes, Tom." The minute the words escaped, she knew she had to grab them back. "I've enjoyed having you for a friend." She turned from his gaze.

"Just say you love Glenn and I'll ride out of your life. But I have to know."

Does she love Tom? Does she love Glenn? She smiled. "Why," she sputtered hoping for understanding, "I love you both."

Tom studied her, then smiled. "Well," he said, "there's still hope for me."

What a ridiculous thing for him to say the day before her wedding! Slowly she lifted her gaze to Tom's earnest face, read love in his eyes, and felt it reach for her. All doubt vanished. *Tom loved her!* She longed to slip into the comfort of his arms, but Glenn's invisible presence held her steadfast.

Tom turned to Tinder, checked the saddle straps, and remarked lightly, "If I'm still in town—" Suddenly, he swung around, pulled her into his arms, lifted her chin, and kissed her.

Her whole being soared. She slid her arms around his neck. This was the way it should be. Unguarded, complete, giving. Tom released her slowly, his eyes clinging to her face. Mary Lou trembled, not only from the impact of his kiss, but the realization that she had betrayed Glenn. Undaunted, her heart kept reaching, stretching for what she could be—Tom's wife. Ironically, for the first time, Glenn's face formed in her mind. She wilted.

"Forgive me, Mary Lou. I shouldn't have done that. But for what I have to do, I had to be sure." He swung into the saddle, touched his hat, and trotted off.

Mary Lou felt abandoned. Had to be sure? Of what? That she loved him? Yes, she loved him. She raised her finger tips to her lips. The walnut trees rustled then stilled. She walked shakily back to the cabin.

Nelda, settled in her rocker mending, looked up when Mary Lou came in. "He's a nice young man. I like him." She poked her needle into a good-sized hole in the heel of Buck's heavy sock.

"Yes, he is," Mary Lou answered. Did that voice belong to her? She tried to escape her aunt's probing eyes. Her own filled. "Even though I love Tom, I can't hurt Glenn. It would be cruel. His love and kindness saved me when Mama died and Pa . . . Glenn loves me, Aunt Nelda. I can't just—"

"So, you finally know which one you love?" She held up her hand to stave off Mary Lou's comment. "And you're willing to give up Tom and marry Glenn?"

"I have to."

"That does not make sense, child. You don't have to marry anyone."

Mary Lou shook her head. "I really don't know Tom that well. I know Glenn. No matter what decision I make, I'll hurt one or the other." Mary Lou's shoulders raised and lowered in a final sigh. "And Tom got a letter today from Laura Shepard, his girl in Texas. She must be accepted by his family, Tom wrote letters to his mother through her."

"It's true some men have girls at both ends of the trail, but that has nothing to do with you. No one should marry out of pity." Nelda's darning needle wove furiously back and forth.

"It's too late, Aunt Nelda. My wedding's tomorrow. Things have gone too far to stop them, and Pa approves of Glenn—"

"Your Pa isn't the one marrying him. He won't have to live with him and be his husband." Nelda dropped her mending into her lap. "There's only one reason to marry a man—and that is you love him so much you can't live without him. When I met Lars, there was not anyone else I could have married."

"Aunt Nelda, do you have something against my marrying Glenn?"

"Against him personally, no. It's you. I think you're trying to tie up too many ends—brotherly love for Glenn plus a duty to your father."

"Like is not enough!" Jenny had cried when Mary Lou first told her of her betrothal. If she could see it. . . .

"Any girl who marries a man she does not love is eventually miserable." Nelda finished her last sock. "I've said my say." She stuffed her needle in the spool of darning thread, shoved it into her basket, and carried it to the shelf.

Mary Lou inhaled deeply to shift the dead weight that had returned to her chest and shook her head. "Pa would not accept Tom."

"You're not thinking straight. Your Pa will have to accept your choice, just like your Grandfather Stafford had to accept Tibby and Ellen's decisions. He lost two daughters and a granddaughter by never forgiving them.

"I remember the letter Owen wrote me after he met your mother. Ellen was a real lady. His biggest worry was that he could not be her kind of gentleman. He loved being a cowboy. My advice was that if they loved each other, they could survive anything. And they did. Owen's accident, your mother's ill health, losing two baby sons. Nothing conquered the love they had. That's why your Pa is so devastated at her death. He's lost half of himself.

"That's the kind of love your pa should want for you. It's the only kind that lasts and makes for happiness. Read again what God says about marriage. There's only one other decision to make that's greater—the accepting of the Lord Jesus Christ as Savior."

Suddenly, Mary Lou felt tired and confused. Her mind bogged at Nelda's defense. And she knew her aunt was right. She rose and kissed her aunt. "Thank you, Aunt Nelda for being honest—and for loving me so much. I'm going to bed." She gave her aunt a hug. "I want to get up early so I can look my best tomorrow." She passed over the determined look on Nelda's face. She needed to be alone on her last night as Mary Lou Mackey.

In her room, she sank into her mother's rocker. Mama, she cried within. There was no answer. She laid her head back and closed her eyes. Her chest ached. Her heart cried dry tears. Where was God? In the cottonwood grove when her heart found a new depth of His love, she thought she would never again have to go through this kind of agony.

Don't worry, My child, everything is going to be all right.

Mary Lou's spirit responded. She got ready for bed, climbed in, and lay staring at her wedding dress hanging on the way. "Thy will be done," she prayed, "not mine."

Chapter Nineteen

Mary Lou stirred, stretched, and caught the sun peeking through her window. Her wedding day. She rose, bathed, and dressed, ignoring an unexplainable heaviness.

Her wedding dress monopolized the room—the blue dress Mama had made. Mary Lou and Aunt Nelda had added a fresh lace collar and cuffs and a slight bustle on the back—Aunt Nelda's idea for style.

Mary Lou fingered her dress, each handmade stitch neat and even, the darts on the bodice sharp and shapely. Her favorite color, blue. Like the color of your eyes, Tom had said.

Determinedly, Mary Lou tossed her head and flung the thought away. She had not think of Tom. She had had her chance; she had made her choice. By supper time, she would be Mrs. Glenn Farrell. Maybe then Pa would look on her favorably. She wrapped her dress in a sheet for transport to Aunt Tibby's, buttoned her shoes, and opened her door.

Aunt Nelda looked up from biscuit dough with a cheery smile. "Good morning. You look rested, and you'll be a beautiful bride."

Mary Lou flushed and hurried about setting the table. By the time Buck appeared, breakfast was ready and they sat down.

Aunt Nelda bowed her head. "Our Father, thank You for another day to accomplish the tasks You set before us. We ask Your blessing on Mary Lou and. . . ." She hesitated, then quickly continued. "And her new husband. Thy will be done. Thank You for the bounty before us. In Jesus' name, Amen."

Nelda dished up fried cornmeal mush with butter and maple syrup and poured steaming cups of coffee. Between sips, she talked excitedly about preparations Tibby had made for the wedding. They had spent all week cooking and baking.

The Bar-B ranch house had grown from its original cabin to a series of rooms. Then Nate had added a whole wing with an upstairs. Tibby, as usual, had all details arranged. Mary Lou would walk down the stairs, meet her father at the bottom, and walk into the parlor where Pastor Miles would perform the ceremony. Mary Wescott had offered to play hymns on Tibby's small organ. Venture townspeople and neighboring homesteaders for miles around had been invited.

Mary Lou looked at the clock. Seven-thirty. She left for the barn to do morning animal chores for the last time. Tomorrow she would be a townswoman. When she reached Dulcie, she put her arms around her and leaned her cheek against her warm neck. "I can tell you the truth." Mary Lou swallowed tears. "I wish it were Tom and I'd be a rancher's wife." She stroked the animal's neck. "At least I'll have you."

Dulcie nickered and tossed her head.

Mary Lou rubbed the horse's forelock, slid her hand down the smooth hair of Dulcie's face, and nuzzled her velvety nose with the palm of her hand.

Suddenly, she had to ride. Blanket and saddle went on quickly. She mounted and they flew out the barn door into the morning wind. Mary Lou automatically reined Dulcie toward Point Lane. She desperately needed the peace of the Lord she had found the other day.

A rider moved through the cottonwoods. Tom? What was he doing here?

He trotted up, a grin on his face. "I found out one thing this morning," he said brightly. "God answers prayers. For some reason, I had to come here."

Had God's Holy Spirit prompted her to come as an answer to Tom's prayers? Mary Lou gazed at Tom. "Until the other day when you said grace, I did not know you were a Christian."

"You don't know my mother," Tom smiled and added, "or my father. Jesus became my Savior when I was four. My mother did not believe a child had to wait until he was grown. You'd like Mother." He lowered his gaze to his saddle horn. "Even as a little boy, I made up my mind to marry a Christian woman just like her."

"I hear most little boys want to marry someone like their mother." Mary Lou fought to keep her voice casual.

"Guess so." He looked straight into her eyes. "Today's the day,"

She glanced away. "Yes."

The cottonwoods could not soothe her. Tom's nearness provoked feelings that disturbed her, feelings not easily dismissed. She swung Dulcie's head. "I'd better get back. Lots of things to do. I just had to take a last morning ride—"

"As Mary Lou Mackey?" Tom finished.

She looked directly at him. "Yes." How did he know? She wanted to stay, but did not dare. "I must be going. Goodbye, Tom." She swung Dulcie's head and jabbed her flanks.

"See you at the wedding."

She halted and turned. "You're staying?"

"For a couple more days. Smitty and the boys have started back. I have some business to attend to."

Mary Lou forced a smile. Words eluded her. She pushed Dulcie into a trot but could not keep from looking back. Tom sat watching her every move. Her heart pounded its protest, but she only waved. "Let's go," she ordered Dulcie. By the time she reached home, she had gained control.

Mary Lou, Nelda, and Buck squeezed into his buggy at one o'clock to go to Tibby's. The Bar-B ranch house buzzed with a festive air. Vases of jaunty cornflowers and blue grass bowered the parlor, and the dining room overflowed with wedding supper preparations.

Mary Lou hugged her aunt. "It's beautiful, Aunt Tibby. Thank you. Mama would love it."

Tibby cupped Mary Lou's face in her hands and smiled knowingly. "Yes she would. But I bet she knows."

Mary Lou walked slowly upstairs to the bedroom. She opened the door. Her dress greeted her from a peg on the wall. Tibby had insisted she send someone for it so it would not get crushed between the three of them in Buck's buggy. She sat down on the bed and smiled. *I hope you see it all, Mama.* She remembered a wedding she and Mama had attended when she was sixteen. Mama had turned to her and said "When your time comes, you'll be a beautiful bride and bless some young man with a good Christian wife."

Please, God, bless our marriage. Help me to love my husband. That struck Mary Lou as an odd prayer moments before her wedding.

Aunt Nelda hurried in to help her into her dress and fix her hair. Small cornflowers were snuggled into the braid over her head. A whole bouquet of them stood in a vase, ready for her to carry when she walked down the stairs.

At two o'clock, Mary Lou was ready and heard a soft knock at the door. When she opened it, there stood her father. "Pa?" He had climbed all those stairs to see her! "Come in."

Her father looked as she remembered him when she was a little girl. Some of the pain had gone from his face. He was handsome in a dark suit with a string tie. This was how he must have looked to Mama when she fell in love with him. Mary Lou did not blame her.

Buck gazed at his daughter. Slowly, he leaned his cane against the door and held out both hands. Mary Lou placed hers in them. He spread their arms, smiled, and shook his head. "You look just like—and as beautiful as—your Mama."

Had he forgiven her at last? Mary Lou breathed a sigh of relief and walked into his arms. A long-awaited peace settled over her. "Pa," she said softly as he held her. "I do love you, Pa."

Buck awkwardly released her and nodded. "Yes." He ran his hands down his string tie. "Be as happy as your Mama and me."

Mary Lou had not heard that tone in his voice for a long time. "Thank you, Pa." This time, her tears fell for happiness.

Buck retrieved his cane. "I'd best be gettin' downstairs."

Was that a mist she saw in her father's eyes? *Thank you, Lord, for Pa's blessing.*

The sound of the organ's familiar hymns floated up the stairs along with Nelda and Tibby. "It's time," Tibby hugged her. "My, you do resemble your Mama. I remember the day she married your father. I don't believe I've ever seen two people more in love." She laughed. "Except your Uncle Nate and me."

Nelda held Mary Lou in her arms lightly to keep from crushing her dress. "You ready?"

Mary Lou reached for her flowers and took a deep breath. "Yes."

Her two aunts scurried out.

Mary Lou settled her bouquet in her arm and slowly stepped down each step, her knees shaking. At the bottom, Pa looked up, smiled, and nodded. Smiling faces of friends and neighbors greeted her. Pastor Miles and Glenn waited in the parlor. When she reached the bottom step, her father tucked her arm into his.

Her father released her when they reached Glenn. Mary Lou turned a fleeting glance at Glenn and caught a seriousness in his eyes. Was he as nervous as she? She turned to Jenny and handed her the flowers. Jenny looked stricken. She felt Glenn's touch. He lifted her hand to his lips and kissed it, sending color to her cheeks.

The organ music stopped.

Pastor Miles cleared his throat and began. "Dearly beloved, we are gathered together to join this man and this woman in holy matrimony." He cast his gaze over those attending. "If there is anyone who deems this marriage should not take place, speak now or forever hold your peace."

The room stayed silent. Someone coughed.

"I do."

Mary Lou gasped. Jenny? Oh, no! But—it was not Jenny's voice!

"I do," the voice repeated.

Glenn? She faced him in disbelief. Spurned at the altar?

A strained smile twisted Glenn's face. Guests, at first silent, recovered. They buzzed and stretched to see what was going on. An astonished Pastor Miles looked from Glenn to Mary Lou, demanding an explanation.

Glenn turned to Mary Lou and gently took her hands in his. "Forgive me, Mary Lou, I shouldn't have waited until now." He bowed his head. "I kept hoping." He looked into her incredulous face. "But we can't be married. You aren't in love with me—at least not enough to marry me."

She fought for meaning in what he was saying. She had agreed to marry him, had she not? "Glenn, why—"

Glenn grasped her arm firmly and propelled her past the crowd of gaping neighbors. Aunt Tibby recovered and led them into Nate's office. Mary Lou heard the thump of her father's cane.

Jenny rushed up and put an arm around her. "Mary Lou, I'm sorry. He said it before I had a chance."

"Before you?" She stared into Jenny's agonized face. She turned to Glenn—to her father. The light of love she had seen in his eyes upstairs had twisted into a scowl. Mary Lou covered her face.

In the office, Pastor Miles stepped forward. "Will someone please tell me the reason this wedding has been made a travesty?"

Nelda spoke up. "It's probably my fault as much as anyone's, but it did not turn out the way we'd planned. Jenny was supposed to object to the marriage."

Mary Lou swung to Jenny. Betrayed by her best friend? The knot in her chest threatened to suffocate her.

"It's my fault, too." Tibby said. "We thought this was the only way to keep Mary Lou from marrying Glenn when she's in love with someone else."

Mary Lou wished she could die. Glenn shook his head and put a protective arm around her. "None of you have anything to do with this and I have no idea what you're all talking about. This is solely my doing." Glenn turned to Mary Lou. "Last night," he said softly, "I saw you say goodbye to Tom."

Mary Lou's hands flew to her crimson face. She looked for a way to flee, but she was surrounded with dismayed faces.

"I love you, Mary Lou," Glenn continued, with the kindest look Mary Lou had ever seen on his face. "But after I saw you and Tom together, I knew you really loved him. No matter how much I loved you, I'd never be able to make you happy."

Buck, furious, faced Glenn. "Do you mean you refuse to marry my daughter?"

"Yes sir. Because I love her and want her to be happy. You should want the same."

If Mary Lou had been the fainting kind, she would have swooned. Instead, her embarrassment gave way to anger. Everyone except her had decided what was best for her life. Did not anyone care how she felt? She had heard enough.

"Wait a minute!" she burst out. "Don't I have anything to say about this?" Everyone turned to her as if she had appeared from nowhere.

Bang! The door slammed against the wall. Tibby walked in, followed by Tom.

Chapter Twenty

"Now!" Tibby shouted. "Let's get this matter cleared up."

Mary Lou swayed. Would it ever stop? Never could she have imagined her special day would turn into the worst day of her life. And Tom?

Nelda slipped a concerned arm around Mary Lou. "This girl deserves an explanation from all of us. She's in shock. Now that I look at it, it was a sneaky, backhanded way to handle things." Nelda kissed Mary Lou on the cheek. "Dear child, I'm sorry we've put you through this."

Tibby nodded. "Forgive us, Mary Lou. But Nelda and I were watching you being pushed into making the biggest mistake of your life." Tibby shook her head. "At the time we planned it, it seemed a good, simple way to correct things, but it's turned out to be the worst." Tibby folded the stunned girl in her arms. "Your Uncle Nate keeps telling me I can't run the world. Can you ever forgive us two old, busybodies? Our honest concern was for your happiness."

The rising anger in Mary Lou subsided. These dear ones loved her more than she deserved and had gone to extreme lengths so that she could marry the man she loved.

Tibby continued. "The plan was to have Jenny protest the wedding. That would give time to get a few lives straightened out—or so we thought. After we got you and Tom to admit your love for each other, Tom would take Glenn's place. But when Glenn stopped the wedding—"

Glenn broke in. "I did not know of your plan. I only knew what I had to do." He turned to Mary Lou. "I've known for some time you loved me only as a friend. I hoped it would grow into more than that. That's why I waited so long. Then I saw for myself—you love Tom. Forgive me for hanging on till the last minute." Glenn hung his head. "I should have told you before the wedding. Instead, I mortified you before family and friends. I'm sorry."

Mary Lou smiled at the young man who loved her enough to give her up. Through all the confusion, Mary Lou suddenly remembered Mama quoting Psalm 37:4: "Delight thyself also in the Lord; and He shall give thee the desires of thine heart." Was God giving her a fresh opportunity to marry the man she loved?

Mary Lou found her voice. "If anyone is at fault, it's me. Until this moment, I never realized how selfish I was. For me to say I loved both Glenn and Tom was cruel and dishonest. The truth is, I love Glenn—"

Mouths dropped open and shoulders slumped.

"As I'd love the brother I never had." She looked deep into Glenn's troubled eyes. "I've never loved you more than I do right now. I'd have been lost without your caring after Mama died. I'll always love you for that." She reached around her neck and unhooked the locket he had given her. "Here, this belongs to your bride-to-be." She placed the locket in the palm of his hand.

Glenn raised Mary Lou's hand to his lips. "Thank you." His open smile released her.

Buck leaned against the door, scowling. Mary Lou ached for him. Upstairs, she had had her old Pa back, the loving father she had known as a child. She had thought he had forgiven her. What could she say to him now?

Suddenly Tom moved across the room to Mary Lou and turned to the others. "This has to stop. Can't you all see what we're doing to her?"

Mary Lou slowly faced him. "But I can't marry you either, Tom."

Disbelieving silence blanketed the room. Mary Lou smiled up into Tom's stricken face and shook her head. "I can't marry you—because you've never asked me."

Tom's eyes filled with relief. A sly grin spread across his ruddy face. He nodded, took her hands in his, and pulled her to face him. "So I haven't. But there's something I don't know either. I've never heard you say you loved me—only me."

All restraints dissolved. "Oh, Tom, I've loved you since the first day you walked into the post office."

Tom stood erect. "Mary Lou Mackey, I love you with all my heart. Will you do me the honor of becoming this cowboy-rancher's wife?"

Love flooded her being. Mary Lou offered both hands. "Yes, Tom, I want very much to be your wife." All anguish disappeared as he locked her in his stalwart arms and kissed her. She slid her arms around his neck and boldly kissed him back, regardless of the audience. She was tired of pretending.

The approving family watched with relieved smiles spread across their faces.

A familiar thump, thump, thump reverberated across the room. Tom clasped Mary Lou's hand and pulled her with him to her father. "Mr. Mackey."

Buck paid no attention.

Tom and Mary Lou caught up to him at the door and Tom took hold of his arm. Buck stopped, eyes cast down.

"Mr. Mackey, I ask you again for permission to marry Mary Lou."

Buck ignored him, walked out, climbed into his buggy, and rode off, waving a tail of dust.

Nelda called them back. "Mary Lou, I know your Mama would disagree with your father. Her first thought would be for your happiness. Owen's felt like a cheated man since his accident. The loss of Ellen did not help. Losing his daughter is another blow. He's forgotten how desperately in love he was with your mother.

"Sometimes things repeat themselves. Your Grandfather Stafford denied

Owen permission to marry Ellen, but your mother married him because she loved him. She was never sorry. She forgave and prayed for her father till the day she died. Forgive him, Mary Lou, and pray for him. I don't think he realizes he's making you and Tom suffer same as he and Ellen did."

Mary Lou looked into Tom's concerned face. Tom had done what he should. Now the decision was hers. She faced him. "Tom, if you'll have me without my father's blessing, I'd like very much to become your wife."

Tom beamed. "Have you!" He enclosed her in his arm and turned to Tibby. "Do you think we could still have this wedding?"

"I don't see why not, and you could stay with us till you're ready to head for Texas." Tibby cleared her throat. "Well, now," she smiled broadly. "We have lots of guests who are probably wondering what happened to the wedding. Some have come a far piece to enjoy this event. Let's go out and start over."

She swung the office door wide and marched out to the parlor. "Get ready for the wedding, folks. Thank you for your patience. We had to change a few things." She ignored the questioning stares and clapped her hands. "Mary, let's have some proper music."

Mary Wescott lifted her hands to the organ keys and familiar hymns again filled the room.

Tom crossed to Glenn. They spoke for a few moments, Glenn nodded, and they shook hands. Pastor Miles hustled Tom to the parlor. Glenn followed and stood at Tom's right. More than a few eyebrows raised, then faces broke into smiles.

Before she left, Jenny threw her arms around Mary Lou. "I'll miss you but I'm happy for you," she whispered, eyes swimming. She started off, then spun around. "I'm still your bridesmaid, aren't I?" Jenny giggled and left.

Nelda and Tibby smoothed Mary Lou's dress, then beamed in approval. Mary Lou kissed each one. These dear women. They had fought hard for her happiness.

Just before Mary Lou started through the door, Tibby handed her the wilting bouquet of cornflowers. Mary Lou walked forward and stopped. She would have to walk alone. She glanced desperately at Aunt Nelda.

"Don't fret yourself. You're marrying the man you love. If Owen isn't happy about it, that's his problem, not yours. Now, go—with God's blessing."

Mary Lou took a wobbly step. Gently, a strong arm slipped through hers. Uncle Nate steadied her, led her forward, placed her beside Tom, and stepped back. The music slowly faded.

Pastor Miles cleared his throat and began again. "Dearly beloved, we are gathered together to join," he hesitated a second. "This man and this woman in the bonds of holy matrimony." Nervously, he paused. "If there is . . . anyone . . . who deems this marriage should not take place, speak now or forever hold your peace."

The room held its breath.

Pastor Miles drew a relieved sigh and hurried on. "God has given us one of the most sacred unions on this earth when He ordained the marriage of man and woman, and it should never be entered into lightly. It is not unlike the union of His Holy Spirit with His people. God is spirit and those who worship Him must worship Him in spirit and truth. And God sent his Son, Jesus, to be joined with His bride, the church.

"In like manner, the true joining of this man and woman is in spirit as well as heart." He turned to Tom. "Thomas Langdon, do you take Mary Lou Elizabeth Mackey to be your lawfully wedded wife, to cherish her, honor and protect her. . . ."

Mary Lou could hardly contain her happiness. She closed her eyes and drank deeply of the joy that coursed through her.

"Will you answer 'I do'?"

Tom's gaze never left her face. He reached for her hand. "I do," he said.

Pastor turned to Mary Lou. "And do you, Mary Lou Elizabeth Mackey, take Thomas Langdon to be your lawfully wedded husband, to cherish, honor, and obey and cleave unto him until death you do part?"

Mary Lou's heart guided her answer. "I do," she said quietly.

Pastor folded the couple's hands between his. "I now pronounce you man and wife, in the name of the Father, Son, and the Holy Ghost. May God bless you, my children."

Mary Lou walked into the arms of her husband. Tom kissed her gently and whispered in her ear, "Thank God. My wife at last." They turned arm in arm to greet a swarm of well wishers.

Maggie Bartlett squeezed Mary Lou's hands. "My, this is a surprise. I was lookin' forward to havin' you and Glenn as next door neighbors. I figured you'd spruce up that old saloon. Sure would make my place look better."

Mary Lou had forgotten that! She smiled. "Thank you. I'm sure someone else will buy it and fix it up."

Sarah George circled Mary Lou with one arm, patted Tom on the shoulder, and leaned confidentially toward Mary Lou. "You married the right one. You never were meant to be a town girl."

Tom smiled broadly. "I'll see to that."

Mary Lou turned to a tap on her shoulder. Ida Hensley's long, sad face moaned, "What's your poor Pa goin' to do with both you and your ma gone?"

Henrietta moved protectively between Ida and Mary Lou. "Buck'll do fine. He has his sister Nelda to look after him." Henrietta hugged Mary Lou. "But I'm going to miss you terribly. You're like one of my own." She turned to Tom. "When are you leaving?"

"In four days."

"Oh!" Mary Lou gasped.

"I'm sorry, dear, but I have to get back," Tom pleaded, then laughed. "This wedding is still full of surprises."

When the last guest left, Tibby gave a sigh and ushered Tom and Mary Lou to an upstairs bedroom. She stood in the doorway, smiling. "It was worth it all," she said and closed the door.

The next four days flew by quickly. Nate gave Mary Lou and Tom a buckboard and a western team as a wedding present to carry Mary Lou's belongings to Texas. Nelda and Tibby fluttered over Mary Lou pouring out guidance for her new life as a wife. Mary Lou hoped she would remember all their good wisdom.

The three women packed everything carefully under canvas in the buckboard, including Mama's rocking chair padded with Mama's quilts.

"A daughter should have her mother's quilts," Aunt Nelda insisted. "We have enough left, and I've got lots of old clothes to make some more."

"Can't send you off to your mother-in-law like some poor relation." Tibby said. She wrapped a globe lamp and tucked it carefully into a basket.

Jenny visited often. They talked and talked, storing up a lifetime of memories before they parted. They reminisced about the hours they had spent as little girls roaming their beloved prairie on foot between the two cabins.

Every day, Mary Lou rode into Venture to the store to see Pa. Glenn said he came in late and left early. "He gave me half-interest in the store if I moved out of the boarding house into the back rooms to run the store. He's a great man, Mary Lou."

"I know. My Mama married him. I hope I see him before I go, but if I don't, will you tell him I'll always love him and that someday, I hope he'll forgive me."

Mary Lou glanced into the post office where she had spent most of her life. In spite of her sadness, she could not resist the freedom and joy she felt. She was now a rancher's wife!

Chapter Twenty-One

Only one day remained before their departure.

Mary Lou planned to spend it with Aunt Tibby, her second mother. Mama had willingly shared Mary Lou with her sister since Tibby had no children of her own. In the last year of Mama's illness, Aunt Tibby had come every day to relieve Mary Lou of some of the burden. They had grown much closer.

Mary Lou stepped into her aunt's familiar kitchen, received a welcoming hug and was suddenly struck by an attack of homesickness. The homey fragrance of bread fostered memories of happy times shared when Mama was alive. Mary Lou expected to yearn for Kansas after they got to Texas. But now? While she was still surrounded by the people and land she loved?

What sparked her sudden emotion was the table. Aunt Tibby's good china was neatly set for a special tea party, and her aunt's arms held her longer than usual. "Don't tell me we're having a special tea party all by ourselves?" Mary Lou asked lightly.

Tibby smiled. "Yes. I'm reminding you to have tea parties with your children."

Mary Lou laughed. "Gracious, Aunt Tibby, aren't you rushing things a bit?"

Her aunt's expression gave her away. She had always planned to join Ellen in being "grandmother" to Mary Lou's children. It hurt to realize that distance would keep her children from getting to know their loving, energetic great-aunt.

Tibby picked up the teapot. "Sit down. Henrietta and Jenny will be here later, but we'll sip a chattin' cup before they come. I need to talk to you anyway."

They sat and Tibby poured.

Special tea parties had begun when Mary Lou was a little girl. Whenever they were together at either home, Mama and Aunt Tibby always had made time for a pot of tea and a lot of talk.

One day, Ellen and Tibby had been at the table, engrossed in their conversation. Three-year-old Mary Lou had climbed on a chair, gotten a cup from the shelf, and carried it to her mother. Then she had shoved a chair to the table and joined the tea party.

Aunt Tibby had taken the hint. Laughing, she had prepared a special cup of tea for Mary Lou. Much later, Mary Lou had discovered that her cup of tea was a small amount of tea doctored with lots of milk and sugar.

It was during winter special teas that Aunt Tibby had taught Mary Lou and Jenny to tat. At first the thread had resembled a tangle of knots. Gradually, both girls had grown proficient.

The next Christmas, Mary Lou had presented a tatted collar and cuff set to her mother and Aunt Tibby and had even sent a set to Grandmother Stafford.

"And don't worry about your father."

Mary Lou jolted back to the present.

"It's ironic," Tibby continued. "Your mother and I went through the same thing. I remember when Nate asked Father for permission to marry me. Father forbade it! When we went counter to his wishes, he refused to speak to us, even to bid me goodbye. Mother was in tears. But I loved Nate and could not bear to have him leave without me. We got married, bid my mother goodbye, and left for Kansas. I was homesick and missed your mama, so I wrote, asking her to visit. Father was aghast! His daughter travelling on stage coaches to that uncivilized country! But Ellen must have read "homesick" between the lines. She came anyway. And she fell in love with a cowboy and married him at our house.

"Father disowned us both. He never allowed Mother to speak about us or mention our names in front of him. He carried that unforgiving spirit to his grave." Tibby slowly sipped tea, staring into memories Mary Lou knew nothing of.

"All this made Mother's life miserable. By cutting himself off, Father cut Mother off too. Your mother and I prayed. We wrote letters telling how happy we were and what wonderful things we were doing, but neither Father or Mother answered."

"How could Grandfather act like that?" Mary Lou interjected. "He was a Christian and so faithful in church."

"The church had his body, but Jesus never had his heart," Tibby replied.

Suddenly Tibby got up, rummaged in a chest, and returned with two packages of faded letters tied together with frayed ribbon. She handed them to her niece.

Mary Lou turned them over and looked up in surprise. One set was addressed in Aunt Tibby's bold strokes, the other in her mother's neat script. "They aren't opened!"

Aunt Tibby's lips formed a hurt smile. "No. They are yours to read. If nothing else, they are the history of our lives after we left Ohio and married cowboys." Tibby emphasized the last word. "Mother gave them to us when we attended Father's funeral. She said when they were delivered, he threw them in the rubbish but she retrieved and hid them."

Mary Lou frowned. "But why did not Grandmother open them?"

"We asked her the same thing. She said she feared she might mention something from them and betray herself."

"But Grandfather died before she did. Why did not she read them then?"

"By that time, Mother could not see. She did not want anyone else to read them to her." Tibby sat swishing the remaining tea in her cup. "If she had, she would have known I lost my only child, Ellen lost two baby boys, and you were born. Having been a teacher herself, Mother was very proud when Ellen became a teacher. She never knew Ellen continued her teaching by having school in your cabin for you and seven neighbor children."

It was unbelievable! Why had not Mama told her some of this? Had she been too much a baby to tell it? A child? Yes, a happy child because Mama wanted it so. Now Mary Lou understood why Mama was so concerned about Pa and his moody, recluse ways. She had been through rejection from her own father and wanted to shield her child from the hurt she had experienced.

"The sad thing is," Tibby went on, "Father not only cheated himself, but he robbed his wife of the joy of her children and grandchildren."

Mary Lou sat amazed that anyone would act as Grandfather. "But Pa won't. . . ."

Tibby shook her head. "It does not make any difference what your Pa does or does not do. That's between him and God. It's what you do I'm concerned about."

Dazed, Mary Lou shook her head. "Mama never said a word."

"That's because your mother was a loving, God-fearing woman. She forgave Father and Mother completely. She never embraced the hurt, anger, and disappointment like I did.

" 'That's all past,' Ellen kept telling me. 'God gives a new day, every day, and tells us we aren't to hang on to yesterday or make big plans for tomorrow. Our most serious work is to find and follow the will of God each day.' "

How many times Mary Lou had heard Mama say that same thing!

Tibby shook her head. "I was not so inclined. I was angry—no—furious with Father. It took years before I finally admitted Ellen was right. She told me hating, holding grudges, unloving retaliations are not of God. Her loving, forgiving example taught me to forgive Father and Mother. Then God was able to lift the terrible, hate-filled weight from my life. I thank Ellen for that."

Mary Lou's understanding opened to a number of things she had wondered about. Mama had shielded her from her own father's anger over the accident that had changed him from a loving father and husband to a resentful stranger. And she had surrounded Mary Lou with love and happy times. Even in her illness, love had radiated from her face and words. *Oh God, help me learn to love and forgive Pa like Mama did.*

Tibby's and Mary Lou's eyes held, relaying a new understanding, not between aunt and niece but between woman and woman.

Tibby rose and poured boiling water into a fresh pot of tea just as Henrietta and Jenny rode in. Everyone shared a cup, then Jenny and Mary Lou excused themselves, stepped outside, and walked toward the stream.

"When are you leaving?" Jenny asked.

"Tom wants to leave tomorrow."

"Oh."

For two girls who had had spent their lives tumbling over each other's words,

Mary Lou and Jenny were suddenly tongue-tied. They walked hand in hand, as they often did. Big Jon had jokingly told them when they were little to hang on so they would not lose each other in the tall grass and flowers. They had believed him. Those early days had not only clasped their hands, but also their hearts.

Jenny giggled. "After you go, I'm going to let Glenn catch me."

"Then you'll have to slow down. Glenn likes things done in order."

"I do too! Guess that makes me the right wife for him."

"You'll make him a good wife, Jenny. You'll make what he needs—a home and a bright, loving spot in his life."

"Oh, I almost forgot," Jenny said suddenly. "Last night Glenn asked me if I wanted to be the new postmistress!"

"Wonderful!"

"He won't have to run very far to catch me, will he?"

Their steps carried them back to the Bar-B ranch. In the distance, they saw a rider coming. Mary Lou turned to Jenny, determined not to cry. "Dear friend, I'm going to miss you so much."

"Aw, you'll have Tom."

"And you'll have Glenn."

By the time they reached the porch, Henrietta was waiting to leave. Last hugs round, then Jenny mounted Missy and rode off with Henrietta.

Mary Lou watched Tom ride toward her. He sat a saddle well, tall and straight. Her heart overflowed with love.

When he reached her, he dropped to the ground, took her into his arms, and kissed her. Tibby, watching from the door, smiled. She remembered when she and Nate were first married. There had been no better place than in each other's arms. It was still true.

Chapter Twenty-Two

That night as Tom and Mary Lou climbed into their comfortable bed at Aunt Tibby's, Tom informed Mary Lou that Smitty and the boys had already left. He grinned. "I told Smitty we were married and swore him to secrecy."

"You did? Did he make any comment about it?"

"Yep, he asked me if you were a pretty lady."

Mary Lou lifted her chin and asked, "And what did you say?"

Tom pulled her into his arms, his eyes reading her face. "I said 'Nope—'"

Mary Lou opened her mouth in a quick intake of breath.

Tom grinned. "I said you were a beautiful lady."

"Thank you, sir," Mary Lou answered demurely. "If I were out of bed I'd curtsey." Instead, she snuggled into his embrace.

The next morning, Mary Lou lay wide awake watching a morning sunbeam across the back of Tom's curly, red hair. A thousand thoughts tumbled in her mind. She was going to a new life, new home, new family. Even a new state! She had never been to Texas but had heard it was a rough and tumble place. Yet Tom lived there. He was a gentleman and from what he had said about his family, they seemed much the same as any she knew in Kansas. Why was it then that most news was bad when surprising and wonderful things were happening all around?

Mama had always said, "God's goodness is around us in far greater quantity than all the evil put together. It's just we aren't looking." Good was all Mama had ever seen.

When Pa had left home after his accident and lived with Jacob Shineberg at the back of the store, Mama had cooked meals and taken them to the store for both Pa and Jacob to eat. Jacob had been delighted and had eaten with relish. "Good! Good! Just like my Frau used to make."

While Mama was there, she had gathered both men's soiled clothes, taken them back to the cabin, washed, and returned them.

Mama. She had to see Mama before she went so far away.

Tom stirred. Still asleep, he reached for Mary Lou. She moved into his arms—into her safe place where she felt loved and protected. What was it Pastor Miles had said? "The true joining of a man and woman is in the spirit and heart."

The back of Mary Lou's neck tingled. As much as she loved Kansas, thoughts of going anywhere with Tom filled her with anticipation. She could appreciate the Bible story of Ruth who left her own country to go with Naomi. Pastor had also said, "Forsaking all others." Mama had done it. So had Aunt Tibby.

Tom peeked through one eye and drawled, "Y'all ready to leave this morning?"

She raised up on one elbow and smiled. "Yes I am." She rumpled his hair and kissed him.

"But there's one thing I want to do before we go."

"What's that?"

"Say goodbye to Mama."

He nodded with understanding, picked up her hand, and kissed her fingers. "We can ride out there after breakfast."

Mary Lou prayed he would understand what she was about to ask. "Tom, I'd—I'd like to just walk out there alone, if you don't mind."

Tom's tender gaze caressed her face. "I'll watch for you and meet you on the way back. After all that's happened, I'm almost afraid to let you out of my sight."

They laughed and climbed out of bed.

The early morning air was crisp, but the sun spread a warm glow over Mary Lou's head and promised a perfect day. She set out toward the family cemetery, across dewy prairie grass that wet the bottom three inches of her skirt.

The ever-constant Kansas wind tugged gently at her hair, and she reached back, loosed the ribbon, and let her hair blow free. Her eyes etched deeper into her heart this land that had been her playground and the only home she had ever known.

Mary Lou stood tall above the flowers, but could remember walking among them when their colorful faces had brushed against her nose. She bent and picked a bouquet for Mama. When she was little, she had gathered wild flowers almost every day because Mama loved them and set them around the cabin.

Mary Lou pulled the cemetery gate open. Four people were buried in the little plot. In one corner, lay Mama and two baby sons, both of whom died in infancy. Mary Lou's only memory of them was that they had cried a lot and Mama had carried them in her arms most of the time. The only time she had ever seen Pa cry was when he lost the sons he had always wanted.

In the opposite corner was a small grave with a bouquet of fresh wild flowers stuck into a quart canning jar that was buried to its neck. During snowy months, the jar held dried weeds and flowers Tibby gathered during the summer.

This grave held the only child of Aunt Tibby and Uncle Nate, a baby girl. Her first name, Elizabeth, was whittled into the small wooden cross. Elizabeth. Aunt Tibby, Mama, and Mary Lou also carried the name Elizabeth in honor of a great grandmother.

Mama's grave was overgrown again with weeds. The wooden cross Pa had made was almost hidden. Mary Lou knelt and pulled the weeds, her eyes battling tears that made small damp spots on the ground at her knees.

She sniffed. "Mama you always said there were two kinds of tears, one for sorrow and one for joy. I'm crying both. I miss you so, and Pa won't speak to me. He did not want me to marry Tom. But I love Tom, Mama, and he loves me. Oh, Mama, I know you'd love him. I did what you told me. I looked for a gentle man."

She lifted her face heavenward. "I know you're glad for me but Pa. . . ."

Mary Lou laid the flowers on the grave. The wind's gentle warmth enfolded her and reminded her of the night on Mama's porch when she had accepted Jesus as Savior. Mama had cupped her face and lifted it to her own. "Now I will never lose you," she had said. "We both belong to Jesus because He's in our hearts."

Mary Lou turned and saw Tom standing a short way off. She waved high over her head and he ran toward her. When they met, they clung to each other, then walked back to the ranch.

Horses, buggies, and buckboards were waiting. It seemed like everyone had come, the friends and neighbors of a lifetime.

Nelda brought bread, a crock of butter, and a couple jars of prairie apple jelly. "To remind you where you came from," she said and tucked in a pan of sour dough starter with enough flour to last till they got to Harness.

Tibby brought a big basket, "with something to eat on the way," and tucked it under the front seat.

Big Jon, Henrietta, and all ten children came to say goodbye. They brought ground coffee, dried beef, and bread pudding with dried apples. Other neighbors brought gifts to "set them up." The buckboard groaned.

A subdued Jenny leaned against the wagon fighting tears. Glenn stood at her side, concerned.

Henrietta hugged Mary Lou and shoved a brown wrapped package into her hands. "We want you to have this."

Mary Lou unfolded the paper to reveal a beautiful crocheted tablecloth. She gasped, knowing the hours and days of work it took to make it.

Henrietta nodded. "It's too fancy for us and I'll have time enough to make another for Jenny when she's married."

Mary Lou's chest tightened. She could not imagine living without these dear people who had been her life. She hugged them all again and hurried to the buckboard.

Tom shook hands with Nate and Big Jon, men he had come to respect. Big Jon reminded him of his father, strong and gentle at the same time. Tom helped Mary Lou into the buckboard and picked up the reins. He glanced into the distance, hoping to spot Buck's buggy for Mary Lou's sake.

"Thank you, Aunt Nelda and Aunt Tibby," he said. "Without you, this day would never have come. Pray us home."

The two women nodded, mopping tears and noses with their handkerchiefs. At last, everyone stepped back.

Tom gave a slap of the reins and called to the horses. The wagon slowly rolled forward.

"Goodbye. God bless you." Mary Lou waved and watched her friends grow smaller. She strained her eyes for her father, her heart heavy. Yet she could not suppress the exhilaration bubbling inside. Beside her sat her husband, the man she truly loved. She had pinched herself all week to make sure it was true. Was it possible to be happy and sad at the same time?

The wagon rumbled past Point Lane. Mary Lou spied a buggy among the cottonwoods. It was Pa.

Tom halted the horses. Mary Lou waved and called, "Bye, Pa."

Buck started to raise one hand, then jerked it back to the reins. Tom swung the wagon toward the grove, but Buck abruptly turned into the trees and disappeared.

Tom stopped. Mary Lou stood, waved and called. "Bye, Pa. I love you. We'll be back to visit." She blew him a kiss and sat down aching with disappointment.

Tom slapped the reins and turned the wagon south. Tinder and Dulcie, tied to the wagon, tossed their heads and trotted alongside. The cottonwood trees in Point Lane waved their fluttery green hands.

Mary Lou turned to the handsome young man beside her. Her heart swelled in gratitude. *Thank you, Father.* She settled into the seat, adjusted her bonnet, and set her eyes toward Texas, leaving behind her girlish cottonwood dreams for the reality of love.

Whispers on
the Wind

Maryn Langer

Chapter One
1844

Brook Savage leaped from his chair and pushed his face within a nose length of Colonel Mallory's doughy profile. "You mean you won't send help to that wagon train, even when you know they're tracking straight for raiding Comanche?"

"You heard me right, Savage. You're paid to scout for the Army here at Fort Leavenworth, not ride out like a white knight to save every greenhorn who decides to break the rules." The colonel bent over a sheaf of papers on his desk, and Savage knew he had been dismissed.

Savage stormed out of the office in a rage. Mallory's penchant for military regulation and his total disregard for protecting human life continually infuriated Savage so that, out of spite, he frequently did all sorts of dumb things. For example, he knew better than to ride alone into the jaws of the Comanche, yet that's what he had to do, seeing as how he was the only hope of survival for yet another wayward wagon train. Furthermore, they probably would not believe they were in serious trouble and would consider his arrival an unwelcome intrusion into their affairs. These stubborn eastern know-it-alls were rarely grateful for help until it was too late and they were in the process of being scalped . . . or worse.

Nevertheless, he rode away from the fort on a May morning that showed every sign of being unseasonably harsher and hotter as the sun moved toward midday. With the sleeve of his buckskin blouse, he wiped at the trickles of sweat running from under the dirty-tan plains hat and down the channels of his smooth-shaven face—a face that bore the faded deep scars of smallpox contracted when he was a child.

Savage turned west and let the smell of the land freshen his soul. Hock-high grass bent and shook, the tips taking on the look of shallow wind-driven waves, turning the prairie into a featureless sea of white sun in an endless blue sky and variegated green grasses rolling timelessly to where they met. This was his country, God's country. Though he had tried to leave it, settle down among his own kind, chain himself to kin and land and belongings, do the things expected of civilized men, he had failed.

Retreating to his childhood haunts in the heart of the Rockies to lick his wounds, he had found a woman who understood him. He had made her his wife, had built a home far from the edge of civilization and filled it with love and little ones. Then suddenly, five years ago, everything had been taken from him in a brutal senseless massacre. He'd searched until he learned who had led the cowardly attack against a defenseless woman and two small children, and one day, when the time was right, Savage would even the score.

Until then, the only place he'd found any comfort was here on the prairie, feeling the touch of the wind on his face, smelling the fragrance of tree and plant it carried down from the mountains, letting the land cry and grieve with him as it tried to draw the sorrow from his heart.

He rarely admitted the fact, but at forty he was lonely. Yet he could not leave the prairie and the Rocky Mountains. The best and essential parts of his soul were bound here. Bound by the work he did.

His thoughts drifted on the wind until, above the crest of a rise in the distance, a puff of smoke rose, quickly spread thin, and vanished. Savage tensed and his stomach knotted with dread. With the Comanche out raiding, there was no telling what he would find on the other side of that hill.

Making himself as small a target as possible, Savage bent over his horse and hung off to one side, Indian style, and rode toward the plume of dust. Before he reached the crest of the hill, he reined in his horse, slid from the saddle, strung his field glasses across his back, and crawled belly first up the grassy slope. The grass, lush and thick this time of year, hid him from any but the sharpest eye, and allowed him to take his time surveying the scene.

Well, there's that fool wagon train that's gotten itself off the trail and into trouble, he thought with some irritation as he looked down into a cluster of wagons tightly circled for the noon break. Lashed to the wagon tailgates, plows and fruit tree saplings with their roots bound in burlap protruded like large disfiguring growths. Water casks and crates of chickens clung precariously to shelves built along the sides of the wagons, destroying the original uncluttered design of the wagon boxes. These people were obviously farmers, carrying with them the basics for a new beginning, but if they were headed for Oregon, they were definitely going the wrong way! Ever since the Whitman party had made their way to Oregon country last year, there had been a steady stream of people eager to join them, but most of those groups had had the good sense to stay farther north along the Platte. Whatever had possessed these people to travel down into Comanche territory?

The dust cloud that had attracted his attention was made by a couple of scouts sent out from the wagons. Watching them ride toward him now with so little skill, Savage doubted they would be able to recognize an Indian were they to see one.

Before riding into the camp, Savage trained his glasses on the surrounding countryside. He could see no signs of Indians, but that meant nothing. The few islands of trees and dense brush that dotted this rolling sea of dark green grass could hide a raiding party from even the most knowledgeable.

Slowly he scanned the domestic scene below. The women were working together, cooking and cleaning up, while the men tended to the needs of the teams and hauled water. The older children gathered buffalo chips for the fires and watched over the younger ones. It seemed like a well-run group—no squabbling, each person busy with some task. Inside the circle of wagons, a group of men was making repairs on a wheel. Except for the fact that there was no lookout posted, he would believe they had purposely left the established trail and knew where they were headed.

Feeling he had seen enough, he was ready to lower the glasses and drop them back into the case, when a halo of ivory-colored hair braided into a coronet swept across his field of vision. He paused and watched the tall, smiling woman. Graceful as lakeshore reeds bending in a gentle breeze, she stood at the tailgate of her wagon, mixing and administering concoctions to the line of people passing by. Her face, serene and loving as she listened to each person's complaints, reminded him of a medicine woman he had known in the Cheyenne tribe. Once, she stopped to tuck several stray tendrils of white-blond hair up out of her way, and glanced in his direction. He nearly dropped the glasses. She had enormous eyes, blue as cornflowers, fringed with honey-colored lashes. Though he was sure she had not seen him hidden behind the hillock, he stared into the clear azure of her wide eyes and felt a strange sense of disembodiment.

He imagined her voice, soft and low, as she crooned to quiet the restless babies thrust into her arms, and a yearning welled in him to hear her voice speaking to him, soft and close. *Savage, you're one big idiot. You're an Army scout and your job is to find out where these people are going and report back to the fort. You don't need this woman or any woman to complicate your life again.* But his lecture failed to help. The longer he watched, the more he wanted to meet her.

He rode slowly, out in the open, his hands visible at all times. The last thing he wanted to do was take nervous greenhorns by surprise. When he finally arrived at the circle, she had finished her work and was standing some distance away from the wagons, alone in an island of cottonwood and sycamore trees, calmly observing his arrival.

There was a peaceful repose about her face that he had seen only on Indian women, and unconsciously he turned to ride toward her.

"Halt!" commanded a strong voice.

Startled, Savage whirled to see a short, heavy-set man with a battered Hall carbine aimed, ready to fire at him. He had underestimated these people. There *was* a guard, he just hadn't been obvious.

"Who are you and what are you doin' ridin' into our camp?" growled the well-muscled, red-faced guard.

The man seemed not the least intimidated by Savage, who was himself a big man, standing well over six feet, with a lean, hard body. Broad shoulders and thick muscular arms, developed from years of hard work in the outdoors, pulled the soft tanned buckskin shirt taut. But there was not the slightest tremor in the hand holding the gun or in the voice, and Savage knew he had better talk fast.

Slowly, he raised his hand and held it out to the side, away from his holstered pistol. "Name's Savage, Brook Savage, and I scout for the Army out of Fort Leavenworth."

"Ain't you got better sense than to ride in to a camp unannounced?" The guard's light blue eyes glinted with the desire to teach Savage that lesson.

Savage had formed a theory over the years—light blue eyes, though faded in color, were invariably sharp of sight and the man behind them, an expert marksman. "Mind if I swing down off my horse?" he asked, keeping his voice even and low. The man was already stirred up enough. He needed only a little more incentive to shoot.

"Yes, I mind. Up there, if you try to run for it, I can shoot the horse out from under you and still have you left for fun." He grinned as if daring Savage to enliven a boring day.

Light blue eyes also signified a short temper, Savage recalled, and he did not plan to provoke the bull-necked defender of the camp. "Mister," Savage began, "I just want to talk with your wagon master. He around?"

Flinty eyes remained locked on Savage, assessing his real business with the train. At last, the guard bellowed over his shoulder, "Enoch!"

"Be right there," called a voice from inside the circled wagons.

"Got us a stupid mountain man wants to talk to you," the guard said to a short, thick-waisted man scrambling his way over a wagon tongue and through the gear, stacked ready to load.

His hat pulled low to shade his eyes, Enoch hurried toward the waiting men. The horse, spooked by the approaching stranger, pranced a nervous side-hop, and Savage concentrated on quieting him, paying the rotund man little mind.

When he got around so he could see, Enoch broke into a wide smile of recognition. "Savage, you miserable cuss!" he exclaimed. "Get down off that there horse and let's have a look at you." He removed the battered felt hat and scratched at his mop of long curly white hair while he surveyed the scout.

Savage swung easily out of the saddle and clapped the wagon master on the shoulder. "Enoch Fisher!" he bawled. "Never expected to see you leading a train again."

"Never expected to, neither." Turning to the guard, the man's face a twist of bewilderment, his gun still trained doggedly on Savage, Enoch reassured him. "It's all right, Barth. This here's Brook Savage, scout from Fort Leavenworth, about fifty miles north of here on the Santa Fe Trail."

Reluctantly, Barth lowered the gun and, grumbling to himself, stalked out into the prairie.

His broad, florid face still beaming with delight at meeting up with his long-time friend, Enoch took Savage by the arm. "Come on over to the fire, you woodsy ol' critter. Let's get you some victuals and you can rest a spell."

Savage dropped the reins, an act his gelding Smoke took to mean "eat," and followed Fisher over to a dying fire. "Enoch, you old coyote, you're fifty-five if you're a day. Why haven't you given up traipsing over this lonely old prairie by now?"

Enoch chuckled and handed Savage a cup of coffee. "Said I would after that last trip, didn't I? Savage, you know me—a sucker for a sad story. These folks was all ready to leave Independence when their wagon master up and disappeared on 'em. They was determined to come, with or without guidin'. Got themselves started right enough, but like most folks headstrong enough to tackle this country, they wanted to think for themselves and took a wrong turn. Heard this was a faster, easier route. When I learned from some drifters they'd seen this train travelin' straight into Comanche country—" He shrugged and looked a bit foolish. "Like I said, I'm a sucker for a sad story. Be on my conscience if I didn't try to undo the damage before something serious happened to 'em." He paused and looked out over the prairie, heat waves distorting the distance, and rubbed the back of his neck. "I can feel them savages out there. Neck itches all the time and I can't smell a thing but Indian. Can't see 'em, though. You see anything?"

Savage shook his head and accepted the plate heaped with crisp fried potatoes and hominy grits. "I get the same crawling feeling you do, but so far I haven't seen signs of Comanche through this area."

Enoch snorted. "Huh! They're hereabout though. I'll be real glad when I can persuade these folks to head north and travel the proven trail to Oregon."

"Oregon! That really where they're headed?"

"So they say, but they're determined to make their own way. Hard-headed a bunch as I ever dealt with."

Savage shook his head in disbelief and began to eat quickly, aware that Enoch was eager to break camp. "I'm on my way back to the fort," Savage said and handed his plate to Enoch. "See what I can do about getting you an escort until you get up onto the Oregon Trail. Cheyenne country's a lot safer."

"For you, I reckon, boy. You're one of 'em. Not likely to be real healthy for the hair of this bunch though. Be much obliged for any help," Enoch said as he tossed the tin plate into the steaming pot of water sitting just off the fire. Then he acknowledged a summons with a wave of his hand. "Pastor Waite's callin' me. Or I should say that sister-in-law of his is. Gives me a right good idee for why she's a widow at such an early age. Bossiest woman I ever had the misfortune to travel with!" He cast a disgusted look in her direction and turned to leave. "Make yourself to home, Savage. I'll try to get back for a quick visit."

"Mr. Fisher, if you *please*, sir," the widow Waite called in an over-sweet voice, the kind that made Savage's skin crawl. "Your help is required here . . . at once!"

"See what I mean," Enoch said and rolled his eyes. "If you'll excuse me, we'll soon be ready to pull out."

Savage nodded and watched Enoch hurry over to where a short, red-headed woman was giving instructions on how to hitch up a team. The tall, stoop-shouldered man ignored her instructions, all the while arguing that this wasn't woman's work. Savage smiled and gave thanks that he wasn't mixed up with the likes of her.

Alone now, he was free to search out the golden-haired woman. Perhaps even talk with her. He looked to where he had last seen her, sheltered and well-concealed in the woods some distance from the camp.

With the sun dappling her faded calico dress, he almost missed her as she stood braiding her hair. Their eyes met and something in her look struck a chord deep inside, silent for years. Savage came alive with the warmth. A force outside himself propelled him toward her, and she took a step in his direction, their eyes still clinging. He felt the pulse beat in his temples and his mouth dry up. Suddenly, he grew shy and he felt a flush redden his neck and creep up into his cheeks. He had forgotten how to talk to a white woman. What would he say? *Howdy ma'am, you're one fine-looking lady.* He smiled at the sound of the ridiculous words in his mind, and she smiled a slow gentle smile in return.

Quickly, he removed his hat and dropped his eyes, lest she read too much he was unable to hide. It was then he saw her feet encased in soft beaded moccasins.

"Savage!" Enoch's gravely old voice hollered. "We need those big ugly muscles of yours over here."

Like a shock wave, the old man's command ripped through Savage. In a way he was grateful. He was not dealing well with the emotions surging through him, and this was the perfect excuse to back away. He could not resist one final look, however, at the gentle, golden beauty, her fingers caught in half-finished braids. Without a word between them, she had stirred a fire in his blood such as he had not experienced for a very long time.

Chapter Two

Esther finished braiding her hair, never taking her eyes from the man Enoch had called "Savage." She knew, with a kind of inner knowing, that he had been about to come to the copse to talk to her when the wagon master unwittingly intervened. Now she'd have to wait to see if the tall scout would try again when he finished helping with the wagon repair.

In the heat, the men, all except Pastor Waite, stripped to the waist to heft the Cranney wagon and slide on the new wheel. Savage shucked his dusty buckskin shirt, revealing his chest, broad and smooth, coppery-tan in the sunlight. The great muscles of his back and arms stood out like ropes under the silky skin.

Excepting for Barth, Savage, with his tremendous strength, put the efforts of the other men to shame, and helped to make quick work of the wagon repairs. Then, gathering up their shirts, the sweaty men loped to the stream to wash. Esther could hear their wild-splashings and wondered if they had undressed and gone swimming with the children. She wouldn't have blamed them.

Esther knew Savage would come, so while she waited, she withdrew deeper into the thicket to a spot where she could rest her back against a pecan tree. Here they would have more privacy. He seemed the sort who, if he had an audience, would do little more than acknowledge a woman with a nod. She intended to make it easy for him.

She felt Savage's presence before the snap of a small stick alerted her, and she jerked her head around to see him standing a few feet away, arms folded across his chest, leaning against the trunk of a nearby cottonwood tree. His untrimmed shoulder-length hair was still damp and curled around his face as he stood motionless, eyeing her intently.

Now that he had finally come, Esther sat, unable to speak, clumsy with fear at the prospect of meeting the first man, white or Indian, for whom she had ever had any stirring of romantic interest. Though she looked in his direction, she could not bring any words of welcome to her stiff lips. Under his steady gaze, she grew embarrassed over the frenzied pattern her heart insisted on beating, and spread her hand over her throat to hide the pulse throbbing there.

She pressed herself back against the tree as though to retreat from his imposing presence. Why had she thought seeing Savage, speaking with him at close range, would be a good idea? She prayed to dissolve into the ground, away from those penetrating gray eyes.

That petition denied, Esther sat stiff as a board, nervously smoothing out the un-ironed skirt of her freshly washed dress, then cupped her hands in her lap as Sister Waite had taught her. Looking down, she stared at the bottom of his fringed leggings and his great feet, shod in moccasins. They were cuffed with a minimum of red and white beadwork along the edge. Dust clung to them, turning the pale leather a gray color and dulling the beadwork on top of the moccasins.

Savage didn't move from the spot where he first stopped, but remained motionless, as if sensing that any movement would send her into flight. Finally, he cleared his throat softly. "I began to wonder if I would ever get close enough to talk with you." He spoke in quiet words, letting his voice flow to her. "Ever since I first saw you through the field glasses before I rode in, I have wanted to meet you."

His voice, deep and soft like the low rumble of distant summer thunder, fell like music on her ears and helped relieve her fears.

He cleared his throat and spoke again, even more softly, "I mean you no harm. Please don't be afraid of me."

He spoke to her as one would a skittish colt, and something in the tone of his voice soothed Esther, relaxed her taut muscles, invited trust. Gradually her heartbeat slowed, and the quivering began to subside.

His was a strange voice—rough, raspy, different from any she had ever heard—but it fit him. Esther found herself listening intently, all her senses alert. It was then she realized how gentle his voice was, understood with a rush of insight that it was filled with a kindness and caring foreign to her. To her surprise, Esther raised her eyes and found herself saying, "Please, come and sit."

Slowly, Savage walked toward her, his moccasined feet making no sound, and with practiced ease, he crossed his legs and, in one flowing motion, lowered himself to the ground in front of her. He sat, not speaking, as though waiting for Esther to begin.

Even under Sister Waite's expert tutelage, Esther had never been able to master the art of small talk. She thought it silly to toss her curls and say, "I do declare, sir, you say the nicest things," when a man paid a compliment. Besides, such superficial chit-chat seemed absurd to use with this wild stranger sitting at her feet.

The silence stretched, like rawhide being pulled to make a bowstring, and every nerve in Esther's body grew taut enough to pluck. Maybe she could mention how warm it was for May, she thought. Yes, that's what she would say. She cleared her throat, a tiny click of sounds, moistened her lips, and drew in a deep breath.

"My name is Brook Savage," he said, relieving her of the responsibility of speaking first. "Folks mostly call me Savage." He chuckled softly, deep in his throat. "They say it fits everything about me."

Relief spread through Esther, and the breath she held came out as a sigh. He was the most gentle savage she had known, but still she hesitated. She had learned through painful experience that the less people knew about her, the better off she was, the safer from hurt. If they knew nothing, they had no weapons with which to wound her. Now, to her amazement, she calmly introduced herself. "Esther is my name. Esther Wheeler."

Though Brook Savage's face remained immobile and closed, his eyes filled with a warm glow. "Pleased to meet you, Esther Wheeler." The strange voice dropped to a raspy whisper, "Mighty pleased to meet you."

Esther had not yet looked fully at the man called Brook Savage. It was not the Indian way. Even now, she found she slipped into those habits whenever she was faced with unfamiliar circumstances. Still, she longed to inspect Savage's features at close range, and this desire tugged at her like a magnet. Slowly she lifted her gaze to his face and watched the harsh mantle of the army scout fall from him. His face altered until a gentleness, a tenderness appeared in place of the hard unfeeling crust. The years seemed to drop away, the deep lines softened, and Savage smiled, warm and friendly. His eyes, filled with understanding and sincerity, shone like gray satin.

Esther found herself smiling back at him, burying her insecurities and self-doubts, withholding nothing, warming to him as she had to no other. "You deliberately snapped that twig, didn't you?" she said at last.

He smiled again. "I had to do something to get your attention."

She returned a quick grin and watched the corners of his eyes gather into tiny folds.

They continued to sit in silence, a comfortable silence. This was how Indian men courted, Esther knew, the couple getting in tune with each other through the senses. White people talked all the time, their words often getting in the way of their true feelings. This was better.

But, as the minutes passed, she began to grow uneasy under the intensity of his gaze. She raised a small, tanned hand and plucked nervously at the wisps of hair curling at the nape of her neck.

Apparently sensing her discomfort, again he broke the silence, and in his rumbling voice, commented softly, "You're wearing moccasins."

Esther looked down at her feet, crossed daintily at the ankles. "I have for years." She paused, trying to decide if she should say more. After all, they had only just met. But the tilt of his head, as if to catch her every word, invited her confidence. "When I was returned from the Senecas by the good pastor and the widow Waite, I was expected to give up all Indian ways," she plunged in. "They purchased fine boots for me, but my feet cried with pain when I forced them into those stiff, heavy shoes. I couldn't keep my balance on the fashionable high heels." She shook her head sadly. "Poor Sister Waite finally gave up and let me wear the moccasins." Esther shook her head and a sadness crept into her voice. "Though I do try to do what she wants and be like the other white women, I don't often please Sister Waite. She makes it plain that she considers me her cross to bear in this life."

Not knowing what to do with her hands, Esther smoothed her wrinkled cotton skirt and waited for him to speak.

He chuckled softly. "Martyrs are hard to live with." Then, as if eager to set her at ease, he changed the subject. "How long were you with the Senecas?"

She tensed. A flush rose up from her neck and spread to color her face. The loathsome term "squaw woman" slipped into her thoughts, but surely Savage, who seemed so Indian himself, would not be thinking it.

Regaining her confidence under his look of acceptance, Esther decided to tell him her story in a condensed version. "A little over ten years," she began, barely above a whisper. "They captured me from the Delaware who took me when I was six." She bowed her head. Plucking nervously at the grass, she snapped it off and rolled it into balls between her thumb and forefinger. A deep frown furrowed her normally clear brow.

"Esther," he said tenderly, "I am aware of the humiliation you must have suffered at the hands of so-called Christian women because of your being an Indian hostage. I understand your circumstances completely and find no fault in you." Savage leaned forward, his expression of approval unchanged. "Tell me about your capture," he encouraged in a gentle rumble. There was no condemnation, no cold withdrawal. Though he didn't yet know that she had never been forced into marriage or ill-used in any way, his words of unquestioning acceptance fell like rain on her parched soul, making it possible at last to talk of those years.

Looking into Savage's sympathetic face, she began. "The spring I was six years old, my family, the Daniel Wheelers, moved from Shenandoah Valley, Virginia, and settled on the Blue River in Indiana.

"One afternoon when we had been there about three months and the men were away helping a neighbor build his winter cabin, the women and children arranged a berrying expedition downriver. When our baskets were full, we children, under the watchful eye of my Aunt Mercy, began a game of hide-and-seek. I chose a hiding place inside a deep hollow at the root of a great tree. That was a sad mistake. A gigantic bear already occupied the hollow.

"Nothing to this day has ever frightened me as much as when that great growling creature rose up out of the ground and lumbered toward me. I froze with the terror of it until the screams of Aunt Mercy, telling me to run, finally penetrated. I fled headlong into the dark tangled forest, paying no heed to where I ran. There were times when I could feel that bear's hot breath on my neck. For a time, I thought I had escaped, but by then, I was thoroughly lost.

"My next clear recollection is of waking up in an Indian lodge. Because I somehow had learned the language, I understood that I had been rescued by a group of warriors returning from a hunting expedition, camped for the night in a cave near where I fled from the bear. The men heard my screams and took me home with them. One had recently lost a daughter, and he took me to his lodge as a replacement for her.

"These people were very good to me, and I lived happily with them until the spotted sickness struck our village, and my Indian family became ill and died. After that, I was taken in by another tribe, and through a series of trades and sales, I became the slave of a Seneca medicine woman when I was twelve. She was also a white hostage who had spent most of her life with the tribe. She had a Bible and taught me to read and write and when we were alone, we spoke English. I served her and learned from her." Esther paused, thinking of those days. "Six months before I was ransomed, I was made her official assistant.

"Then the soldiers came to free me. Since it would require such a long time to locate my white family, if indeed they were even still alive, I was taken to a mission home. Because Pastor Waite was experienced in dealing with newly found hostages, they placed me with him. When he learned I was a healer, he permitted me to assist him. He also found for me the latest books on medicine and allowed me time to study. I took everything in the medical books that fit the way I believed. Now I practice my own brand of medicine, combining the best of everything I have learned . . ." She paused, measuring Savage with her eyes— "and submitting it, with much prayer, to the Great Healer."

Silence filled the thicket when she finished, and Savage reached out and took her hand, holding it gently in his large work-calloused palm. With the physical contact, her heart again jumped skittishly, and Esther dropped her eyes as a blush burned hot on her cheeks.

Savage gazed at her with unabashed admiration. "From the hill yonder before I rode in, I watched you through the field glasses as you ministered to the needs of these people. They came willingly to you with their medical problems. They trust you. That is a wonderful gift."

Bestowing a gratified smile for his compliment, she said, "I've done all the talking so far. I would very much like to know about you. You are also wearing moccasins, and you tread with Indian steps, noiseless and swift. Does that mean that, like me, you have spent much time with the People?"

He nodded and pursed his mouth. "Mine is also a long story—" He cast an eye at the wagons, the teams hitched, and hesitated—"But there is not time to tell it. I think the train is ready to roll. I promised Enoch I would ride back to Fort Leavenworth and bring a military escort to see your group through to the Missouri River and onto the Oregon Trail. I will make certain I am part of that escort. We will have plenty of time then to talk."

"I understand," she said simply. "I will wait to hear more of your time with the Indians."

In the manner of nobility, he lifted her hand and kissed her fingertips, then held the hand and rose effortlessly to tower above her. With his assistance, she stood before him, the crown of her head coming just under his chin. Their eyes searched, locked, making silent promises.

"Enoch says Abigail Cranney's birthing time is soon," Savage managed. "Says, though the rest of the train will move on, the Cranneys are planning to stay put until she has her baby."

"Yes, that is their request. Abigail is in a very weakened condition. She may not survive even then. If there is no danger, perhaps they can stay even a few days more so she can have a bit more time to recover before being jounced in that wagon again." Esther heard a calm unemotional stranger talking and scarcely recognized herself. Such cool impersonal tones could not possibly be coming from her, not with the turmoil raging inside.

"Are you going to attend her?"

"The Cranneys do not look kindly on my kind of medicine nor on my background. I will stay with her only if I am asked."

He nodded. "I'll be back tomorrow afternoon with the troops. Whether you're with the Cranneys or with the train, I'll come for you. Watch for me." His eyes begged for her promise.

She smiled. "I will watch."

Looking down into her face, he said softly, "If I'm not here by afternoon, don't give up. I'll come . . . no matter what."

Quite unexpectedly, tears of happiness pricked the backs of her eyelids and she turned away. Together, they walked from the copse to where his horse, having eaten his fill, stood hip-shot, waiting.

"Tomorrow," he whispered as he urged her face around to look at him. Seeing the tears, he ran trembling fingers over her cheeks and wiped them away. "I'll come. Nothing will keep me from coming back to you. Nothing!" Then, he turned his back, stepped easily into the saddle, and rode away without looking at her again.

Through her tears, Esther watched until he rode to the top of the small hill. He reined up, turned and, silhouetted against the horizon, waved to her. Then, spurring the prancing gelding, Savage galloped out of sight over the ridge. Small puffs of dust drifted to the horizon to remind her in which direction he rode.

Standing there, suddenly bereft, she wondered if he was aware of the extra weight he carried away with him. For, in their brief encounter, she had given him her heart.

Chapter Three

Running Elk, wearing only a breechclout and moccasions, rested in the brilliant afternoon sun. Rested for the first time in days and let his mind drift.

He was a handsome man with features that seemed chiseled from fine-grained mahogany and polished to a satin luster. Yellow paint ran in carefully applied streaks on his forehead, across his high cheekbones, down over a firm jawline, making him look fierce enough to frighten the most stout of heart. Still, though ringed with black paint, his deep-set dark eyes continued to reflect wisdom and generosity, traits that made men trust and willingly follow him on raids year after year. His silver-threaded black braids, wrapped in soft strips of beaver fur, hung long and thick over his shoulders. Though solidly built like his brothers, he was unusually tall for a Comanche and equally graceful on the ground or on horseback.

Running Elk carried few tokens of his coup, yet the People knew he always gathered more than any man in the raiding party. At twenty-one, he had been the youngest member of the Kaitsenko, the Society of Ten, the Kiowa's highest honor. Now, at thirty-three, he was their most honored war chief.

They had just completed the first foray of the summer season and again Running Elk, as their war chief, led them. The raids had been a great success, and the warriors had much plunder to take their women. Now they rested in the grove of tangled underbrush and cottonwoods by the river and divided the goods among themselves.

Running Elk, from his vantage point above the camp, looked out on the grassy softness just beneath the crest of a low hill. Looked north at the sun-drenched prairie unrolling before him. There was no sharpness in the landscape, no abrupt bluffs to break its flatness, no rocks heaved up to make a jagged skyline. The land flowed and curved and way off to the north, the cloudless sky curved and flowed to meet the greening land, soft and rounded like a woman.

He had been gone too long from his land, hard and bold, full of strength. Though the mountains were solitary, there was a majestic lack of symmetry in their ruggedness that relieved the eye. With each journey up or down the craggy peaks, there was a new path, a hidden magic to be discovered, ever changing, ever new.

Here in this place, the timeless, unceasing prairie wind, carrying with it the sadness of the long-reaching silent land, blew through his soul, leaving behind it the grieving feeling of something lost forever.

With apprehension, he studied the islands of trees and bushes dotting the plains, and suddenly he felt restless, uneasy. The wind seemed to talk through the trees, moaning with the voices of lost souls. The thick bushes growing under the trees were the friends of the enemy, giving them too many places to hide. A cold chill ran through him, and he shivered.

Turning his back on the undulating sea of grass before him, Running Elk shook off his melancholy musings and gazed down to where the men of the three Comanche tribes were busy changing the surcingles that held the packs and transferring them to fresh ponies. He sized up the large herd of stolen horses grazing along the slow-flowing river that snaked across the prairie. The People would make good trades with such fine animals.

When the chiefs of the other two tribes finished dividing their share of the spoils and climbed the hill to join Running Elk, one of them motioned to him.

"Do you see the dust cloud in the distance?" Tall Lance asked, folding his long thin legs under himself and dropping to the ground.

"I have been watching it," Running Elk answered. "When the wind blows right, it will clear the dust and then, with these 'magic eyes,' I can see everything." He held up the field glasses he had taken from the body of a Texas Ranger last week and handed them to Tall Lance.

Tall Lance examined the two metal tubes bound together in the middle. The ends were blocked with thick glass. He rubbed curious fingers over the slick surface and licked his lips in anticipation as he placed the two rings against his eyes. He moved the glasses up to the sky and down across the prairie, then over to the dust cloud with the wagon train underneath. All the while he looked, he kept up an excited running commentary on what he saw. "If only the dust would clear. I want to see more of the train of wagons. Will you let me look again?" he asked Running Elk.

Upon being assured that he could look through the magic eyes when the train became visible, he relinquished them to Ugly Owl.

Ugly Owl gripped them in his pudgy hands, turned noticeably pale, hesitated, then squared his fleshy shoulders, and set the glasses to his eyes. "Oh!" he gasped and lost himself in exploration.

"Running Elk, my brother," Tall Lance began, "I hope these white people keep coming west so we can raid them often. They bring such wonderful things, and they are easy to plunder—soft like newborn pups." Tall Lance, from the Staked Plains Comanches east of Santa Fe, glanced again in the direction of the slow-moving line of wagons. "My people do not see things like this. With such riches for the taking, I may spend more time here in the east." He caressed the fine new rifle he had taken.

Ugly Owl handed the field glasses back to Running Elk and reached into the fringed bag slung over his shoulder. "I agree with our brother, Tall Lance. See what I have." He pulled out a small round mirror and, with his fingertips, explored the back decorated with intricately intertwined flowers and leaves etched in the silver. Turning the mirror over, he stared for a long time at his reflection, then handed the mirror to Running Elk.

Cautiously he took it, running his finger lightly over the cool, smooth surface of the glass. On occasion Running Elk had seen his reflection in still pools, but the image had been indistinct, broken by slight movements of the water. Now his large luminous eyes with their heavy fringe of black lashes stared back at him, unblinking in their intensity. The clarity of the reflection made Running Elk feel detached, as though he was outside of his body, observing his face from a distance.

"The one who made this has medicine, powerful medicine," Running Elk said, with a slight tremor in his voice. Handing back the mirror, he stared at Tall Lance's gun and continued in a faraway voice, "You are wrong, Tall Lance. The white people are not soft. A soft person could not make the new firestick you now carry. Always, with each raid we learn to our sorrow that they have new and better weapons. The white eyes are like the wind, never still, always changing." He held up the field glasses. "The people who make these things are not soft or stupid—" He paused and his eyes narrowed as he looked into the distance. "Unlearned about a new land, but not stupid."

"You talk as though you are afraid," Tall Lance taunted.

Running Elk stared hard at the wagon train. "I only wonder what the White Eyes you call pups will be like when they grow into wolves." He turned and his gaze pierced Tall Lance. "And never, never believe for one moment that they will fail to learn as they grow."

Again placing the field glasses to his eyes, Running Elk followed the slow progress of the wagon train. After a time he said in a voice almost too soft to hear, "Then we shall see who is the victim and who is the prey." Though the sun was four hours in the sky and already hot, he shivered again and slowly lowered the glasses onto the grass-carpeted ground.

"Do you want to raid the wagon train?" Running Elk asked the other two chiefs.

"Since you saw the train of wagons first, Running Elk, it is yours if you want," Ugly Owl said in a generous gesture of friendship.

"I agree," Tall Lance said. "We have been lucky so far and have much goods. My brothers are getting anxious for the warm beds of their women. There is no need to get greedy and make them weep when we do not return."

"I thank my brothers for their generosity. I accept the wagon train." Running Elk held out his hand and clasped the wrist of each war chief.

"We will continue to rest here until evening when it is dark and cool, then we will ride like the wind toward home," Ugly Owl said. "If we are favored, we will be home in two, maybe three sleeps."

Tall Lance nodded and, like young boys, he and Ugly Owl loped down the hill to tell the men of their decision.

Running Elk lay without moving a muscle. He propped his elbows on the soft earth and looked again through the glasses at the dust cloud. Just then, the late afternoon breeze came up and blew the dust away, revealing a long line of swaying white tops. Through the glasses he could see the women and children walking beside the wagons. Some of the men drove the teams, while others rode ahead as scouts. Even with the glasses, all these things looked no bigger than bugs. He would wait until they grew larger before calling Tall Lance for another look.

There was nothing new or different about this train to set it apart from all the others he had watched and raided. Today, however, he did not feel the urge to raid. He laid the glasses down and rested his head on the cool grass. He and his men would also stay here during the day and tonight continue their homeward ride north under the moon. The sun was still high enough in the sky to warm his back and make him drowsy. With no reason not to, Running Elk slept.

The train created its own music as it moved, a cacophony of wheels creaking on the hard ground, white tops flapping in the constant wind, harnesses squeaking, and the plodding teams grunting and wheezing with the strain. There was an uneven rhythm that soothed the civilized ear. To Running Elk, however, the sound and rhythm grated along his back, and he woke with teeth clenched.

Signaling to Tall Lance to hurry, Running Elk grabbed the glasses and looked down the slope in front of him at the passing caravan.

Tall Lance arrived panting, crawling at an incredible pace on his stomach so his silhouette would not be seen from below. Silently, Running Elk handed over the glasses and Tall Lance accepted them, his hands trembling with eagerness. He swept the glasses swiftly along the length of the train, murmuring his discoveries to Running Elk.

"I see a woman with nearly white hair braided high on her head, but she is young and beautiful. She walks proud, solitary, like a chieftain's daughter. You will like to watch her, my friend."

"Why will I like watching her more than you?" Running Elk asked, feeling a bit irritated that Tall Lance should think to choose a woman for him.

"My tepee is full and warm. Two wives take care of my needs. Besides, I like roundness in my women. This one is too skinny. It is you who need a woman to warm your bed and take care of you. This one is tall and slim. You like that kind, I have noticed." Just then Tall Lance paused, slid the glasses backward, and held the position. "Ah," he breathed, "here is one for me. Her hair is the color of new copper and it shines in the sun like fire. She is not very tall, and she is round in the right places." He took the glasses from his eyes and handed them to Running

Elk. "Here, see the golden one for yourself. She walks near the front."

Slowly, Running Elk moved the glasses up and down the line of wagons. It delighted him how clearly he could see even the smallest detail. He watched the children playing tag, and the mothers hurrying them along when they fell too far behind. *How little difference there is between my people and the white eyes,* he thought. *And yet, we will not stop warring until one of us has won and driven out the other.*

He found the golden-haired one beside the last wagon walking alone as Tall Lance had described. Much as Running Elk was loathe to admit it, Tall Lance was right. She did take his eye, and he held the glasses steadily on her. She walked with long graceful strides, the kind that ate up the miles without tiring the body. Unlike the other women, she wore no protective bonnet, and the sun shone full on her clear tanned skin. Her gold-white hair was bound in two thick braids wrapped high on her head and it shone like a halo. She wore the usual calico dress, but when he looked at her feet, he saw she walked in moccasins. His heart stopped. She was fair as a spring day, not a drop of Indian blood. What did the wearing of moccasins mean?

"Ah, you found the golden-haired one. I can tell," Tall Lance crowed, his wide mouth pulled into as much of a smile as the long scar across his cheek allowed. "She is a fine one. But look for the red-haired one near the front of the wagons."

Dutifully, Running Elk swept his lenses up to the front. It was easy to spot the one who caught Tall Lance's attention. She was nothing to look at, short and dumpy, and she never stopped talking for a minute, even when the dust caught in her throat and choked her. *Foolish squaw!* he thought disdainfully. Her throat would turn raw and bleed in another day or two if she did not stop coughing and drink little sips of water instead. Running Elk conceded that her hair was striking, but nothing else about her appealed to him. "If you want her, we will raid and take her," he told Tall Lance.

Tall Lance shook his head, reached for the glasses again, and followed the woman a bit longer. "No, I shall only dream of her," he said as he handed back the glasses. "My other wives would make her life one great misery if I brought her back. I would get no enjoyment from her." He looked at the train with sad eyes, sighed over the lost dream, then walked slowly back down the rise to the river.

Running Elk fastened the glasses again on the tall woman and watched intently. Studying her as she walked, he learned much about her. No children flocked around her, and while the other women chattered like magpies, no one spoke to her. Nor did she speak. Once, she put up a hand to shield her eyes from the sun and looked directly at him. He knew she could not see him, but looking into her eyes gave him a strange feeling. On her hand, she wore no gold band that showed that a white woman was pledged to one man. Running Elk did not understand why. From what he could see, she was without flaw.

At that moment, a gaunt, raw-boned man rode up and talked briefly with her, then urged his horse on along the line of wagons. And once again she walked alone.

As though in answer to Running Elk's wishes, she stopped just below the rise where he lay and stretched as though reaching for sunbeams to put in her pocket. A brisk west wind picked up her skirt and billowed it out. She did not bother to catch it, and the rising hem revealed strong straight legs, bare and well-muscled.

Running Elk could not get his fill of looking at her and followed her with the glasses until the train passed by and out of sight behind a hill on the horizon. When she disappeared and he knew he would not see her again, an icy void filled the place where his heart beat. Tall Lance was right. His bed had been cold for too many years.

Closing his eyes, Running Elk remembered the long ago when he returned to his camp from a hunt. At the memory, the stench of burning flesh still filled his nostrils. His skin crawled at the silence smothering the village, and he saw his heart's joy lying in front of his lodge, her soft white deerskin dress covered with dried blotches of blood.

Though he had attempted to appease his grief by wreaking equal acts of pain and devastation on the white man, hate grew inside him, dried his tears, and filled his heart. Her memory still brought the bitter metallic taste of hatred to his mouth, and Running Elk had, until this moment, looked without pleasure on other women, preferring to remember his beautiful bride.

Today, however, this tall, golden woman touched him, made him warm inside again. Perhaps it was time.

Chapter Four

Darkness fell and the breeze died away. Mosquitoes whined around Esther's face as she felt her way out from the circle of wagons and along a tentative path, worn to the bank of the slow-moving stream. With the thick darkness between the last of twilight and the rise of a full moon, a hush settled over the land. Even the fretful cries of the children, exhausted from long hours of walking in the hot sun, quieted, and the murmured conversation of the men around the brightly burning fire ceased for the moment. Only an occasional cricket chirp punctured the stillness as though the little creatures were testing the air for the proper moment to begin their nightly concert.

Esther sank onto the grass-carpeted ground. It had been a long day for her, too, a day full of promise, and she wasn't ready for sleep. She craved, instead, a few minutes of solitude to savor her time with Savage before she had her evening prayers and returned to the wagons circled and chained tightly together. Besides giving fort-like protection for the people, the circled train provided an enclosure for the stock, beyond the easy reach of prowling Indians.

Because Abigail Cranney was in such pain with her impending delivery, the train had stopped early. A large tent had been pitched in the center of the wagon circle, a tent Esther had not been allowed near so far. A bent old woman threw back the flap and stepped outside. The firelight picked up the snowy white of her hair, highlighting the fluffy crown as she bobbed her way across the circle and out between the wagons into the darkness, while another woman with the vitality of youth, took her place.

A few yards from the tent, the fire burned bright and hot, and the scattered forms of blanket-wrapped children, bedded for the night, lay close around to gather warmth from the blaze. All the men, save one, hunkered down around it, visiting quietly. Out of reach of the flickering light, in the shadows behind the tent, a young giant of a man paced. This was Abigail and Joseph Cranney's first child and Joseph, in the tradition of the white people, was forbidden to be with his wife during the birthing, or even to know how things were going with her. As he paced, he nervously raked thick fingers through a mane of shaggy brown hair.

Esther wished she dared speak a few words of comfort and explanation to him, but she might as well be a leper, she thought, so repugnant was she to the others. Though they did not speak of it, she knew that the other women considered her soiled because of her Indian captivity, and seemed to draw back almost visibly whenever she came near. Consequently, she spoke to no one unless spoken to. Only with Pastor Waite did she feel remotely comfortable, and they talked only occasionally of mission work to be accomplished in Oregon when they joined the Whitmans.

One reason she had been so eager to travel across the uncharted continent was the hope that, in the West, she could leave behind forever the taint of her Indian life and be accepted for herself. Here among the women of the wagon train, however, Sister Waite had quickly spread the word of Esther's past, and any hope of her belonging had been rudely dashed. Though all but the Cranney family came regularly to Esther for cures for sickness, everyone remained cold and aloof, choosing to ignore her except as manners dictated.

Another scream pierced the air, split the silence, then left an echo wafted off across the plain. Esther clenched her hands and knelt to pray. *Dear Lord, please bring about some way that I can help Abigail in her time of need.* Esther paused and wondered if she should mention Savage. But her heart was too full not to. *And thank you for sending Savage,* she prayed. *It seems as though You prepared him to understand me, to accept me just as I am . . . the way You do. But even if he never becomes more than a friend, I will feel richly blessed.*

Esther stopped and pursed her lips. This next part of her nightly prayer was always difficult. *Lord, please soften my heart toward Sister Waite. She judges me so harshly when she knows so little about me.* Again Esther paused and a deep sigh escaped.

Another agonizing scream, this time more piercing and lingering, shattered the night. Those by the fire jumped up, and the children on the ground threw back their covers and leaped, trembling, to their feet. Women, wiping their hands on their aprons, came running from all the wagons and clustered around outside the opening of the tent.

Still another wrenching scream hard on the heels of the last brought Esther to her feet. Would they ever let her go to Abigail?

Joseph pounded up to the tent entrance just as Delia Cranney threw back the flap and stepped out, her eyes great dark holes in a white face. "I don't know what to do," she cried, wringing her hands.

The children cowered together, and the men and women looked at each other in helpless frustration until Joseph whirled and searched out Pastor Waite. After a quick conversation, Pastor Waite nodded. "Esther!" his voice boomed. "Sister Cranney needs your help."

Esther gave quick thanks. She had prayed all afternoon that she could be of service. The women assisting Abigail had only borne babies. They knew nothing about delivering them. But from the age of twenty-one, she had been recognized as a healer by the tribe with whom she lived, the Seneca. It was a rare gift, she knew, bestowed by God on very few. Even after her return to the white man's world she had not taken the sacred gift lightly, nor did she ever refuse to use it when called upon.

"I'm coming," she answered, not looking forward to her reception at the birthing tent.

As Esther stopped by her own wagon to pick up her chest of supplies, Enoch Fisher stepped out of the flickering shadows near the lead wagon and fell into step beside her. "See if you can do somethin' about Miss Abigail's unbridled screaming. I realize birthin' ain't easy, but this moon ain't called a Comanche moon for nothin'. They cotton to raidin' at night under a full moon. I can't see no Indians, but I can smell 'em everywhere."

Esther nodded and hurried on. Arriving at the tent and kneeling beside the birth pallet, she placed her hand on the young woman's swollen belly. "Abigail, listen to me," she said quietly, "if there is an Indian within a hundred miles, he can hear you. This early in the birthing, please try to exercise some restraint and not bring down all the Comanche tribes in the territory on us. You'll have plenty to yell about later on."

Abigail opened her eyes and shot Esther a venomous look, but she pressed her lips together and tried to smother the next scream. Despite her efforts, however, the cry forced itself out as the contraction intensified. A low moan built in her throat, rising higher and becoming louder behind her clenched teeth, until she could contain it no longer. It burst from Abigail's lips in a shrill, dissonant shriek.

As the scream died away, Widow Waite slipped through the doorway, unannounced. "I know a bit about these things. You're going to need some help, Esther."

Esther looked up into the clear green eyes and wondered what on earth had possessed Jasmine Waite to volunteer to work with her. Sister Waite, as she liked to be called, rarely spoke directly to Esther, unless it became necessary to correct her manners or speech and thus civilize her. Even though Sister Waite had taken her into the home she made for Pastor Waite, had taught her how to dress, and trained her in proper manners and housekeeping skills, she'd never treated Esther like an equal, had never discussed anything of a personal nature with her. Maybe now things would be different—

"I would be most grateful for some assistance," Esther said, trying to conceal her surprise at the offer.

Then she understood. It wasn't Esther the woman wanted to help. It was just that this event was the most interesting at the moment, and Sister Waite had to be a part of it, even if it meant sharing close quarters with someone she disliked.

Without further words, Sister Waite knelt, took the rag Esther had just used, and dipped it into the water basin. Wringing it out, she wiped Abigail's face with the cool cloth. In the light of the lamp, Sister Waite's hair, carefully parted in the middle and dressed into two thick coils in back, burned a hot copper as she bent over Abigail.

The contractions were still coming a considerable distance apart, and with Jasmine doing the only thing that could be done at the moment, Esther took the opportunity to rest and gather her energy for later. She sat back on the pallet and watched Sister Waite attacking the chore assigned her with the dedication and thoroughness with which she tackled everything, but with no joy.

Though round in shape, Jasmine's pinched face, the petulant set of her mouth, her green eyes darting everywhere into other people's business, coupled with a bossy manner, made her almost as friendless as Esther. But if Jasmine Waite was aware of the people's opinion of her, she never let on. Talking nonstop, she pushed herself into conversations, gave advice by the bucketload, and lamented loudly when it wasn't followed. She ran from morning to night, up and down the train, "doing her Christian duty," as she called it.

Esther often wondered how Pastor Waite endured his sister-in-law, particularly when it was she who was responsible for his losing pastorate after pastorate. As far as she knew, the only one he had ever left willingly was the ministry on the streets of New York when he decided to travel to Oregon.

Through the hours of Abigail's deepening labor, Esther continued to study Jasmine carefully, determined to find something praiseworthy about the woman. Then Jasmine lowered her head to peer more closely at Abigail, and the lamplight turned her hair to a burnished russet. Naturally curly, Sister Waite's hair was the most beautiful in the company, to Esther's way of thinking. If one looked only at her hair and didn't listen to her incessant drone, Jasmine was quite striking, so Esther concentrated all her attention there.

A moan as Abigail's contraction deepened, and Esther forgot the Widow Waite. "I am boiling some herbs for you to drink, Abigail," she explained. "It will help ease your pain."

Abigail's mother, Veraleen, gave Esther a studied look. "You delivered any babies when you was with the Indians?"

Esther winced at the reference. "Yes. Several hundred. Then, when I worked with Pastor Waite in the mission in New York, I delivered several hundred more. And I used the same herbs I'll be giving Abigail. Needless pain will only sap her strength."

Veraleen continued to regard Esther with suspicion. "Well, I say it's natural to hurt when a woman has a baby. Woman's burden is pain, and if the Good Lord hadn't a wanted it to hurt, He wouldn't a made it hurt. He said to Eve right in the Good Book that we was to bring forth young'uns in sorrow. And the way I see it, it ain't proper to tamper with the Lord's way."

It amused Esther that Veraleen resented the idea of Abigail not having to suffer, and she suppressed a slight smile. "Veraleen, God made people with legs and feet for walking, but we ride in wagons or horses every chance we get," Esther said easily. "It saves our energy for more important things."

Granny Cranney laughed boisterously, slapping her thighs with delight. "She's got you there, Vera!" she cackled. "She's sure got you there!"

The others smiled and chuckled, and Veraleen's thin pale features contracted into a dark frown and flushed an angry brick color. She turned and looked out the entrance, pretending to study something outside, then she closed the flap, shutting out any cool air.

Esther made a mental note that the drawn look of Veraleen's face and the way she sat with her shoulders hunched indicated a chronic stomach complaint. In fact, no doubt the older woman's gut was probably burning right now, like she'd swallowed a hot coal.

"Your stomach bothers you a lot, doesn't it?" Esther said, feeling a boldness she had not experienced in the nine years since her rescue.

At the mention, a spasm hit, and Veraleen's hand knotted into a fist and ground at the spot just below her ribs. A glaze of sweat stood out on her upper lip, and her already sallow complexion turned dough-colored.

"You can really do somethin' to help this?" she asked in a pain-weakened voice.

Esther nodded. "After Abigail and her baby are comfortable, I'll stir up some herb tea for you."

Startled, the women exchanged glances. Granny peered into Esther's face. "How'd you know 'bout that? Vera don't complain none. We know 'cause we're family. But you, you ain't said more'n two words to any of us since you and your good Pastor joined the wagon train in Independence."

Esther restrained the temptation to remind them that it was they who had avoided her, and said instead, "I'm a healer, trained in the ways of herbs and massage. I can tell when people are in pain by the way they sit or walk or stand."

Veraleen stared at Esther, weighing her words, then with a tight smile, she said, "Then I'd be much obliged for somethin' to stop the burnin'. Been naggin' me a bit more lately than I'm used to," she confessed.

Esther gave a brief nod, then turned her full attention to Abigail. The skepticism with which the women regarded Esther slowly vanished and, silently, they looked from one to the other as though asking permission to speak. Finally, Delia said, "My youngest has a diaper rash that's turned to sores and blisters. Could you take a look at him?"

Esther raised her head and a shadow of a smile lifted her lips. "I'd be glad to. Show you how to wash your diapers to keep the rash away, too."

Ruth, a sister to Veraleen and married to a Cranney brother, moved self-consciously and cleared her throat. "My girl suffers terrible with her woman's time. Cramps and gets so weak and sick she cain't keep up on the trail and has to ride."

"I have just the thing for her. Make her forget her time's even here."

Granny cast a hesitant glance at Esther. "My good Mister's got such a crick in his back some days he can hardly hobble along, and he don't sleep much nights. Real wearin' on him, and I'm right worried he won't be strong enough to make it to Oregon." She dropped her eyes and smoothed at her stained apron. "My back hurts a mite, too, now and then."

"I imagine it hurts more than a mite," Esther said. "From the way you hitch along, I'd say it hurt a lot most days. I have something that will ease the pain. Won't cure your problem, but it will give relief."

Squinting her eyes and sizing up Esther carefully, she asked, "And what do you charge for all this kindness, Missy?"

Esther chuckled deep in her throat. "The charge is what you can afford. Supper and thanks have been my pay more often than not."

Granny smiled, showing wide gaps between her remaining teeth. "If you can deliver all the relief you say you can, I'll gladly give you supper and thanks here on the trail. But when we get to Oregon, I'll do better'n that!"

Veraleen grunted and heaved herself to her feet. "There ought to be some coffee left if the men ain't drunk it all. I'll go see if I can't scrape together a cup fer you and Jasmine. It's gonna be a long night from the way that girl's restin' between cramps."

While she was gone, the contractions picked up, each one harder than the last. It was time to gentle Abigail's pain.

Esther poured a dark liquid into a cup. "This tea will help," she promised. "I want you to unclench your teeth now so you can drink."

"Yes, Abigail, do as Esther says," Sister Waite spoke up, helping the laboring girl to a half-sitting position. "She's a healer, and we all believe in what she's doing." Her eyes narrowed dangerously as she turned to demand support from the women looking on with rapt attention.

Esther nearly fainted from the shock. Has God wrought a miracle after all these years?

While Abigail slowly sipped the bitter brew, the women relaxed and talked quietly among themselves. Then, after carefully returning the cup to the herb chest, Esther placed her hand on Abigail's thigh, feeling the tension drain away.

With Abigail relaxed for the moment, Esther leaned back in a more comfortable position and smothered a yawn, then blinked her eyes to resist the sleep threatening to close them.

Soon, another contraction began, and Esther sat forward. The pain built in intensity, and Esther rose to her knees and again rested her hand on Abigail's stomach to feel the rhythm of the spasms. Bending down close and speaking in a hushed voice, she instructed her when to breathe and when to push. When the contraction passed, Abigail collapsed like a rag doll.

"How long is this going to take?" she asked, gasping for breath, then letting out a healthy yell with the next contraction.

"You're coming nicely, Abigail," Esther reassured her. "You're doing just fine."

Just then, the tent entrance flapped open and Veraleen stepped through, carefully balancing two cups of steaming coffee. She handed one to Esther and the other to Sister Waite. "Sounded like a right good one that time."

Grateful, Esther accepted the cup. "Yes, it won't be long now." Taking a sip of the fragrant brew, her head jerked up in surprise. "This is freshly made."

Veraleen blushed slightly and squirmed in embarrassment. "Tried to pour that stuff the men was drinkin'." She held her stomach and grunted as she lowered herself back onto the rock. "So strong it kinda oozed outta the pot like molasses. Were too thin to eat and warn't fit to drink."

Esther laughed and took another sip. "Sister Waite and I are much obliged to you for the trouble."

"Afraid it's us that's obliged to you. I don't know how little Abigail woulda done, this bein' her first young'un, if you hadn't a been willin' to help out."

Taking another sip of the scalding coffee, Esther smiled her gratitude.

Silence again settled over the tent, but it wasn't a restful silence. Esther sensed an agitation beneath it. Except for Granny who dozed with her chin resting on her chest and her lower lip drooping, the women were all alert.

Finally, Veraleen gave the little grunt that prefaced her every act and said, "We was uncommon rude to you, Esther, and we need to apologize."

"That's not necessary," Esther murmured.

"Oh, yes it is," Ruth and Delia chorused.

Their sincerity touched Esther deeply, and she fought to hold back the tears. These were the first white women in the years since her rescue who had reached out to her, had accepted her as anything but a healer to be called in time of need. "Thank you," she said in a trembling whisper, not trusting herself to say more.

Veraleen glared at Sister Waite and worked the muscles of her jaw. Finally, she could contain her resentment no longer. "And while I'm about it, Sister Waite, I'd like to know how you'd get along with the Indians, was you to be took sudden into their midst?"

Sister Waite sat back on her heels and scowled. "I can assure you, I would not permit one of those filthy heathens to touch me." She paused in her tirade and glared sharply at Esther. "And as for a savage making me his wife, I would kill him or myself to prevent such a thing."

"But, Jasmine, dear, it's against the laws of God to take your own life or the life of another," Ruth reminded her gently.

Delia's young eyes grew wide. "I just can't think what I'd do if some Indian carried me off and threatened to—" She shuddered at the unspoken horror.

Granny, apparently feeling enough had been said on the subject, turned to

Esther, and asked, "Tell us, child, 'bout your capture."

Since the women seemed genuinely interested in hearing about her ordeal and since she knew it would help pass the time for all of them, Esther told them much the same story she had shared with Savage earlier in the day. When she finished, she sat quietly observing Abigail.

"Ya got real sad eyes," Veraleen commented. "Ya sorry ya got rescued?"

Esther pursed her lips in thought before she replied. "It's painful to be considered an untouchable. People even refused to sit near me in church, so I often sat in a corner by myself. The only ones who didn't mind conversing with me were those who didn't know about my background and the women of the street where I worked with Pastor Waite. But when they learned I had been brought up by savages—" She paused, thinking of her new friend—the gentle man who bore that name—"then even the poorest souls in New York held themselves aloof from me as though I had committed sins that might rub off and poison them."

"Well, have ya?" Veraleen asked bluntly.

Esther couldn't hide her smile. "As an apprentice medicine woman, I was kept far too busy to get into trouble. I can lay claim to no more than the usual sins everyone is guilty of."

Sister Waite looked up, startled by Esther's story. "You never told us any of this."

"You never asked," Esther said softly and watched an ugly red stain creep up Jasmine's neck.

Handing the empty coffee cup to Delia and sitting forward again, Esther watched as Abigail tensed with the onset of another contraction. Every muscle in her body became rigid with the effort and a shrill, piercing scream filled the tent once more.

"Glory be!" Veraleen exclaimed, her eyes wide with delight. "That screech were pure beautiful."

"It hurts so," Abigail panted. "Is everything all right?"

"Abigail, you're going to deliver a healthy baby very soon," Esther said with a reassuring smile. "Be strong."

Two more contractions, a quick, competent move by Esther, and Ruth held up the lantern so all the women gathered round could see the newest little soul.

"Oh, Abigail, you've got the purtiest baby boy I ever seen!" Veraleen babbled.

Abigail gave a tired smile. "A boy," she sighed and relaxed.

The small face twisted, the mouth opened wide, and tiny arms flailed the air. He drew in his first breath, a deep gasp to expand the lungs, and expelled the air in a loud wail. He drew in another breath and wailed even louder, a lusty bellow that filled the tent and spilled out into the night, and his firm little body flushed pink with life and health.

A cheer went up outside as the men and children recognized the sound, and a deep voice bawled against the wall of the tent. "What we got in there?"

Veraleen stuck her head through the tent flap. "We got us the finest boy I ever seen, that's what we got. Joe, ya got yerself a son!"

Chapter Five

Glad to be useful at last, the Cranney women washed and dressed Abigail in her fresh shift and moved her to a clean pallet, while Esther gathered her things and left.

Seeking a quiet moment alone, she walked out into the cool evening air. The stars hung bright along the horizon, but in much of the sky, they were washed to nothingness by the brilliance of the Comanche moon. Esther did not recall ever being quite so aware of a full moon. It was bright enough to see the tiny feeding night creatures. Bone weary, she gave a prayer of thanks for the safe delivery of another baby, then slowly walked back to the camp.

Sinking onto her bed underneath Pastor Waite's second wagon, Esther tried to sleep. In spite of her numbing weariness, all she managed to do, however, was to think of other bright moonlit nights and to grow homesick for her Indian family. When she had been in unfamiliar territory in New York City, the strangeness had kept such thoughts at bay. Here on the prairie, she found herself drawn more and more to thoughts of her early life with the Delaware.

Giving up on sleep, she took her mat and, seeking the peaceful serenity of the woods, carried it into the tangle of trees near the camp. Finding a level place under some berry bushes, she stretched out the pallet. This time before she lay down, she knelt in prayer. A deep sense of gratitude stirred in her at the latest miracle of childbirth, and she gave thanks, too, for the change in attitude among the women of the Cranney family. They would spread the word, and perhaps Esther would be accepted by the rest of the women in the train. Wearily she curled onto the pallet as sleep swept her away on gentle arms.

Hidden by the thicket of berry bushes at the foot of pecan and walnut trees blooming their promise of a bounteous fall harvest, Esther awoke, taking a moment to remember where she was and why. In these few minutes of respite before she rose to see how Abigail and the baby had fared during the remainder of the night, Esther savored the fragrance of the blooms mingled with the new grass. Solitude was frowned upon when there was work to be done, and there was always work when the wagon train halted.

Enoch had said that if they went the night without being attacked, they would stop here to allow Abigail time to recover a bit and wait for Savage to return with the army. Because there was wood and water, they could wash their clothes and themselves, and repair the wagons and harnesses in readiness for the hard trail ahead.

Esther closed her eyes and let the fragrant breeze blow over her, felt the tender shoots of grass caress her cheeks, allowed her tired body to sink into the bed of last fall's leaves, growing pungent with the warming of the early May morning. Her thoughts drifted off on the shredded clouds, floating in tattered wisps across the azure sky. Times like now when she gave her mind free rein, her memory stirred with visions of those warm, carefree times with Walking Bear and her Indian family, when she had felt completely loved and fully accepted.

Hearing something, Esther stiffened. The sound was not like anything she normally heard. This sound traveled from a great distance and vibrated against her ear next to the ground, like a great drum beating inside the earth. All her senses came alive, and she pressed her head more tightly on the hard-packed dirt. The sound thrummed with pulsing regularity, growing closer and louder as she listened. What could it mean?

In this strange new land where tall grass rolled on forever, pushed into waves dappled with primroses by the eternal wind, Esther had come to expect anything. But this throbbing earth was different, frightening. Should she sound an alarm? And if so, what would she say? The ground beats beneath my ear? Pastor Waite would laugh and make fun of her for a week over such nonsense. No, she would not risk such ridicule. Better to wait until she had something visible to report.

With body taut and every nerve tingling, Esther listened as the drumming sound rolled deeper and louder in the direction of the circled wagons. Now the ground under her began vibrating ever so slightly with the rhythm, making cold chills prick along her arms.

Suspended in a web of growing fear, time held little meaning, and Esther had no idea how long she remained motionless until the sound waves began traveling through the air, also. At first it imitated distant thunder, but as the rumble drew closer and louder, the vibrations took on an increased intensity and a chant of voices rose above the thunder.

"Indians!" a woman's terrified scream richocheted through the camp.

Suddenly everything came together in a crescendo of noise and light. Galloping hard over the low hills behind the copse of trees and into Esther's view was a band of Indians on horseback.

Quickly, she raised herself to a sitting position, ready to run. Then she shrank back down. Too late! For fear of ridicule, she had waited too long. Bedlam broke loose in the camp as mothers screamed for their children still playing down by the river, and men raced for their guns.

Without any visible signal to the animal, the chief stopped his raven-black pony and turned so that Esther, still hidden in the bushes, could see his face slashed with bright yellow paint extending down onto his breast. Circles of black around his eyes, accented with smaller smears of red, made his face terrible to behold.

The Indian sat atop his quivering black stallion with a relaxed grace acquired from years of riding, his long lean legs encased to the tops of his naked thighs in soft, tan leggings decorated with deep fringe and tinkling brass bells. Except for the quiver of arrows strapped across the smooth thick muscles, his buttocks and upper body were bare. A wine-colored breechclout fluttered behind him in the hot wind like a bloodied flag.

Tall and lordly on his sleek horse, the war chief rode up to the first wagon where Enoch stood, looking no less frightened than the greenest of his charges. Dangling from the chief's left hand was a soiled white scrap of fabric, nearly dragging the ground and rippling weakly in the slight breeze. At least, Esther thought, this symbol meant they came in peace.

Scores of painted Comanche warriors on winded ponies joined their leader and milled behind him, churning the prairie to dust. Sullen and suspicious, their heads constantly swept from side to side, their sharp slitted eyes missing nothing.

As the band of marauders fixed the group with their venomous looks, all activity and sound ceased. People froze in place—a large hammy hand reaching for the gun leaning against a wagon wheel remained poised in mid-air; a mother attempting to hide her small child under her skirts paused with the skirt raised nearly to her knees, the little boy crouched at her feet, unmoving.

Esther, well hidden in her woodsy retreat and unseen by the invaders, remained fixed, looking to the tent where Abigail lay helpless. The leader raised his left hand and opened his fingers. Esther's eyes fastened on the white flag as it fluttered slowly to the ground and disappeared into the dust under the prancing feet of the leader's nervous mount. They hadn't come in peace, after all. Her heart thundered with panic.

The warriors watched in silence as Enoch Fisher stepped forward toward the waiting war chief. Foreboding welled in Esther's chest, scarcely giving her heart room to beat. But beat it did, pounding in her ears, rocking her body with its force. While she was not satisfied with her life as a former Indian hostage, she did not relish the thought of being captured again. The first time she had been a child. Now, as a woman, her treatment would be quite different.

Inside the circle, Pastor Waite disengaged himself from the frightened flock clustered around him and walked slowly from between the wagons, joining Enoch. Together, they moved with slow deliberate steps toward the waiting Indians.

The heavy silence, broken only by the occasional stamp and whinny of an impatient pony, drew nerves taut. Suddenly, the tent flap swished open and Jasmine, who had been left to tend Abigail and her baby, stormed outside. "Where's that bucket of wat . . ." she began and swallowed her words. Her face paled until, under the blazing sun, she appeared to have no features at all except for her great wide eyes. She froze in mid-step, staring in terrified silence at the hideously painted and fully armed Indians.

The ponies, having caught their breath, quieted. No one spoke and, with the passing moments, the silence grew thicker and thicker, like syrup boiling down.

The chief peered intently at each woman, apparently searching for someone or something. Esther shrank farther into the shelter of the shadowy bushes under which she had slept and prayed he would not see her there. *But Thy will is mine, O Lord.*

The breeze stirred, twirling the feathers on the Comanches' slender lances, raised in a nonthreatening position. A war pony whinnied and, from inside the wagon corral, Pastor Waite's sorrel answered. The Indian pony danced at the response causing the small brass cones on his rider's leggings to jingle merrily.

A movement inside the wagon circle caught Esther's eye. She clenched her hands into fists, pressing them against her lips to keep back the scream threatening to erupt as she recognized Joseph Cranney easing along the circle. He carried his new breechloader, a wonderful new weapon he could load over three times in one minute. Ever since leaving Independence, Joseph had practiced continually for just such a moment as this.

A hundred Indians, and he could kill three a minute! With the ludicrous thought, the urge to scream died and Esther fought against hysterical laughter bubbling inside.

At last, Pastor Waite stepped forward, and he and the Comanche war chief, still sitting in regal disdain atop his horse, began talking. When neither could understand the other, Enoch stepped up to intercede. Using the sign language of all the Plains Indians, he explained who the people in the train were and what they were doing here so far off the usual wagon routes.

The chief considered Enoch's information, then turned and spoke to his men in short clipped words. They seemed to be pondering their course of action.

At last, the leader signed to Enoch to gather all his people before the Comanches. Enoch knew all about these wildly painted savages and their warring raids on the Texas settlements, and he hesitated. The lances dropped with swift precision to striking position.

Give them what they want, Esther pleaded silently. *If you don't give them what they desire, they will surely take it and give no thought to the cost.*

Pastor Waite gave the signal and, slowly, people came from all directions. The older children grouped together into a frightened huddle near the wagon. The men filed in from various places about the encampment to stand in back of Enoch and Pastor Waite. The women, clucking at the little ones to hurry along, formed a ragged line behind their men.

"Is this all?" the war chief signed.

Pastor Waite turned and looked over the assemblage. "Joseph!" he called.

"Esther! These good men mean us no harm. Hurry along, now."

Reluctantly, Joseph slid through a break in the circle between the two front wagons, the unplaned wood of the wagon boxes plucking at his thick cotton shirt. Then he stopped, glaring his hatred of the large band of savages assembled before him and fingering the blue-black trigger of his weapon.

"Joseph, come here at once," Enoch insisted, ignoring the young man's hesitation.

Obediently, Esther rose from her spot in the island of trees and gathered up her pallet. No one took notice of her, camouflaged as she was by dappled sunlight and swaying shadows. All eyes were fixed on Joseph's gun.

The war chief reached out a hand, gesturing that he wanted the rifle. But Joseph pulled the weapon tightly against his chest. A dangerous twist curled the chief's lips and his eyes took on a deadly glitter.

Seeing the chief's ominous expression, Enoch stepped toward the towering young farmer. "Joseph, give the man your gun," he ordered as if speaking to a wayward child.

Still Joseph clutched the weapon to him, giving no indication that he had any intention parting with his most precious possession. The war chief remained motionless, hand extended.

To the chief's left, a tall man with a jagged scar carved across his face, glanced first at his leader, then at Joseph. When Joseph showed no signs of relinquishing his rifle, the warrior pulled back his lance. In the brilliant sunlight, the taut muscles bulged and flexed as he shifted his fingers along the long thin shaft to locate the perfect balance. Joseph, unmoving in his terror, stared transfixed at the tip of the delicate weapon aimed at him.

Reaching out, Enoch jerked the gun from Joseph's grip and handed it up to the war chief. Looking it over carefully, the chief signed for instructions on how to use the weapon and, reluctantly, Enoch took back the rifle and demonstrated. Joseph looked on helplessly, fury twisting his face as the war chief slipped the strap over his shoulder and gave the gun an affectionate pat.

Driven to desperation, Joseph leaped toward the Indian. But at that moment, Enoch Fisher's hand shot out and caught the younger man across the chest, sending him spinning to the ground. Then, to make sure he stayed there, Enoch placed a foot in his mid-section, pinning him down. Thoroughly humbled by his spread-eagle position, Joseph lay still, but his eyes flashed pure hatred.

"Esther!" Pastor Waite called again.

She stepped from the sheltering copse and all heads turned to watch her slow progression across the prairie, her tall, lithe body flowing with an untaught grace. The Comanche leader's eyes narrowed to slits as she walked, head erect and shoulders squared, moving in long easy strides toward him.

Having just awakened, Esther had not had time to braid her hair and anchor it to her head. Flaxen strands of silk cascaded over her shoulders and down her back, rippling in the morning breeze.

Head still high, she came to a halt beside Enoch and a discreet distance from the powerful black horse. Her eyes never wavered from the chief's face as she stood, mute, before him. Though she was quaking with fright on the inside, Esther had learned in her fifteen years with the Indians that showing any fear often provoked the creation of ingenious tortures. So her own expression remained mask-like.

The war chief handed his lance to one of his men, swung his leg over the horse's neck, and slid easily to the ground, flexing gracefully up on his toes. Then he sauntered casually up to Esther, his hooded black eyes piercing in their intensity. Everyone, white and Indian alike, seemed to hold their breath as they watched the meeting between the two. Presently the chief signed something.

"Says his name is Running Elk," Esther translated, paling noticeably.

"That means something to you, doesn't it?" she asked, keeping her voice low.

Enoch wiped a trembling hand over his mouth. "Means he's the most powerful of the Comanche war chiefs."

"How fortunate," Esther said, attempting a smile. "At least we don't attract the socially undesirable."

Despite the situation, Enoch gave a weak chuckle. "You got guts, girl. I'll hand ya that."

"You forget that I've been captured before, if that's what they're planning."

Her reminder had an instant sobering effect on Enoch. "I'm plumb sorry, Miss Esther. Didn't mean to make light."

"I did. When you're scared to death and hope seems remote, laughter sometimes drives out the fear."

All the while she and Enoch bantered, Running Elk was appraising Esther, omitting no part of her person from his intense scrutiny. Then he stepped next to her and ran strong fingers through the soft strands of her hair. She froze. Did he mean to scalp her? Without warning, he gave a tug.

Esther's eyes flashed. She grabbed his hand and flung it away from her. "What do you think you're doing?" she demanded with far more bravado than she felt. She would let Enoch sign her words.

At her rash action, a gasp went up from the crowd.

A slow grin, parting strong white teeth, altered the chief's countenance. He signed.

"Just wanted to see if it was attached to her head," Enoch explained to the stricken group. "He didn't mean to cause her no pain."

Esther let her eyes stray to the fresh scalps twisting from the lance poles. "Do you have a painless plan for scalping me?" she asked, making her voice calm and cold.

The smile faded from Running Elk's face, and he demanded of Enoch to know what she had said. When Enoch told him, Running Elk let loose a roar of laughter.

He signed, "I have no wish to have your hair any place but where it is. It floats about you like moonlight. I only tested to assure myself it was real."

Intently, he watched for her reaction to his words, and it gradually occurred to Esther that the man had shown no interest in anyone but her. In some way she was responsible for this raid, and suddenly she knew that she held the key to the safety of everyone in the entire wagon train. Her insides knotted with the dread realization that she was to become an Indian hostage once again.

The rest of the Comanche raiding party sat silently on round-bellied ponies, stomping their restlessness into the dirt. The wind riffled the brightly colored feathers and pieces of cloth attached to the warriors' shields and lances, lending a strangely festive air to the deadly moments. Esther lost track of time as Running Elk, without speaking further, gently fingered her hair and let his eyes roam her face and form, drinking in everything about her.

When it appeared that they were going to stand thus through the day, one of Comanches spoke briefly in the hard chunking syllables of their language.

Acknowledging his warrior, Running Elk nodded and motioned Esther toward his horse, in much the same manner a gentleman would indicate the carriage was waiting. Esther, not quite resigned to her fate, stumbled in her first step, and he reached out a hand to steady her as she walked with slow measured tread into an unknown future.

Lifting Esther onto the horse with no more effort than if she had been a child, Running Elk sprang up behind her and wrapped a possessive arm around her waist, pulling her tightly against his chest. "You stay quiet and not move," he said firmly to her in Comanche.

Though she did not understand all the words, his meaning was clear. She nodded and sat stiff as a pole in the saddle.

Satisfied that Esther understood what he expected of her, Running Elk signed to the group.

"What did he say?" Pastor Waite asked when the message was finished.

Enoch turned so all the company could hear. "Running Elk says all he wants is the golden-haired one. They've raided enough and are itchin' to get back to their warm lodges in the north. If we won't make no foolish moves, they'll leave peaceful-like." He turned anguished eyes on Esther, and his shoulders drooped with the helplessness he felt. "I'm plumb sorry, Miss Esther."

Though inside she felt a chill, Esther kept any emotion from her face as Running Elk slid off the pony and tied her ankles with a rope passed under the horse's belly. "If my capture will spare the lives of but one of you, I go willingly," she said. "I do have one request, though. Enoch, go get my Bible and my herb case, please."

His anxious eyes on Running Elk, Enoch signed her request. Running Elk nodded and said something to the tall scar-faced warrior next to him. The man leaped from his pony and strode up to Enoch. More signing.

"Where do you keep those things, daughter?" Pastor Waite asked, keeping a wary eye on the Indians.

"In my trunk in the second wagon."

Before anyone else could move, there was a blur of calico, and Esther watched Jasmine dash toward the wagon. The Comanche warrior sprinted after her, snaked out an arm, and hauled her up short. Jasmine landed a solid kick on his shin. He let out a roar of pain and threw her to the ground. Frantically, Enoch signed that Jasmine was only going after the things Esther had asked for. Though Running Elk nodded in understanding, he growled his displeasure of Jasmine's treatment of the Indian, now limping about on his injured leg.

Without further ado, Jasmine clambered over the tailgate and into the wagon. A few seconds of rustling and she reappeared, holding the small trunk out for the Indian to take. Grudgingly he reached up and grabbed it, then waited for Jasmine to climb down. They stood eyeing one another, but Jasmine didn't drop her gaze.

Good for you, Esther applauded silently, recognizing a side of the red-haired woman that she nor anyone else had ever seen. Their amazement registered even over the fear on their faces.

Clipped words from the warrior, and Running Elk nodded again.

Carrying Esther's trunk, the warrior handed it to one of the other men. "Please be careful," she signed. "There is much magic in that case."

A flicker of alarm altered the expressions of the Indians, and the unfortunate brave who was holding the case at the moment started as if he held fire in the palm of his hand.

"No, no," Esther signed quickly. "It is good magic. Magic to take away sickness and pain."

The raiding party relaxed visibly, and cheered by Esther's smile, the brave sat tall, pleased with the honor of guarding the precious container.

A shrill scream split the silence, and Esther whirled to see the Indian who had followed Jasmine, packing her like a sack of flour toward his horse.

Pastor Waite blanched and thundered, "Unhand her, you heathen savage!"

"What do you think you are doing?" Esther flared at Running Elk, signing her words. "It is one thing to take me. It is quite another to take Jasmine hostage."

He laughed and signed, "Tall Lance is as attracted to Jasmine as I am to you. I cannot deny my warrior a love to keep him warm in the cold winter."

Tall Lance dumped Jasmine on his horse, where she immediately fought to get down. Seeing her struggle, several warriors dismounted and helped Tall

Lance lash Jasmine's ankles together with ropes passed under the horse's belly in the same manner Esther was tied to Running Elk's horse. All the time they worked, she flailed at them with her fists and screamed at the top of her lungs.

Her feet secured, Tall Lance produced a leather thong, bound her wrists together, and fastened that to the saddle. Jasmine continued screaming and hollering dire threats while he worked. In her exertion, her hair worked loose and now fell over her shoulders and down her back in a flaming fall of satin.

Tall Lance stood with his hands on his hips, staring at her. Then, he looked at Running Elk, smiled, and made a guttural comment.

Running Elk laughed, then sobered immediately. He began signing, this time with an emotion Esther understood well.

"The Comanche have what they come for and are leavin' now," Enoch translated. "There won't be no trouble 'less we make it. Still if any of ye want war, I expect they'd be glad to oblige." He stopped and fixed the company with a glacial stare. "I say that if any one of ye plans on bein' a hero, ye'd best be prepared to sentence the whole shebang to a grisly death. If these fellers look calm, it's only because they've gotten their fill of blood . . . for now. But that don't mean they couldn't turn cruel without warnin'. They're also tellin' us to break camp and move on. At nightfall, Runnin' Elk will send back a scout. If he find us, they'll attack."

Wordlessly, fear-glazed faces nodded their agreement to the terms, and Enoch turned and signed their intent to let the Comanches ride peacefully away.

Esther settled in front of her captor on the horse and smelled the familiar combination of smoke and tallow and leather emanating from him. A flood of memories swept over her, memories she had buried deep as she tried to forget her other life.

Making her backbone ramrod stiff, she held herself away from his bare body, glistening with sweat and oil. But when he quirted his horse, she lurched. Once more he wrapped a sinewy arm around her waist and pulled her tightly against his chest.

Not trusting the white men, the warriors regrouped around Running Elk and Tall Lance. Then, bending low over their mounts, they galloped through hock-high grass and flowers to the northeast, up to the crest of a hill. There, Running Elk paused for one brief moment against the skyline.

Esther looked back at the big circle of white tops. From this distance, the people resembled ants as they scurried to break camp.

Dear Lord, she prayed. *Please go with Jasmine and me, and be with Savage as he comes for us.* Without question, she knew neither of them would disappoint her.

A quiet stole into her heart, leaving Esther free to concentrate on sitting with rigid spine, as far away from any contact with her abductor as she could manage.

Sensing her distaste, Running Elk pulled her hard against him, nearly squeezing the breath from her. Then, the great Comanche war chief sent his steed plunging over the hill and, for the second time in her life, Esther disappeared into the world of the People.

Chapter Six

Fort Leavenworth, standing alone on the west bank of the Missouri River near the mouth of the Little Platte, broke the monotony of the rolling prairie, drawing the eye of the traveler and holding it like a rare coin in the palm of a hand. But today the sprawling encampment more nearly resembled a mirage, shimmering in the unseasonable heat of the May afternoon. Though the mountains, too far west to be visible, cooled the breeze sweeping across the plain, the sun-baked ground warmed it again before it had traveled any distance.

Lulled into lethargy by the mounting temperature, the guards on duty inside the gate lounged against the rock wall enclosing and securing the fort until the drumming of hooves in the distance brought them to life. Racing to the gun slits facing the plains, two young recruits shoved their Henry rifles through the openings and pulled back the hammers. Shivering in spite of the heat, they waited in tense anticipation.

"Open the gates!" shouted the sentry in the watchtower.

Quickly the soldiers swung wide the gate to Fort Leavenworth and stepped aside as the lone rider streaked in a straight line for the opening.

"Trouble!" one said.

"How do you know?" asked the other, new to the frontier.

"Indian signal for sounding an alarm is a rider aiming straight for the village. If there's no problem, he'll zigzag his way in. Savage always uses it."

"Couldn't ride any straighter than he is today. Wonder what's up?"

"We'll ask him when he dismounts."

But the Army scout, his buckskins covered with sweat, galloped past the guards in a cloud of dust and up to the hitching rack in front of the headquarters building. He jumped off his still-moving horse and raced up the stairs, forcing his way past Sergeant Major Archibald Haskell's deck in the outer room.

With a loud protest, Sergeant Haskell leaped to his feet and followed hard on Savage's heels. Ignoring the irate sergeant, Savage continued across the room with long quick steps, threw open the door, and marched unannounced into Colonel Mallory's office.

The tall slightly round-shouldered colonel looked up over a sheaf of papers, an angry red flushing his pale cheeks. "What is the meaning of this intrusion, Sergeant?" Colonel Mallory asked sharply, ignoring Savage. "I gave specific orders not to be disturbed until I complete this field report for Washington."

"Yes, sir. I know, sir," Sergeant Haskell hastily agreed. "But Savage took me by surprise, sir. Do you want me to show him out?" The sergeant glared his annoyance with the interruption. "I can boot him into the parade ground for you, sir."

The sudden unexpected sound of chuckling drew their attention to the dust-covered, foam-flecked scout leaning against the wall, his arms folded across his massive chest.

"When you two get through deciding if you'll hear my story, let me know." Savage shoved off from the whitewashed wall with calculated deliberation, leaving a stain where his shoulder had rested. Then, as he sauntered to the center of the room, he brushed against the fastidious sergeant, marking his dark blue jacket with a smudge of dust.

Sergeant Haskell, a large burly army regular in the last years of his service, bristled and flicked the dust away in Savage's direction.

The Colonel drew himself inside his own meticulous dress uniform, narrowed his eyes, and squinted his displeasure at Savage. The man defied all sense of order and decency, he thought. Why, in those dusty buckskins, he looked more Indian than military. He spoke his mind without deference to rank, took exception to his superior's orders any time it suited his fancy, and probably even indulged in all manner of sinful practices in his off-duty hours as well. Brook Savage was utterly contemptible!

Clasping his saber meaningfully, Colonel Mallory spoke from between clenched teeth. "You know, Mr. Savage, the only thing that makes your insolence the remotest bit tolerable is the fact that you are the best scout west of the Mississippi. If it weren't for that, I would find countless reasons to have you court-martialed."

Savage broke into a rich full laugh. "I'd have to be a member of the Army for you to do that," he taunted. "So you'd better prepare to wait 'til Judgment Day!"

The Colonel glared at Savage, swallowed over a fierce frown, and opened his mouth to speak again. But, when he caught sight of the mocking gray eyes, he apparently thought better of it, for his jaws snapped shut. Although the colonel was not a man ruled by his emotions, he came as close today as he ever had to hating Brook Savage.

He drew a deep breath, compressed his lips into a tight line, and continued to glower. "There is no excuse for such unmilitary behavior, Savage," he said in a thinly controlled voice. "You *were* hired by the U. S. Army. That makes you an employee of the government, *my* employee."

Ignoring the colonel and the sergeant, Savage strolled the rest of the way across the room and pulled up a stiff-backed chair near Colonel Mallory's desk. Swinging his leg over the top, carelessly he dropped into it. He removed his tan plains hat and beat it on the leg of the chair, then replaced it at an angle down over his eyes. Dust flew in clouds, settling in a gritty film on the writing paper strewn over the desk.

Seeing his precious report sullied, the colonel stopped pacing and dashed to rescue the once-white sheets, shoving them for safekeeping into a drawer. Then, shutting the drawer with some force, he sputtered, "Well, what did you want to tell me that was so important you couldn't wait to be announced."

When Savage didn't respond, Colonel Mallory gave the desk a sharp rap. Savage opened one eye and peered out from under his hat as the colonel sat in the chair behind the desk, winced, and with long graceful fingers, pressed his temples.

Poor dumb biscuit, Savage thought in a rare moment of compassion. *He makes life unnecessarily tough on himself, and then when he can't handle the mess he makes, he gets a sick headache so he can escape to the safe world inside his darkened bedroom.*

"Mr. Savage, are you, or are you not, going to tell me what message you bring?" The colonel drummed his fingers on the polished mahogany of the desktop.

Savage tipped his hat back and sat forward. He had had his fun, and there wasn't any more time to waste or it would be too late. In a voice raspy from dust and lack of sleep he said, far more calmly than he felt, "The young bucks on both sides are restless after the long winter. The Comanche and the Cheyenne have cooked up some imagined insults and are planning to defend their honor in a couple of days."

Colonel Mallory slapped the desk with the palm of his hand and jumped to his feet. "Good heavens, man! You surely didn't ride here in a frenzy to tell me that bit of news, if news it be. That's a normal day in the lives of those heathens."

His flash of charity gone, Savage ached to tell the colonel what he really thought of him, but now wasn't the proper time. If the pompous donkey would only listen, Savage might manage to hold his temper and chalk up another day without their coming to blows. "I agree there's nothing shocking about Indians warring among themselves, but I thought you might like to know that the wagon train I told you about earlier, possibly a hundred people strong, are camped smack in the middle of the proposed battleground. They're waiting on a birthing and, with water close by and the weather warm, they don't seem to be in much of a hurry to move on."

Colonel Mallory creased his untanned forehead into deep furrows and rubbed his temples again. "This news comes at a most inopportune time. As you know, most the men are on scouting missions, and we are severely understaffed."

Savage leaned forward. "If they're doing any scouting at all, they're going to see the gathering of the warriors and get back here on the double."

"I expect them before nightfall."

"Colonel, that could be too late. The moon will be full tonight, and you know what that means to the Comanche. Are you willing to gamble the lives of all those people?" Savage paused, feeling a twinge of pain. He cared about the others, but it was Esther he didn't want to lose, not when he had just found her.

"Did you talk to the wagon master and tell him of the danger?"

The colonel's sarcastic question jerked Savage back to the present, and he ground his teeth to keep his temper in check. "I spoke to him," he managed to say in a quiet conversational tone, though the blood pounded in his temples from the desire to slam out of this stuffy little office and never come back. "Name's Enoch Fisher. But I didn't know about the gathering of the tribes until I was on my way back here. If I had known, there still wasn't anything I could accomplish there alone. They need a troop escort."

Colonel Mallory picked up a book of Army regulations, leafed through a few pages, then flung it down. "It's no secret around here that I run this command post by the book. My first duty is to protect the fort . . . you know that, Savage. There *is* a purpose for rules and regulations."

"And some rules are made to be broken!" Savage snapped, tiring of their perpetual verbal swordplay. He felt sorry for the inept man, but he wasn't going to let the colonel "regulation" his way out of this one. "If any harm befalls those people in that wagon train, Colonel," he continued in a menacing tone, "I guarantee that you will be held personally accountable. Wouldn't look good on your record when you come up for promotion, now would it? Wouldn't look good at all." He waited, allowing the significance of his implication to sink home. "I really think you ought to send some troops out as soon as possible."

The colonel's face turned an unhealthy purple, and his eyes bugged dangerously. Dropping into his high-backed wooden chair, he sat stiffly on the edge of the seat. "Mr. Savage," he began icily, his Adam's apple bobbing with agitation, "*I* am in charge here. The men will leave when and *if* I say so and not one second before. I repeat, my first duty is the safety of this fort. If the Indians are going to war, I will not risk leaving the fort unprotected. We will wait until all the men have returned."

"That your final word?" Savage asked quietly, though he knew it was.

"Good day, Mr. Savage," Colonel Mallory said firmly, and retrieved his report from the desk drawer, thus dismissing both Savage and Sergeant Haskell.

It was late afternoon by the time Sergeant Haskell could talk the colonel into releasing the troops. At dusk the cavalry set out with Savage in the lead. He turned and looked over the sullen soldiers trailing out behind him. They had ridden most of the day, seen nothing, and come back to the fort anticipating a hot supper and some shut-eye. At Savage's insistence, they had been forced into this night ride. He'd be lucky one of them didn't shoot him in the back before it was over.

Savage squinted into the last rays of the dying sun, took a deep breath of the dry air, and choked. His throat felt tight, constricted. In another man, such symptoms might signal the onset of a cold. To Savage, who had never had a cold in his life, it meant death stalked his heels. He knew that what he felt, sensed, tasted was raw instinct, something most white men knew nothing about.

It was thanks to the Sioux and Cheyenne that Savage understood how necessary instinct was for survival. Years ago he had learned to listen to his instincts. They were given of God to protect His children, and though Savage wasn't big on praying, he did give daily thanks for the preservation of that gift.

His eyes began to burn, and he rubbed them with sweaty palms. He cleared his throat and took a swig of cool water from the canteen tied to the side of his saddle. Nothing eased the burning. He tried clearing his throat again and told himself how stupid Colonel Mallory was. The man was a coward and a donkey. He would let a wagon train be needlessly massacred and stay in his office making a report about it rather than face up to his responsibilities.

On they rode. Savage sighed, and wiped beads of perspiration from his forehead with the sleeve of the cotton shirt he had changed into out of deference to the heat.

Why did the Army always promote the most inept? he fumed inwardly. They came West, spewed out of the Academy, all alike from their starched uniforms and book-learned field tactics to the ambitious gleam in their eyes. With no exceptions, they were inexperienced, lacking understanding of the problems they faced, and with no desire to learn. All they cared about was upholding their precious traditions, following regulations to the letter. No deviations regardless of the circumstances.

And then they met Savage. He had to admit he enjoyed frustrating them. It was his way of getting even for their insensitive handling of delicate situations, their total ignorance of the problems to begin with. Savage had a much deeper reason for tormenting the officers, however. He was an individualist and restrictions infuriated him. The army was no place for him. If he had not made a pledge to his dying adoptive Indian mother to help keep the peace, he would never again enter a fort.

Having been born in the West when few white men were even aware it existed, he felt uncomfortable even in the small settlements beginning to spring up along the eastern edge of the territory. Given his preference, he would never choose to leave the majestic snow-capped mountains where he had learned the frontier skills with his father, one of the most knowledgeable of mountain men. In the land of the Cheyenne and Sioux, the pine-scented air filled his lungs and blew cool against his beardless cheeks. By the time he was eight, he had even learned to speak reasonably well the language of the People and could sign with great skill.

Then, to the boundless joy of his New York-born mother, when he was ten, they had found a small white settlement and moved into their first permanent house. Savage rubbed the tips of his fingers lightly over the scars on his face, remembering the terrible sickness that had snatched her away forever and nearly killed him.

After he recovered, he and his father had traveled the high country together until the fall of his eleventh year, when his father had been shot by the Sioux during a war between the tribes, such as was now brewing. Savage was captured.

He learned a great deal about the wilderness from the Sioux, and the Cheyenne taught him the rest—at this point, his memories grew more obscure, more resistant to being called forth from the recesses of his mind. Even after all these years, he could not think of Smiles Alot without grieving for his Indian wife, his two beautiful children—nor had he considered taking another wife . . . until he looked into the eyes of Esther Wheeler this morning.

With every thought, Savage ached with the loveliness of her, this princess of the prairie he had come upon so unexpectedly, all gold and ivory and azure blue. Those eyes—large and luminous and vividly blue—reminded him of a crisp, clear autumn sky, and they were as distant, as ancient, as inscrutable. He guessed that when she chose, those same eyes could turn to glittering ice or to blue fire. . . .

Sergeant Haskell uttered an oath, bringing Savage back from his musings with a jolt. It had grown dark hours ago, but the moon made tracking at night easy. They had just ridden over a hill Savage had described in considerable detail as a likely place to camp if Abigail decided to have her baby and the train was forced to stop for some time. But there was no wagon train to be seen.

Savage set spurs to his horse, and he and the sergeant raced to the site. Swinging out of the saddle, Savage knelt to survey the pulverized earth.

"Looks like they were here and pulled out in a hurry," Sergeant Haskell observed as he kicked at an abandoned crate of chickens clucking wildly.

A blind man could have arrived at that conclusion, Haskell, Savage thought sourly as he tossed a buffalo chip into the firepit and watched tiny red sparks spin off into the wind.

Using the firepit as the center, he began walking in ever-widening circles until he found what he was looking for. A large number of unshod horses had milled around this spot, but there had been no struggle. He removed his hat and scratched his head. The men in the train were armed, and they weren't cowards, that much he knew. If they had been threatened, they would have put up a fight, yet there was no sign of a struggle.

Then, he saw it . . . a once-white piece of cloth trampled into the dirt by sharp hooves. He picked it up and shook out the shredded flag of truce. His shoulders sagged as he tried to piece together what had happened. Riding into a camp under the peace flag was an old trick, but then the Indians usually went wild. Obviously, this group had not done that.

Savage found the footprints where the children had clustered, the line of tracks made by the women and men. He even located two sets of prints at the front, set apart from the group. Most likely Enoch and that Pastor what's-his-name.

Nothing made sense. All the Indian pony tracks headed northeast, but the wagon train continued on northwest. The settlers had not been followed.

Then something hit Savage in the pit of his stomach. It drove through him, sending him into a frenzy, a feeling he couldn't ignore . . . not when he had ridden all day with the smell of death nearly choking him.

"All right, Sergeant, have the men mount up," Savage ordered. "Let's go find that wagon train . . . if there's anything left of it."

Chapter Seven

Esther forced everything from her mind, refusing to think of the ride ahead, of the night at the end of the day, and of what was surely in store for her. She concentrated instead on mundane things like the sun beating hot on her unprotected head and the growing thirst that gradually was becoming a torment. She wondered how Running Elk stood it, for though he had an army canteen tied to his saddle and she could hear water sloshing inside, he never touched it. At least, as a captive of eastern Indians, there was always water, and one was allowed to drink if one gave no trouble. Here, it seemed, no one, not even the most powerful of the warriors, quenched their thirst.

Jasmine continued behaving badly. Her hands, bound to the rounded pommel of the saddle, chafed and bled in her attempts to free herself. She alternately screamed and cried until Tall Lance, his disfiguring scar growing white with anger, finally tied a noose around her neck to silence her. Choked by the thin leather line, Jasmine's face turned a frightening shade of purple as she gagged and gasped for air. Each time she seemed about to lose consciousness, Tall Lance would loosen the thong. But instead of being grateful, Jasmine railed at him until he was forced to cinch it tight again, leaving the noose so she could draw in only enough air to sustain life.

Esther could see the coarse horsehair lariat that bound Jasmine's feet and left harsh red circles around each ankle. Blood trickled over her bare, swollen feet. Esther was sure her own feet and ankles must look the same, but since they had long ago gone numb, there was no way to tell for sure.

They rode like this for hours, it seemed. Then, without warning, a shrill, gurgling scream pierced the stillness. It was Jasmine. Apparently the leather of the thong around her neck had become sweat-soaked and stretched, for suddenly she launched into another violent tirade.

Pulling the horse they shared to a halt, Tall Lance leaped from the saddle and began striking Jasmine with his quirt. He rained blows on her until the bodice of her dress hung in tatters from the shoulder seams, and her back and arms were laced with angry purple welts.

"Stop!" Esther cried, turning to Running Elk. "Stop him!" Her eyes brimmed with tears as she spoke in a mixture of sign language and the Delaware dialect of her childhood Indian home. "Please, make him stop beating her!"

Running Elk's eyes widened ever so slightly, and he answered her in Comanche and in sign language. "I cannot interfere. She is his woman and deserves to be beaten."

"May I speak to her?" Esther signed in return.

Running Elk looked intently at Esther, then nodded. "Tall Lance!" he said, his voice issuing the name as a command.

His arm in mid-air ready to strike another blow, Tall Lance glanced over his shoulder, his puzzlement at the unexpected interruption showing in his twisting mouth and the questioning look sparking behind black eyes.

"The golden-haired one requests to speak with your woman. Perhaps she can make her behave."

Tall Lance took the measure of Esther, letting his eyes penetrate deep into hers. At last he nodded. "Let her know that I will put up with very little more, then I become angry," Tall Lance signed, his face flushed dark red under the pecan coloring.

Esther wondered what he would be like if he weren't making some effort to control his temper. "Jasmine!" she shouted above the woman's screams. "Listen to me!" she ordered sharply.

Jasmine paid Esther no mind, but continued to wail in deafening volume.

"Jasmine, you are going to be killed if you don't hush this minute!"

Jasmine stopped and sucked in a deep breath that rattled over her swollen throat. "Let them kill me." She spat the words in a hoarse croak and glared at Tall Lance with eyes moss-green with hatred. "It will be preferable to what I am suffering," she ended in an ear-splitting wail.

Esther felt a great urge to shake the silly woman. "Jasmine, you don't begin to know what you are saying. You won't be killed with the neat stroke of a knife or arrow. You'll be assaulted by every member of the party who desires to, then Tall Lance will . . . well, you don't want to hear what *he* will do." Esther paused and saw the fury seething in Tall Lance's eyes, waiting for her words to sink into Jasmine's head.

Apparently Jasmine heard and believed, for she stopped screaming, and the very air seemed to sigh with relief. Then, unexpectedly, she let out such a shriek that Esther felt Running Elk tense. The unearthly noise startled the horses, and they pranced nervously, their heads rearing. It took a minute to quiet them before Jasmine croaked in angry ragged sounds, "They wouldn't dare! I'll bite and kick and scratch—"

Esther glanced with despair at Running Elk, before she tried one last time to reason with the woman. "Jasmine, listen to me and hear what I say. You do not understand these people."

"And you do, Squaw Woman? You understand because you *like* their heathenish ways. You never tried to fit in with the white people. You resented my trying to civilize you. You *belong* here. I *don't!* And I won't give myself to them . . . no matter what!"

"Enough!" Running Elk commanded.

"Please?" Esther begged. "Just a minute more."

With a quirk of his eyebrow, Running Elk looked at Jasmine, alternately beseeching God to save her and hurling defiant insults at Tall Lance. Her behavior was incomprehensible to the war chief. He shrugged and shook his head, a look of contempt twisting his mouth.

"Jasmine, listen to me!" Esther waited for Jasmine to quiet again before she continued. "You will be staked to the ground and bound, hand and foot, and you will be helpless to save yourself. Look into the eyes of every man here and consider what they could do to you. Look at them!"

At last, Esther's words broke through Jasmine's hysteria. Though her mouth remained open as if to loose another volley, her eyes cleared, and she studied the cold faces of the twenty warriors who rode up to investigate the commotion. When her appraisal reached Tall Lance, her eyes widened, and she recoiled under the pure fury radiating from him.

Recognizing the meaning in their looks, she paled, and her eyes darkened with the realization that Esther spoke the truth. "What must I do?" she asked frantically.

"You must do exactly as he says, and not make another sound. You have humiliated him in front of his friends and his leader, and it will be awhile before he forgives you and looks with favor on you. To gain his respect again, you must bear your punishment with strength and make him proud that he selected you. Otherwise—" Esther's voice trailed away, but there was no mistaking her implication.

"I don't *want* his favor," Jasmine hissed, "and I don't care if he respects me or is proud of me. That's the silliest thing I ever heard—wanting a heathen savage to be *proud* of me. I didn't ask him to take me, and I'll make him sorrier every day he keeps me." She sneered at Esther. "I have no intention of surrendering to these animals . . . like you!"

Esther's shoulders sagged. "Jasmine, you are a fool. You have seen women who've returned from captivity. They didn't come back toothless, scarred, mindless crones for no reason. Do you want to be like them?" Esther looked at Tall Lance, growing impatient for their conversation to end, running his bow across the palm of his hand, and glaring at Jasmine from beneath hooded eyes.

Jasmine turned wild eyes on Esther, then slumped in defeat, her shoulders rounded and her head drooping on her chest.

Tall Lance scowled at Jasmine for a minute more, slung his bow over his shoulder, and sprang into the saddle behind her. He dug his heels into his pony's ribs and the two of them took off, leaving a trail of dust as they streaked over the prairie.

"I hope she has the good sense to listen to you," Running Elk said softly and urged his horse forward to join the rest of the warriors as they moved on. "She is a fortunate woman to have you for a friend."

In silence they rode swiftly toward the cool shade of pecan and sycamore trees clustered along the river. At first glance, the tree-sheltered thicket on the bank seemed empty, filled only with an eerie silence. Then from the deep shadows, two boys of about fifteen emerged, leading a string of spirited ponies. So well concealed were the horses that a sharp whinny was the only clue that anything was there. Strong hands worked with practiced precision to remove the leather surcingles binding the saddles to the weary ponies and transfer them to fresh animals.

The goods stolen in the Comanche raids on settlers and wagon trains were packed and padded to muffle any noise and lashed to pack animals hidden in the thicket.

Out of the shadows stepped the warrior holding Esther's Bible and herb chest. "Do you want me to carry these things all the way?" he asked Running Elk.

Running Elk looked at Esther and pointed to a heavy leather pouch hanging like a large brown scab on the side of one of the pack horses. She nodded and watched as the Indian gently lowered her precious items into the pouch.

A sharp, short shriek bit at the air . . . then silence. Esther's heart leaped in her chest. Jasmine! What was Tall Lance doing to her now?

Running Elk slipped over the rump of the sweat-stained black horse and began untying Esther's chafed ankles. She sat mute, making herself as unobtrusive as possible. She understood only too well that her survival depended on her behavior in these first few days. *Lord, please let Your Spirit be with me. Enfold me in Your loving arms. Help me bear with dignity what I must.*

As she finished praying, Savage's face rose unbidden in her mind's eye. A sob caught in her throat. What would he think when he learned of her capture? Would he come after her? Would he even care? There was no reason he should risk his life on so dangerous a mission. After all, they scarcely knew one another. While she had lost her heart to him, they had spoken no words beyond polite conversation. He was bound in no way to her. But he had promised, and she held that promise in her heart like a talisman.

Running Elk pulled Esther down from the horse, jerking her back to reality. "Go," he said and pointed to a thick clump of bushes. Understanding that he was granting her privacy to tend to her personal needs, she managed a thin smile of gratitude and hurried off. In the copse, she came upon Jasmine sprawled on the ground, her face ground into the dirt. Tall Lance's foot in the middle of her back held her fast.

Esther paused and regarded the struggling woman. "Jasmine, you are most foolish. You will live to regret your folly if you don't soon cooperate."

Raising her head and fixing Esther with an icy stare, Jasmine croaked through her tortured throat, "At least I am a moral Christian woman, and I will go to my grave knowing I fought with my last breath to preserve my virtue . . . not like someone else I know." Her lips tightened. "And to think I believed the story you told about your previous captivity."

Esther sighed and disappeared into the privacy of the brush. Poor, stupid Jasmine. Esther prayed she wouldn't have to be present when Tall Lance lost his patience completely.

When Esther returned, Running Elk helped her onto a different horse, a mean-tempered roan whose immediate goal was to take a healthy nip from the nearest person. A young boy jerked the big head down and held the reins tightly while Running Elk retied the lariat around Esther's raw ankles.

Another of the boys brought a rounded leather pouch that looked like the stomach of some large animal, not dissimilar to the one in which Esther's chest and Bible were stored. This one, filled with water, sloshed as he offered it to Running Elk. Accepting the vessel, the war chief balanced it lightly in his hands, toyed with it as though denying his great thirst. Then, before he drank, he looked hard at her.

For the first time since he had hoisted her onto the horse back at the wagon camp, she looked directly into his eyes. They were black bottomless pits registering no emotion. She kept her own expression neutral. She would not let him know of her great thirst, would not give water a thought. Would, in fact, watch with disinterest as he took long, gulping swallows.

How strange to be thinking like an Indian again. It all came back so easily. Perhaps Jasmine was right. All her efforts at civilizing Esther had merely laid a veneer over the real person, the Indian person underneath.

Something softened in Running Elk's eyes. Did she read admiration there? Finished, he raised the pouch to her lips. Avoiding his eyes, Esther took a small amount of the precious liquid, then returned the pouch to him.

Tall Lance walked over and Running Elk passed on the water pouch, his gaze never leaving Esther's face.

Tall Lance drank deeply, making sure he stood where Jasmine would see him. A longing look compressed her features, and she ran a dry tongue over cracked, bleeding lips. Having slaked his thirst, Tall Lance knelt as if to give Jasmine a drink. She raised her head to receive it, but when her mouth was but inches from the pouch, Tall Lance slowly poured her share on the ground, letting a tiny stream of water trickle into a muddy stain just out of her reach.

Jasmine stared in disbelief, then lowered her head into the dust and whimpered.

The Indians divided into small groups, each party taking a share of the spoils. In short order they were all mounted and riding off in different directions.

Here, Running Elk and Tall Lance separated, with Running Elk and Esther heading northwest toward the headwaters of the Arkansas River. Through the late afternoon hours and into the sunset, they rode, giving Esther reason to regret the fact that the eastern Indians with whom she had lived did not have horses, for she was not a skilled rider and was forced to grip the pommel with whitened fingers as the great beast surged over washes and hummocks. With each flying leap, she gave thanks that, at least, she was securely tied to the horse and braced by Running Elk's strong arm.

By the time darkness fell, Esther's only thoughts were concentrated on the rhythmic motion and unending pounding of the horses and the pain wracking her body. Clamped to the war chief's chest, she was drenched in sweat and bore the brunt of wind and sun as well, her face burned raw from the abuse.

They did not stop again, and Esther decided no mortal, man nor horse, could run like this for hours over the broiling prairie. Yet on they galloped. To save their mounts, the Indians alternated the pace from a lope to a fast walk, from a canter to a bouncing trot. Esther felt bruised, inside and out.

As the sky darkened, a brilliant moon rose in front of them, spilling light and shadows over the rounded hills and into the valleys. The sea of grass, green in the daylight, became a silver sea, shimmering in the press of the wind rippling through it. Variegated night hawks, silhouetted against the bright face of the moon, swooped and darted through the sky. In the distance, a wolf howled a lone mournful plea, and Esther's skin crawled.

Somewhere in the night, they met Tall Lance. Jasmine rode behind him, her hands unbound and her mouth free of a gag for once. She kept her balance by clutching the saddle. She traveled with her eyes closed, seemingly unaware of her surroundings.

There had been no sound from Jasmine since Tall Lance rejoined Running Elk. Perhaps she had decided to stop fighting and live.

To block out the endless bobbing sameness of the land they crossed, Esther followed Jasmine's lead and closed her eyes. She rode unseeing, thinking of Savage, remembering each detail of his face, each moment of their time together.

If he had done as promised, he would have returned to the wagon train by now and discovered her gone. She prayed he would come soon.

Chapter Eight

"We'll camp here and get a little shut-eye," Sergeant Haskell announced as Savage swung back into his saddle after concluding his tracking.

Savage whipped around and faced him. "*You* say! And *I* say we're riding after those wagons. Now!" He lashed the horse's rump with the reins.

Haskell's hand shot out and grabbed the bridle of Savage's horse, jerking it around. "The Indian pony tracks went off in the opposite direction from the wagon tracks," he said, his voice cold and shockingly forceful. "If they did circle back and attack the wagons, there ain't one thing we can do for 'em now." The bright moonlight cast few shadows, and he studied Savage carefully. "I don't know what's eatin' you, but don't take it out on these men. They rode a full patrol, then with only a break for fresh horses, they followed you out on this trek. It's after midnight. They've been in the saddle over eighteen hours and done precious little complainin' about it." Haskell swung his leg over the cantell of his saddle and stepped to the ground. "You can do what you like, Savage, but the rest of us are bivouackin' here tonight."

Savage opened his mouth to blast Haskell as a cowardly has-been, finishing out his army time pandering to a washed-up colonel. But something had changed in the sergeant. His jaw was set like granite and a defiant look sparked in his eyes.

Haskell raised his hand for silence, and Savage slowly closed his lips over the biting words he had ready.

In that unfamiliar commanding voice, the sergeant continued, "In the mornin', after a good breakfast, we'll track your wagon train."

In his heart, Savage knew Haskell was right. He had been in the saddle even longer than the troops. Not normally a rash man, Savage usually didn't rush into danger until he sized up all sides of the situation. Tonight, he had to admit to being overly tired. And that fact, coupled with his emotional involvement—a factor he hadn't reckoned with until this moment—added up to poor judgment.

Relenting, Savage gave Haskell a curt nod. "Take care of 'em, then," he snapped and rode across the trampled ground and into the thicket where he and Esther had talked in the early afternoon. Had it been only twelve hours since he sat here holding her hand? He looked at a spot, still matted from a sleeping pallet, bathed now in the Comanche moonlight, and a rush of pure fury at his helplessness pressed against his temples. *Savage, get hold of yourself. You won't be any use to her like this.*

Bone weary, he eased out of the saddle and tethered his horse at the foot of the giant old cottonwood he had leaned against when he came up from the river to find Esther. Spreading a blanket on the spot where they had sat, he stretched out and let her face drift into his mind, let the soft night wind carry her scent to him—a mixture of herbs and roses—heard the softness of her voice, husky and low, as she told him her story. He could listen to her talk for the rest of his life and never grow tired of so musical a sound. He wondered what her laugh would be like, guessed she'd had little to laugh about, and that it would be a long time before he heard that sound . . . if ever.

The thought of those prancing Indian ponies stirred through his mind, and he balled his hands into fists. He couldn't seem to put to rest the feeling that Esther had been taken captive. Rolling on his side, Savage tried to sleep, but her face remained before him. He saw muddy tears streaking her pale cheeks, and her long golden hair streaming out around her, matted with dirt and twigs. In his imagination, she lay limp, sprawled like a child's doll, against the trunk of a tree. The scene grew inside him until it became so real that cold sweat beaded on his forehead and his stomach grew queasy.

Levering himself up onto his elbow, thinking to mount and ride, he raked icy fingers through the tangle of sweat-dampened hair and recognized the futility of trying to follow a trail even in such bright moonlight. If the Comanche had taken Esther, and not circled to attack the wagon train, they could have ridden an incredible distance today, removing themselves as far as possible from the soldiers. Savage pounded his frustration into the ground with his fist. Grief would accomplish nothing.

Slowly he lay back down, resigning himself to the fact that he could not act until morning. He laced his fingers behind his head and stared up at the moon, transformed into a backlight behind the fluttering leaves of the trees silhouetted against it. Unable to sleep, he relived every second of the time with Esther, fixing the tiniest detail firmly in his heart and mind. Sometime toward morning, he acknowledged that he loved her, would devote the rest of his life to rescuing her, and avenging any desecration of her.

At first light, Savage pulled himself upright, shook his head to clear it, and gazed for a brief moment at the small fire crackling in the pit used by the wagon people. Drowsy soldiers were dragging still-weary bodies out of bed and down to the river. Haskell, appearing amazingly fit and already dressed in a uniform that looked like it had just been freshly pressed, stood with his hands on his hips surveying the scene. "All right, you lazy sons of proud mothers," he bawled in the tough voice sergeants seemed born with, "get your blankets stashed and mount up. You can breakfast on biscuits and jerky while you ride."

A chorused groan rose from the shapeless, blanket-covered mounds, still trying to catch one last wink of sleep.

Savage rolled up onto his feet and moved with silent steps to untie his horse.

Leading him to the river to drink and then up to where Haskell was putting out the cooking fire, Savage growled, "You finally ready to break camp?"

"In a minute" was the infuriating reply.

Savage heard the sizzle of water as it hit the flames, and every nerve snapped. "You also planning to sweep and dust before you leave?" he roared.

With the patient look reserved for recalcitrant children, the sergeant said calmly, "Perhaps, Mr. Savage, you would like to leave the fire burnin' so it can set the prairie ablaze."

Blast! The man was right, but Savage found his cocksureness almost beyond enduring this morning. Not bothering to reply, Savage swung into the saddle and settled himself.

Haskell gave the signal and waited as the line of soldiers moved slowly out along the tracks left by the wagon train as it rolled north.

Savage's horse danced in its eagerness to be gone and Savage shared the same eagerness. "Haskell," he said as he rode up next to the sergeant, "are you ready to ride, or take a Sunday canter through the park?"

Haskell looked straight ahead. "I shall proceed at a sensible pace. If that don't meet with your approval, maybe you should ride ahead. When your horse drops dead from abuse, you'll make excellent time walkin'."

Savage hesitated, looking up along the trail cut through the waving prairie grass, the trail made by the Comanches. Esther's voice seemed to call to him. He even went so far as to allow the horse a few steps in that direction, then bowing to logic, he laid the reins against the sturdy animal's neck and turned him in the direction the troops were taking.

Before he rode away, however, Savage looked again at the berry bushes and the blooming nut trees and imagined Esther sitting on the edge of a clear stream, dangling long firm legs in the cool water, letting the wind toy with the corn-silk-colored cascade rippling down her back. He felt the soft strands running through his fingers, tried to imagine her full soft lips on his, heard her voice as it murmured in harmony with the water, saw her gentle smile as she drew the cold knot of grief and revenge from his heart and filled the spot with warmth and love.

Savage, you poor lost soul, dreaming such things about a woman you've scarcely met!

Nevertheless, his feelings were real and would not be denied. He could not ride at such a pace as Haskell set. Shouting a farewell to the troops, he bent over Smoke and gouged the gelding with spurs. Not used to such treatment from Savage, the startled animal leaped into a gallop past the slow-moving line of soldiers.

Savage reset his hat low on his forehead and clenched his jaw. If something had happened to that wagon train and his woman had been hurt, Savage promised himself he'd ride back to the fort as if all the demons of hell were after him and gut that mealy-mouthed coward of a regulation colonel!

He rode hard, covering the miles with little awareness, the image of Esther in need, the force driving him on. Having lost all sense of time, he was startled when a wisp of smoke signaled some kind of action just over the next rise. Crouching low over the sorrel's back, he topped the crest of the small hill and came upon the wagon train, stopped for their nooning near a grove of cottonwoods.

Savage lost no time in making camp, searching out the one face that had filled all his dreams. But it was Enoch Fisher's craggy features he saw first after he'd dismounted. And in the grim set of the wagon master's shaggy white head, he read the message of defeat.

"She's gone, lad. Warn't nothin' I could do."

A deep pulsing fury replaced the hope of the last hours. The fury was self-directed. Against Savage's better judgment and all his instincts, he had let Haskell talk him into camping for the night. If he had ridden on as he'd wanted, he could have reached Esther this morning. The thought seared his soul, and he slammed his gloved fist against the wagon box, trying to relieve the tension twisting his insides.

Now a single thought consumed him like a raging prairie fire: he must find Esther and bring her back before those oily snakes could violate her.

"I'm riding," he said shortly, whirling to remount Smoke and be off.

But Enoch put a restraining hand on Smoke's bridle. "One man against an army of Comanche on the warpath? Don't do it, boy. Wait for the Army. Judgin' by their dust," he said, eyeing the southern horizon, "they'll be along in another ten minutes or so."

Savage looked, then scowled fiercely. "Can't wait."

Enoch thrust a mug of hot coffee at Savage. "Can't afford not to. Take a few minutes, eat, and wait for reinforcements. Gather your strength, boy. Don't try to go it alone."

Knowing Enoch was right, Savage permitted himself to be talked into waiting and swung down out of the saddle. He accepted the coffee and walked over into the shade of a tall wagon to sip the potent brew.

Was he getting soft in his old age? Allowing himself to be delayed when he knew he should be riding wasn't like him, and Savage pondered this with some uneasiness as he waited for the troops to arrive.

He didn't have long to wait. Haskell, leading the line, cantered up in front of Savage and dismounted. "What did you find out?"

Pitching the dregs of coffee into the dust, Savage tossed the cup into the back of the wagon and quickly recounted the story of Esther and Jasmine.

When he finished, Haskell exclaimed, "Well, I'll be! You've had a hunch all along, ain't you?"

Savage nodded.

"What are you goin' to do?"

"Go after them, of course."

"By yourself?"

"Do I have a choice? You going to let me have some men?"

Haskell fidgeted with his reins and looked down where the toe of his boot scooped the dust into little mounds. "I'd like to let 'em go, I really would. If it was up to me, there'd be no question. But you know our orders as well as I do. No ridin' after Indians without the colonel's permission. And he ain't likely to give any such command."

"Then I'm just wasting more time." Savage moved away to water his horse and reset the saddle.

Before they could talk more, Enoch came up to greet Haskell. "Mighty comfortin' to have you and your men along." He paused and cast an anxious eye at Savage. "Unless, of course, you're plannin' on givin' that boy a hand."

Haskell shook his head. "Can't. Orders are to escort you folks up to the Oregon Trail, then head back to the fort. Boys would like a chance for a little action, but none of 'em is hankerin' to be court-martialed as a reward for a few scalps."

Pastor Waite, looking even more wraith-like than usual, brought a sack of food and handed it to Savage. "It's not much, but then I thought you'd be wanting to travel light."

"Much obliged," Savage said as he tied the bundle to his saddle.

Enoch stuck out a meaty paw. "Good huntin', son."

Savage took the old man's hand, wondering for an instant if either of them would be alive to see the colors of fall.

"Anything you can do to bring Sister Waite and Esther back to us will not go unrewarded," the pastor promised.

Savage nodded. Then, swinging into the saddle, he touched the brim of his hat with his fingers in a quick salute, and nudged his pony into a canter toward the northwest.

Savage didn't know when he had been this tired. But worse than his weariness was the feeling of emptiness. Just when his life had started to have meaning again, everything had been swept away. It had been a long time, but the urge to pray edged in around the corners of his mind. However, when he tried, he couldn't find the words and the sense of loss turned icy.

Savage, you know better than to keep thinking this way. Can't find your woman unless you get hold of yourself. Being a practical man, he forced Esther from his mind. Torturing himself would accomplish nothing. Her rescue, which would motivate his every act from now on, was going to take time, maybe a lot of time—weeks, months, maybe even years. A man alone was going to have to plan carefully, take his time, do nothing rash.

The moment for surprise was long gone, the need to hurry over. Savage cut across the open rolling prairie in a straight line, hoping to intercept the trail of the Comanche. They should be riding north, but with a war brewing, it was hard to tell what they would do.

The sun was casting shadows on the trail when he heard galloping hooves coming up behind him. Quickly, he looked for shelter. There wasn't a tree or rock anywhere. He was caught in the open with no place to hide, and he'd have to take his licks if he couldn't talk his way out of trouble.

He pulled up and turned to face the approaching horseman, leaving his hands spread at his sides in full view. "Well, I'll be—" Savage said under his breath as he watched the uniformed figure riding toward him.

When he was close enough to hear, Savage shouted, "Haskell, you lost or you out recruiting scouts?"

A wide grin split Haskell's sunburned face as he drew to a halt. "Got to thinkin' as I was ridin' along beside that wagon train that I ain't had this much fun in years, ever since I started takin' the safe route. Don't have no family. Not a soul in this world cares whether I live or die but me. Kept thinkin' about going back to that office and six more months of doin' reports from the yellow-bellied colonel. Didn't hardly seem the way to close out a long and honorable career." He gave Savage a sheepish grin. "I'd like to ride along, if you'll have me."

"But what about your pension and all you've worked for? This little sortie could take more'n six months. They'll get you for desertion and you'll be left high and dry."

"Naw, not with my record. Put the troops under a leathery old corporal who's been busted from sergeant more times that he can remember. He'll tell the colonel I went out to scout the country and didn't come back. He can only presume I got captured, but with orders not to chase the Indians, wasn't a thing he could do for me. Now that ain't a lie." He laid the reins in a show of turning his horse around. "Of course, if you don't want me along—"

Savage reached out and clapped the man on the back. "You sure put on a good show back at the fort, Haskell. Never would have guessed desertion lay black and dark in your heart. Sure, I want you. Two can do a lot more than one and you know it."

Haskell removed his hat and, using the sleeve of his once-spotless uniform, wiped the stream of sweat seeping down in front of his ears. "Well, if you're ready, I am," he said. "Let's go get me some Comanches, and you a wife."

Savage looked at Haskell from beneath the low brim of his hat. "Who said anything about a wife?"

Haskell gave a hard chuckle. "Boy, you been lookin' like a moon-eyed hound dog ever since we got back to where that wagon train was supposed to be. Nothin' brings that out in a man but a woman."

Savage didn't bother to deny Haskell's words. Suddenly, the air seemed clearer, the wind fresher. A brisk gust rippled the brim of his soft hat as he turned back to the east. He bent his head, and glanced at Haskell. The big man was looking at him, a grin crinkling his face.

"So, you want to help me get my woman back, let's ride." Savage urged his pony into a brisk canter and the two men, heads high, set their course.

Chapter Nine

Before dawn, on the morning of the third day of her capture, Esther opened her eyes. The aroma of stolen coffee brewing in a large copper kettle wafted over to her, and she looked with hunger-widened eyes at fileted buffalo steaks draped from long, sharpened sticks planted around the cookfire. The sizzle of the juices dripping into the flames and the rich aroma of the roasting meat made her mouth water and knotted her empty stomach.

Crouched on his haunches before the fire, Running Elk chomped on hunks of the steak, wiping the grease on his leggings and talking in low, guttural tones with some of his men.

As he visited, he reached out casually with the tip of his knife and nursed an especially delicious-looking piece of meat. When he was satisfied that it was done, he eased the strip from its skewer, rose unobtrusively, and walked away from the circle, past where Esther lay. He paid her no heed, but just before he disappeared into the trees, she heard a plop in the leaves above her head.

Pretending to be asleep, she rolled over onto her stomach. Resting her head on her chin, Esther found herself staring at the succulent meat. Trembling fingers darted out, grasped it, and dropped it just as fast. She licked the juices from her burning fingertips, then judiciously blew on the meat to cool it.

Thank you, God, for touching Running Elk's heart, she prayed, and restrained herself from wolfing down the first food she had had in three days, so tender that she tore it to bite-sized pieces with her fingers. Exercising great restraint, she forced herself to chew each bite thoroughly, lingering over the tasty meal.

Finished at last, she pushed herself into a sitting position and wiped the last traces of grease on the tattered remnants of her skirt. Wishing fervently for water, both to drink and to wash in, she scanned the busy camp. Here, without their women to do the menial tasks, the men, with surprising efficiency, had taken over the preparing of the meat from their hunt and the cooking of it. They had also set up and struck the camp with practiced ease, each seeming to have an appointed task in the overall scheme.

Suddenly, a thin, croaking wail disturbed the orderly clamor of preparations to leave. Jasmine, her haunted, red-rimmed eyes sunk deep in their sockets, staggered out of the trees across the clearing. She walked with shuffling steps, jerked along by the leather cord Tall Lance still kept around her throat. As they passed the men packing the last of the supplies and equipment, the laughing warriors stopped their work and formed an aisle. They pinched and slapped Jasmine, shouting loudly to her as Tall Lance pulled her through the gauntlet to a waiting horse.

Esther, distressed but helpless, shook her head at Jasmine's plight and offered a brief prayer for the poor woman. If only they would soon arrive at the main camp, perhaps Esther would be permitted to talk with her and offer her some hope. Tall Lance must care greatly for her not to have tortured her to death before now. She must make Jasmine understand that.

Weaving his way through the milling crowd, Running Elk crossed the clearing, a head taller than all the others. Approaching Esther, he hunkered down before her. He had washed off the war paint, revealing the sharp angles of high cheekbones and a finely chiseled nose. His intelligent eyes, spread wide apart, looked at her with cold indifference as he worked at the knots around her blood-scabbed ankles.

Determined not to let him intimidate her, she signed, "Thank you for the food," and forced cracked lips into a crooked smile.

For a brief moment the cold mask dropped from his face, and the warm glow in his dark eyes stunned Esther. She went rigid. Why had it failed to occur to her before that he had captured her to make her his wife? The signs were now most obvious, particularly when she recalled that the warriors had ridden away peacefully and made no attack on the wagon train.

But then perhaps she should not condemn herself, Esther thought. No doubt in these past three days, her discernment had suffered in her preoccupation with Jasmine's treatment and her own desire to spare herself most of the abuse normally rained on white captives.

The last knot slipped loose, freeing her feet. Fierce needles of pain raced up her cold, bloodless legs, and she almost wished for a return of the numbness.

Slowly, Running Elk withdrew his scalping knife from the leather sheath strapped to his thigh.

Esther held her breath and stared, trance-like, at the thin blade glittering in the first rays of morning sun.

He placed the flat of the knife against her lips. Then, moving the blade to the hollow beneath her right ear, he lay the fine tip against her skin and drew it skillfully in a light line under her chin, and up to her other ear. There he held it, gave a quick twist, just enough to draw blood, and with a trembling hand, returned the red-tipped instrument to its sheath.

"If you do not try to run away, I will leave you untied," he said, his voice unusually husky.

His meaning was clear. He did not want to, but he would kill her if she forced him. Esther shrank back, nodding her understanding.

Suddenly Esther was aware that the bustle of the busy camp had subsided. She looked past Running Elk, observing that most of the warriors had paused to watch their chief with his prisoner. Glancing at their stern countenances, he gave a deep sigh and reached into his bag, bringing out a noose similar to the one Tall Lance used to lead Jasmine about. Slipping it over Esther's head and tightening it around her neck, he stood and jerked her to her feet by the cord, sending a shower of stars behind her eyes. Grim lines altering his handsome features, he stalked away and Esther, staggering and stumbling on her still numb lumps of feet, trailed meekly along behind him.

Seeing her thus secured, the men finished packing away the makings of the overnight camp and strolled off to claim their horses.

While Running Elk held her neck thong loosely in his hand, she followed him in the direction of the staked horses and stared at his well-muscled back, rigid and forbidding. She understood that Running Elk had to test her. If she were not strong and brave, worthy to be the wife of a powerful war chief, he must know it now. Still, watching the slack of the line around her neck nearly drag the ground, she knew he would permit only the most necessary trials to be inflicted on her. She lifted her head resolutely and pledged to bring no shame to him.

She knew she was lucky to have been captured by one such as Running Elk since she would spend her life as an Indian. For she did not want to return to the white world after a second season of bondage to suffer greater humiliation and rejection than she had experienced the first time. There would be no other as understanding as Pastor Waite.

Though she had heard that people in the West were more understanding, she did not believe it. People were people wherever they lived, and those who had not experienced the trials of captivity lacked any real sympathy for the captive.

No, Running Elk, she vowed silently. *I will not try to escape.* Unless a miracle occurred, this man would likely be her husband for the rest of her days on this earth, and she would do well to please him.

Then, deliberately, she conjured the image of Savage's face, tracing his every feature mentally, feeling his presence strong around her. As she concentrated on the brilliant morning star just above the horizon, it seemed to act as a bond linking the two of them together. With the coming of dawn, slowly the image of his face slipped, blurred, and disappeared as though he had stopped thinking of her.

Esther sighed. It was probably just as well. It was not wise to dwell on an impossible dream, and so she forced all thought of him away.

When she and Running Elk arrived at the thicket where the horses milled about, a young boy handed him the reins to two fine-looking ponies already saddled. The war chief nodded his acceptance of the horses. Turning to Esther, his face now an immobile mask, he gave her the reins to a sorrel dancing in a circle around them.

With a dignified tip of her head, Esther nodded her thanks and accepted the lines. She decided at that moment that, if she was to ride alone, she would not be tethered to Running Elk. Since the Indians admired independence in their women, she hoped this was the proper time to demonstrate hers. Keeping her eyes fixed on him, she reached up with deliberation and slipped the noose from her neck and handed it to him. Her fingers trembled slightly at the daring of her act, but she pushed down the thoughts of possible consequences if she proved to be wrong. She thought she saw a twitch of amusement at the corners of the Elk's mouth, but it was so fleeting she could not be sure.

Her heart pounding erratically as she walked around to the right side of the horse, Esther mounted the powerful sorrel with some expertise gained over the past three grueling days. Seeing she was safely in the saddle, Running Elk leaped onto his stunning black stallion, now brushed and shining, and galloped to the head of the line of warriors.

Attempting to imitate his manner of communicating with a horse, Esther pressed her knees into its ribs, and the pony sprang forward, nearly unseating her. Until today she had been tied to the saddle, and only now could she appreciate the safety that had afforded. But by clasping the pommel in a death grip, Esther managed to arrive in line behind Running Elk without losing her seat.

With the freedom of her own horse, she should have enjoyed the day, but as they rode away from the camp, she felt eyes on her, unfriendly eyes that over the next hours grew increasingly hostile. Trying not to appear obvious, she searched the group, but no one seemed to be paying her the slightest attention.

Tall Lance rode at the rear of the group with Jasmine in front of him, hands bound to the pommel, body so slumped her head rested nearly on the horse's neck. Tall Lance looked straight ahead, his face an angry mask, the ferocity of his feelings accented by the white scar twisting across his left cheek and into the corner of his mouth. Over the days since the women's capture, Tall Lance had changed. His eyes had taken on a hard glitter. Apparently Jasmine brought out the violence in him and kept it boiling. Esther shuddered when she thought of the woman's future.

The sun crawled high into the sky, then having reached its zenith, began the hot descent toward evening. The hours of the afternoon blended into one another and would have been as monotonous as the other days had it not been for the crawling feeling running along her back. To escape, she urged her pony into a canter and rode up beside Running Elk.

Surprise flickered over his face and he stared at her with an intensity she found unsettling. She lowered her eyes, only to have him reach over and roughly tip her chin up and around, forcing her to look at him. It took a moment to register that he wanted to see her eyes. She had forgotten the fascination her brilliant azure eyes held for an Indian. Now, it seemed, they drew Running Elk like a magnet, and she watched desire for her flame in his face.

Esther wanted desperately to turn away, but knew she dared not until he chose to dismiss her. He took her hand, and it was at that instant that she felt a bolt of loathing strike her as if it were a physical blow. She winced, and he dropped her hand.

Realizing she had offended him, she paled and signed quickly, "I apologize. I find your hand comforting, the more so because someone behind is sending hate-filled thoughts to me. I cannot see who it is, but I feel the anger."

Running Elk did not answer at once, in fact, rode for some time as though he had not heard. Then he asked, "Do you still feel it?"

Esther nodded.

"We will drop back a little at a time until you are no longer aware of the feeling. It will not be hard to tell who it is." He slowed and Esther followed his lead, letting those in back ride past. The closer to the rear they moved, the more intense the feelings became until Esther expected at any minute to be stabbed or shot. Whirling about, she found herself looking directly into Tall Lance's black, glittering eyes, eyes that continued to discharge his venom at her, making no attempt at concealment.

There was no way she could tell Running Elk of her discovery. He and Tall Lance had ridden side by side until today, when Jasmine had forced Tall Lance to retreat to a place of low esteem. Perhaps he hated Esther, she guessed, because she brought no such shame to Running Elk.

Finally, she and the chief rode at the back behind Tall Lance. Once more, Running Elk looked to her, awaiting confirmation, but she shrugged and signed, "I cannot be sure."

He nodded and sent his pony racing forward. Esther joined him, glad to be in front again, out of the dust. Looking back from time to time, she always found Tall Lance staring at her with his bead-black eyes.

In the late evening, just as the last light turned the sky pearly, they returned to the camp they had left that morning. The Comanche must feel danger, Esther decided, and were splitting into small groups, making many tracks, circling, creating an impossible trail to follow. Tonight many fewer people sought shelter in the woods. There was no fire and no visiting. While their captives huddled in miserable heaps, the warriors ate cold meat and loudly slurped their fill of water. Running Elk tied Esther securely, feet and hands, and gave her nothing.

On this night, Esther lay staring up at the stars flickering like tiny candles in the inky blackness of the sky, still moonless. In spite of her vow, she thought of Savage. She knew it was a futile and needless torture, but she drew a measure of comfort from remembering his soft gray eyes as they studied her face, the notch in his chin he rubbed when he was thinking, his deep rumble of a voice that gentled when he spoke her name. He seemed so near, as though the stars were his eyes. Then, once more, her awareness of him slipped away.

She huddled into the leaf mold that made her bed and shivered with the cool breeze blowing across her uncovered body. Her teeth grated on the dust and the insides of her eyelids scratched like fine sandpaper.

Mounds of warm buffalo robes scattered around the clearing told where the men slept, though a few of the warriors were restless and wandered to the edge of the trees to gaze out over the undulating prairie, silvery-white under the newly risen Comanche moon. Twice, Tall Lance rose, walked close to Esther, his look sending chills through her body as he passed by.

She lay listening to the night sounds. The distant howl of a wolf, the yipping of a lone coyote, the never-ending crickets sawing at the air, the eerie cry of the screech owl all conspired to overwhelm Esther with the hopelessness of escaping this hostile, featureless world. Besides the wild animals and snakes to keep her prisoner, hunger and thirst and slow death guarded her well. She bit her lip until she tasted blood. Tightly shutting her eyes and concentrating on Savage's face, she managed, for a few fanciful minutes, to create a measure of comfort and hope.

But always, invading her last conscious thoughts and stealing her small scrap of peace was the image of Tall Lance, spearing her with his black and fearsome gaze.

Chapter Ten

The Comanche called the Colorado River, Talking Water River for good reason, Esther knew. Its rumble could be heard for miles before one could ride close enough to see into the great canyon beyond the high bluff. Racing, leaping rapids churned over the rock-strewn bed, making conversation impossible.

Today, the party rode for several miles along the north canyon edge overlooking the rich, narrow bottomlands. Late in the afternoon they stopped at an imposing pile of boulders, dismounted, and began riffling through their packs.

When the warriors pulled out their war gear, Esther's heart jumped at the sight. Were they going to attack a lonely cabin of defenseless people? Was there a settlement hidden away here in this wilderness? Though she had not seen the aftermath of a Comanche raid, she had heard of little else since leaving Independence.

Please, God. Don't let them raid and massacre helpless people.

While the men dressed, pulling up their fancy beaded leggings heavy with fringe and tying them to breechclouts, Esther moved her horse to the outside of the trail. Here, though she was still close to Running Elk and in his line of vision, she could see into the valley.

The warriors painted themselves, then greased, rebraided their hair, and wrapped the heavy braids in strips of beautiful furs—otter, beaver, and ermine. Sliding their war shields carefully from their protective soft leather cases, the warriors shook and straightened the feathers rimming them. Running Elk tied up the black's tail as for war, and braided feathers and bells into his mane.

While everyone was thus occupied, Esther searched the valley frantically for signs of settlers. She determined that if necessary, she would scream a warning and keep screaming until her captor killed her. If she saved even one life, her death would not be futile.

As though reading Esther's mind, Running Elk halted in his battle preparations long enough to slip the noose around her neck and tie the other end to his wrist. He gave her a stern look, indicating that she was to follow and give no trouble. Even Jasmine had the good sense to remain silent.

In their war finery, the Comanche mounted their gaily decorated horses. The warriors, their bows and quivers strapped to their glistening backs and shields hanging from tough sinewy left arms, rode with streamers fluttering and lances held at the ready.

They rode along the river bluff westward into the setting sun until, in the afterglow just before dark, a settlement appeared. Not the white settlement Esther had expected, however, but hundreds of squat conical tents scattered among the cottonwoods, rising tall along the river bank.

A roaring fire in the center of the village sent tortured shadows writhing across the pale tan curves of the nearest lodges. Running Elk gave a long, howling cry that was picked up and echoed by his men. Below, hundred of throats took up the call until the low, wide canyon echoed with the sound.

War ponies raced over the edge of the cliff and plunged headlong down the steep night-darkened slope. Small avalanches of stones and dirt clattered and snapped as they rumbled to the bottom, reaching there only seconds before the riders.

Running Elk waited until all his men were down, then he plunged with equal fury over the edge. Esther, terror pumping through her, clamped her eyes shut and sent her pony over the edge. Concentrating on staying in the saddle and not pitching off head-first into the dense clumps of prickly pear cactus dotting the ground, she rode her way down.

The horses smelled home and, once her pony struck level ground, he reared, gave a sharp whinny, and joined the others in the race for the village. Arriving at the outermost tents, the warriors reined in the ponies and, with Running Elk back in the lead, paraded slowly and with solemn dignity through the narrow streets.

Not much different from a Delaware or Seneca homecoming, Esther thought, *except the Comanche make their entrance on horseback.* From times past, however, she knew what lay in store for the women of returning warriors, and the knowledge drained her of any pleasure in the colorful return.

Kin and friends surrounded the heroes, chanting and yelling their excitement and joy at a safe return for their men. A cluster of small boys fell in beside them, imitating the war whoops and waving their small bows and lances, duplicates of those the warriors carried.

Arriving at the huge bonfire that had been built in the center of the village, everyone dismounted and fell into the welcoming arms of loved ones. Running Elk hugged a withered old woman, her face wreathed with smiles. In the background stood a beautiful young woman, wearing an elaborately decorated green chamois dress. Her wide dark eyes fixed only on Running Elk, her face aglow with her feelings. He paid her no mind except for a casual nod, but she continued to smile a genuine undimmed smile as though his scant attention was enough.

With shuttered eyes, Running Elk regarded Esther, still mounted on her horse. Roughly he jerked the line around her neck, pulled her from the horse, and sent her sprawling into the dust. Leaving her there, he walked away, abandoning her to the mob.

As the night stretched on, the celebration built in intensity. A blur of blankets, leather fringes, buffalo robes swirled around Esther. Hands attached not to bodies but to evil faces reached out like writhing snakes and plucked her to her feet, only to pinch, slap, then shove her down into the thick dust. All the faces looked the same, round and cruel, with hard beady eyes glittering their hatred.

Someone grabbed a piece of her bodice and ripped it away, waving it overhead in triumph. Then, everyone wanted a sample. Hooting and laughing, they began tearing strips from the tattered remnants of her dress until she was barely clothed. Somebody else grabbed a hank of her hair and held it up for all to see. A knife flashed, and she felt a strand leave her scalp. Others wanting a lock of the golden hair reached out to snatch it, but she fought back, shrieking as fiercely as they.

Grabbing the first dark head of hair that came into view, she held on with the tenacity of a wolverine defending her newborn cub. Pulling and kicking with complete abandon, Esther was scarcely aware when everyone but the person she held captive backed away and grew silent and she found herself staring at leather leggings planted wide apart in front of her.

"Let her go," Running Elk ordered.

Slowly, Esther untwined her fingers from the hair she held and found herself looking into the lovely face of the green-robed woman. Running Elk jerked Esther to her feet, whirled her around, and gave her a vicious shove. The force propelled her down the street.

"Go!" he commanded and followed some distance behind.

Still clutching a handful of long black hair, Esther staggered along the dusty roadway past dark vacant lodges, their inhabitants silhouetted against the firelight.

What is he going to do with me? she agonized, her insides knotting with dread. Was he taking her to his lodge or—and this thought was more frightening still—would he give her over to others?

Her heart pounding wildly and terror nearly blinding her, Esther stumbled on in the direction he had shoved her. As they passed each lodge, he gave her another push that staggered her and nearly sent her plunging to the ground. Finally, they arrived at a lodge in a quiet section of the village.

"Here!" Running Elk growled and threw aside a hide flap covering the door and called to someone inside.

"Makes Medicine, I have brought you a gift. I had to save the People from her. Star Flower was in danger of being scalped!" He looked down at the black hair Esther still clutched in her fist. "This one's name is Esther, and she makes good medicine. I watched her prepare herbs for the sick on the wagon train. She will be your legs and be much help to you."

"Thank you, Running Elk," came a low gentle voice from the darkness inside the lodge. "But are you sure you brought this child for my use?"

Peering inside, Esther recognized the bent little woman who had hobbled out to greet Running Elk upon his arrival. Now her broad, flat face wrinkled with smiles of delight.

Giving her full attention now to Esther, Makes Medicine's little black eyes examined her carefully. "When she is dressed, she will be beautiful. It is time you took a wife. You need sons." She circled Esther, squinting closely, not missing a single detail. "She make you *fine* sons . . . strong, tall."

Running Elk squirmed and shuffled his feet in the dust. "We shall see, little mother," he said without looking at Esther. "But until I decide what to do with her, I would like her to stay here and help you." He sent Esther a meaningful look. "She will give you no trouble."

Makes Medicine reached out talon-like fingers and clutched Esther's arm. "Yes, yes, I think she understands our ways. Right now, though, she looks weary. Leave her and go back to your celebrating. You have earned this night."

Running Elk gave Esther one final piercing look, a warning that she had no intention of ignoring, then strode off in the direction of the fire and clamor.

Guiding Esther inside the tent, Makes Medicine left her standing on the hard-packed dirt floor and scurried off toward a pile of buffalo robes. There, in the great untidy mound, she searched for something. The warm close air, heavy with a wild blend of odors, seemed to smother Esther and while she waited, she swallowed waves of nausea. She concentrated on giving grateful thanks for being spared more abuse, but nothing would stop the sudden swaying on aching battered legs, weak from lack of food. For a moment she feared she would faint. But this would surely anger Makes Medicine.

Esther wondered what her life would be like with Makes Medicine. Wondered how she would be treated, wondered if Star Flower was a wife to Running Elk, then decided she was not but would like to be. Wondered . . . a wave of heat swept over her, bile rose in her throat, and though she fought the inevitable, Esther's knees buckled. Slowly, she sank onto the floor, her mind hovering at the top of the tent. Then everything went black.

Sometime later, she was not sure just how long, Esther felt strong hands lift her and stretch her out on a soft bed. A warm cover dropped over her and she sighed. Tomorrow would come, but for now she could sleep, warm and comfortable. Gentle fingers stroked her hair back from her face, and she fluttered her eyes open for a second. Running Elk crouched next to her pallet, his attention fixed on something Makes Medicine was saying.

Esther relaxed, knowing she had nothing more to fear from the People. Running Elk would protect her.

Then, silently, in the doorway and unseen by Running Elk, Tall Lance appeared, his scarred face twisted into a cruel leer, and the look he pinned on

Esther sent cold chills shuddering through her.

Yes, Running Elk would protect her from that which he could see, but he would never suspect Tall Lance, his friend and companion, of wishing her harm. The cold hard knot of fright returned to her stomach and, though Running Elk stayed by her side through the night, it was daybreak before Esther drifted off into a troubled sleep.

Chapter Eleven

This morning began like every other morning since Esther's arrival in the Comanche village four months ago. Peering from under the warm buffalo robe, she watched the smoke from the cooking fire spiral upward to be sucked out through the hole fifteen feet above the floor. The thin leather tepee, a large cone shape, was staked over hard dirt still spiked with tough buffalo grass. Motes of dust filled the shaft of morning sunlight until it appeared as a solid object slanting in through the open door to spotlight the jumble of furs and buffalo robes on the two raised bedsteads against the far curved wall.

With the men still away hunting and raiding most of the time, there was a minimum amount of work for those left in camp. So they spent the long cool evening hours of September visiting, and even the children went to bed at no appointed hour. Because of this, the village awakened slowly to the day.

Now, the late morning sun seeped through the translucent walls and washed the heaped bags and bulging rawhide boxes with a warm, golden haze. Today, however, the camp churned with the clank of pots and talk. Esther threw back the robe and sat up, listening intently with her ear against the wall of the lodge. Word had just come that the men would be home this evening.

Quickly, she slipped into her moccasins and hurried outside. Bent over the big copper kettle Running Elk had brought as a gift when he gave her Esther, Makes Medicine looked up. "Good morning, daughter."

Esther smiled. "Good morning, Makes Medicine." She peered into the pot hanging on a tripod over the fire. "Why are you cooking out here?"

"You needed your sleep after helping Waving Grass get her baby here. Slow Walk says, without you, the child would not be alive."

Esther, still unaccustomed to such lavish praise, blushed, picked up a knife and began cutting the tops off a bunch of wild onions before she dropped the whole bulbs in the pot. The aroma curling in the air mixed with that of the hot coffee at the edge of the fire and reminded Esther how hungry she was. With Waving Grass only fourteen and small, it had been a long night and a difficult birth.

Finished with the onions, she took the flat wooden stir stick and fished out a piece of meat. While it cooled, she poured a cup of coffee, added some water to dilute the strong brew, and sipped it. "How else may I help?" she asked Makes Medicine.

Straightening, the old woman passed the back of one hand over her sweaty brow and with the other, made a fist and pushed a kink from her back. "You can tend to the sick today while I cook. I will not have you around much longer to do that for me."

Esther drew up sharply. "What do you mean?"

Makes Medicine looked carefully at her. "You do not know?"

Esther shook her head.

"Running Elk has been collecting a large number of horses to trade for you. He knows you are the finest woman in the tribe, and he must not insult you by offering me too few ponies. Rides Fast came this morning to tell us that Running Elk and the men are successful in their raids and have many horses." Makes Medicine smiled a toothless smile and smacked Esther across the rear in a show of affection. "He will take you from me now to warm his bed for the winter."

Hoping her face did not betray her alarm, Esther absorbed the news like the kick of a mule in the pit of her stomach. With Running Elk away most of the summer, she had been safe and serene and almost happy here in the village, making herself useful and getting to know the Indian women and the old men who could no longer fight or hunt. Still, she had expected Savage to appear and take her away by now. Her mind raced with only half-formed plans for her escape.

"I am greatly honored, Makes Medicine," she said as calmly as she could manage. "When do you expect him to come with the horses?"

"The warriors will council tonight and maybe tomorrow night." The old woman paused and stared off across the valley. "I think he will come in three days. He is getting very anxious to take you from me."

"How do you know that?"

Makes Medicine's eyes widened and her mouth dropped open. "Don't you know he has much feeling for you . . . here?" She clasped her hands to her sagging bosom. "His eyes follow you everywhere."

Esther's face grew hot under Makes Medicine's scrutiny. "But does he not see Star Flower's eyes following him? She is the one he should be honoring with all those horses."

Giving the stew one last stir, Makes Medicine laid aside the stick and shuffled toward the lodge. "I agree." She turned her wizened face to Esther, nodding solemnly. "Star Flower has loved Running Elk since she was a little girl. There has never been another in her eyes. But a man cannot control his heart. You have taken his heart prisoner, and he is helpless."

"I have made no move to do that thing," Esther said, appalled that Running Elk's intentions toward her were the talk of the camp.

"Perhaps that is why he finds he cannot live without you. He is very handsome and powerful and all the maidens make eyes at him. But there is no thrill of the hunt in that. You give him nothing, and he craves you. That is the way of it." She shrugged matter-of-factly. "Do you feel no love at all for him?"

Would Makes Medicine talk among the women if Esther told her how she really felt? Running Elk had been very kind and gentle with her. Because the Comanche respected a woman's virginity, he had never made an improper advance toward her. He had spent time teaching her the fine points of riding, hunting, and tracking. In the few days he had been in camp, they had had good times together. He had been particularly impressed when he learned of her years with other tribes and asked many questions. For all the good in him, Esther loved Running Elk like a brother.

But Savage was never far from her thoughts, and each day she grew more certain he was the man she must marry. Perhaps today was the day he would come for her. From habit, she stopped a moment and scanned the high bluffs. But there was nothing there but worn denim sky.

Holding back a sigh of longing, Esther looked into Makes Medicine's eager face and decided against confiding in her. "How could I not feel something in my heart for him? As you say, he is most wonderful."

The answer pleased Makes Medicine, for a wide smile wrinkled her old face and she chuckled happily as she hobbled back inside the lodge.

The sun was drifting past noon, when Esther set out for her daily visit to Jasmine. She hurried across to the other side of the village, where Tall Lance lived with his three wives. Still some distance away, she could hear the commotion. Breaking into an easy run, she hurried in the direction of the ruckus.

Esther arrived to see Jasmine, a thick piece of kindling in one hand and a quirt in the other, encircled by neighboring women and children keeping a healthy distance. Inside the circle, Digs Much, one of Tall Lance's wives, was scrambling about in the dust on hands and knees, trying to escape Jasmine's flailing weapons.

Esther knew that Digs Much was selfish and lazy and not well-liked by her neighbors. Now they gathered to make sport of her, laughing and shouting and placing wagers on the results of the fight. There had not been this much excitement in days, and even such an event as this was a welcome break in the monotony of their lives as they waited for the men to return.

Tall Lance's second wife, Whitewater, a much larger woman than Jasmine, stepped out of the crowd and wrenched the club from her hand. Throwing it far out of reach, Whitewater grabbed the quirt, but before she could land a blow, Jasmine spun and, spreading her long fingers like talons, struck at Whitewater's bulging eyes, while Digs Much set up a steady howl. The crowd cheered as the intensity of the fight increased.

With eyes wild and hair streaming down her back in a tangled mat, Jasmine hissed ominously, stooping to scoop up a handful of dust. Esther moved forward, crying out for the violence to cease. But the general uproar blotted up her words, and they went unnoticed.

When Whitewater approached Jasmine once more with the upraised quirt, Esther forced her way into the circle. "Whitewater!" she shouted. "Put down that whip. You know Digs Much has been unfeeling and cruel to Jasmine ever since Tall Lance brought her here to help you. She is just trying to defend herself."

"The white slave has been no help!" Whitewater retorted. "She only causes trouble!"

Esther fixed a firm eye on Jasmine, who opened her fist and let the dirt sift through her fingers. Turning to Whitewater, Esther spoke quietly. "I agree with you. Jasmine has much to learn, but Tall Lance will be furious with you if he comes back and finds her disfigured and ugly. You know how he takes pleasure in her red hair."

Grudgingly, Whitewater tucked the quirt in the band of her skirt and stomped back to the river where she had been washing her cooking pots.

Digs Much scuttled into the lodge and, the show over, the neighbors, except for the wounded—those who had ventured too near Jasmine's weapons—went back to their preparations for the returning warriors.

Now the victims of the altercation gathered around Esther, pointing to their various cuts and bruises. As they passed by the still-prone Jasmine, each in turn planted a kick on her for inflicting the injury.

"If you will bring your herbs, I shall mix them and apply them for you," Esther said. And for the next few minutes, she ministered to their needs. Finally, however, she and Jasmine were alone.

The woman still lay sprawled in a heap in the dirt, a gaunt shadow of her former plump self. There were purple bruises around her sunken lusterless eyes, not only from beatings, but from exhaustion and malnutrition, Esther suspected. Dressed in scraps and patches gleaned from rags and leftover pieces of buckskin and sewn into a crazy-quilt pattern, Jasmine looked like a scarecrow. When the light breeze picked up her tattered skirt and flapped it against her thin body, Esther could see the cuts and bruises covering the woman's arms and legs, and her once lady-like hands were filthy and calloused.

The thick copper-colored hair she had always kept styled with such pride hung in matted ropes, greasy and snarled beyond the ability of a comb or brush to untangle. Esther knew that Jasmine bathed seldom and made every attempt to be personally repulsive, thinking to keep Tall Lance at a distance. Nothing she did, however, discouraged him. And Jasmine, only two weeks older than Esther, looked all of a hundred.

From her prone position, she watched Esther sink gracefully to the ground beside her. "You heard that the men are returning this evening?" Esther asked.

Jasmine did not reply, but picked up another handful of dust and let it sift through her fingers.

"Is that why you started beating Digs Much? In your heart was it Tall Lance you wished to hurt?"

Again Jasmine was mute, retreating into some safe corner of her mind.

But Esther persisted. "If you fear him so, why don't you try to please him for a change? He might even be gentle with you."

Still no reply.

"On the other hand, Makes Medicine says the men will sit at the council table much of tonight and tomorrow night as well. Tall Lance may not come home for some time yet." She watched Jasmine carefully, gauging the effect of her words. Encouraged by a flicker of response, Esther continued her monologue.

"You have suffered much, but let me tell you my story. The Lord blessed me when I was first captured by allowing me to be taken in by a family with a fine Christian woman as a slave. She talked with me about the Lord and let me speak English as well as the language of the People. Then, when the Seneca captured me from the Delaware, I was given to the medicine woman of that tribe. She was also a Christian. So I have never been abused as you have, Jasmine. My faith has not been tested under such terrible circumstances—" She paused. "You see, you are really quite strong to have endured so much without breaking." Esther breathed a quick prayer for direction. Only the eyes of the Lord could see into Jasmine's twisted mind, her wounded spirit, and could guide Esther's words. "God has placed a strength within you that you have not begun to tap."

Again she waited for a sign that Jasmine was receiving her challenge before going on. "If I did not believe that, Jasmine, I would not be sharing with you now. Listen to me—" She paused once more, dropping her voice lest a passer-by might overhear them. "There is a man . . . a good man . . . who is searching for us. There is a very good chance that we will be rescued soon. But even if we are not, you must not give up. God is here with us. All you have to do is trust Him. He understands what you are suffering better than anyone else, and He will not hold anything you have done against you. But you will surely lose your mind and desire to live if you dwell on your circumstances—"

Jasmine's face lost a little of its despair, and a tear formed, spilling down her cheek and mixing with the dirt to leave a tell-tale track down her cheek.

"Jasmine," Esther leaned forward and whispered in her ear, "I have a plan . . . a plan to escape—"

This time Jasmine pulled herself into a sitting position and pinned Esther with a searching look. "Escape?" she croaked.

"Hush now!" Esther put a warning finger to her lips. "Someone may hear us. But if you'll listen, I'll tell you as much as I can." Satisfied that Jasmine was alert now, she sketched the barest outline of the proposed getaway, keeping it simple so the woman could follow.

"I have packed food for both of us," she went on. "I'll come for you tonight . . . while the entire village is celebrating the warriors' return. We can be well away from here by the time anyone misses us. Do you understand?"

"Y—yes, I understand." Jasmine's cloudy eyes cleared and she grasped Esther's hand with both her filthy ones, as a drowning person clutches a lifeline.

Esther gave her a long look. "I know you've never liked me very much, Jasmine. But you must trust me now and do exactly as I say if we are to survive."

Chapter Twelve

High up on the bluffs above the camp, Esther paused along the trail to slip out of the dress she had worn to the tribal celebration feast for the triumphant return of the warriors.

Jasmine curled against a rock, her head drooping onto her chest, still heaving from the exertion of the climb.

"Jasmine, are you all right?" Esther asked, using the brilliant moonlight to examine the deathly pale face. Still, she was relieved to see, the woman's appearance had improved drastically with the advent of hope, plus a thorough cleansing with lye soap in the river.

"No. I'm terrified of what they will do to us when they learn we are gone. I'm sick all over with fright." As if on cue, a shudder rippled through her body, and the hollow eyes regarded Esther through a glaze of fear and fatigue.

"They will not miss us for a long time," Esther said with a bold show of confidence.

Looking down on the brightly moonlit camp from this vantage point, the village appeared as a miniature on a tabletop. She could see the great fire and the tiny figures silhouetted in a circle around it. "See, Jasmine, the whole village is still dancing. The warriors continue riding into the fire circle to tell of their coup. Who counted coup and how many hasn't been decided yet. None will go back to their lodges until that decision is reached."

Esther carefully folded the cream-colored ceremonial dress and soft beaded moccasins and stored them in the pouch tied to their pack horse. Then, slipping into her comfortable, worn buckskins and heavy work moccasins, she tied a knife sheath around her waist. From habit, she tested the sharpness of the blade that had begun as a small kitchen utensil. She had ground it down from the original shape until it was thin as a stiletto and beveled only on one side, well-oiled and razor-sharp. Satisfied with its edge, she slipped the blade into the sheath and fastened her bow and the quiver filled with arrows over her shoulders.

"Jasmine, are you ready to ride?" Esther asked.

There was a puzzled frown on her companion's face. "Do you really think it safe? I don't mind walking, really I don't." Jasmine eyed the large sorrel thoroughbred mare, the blood of centuries of strong, fleet Arabian horses flowing in her veins, and drew away.

Esther managed a tight smile. "I know you don't like horses and you don't like riding, but we can't *walk* all the way."

"All the way . . . to where?"

"Jasmine, I don't know to where." Esther struggled to steady her voice, lest she reveal her own fears and impatience. "Just away from the Comanche. From Tall Lance and his cruelty to you . . . and his determination to kill me."

Jasmine's head bobbed up. "Kill you? Esther, you imagine it. With Running Elk and Makes Medicine sheltering you, no one would dare harm a hair of your head."

"That's the only reason I'm still alive, of course," she admitted. "But Tall Lance just hasn't figured a way to get rid of me yet without the deed being traced to him. But he will, and knowing that Running Elk is planning to make me his wife gives Tall Lance only two more days. I'm convinced that he will try to kill me soon. In fact, he will probably be the first to learn of our escape . . . and then our time will be short."

"You never told me he had threatened you."

"Haven't you noticed the way he watches me? If looks could kill, I would have been dead on the third day of our capture."

"But why would he want to kill *you*?"

"I can only guess." Esther said no more, but privately she blamed Jasmine herself.

Even with two wives, Esther knew Tall Lance was lonely. One wife was hard-working but ugly. The other was a cranky, evil-tempered, lazy crone Tall Lance had married before he knew her disposition. Not only that, but Esther had overheard him confide to Running Elk that he truly longed for a fair woman to love. She suspected that he would have been good to Jasmine if she hadn't angered him so. To further insult his pride, it now appeared that Running Elk was getting the better end of the bargain—marriage to Esther who was well-versed in Indian ways—while Tall Lance was stuck with Jasmine, who grew uglier and more undesirable by the day.

Yes, Tall Lance wanted to kill her. But when she had tried to discuss his intentions with Running Elk, the war chief had dismissed her fears as those of a silly woman, unworthy of her.

"Esther, can't you please tie me in the saddle like Tall Lance did when he brought me here?" Jasmine asked, clutching the cantle with knuckles whitened from the intensity of her grip.

Her request jerked Esther back to the lonely trail with a start. Quickly fishing out a rope from the pack, she looped it around Jasmine's ankles and pulled her feet tightly against the sides of the horse. Knotting the rope, she slipped the ends under the surcingle holding the spotted cat skin and saddle in place.

"There. Feel more secure?"

"Yes, thank you."

The drums, silent until now, began pulsing through the night air with a steady spellbinding beat, signaling the end of the tales of coup. Now the impartial warriors would weigh the evidence and decide who could and could not count coup.

That would take much time. She and Jasmine were safe from discovery for a few hours yet.

Effortlessly, Esther swung into the saddle and gathered the reins. With a departing look over the cliff at the camp, Esther urged the horses up the trail. Very shortly, the path turned into the pass that led out onto the plateau, and the camp disappeared. Only the faint beat of the drums followed them. And as they rode steadily through the night, Esther couldn't tell when she ceased to hear the beat and when it only pulsed on inside her brain, though she continued to move to its rhythm until sunrise.

The moon was setting as the sun came up. "We must find a place to hide," Esther said. "If we travel at night and rest during the day, our chances of being found are much less."

"Don't you think Running Elk will track you at night?"

"He will, but we must be more clever than he."

Jasmine moaned. "There is *no* one more clever than he. That's why he is the chief."

"Jasmine, where is your faith?" scolded Esther. "God has brought us this far. He won't let us down now if we trust Him. If it is not His will that we stay with the Comanche, He will lead us to safety."

"If it's not His will that we stay with them, then why did He let us be captured in the first place?"

Esther sighed a long sigh. "I've thought a lot about that. Perhaps we both had some lessons to learn that could only be mastered in this manner."

"What lessons? How to endure rape, beatings, hunger, hard work?"

"Yes, and you have come through it all like Job, with your faith in God strong and shining for all to see."

A bitter laugh exploded from Jasmine. "Don't be too sure, Esther. Don't be too sure."

"I *am* sure, Jasmine. You don't know it yet, but I do, else why would you bother to risk everything to escape with me?"

"I keep asking myself that question. I feel the same terror, the same sickness I did when I rode here with Tall Lance. I can't pray. I've given up trying. How can I go to God in my unclean state? " Jasmine's voice dropped to a whisper and her words ended with a low moan.

"Jasmine, you are the only one condemning yourself. God isn't. And I am not. You have done nothing wrong."

"Oh, but I did! I was such a coward that I let myself be used by every man Tall Lance invited, knowing I was wrong to do so." Deep sobs told of Jasmine's anguish. "I could have fought them off harder. I could have *died* rather than submit to such degrading treatment." Her body sagged against Esther's back with the force of her lament.

"How could you have done differently? You were helpless."

"But no decent man will want me . . . not when he knows."

"The right man will."

"Esther, you are naïve. There isn't a man on this earth that would want a woman who has been ravaged as I have been. At least, not any man *I* would have."

Esther's heart lifted with this evidence that the dead hopelessness in Jasmine's voice was gradually being replaced by a bit of her old spark. "Don't worry, Jasmine. There is such a man and we will find him."

Thank you, Lord, for guiding us and restoring Jasmine. I ask You now for a secure place to spend the day, knowing that You are with us, protecting us from all harm. As Esther finished her prayer, she spotted a dim game trail twisting down the face of bluff to the river. Quickly, she threw her leg over the horse's neck and slipped to ground. "Hang on tight, this path is steep. Here is where we will lose the trackers. Our trail won't be visible for long. The animals going for water will soon wipe away any trace of us."

Esther knew all this for a fact, and her heart sang in thanksgiving.

Late on their fifth night of travel toward the east, Jasmine slept with her head resting against Esther's back, while Esther rode, tense and alert. Besides their extra horse threatening to grow lame, a prickling feeling running along the back of her neck told her that something was different. She didn't get the impression of danger; nevertheless, she traveled with considerably more caution than on previous nights.

They were out on the flat prairie now, with no protection except for occasional islands of trees. Tonight large dark clouds scudded across the shrinking moon, blacking out the landscape for periods of time. It was during one of these blackouts that she spotted it—a small wooded area in the distance, with a campfire flickering at the edge.

"Wake up, Jasmine," Esther whispered.

"Uh?" the woman startled.

"There." Esther pointed toward the woods.

Instantly awake, Jasmine's face was a mask of terror. "Oh, Esther, who . . . or *what* do you think it is? We have seen no other humans in five days."

"You stay here with the horses and keep them quiet. I'm going up to see."

"You can't go and leave me alone," Jasmine wailed softly.

"I can't stay with you, either. And we can't take the ponies any closer. Whoever it is will hear their hooves. You're going to have to stay here." Esther looked into wide green pools of fear. "This is the time to pray, Jasmine. The Lord will hear you and give you strength."

"I—I can't."

"Yes, you can," she insisted. "You just haven't tried for a long time. Get down on your knees . . . but don't forget to hold the reins tight while you do." With those words, Esther, giving thanks for the cover of velvet blackness, crept off toward the fire.

Staying low to the ground and moving with cat-like stealth, she crept across the prairie, covering the distance quickly. Finding a large clump of buffalo grass, she crouched behind it and looked into the camp. Seated cross-legged facing the fire were two men. One, sitting with his back turned to her, wore the uniform of an Army officer, with many stripes on his sleeve. Since his large frame hid the face of the other, Esther crawled on her stomach until she could get a better look.

Savage! She bit back the urge to cry out to him. Though she had thought of him almost constantly, to find him sitting by the fire, relaxed and pensive, seemed like a dream. He was more handsome than she remembered. His face no longer reflected the bitterness she had seen that day in the wood so many months ago. Now, the classic profile, outlined in the fire, held a peaceful look. The flames showed a burnished copper tan from months in the sun. He looked incredibly Indian sitting there, quiet and calm. He was a man totally at ease with himself and the world around. She had been right to love him, right to hold to the hope that he was hunting for her and would find her. Only it was *she* who had found *him*.

The problem now was how to let him know she was here. She didn't dare rise and run to him. His reflexes were lightning-quick, and he might shoot her before he realized who she was.

Finally, she found a small rock and pitched it so it landed on the ground next to him. She had been right. In an instant, he had his rifle up and pointed in her direction. Hugging the ground, she called, "It's me, Savage, Esther."

She watched the big man flow to his feet and race in her direction. She only had time to get to her hands and knees before he dropped to the ground in front of her.

"Esther," he whispered and pulled her into the circle of his arms. "Oh, Esther." She felt his sobs, rather than heard them, as he smothered her against his chest in a great crush. "We've hunted for so long and found no trace," he choked and put her away from him.

"My heart sings to see you," she said softly as she wiped the tears from his cheeks. "The prairie is vast, and they left no clues. I watched them circle and retrace their route until everything had been blotted out. No tracker, no matter how good, could have followed us for long." She looked up, staring at him, swept into the depths of his warm gray eyes. "But I knew you were looking," she assured him. "And I knew you'd never give up."

His body was leaner, the angles of his face sharper, more angular than in May, the planes finely etched, revealing firm, strong bones. "You're right about that. Haskell over there was ready to ride back to Fort Leavenworth tomorrow, but he was going alone." His eyes roamed over her, drinking in everything about her. Tension vibrated between them like a plucked bowstring. Her heart rose into her throat and she could barely breathe.

"You're beautiful, Esther Wheeler, more beautiful even than I remembered," Savage whispered in her ear. He put his hand lightly on her hair and captured a stray lock that had escaped its confining braid.

A soft whinny and in a flash, the spell broken, Savage's head whipped around and he reached for his pistol. "Were you followed?"

"I'm sure we have been, but that was my horse you heard. Jasmine is tending her."

"Jasmine is with you?"

"You surely didn't think I would leave her behind?"

"I didn't think about her at all," he confessed. Turning, he called over his shoulder, "Haskell, there's a lady out there tending a horse. How about going to the rescue?"

Haskell, heaving himself to his feet with a series of grunts, strode off in the direction of the prairie.

"Jasmine, we've found Savage!" Esther called. "Sergeant Haskell is coming out to bring you into camp."

Esther gave thanks that days earlier she had hacked off Jasmine's hair. It now curled over her head in ringlets, clean and unmatted, giving her the look of a thin pixie. Though the travel had been hard, five days with regular food and no beatings had already improved Jasmine's looks considerably. Tonight she could be seen by the sergeant and Savage without embarrassment.

Savage helped Esther to her feet and guided her toward the fire. "How much time do we have before you figure Running Elk will be here?"

"Not much. I've sensed Running Elk very close several times. We rode in water tonight. There were several streams to choose from, so it will take some time for them to decide which way we went. He isn't alone. He will have the best trackers in the tribe with him."

Savage quickly doused the fire. "That will help some. And there's a storm brewing to darken the moon." He looked up as Haskell and Jasmine arrived in the small clearing. "Esther says the Comanche are hard on their trail. We can't stay here. It will be more confusing if we split up and ride for the fort separately."

Feeling like she was being pulled apart, Esther sank slowly to the ground.

Quickly, Savage knelt beside her. "What's the matter. Are you ill?"

"Yes and no," she said in a trembling voice. "If we ride to the fort, Running Elk will make war to take me back. He and other good men, both white and red, will surely be killed. Let Jasmine and the sergeant go to the fort. Let us track off in another direction. Running Elk knows my pony tracks by now and will follow us. Perhaps we could outrun him."

Savage thought for a few minutes. "I have some ideas," he said at last. "We aren't that far from the Cheyenne. We will be safe once we're in their stronghold."

"Good," she breathed.

Haskell stared at Esther, his undisguised admiration showing in his face. "Name's Haskell, ma'am, Archibald Haskell, late of the U.S. Army."

Esther nodded. "Much obliged for your help in finding us." He was a good man, probably in his late forties or early fifties.

"Seein' you, ma'am, I can sure understand why Savage has tracked you night and day." Turning to face Jasmine just as the clouds uncovered the moon, he bowed, "And you too, ma'am. Nobody told us we'd be findin' *two* beauties."

Jasmine regarded him coldly. "Sergeant Haskell, let's have an understanding right now. I was a slave, used by half the men in the tribe. I have been beaten, starved, worked, and abused in every imaginable way. I am not fit—"

"Mrs. Waite," he interrupted, "I know how Indians treat their white slaves. That you have escaped with any kind of sanity a'tall bespeaks the high type woman you are. I am returnin' to Fort Leavenworth pronto. If you'd like to make the trip with me, I'd be most obliged to have your comp'ny."

One thing Jasmine had learned through her ordeal was to hold her tongue. She stood quietly watching Haskell as he turned a brick red and wiped the sweat from his upper lip.

"Well, Mrs. Waite, what I'm tryin' to say is, I'm an old dog ready to retire. I got no family, no home. I'm lookin' to set up a place and, if after we get to know one another better—" His voice trailed off into an embarrassed silence.

Not a flicker of emotion altered Jasmine's features. She regarded the nervous man for some time before she said, "Sergeant Haskell, I appreciate your offer of an escort to the fort. I will not hold you to anything more. Given time, we shall see about the rest."

Clouds settled over the moon again and flicks of lightning pierced the heavy black clouds. Rumbles of distant thunder beat on the air and a cool wind began blowing. "Looks like a good time for us to move out," Savage said.

"Our pack horse is lame," Esther said. "I don't think he'll stand riding."

"I've a good extra mount," Haskell said, turning to Jasmine. "We can ride double. That is, if you don't mind, ma'am."

She regarded him with heavily lidded eyes. "My name is Jasmine, and I wish you would call me that, Sergeant." Having made the point of her name, she seemed to mellow a bit, and she took a step toward the sergeant. "And no, I don't mind. I'm no horseman, and I find riding alone a terrifying experience."

The sergeant took Jasmine's hand and, as though escorting her to a fancy ball, he led her to his horse. "Since we're goin' to become more than acquaintances, my name is Archibald."

Jasmine smiled the first sweet smile Esther had seen cross her face in months. "A most fitting name for so fine a gentleman."

Esther followed, and the two women embraced with a genuine caring born of months of shared suffering. "Take care of yourself, Jasmine. I have a strong feeling your life is going to take a decided turn for the better."

Jasmine smiled. "Thanks to you and the Lord, I may have a life to live after all. And, Esther, I must ask your forgiveness for all the things I said about you—" Choked with emotion, she could not go on.

"Have a safe trip, and God go with you." Esther gave her a final hard squeeze and turned away so Jasmine wouldn't see the tears.

Squaring her shoulders and with a dip of her head, Jasmine placed her foot in the stirrup. "Archibald, with a bit of help, I am ready to mount this animal."

Haskell set Jasmine on the skirt of the saddle and climbed on, awkwardly swinging his leg over the horse's neck. Esther handed Savage Jasmine's pitiful little pouch containing her belongings, and he tied it to the saddle. Then, scrounging a blanket from his pack, Savage wrapped it around Jasmine's thin shoulders. She smiled her gratitude and clutched the folds to her.

"Looks like you're ready to ride," Savage observed. "Have a safe trip."

Haskell looked down at the big man, real affection in his eyes. "It's been a great experience, Savage. One I wouldn't have missed for the world. Take care of yourself wherever you and the lady decide to go. Just might run into you one of these days."

Savage held out his hand and the two men clasped wrists. Reluctantly, they drew apart and Haskell placed Jasmine's arms around his waist. "You hang on tight, now. We're gonna make tracks for civilization."

Haskell set his heels against the horse's sides and it took off at a good pace. The thunder covered the sound of the hoofbeats, but lightning, streaking the sky in eerie flashes, occasionally lit the pair as they disappeared into the vastness of the prairie.

Savage put his arm across Esther's shoulders. "Ready?"

"Ready," she said and swung effortlessly onto her horse.

Savage leaped onto his pony, Indian fashion, and turned its head into the wind and the storm. "We'll ride north into Cheyenne country. Pray your Comanche friends have had all the war they want this season and don't follow us."

Esther didn't tell Savage that Running Elk would be as determined to have her back as Savage had been to find her. Tracking her into Cheyenne country would only slow him down. It would not stop him.

Chapter Thirteen

The storm that began so ferociously was a false alarm and passed with nothing more than a spectacular fireworks display. Though it had been a long time since rain and moisture was sorely needed, Esther gave thanks that there hadn't been a heavy downpour to soak them as they traveled.

They rode in the pale morning light, the weak sun barely penetrating the heavy cloud cover, up the rocky bottom of a wide flat canyon. But it was light enough now for Savage to see her skin-tight buckskin breeches meeting the tops of her high moccasins, a fringed shirt, and her hair braided in two heavy braids wrapped Comanche style with otter skin. Savage looked . . . no, *studied* the effect.

His eyes kept returning to the red paint down the part in her hair. "You turn completely Comanche?" he finally asked.

Though the words seemed innocent enough, she didn't like their implication. Her eyes narrowed as she probed his face. "What are you asking?"

"Painted your part. Means you're married."

"First time I've known you to be wrong, Cheyenne man. You obviously don't know what it means." She searched hard inside to find a balance in her words and voice—enough force to let him know it mattered to her, but not so much intensity that it forced him to defend his words. They knew so little about each other and yet they knew so much. Right now, either one could say something to shatter their fragile love before it matured.

Cautiously, in a more gentle voice, she continued, "All Comanche women and girls paint their parts for ceremonial events. The red line signifies the long trail I will travel during my lifetime, and asks the Great Spirit to make me fruitful."

She gave him a sidelong look and saw that his profile had relaxed slightly. And since he continued to ride by her side, she was satisfied that he was not angry and had accepted her explanation.

Esther would have liked to talk more with him. There was so much to say, but he seemed drawn within himself, listening, sensing the very air about them. She knew that while he listened politely, until they were safe, she would have only a small part of his attention. Still, she was selfish enough to want it all.

"This valley is the understood border of Cheyenne territory," he was saying. "We should be reasonably safe here. Safer," Savage went on, "than trying to find shelter for the daylight hours inside Comanche country."

As they rode, however, he kept turning to look back over his shoulder.

Growing more nervous by the minute, Esther could not resist asking, "Do you see something to cause alarm?"

"No, but I have an ugly feeling, and I can taste death. It crawls up and closes off my throat."

She felt the color drain from her face and a hollow open in the pit of her stomach. "I guess I'm grateful for your honesty, but what are we to do? Do you think Running Elk knows we are here?"

"I don't think it has anything to do with Running Elk or the Comanches. I don't know what's the matter, but it's very bad. Stay close and do exactly as I tell you . . . when I know what that is." He sent her a rueful smile and his eyes softened as they met hers.

She drew them to her, held them, watched as they traced her face, seeing her heart-shaped browline, high cheekbones, straight nose with finely flared nostrils, lingering on her full mouth and firm chin. His hands flexed and Esther felt his need to touch her. She reached out to him, and he took her hand, holding it as they rode with fingers entwined, letting their love flow and mingle.

They rode awhile in the warm glowing silence, then she asked, "Do you still sense something wrong?"

"Yes." This time when he spoke, his eyes and voice suddenly turned hard as flint. "Only it's much worse than I thought."

She pursed her lips and turned around. There was nothing in the canyon but the stream flowing deceptively smooth, gurgling as it bumped up against rocks in its path. "It disturbs me that I feel nothing. I am usually the first to grow uneasy."

"Do you doubt me?"

Her eyes widened. "No. Only myself. If such a great danger exists and I am unaware of it, then I am dangerously vulnerable."

He allowed himself the ghost of a boyish grin, easing the long tension. "Means you'll have to stay close to me at all times."

They stopped to rest at the water's edge and let the horses drink. The water ran dull, reflecting the leaden skies overhead. Crows wheeled like black messengers in and out of the low clouds, cawing crossly at one another. The rest of the land seemed unnaturally quiet. She and Savage made no attempt at conversation. He still seemed to be listening and looking for the unseen danger.

Mounting up again, they rode on up the barren valley. Only random clumps of grass held the sand in place. But it was so tough and old, the horses made no attempt to snatch any as they walked by.

Esther heard the pounding hooves before she saw the lone buffalo stagger into the canyon, fall, struggle to its feet and crash on again. "Look!" she cried.

Both wheeled their horses around and watched the animal weaving an erratic pattern—stumble and fall, rest while it gathered strength enough to rise, then lurch on until something tripped it up and, helplessly, it crumpled again to the ground.

Savage set his heels in Smoke's ribs and they rode back until they could see the buffalo clearly. The hair had been singed off the animal's back, revealing shriveled skin like dried grapes. Its knees were bloodied, scraped raw by repeated falls as it ran in blind circles over the prairie.

"Look, Savage, his eyes are swollen shut and his face is blistered. Looks like he's been burned."

"The lining of his nose has been seared, and he can't smell. That explains why he's letting us get so close to him."

Esther gave Savage a stricken look. "Poor thing, what can we do for him?"

"He's doomed to attack by wolves or coyotes and, blind as he is, he can't defend himself. Shooting him and putting him out of his misery is the kindest act."

Though she knew Savage was right, Esther didn't want to watch. She pressed her hands over her ears and lifted her eyes, looking out the mouth of the canyon to the prairie beyond.

There, reflected by the low somber layer of clouds, was a reddish glow spreading across the horizon. At night around the campfire, Enoch Fisher and others had told of sweeping prairie fires, but their most vivid descriptions had not begun to prepare Esther for the eerie magnificence of this destructively spectacular act of God. Though she jerked at the sound of Savage's rifle, her eyes remained fixed in dazed fascination as the tinted sky grew rapidly brighter.

"Fire!" Her voice was a keening wail.

Savage gave a low moan. "So this is what I've been fearing. Here in the canyon, the wind's been blowing the smoke past us." His broad shoulders slumped and his head bowed. "This could be the end for us," he said and looked at her with tortured eyes.

She nodded her understanding and reached out for his hand.

While they watched, the wind picked up, chasing the flames ever higher before it, sending them roaring into the mouth of the canyon. Too late to escape through the entrance, they were sealed inside, waves of heat beating against their faces. Towering tongues of fire licked at the foreboding clouds turned an orange-red, and filled the canyon with gigantic shadows flickering in grotesque shapes over the red-stained cliffs.

Savage looked at her for a minute, roused from his state of hopelessness, took out his field glasses and searched the walls of the cliffs holding them prisoner. Game, fleeing before the advancing fire, began trickling past. Then the trickle became a flood. The animals that were fleeter of foot—deer and pronghorn sheep—arrived first, racing up along the river, scrambling in terror over the rocks of the cliffs to the high plateau at the head of the canyon.

"Can we follow the animals?" she asked and coughed as the black smoke rolled over them, stinging her eyes and nose. The roar and crackle of the flames echoed against the rocks and still they didn't move. "Can't you find some place for us?" she pleaded between coughs.

"Maybe—" He slipped the glasses into their case and pointed to a ledge. "There's a narrow game trail up there and I think I can see a cave. Come on. Let's try to make it."

Seeing her hesitate, Savage reached out and pulled her onto his horse, holding her in the saddle in front of him. Setting his heels in the ribs of the big sorrel, he raced toward the cliffs, towing Esther's horse by its reins.

At the beginning of the rock-strewn trail, Savage reined to a stop, and dismounted. "We'll have to hike up. Trail's too narrow to ride. If a horse spooks, it'll go over the side before one of us can stop it."

Dumbly, she nodded. The narrow trail, steep and rocky, wound between crevices and around huge boulders, dislodged centuries ago from the bluff walls. It took all Esther's concentration to keep her balance and lead the horse. Savage set a grueling pace and she struggled to keep up. She set her jaw, however, and vowed she would not give him the satisfaction of having to stop for breath before he did. The higher they climbed, the more agonizing grew her need until finally only the dull thuds of the horses' hooves echoed over her deep gasps for air.

Esther thought her lungs would burst, but Savage marched on with dogged determination. What on earth made it so necessary that they reach the ledge without stopping? If she had any breath to spare, she would have asked him, but that would have necessitated stopping, and something in the set of his jaw told her he would not do that. Her only consolation was that his breathing was as labored and ragged as her own.

Fire burned through her legs and flowed into her lungs and parched throat. Like it or not, Esther was going to have to stop or fall on her face in the trail.

"Don't . . . think . . . 'bout . . . stopping," Savage read her thoughts. "We're . . . almost . . . there."

"Why can't . . . we rest?" she pleaded.

"I can't be sure . . . and don't want to take the time to look, . . . but I thought I saw a glint of light . . . from the bluff across the canyon. May not be anything and then again—"

Worn from the pace she had set to escape from Running Elk, she had very little left to give, but his words frightened her enough to plod on a bit farther. She bowed her head and looked only at the trail before her. It took every bit of reserve strength she had to pick up her feet and set them a few inches farther along the path. They began to feel like lead weights at the ends of her legs and, when she stumbled and nearly plunged over the side, she was sure she could not take one more step. She lacked the strength or the voice to call to Savage, but looking up she saw the sharp turn the trail made onto the shelf he had described seeing from the ground.

On the ledge, she started to collapse against the bluff wall. Strong fingers dug into her arm and Savage half-dragged her into the cave. Once inside, she slid slowly to the ground, closed her eyes, and curled into a pain-washed heap. She lay like that for many minutes, weaving in and out of consciousness, recovering her wind.

"You all right?" Savage finally asked in a thick croak.

Esther raised her head to answer and saw him slumped against the jagged rock wall, his face gray and strained, his eyes watching her. In one hand he held his field glasses and in the other, he held out the canteen to her.

"Thank you," she said and drank greedily. Wiping her mouth with the back of her sleeve, she handed the nearly empty container back to him. "I was so thirsty, I imagined I heard trickling water."

"Wasn't your imagination." He staggered to his feet and crossed the hard uneven floor to where a thin stream of water spilled over the rocks and collected in a small pool at the base. He filled the canteen and slaked his own thirst, then filled the flask again.

Moving past her, he brought the horses inside and led them to the pool. They drank in great noisy gulps. Then, he led them into the back of the cave. Fishing around in a pack, Savage returned with something wrapped in oilcloth. "Our meal won't be the most memorable. All we have is some pemmican and hard biscuits."

"I won't complain," Esther said and accepted her portion gratefully. "I've eaten worse."

While they ate in silence, Savage played his glasses across the plateau across from them and Esther stared into the valley below. For want of fuel, the fire had burned itself into smoldering ruin. "See anything?" she asked at last.

He shook his head. "Could have been the fire glinting off a piece of mica." But he didn't sound convincing.

The promised storm arrived, the chill breeze stopping briefly to switch directions and return with renewed force to whistle around the cave entrance. It carried with it the acrid scent of the dead fire. A close-by crack of lightning sent the horses dancing against their tethers, and Esther shivered.

Unfolding his long frame, Savage got up and brought the horses closer to the entrance. "Since we don't have wood for a fire, the horses will help keep us warm." He took their saddles off, stacked them together to provide a back rest, then brought the soft wildcat skin that protected Esther's mount from the saddle and handed it over to her. Turning the fur side in, she wrapped it around herself.

"Thank you, Savage," she said simply. "And thank You, dear Lord," she prayed aloud, "for providing for all our needs again."

"More than you realize," he said. "The fire and now the rain will remove any trace of our tracks. The best tracker in the world will never know what direction we took."

With a deep sigh, she turned to him and found his eyes, wide and shining, gazing at her. "And so, my beloved, we are safe, at last," she said softly.

Tucking the wrap around her snugly, he moved to cup her upturned face in his hands. She closed her eyes, relishing his nearness, and he kissed the delicate lids, the smooth skin of her forehead, and she smelled the slight scent of salt still clinging to his skin. Then he drew her close against him and tenderly stroked her hair, pulled tight at the temples into the thick braids.

Her head nestled in the hollow of his neck, she could feel the quickened beat of his heart as he whispered, "My beloved."

Such an endearment had never been uttered to her, and she trembled with the delight of it, the promise it bespoke.

"You are my beloved, Esther," he said deliberately as though to impress the fact upon her. "I love you as I love life, Esther Wheeler."

"Oh, Savage," she breathed against his lips, "and I love you."

He kissed her then, and she was lost in the wonder of being with him, of having his strength to stand guard over her, of seeing the gray of his eyes turn from cold granite to warm blue-gray, shining with his love. With him, she knew she would never have to face the world alone again.

For one moment more, she kept the other thought at bay, kept him close to her, kept their love whole around her. But Running Elk's face would not be put aside. It rose before her in all its dark intensity, blotting out Savage.

She stirred and he held her away from him. "What's the matter?" he asked sharply. Then, without waiting for her reply, his voice softened. "I know you have been through much, but you're safe now. Let me do the worrying for a while."

She turned from his arms, and the fear flooded back, draining her, pulsing through her. "Savage, Running Elk won't give up until he's found me. He's a dangerous man, clever and ruthless when he wants something."

"So am I," Savage said, a harsh edge in his voice.

Esther saw the truth of his words born in the change that instantly came over him. His eyes turned cold and deadly under slitted lids, his face again assumed the hardened planes and angles of a killer, and it frightened her.

Then, like a chameleon and as quickly, he again made himself gentle for her. "I must settle one thing before we move on in the morning. Will you marry me?" His voice was soft, but the intensity told her how much her answer meant to him.

"Oh, my dearest, I can't imagine living without you as my husband." She drew his head down once more and kissed him.

They held each other so for long moments. Then, weary from the long days of strain, they slept.

Chapter Fourteen

The autumn air, crisp and cold, flowed past them in a gentle morning breeze. A bright blue sky with only a few straggling dark clouds was all that remained of yesterday's storm. Outside the cave, the prairie stretched in the distance, black and lifeless, as far as the eye could see.

"What is your plan?" Esther asked, scanning the horizon in all directions.

Savage leaned with his forearms resting on his saddle horn, using his thumb to push back his hat, and let his eyes drift to the north. "We have two choices, maybe three, as I see it. We can keep on north, hope to find a late wagon train with someone to marry us. We can go east and get married at the first settlement we come to. Or we can turn south for Santa Fe. Your decision."

"South is Comanche and Apache country. That would be too dangerous, even if we weren't trying to avoid Running Elk. East means civilization, and one thing this adventure has taught me is that I'm not cut out for settlement living." She cocked her head at him. "You knew I'd choose the north, didn't you?"

He grinned a slow grin. "Hoped you would. North is Cheyenne territory, home to me. And I don't think it will be hard to waylay a train. There's always somebody along to do marrying."

"Then let's move out," she suggested. "I've been alone long enough."

With each passing day and no sign of Running Elk or the Comanche, Savage grew less tense. Finally, he agreed it was probably even safe to travel by daylight and, this morning, Esther was seeing for the first time the rugged mountains he had told her so much about. Distorted in a blue haze and at a distance of several days journey to the West, they still looked imposing.

"At the foot of yonder tallest peak, in the most beautiful canyon you ever laid your eyes on, I had a snug little cabin," he began softly as they stopped to rest the horses. "Had me a fine woman and two babies. Life was sweet and full of promise until five years ago. Came back from a hunting trip to find the Comanche on the warpath—" She listened as his voice grew as hard as the muscles in his clenched jaw. "Burned the cabin to the ground and killed my family. I rode in as they rode out. I won't rest until I get the Indian that did it."

"Do you know who it was?"

"I don't know his name, but I'll never forget his face. He turned around and we both got a good look at one another before he rode away."

"You mean a single warrior attacked your family?"

Savage nodded.

"Isn't that unusual?"

"I've thought a lot about that. But why he did it doesn't matter. He did it, ugly and brutal, and he's going to pay if it takes the rest of my life."

"Why did you wait until now to tell me about this?" Esther asked, bewildered. Then after thinking about Savage's omission for awhile, anger surged in her, and she flared at him. "Brook Savage!"

He turned to her, shock at her anger registering in his widened eyes.

"Hunting down a nameless Indian isn't how I want to spend my life. I love you, but not enough to watch you waste your life and mine on senseless revenge."

"Now wait a minute," he said in a smooth calming voice. "I didn't say I was going to make that my sole reason for living. Just that when the time comes right, I'll get him, and I thought you ought to know." His face paled in the bright sunlight and he looked weary.

"Hard thoughts are heavy burdens," Esther said with determined force. The weight of her words slammed against him and he moved out in front. She followed, still pondering his words. It wasn't right for a man to carry enough hate in his heart to kill with and yet, she didn't know what to do about it. This was something she was going to have to discuss with the Lord. In fact, they would probably have many discussions about this.

She and Savage rode in silence for some distance, then he turned, his face a mask, and asked, "Have you ever heard from your white family?"

His question caught her by surprise and she gulped. "No," she managed evenly. "When I was ransomed in New York, the officials said they would try to get word to my parents. They found out they both were dead, and nobody along the Blue River in Indiana knew what had happened to Saba and Phelan—but the one I really miss is my Aunt Mercy. She was more like a mother to me than Mama. Chances are she's dead, too. Twenty-four years is a long time."

"Two of a kind, aren't we? No family but each other." He reached out and took her hand. "I promise never to give you any cause to be sorry after we're married."

There it was again. She couldn't run from it this time. "You've made two promises today, Savage, and you can't keep them both. You have to give up your vow to kill the Comanche, or you will cause me sorrow."

He didn't look at her, but dropped her hand and rode on ahead. After a long time, he fell back and rose along beside her once more. "I can promise I won't go looking for him. But . . . if he comes across my path—" Savage paused to see how she was taking it—"I'll have to kill him. Something in me won't let him live after what he did to my family—" He flexed his jaw. "I can't let that . . . atrocity . . . go unpunished."

Perhaps the paths of the two men would never cross. She could always pray for that. "I don't like what you're saying, but I don't want to live without you either." Was she going to be sorry she didn't take a stand over this, make him promise to give up his vendetta? She wasn't sure she would win. He could possibly live his life without her. But, to her, life without Savage was unthinkable.

A slight smile altered his stern features. "Probably such a bad Indian, he's already been done away with by some enraged settler. The coward's bones have most likely been picked clean long ago by a flock of vultures."

"I can hope . . . and pray," she said softly.

They camped this night in a deep ravine and Esther felt safer than she had since the night in the cave. When an arrow hissed through the air and buried itself in the muscle of Savage's upper arm, he made no sound beyond a sharp grunt.

Shocked awake, she stifled a scream and crawled from her side of the flickering fire to where he lay. "Hold still. Let me see," she whispered.

"Leave it," he ordered in a low rumble, pain weakening the usually rich timbre of his voice. "Let him think he killed me. He'll come closer to have a look. Then I'll shoot the miserable cur."

"You could bleed to death before then."

Another arrow whirred through the silent night, landing just above Esther's head. Slowly, moving only her eyes, she looked around. "We're in deep shadows. I don't think anyone can see. I think they're shooting in the general direction of the horses and getting lucky."

"Any luckier, and we're going to be dead." Savage reached up and pulled the arrow out of the dirt.

Esther gasped and grabbed it from him. The base of the shaft was marked with two narrow red lines. "Running Elk! He's found us. This is his brand on the arrow."

"You're going to have to run for it!" Savage whispered to her. "I'll hold them off."

"No, you don't know how many are out there. I'm staying with you."

"I've had one woman cut to ribbons by Comanche, I'll not have another, no matter what the cost. You've got no chance at all if you stay." A tender look of pleading filled his eyes. "Please go."

"I can't leave you alone, wounded and helpless. Don't ask me to."

"Esther, listen to me. They don't do to men the things they do to women, you know that. This is our only chance to get out of here alive—" He grimaced with pain. "I have plenty of ammunition and water. They're not going to do anything until morning, so I can last until you bring help. If you ride straight to Bent's Fort, you'll be back long before things even get interesting."

"Well, I'm not going until I fix that arm."

He sighed. "You are a stubborn woman."

When she had broken off the shaft and pulled it through, she saw that the arrow had only grazed Savage's arm. He wasn't too badly hurt, and she offered continuous prayers of thanksgiving while she packed his wound with herbs she had brought with her in her flight.

"Cover your hair with my hat. That white mane of yours reflects moonlight as well as sunlight." He kissed her hard, letting his longing for her speak volumes. "Now, go!"

Esther clamped Savage's plains hat on her head and crawled to where the horses were tethered and still saddled. A few stray wisps of cloud briefly darkened the moon and, leading her horse by the reins, she set off in darkness through the night. The trail was too steep and treacherous to ride and, on foot, it seemed hours before she broke out on top and could mount up.

Once on horseback, she fled through the hollow of a hill, then struck out across the gently rolling plateau. The moon, though not full, still gave light enough to see by. The cool air of the night, the slow sweep of stars overhead, their slight swaying as she rose and fell in the pulsing rhythm of the gallop, reassured her, little by little.

She was going to get away and bring back help. She was. Glory be to God, she *was*! She gave the pony her head and they rode on like an arrow, straight and true. The hills swept by, an occasional tree whirred past, the pounding hooves of the pony struck sparks from the rocks, here and there.

When, at last, she could feel the sorrel's sides heave in great waves as she sucked in air and her head bobble slightly, Esther knew the pony was used up. She pulled in on the reins. Gradually, the little animal's stride slowed from a full gallop to a stumbling walk. It was then Esther heard the beat of hooves well behind her. Her heart stopped. Had Savage made a break for it and followed her? Inside, she laughed bitterly at her wishful thinking.

Perhaps it hadn't been Running Elk following them, after all. It could be a bunch of renegades. But if so, she was in worse trouble. How did they get Running Elk's arrows? The only obvious answer was that they had killed him and taken them. Fear pounded in her head and dried her mouth. She must find a place to hide and find it quickly.

A small thicket appeared ahead. Probably growing around a spring, she thought. It would have to do. There was nothing else on the flat rolling landscape to offer any kind of protection.

As Esther rode closer, she heard the trickle of water. Dismounting, on moccasined feet she walked silently until she found a small stream that pooled itself conveniently in the lap of a sunken boulder, well hidden by a tangle of brush. Esther led the horse inside the willows and tethered him. Looking and waiting, she listened intently to see if she really was being followed, or if what she had heard was only the product of an active imagination. Though she heard nothing more, that gave her no comfort.

They both drank, Esther and the pony, letting the cool liquid ease down and relieve raw parched throats. Making no sound, she stood against the animal and listened again. If there had been hoofbeats, they had stopped. There was no sound except the occasional howl of a wolf, lonely and far away.

At last, she slowly sank to the ground and rested her head on a stump-sized rock. The fright gradually drained away and, exhausted, she nodded, almost asleep, until something startled her wide awake. She listened, holding her breath, but the only sounds close by were the pony's breathing. Yet, she felt warned of danger, as though an invisible guard posted near her had heard what her sleep-dulled senses had failed to register.

Fear gripped her again, rendering her immobile, a motionless statue. She raised her head a bit at a time. And then she saw an indefinable form glide through the shadows straight toward her. On all fours, it was impossible for her to distinguish what or who it was. Too late to run, she clenched her fists and waited, a cold smear of perspiration beading on her forehead and in the palms of her icy hands.

She didn't stir, didn't move a muscle. Even the pony seemed to know something was amiss, for he stopped eating the tender ends of the willows and stood, unmoving.

Without warning, a hand dropped like a mask over her face, a hard, damp hand like cold stone. Her jaws locked. She could neither move nor cry out. For the tenth part of a second she prayed it was Savage, then the familiar scents of smoke, rancid grease, and sweat told her it was not. His other hand, with fingers like steel thongs, pulled her up hard against his tall lean figure and held her so tightly she could barely drag in enough air to keep from fainting. As she weakened, she felt the grip loosen and he spun her around and dropped his smothering grip.

Running Elk! How had he known where to find her? Had he killed Savage? She refused to consider that possibility. Other questions darted through her head like bats in the twilight, but she didn't dare ask.

"I am sorry I frightened you," he said surprisingly tenderly. "I did not know it was you for sure. With your hair covered and dressed in buckskins, you looked like a man. I have come to take you home." He spoke without rancor.

Esther did not know how to answer. But she must deal with him honestly. Best to get it over with, cut quick and clean like a sharp knife. "Running Elk, the White Eyes did not capture me. I willingly went with him. I love him."

The only indication that Running Elk had even heard her was a slight narrowing of his eyes. "You are mine. I gave many horses to Makes Medicine for you. He is white, you are Indian. He cannot make you happy."

"Please, Running Elk, you have been very good to me and I care greatly for you, like a sister for a brother. But it is Savage I love."

"You cannot be sure of that. Away from here, you will forget him and be happy with the People." He untied the reins of her horse and took her by the wrist. "Come, you walk first. I will come behind and lead your horse." He continued to talk to her smoothly, gently, as one would quiet a startled animal.

She obeyed, not wanting to inflame his wrath, but her brain struggled desperately. She must think of a way to escape and get on to Bent's Fort. Other people had been in situations as desperate as this and devised ways out. She had to think, keep calm and think. *Please Lord, let me know a plan that I may save Savage and escape from Running Elk. And let there be no bloodshed.*

From behind, Running Elk directed her over the prairie, first to the left, then to the right, until they came to another clump of trees. Tethered inside were three magnificent horses. She immediately recognized the one wearing a saddle as Raven. The other two carried small packs. She brushed an aimless hand against Raven's shoulder, rippling and hard with muscles.

"What do you plan to do?" she asked, facing Running Elk.

"Does this man you call Savage love you, also?" Running Elk asked with a serious face.

"Yes, he does."

"And you find only the love of a brother for me?"

"You know I find you very dear. But I cannot make my heart feel what it will not."

Slowly, he nodded. "If that is all you have in your heart to give, I will not ask more. Someday, perhaps, you will come to love me as a woman loves a man. I can wait. These last days have shown me I cannot live without you. Even the crumbs of your affection will serve to keep me warm."

Esther started to speak, but the hard look in his eyes silenced her.

"We will lay a trail that Savage will have to follow."

Her heart leaped with gladness that her beloved was alive, then Esther frowned as the meaning of Running Elk's words came clear. "You are using me to bait a trap for him?"

"You will never love me while he is alive."

"And I will never love you if you kill him."

"It will be a fair fight. The victor will have you for himself."

"Running Elk, that is barbaric!" she exploded. "I will not be the spoils won in battle."

He looked with great tolerance at her. "You have no choice."

"Savage will not come after me," she said, gambling that perhaps he would stay put until she and Running Elk were too far away to track.

The corner of his mouth lifted, and fine lines of amusement deepened around his eyes, telling her how ridiculous he thought her words. "If this is a real man who loves you, nothing will keep him from tracking you for as long as it takes to get you back. He is going to come in a rage, blaming himself for letting you go for help. Oh, yes, my beautiful Esther, he will come. And his rage will be grand to behold!"

Chapter Fifteen

Late in the afternoon, Esther and Running Elk came off the shoulder of the plateau and saw before them the western pass between granite peaks. The walls stood close together on either side, making a thin slit in the mountain. As they entered the pass, Esther had the feeling they crossed a threshold over which neither of them might ever return.

They rode slowly, Running Elk making no attempt to cover their tracks until they came to the creek. From the upper rim of the nearly sheer walls of the canyon it had cut, they looked up and out across naked rock. With difficulty now, for the stream descended rapidly through a series of box canyons, they followed it down from the pass.

Esther would never have guessed it possible, but they worked their way down one after another of the precipitous walls that bordered the creek until, in the canyon below, they came to fine level meadows and groves of lofty pines. Some of these great ancient trees, their fragrance released by the day's heat, lifted their dark green heads above the top of the valley walls.

Esther drew in a sharp breath of delighted surprise at the scene spread before her. A cool green valley rested, gem-like, in a setting of ragged mountains and blue strand of river that flowed through its length. Though she was touched by the view, it was the sound that held her conscious attention. It hung continually in her ears, at first only a thin murmur in the distance, growing deeper, fuller like the deep rumble of drums or the trampling of thousands of buffalo in stampede as they drew near.

Running Elk turned to her. "At the other end of the valley, the river drops in a small rapids, pauses a moment on a wide rock ledge, then falls a great distance."

Esther nodded her acknowledgment. "It grows dark. Is it safe to travel this canyon in so little light?"

"Only a little farther, then you will see."

They rounded a protruding rock and came into a spacious canyon spread with a carpet of thick grass, interrupted by small groves of tall trees. In a gap in the trees stood a log cabin, the sawed ends of unpeeled logs still showing traces of unweathered yellow. Esther's heart leaped. People! Perhaps she could tell someone her plight and they could help her. Slowly, she shook her head. For the sake of the occupants, she should pray that the cabin was empty. In Running Elk's present mood, he would be more likely to kill them for sport.

They hid the horses well back among the trees. "Will you go with me as an Indian, or run screaming a warning as a White Eyes?" he tested.

Here it was again. Would she always have to face this question? How comforting it must be to have clear, undivided loyalties, never to question which side was right, never to know the torment of being torn between two worlds. Would she ever have even a measure of peace? She would not warn the people, she told him, and prayed no one was home.

Running Elk led the way, his noiseless steps pressing down the pine needles without so much as a whisper. Cautiously Esther followed him, taking care that her feet fell in the same spots, across the open ground and into the grove of smaller trees that surrounded the house.

Without challenge, the two of them emerged into the clearing where the cabin stood and found that the cleared area continued, unobstructed, to the edge of the river. Here, the water seemed to slow and widen, creating a calm surface that reflected the gold of evening. Close to the shore, however, the current constricted in a narrow channel and poured with undisguised speed toward the unseen cataract.

Part of the shoreline was clear of brush, forming a small beach where a small canoe rested, turned bottom-side up. A pile of rugged rocks thrust up close to where the trees began again. A perfect place to keep watch, Esther thought.

Fading off into the trees on their left, they continued on toward the cabin. Running Elk held his rifle, Joseph's rifle, and motioned for Esther to look in the windows of the one-room cabin. Crouching along the wall, she crept up and peered in. She could see only shadowy forms of furniture. The room was empty, she signed to him.

Slowly, they inched their way around to the front door that faced toward the water. Stationing himself on one side of the door and her on the other, he nodded for her to lift the latch. With fingers numb and rigid with fear, she grasped the latch and raised it. The door creaked open, the sound drowning out even the roaring of the falls in Esther's ears. Frozen, she hugged the wall until Running Elk dashed inside waving his rifle.

She could hear him poking around, then he stuck his head outside. "It is empty. Come in."

Still unsure, she stepped into the doorway and surveyed the small room. Even in the afterglow, she could see the furnishings, sparse but neat. She ran her finger over the table to test for dust. There was only a thin covering. She eyed the cold fireplace.

"Do you want a fire?" she asked and picked up the poker.

Indecision flickered in Running Elk's face.

"If we are being followed, and I doubt it," she reasoned, "you have the advantage of being inside the cabin. Unless the owner returns and becomes unhappy at our presence in his home, I don't know why we should not be comfortable."

"You have a silver tongue, Golden One. Build your fire."

It took little to shave some wood curls and place on some wood from a neat stack at the side of the rock fireplace. Soon the fire crackled and cast flickering light through the room.

A narrow bed stood against the far wall, covered with a neatly spread khaki blanket. The earthen floor pounded hard was swept, but bare except for a small, round rag rug next to the bed. A plain undecorated washstand held a thick crockery bowl and pitcher, empty of water now. In the center stood a small square table with two chairs drawn up across from each other. An unlit lamp filled with oil waited in the center of the table to be lit. The most uncommon thing, however, was a small shelf of books on the wall above the bed. Whoever lived here was a person of exceptional taste.

"I will bring the horses up and stake them behind the cabin. When Savage comes, he will not see them," Running Elk said.

"You are so sure he will come. I do not think he will."

Running Elk gave her a disdainful look. "If you speak true and he loves you, he will come. Nothing will keep him from you, just as nothing has prevented my tracking you to the ends of the earth to reclaim you. He and I think much alike."

Without reply, she gathered the water pail from inside the door and followed Running Elk out, each attending to their separate errands.

The fire blazed warm and cheerful, and Esther raked some coals to the outside and set a spider to heat. From the supplies in the packs, she set out the makings of fry bread, but before she began, something drew her to the doorway. Looking out, she watched Running Elk mount the pile of rocks. Then he sat absolutely still, the rifle resting across his knees. The last golden rays of daylight played over his magnificent body and turned him to bronze. The only movement was his lone eagle feather riffling slightly in the evening breeze, From the top of the rock heap he could survey the upper reaches of the river, the clearing, and the cabin itself.

In spite of herself, Esther looked on him with an odd feeling of admiration and awe comingled—admiration for his steadfast devotion to those for whom he felt affection, and awe for the lengths to which he would go to preserve his extended family. He frightened her much of the time, for he hardly seemed human, moving soundlessly, appearing like an apparition out of nowhere, looking so fierce in his war paint.

She sensed the man before she saw his shadow glide, unveering as a compass point to north, across the clearing toward the rocks and Running Elk. *Savage!* She slammed her fist against her mouth to stifle a cry as Running Elk leaped up with a shout and dropped back out of sight among the rocks of the stone heap.

Savage, as though at a signal, sprinted straight forward. Esther clasped her throat and hugged herself to still the trembling. Stripped to the waist, he attacked Running Elk, though she could see no sign of a weapon as he raced toward the warrior.

Running Elk's rifle rang out. Esther shuddered and half-closed her eyes. When she recovered enough to look again, she saw that Savage had not fallen. Instead, he sprinted on until he crouched in the shelter of the steep-sided rocks to catch his breath.

Then, barehanded, Savage swarmed over the barrier with the sure-footedness of a panther on toward where Running Elk waited, armed. The rifle spoke again. Esther shut her eyes and with her knuckles pressed her lips against her teeth to drive back the screams. At such close range, it was impossible for Running Elk to miss.

Hearing nothing, she squinted again at the scene. Savage was still working his way toward the crest of the rocks. Running Elk must not have had a chance to properly load and aim the rifle. She knew he longed for his reliable bow and arrows strapped securely to Raven's saddle. With them, there would have been no missing, and Savage would be dead.

The man was mad to expose himself like that. A few more inches, and he would be in full view of Running Elk. One well-placed bullet . . . Esther dared not think, dared not imagine the burning passion that had mastered Savage, whipped him into such a state.

His towering rage was not spawned by any treatment she had received at Running Elk's hands, for Savage knew that the chief had never been anything but kind to her. Some unspoken fire must burn deep inside him, a driving flame that Savage believed only Running Elk's violent death would quench.

A dark outline rose up on top of the rocks, silhouetted a moment against the turquoise of the darkening sky, then Running Elk's powerful figure joined Savage. The two grappled fiercely, twisting and turning, roaring and snarling above the sound of the falls like two maddened lions. She could not even guess which throat uttered which sound, they were so much alike.

Forward and backward, the closely entangled bodies swayed, and then she saw them lean out, stagger, and fall down the sheer face of the rock into the current of the river!

Unable to stand the uncertainty, Esther threw caution to the wind and dashed across to the clearing. Rounding the side of the rock, she expected to see them both knocked senseless. To her amazement, she found them still struggling. Even in the icy water, as the swift current swept them downstream, they fought, twisting over and under the water, rising to surface and hammer at each other again.

It was as if two mountain lions had gripped one another, and rather than relinquish the win to the other, would allow themselves to be swept to their deaths.

And death lay straight ahead for them both.

Perhaps a hundred feet below the rock, the river disappeared into a raging cataract. Here the water dashed around and over sharp rocks, dove into pools, and swirled out again to pound itself into white foam against more rocks lower down. It was sufficient to grind life from even the strongest.

Paying the danger no heed, the pair, ignoring the current and their impending doom, struggled on. Esther raced ahead and stood at the verge of the plummeting water, looking in horror at the arching water, felt the spray fly against her face, heard the hungry roar pour upward and fill her ears with a death chant.

"Savage!" she screamed. "Running Elk!" Her words, battered and distorted by the river's fury, fell impotent at her feet.

Just above the brink of the falls was a foam-rimmed shoal in the middle of the current. Somehow the two struggling figures were thrown up on it. They rose up out of the water, boiling about their knees, and weaved uncertainly as they stood on the slick rocks. If they took even one step and staggered in the slightest, they would be swept over the precipice. The river pulled and churned around them, struggling to carry them down.

But they fought on, heedless of the danger. Death was in their hearts, one for the other, and it left no room for fear or mercy.

Esther stood watching the fighters twist and turn, grappling, swaying, first one giving, then the other. Reason fled as she watched and her heart spoke. She must try to stop them, and she waded in. When the cold water reached her waist, she sucked in her breath.

Savage was the first to spot her. A look of terror rearranged his features as he froze. Seeing his opponent stricken, Running Elk's gaze followed and registered a similar emotion as he watched Esther struggle toward them.

The men let go each other and reached to drag her up on the shoal.

The first to regain his voice, Savage screamed at her. "What in the name of all that's holy are you doing? You want to get yourself killed?"

"What is life without you in it?" she gasped out. "One of you will not leave this place alive. Maybe both of you!"

"You don't understand!" Savage shouted, turning to face Running Elk. "This is the man who killed my wife and babies! He didn't wait until I was around to make it a fair fight. He came while I was away hunting and butchered 'em. Their bodies are buried right over there—" Savage clenched his fists and pointed to the copse of trees behind the cabin.

So Savage had lived here. This was his home.

Then he spat his contempt of Running Elk. "I swore I'd kill the man who did those things. It's taken me five years to find you, Running Elk, to be sure it was you who slaughtered helpless women and children—"

Esther felt the color drain from her face and her stomach rolled over. A slow sick horror rose inside and filled her. In her short time with the Comanche, she had seen such attacks as Savage had described, but she also had seen what white men could do to Indian villages.

"I can understand Savage's hatred, though I do not approve," she told Running Elk in her limited Comanche. "But why do you fight *him* with such venom?" she demanded. "I know there is something more than your attraction to me."

Running Elk's face twisted into a grimace of defiance. He spoke in clipped sentences, making his meaning clear with signs and gestures. "We were hungry. The buffalo did not come and we had to hunt far from our usual places, too close to White Eye settlements. We left the main camp and made a small camp closer to the buffalo, but the White Eyes watched our camp. When they were sure all the warriors were gone, they attacked. There were only seven warriors in the camp. The rest were old men, boys, women, and children. The White Eyes were not content to kill those in the camp, they ruined all the meat, too. Many more of the People died of hunger that winter, slain as truly as if White Eyes had taken knives to their throats."

Esther felt the blood rush from her head, and she swayed. "Were you there?" she asked Savage in a thick voice.

"I was not there," he snorted. "Though the Cheyenne are enemies of the Comanche, I would not commit such a coward's act."

Running Elk did not waver in the intensity of his speech. "When I returned from the hunt, I found all my family dead. My mother . . . my bride of a few weeks—" He paused, shaken by the gruesome memory. "In grief, we rode out, scouring the countryside for any White Eyes we could find. We killed and killed. I do not know where or who." He turned for the first time and lifted glazed eyes to Savage. "I do not remember ever being here before."

Savage stared back. "I don't believe you. You came to this spot today straight as an arrow. You did kill my family, and you remember it. And just as surely, I will kill you."

Esther grabbed Savage's arm and looked full into his face. "Have you ever deliberately killed a man?"

"In war, a few, and I've shot some Comanche and Sioux."

"But not this way. Not toe to toe, with your bare hands, strangling the life from a man."

"No. I've been lucky."

Her eyes widened in surprise. "*Lucky*! You say you are lucky because you have not killed a man in cold blood. How strange to put it that way."

"And why do you think it isn't luck?"

The cold from the water began seeping into her bones. Through chattering teeth, she said, "It could be compassion. It could be righteousness."

A violent laugh exploded from Savage.

"I noticed the Bible on your bookshelf. I think your luck is conscience. Thou shalt not kill!" She dropped her hold on his arm. "Savage, if you do this thing, it will be murder. You will live with murder in your heart, a useless murder that will not bring back your wife or your children."

She turned to Running Elk, speaking haltingly in his tongue. "And killing Savage will not bring back your bride. This barbaric act will accomplish nothing for either of you."

Savage leaned toward her slightly. Without touching her, he searched her face. Esther filled her eyes with all the pleading in her soul, her lips trembling with her desire to speak the words that would free him from his vow.

"You don't understand. You can't know what was done to her, to my children. The mutilation—"

Then Running Elk exploded. "Shall we compare torture for torture, that of the heathen Indian against the civilized White Eyes? Strange that *you* are the man called Savage."

Savage looked at Running Elk. "I will not change my mind. I searched until I found the man who took his vengeance on my family. You could have done likewise. But, instead, you spilled the blood of innocent people. For that, Running Elk, I will kill you."

Each word Savage spoke dropped like chips of ice into Esther heart. "That is your last word?" she asked.

He nodded.

"Then, hear me well. If you do this thing, I cannot marry you. This thing that has no righteousness in it would always stand between us. There is not enough love in any marriage to live with murder. If you love me—" Her voice filled with anguish so deep she could not continue for a moment. She drew herself tall and held rigid against the pounding of the current against her thighs. "Love," she said and her voice broke, "love ought to guide you."

Savage did not move. His shoulders grew slack as with a heavy burden, and a tired look swept his face. When he spoke, his lips moved stiffly. Esther could not tell if it was from cold or emotion.

"I wish it could be different." He gazed at Running Elk's limp figure, for the moment drained of fury. "He understands and would do the same in my place."

Running Elk nodded. "We will not fight more in your presence, but Savage is right. It must be done."

She looked helplessly from one to the other. "You are crazy, both of you. You do not want to kill each other . . . and yet you will." The pain of it at last crumpled her, and she fell sobbing onto the wet rock.

Savage fought upstream against the current and onto the bank. Finding a rope from his pack, he cast it to Running Elk who tied it around Esther's waist. With Running Elk to guide her and Savage to man the rope, they made it safely to shore.

With scarcely any effort, Running Elk picked her up and carried her to the cabin. Savage produced a towel while Running Elk built up the fire. Numbly, she watched Savage turn back the covers on the cot, and both men left the room. Struggling, she stepped out of the soggy buckskins. She toweled dry and slipped between clean blankets.

Exhaustion quickly overtook her, but her last conscious thoughts were of two men working together to save her life. How was it that they could still plan to fight to the death tomorrow? One thing Esther knew for a certainty. She would not be here to witness it.

Chapter Sixteen

When Esther awoke the next morning, she realized that it had not been early enough. In the first light, she could see fresh clothes laid over a chair—a pair of Savage's buckskin leggings, a shirt she recognized as Running Elk's, and a pair of knee-high fringed moccasins she had left in the village. She tried to imagine Running Elk slipping past Savage, into the cabin, and carefully, lovingly placing her things on the chair.

Maybe they had already had their fight and Running Elk had won!

Throwing back the blankets, she leaped to her feet. The air was unnaturally warm, and she looked at the fireplace. A small fire burned quietly on the hearth, enough to take the chill from the room, and on hot coals at the side of the fire box, a pot of water steamed. When she approached it, there on the table sat a tin plate, the kind Savage carried. On it were two biscuits and a rounded heap of blackberries for her breakfast.

Her heart raced, pulsing blood into her temples so that she could scarcely hear or see. Savage was not dead! Had they, during the night, worked out their differences, called a truce? Were they now friends? Though that was highly unlikely, Esther still prayed so as she quickly washed and dressed.

She looked a moment at the food, considering it, but her throat constricted and she knew nothing would go down. Opening the silent, now-oiled door, she stepped into the morning and looked upriver across the clearing.

Like duelists, they faced each other.

A chill dawn mist rose off the river, coiled around and through the dark branches of the guardian pines. The dawn sky turned pearly as the sun washed the darkness away, and the dark river hissed along its channel as it hurried into foaming ruin over the cataract.

The two men, stripped to breechclouts and armed with knives, stood slightly crouched, taking the measure of each other.

Esther's Indian upbringing took over. Though thoroughly confused by the scene she had awakened to, she well understood what was happening at this moment. Having made a truce earlier to care for her, they were now going to continue their duel to the death, the duel she had only succeeded in delaying last night.

They had certainly chosen the best time of day for it. The sun, not up yet, would not shine in a man's eyes and the air, still crisp from the cool of the night, kept a man's senses sharp and alert.

Slowly, they circled. Savage stood, balanced on the balls of his feet, his right hand holding his knife waist-high, his left hand stretched out to the side, the fingers spread slightly, the hand weaving in small circles. He shifted lightly in response to Running Elk's movements, circled one slow step at a time, moving sideways, keeping just out of reach, then back to the other side, stepping as gracefully as a ballet dancer.

Hugging the wall of the cabin, Esther wanted to run, to leave forever this place of death, but she could not move. Deliberately, she was being drawn into their battle until it seemed she became a part of their circle, found her body moving slightly with the rhythm of their maneuvering. A rhythm as strong and irresistible as if it were being guided by drums.

Strange, but she did not feel hatred flowing between the two men. Not like last night when the air hung thick enough to taste, permeated with their hostility. Esther scrutinized the scene through narrowed eyes, but with surprising calm, her head to one side, as she tried to understand. Involuntarily she licked her lips to taste the air. It held only the scents of autumn—leaves colored and falling, the last berries ripening, the touch of smoke from the fire inside. Downwind from the men, there should have been something radiating from them—hate, fear, anger.

When the reality hit her, she rocked slightly. They did not want to fight each other! Somewhere between last night and now, they had lost their hatred, their desire for vengeance. Savage and Running Elk were only going through the motions, trapped, not knowing how to renounce their vows and still save face.

Esther passed her hand over her brow and shut her eyes. Stopping them was up to her, and she had not the faintest idea how to go about it. *Help me to know, dear Lord,* she pleaded.

At a slight shuffling sound, her eyes flew open. A blade streaked out like the tongue of a snake, and the tip pricked Savage's arm, drawing blood. Esther clapped both hands over her mouth to smother the scream rising inside.

Slowly, the two warriors continued to circle, then a brief glitter, and a small stream of blood trickled over Running Elk's chest.

Think, Esther, think! You must think of something and be quick about it. Lord, where are you? What am I to do?

All the beginning feints were made, and both men had drawn blood. Having taken the measure of each other, what came now would be final.

Running Elk shuffled around an imaginary pivot point. Savage followed him. The Comanche warrior feinted, then leaned in quickly, his knife ripping upward in a strong, swift motion. Savage knocked the glittering blade away, and Esther watched Running Elk draw in his breath, saw the knife flash briefly as he bent to recover it. Then, he stepped forward and thrust, narrowly missing Savage's thigh.

She could watch no more. Her mind, numb with despair, refused to conjure up a way out for Savage and Running Elk, and she could hear no directions in her heart from the Lord. The two people she loved most on this earth were intent on killing each other, and she was helpless to stop them.

For the first time, she understood the Indian custom of chopping off a finger to ease the pain of grief. Any kind of physical pain right now would have been welcome. It could not begin to hurt with the intensity of the clawing, tearing, shredding her spirit and heart were experiencing.

Their total concentration on each other made Running Elk and Savage oblivious to anything beyond their circle. With the mist still shrouding the clearing, she easily made her silent way to where the horses were tethered. It wasn't until Esther brushed her face as she reached into a pack for food and felt her damp cheeks that she realized she was crying.

She had not felt this lost and lonely since she was six and had awakened in the bottom of a canoe, an Indian captive, realizing she would never see her family again.

Making no effort to stem the flow, tears dripped off her jaw and wide splotches spread across the delicate dress. Esther didn't care. She really wanted to die. Then she looked at trembling fingers fumbling to tie food and water to her saddle and knew that wasn't true. She wanted desperately to live, and she wanted both Savage and Running Elk alive, too, unharmed and forgiving.

As she led her horse along a faint path away from the river, she came to three graves marked with freshly painted white crosses. He had done that this morning.

Kneeling, she read the inscriptions. This was the resting place of Savage's wife and two sons. Would there be another grave in the small plot by tonight? A family united in death?

No longer able to hold back the sobs, Esther rested her head on the larger cross and cried, deep, wrenching sobs that shook her body and tore at her throat.

Men! They were the most impossible creatures on this earth. Whatever had God been thinking of when He created the unreasonable things? There was no understanding them and no way to stop loving them.

Wiping at the decreasing flood, Esther mounted the patient little pony and continued on along the shadow of a trail nearly invisible in the mist. This must be the way Savage had come last night. When she and Running Elk had arrived at the cabin, she knew there surely had to be an easier trail than the one he led them down yesterday.

Breaking free of the trees, Esther could see a switch-back trail along the face of the mountain. The horse, sure-footed and sturdy, climbed up out of the autumn-touched valley. Though she could see for miles, she forbade herself to look down into the clearing. She had enough terrible memories. She didn't need to see one of the dueling pair lying on the ground, his bright shining life draining away in a river of red pooling at the feet of the victor.

She meant it when she had said she loved Running Elk like a brother. But Savage—he was different. She loved him as a man, deeply. She had trusted him completely. How could he throw away their life together in order to satisfy a futile grudge, one he no longer even cared about? Her head hurt from trying to understand.

Stopping her horse on the rim of the canyon, she put all her frustration, grief, rage, and love into a chilling Delaware war whoop. It rang through the canyon, echoed over the roar of the falls, drifted over the clearing. Again Esther let the cry rip from her throat, sat ramrod-straight, staring across the canyon to the west. Then, still without looking down to the valley and clearing below, she turned east toward the prairie.

Unable to bear more grief now, she shut down her mind and sat huddled in the saddle, mute and staring, just riding.

Esther rode like this through the day, some of the time letting the horse have its head, at other times coming to life and in a frenzy of grief, galloping over the canyon-cut plateau like a person crazed.

In the late afternoon the sky clouded over and, with the coming of night and no moon, it grew too dark to safely travel longer in unfamiliar territory. Hearing water, she searched until she saw a glint through the trees and rode up to a pool of clear water.

With a weary sigh, she slid from the saddle and let the tired horse drink. Then she knelt on the stiff dry grass beside the pool. After drinking and splashing the cool water over her burning face, she felt better. Not enough, however, to be hungry. She tethered the horse on a long rope and spread a blanket on the ground under some scrubby evergreens. She took another to spread over herself. Crawling between the scratchy wool, she longed for the soothing fur of the wildcat skin under her saddle. But, if necessary, she wanted the horse ready to ride immediately. With a deep sad sigh, she curled into a ball, more miserable than she had ever been in her life.

God, I've been praying all day and You haven't heard a word I've said. Please, help me. Help them. Let me know You are listening. I can't stand being cut off from You this way. Esther continued to plead for guidance and couldn't remember when the words stopped going around inside her head.

Shocked awake by the thunderous blast of cold wind-whipped rain slamming into her, she sat bolt upright and denied at first that she had slept. Shaking her head to clear it, she wrapped the blanket more tightly around herself and huddled against the storm.

Icy rain puddled around her until she was thoroughly soaked. *Might as well ride,* she decided. *It won't be as miserable as sitting here without shelter.*

The blanket on the ground was too heavy with water for her to lift and she left
⁀he struggled into the saddle, keeping the other blanket for protection,

though it dripped its burden of rain. Grateful she had left the horse saddled, she rode into the black of the storm.

Having no destination, she gave the horse his head. The Arabian was strong and plodded on gallantly even when the sodden ground slipped treacherously away beneath his hooves. Despair beat against her more fiercely than the rain. Her mind backtracked to the canyon. Had she done right to leave? Maybe if she had stayed . . . *Esther, you could do nothing. Now, stop thinking. You will surely go mad if you don't. If you believe in the Lord, really believe, you are going to place this whole sorry mess in His hands. He is the only one who can solve it.*

Strangely, the listless non-caring eased away and, when dawn finally lightened the sky, Esther found herself straining to see, straining until her eyes ached. What or who was she looking for? Why did she think those two unreasonable men would stop fighting and come looking for her? *Esther, stop! You promised yourself and the Lord not to consider that subject further.*

Wrapped in the cold, sodden blanket and soaked to the skin, Esther began to shiver and her teeth started to chatter. The longer she rode, the more intensely she shook. Then, when the chills became almost unbearable, she began to grow drowsy. Her breathing became shallow and she felt light-headed. Swaying in the saddle, she caught herself just before she slid off. Finally the effort to ride was too much, and exhausted, she kicked free of the stirrups. Numb with cold, she hardly felt the jar as she hit the ground.

Instinctively she curled into a ball and drifted away to a sandy bank by a gentle stream, a place where the sun shone hot and bright, warming her. She sighed with contentment and slept.

Savage let the tears course down his cheeks. In the dark and mixed with rain, Running Elk would never notice, so Savage made no effort to stem the flow. *Oh, God, let Esther be alive!* His mind cried words he hadn't thought to use in five years, years in which he had led a godless life. How dare he call on God now?

He looked helplessly across the rain-drenched plateau, the blackness shattered by the blue-white flashes of lightning, casting a brief eerie, unholy glow over the bleak landscape. There was nowhere else to turn. He and Running Elk had ridden for miles, but the rain had washed away any trace of Esther's horse. The farther they rode, the more intense grew the foreboding that something had happened to her.

He felt and could almost see her hovering between life and death. If they delayed much longer, she would be dead.

Dawn brought with it no sun, only a half-lit world dissolved into distorted shapes by the ceaseless rain. A quick look at Running Elk showed his agony in the twisted features of his face. He was crying, too, and making no more effort to hide it than Savage was.

The depth of despair that flooded Savage now was unlike any he had ever encountered. When he found his family dead, he felt guilt and grief, but there was nothing he could do to bring them back. This trek was different. Esther still lived . . . if they could but reach her in time.

"Running Elk, there has to be a clue," Savage signed, "something we're missing." He roared into the morning, giving vent to the anguish building in his heart. Then, before Running Elk could answer, they both spotted the mud-encrusted blanket hugging the ground.

The two men wheeled off their horses and crouched over the indistinct tracks of Esther's horse. In the rain-softened earth, the big stallion had left pock marks now filled with water. Leaping onto their horses, Savage and Running Elk hung out of their saddles, riding beside tracks that wandered aimlessly away from the blanket.

It was the better part of an hour before they saw the riderless horse standing in the distance, silhouetted against the dark sky. Though it went against every instinct, Savage kept reminding himself not to push his horse too hard in the unstable ground, and Running Elk took the same precaution. It would do Esther no good if they were injured and unable to reach her.

A soft, nervous nicker of welcome from Esther's horse was answered by the approaching ponies. It wasn't until they were nearly upon the pony that they saw an irregular heap on the ground, wrapped in a sodden, muddied blanket. The faithful animal was standing over Esther, making an effort to shield her body from the storm.

Both men leaped from their horses and raced to where Esther lay. "We've got to have a fire," Savage signed and shouted over the storm at Running Elk.

Running Elk nodded his understanding and Savage gave no more thought to him. *Dear Lord, don't let her be dead,* he pleaded as he stripped the blanket back. *Please don't let her be dead.*

His fingers felt her throat for a heartbeat and found a thin, reedy pulse. Her breath was irregular and shallow. "She's alive!" he shouted to Running Elk. Then, gently, Savage picked up the limp body.

"Bring her over here!" Running Elk answered back.

Savage slipped and slid his way toward a small shelter Running Elk had hastily constructed of oiled skins.

"I cannot make a fire in this rain," Running Elk moaned. "What do we do for warmth? She will die soon without it."

Savage stripped the wildcat skin from Esther's horse and shook off the water. He wrapped it around her, fur-side out. The shelter wasn't big enough to shelter them all, so the two men knelt in the pouring rain and massaged the circulation back into her legs and arms.

At last, the storm roared over and beyond them, leaving a clear blue sky in the west and the promise of sun in a little while. The quiet after the fury was strange and terrifying, for now they could hear the pauses growing longer between Esther's gasping breaths.

Savage felt again for her pulse and found it weaker. "She's dying," he sobbed and made no effort to disguise it. He picked up her slight body, feather-light in his arms, as if the spirit that gave it grace and strength had already fled beyond them. He clasped her to him, sobbing as he had never done, seeing the years without her stretch out like black beads on an endless chain. They had had so little time together, had never shared a bed or fulfilled their love or brought children into the world. They would never grow old together—

Then an unreasoning fury filled him. "Esther!" he shouted at the top of his voice. "If you die on me, so help me, I'll—I'll finish the fight with Running Elk, slice him to ribbons, hang his hair out to dry, and marry his Comanche princess in your place. I swear I will, my beloved, I swear it!" The words issued forth in a babbling scream of rage, fear, and love so garbled they were barely understandable.

Esther, however, understood, for a ghost of a smile curved her still blue lips. Savage bent to hear her words, faint and slurred, "Then . . . you'd better . . . start collecting . . . horses—"

"Oh, God, thank you," he breathed. Cradling and rocking her slowly in his arms, he crooned to her as one would a baby until her breathing grew deeper, more regular and her pulsebeat stronger. Then, gently, he laid her down.

Savage felt Running Elk's eyes on them, heard the splashing in the puddles as the rain-soaked warrior came leading his horse up to the shelter. "It is time I go," he signed. "The Golden One has made her choice. Sometimes what is too near is not easily seen. The beautiful, loyal Star Flower waits for me, has always waited. I will go to her."

"You are a brave and wise man," Savage signed. "We will not fight again."

"I wish that were so, but with you leading the army to the Comanche, we will meet as enemies. The next time there will no Golden One to bring sense to our heads. We will kill each other, for I will never stop again until you are dead."

Savage eyed him through slitted eyes. Running Elk was right. If they ever met again, with Savage as an army scout, it would be a duel to the death. "You have nothing to fear from me, my brother. I will not lead the army to you and your people. I will not lead the army again, ever. I am taking Esther away from here to a place that will make her very happy."

Running Elk looked down into Esther's bloodless face. "If you can hear me, my Golden One, know that if you are ever in need I will know and I will come to you." He leveled a stunning look at Savage. "If you do not make her happy . . . I will meet you sometime, somewhere and you will pay."

The chief extended his hand. Savage grasped his wrist, and the two men welded a bond between brothers.

Then, like a graceful shadow, Running Elk sprang on his pony and was gone, the receding thuds of Raven's hooves sounding a melancholy tattoo over the deserted hills.

Chapter Seventeen

Staring back from the borrowed mirror was a stranger. She was dressed in white ruffles and a flowing veil, her ivory hair curled in ringlets and held at the sides with fashionable combs. But something was wrong.

Tears welled in the azure eyes. *This isn't me*! Esther wanted to shout, *I can't get married looking like this*! But seeing the glowing faces of the delighted women of the wagon train, she couldn't bring the words to her lips.

Riding northwest, she and Savage had found a late train along the Oregon Trail, as he had predicted they would. And traveling with the wagon train was a preacher, also predicted. What was not as easily foretold, however, was the enthusiasm with which the weary travelers had halted in their journey to help the young couple tie the knot. Eager for something to celebrate, the pioneers had circled their wagons and pooled their finery to make this a memorable wedding day for Esther and Savage.

Dear Lord, what am I to do? she moaned silently, regarding her reflection with anguish.

As if in answer to her prayer, a small girl stepped forward shyly and handed her a bouquet of prairie grasses and weeds, tastefully arranged inside a ring of evergreen sprigs. Following behind the child was the young mother, her eyes wide with worry.

"I'm Anne Conklin," she said, introducing herself. "I'm so sorry, but this is the best we could do. We couldn't find a flower blooming anywhere." Her eyes flew around the tent as she stiffened her back, bracing herself for the condemnation of the other women.

Before anyone could speak, however, Esther said, "This is a lovely bridal bouquet! I'm delighted. Thank you."

Anne and her daughter exchanged grateful smiles.

"Well, it certainly doesn't go with the rest of her lovely things," said the matriarch of the group, with an irritable snort.

"I have a solution for that," Esther put in. "Since there are no flowers to be had, I have something that will fit the bouquet."

Quickly, she removed the veil, stepped out of the layers of clothing, and ended with the removal of the high-heeled, pointed-toed shoes. With the shedding of each layer, the women's faces dropped a little until, by the time she had stripped away the last petticoat and stood in the fine muslin undergarments, they all looked thoroughly miserable.

"I know you think me ungrateful, but I am not used to such finery. I will be much more comfortable in my own clothes. In my pack there is a dress I think will be suitable."

Before Esther could say more, Anne dashed from the tent. An uneasy silence hovered over the proceedings as everyone waited for her to return. Within minutes, she came lugging the heavy pack. "Is this what you wanted?"

"It is. Thank you, Anne."

Esther handed the bouquet to the child for safekeeping, reached into the leather pouch, and brought out a carefully wrapped garment. She slipped the dress over her head. Makes Medicine had made the doeskin soft by tanning and chewing it for hours, then smoking it until it was as dainty as linen, as soft as velvet, and the palest of yellows, like rich, frothy cream. Thick fringe hung from the neckline and shoulders, brushing against her legs at the hemline that dipped long on the sides, and scalloped up over her knees in front and back. Dozens of small, metal cones fastened in clusters at the side seams and yoke, tinkled when she moved.

Anne then handed Esther a pair of thigh-high fringed leggings, painted a soft blue, beaded and belled. She tied the tops of the leggings to her breechclout. Beaded garters, worn just below the knee, held the leggings firmly in place. Finally came the high-topped moccasins—soft, fringed at the calves and running down the single back seam.

Esther stepped away from the mirror, and the heavy fringe swayed as she moved, accentuating her long legs.

"You intend to wear *that* heathen thing to be married in?" The matriarch quirked her right eyebrow and sniffed her displeasure into a linen handkerchief.

Esther smiled gently. "I do believe it suits the bouquet, don't you?"

Removing the combs from her hair, she allowed the white-gold mass to tumble over her shoulders and down her back in a lush mane, shiny as an iridescent pearl.

When she turned, a quick intake of breath from the onlookers told Esther all she needed to know. Retrieving her bouquet, she announced in a soft, but determined voice, "I think I am ready."

"For a scalping party, not a wedding!" the matriarch huffed under her breath.

"Effie, do be quiet," Anne said crisply. "It isn't *your* wedding. Besides, Esther looks as lovely as any bride I've ever seen and lovelier than most."

Anne held the flap of the tent open and the women, murmuring their good wishes, filed out. Another glance in the mirror, and Esther, too, stepped into the sun shining from a pale blue sky dimmed by thin high clouds. A cool breeze blew wisps of hair around her face as she walked toward the gathering crowd.

She gave the people and the nervous preacher only a cursory glance, for awaiting her arrival was Savage, looking more magnificent than she had ever seen him. Standing proud as the pines surrounding them, he wore a long leather hunting shirt scraped thin and dyed a pale cream color over dark blue leggings.

His hair, shining in grizzled splendor, had been neatly trimmed, and a band of leather strung through beaten silver disks held it in place.

A look of delight swept over his face when he saw Esther, and his mouth tilted in a welcoming smile. Thick clusters of tiny metal cones sewn into the long fringes of his leggings jingled softly in rhythm to his moccasined steps as he walked to meet her. Somehow the sound was intensely masculine to Esther, and it stirred a warm, safe feeling deep inside.

Savage held out his hand, and Esther placed her own in his open palm and watched as the long sinewy fingers closed over it. With slow steps, he guided her to a position in front of the little preacher, who was flipping nervously through a large worn Bible.

Having found what he was looking for, the preacher began reading, but Esther heard little he said. In awe, she studied Savage's classic profile silhouetted against the sky, the morning sun bronzing his strong face. His expression was that of a man at peace with himself and his God.

Oh, thank You, Lord, for giving me this man, Esther prayed. *With him beside me, I can walk tall and free, with my face to the sun. I can meet life with faith and hope and hear Your whispers on the wind, for I will no longer walk alone.*

Turning his head toward her, Savage looked deep into her eyes, now shimmering with tears, and sent a prayer heavenward. *Thank You, Father, for taking back a trail-hardened old sinner like me and giving me an angel like this woman. . . . It's hard to believe You could forgive me for all my black thoughts and deeds. But you've taken away the hatred and filled my heart with love. Now my life . . . our lives . . . are Yours.*

"And do you, Brook Savage, take this woman to be your lawfully wedded wife?" the preacher prompted.

With his eyes on Esther, Savage spoke. "Yes," he said, his voice husky with emotion.

"Then keep the commandments, children, and live with the Lord. You are now husband and wife." The deep booming voice of the preacher rolled over the hills, and the gathered witnesses let out a great cheer.

Underneath it all, however, Esther heard soft stirrings. All nature, which had appeared to be holding its breath until the sacred pronouncement, now erupted in a veritable cacophany of sound and motion. The playful breeze picked up, sighing through the evergreens. Crickets and other tiny woodland creatures chirped their delight. And eagles circled and plunged to earth in a breathtaking spectacle of flight.

At day's end, when they had ridden many miles along the trail into their future, and Esther sank, exhausted, into the sweet, soft boughs Savage had gathered for their bed, she held out her hand and bade him come near. "It is the Indian way . . . wherever we are together, it is home."

In the golden glow of autumn, they rode at a leisurely pace for the better part of two weeks. Despite Esther's entreaties, however, Savage had not told her their destination.

"Won't you say where we are going?" she would ask. "I would like to know something of my future."

"You will know in good time," was his only reply as silver glints lit the gray of his eyes.

This afternoon on the great Plain, with no shelter in sight, the sky was growing steadily darker, filling with great thunderheads that threatened a downpour at any minute. A chill breeze brought the scent of rain from the north, and the first crack of thunder sent Esther's horse skittering sideways in small leaps of panic.

Quickly, with quiet voice and firm hands on the reins, she brought the mare under control, but not before looking up to see a worried frown creasing Savage's face. "If you look like that every time I trip or my horse misbehaves," she teased, "you will be an old man before your time."

Though Savage gave a thin smile, the worry did not leave his face. He had not felt this tremendous weight of protective responsibility with his first family, and he could not help feeling that if he had, they might be alive today. Though it was foolish thinking, it weighed on him.

When the skies opened and the rain began, Esther turned up her face to catch the first drops. "I love rain," she said softly. "It was the rain that brought you to me."

She laughed gaily, and it was impossible to resist her mood though they were soon drenched.

When the misty shroud lifted for an instant, it was Esther who caught sight of the cabin. "Look, Savage! Surely whoever lives there will shelter us for the night."

The rain poured down again, blotting out the landscape, but they rode toward the spot where they had seen the building nestled in a grove of bare-branched trees. Savage seemed to be leaning forward in his saddle as though anticipating something.

"Is there danger?" she asked uncertainly.

"I don't think so."

Nevertheless, his body went rigid, and Esther swallowed against the fear that rose and tightened her throat.

Behind them an unexpected break in the clouds sent a shaft of sun through the gathering darkness. It spotlighted the meadow and created a brilliant sweeping rainbow that seemed to end at the front door of the small, tidy cabin. Esther gasped, speechless at the sight.

Pulling the horses to a stop at the front door, Savage motioned her forward.

"I'll take care of the ponies. Why don't you knock and see if they will take us in?"

Since strong healthy men didn't normally send their women to a stranger's door, Esther's eyes darted quickly to his face, but nothing in his expression suggested that anything was amiss. She opened her mouth to protest, then decided he must have a good reason for the unusual suggestion, and clamped her lips shut.

Sliding off the sturdy mare, Esther sloshed her way to the weathered slab door. Before she could raise her hand to knock, however, the door opened wide and Esther found herself looking down into the face of a tiny bird-like woman.

The woman's once raven-black hair, streaked with silver-white, was pulled back from the translucent skin of a scarcely wrinkled forehead and held with a red scarf. One-half the woman's face was a vision of delicate beauty, but a rough disfiguring scar marred the other half.

Esther felt the strength drain from her body and she went numb. Whirling, she looked at Savage who stood at a distance, holding the reins of their horses and grinning widely. So he had known all along and had planned this as a wedding present!

Delirious with joy, she clasped the little woman in her arms and sobbed, "Aunt Mercy! Oh, Aunt Mercy!"

Esther had come home.

A Place to Belong

Tracie J. Peterson

Chapter One

The Kansas heat was enough to wilt the sturdiest flower. Humid air hung thick and heavy, but certainly no heavier than the atmosphere inside the Intissar parlor on that June day.

"I won't go!" Magdelena Intissar announced at the top of her lungs. She stamped her small foot, just in case her words weren't enough to make her decision clear.

"Maggie, lower your voice," Sophia Intissar said patiently. The stately old woman was used to her granddaughter's temper. The only other person in the parlor was the subject of Maggie's displeasure.

"I won't go with that man, Grandmother. And that's final!" Maggie's blue eyes blazed at Garrett Lucas. He shifted uncomfortably.

Sophia smiled sympathetically at the young man. He had appeared on her doorstep only hours earlier, and with him had come the news that Maggie's father was sending for his daughter.

With a swish of her English afternoon dress, Sophia moved gracefully to a chair and took her place. "I suggest you sit, Magdelena," she said, pointing to a brocade parlor chair. "This issue will not be easily dismissed. We must talk."

Maggie never took her eyes off Garrett Lucas as she followed her grandmother's instructions and sat down.

"Please continue, Mr. Lucas," Sophia requested.

"As I said, ma'am," Garrett began. "Your son, Jason Intissar, instructed me to come to Topeka and return to New Mexico with his daughter. I have two train tickets." He pulled the tickets from his vest pocket and held them up for both women to see.

"So what! You have two train tickets," Maggie interrupted, enraged at the presumption that this should make any difference.

"Grandmother," she said turning to Sophia Intissar. "You can't trust him. Anybody can buy train tickets. He's probably some kidnapper who thinks Father will pay a high price for my return."

Garrett chuckled, but Maggie ignored him.

"Grandmother, it wouldn't be appropriate for me to travel unchaperoned with this man. What would our friends say?" Maggie knew she was grasping at straws. Neither she nor her grandmother had ever given much thought to neighborhood gossip.

Sophia took the tickets, reviewed them, and returned them to Garrett Lucas's well-tanned hand.

"I also have this letter," Garrett said. Reaching into his pocket, he pulled out a sealed envelope.

Sophia took the letter and used it to fan herself for a moment. The high collar of her gown framed her thin, aged face. Signs of quality were evident from her gleaming white hair to the sweep of her elegantly tailored gown. Lifting her chin slightly, she drew a deep breath.

"I believe you are who you say you are, Mr. Lucas. I believe this letter will explain that my son has sent you to retrieve his daughter. We all know that he's tried many times before. What I don't understand is why you must leave today on the four o'clock train."

"The letter will explain, ma'am. Mr. Intissar was afraid that his daughter might react as she had before and run off."

"How dare you!" Maggie could take no more. "How dare you talk about me as if I weren't even here! You don't know me. My father doesn't know me. He deserted me to my grandmother's care when my mother died. I was eight years old, and I've only seen him twice since then!" The bitterness in Maggie's voice was not lost on her listeners.

"Maggie, remember your manners," Sophia interjected firmly, but not without gentleness. She'd known the pain of that eight-year-old girl as she knew the pain of the young woman who sat angrily before her. "Mr. Lucas does have a point," she continued.

Maggie knew that her grandmother was right. Her father had sent for her on a dozen other occasions, but always Maggie had managed to be away from Topeka or hiding out with friends when he had arrived to take her home. She'd never been able to get past the pain of being left behind, and in her heart, Maggie had held an anger toward her father that seemed to grow each year.

Now, Garrett Lucas had arrived. If she were forced to leave with him, Maggie knew it would not be easy to escape and return to her grandmother. But no matter how difficult flight might prove to be, Maggie was determined to defy her father's wishes. She had no desire to face him or the wounds that stood between them.

"It seems that your father has outwitted you, my dear," Sophia was saying. Maggie jerked her head up.

"You'll have to drag my dead body to that train!" she shouted, jumping to her feet. Garrett's lips drew back in a wide grin. The girl had spunk, and he had to admire her ability to stand up to people.

Maggie noticed the smile and felt her heart skip a beat. Garrett Lucas was quite handsome, especially when he smiled. His skin was tanned from many years spent outdoors, and Maggie lost herself in his intense blue eyes. Just then she remembered that he was grinning because of her.

Maggie raised herself to her full height. "I mean it. Go back and tell my father that I refuse to come to New Mexico. I have friends and family here, and that's enough for me. Furthermore, in less than two months I will be eighteen years old. I think I am more than mature enough to make my own decisions, and my decision is to remain here."

As Maggie's tantrum played out, silence fell over the parlor. Sophia quietly read her son's letter. From time to time, a faint breeze fluttered the lace parlor curtains, bringing with it the sweet scent of honeysuckle.

Maggie refused to look at Garrett, but she was well aware that he studied her intently. How she wished she could run from the room.

Sophia let the letter fall to her lap. It confirmed that her son was determined to form a relationship with his child. Pity he'd allowed Maggie to have her way for so many years. There were so many miles and scars to overcome. But Maggie must face her father's decision. Scars or no scars, it was time for her to go home.

Sophia broke the silence. "Maggie, I have no choice. You will go with Mr. Lucas."

"What? You can't be serious, Grandmother. You would trust this man, this . . . this devil?"

"Magdelena!" Sophia admonished, and Garrett Lucas broke into a hearty laugh, causing both women to look at him.

"Excuse me, ma'am," Garrett said to Sophia. "I meant no disrespect."

"I apologize for my granddaughter, Mr. Lucas. She doesn't yet understand that being grown up often means making unpopular and unwanted decisions."

Maggie came to stand in front of Sophia. "Grandmother, what are you saying? Will you really let him take me away?"

"Maggie, I must. Your father has made it very clear in this letter. He has his reasons, and now I have mine. Run upstairs and pack your things."

"She doesn't need to take too much," Garrett offered. "Jason's bought her quite a bit already. She'll have enough clothes to be the envy of any woman in the territory."

"Clothes? Pack my clothes? Has everyone lost their minds?" Maggie questioned, her voice nearing hysteria. "What's in that letter? How could you send me off with a stranger to a man who cares nothing about me. He walked out on me, remember? He left me when I needed him."

"Maggie," Sophia took her granddaughter's youthful hand in her own weathered one and patted it gently. "You must be brave, my dear. You must listen to me and do as I say. I am an old woman, and I don't have many years left in this world. God is in this change."

"Don't say that," Maggie interrupted curtly. "God can't possibly care about me, or He'd have kept Garrett Lucas in New Mexico. God has never cared about me, or He would have given me a father. One that would stay and do the job, rather than leave it to someone else to do."

"Maggie, that's not fair. Please hear me out," Sophia pleaded, and Maggie grew frightened. It wasn't at all like her grandmother to take on an air of frailty. Maggie's eyes darted in the direction of Garrett Lucas, but she could see he was fidgeting with his coat button, trying to leave the two women some privacy.

"I don't want you thinking that I don't love you anymore. Nor do I wish for you to believe me cruel and heartless in this matter. You're seventeen years old, and your father feels it's time for you to consider marriage and settling down to your own family."

Sophia stopped to see the impact her words were having on Maggie. She could see tears brimming in her granddaughter's eyes and knew that her own weren't far behind. "Your father has found a husband for you, child. He has that privilege and right."

"A husband? I guess I could've guessed he didn't want a daughter. He just wants a son to replace the one he lost." Maggie's bitterness was clear.

"Now child, be fair," Sophia implored.

"What would I want with one of Father's old cronies? He probably has some ancient man lined up. I won't do it. I can't!" Maggie sobbed the words. She fell to her knees, hating herself for breaking down in front of Mr. Lucas.

"Child, you must understand. Your father is not a well man. The letter makes this clear. He wishes to leave his estate to you. And," Sophia added most reluctantly, "he wants to have a say in who will share that responsibility with you."

"Let him find someone to give his empire to. I don't want it. I want to stay here with you, Grandmother. I don't want to leave Topeka."

Just then the hall clock chimed two. Maggie turned terror-stricken eyes first to her grandmother, and then unwillingly to Garrett Lucas.

Garrett hated being the cause of the fear he saw in Maggie's eyes. She was easier to handle when she was defiant. He wished he could assure her that he was only here as a favor to Jason, but he knew she'd never listen to him. No, it was best that he let the two women work through this together.

"If God loves me so much, why is He allowing this to happen? Better yet, why are you?" Maggie knew her words tortured her grandmother, but she had to make her grandmother see her pain.

"Maggie, I have little choice. I would love to have you here for the remainder of my life, but your father has set his mind."

"He doesn't care about me, Grandmother. It's just his land and his business ventures. Don't you see? If he cared about me, he would have come home to Topeka. He wouldn't have jeopardized my security by forcing me away from all that I know and love. He wants a land baron, not a daughter. He's always hated me for what happened to mother!"

"Nonsense, child. You listen to me and listen well. I was there when your mother died. She struggled to give birth to your brother, but we all knew that neither one of them was going to make it." Sophia's eyes clouded with tears.

"Typhoid fever had been fierce in town. Your mother was well into her pregnancy when you came down with the fever yourself. Before I knew what had happened, your mother was sick as well."

Maggie felt tears fall hot upon her cheeks. She buried her face in her grandmother's lap. Sophia gently stroked the long auburn curls. "Your father always blamed himself. He couldn't live with his grief, nor with the child that reminded him so much of his wife. You were a constant reminder of what he had lost. I love my son, Maggie. I never faulted him for leaving you in my care. I saw the necessity of it then, just as I see the necessity of this now. God has always been here for us."

"Father left because he blamed me for Mother's death. He hates me, and I don't care!" Maggie exploded.

"That is absurd, Maggie. You didn't give your mother typhoid, and your father didn't blame you then or now." Sophia lifted the letter to fan herself, succumbing to the heat and stress. Her face paled.

"Grandmother!" Maggie cried, reaching out to steady her. Garrett was beside Sophia in a moment.

"Get her some water," he commanded. Maggie raced to the kitchen and returned with a glass.

"It's not very cold, " she said apologetically.

"It will be fine, child," Sophia assured her. "I'm feeling better now. It's just this insufferable heat. If this is any indication of what the rest of the summer will bring, I'm not sure how I'll stand up under it."

"See, you need me," Maggie said pleadingly. Then she whirled to face Garrett. "You can't expect me to leave her here alone!"

Garrett was standing close to Maggie. Close enough that she could smell the cologne he wore, musky, yet sweet. He looked down at her with soft eyes and opened his mouth to speak.

"It isn't my decision, Miss Intissar. I'm only doing what I promised your father I'd do."

"I'm fine, Maggie," Sophia insisted.

She did look better, Maggie decided, but the girl feared that neither of them would be able to bear the separation.

"I don't want to leave you." Maggie threw herself to her knees again and hugged her grandmother tightly.

Sophia brushed the damp hair away from Maggie's forehead. "I don't want to see you go. I love you, child. But you must do this for me." Sophia raised Maggie's face to meet her own. "You must go with Mr. Lucas. Promise me you will go upstairs right now and pack your things."

Suddenly there was no room for further discussion. Maggie stared intently at her grandmother's wearied face and then looked up at the towering stranger. She lowered her head and with a voice of complete dejection whispered, "Yes, Grandmother."

"And Maggie, remember that God will always see you through the storms," Sophia added. "He's there for you Maggie, but you must come willingly. Don't put God off simply because you fear He will desert you. He won't." Sophia had prayed so often that her granddaughter would turn from her bitterness to accept Jesus as her Savior.

Maggie got to her feet and brushed off the skirt of her gown. "I will take my leave now, if I may," she said ignoring Garrett's closeness. Sophia nodded, and Maggie moved from the room.

As Maggie reached the oak staircase, she turned and made the mistake of meeting Garrett's unyielding eyes. Maggie sighed and began to climb the stairs, when a thought came to her. *Lillie! I'll sneak out of my room, down the trellis, and run to Lillie's house.* Maggie hiked her skirts and fairly flew up the remaining stairs. She was safely behind her bedroom door when Sophia Intissar rose slowly to her feet in the parlor below.

"If I know my granddaughter, Mr. Lucas, and I believe I do, I can count on her trying to leave this house without your knowledge. I would suggest you keep your eyes open. We have a staircase in back as well as the one in front."

Garrett nodded. "I understand. I'll keep track of her. You just rest." Garrett turned to leave, but Sophia placed her hand on his arm.

"Please be gentle with her, Mr. Lucas. Life has not always treated her kindly."

"I'd venture a guess that it's been rough on all of you. Please don't worry. I'll be a perfect gentleman. I'll do as Jason instructed me, and nothing more than is necessary to fulfill his wishes." With that Garrett walked out the front door of the Intissar house.

Chapter Two

Maggie gazed around the room. She wondered if she should bother to take anything with her. No. She could always borrow clothes from Lillie. Nervous excitement washed through her body. It would be a pleasure to defeat Garrett Lucas and to show her father once again that she wanted nothing to do with him.

It was odd how days, even weeks, passed when Maggie didn't think of her father. God, on the other hand, could never be outrun.

Putting such uncomfortable thoughts aside, Maggie went to the window. She touched the powder-blue Priscilla curtains and remembered making them with her grandmother. Maggie held the soft folds against her cheek. She thought of how she and Grandmother had gone downtown to pick out the material and wallpaper for their new home in Potwin Place.

Maggie threw open the window. "I won't be forced to give up all that I love. It's just not fair!" she cried out loud. "Father can't force me to leave Grandmother and marry someone I don't know."

There was a light rap at the door. "Maggie, do hurry along child. We've only a few minutes before we leave," her grandmother called softly.

"In a minute," Maggie responded. She hurriedly reached out the window to take hold of the trellis. Her skirts were quite cumbersome as she struggled to put her foot out the window. Gingerly, Maggie climbed onto the delicate wood frame sharing space with the climbing roses. The trellis shook vigorously for a few moments and then settled under her weight.

"If he thinks that he can just come in here and take me away, he's got another thing coming," Maggie muttered to herself as she fought her skirts and the trellis. "He's got to be twelve kinds of fool to think I'd go anywhere with—" Her tirade ended abruptly as she was wrenched from the trellis into the arms of Garrett Lucas.

A look of amusement played in Garrett's eyes, and Maggie couldn't help but notice how effortlessly he carried her, squirming and twisting, back to the front door. "You were saying?" he questioned sarcastically.

"Oh, you are insufferable! Put me down!" Maggie said, suddenly finding her voice.

Garrett carried her through the etched glass double doors of her Queen Anne home. He took the stairs two at a time and didn't stop until he reached the upstairs hallway.

"Which room?" he questioned.

"Put me down! Grandmother!" Maggie yelled.

"Unless you want me to help you pack, I suggest you settle down and do what your grandmother told you to do. I'm going to be watching this house the whole time, so no more tricks. Do you understand?" Garrett's words left Maggie cold. "Do you?"

Maggie nodded slowly.

"Very well," Garrett said as he set Maggie on her feet. "Now get your things together and be quick about it, or I'll come in and help you!" With that he went downstairs and left Maggie to watch after him in total amazement. Who was this man?

Maggie hurried to the sanctuary of her room. There was no more time for memories or escapes. If she couldn't get away from Garrett at home in Topeka, would it be possible to flee while on the train?

Suddenly a plan began to form. "If Father thinks he's won this round, he's wrong." Maggie said, pulling out a drawer from her writing desk. She dumped the contents onto the desktop. Coins and trinkets spilled out. "I'll show him," Maggie muttered to herself as she counted the money. Finally, thirty dollars and some change was counted out. "I wonder if this is enough to buy a train ticket home," Maggie mused.

Next, she pulled out a piece of writing paper and jotted a note to her best friend, Lillie Johnston. She tried to explain what was happening and that, somehow, she'd be back. She sealed the envelope and left it in the middle of her desk, knowing her grandmother would find it and have it delivered.

Quickly, Maggie pulled off her gingham day dress and took out a green linen traveling suit. The day was too hot for such an outfit, but Maggie knew it would be expected by the matrons of society.

Maggie herself often scoffed at the rules and regulations that the women of Potwin Place had made for themselves. But they were rules that were followed by the genteel of society everywhere, not just those in this upper-class neighborhood.

Maggie pulled on her petticoat and then eyed herself in the mirror. She was only seventeen, not even an adult. Still, many of her friends were already married. Some even had children. She was woman enough she decided, but for what?

She labored with her shirtwaist and the faux lace collar that tied at her neck. Securing the collar with a velvet green ribbon, Maggie turned her attention to the skirt.

Within twenty minutes, Maggie stood at the base of the oak staircase, dressed in her green suit with valise and purse in hand. She was an alluring picture with her long auburn hair put up and a green hat pinned jauntily to one side.

Her appearance was not lost on Garrett. "Let me take that, Miss Intissar," he said as he stepped forward to take the valise from Maggie's hands. Maggie glared at him but said nothing. He took the bag and stepped back.

"You must be stronger than you look. This thing weighs more than a yearling heifer," he drawled.

"I am a great many things more than what I appear to be, Mr. Lucas," Maggie answered, refusing to allow him the upper hand.

"Somehow, ma'am, that doesn't surprise me." His eyes pierced her soul, and Maggie felt as though she'd just been put in her place.

"Oh good, you're here at last," Sophia said as she entered the room carrying another small bag. "I had Two Moons pack you some things to eat." Sophia referred to her Indian housekeeper who had been with her since she'd been a young girl.

"That isn't necessary, ma'am," Garrett began. "Mr. Intissar sent along plenty of money for the two of us to eat along the way."

Maggie thought of at least a dozen retorts, but kept her tongue in check for a time longer. Once they were on the train, Garrett Lucas would discover just how difficult his trip was going to be.

"I only thought that you might need something extra. I suppose it's the mothering instinct in me." Sophia started to discard the bag, but Maggie reached out and took it.

"Nonsense, Grandmother. It was a wise idea," she said gently, while flashing a look at Garrett Lucas that made it clear he'd overstepped his bounds. "One can never tell when the food will be unsatisfactory. Why, Lillie told me just last week that the food offered on their trip to Omaha had been appalling."

"Of course, ma'am. It was very thoughtful of you." Garrett spoke politely, all the while returning Maggie's blazing stare. He raised one dark eyebrow slightly, as if contemplating a further reply, and then changed his mind. "I suggest we be on our way. It's already three o'clock."

"Very well, Mr. Lucas." Sophia allowed him to take her arm and lead her to the carriage.

Maggie lingered for a moment, trying to drink in every inch of the house. Standing at the foot of the stairs, she could look into three different rooms. They held comfort and good memories. Suddenly she wanted to embrace it all, fearing that she'd never see her home again. Why was God punishing her? Hadn't she paid enough?

Maggie choked back tears and steadied her nerves. She'd make it back, she vowed to herself. All the Garrett Lucases and Jason Intissars in the world would not keep her from her home and Grandmother.

"Come along, Maggie." It was Grandmother, calling from the carriage.

Maggie stepped onto the porch and shut the door behind her. She turned to find Garrett Lucas at her arm.

"I would suggest, Miss Intissar, that you make this matter as easy on your grandmother as possible." Garrett's voice was deadly serious. "She has done nothing but care for you and love you. You are a spoiled and selfish child." He paused to search her eyes. "I will not allow you to cause her further grief by a display of childishness at the train station."

Maggie's mouth dropped open in shocked surprise. "How dare you—" Her words were cut off by his stern expression.

"I'm not the enemy here, but you are going to get on that train if I have to rope you and tie you to the seat. Everyone, including that sweet, old woman, has danced to your tune long enough. You are now in my care, Miss Magdelena Intissar, and I am quite capable of dealing with you."

Maggie was stunned. She could barely work her legs to walk down the porch steps. It wouldn't be as easy to give Garrett Lucas the slip as she'd hoped. Mutely, Maggie allowed Garrett to lead her along the board walkway to the carriage.

Topeka of 1888 was bustling with life and activity. It was the capital of Kansas and in its own right demanded grandeur and charm. Potwin Place was the high point of residential Topeka, although it desired to become a city in its own right.

Potwin Place homes, while fairly new, were elegant and stately. They were surrounded by well-manicured lawns. Young trees had been planted along the avenues. Maggie was well aware that she had lived a privileged life. Now she could only stare longingly as the carriage took her from the place she loved to an uncertain future.

Maggie had always loved the hubbub of the city, but even that simple pleasure was lost on her as she brooded about the future. The carriage passed the large stone church which Sophia insisted her household attend every Sunday. Maggie thought momentarily of God. He was up there somewhere, she decided as she looked into the fluffy clouds. Somewhere up there, but certainly not with her.

Soon, the two-story depot came into sight. Maggie realized the moment of truth was nearing. She toyed with the idea of causing a scene. Maybe there was some way to discredit Mr. Lucas so that her grandmother couldn't possibly send Maggie with him.

Maggie shot a quick glance at Garrett Lucas. He narrowed his eyes slightly as if reading her mind. The look on his face was adamant, his message unmistakable.

"I must say, Mrs. Intissar, you have a lovely city," Garrett observed, breaking the silence that had lasted the duration of the carriage ride.

Sophia roused herself. "Yes, I suppose it is one of the more lovely times to be here. The flowering trees, the honeysuckle and lilacs. Topeka is a sweet smelling town. However, we have some nasty storms. Cyclones, you know." She spoke with a heavy voice, and both Garrett and Maggie knew her mind was far from thoughts of the weather.

"Yes, ma'am," Garrett replied, "We have them out West, too. Sometimes they come in a series of storms that last all day."

Sophia nodded. "I've seen storms like that. It's always been the thing I've disliked most about our fair state. Of course," she added rather absentmindedly, "if not cyclones, then something else."

Maggie sat in silence, trying to formulate a plan. There'd only be one chance to make it work. She thought of the various junctions and water stops on the Atchison, Topeka, and Santa Fe Rail Road lines. She'd traveled with her grandmother as far as Newton, but beyond that, she was rather uncertain about the route. She'd have to escape before they reached Newton.

The carriage ride came unceremoniously to an end at the depot entrance. Garrett jumped to the ground before the driver could announce their arrival.

"Allow me to help you, ma'am," Garrett said tenderly, reaching up to take hold of Sophia's waist. "Forgive the familiarity, but I fear this heat might grieve you if I allow you to exert yourself."

"You are very kind, Mr. Lucas. My son has always been a good judge of a man's character. I see his judgment is still sound."

Maggie rolled her eyes, not realizing that Garrett could see her. "Yes, Father is quite knowledgeable about men and horseflesh, cattle and land grants. It's women who seem to escape his understanding," she said sarcastically. She refused to take Garrett's offered hand and nearly fell from the buggy as she tried to dismount.

Garrett flashed her a brief smile and returned his attention to Sophia. The heat was nearly unbearable for the older woman.

"June isn't always this hot. Some years, we're still enjoying cool temperatures at this time. Why by all the means of Kansas, we could be quite chilled tomorrow. We have a saying about the weather here, Mr. Lucas, if you don't like it, wait a day and it'll change," Sophia murmured. She stumbled slightly, leaning heavily against Garrett's offered arm.

"Ma'am, I know you wish to see your granddaughter safely on the train, but the truth is it would be better if your driver took you home. I don't want to worry about you having to make it back to the carriage without help." Garrett's command of the moment went unquestioned. Sophia allowed him to place her back in the buggy.

"Maggie, listen to me," Sophia said leaning down from her seat. "Don't cause Mr. Lucas any trouble. Just do as your father wishes, and perhaps in the fall, I'll come and visit you."

Maggie felt tears on her cheeks. She hated appearing weak in front of Garrett, but perhaps it was what he needed to see. He should understand how miserable he was making her.

"Grandmother, I simply can't bear to leave you." Maggie began to cry. "I don't want to go." She held tightly to her grandmother's arm.

"It will be all right, child," Sophia murmured, gently stroking Maggie's face. "God sometimes sends adversity to strengthen and teach us. You'll grow stronger from this. Now remember the things you've been taught. Never forget you are loved."

"I'll remember," Maggie promised.

"It's time to go, Miss Intissar," Garrett said softly, extending his arm for Maggie.

"I'll see you soon, Grandmother," Maggie said standing on tiptoe in order to reach her Grandmother's ear. "I'll pray every night that God will bring us together again." She wondered if she had added that last statement more for herself than for her grandmother.

Maggie allowed Garrett to lead her away. As they passed through the depot entrance, she paused to look back. Her grandmother was waving weakly. Maggie returned the wave until Garrett firmly propelled her to the other side of the depot and onto the boarding platform.

Oh, Grandmother, Maggie thought. *Somehow I will return to you. Somehow.*

Chapter Three

"All 'board!" the conductor called as a stern-faced Garrett approached, pulling a willful Maggie behind him.

"Afternoon to you, Mister," the conductor said without breaking his concentration on the pocket watch he held tightly in his hand. "Missus," he added, touching the brim of his blue cap. Maggie stiffened at the comment, causing a smile to play at the corners of Garrett's mouth.

Maggie tried to pull away, but it was no use. Garrett only smiled broadly, and raised a questioning eye from beneath his black Stetson.

"Tickets, please," the conductor requested.

Garrett pulled two tickets from his vest pocket and handed them to the older man.

"Um, I see here you're in number fourteen. That'd be the second car down," the conductor said, motioning to a porter.

"Y'sir," the porter said with a nodding bow of his head.

"These passengers have seats in number fourteen. See to it," the conductor instructed. "And be quick about it. I'm about to call final 'board."

"Y'sir," the porter smiled and offered his assistance. "Do you have bags, sir?" he questioned Garrett.

"I've already checked them," Garrett answered. "Except for this one. We'll take it with us." Garrett motioned to the carpetbag Sophia had packed. Maggie clutched the bag as if it were all she owned.

"Very good, sir. Right this way."

Maggie felt herself being pulled along at such a pace that when Garrett stopped, she nearly fell headlong onto the tracks. Garrett steadied her and gently handed her up the steps of the train. Maggie was amazed at how light his touch could be when he wasn't bullying her along.

The porter led them down the narrow train aisle. "Seats twenty-three and twenty-four, right here, sir," the porter said. "I'll show you to your sleeping compartments this evening."

"Thank you," Garrett replied, handing the man a coin. The porter smiled broadly and nodded his head to the couple.

"Take the window seat, Miss Intissar," Garrett stated matter-of-factly. "I believe the train is about to pull out, and it would do little good to have you sprawled in the aisle."

Maggie stepped meekly to her seat. Garrett, although surprised, said nothing. Instead, he took off his hat and coat and, before sitting, removed his vest as well. Maggie's discomfort became evident as Garrett pulled his necktie off and unbuttoned his shirt collar.

Garrett noticed Maggie's flushed face. She quickly turned away, and he couldn't help but grin. "I'm finished, if that's what you're wondering," he teased. "It'd do you some good to get out of that jacket and open up a button or two yourself."

"I'm fine for the time being," she lied, wishing she could do just as Garrett had suggested. The worst heat of the day was only heightened by the closed, cramped quarters of the train.

"As you wish, but remember we're traveling south. The heat will only get worse once we leave Topeka," Garrett said with a shrug of his shoulders.

His words only reminded Maggie that they were leaving her home. A further reminder sounded loud and clear as the train whistle gave two long blasts. Maggie felt the color drain from her face. It was all she could do to keep from fighting Garrett in an attempt to get off.

The train gave a bit of a jerk, as if it needed help to start moving down the tracks. Finally it started pulling slowly out of Topeka's Santa Fe Station. Maggie watched as people on the platform waved. One older woman, sending a kiss with her gloved hand, reminded Maggie of her grandmother. Maggie bit her lip to keep from crying, but her eyes held betraying tears.

Long after there was nothing but outlying farms and scenery to look at, Maggie continued to stare out the window. She remembered several years earlier when she had gone with Lillie to see the circus. The two girls had watched the animals get loaded on the train after the final performance. Maggie had felt sorry for the animals in their barred cages. Now, she felt caged.

After nearly fifteen minutes of strained silence, Garrett spoke. "We should talk before this situation gets worse," he began. He leaned back against the padded leather of the seat and crossed his arms behind his head.

Maggie stiffened and moved closer to the window. She was hot and sticky, and the humidity made it nearly impossible to breathe. She wanted to lower the window, but the smoke and cinders from the train's smokestack would only worsen things. Either way, Garrett Lucas was too close, and she wished desperately to put some kind of distance between them. She sighed deeply.

"Did you hear what I said?" Garrett questioned.

"I heard you," Maggie barely whispered the words. "I simply chose not to argue with you."

"I have no intention of arguing with you, Miss Intissar, and begging your pardon, but I believe I will call you by your first name." Garrett's voice told Maggie he'd settle for nothing less.

"Whatever you feel is necessary, Mr. Lucas," Maggie replied with a coolness to her voice that surprised even her. "It is of little consequence what name you call me by."

"Dare I believe you are offering to cooperate with me?" Garrett questioned sarcastically. He turned his body slightly toward Maggie, which only made her more uncomfortable.

A woman with two children occupied the seats across the aisle, and she leaned toward Garrett and Maggie to catch pieces of their conversation. Maggie detested the woman's prying attitude and lowered her voice even more.

"I've already agreed to go with you to wherever it is my father calls home. I don't care what you call me, and I don't care where you take me. Now, what more is there to discuss?" Maggie felt rather proud of her little speech.

"I see. What, may I ask, brought about this change in the wild-eyed child that I had words with earlier?" Garrett questioned, intently studying Maggie for some clue as to what she was planning.

Maggie bit hard on her lower lip, and Garrett smiled, letting Maggie know he was aware he'd hit a nerve.

"You have your father's temper. Are you aware of that?" Garrett asked. Maggie said nothing, but she noticed over Garrett's shoulder that the woman had leaned even farther into the aisle. Garrett turned to see what Maggie was looking at.

"Have you lost something, ma'am?" Garrett asked the embarrassed woman. The woman shook her head and quickly turned her attention back to her children. Garrett chuckled and continued his analysis of Maggie.

"You have his eyes too." Garrett's voice sounded low and melodic. Maggie felt herself relaxing against her will.

"I suppose one would have to share certain characteristics with one's parent. It isn't necessary to live with a parent to look like one. I also look a great deal like my mother, and she died nine years ago," Maggie said rather stiffly, refusing to fall under Garrett's spell.

"Yes, I know. Your father showed me her picture. She was a beautiful woman, and you are the very image of her."

"Am I mistaken, or have you just complimented me?" Maggie questioned curiously.

"And the lady is intelligent too!" Garrett drawled sardonically.

Maggie could no longer play her part. "You're insufferable!" she huffed and turned back to the window.

"Ah ha! I knew the temper was still there. Don't think that you can set my mind at ease by playing the prim and proper lady. I will not trust you on this trip, and you might as well know my terms right up front," Garrett said firmly.

Maggie stared incredulously as Garrett sat up and reached over to pull her to the edge of her seat.

"Now, off with the jacket before you pass out. And take off that collar," he ordered. He reached out as if to undo the buttons himself.

Maggie noticed the widening eyes of the woman across the aisle. Garrett turned to the woman briefly. "I can't believe you women actually travel comfortably in these getups you call traveling clothes." The woman turned crimson, but Maggie noticed she didn't pull back like before.

"Take it off," Garrett commanded a stunned Maggie.

"I've never been so insulted!" Maggie tried to jerk away, only to find Garrett's firm hands holding her upper arms.

"I'm sure no one has ever dared to cross you, Maggie. But this time, you've met your match. Your father didn't send me without considering the type of person this job required. Now do as I say." Garrett loosened his grip as Maggie obediently began to unbutton her jacket.

"This is totally inappropriate," she muttered under her breath. "I'm a lady, and I demand that you treat me as such."

"Perhaps when you start acting like one, I'll be more inclined to treat you differently. Fashion or no, I can't see having you passed out from heat. I'm truly thinking only of your comfort. Now let me help." Garrett's words were so precise they sounded rehearsed.

Maggie allowed him to help her out of the traveling jacket. She had to admit, at least to herself, that it was an immediate improvement. She leaned back and sighed. Why was this happening? Did God hate her so much? Why couldn't she live with her grandmother? Was it because she refused to hear God's calling?

"Now, as I said before, we really should talk." Garrett's voice intruded into Maggie's thoughts. "I know you're feeling badly. I know you don't want to go, and I know that you're afraid."

"I'm not afraid of anything!" Maggie exclaimed, raising her voice slightly. When several of the train passengers joined the nosy woman in turning to see what the commotion was, Maggie immediately stared out the window.

"You were saying," Garrett whispered pressing close to her ear.

"Get away from me," Maggie hissed. "I may have to suffer through your deplorable presence, but I will not have you accosting me."

Garrett laughed loudly, causing people to stare at them once again. The woman across the aisle was thoroughly enjoying the scene.

"Will you be quiet?" Maggie whispered angrily. "I won't have the entire train watching me. One nanny is entirely too many, but now you'd saddle me with a dozen more," she said waving her arm at the people who stared. Everyone with the exception of the nosy woman turned away quickly.

"Look, little girl," Garrett said in the authoritative tone Maggie had grown to hate. "You're spoiled and selfish, and a woman, you're not!"

Maggie felt her face grow red with embarrassment. Garrett Lucas was impossible. It made thoughts of escape seem that much sweeter. She struggled to regain her composure.

"Mr. Lucas," Maggie began when she could trust her voice. "I am tired of your insults and tired of trying to make sense out of this situation. I don't suppose it's possible for you to understand what I'm going through, therefore I don't see any reason to continue this conversation."

"Maybe I understand more than you give me credit for," Garrett answered gently.

"I suppose anything is possible," Maggie said wearily. "But I don't believe you appreciate my position. I am seventeen years old. I've lived all my life in Topeka. What few friends I have are ones I've spent a lifetime making.

"Why, Lillie Johnston from next door has been my companion since I was a very small child. Her father and mine invested in the railroad together. Her parents and mine were good friends. When Lillie's parents decided to build a house in Potwin Place, my grandmother arranged to build there so we could remain close. I was to be in Lillie's wedding later this month. So you see how little you or my father know about me."

"I've learned a great deal about you through your grandmother's letters to your father," Garrett said noting the surprise on Maggie's face.

"I see," Maggie replied, knowing that her grandmother had written long, detailed accounts of their life in Topeka. Maggie decided that by sharing those letters with a stranger, her father had betrayed the family once again.

"I know that, except for times when Lillie prodded you to attend social events, you've lived a cloistered life," Garrett continued, much to Maggie's dismay. "I know that you've refused gentleman callers, telling your grandmother that men were more trouble to deal with than they were worth."

Maggie blushed a deep crimson. "My father had no right to share that with you. In fact, my grandmother had no right to share it with my father. But," she paused, gaining a bit of composure. "I suppose that is all in the past."

"Your father has every right to know about you. He's tried for years to get you down to New Mexico with him. Seems to me that it's you, not him, who refuses to put the past aside. I can't imagine a living soul disliking Jason Intissar, much less hating him the way you do." Garrett's words were like a spike driven into Maggie's heart.

"You have no right to talk to me like that! I demand that you have the porter show me to my sleeping compartment so that I might retire for the evening."

"I see. And if I refuse?" Garrett questioned in a cautious tone.

"I can't very well force you, now can I? I am, after all, just a spoiled little girl. But, I am not feeling well, and I am asking you," Maggie continued at nearly a whisper. "to let me go."

Maggie hoped her case sounded believable, but just in case, she quietly held her breath, a trick she and Lillie had learned as young girls. If she held her breath long enough, she'd grow faint. She and Lillie had done this on more than one occasion to get out of school. If Garrett expected childish behavior, then that's what she'd give him.

Garrett eyed her suspiciously. She was incredibly beautiful and looked nothing like the child he'd accused her of being. He liked her spirit, but he had to admit that she didn't look well.

"All right, Maggie." Garrett agreed and signaled for the porter.

"Sir?" It was the same porter who'd shown them to their seats.

"Please show Miss Intissar to her sleeping compartment. I'm afraid the heat's been difficult for her," Garrett said as he stood and helped Maggie to her feet.

Maggie slowly exhaled, but found herself dizzy from her antics. She fell against Garrett's arm. The woman across the aisle gasped loudly, but Garrett ignored her.

"Maggie?" he questioned, quite concerned. Maggie kept her face down and smiled to herself. *Good,* she thought. *Let him worry.*

"I'm so sorry," Maggie said aloud. "I'm afraid I'm feeling worse than I thought."

"Porter, lead the way. I'll bring Miss Intissar," Garrett directed, and the porter headed in the direction of the sleeping car. Garrett pulled Maggie tightly to him. "Lean on me, Maggie. I'll help you."

The fact that Maggie willingly accepted his help caused Garrett great concern. She would never allow him to touch her if she were strong enough to do otherwise. When they reached Maggie's room, Garrett instructed the porter to bring fresh water and a glass.

"I want you to drink this," Garrett said to Maggie as he poured the glass full of water. "Then I want you to undress and get some rest."

Maggie raised an eyebrow this time. "You seem intent on speaking on very familiar terms with me. I'd rather you leave this relationship as unfamiliar as possible. Neither one of us has anything to gain by doing otherwise."

"On the contrary, Maggie. We have a great deal to gain by working through this antagonism—if not for our sakes, then for the sake of your father," Garrett replied as he pushed the glass into Maggie's hand.

Garrett's fingers touched Maggie's hand and sent a searing charge up her arm. She made the mistake of looking into his eyes. They were steely blue, and yet there was something more. They seemed to hold a glint of something that

Maggie couldn't quite comprehend.

She pulled away from his hand, and the glass of water. "Wha . . . what?" she stammered. "What could this possibly have to do with my father, and why should I care?"

"Because your father has gone to a great deal of trouble for you. He cares very deeply for you, and he wants your happiness," Garrett said placing the water on the dresser of Maggie's compartment. "And, despite what you may think, his plans for you are better than your own."

Maggie stamped her foot. "My father doesn't even know me, Garrett Lucas! He's making arrangements for me to wed a man I don't know. A man who doesn't know me or what I care about in life."

"Your father knows more about you than you give him credit for, Maggie," Garrett stated as he walked to the door. "And, I might add, so does the man he's chosen to be your husband."

Maggie grew furious at this. "And just how would you know?" she asked, crossing her arms in front of her.

"Because, Maggie," Garrett replied dryly. "I am that man."

Chapter Four

Garrett returned to his seat with the porter close behind him. "Will you be needin' anything else, sir?" the porter asked in a low voice.

"No, thank you," Garrett replied rather distracted.

"What about your missus, sir?"

"No. Nothing." Garrett stated firmly.

When the porter had walked away, Garrett punched his fist against his leg. *I never should have told her like that,* he thought. He stared out the window at the open expanse of Kansas grasslands flashing by. The train was traveling at nearly seventeen miles an hour.

Garrett closed his eyes and remembered Maggie's expression as he had told her that she was to marry him. Her look of terror had done little to assure him that he was doing the right thing.

Things had seemed much simpler back on Jason Intissar's ranch. His mind flashed back to the day Maggie's portrait had arrived. Jason was intensely proud of his little girl, as he always referred to Maggie, but Garrett had seen a woman behind the little girl's eyes.

"She's a beauty, but wild, like a green broke mustang," Jason had announced as both men studied the portrait. Maggie had put up quite a fight over the portrait sitting, agreeing to it only after Jason had given his word that she could stay another year with her grandmother.

The promised year had come and gone. Throughout the weeks and months, Jason and Garrett had found themselves paying homage to the portrait. Garrett remembered the day Jason had found him in the library studying his daughter's likeness.

"I've had some time to reflect on matters," Jason had begun. "It seems to me that a ranch the size of mine will need more than a wisp of a girl to run it. I've worked hard to train you in every area of my holdings. Seems only fitting that you reap the reward."

"Meaning?" Garrett had questioned.

"Meaning Maggie. She'll need a strong man. A good man. A Christian man." Garrett had said nothing, afraid to believe what he was hearing. Jason had continued, "I want you to marry Maggie. That is, if what I think I've read in your eyes is true. You do love her, don't you?"

Garrett had found the thought startling, almost unsettling. But he'd known it was true. Everything Garrett had learned about Maggie in her grandmother's letters had filled him with a growing love.

"It won't be easy," Jason had explained. "She has a temper to beat all, and she won't take lightly to my choosing a husband for her."

Garrett had agreed to Jason's plan, certain that, in time, Maggie would come to feel for him the love he already felt for her.

The blast from the train whistle brought Garrett back to reality. Indeed, Maggie hadn't liked the idea of her father choosing either a husband or a home for her.

Garrett could understand Maggie's pain, but not her hatred. From their first encounter when Garrett was only fifteen, Jason had never been anything but kind to him. He had looked past the angry, pain-filled young man and seen potential that Garrett hadn't known existed. There was a kindness about Jason that brought people from the farthest reaches of the New Mexico Territory to seek work or assistance. Having known what it was to be in need, Jason never failed to feed the hungry or help the hurting.

Jason had been successful in a little bit of everything, and Garrett couldn't think of a wealthier man in the territory. Knowing that he was dying, Jason's fondest wish was to leave his empire to the two people he loved most, Maggie and Garrett.

Garrett sighed. "I can't blame her for hating me. Jason and I knew this wasn't going to be love at first sight."

Garrett hated the thought of hurting Maggie, and yet he'd had to create an attitude of uncompromising firmness between them. He'd had to act the ruffian and cad in order to drag her from the care of her beloved grandmother. But Garrett was determined to bring Maggie back to Jason and put an end to her father's continued heartbreak.

Garrett glanced at his watch. Soon they'd be stopping for supper. At least Fred Harvey's restaurants, known as Harvey Houses, were at virtually ever major stop on the rail.

Garrett remembered past meals with fond satisfaction. Fred Harvey allowed only the finest foods to be served in his restaurants. So meticulous was Harvey that he had water hauled in steel tank cars to every restaurant. Harvey had announced that this way, no matter where one traveled on the Santa Fe line, the coffee would taste the same. A wise decision, Garrett surmised, knowing that the farther west they traveled, the heavier the alkali content in the water.

The car door opened, admitting the conductor. He announced loudly their arrival in Florence, the supper stop. Those who planned to dine in the Harvey House had given their meal choices to the porter back in Emporia. Their selections had been wired ahead and would be waiting, piping hot, for them to eat.

Garrett sighed. As much as he hated the idea of disturbing Maggie, leaving her alone on the train was out of the question. She was likely to run away, as she had other times when Jason had sent for her.

Meanwhile, Maggie was pacing in her sleeping compartment, ranting and raging against her father, Garrett, and even God.

"The arrogance! The absurdity! If my father thinks for one minute that I'll allow him to marry me off to the likes of Garrett Lucas, he's out of his mind!" she shouted. She grabbed her glass of water and threw it against the door.

When her tantrum had played itself out, Maggie sat down on the edge of the bed. The entire room was only a few feet across, and eight feet long. There was a window, a bowl and pitcher sitting on a tiny dresser, and a small wooden commode. The bed itself was barely wide enough for one person, and Maggie wondered if her feet would hang over the edge.

She sat in silence for a long while and contemplated Garrett's final words. He was to be her husband! "Oh God," she breathed. "Why do You hate me so?"

A clouded memory appeared. Her mother's loving face bent over her in care, and then nothing. "You do hate me," Maggie murmured in utter despair.

Maggie caught sight of her grandmother's carpetbag and pulled it close. She felt a lump in her throat as she thought of her grandmother sitting alone in the big Queen Anne house.

"Grandmother, I love you so. Please God, even if you can't forgive me, take care of Grandmother until I can get back to Topeka," Maggie murmured.

Her mind was overwhelmed with the events of the day. It had all happened so fast. Her father had been wise to handle the situation as he had, for she would have gone into hiding if she had she known of his plans.

In his own way, he had probably tried to tell her. Maggie's mind wandered back to an unopened stack of letters collecting dust in the attic back home. She had heard nothing from her father for two years after he left. When at last a letter had arrived, Maggie had refused to read it. Grandmother had been understanding, Maggie remembered, but she had also engaged her granddaughter in discussions about forgiveness and God's overall plan.

"Oh, Grandmother," Maggie sighed.

She opened the bag and removed its contents one by one. There were a dozen or more biscuits, and Maggie knew they'd be the lightest, finest soda biscuits ever made. Next she pulled out several pieces of fruit and a large chunk of cheese that her grandmother had lovingly wrapped in an embroidered tea towel. Maggie reached down deep and touched something quite familiar. She began to sob. It was her grandmother's Bible.

Maggie hugged the Bible to her chest and cried. Her pain grew more intense. She allowed the Bible to fall open. The final verse of the Old Testament loomed prophetically across the page: "And he shall turn the heart of the fathers to the children, and the heart of the children to their fathers, lest I come and smite the earth with a curse" (Malachi 4:6).

"But this can't be right," Maggie said aloud, snapping the book shut. "Grandmother needs me, and I need her. My father hasn't turned his heart to me, and I certainly won't turn mine to him. Will You curse me without considering my side of the matter?"

Just then a knock sounded at the door, and Maggie began to tremble uncontrollably. Was it Garrett? What would she say?

Silently, Maggie placed the food in the carpetbag and set it on the floor. Then she eased down to the mattress, pulled her legs up under her, and feigned sleep. The knock sounded again, and then the soft voice of the porter called her name. Finally, there was nothing.

Afraid to move, Maggie succumbed to the weariness that possessed her body and drifted into a fitful sleep. The day's events combined with the heat had been too much.

Maggie dreamed of a field of prairie flowers. Tall Kansas sunflowers waved majestically above the knee-high prairie grass. Bachelor buttons and sweet williams dotted the landscape with vivid purples and blues. She was running and running across the prairie until she could feel her legs ache from the strain. She pushed herself to continue until the pain in her legs became unbearable. Maggie felt herself falling in slow motion. Down she went to the velvety softness of new prairie grass.

Someone was calling her name, and when she opened her eyes, she met the bluest eyes she'd ever known. Garrett Lucas!

Maggie struggled to move away from Garrett, but it was no use. Her legs were badly cramped and the pain she'd felt in her dream had become a very real sensation.

"Don't touch me!" Maggie winced in pain as she tried to move her legs.

"Stop fighting me. I'm not going to hurt you," Garrett said gently as he tried to help Maggie sit up.

"I don't want your help, and I don't want you here. Why are you here?" she suddenly questioned, forgetting her fear.

"We're in Florence. It's a supper stop. I've only come to wake you up and take you to supper," Garrett reasoned.

Maggie laughed nervously. "Supper? You think that I'm interested in eating? You waltz into my life, take me away from everything I love, tell me I have no choice—no say, and," she paused, drawing a deep breath to steady her nerves. "You top it off by telling me that you—you, Garrett Lucas—are to be my husband. And now you act as if nothing has happened and come to take me to supper?" Maggie tried to pull away from Garrett but found herself pinned against the wall of her compartment.

"I told you to stop fighting me. I'm not going to hurt you. I have the highest respect for your father, and for you," said Garrett in a hushed whisper. Maggie could barely hear him above the noise of her own ragged breathing.

His face was only a matter of inches from her own. Maggie swallowed hard and felt her face flush. She stopped fighting and matched Garrett's stare with one of her own.

Neither one said a word. Suddenly, Maggie knew her life would never be the same. By some means, her father and Garrett would have their way. What made it worse was that Garrett sensed this understanding in her.

Garrett moved his face closer, and Maggie closed her eyes, certain that he would kiss her. She'd never been kissed before, and part of her wondered what it would feel like.

When nothing happened, Maggie opened her eyes to find Garrett had pulled away. He looked at her with smug satisfaction, and Maggie wanted to disappear. How could he stir such intense feelings that her anger melted away, leaving her helpless to fight him?

"Shall we go to supper?" Garrett drawled, enjoying the upper hand. He helped Maggie to her feet and steadied her as she waited for the blood to return to her legs.

"I suppose I have no other choice," Maggie said soberly. "Lead me where you will, Mr. Lucas."

Chapter Five

Maggie went through the motions of eating dinner. She said very little, even though the food was some of the best she'd ever enjoyed. Maggie had never eaten at a Harvey House. She and her grandmother had always intended to do so but had never gotten to it.

Garrett had ordered the English-style baked veal pie for himself as well as Maggie. Accompanying the veal were fresh vegetables and a selection of salads, one of which was made with lobster brought in from the East.

Maggie wanted to show as little interest as possible, but her curiosity got the best of her once or twice. When the Harvey girl brought out dessert, Maggie nearly moaned.

"I don't know where I could put another bite," Maggie said to the young woman. "Just look at this piece of pie!"

Garrett smiled to himself, happy to see Maggie talking, if only to the Harvey girl.

"It's a quarter slice, ma'am. That's the way Mister Harvey says it's to be done. He doesn't want his customers leaving the Harvey House hungry." The girl curtsied.

"No chance of that," Garrett joined in good-naturedly. The Harvey girl smiled appreciatively at Garrett, and for some reason, Maggie felt angry.

"If you'll excuse me, Mr. Lucas," Maggie said, getting to her feet. "I will have this young woman show me where I can freshen up."

Garrett's eyes narrowed. They sent Maggie a silent warning, but she merely tossed Garrett a smile over her shoulder and followed the Harvey girl from the room.

"You'll find provisions to wash up at the end of the hall. The rest is out the back door," the Harvey girl pointed. "I've got to return to my station now."

Maggie lingered several minutes at the back door. It would be easy enough to slip from sight, but to where? If she left, Garrett would be right on her trail, and there would be no chance to escape before he found her.

She turned her attention to the pitcher of water on the alcove table. She poured a small amount into the bowl and took a fresh wash cloth from the stack beside the pitcher. Dipping the cloth over and over, Maggie managed to wash away most of the day's grime. Taking a comb from her bag, Maggie tried to put her hair back in order. She'd lost several hairpins.

Convinced that she had done her best, Maggie started back down the hall. As she neared the entrance to the dining room, she noticed a large map of the state. The rail line was clearly outlined, including the many spurs that ran from the main line to a variety of small Kansas towns.

Maggie traced the route. There would be a variety of whistle stops in between, but Newton would offer her the best chance of getting home. A smile played on her lips. "We'll see just how smug Garrett Lucas is when he wakes up in western Kansas and I'm gone," Maggie whispered under her breath.

In the dining room, Garrett was finishing a cup of coffee. His relaxed appearance gave no hint of his inner turmoil. Four times, Garrett had checked on Maggie, making sure she hadn't disappeared. Now as she took her seat across from him once again, he was captivated by the beauty he saw. Although he'd accused her of being a child, it was increasingly clear that she was a young woman.

"The train's been delayed," he told Maggie. "We can wait it out here or on board. What's your choice?"

Maggie said nothing, pretending to take sips of tea. Pushing the fine china cup back to its saucer, she forced herself to meet Garrett's eyes.

"It is of little consequence to me, Mr. Lucas. I leave the matter entirely up to you," she said icily. Each word had been carefully chosen and delivered.

"Very well. Let's return to the train." Garrett motioned toward the door. He left a generous tip of thirty cents and helped Maggie from her chair.

Maggie waited patiently while Garrett paid for the meal with money her father had provided. She felt angry at the thought of her father's scheming, but said nothing as Garrett lead her back to the train. Outside, the weather had turned chilly, and Maggie was glad she'd worn her heavy traveling suit.

Garrett walked slowly and made small talk about the town of Florence. Maggie feigned interest and even glanced north at the main part of town, but she breathed a sigh of relief when Garrett finally led her back to the train.

"You've been awfully quiet," Garrett drawled, making note of Maggie's sigh. "I don't suppose you'd give up this play acting and talk to me."

Maggie raised an eyebrow and lifted her face to meet Garrett's inquisitive stare. "I don't know what you want me to say, Mr. Lucas. I'm tired and confused, and as a spoiled and selfish child, I can't imagine having anything to say that could be of interest to you."

It was Garrett's turn to sigh. "Maggie, that's not true. First off, I wish you'd call me Garrett."

"First? What next?" Maggie questioned in a sarcastic tone.

"Frankly, I wish you'd sit a spell with me. It's early, and you'll have plenty of time to rest later." Garrett was as polite and considerate as Maggie had ever seen him.

"Very well—Garrett. I will sit with you," Maggie said, trying to put Garrett's mind at ease. It was important to make him believe that she'd accepted her fate.

Garrett felt his chest tighten when Maggie said his name. He grinned broadly as he helped her board the train and led her down the aisle to the window seat.

For a moment Garrett stood, admiring Maggie's profile. The lanterns above the aisles threw a mysterious glow. In their gentle light, Maggie looked more a woman than her seventeen years.

Maggie grew uncomfortable under Garrett's detailed scrutiny. "What was it you wanted to discuss, Mr. Lu . . . , Garrett?" Maggie questioned, hoping he'd stop examining her face.

"Maggie, you don't need to be afraid of me," he said softly, taking the seat beside her.

"I'm not, . . ." Her words trailed off. There was no sense in lying. "I guess it's just a natural reaction," she finally admitted.

"Of course," Garrett agreed. "I wouldn't expect anything else, but I want to put your mind at ease if I can."

Maggie wished she could freeze the moment in time. The muted light of the train, the star-filled sky beyond the windows, and Garrett Lucas looking at her in a way no other man had ever done.

Garrett closed his brown, calloused hand over her small, soft fingers. Maggie's breath caught in her throat. She tried to will herself to pull her hand away.

"I wish you wouldn't do that," she whispered without daring to look into Garrett's blue eyes.

"Is that the truth, Maggie?" Garrett inquired, daring her to face her feelings. He knew playing upon those feelings might jeopardize the progress that had been made, but human nature urged him on.

Maggie touched her free hand to her forehead. "I can't think clearly when you're close by."

Garrett laughed out loud, causing several of the train passengers to lift their eyes from newspapers and embroidery work. Maggie was grateful that their nosey train companion had departed. Garrett gave Maggie's hand a squeeze.

"That's a good sign, Magdelena, mi quierda." he murmured, so low that Maggie could barely make out the words.

"What does that mean?" she questioned, not certain she wanted an answer.

"I'll tell you later," Garrett grinned. "I don't think you could appreciate it right now."

Maggie spoke out boldly. "A term of endearment, no doubt." The warmth of Garrett's hand seemed to radiate up her arm.

"Would you hate that so very much?" he inquired.

Maggie didn't trust herself to answer. She lowered her face as she felt blood rush to her cheeks.

"I'm sorry," Garrett said. "I shouldn't have pressured you with something so intimate."

"No," Maggie whispered. "You shouldn't have." Silence fell like a heavy blanket between them. Maggie wished Garrett would remove his hand, but he didn't.

"Don't you have any questions about your father?" he asked. He hated to break the moment of intimacy by bringing up Jason's name.

"I suppose I am curious," Maggie said thoughtfully. She pulled her hand from Garrett's, pretending to loosen the lace collar at her neck. What she said was the truth, and it couldn't hurt to listen.

"Good. What would you like to know first?" Garrett questioned her as easily as if they'd been lifelong chums. This feeling of familiarity bothered Maggie.

"Start anywhere. I don't know much at all. Grandmother used to share bits and pieces with me, but she knew how uncomfortable it made me," Maggie replied absentmindedly.

"Why, Maggie? Why did it make you uncomfortable to hear about your father?" Garrett pried, hoping Maggie would answer truthfully.

"Because he'd hurt me so badly," Maggie blurted out. She couldn't help the tears that formed in her eyes. She turned her face to the window, but Garrett reached across, compelling her to face him.

"Sometimes it's necessary to open up a wound, to clean it out and let it heal. Life's like that too, Maggie," he said softly.

Maggie wiped a single tear away as it slid down her cheek. "Some wounds never heal, Garrett."

"They can with God's help. 'My heart is sore pained within me: and the terrors of death are fallen upon me.' That's from Psalms," Garrett offered.

"You know the Bible?" Maggie questioned in disbelief.

"Not as well as I'd like to, but I suppose more than some. I found religion a way of life when I was young. But it wasn't until after I lost my parents that I learned what a relationship with Jesus Christ was about," Garrett answered.

"I didn't know your parents were dead. What happened to them?" Maggie questioned, steering the conversation away from the issue of salvation.

"Their wagon overturned on a mountain road. They were hauling goods back from Santa Fe and never came home. I was twelve at the time."

"How awful," Maggie gasped. "What did you do?"

"I did the only thing I could do," Garrett shrugged. "I mourned their passing and was packed off to Denver to live with an aging aunt."

"You had no other family?" Maggie was suddenly quite interested.

"None. My mother's sister was quite a bit older. She was the only living relative I had in the world. Life out West isn't easy on people," Garrett reflected. "My aunt died two years later, and I took off on my own."

"Where did you meet my father?"

"I'd wandered down to Santa Fe," Garrett said, smiling sadly. "I was nearing my fifteenth birthday and feeling pretty sorry for myself. Here I was, a young man alone in the world. I was just existing, not really living. I felt God had deserted me. That's when your father came on the scene.

"I was sweeping out a livery stable for a man in Santa Fe. He paid me twenty cents a week, and let me sleep in the loft. It wasn't much, and I was getting pretty tired of it. My parents and aunt had left me some money, but I couldn't touch it until I turned twenty-one. Since my fifteenth birthday was coming up, I figured I'd take my week's wages and blow it at the saloon.

"I'd never been to a saloon, but I guzzled down as much rotgut as I could buy. I sat there nursing the last few drops in my glass, when it hit my head and stomach at the same time. I made a mad dash for the back door and the alley. That's where I met your pa."

"My father?" Maggie asked surprised.

"He happened to be walking down the alley just then. Most nights he'd walk for hours by himself. You have to remember, he'd just come to this territory. He'd lost your mother and a baby son and had had to leave behind a baby daughter. If I had been five minutes later to the alley, I'd have missed him all together."

"What happened?"

"I thought I was dying, but your father helped me, and when it was all over, we shared our troubles. Your father offered me the use of his hotel room, and we fast became friends."

"My father was depressed because of Mother's death, wasn't he?" Maggie asked, picking at imaginary lint on her skirt.

"Not really. Jason, your father that is, said he believed his wife was safely in heaven with your brother. He showed me where the Bible said there'd be no sorrow in heaven, so he knew she was happy. What he couldn't abide was his need to separate his life from yours."

"Me? I was the reason he was so unhappy?" Maggie wanted to change the subject, yet in her heart she wanted to understand the years that had separated her from her father.

"He told me that all he wanted to do was work so hard that he could go to sleep without seeing your face. He told me how you'd stood at the gate, tears streaming down your face, calling for him over and over," Garrett paused knowing that Maggie was filled with the pain of this memory. He reached his arm around her shoulder and pulled her close.

Maggie allowed Garrett to hold her. She no longer hated her father for leaving her. What else could he have done? She had deserved to be left behind.

After a few minutes, Maggie composed herself and pulled away from the sanctuary of Garrett's strong arms.

"He just kept walking. He never looked back," Maggie began. I ran the length of the fence calling him. I knew he blamed me for my mother's death. I needed so much to know that he still loved me, but he said nothing."

"He couldn't, Maggie. Not and still walk away, and if he'd stayed, he knew he'd be forever lost in his remorse and sorrow. It couldn't have been an easy decision," Garrett answered gently. "I can just see you as a little girl, standing there waiting for him by the gate, day after day."

"How did you know?" Maggie's surprised expression matched her tone.

"Your father told me, and I would imagine that your grandmother told him. Maybe she thought it'd make him come home. Maybe she thought it would turn him around."

"But it didn't," Maggie said sadly.

"No, it didn't, but there is another reason your father sent for you rather than traveling to Topeka himself," Garrett said in a way that demanded her attention.

"What?" Maggie questioned.

"If you'll recall, your grandmother mentioned that your father hasn't been well."

"Yes," Maggie murmured.

"Your father always intended to make things right. He thought that if he gave you enough time, you'd outgrow your hatred. But now he doesn't have that luxury."

"Why not?" Maggie asked.

"Because he's dying, Maggie."

"That isn't possible! He's not an old man, and he has plenty of money for doctors and medicine. He can't be dying," Maggie stated in disbelief.

Garrett's eyes softened. "All the money in the world can't buy you a new heart. Jason's heart has worn itself out, and there's no way to make it right again. He's aged rapidly, lost a great deal of weight, and spends most of his days in bed."

Maggie let the news soak in. "How, how long . . ." Maggie couldn't ask the question.

"How long does he have?" Garrett filled in the words.

Maggie nodded.

"Only God knows for sure."

Maggie felt more tired than she'd ever been before. She could no longer deal with her painful past.

"Garrett, I believe I'd like to retire. I'm completely spent."

"I understand. Let me walk you to your sleeper." Garrett stood and offered Maggie his hand. For a moment she hesitated, but her heart reasoned away any objections. She placed her hand in Garrett's and allowed him to lead her down the train aisle.

The lantern in Maggie's sleeping compartment made the room look warm and inviting. She paused in the doorway.

"Goodnight, Garrett," she said. She tried to think of something else to say, but the intensity of Garrett's stare banished rational thought. Maggie could feel her heart beating in her throat. Garrett was too close, and his hand was still firmly around her arm.

When he leaned down and gently pressed his lips on hers, Maggie went limp. She'd never been kissed by anyone on the lips, and now she was letting a man she'd known only hours do it.

The kiss lasted a heartbeat, but to Maggie it seemed like a lifetime. When Garrett raised his head to speak, Maggie kept her eyes lowered. "Goodnight," he said before retreating down the narrow train aisle.

Chapter Six

At midnight, the train entered Newton, Kansas. Maggie was jerked awake by raucous laughter and drunken singing. As she struggled to sit up, she remembered Garrett's kiss.

"I've got to get away from here," she said in a hushed whisper. The sound of breaking glass outside drew her attention, and she peeked out from behind the window shade. The depot's large white letters read, "Newton."

Surely, Garrett's asleep at this hour, Maggie thought. *I should leave now.* The girl rushed to find her clothes. She reached into the inner pocket of her jacket and found her money still safe.

The lantern burned very low, and Maggie hurried to the mirror and did her best to pull her hair back. She tied it with the ribbon that had held her lace collar at the neck of her blouse. "It'll have to do," she conceded, not totally satisfied with the results.

Maggie grabbed the carpetbag and pulled her coat on quietly. Gently she edged the door of her sleeping compartment open and checked the hallway for any sign of Garrett. There was none.

As quickly as she could, Maggie maneuvered through the shadowy corridors of the train car. At last she was rewarded with the exit door.

"Well, Miss, if you're getting off here, I'd suggest you hurry. Train's pulling out directly," the conductor told her in his disinterested manner. Maggie prayed that he wouldn't question Garrett's whereabouts.

"Thank you, I will," Maggie replied. "Can you tell me where the nearest hotel is?"

"That whitewashed clapboard over there," the conductor said, eyeing his watch. "Sorry ma'am. We're pulling out. Are you staying?"

"Yes," Maggie managed to say. She took a last look at the train. The laughter had died down, and there was just the muffled noise of several other passengers walking away from the railroad station. The conductor returned the steps to the platform of the train and waved his brass lantern to signal the engineer.

As the train groaned and jerked down the tracks, Maggie thought of Garrett. She was almost sorry that she'd outfoxed him. She chuckled to herself as she walked toward the hotel.

Maggie found sleeping quarters with only moderate difficulty. As tired as she felt, she would have gladly slept in the barn. The manager had given her a candle, and Maggie didn't bother to inspect the room other than to locate the bed.

She undressed and, with a quick breath, blew out the candle and settled into bed. Maggie thought about all the things Garrett had told her. A part of her wished she could break down the barriers between her father and herself, but Maggie was certain he would never forgive her. Loneliness filled her as she again saw herself as a child. She struggled to remember something, but it passed away quickly in the cloudiness of sleep.

Several hours later, Maggie woke with a start. She couldn't remember where she was. The sun was just starting to shine through the lace curtains of her hotel room window.

Maggie swung her legs over the side of the bed, newly aware of her surroundings. The room wasn't much to look at, but it was clean and safe. The girl shivered from the cold wooden floor as she crossed to the window.

Careful not to reveal that she was dressed only in her camisole and petticoat, Maggie pulled back the curtain. Most of Newton still slept, and she wondered what time it was.

It must be early, she thought to herself. Realizing she was hungry, Maggie placed the carpetbag on the bed and pulled out a soda biscuit. As she began to eat, she remembered the evening before when she'd dined with Garrett in Florence. The heady aroma of the Harvey House food lingered in her mind, making her biscuit seem inadequate.

She also remembered the intimate conversation, Garrett's touch, and their kiss. Maggie shook her head as if to dispel the memory, but it was no use. Dancing blue eyes and a gentle smile were all she could remember. That and the fact that she was supposed to become Garrett Lucas's wife.

Within an hour, Maggie was dressed. Her traveling suit was hopelessly wrinkled, but there was no use worrying about it. She took the carpetbag and headed downstairs.

"Morning, Miss." The same man who'd given her entrance the night before was greeting her as though he'd woken from an undisturbed night. Maggie couldn't help but smile.

"Good morning," she answered politely. Just then, half a dozen children came running through the lobby. They were laughing and playing tag.

"Now children," the man began. "You know the rules about running inside. Go on out if you're going to run." The children stopped long enough to acknowledge their father, and then rushed through the hotel door out onto the street.

"Now, Miss, what can I do for you?" he asked, turning his attention back to Maggie.

"When will the next train for Topeka be through?"

"Well, that's hard to say. Usually, the train you were just on transfers its passengers at Great Bend. Then it comes on back and picks up eastbound passengers," the man told her.

"Usually?" Maggie held her breath.

"They've been having trouble with the Arkansas River. Rains are causing grief with the flood levels. If there's much more rain, the Arkansas is going to be out of its banks, and then there won't be any trains through for a spell."

"If it doesn't flood," Maggie began in a hopeful tone, "when will the train be back through?"

"This afternoon."

Maggie bit her lower lip as she thought. Garrett was bound to know she was gone by now. If not, it wouldn't be much longer before he found out. She couldn't risk staying in Newton long enough for Garrett to return on the afternoon train.

"What about a horse? Where could I buy or rent a horse?" Maggie questioned innocently.

"You could check at the livery stable, but I wouldn't get my hopes up. Horses are hard to come by out here. You won't find too many people willing to rid themselves of one. Besides," the man answered noticing Maggie's attire. "You aren't really dressed for riding."

Maggie tried to smile, but her mind was in a frenzy. If she couldn't get out of Newton within hours, Garrett would find her.

"What about the stage? Will there be a stagecoach or freighters leaving for Topeka today?" Maggie knew she was appearing desperate.

"I don't know what's chasing you, little lady, but the answer is no. Stage isn't due through here for another day," the proprietor said sympathetically. "I'd check with the livery stable first, but I'd say if you're going to leave Newton today, it'll be on foot."

Maggie nodded and thanked the man. She walked to the livery stable, where the livery owner told her there hadn't been a horse available for sale since February.

"Where you want to go, little lady?" a foul-smelling man asked Maggie.

"I'd rather not discuss it," Maggie said, growing increasingly uncomfortable as the man's friends joined him.

"She ain't your type, Jake," one of the man's filthy friends offered. "You're more my type, now ain't you?" The other men laughed and ribbed each other with their elbows.

"You saddle tramps git out. You hear me? Now git!" the livery owner bellowed. When the men begrudgingly walked away, Maggie turned to thank the man.

"I appreciate your help. I don't suppose there's any hope of someone hauling freight out this morning?"

"Nope, I'd know if there was. As far as I know, you're stuck here at least until tomorrow, probably more like next Friday. I don't think the train will get past the Arkansas River crossing."

A discouraged Maggie walked to the Harvey House and sat down for a hot breakfast. Her money was going fast, but if she did have to walk out as the hotel manager had mentioned, she would need proper nourishment.

While eating breakfast, Maggie learned the train she'd been on the night before had already turned back in the direction of Newton. The Harvey girl informed her that they expected the train for the lunch meal.

Maggie wondered what she should do. She could try to hide out in Newton or get on the train after Garrett got off. She toyed with several ideas while absentmindedly stuffing food in her mouth. She was surprised to find herself nearly finished with her meal when the Harvey girl appeared at her table to see if she needed anything else.

By eight o'clock, Maggie had decided to walk to Florence. The town was a main hub for the stage, and freight was being hauled out every day. Maggie didn't know how long it would take to walk the thirty miles to Florence, but putting space between Garrett and herself was the only thing that mattered.

After paying for her breakfast, Maggie got directions to the general store and went in search of supplies.

A cheery bell rang on the door of the store as Maggie entered. She was greeted by an elderly woman who eyed every stranger suspiciously.

"Where did you come from?" the woman questioned rudely.

"I'm from Topeka," Maggie answered, hoping that her honesty would quell the woman's curiosity.

"Topeka? You came here from Topeka? When?"

"I came in last night, and now I'm getting ready to leave. I have a few things I need, and if you don't mind, I need to hurry," Maggie retorted rather harshly.

"You running from the law, girl?" the woman continued to pry.

"Absolutely not!" Maggie exclaimed.

Quickly, Maggie located the things that she needed for the walk. She was grateful she'd had the sense to wear walking shoes. She located a canteen and some dried fruit and placed them on the counter.

"I figure you must be planning on walking somewhere. I'd be mindful of the weather if I was you," the older woman said, seeming to soften a bit. "My big toe has been aching all night from the chill in the air. I figure a powerful storm is brewing, and we'll be due for rain tonight." Maggie nodded and paid the woman.

"You aren't going to walk far in that outfit are you?" the woman asked, smoothing back a strand of gray hair.

"It'll take me as far as I need to go," Maggie replied and walked out of the store.

Maggie knew that following the train tracks would be the wisest thing to do. She also knew that it would be the first place Garrett would look for her. She walked several yards before deciding to parallel the tracks as best she could without being seen. The prairie stretched out endlessly before her. Only an occasional stand of trees broke the monotony.

Remembering the old woman's warning, Maggie looked to the skies. Clouds were building to the west. Probably the same storm that had flooded the Arkansas River, Maggie surmised.

For a moment she thought better of her decision to walk to Florence. She turned to survey Newton once again. Surely it couldn't be that hard to find a hiding place.

She looked skyward again, and her mind turned to thoughts of God. Where was He in all this? Maggie couldn't help but wonder what God would want her to do. She'd spent so much of her life ignoring God's direction that now she felt ridiculous for her concern.

But maybe God wanted to use something in this to help her find her way. A place where Maggie could finally belong. She sighed. Why would God care about her? After all, she'd done nothing but turn her back on Him. No, Maggie decided, God certainly wouldn't listen to her now.

Calling upon every ounce of courage she possessed, Maggie moved north, away from the tracks. She knew she'd be able to see the telegraph wires from quite a distance, and the added space gave her a slight feeling of security. When Maggie felt confident that she was far enough away from the tracks to be hidden by the tall prairie grass, she turned east. Determined to reach Florence as soon as possible, Maggie quickened her steps.

"Soon I'll be back where I belong," Maggie said aloud, trying desperately to bolster her sagging spirits. But in truth, Maggie wasn't sure where she belonged.

Chapter Seven

By ten o'clock, Maggie knew that leaving Newton had been a mistake. Her feet hurt and her back ached. Sitting down, Maggie took off her shoes and surveyed the terrain around her. It was pretty enough, she thought as she rubbed her blistered feet. The fields were covered with tall, thick prairie grass. In the distance, rolling hills were covered with soft greens and purples.

Returning her shoes to her feet, Maggie stood and brushed the grass from her skirt. If only it were that easy to brush off the emptiness that filled her heart!

The air felt heavy and sticky. The farther Maggie walked, the more desperate she felt.

"But I had to leave," she reasoned aloud. "I couldn't go on with him—with Garrett." Just saying his name reminded her of the tender way he'd kissed her.

Growing up in Topeka, Maggie had avoided both boys her own age and older men who found her prime wife material. It was the age of the mail-order bride, and Maggie couldn't help but laugh out loud as she remembered one particular encounter. Harley T. Smythe, a local bride broker, had come unannounced to the Intissar home.

Maggie could still remember the stunned look on her grandmother's face as Mr. Smythe had explained his intentions of arranging a marriage for the older woman. Sophia had listened patiently, but not without discomfort. When at last Mr. Smythe took a breath, Sophia had interrupted and led him back to the front door.

"Mr. Smythe," Sophia had stated as she fairly pushed him through the portal. "I have no intention of remarrying." With that she closed the door in Harley T. Smythe's astonished face, and let out a laugh that matched that of Maggie's.

Maggie felt tears in her eyes. "I love you so much, Grandmother. You were always there for me, and you always made me happy." Maggie continued talking as if her grandmother walked beside her. Somehow it made the miles pass more quickly.

She had walked some distance when the grasslands started giving way to rockier scenery. The rocks were a nuisance, but there was no avoiding them.

Soon Maggie came to another obstacle. A wide ravine, apparently a dry wash or creek bed, cut deep into the ground. Maggie considered her plight, but within seconds her mind was made up for her. The sound of riders caught her attention.

"Garrett!" The name caught in her throat. Three mounted horses were kicking up a fury of dust in the direction Maggie had just come from.

Without thinking, Maggie started down the edge of the ravine. The rocky gravel gave way, causing her to slide halfway into the small canyon. The ravine was deep and ran for miles either way, with small caves and inlets hidden in the rock walls. As she reached the bottom, Maggie hurried in the direction of the railroad tracks.

She kept straining to hear the sound of hooves. She knew the men must have seen her, and she began to run, tripping over larger rocks. She heard rumbling in the distance. The sky had grown dark. Her side began to hurt and her legs were cramping, but Maggie knew she had to continue running.

The ravine grew deeper and began twisting and turning. Maggie could see where the railroad trestle crossed the ravine. If she could make it to the trestle, she might find a place to hide. She hiked her skirts up higher and put all her strength into running. As she approached the trestle, her eyes darted back and forth. No sanctuary revealed itself.

Quickly, Maggie scurried under the trestle and continued down the ravine. Rain started to pour, and Maggie grew desperate as she heard a horse's whinny. The riders were very close.

"Deliver me in thy righteousness, and cause me to escape: incline thine ear unto me, and save me." She murmured the Psalm, surprised that she had remembered it. She thought about praying, but changed her mind. She never could abide the attitude of calling on God when one was in trouble, only to go one's own way when things went well.

Just when Maggie found it impossible to force herself any farther, an opening in the ravine wall revealed itself. It was scarcely more than a two-foot-wide indention, but Maggie could hug her rain-drenched body against the rock and avoid being seen by the riders above her.

A flash of lightning startled the girl, and she bit her lip to keep from crying out in surprise. The boom of thunder so soon after the lightning let her know that the worst of the storm was nearly upon them. The wind picked up, muffling the riders' voices.

"I don't see her, Jake," one of the men called out. "Let's go back to town and out of this mess."

Maggie tensed. It wasn't Garrett after all, but the ruffians from the livery stable at Newton. Remembering the look in Jake's eyes caused her to freeze in fear.

"I guess you're right. I'm pert near soaked to the bone already."

Maggie recognized Jake's grizzly voice. Another flash of lightning caused Maggie to jump. Overhead, the horses snorted and stamped.

"Come on. Let's git," Jake called to his companions. "Another day, little lady," he yelled in the direction of the ravine. Maggie shivered at the thought.

The men rode away, but with the storm growing stronger, Maggie stayed against the ravine wall. Thunder continued to boom out answers to lightning, and the sky grew even darker. Maggie noticed water collecting in the ravine bottom.

After another ten minutes, the lightning had lessened, but not the rain. The water was nearly to Maggie's ankles, and it continued to rise.

I've got to get out of here, Maggie thought. She began to wade toward the railroad bridge. The weight of her water-drenched skirts threatened to drag her down, but she held her skirts up above her knees and kept wading. She got to the trestle, thankful that the skies had lightened a little.

Maggie rested against one trestle support after another until she'd worked her way out of the ravine. At the top, she rested under the bridge and considered what to do next. The water had risen even higher and resembled a small creek.

Suddenly, Maggie became aware of what a sheltered life she'd led. Someone had always been close at hand to help her out of trouble. While she'd learned many social graces and home skills, she was just as Garrett had said: a spoiled and selfish child.

When the rain let up, Maggie continued her journey toward Florence. The sky was overcast, but the sun was beginning to heat things up. Maggie felt sticky and uncomfortable in her clothes.

The clouds began to build again, and huge thunderheads were lining the horizon to the west. Maggie recognized signs of another storm. She picked up her pace, but because of her blisters, she just as quickly slowed down again.

Tears welled in Maggie's eyes. All she wanted to do was go home, care for her Grandmother Intissar, and be happy. Why would God begrudge her that? But Maggie already knew the answer. God was not making war on her. She was making war on God.

Refusing to deal with the issue of God and her need for Him, Maggie concentrated on each step. "I'm one step closer to Topeka. I'm that much closer to home," she murmured as the soggy ground mushed up around her feet.

The sky grew darker as the squall line neared. Maggie felt even more vulnerable than before. Part of her wanted to sit down on the waterlogged ground and cry, but she knew that she had to find shelter.

Maggie could see very little that constituted a safe haven. Ahead to the north was a small stand of trees. They weren't likely to offer much protection, but perhaps they would buffer the wind. As Maggie pushed forward, she remembered her grandmother's warning about trees and lightning. She knew she was being foolish, but the alternative of open prairie seemed far less appealing.

Maggie barely reached the trees when the first huge raindrops began to fall. The sky had taken on a greenish hue, a sure sign of hail.

The trees offered little cover. The brush around them was laden with dead leaves, grass, and twigs. Maggie chose a spot surrounded on three sides by young trees, hoping that if lightning proved to be a problem, it would strike taller, older trees.

The wind picked up and chilled Maggie to the bone. Rain pelted her from every direction. Maggie hid her face in the carpetbag, refusing to watch the violence around her.

After what seemed hours, the storm played itself out, leaving colder temperatures behind. Maggie began to walk, no longer able to bear the pain and cold of sitting crouched against the trees.

There was little hope of reaching Florence before night, and Maggie began to wonder how she would endure a night on the prairie. If she continued walking after dark, there would be no way of knowing where she was. But if she stopped, she'd have to sleep out in the open.

Maggie walked on in the fading light. Every part of her body was saturated from the rain, and the weight of her clothing was slowing her pace to a near crawl. Finally, as the last bit of light slipped over the horizon, Maggie dropped to her knees in the soggy prairie grass.

The prairie sky filled with stars, and the moon darted in and out from behind clouds. Maggie huddled shivering on the ground below. Her senses were dulled from the cold, and her mind was groggy with sleep. The last thing she remembered was the distant howl of a coyote.

The next morning dawned bright and clear, but the wind was still cold. Typical of Kansas weather, summer didn't guarantee warmth.

Maggie pulled herself to a sitting position and waited for her head to stop spinning. When the dizziness refused to subside, she began to panic. She shook her head and felt blinding pain.

Slowly, she got to her feet and tried to get her bearings. There was no sign of the railroad or the telegraph poles. There was nothing to do but walk in the direction of the rising sun. At least that would put her in an eastward direction.

Minutes worked into hours, and Maggie still had no indication that she was where she ought to be. She strained her eyes to catch some sign of life but saw nothing except hills and rocky fields.

When the sun was nearly overhead, Maggie stopped and ate some of the food from her carpetbag. It satisfied her hunger but did nothing to clear her head. She rested on the grass for a moment, fighting dizziness. Mindful that precious time was escaping, Maggie summoned all her strength in order to push on.

She got on her hands and knees and tried to stand, but immediately fell back to the ground. She tried again and again, but it was no use. Finally, Maggie gave up and let her body slump to the ground.

"I give up God!" she cried to the heavens. "I give up. Whatever it is You want, I accept. I won't fight anymore. If marrying Garrett Lucas and living in the New Mexico Territory are best for me, then so be it. I will not defy Your will any longer. But, please, please help me now. Show me what to do, where to go! Please!"

Maggie was unable to keep her eyes open. She dreamed of warm fires and her grandmother's hot chocolate. She was vaguely aware of a dull ache in her head and chest, but she couldn't rally enough strength to figure out why she hurt so much.

When next she opened her eyes, the sun was just setting on the horizon. Or was it rising? Maggie tried to get some sense of the time of day, but her mind refused to register anything but pain. She coughed until she nearly passed out. The intense cold made her shake violently.

At one point, Maggie opened her eyes and thought she saw people in the distance, but when she squeezed her eyes tight and opened them again, she realized it was just her imagination.

The sky grew dark and the ground grew colder than ever. Maggie's teeth began to chatter uncontrollably. She didn't hear the approaching sound of horse hooves, and she barely felt the hands that gently turned her over and helped her to sit. When she opened her eyes, she could only gasp one word before falling back against the offered support.

"Garrett."

Maggie saw tears in Garrett's eyes as he cradled her in his arms. They couldn't be real, she decided. Nor could the words she heard him saying.

"Maggie, my Maggie. What would I do if I lost you now? Please, God don't let her die!"

No. Those words were only her wishful imagination, Maggie decided as she drifted into sleep.

Chapter Eight

It seemed only moments had passed since Maggie had last opened her eyes. But looking above, she was dumfounded to find mud, thatch, and sod hanging over thin poles. Where was she? Maggie struggled in vain to remember what had happened on the rain-drenched prairie.

Mindless of the pain in her chest, Maggie sat up and began coughing violently. A bearded Garrett Lucas rushed into the room to her side.

"Try to take a sip of water," he said, gently supporting her back while handing her a tin cup. Maggie did as he said, and found her cough abated somewhat.

"What happened? Where are we?" Maggie hoarsely whispered. She was puzzled that Garrett wore a beard and that his attire had so drastically changed since last she'd seen him on the train.

Garrett went to the small cook stove and returned with the cup.

"Drink this," he instructed.

Maggie took the cup and looked inside. It held a thick black syrup." What is it?" she questioned skeptically.

"It's medicine to clear out your lungs," Garrett replied, concern hanging thick in his voice.

"Your stomach too, I'd venture to say," Maggie said, trying to lighten his mood.

Garrett laughed at Maggie's words. It was so good to hear her speak, even if to question his actions.

"I'm glad I amuse you, but what in the world has happened? I remember walking out of Newton, and the terrible storms, but after that . . ." Maggie paused trying her best to remember.

"Drink first, and then we'll talk," Garrett said, pointing to the cup. Maggie screwed up her face at the thought of drinking the medicine but did as Garrett instructed. The blend wasn't so bad. Maggie finished it and held the empty cup up as proof.

Garrett set the cup aside and pulled up a crude wooden chair. "Now, I believe we have some things to discuss." His dark brown hair was a bit wild, and the beard made him look older.

Maggie was captivated by the way Garrett looked, but she refused to acknowledge the slightest admiration. She waited for Garrett to continue.

"I don't know what in world you were thinking, getting off a train in the middle of the night," Garrett tried unsuccessfully to sound stern. When he looked at Maggie, even in her sickly state, she was all he'd ever wanted. She was beautiful, intelligent, hardworking, and resourceful—although he would have to teach her a bit more about that last quality.

"I wanted to go home to my Grandmother," Maggie offered lamely.

Garrett ignored her remark. "I went to let you know that the train was turning back because of the flood waters. I had the porter open your door when you didn't answer, and—" His voice caught. "I felt like dying inside when I saw you were gone."

"Father would have been quite miffed with you, eh?" Maggie teased, still refusing to acknowledge the seriousness of the situation.

"Don't you know how close you came to dying?" Garrett's face contorted painfully.

"I suppose very close."

"You suppose that, do you? Well if I hadn't come riding up when I did, you wouldn't have lived another hour. You were drenched to the bone and nearly unconscious. I was lucky enough to locate a doctor. He and his wife agreed to let us stay here in their dugout."

"So this is a dugout?" Maggie murmured while looking around the small room. Everything seemed to touch. What little furniture she could see was poorly put together, not at all what one would expect a doctor to have. The dugout had been dug by hand, some six or eight feet into the earth. The roof rose above the prairie only two or three feet.

"Yes, this is a dugout. But that isn't the issue. Maggie, please promise me you won't run away again. I can't imagine returning to your father or grandmother and explaining that you got yourself killed."

Maggie could sense the genuine concern in Garrett's voice. *Why did he care so much? He hardly knew her.*

"I'm sorry, Garrett. I shouldn't have run, but I was scared. I kept thinking about never seeing Grandmother again. Then I thought about having to face my father and his condemnation. All that along with what it would be like to . . ." Her words faded as she nearly mentioned the idea of becoming Garrett's wife. Embarrassed, Maggie lowered her face.

"I put a great deal of pressure on you," Garrett apologized. "I'm sorry for that. Back in New Mexico, the plan seemed so right."

"I guess sometimes we only seek our own way," Maggie said softly. "I don't think I've ever done as much praying as I have in the last few hours. Not that I really expected God to listen to me."

"Last few hours? How long do you think we've been here, Maggie?"

"I was just going to ask you that."

"Five days," Garrett replied dryly.

"Five?"

"That's right." Garrett leaned back against the chair. "Five days of wondering and waiting. Praying that you'd live but feeling so helpless. That's part of what I wanted to talk to you about."

"I can't believe it's been that long. It seems like just hours ago I was bartering with God for my rescue, and here you are."

"Oh, Maggie. I wish it was that simple. I found you, brought you here, and waited. Doc said he'd done all he could. We took turns watching over you. I told God if He would make you well, I'd never force you to marry me." There. He'd finally said the words.

Maggie burst out laughing, and with the laughter came the cough again.

"Maybe we should wait. Maybe you aren't up to this," Garrett hastily suggested, concerned that she was becoming hysterical.

"No, pl . . . please," Maggie sputtered the words, trying to contain her cough. "Don't take offense. I'm only laughing because I made a similar deal with God myself. I told him I'd do whatever He wanted me to, even if that meant marrying you and living with Father. I said if God would rescue me, I'd stop fighting Him."

"I see," Garrett said thoughtfully, realizing that Maggie had said nothing of a commitment to Jesus. "Seems we've both been bartering with God."

"Grandmother would chastise me," Maggie admitted. "She used to say,

'Never offer God anything you aren't ready, willing, and able to give.' "

"And now, Maggie." Garrett's voice was barely audible, "Are you ready, willing, and able to follow God's direction for your life?"

"What about you, Garrett Lucas?" Maggie avoided the question.

"It seems to me, God saved us both in spite of ourselves. I don't think we thought too clearly. I'd hate to be rash with any decision, but I did promise God I'd leave you be."

Maggie tried not to show her disappointment. Part of her was starting to like the idea of becoming Mrs. Garrett Lucas.

"I promised God I would do anything, even live with my father and become your wife. I can't break a vow to God," Maggie answered honestly.

"I'd say there's something important to learn from this. We need to seek God's will over our own. He'll guide us, but He can't if we're always trying to lead," Garrett reflected.

"I believe that's true. I guess I'm ready to try harder at trusting Him," Maggie added.

"Even with your life?"

Maggie lowered her eyes and fingered the sheets nervously. "I don't know. I don't want to make that kind of decision lightly, and I don't want to make it simply because I'm scared. I want it to mean more than that."

Garrett nodded. "I wouldn't presume to rush you. You'll make the right choice when God's timing is complete."

"Thank you for understanding," Maggie whispered. "I appreciate that more than you'll ever know."

"I wonder, Maggie," Garrett mused, leaning toward her from the edge of his chair. "I wonder if we could start over."

"Start over? What do you mean?"

"I'd like to be your friend, even if I never become your husband. Although," Garrett added with a wry smile, "I'd like to be that too."

Maggie blushed.

"I believe," she replied after a thoughtful moment, "that we could be friends. I will be your friend and I will go to my father's ranch willingly. On that I give you my word."

Garrett gently lifted Maggie's chin. He studied her delicate cheekbones and dainty lips. When he looked into Maggie's eyes, he found a sincerity that he hadn't dared to hope for.

"I know it will please your father, and if it means much," Garrett added, "it pleases me."

"Garrett, please don't rush me about my father. I still feel uncomfortable about this whole thing. I won't lie and tell you otherwise. I feel trapped, but I know that going to him is the right thing." Maggie tried to clear the hoarseness in her voice. "I can't pretend I feel anything but pain about the past and my father."

"I understand. I just love Jason so much. He's been like a father to me." Garrett immediately regretted the words.

"I wish he'd been a father to me," Maggie breathed.

"I wish he could have, too. Selfishly, I'm glad he left Topeka. I'd be a far worse man if I'd never met him. But because I care for you, I'm sorry he had to leave you."

He cared for her. Maggie warmed at the thought. Refusing to get carried away, Maggie pushed the feeling aside.

"There are a great many things I wish I could change," she finally said, looking up at the sod roof. "But wishing doesn't make it so. It doesn't bring people back to life, or give you a place to belong."

"Maggie, you'll always have a place to belong. You belong to God, but you just don't know it yet. You belong with your pa, but you can't get past the mistakes. And," Garrett sighed, "I'd like to think you belong with me."

Maggie offered a gentle smile. "All I can do is try," she replied. "But it's going to take time, and I'll need your understanding."

"I promise to help in whatever way I can." Garrett whispered the words although he wanted to shout in triumph. With God's help, he had broken through the wall of protection Maggie had built around herself. The foundation for friendship had been laid.

An hour later, a white-haired woman came bustling through the door and down the dirt stairs of the dugout. She huffed as she struggled to carry in a basket of vegetables.

"Well look who's awake," she said, spying Maggie.

Garrett smiled broadly. "We've already had quite a lively conversation. I gave her some medicine and made her stay put."

"I must say, child, you gave us quite a fright. Doc will be mighty happy to see you've pulled out of it," the woman remarked, stepping to Maggie's bedside.

"Maggie, this is Dottie. She's the doctor's wife," Garrett introduced. "She and Doc have allowed us the pleasure of staying here until you get well enough to travel."

"It's a pleasure to meet you," Maggie said sweetly. "It's so kind of you to let us stay here."

"Ain't nothing at all. I was glad for the company. Doc doesn't always make it home very early, and it gets mighty lonesome out here on the plains. I was glad to have you both, 'specially this one," Dottie nodded toward Garrett. "He's been a Godsend—brings me fresh water for the garden and totes and fetches just about anything else I need."

"If she'd waited, I would have carried in those vegetables, too," Garrett added with an admonishing look.

"Weren't that heavy. Didn't see any reason to go bothering you." Dottie waved him off. "Now how about you, Missy. Hungry?"

"I think I am," Maggie replied, realizing she wanted something to eat.

"Good. I was just about to get us some lunch. Broth for you and stew and biscuits for us." The older woman pulled on a clean apron.

Maggie wrinkled her nose. She'd hoped for something more substantial. Nonetheless, she felt very fortunate and cared for. She pushed aside the nagging thought that God had watched over her.

Day after day flew by. As Maggie grew stronger, she spent more time contemplating her life. She also developed a real love for Dottie and Doc. The older man had infinite patience and entertained his patient with humorous stories from his practice.

Maggie enjoyed watching Doc and Dottie as they playfully bantered words. Doc teased Dottie as if she were a young school girl, and Maggie noticed Dottie blushing on more than one occasion. *It must be wonderful to love each other so much after so many years of marriage,* Maggie thought.

Eager to be up and around, Maggie talked Doc into letting her get out of bed at the end of the first week. As the end of the second week neared, she and Garrett began talking about the trip back to Newton.

"With the horse I bought in Newton, we can make it back to town in a matter of hours," Garrett began, as he and Maggie strolled along the outside of the dugout. The sky threatened rain any minute, and Garrett wouldn't allow them a longer walk. "Or Doc could drive us in his buckboard. I thought I could leave him the horse as partial payment for all he and Dottie have done. They don't have a good saddle horse."

Maggie remembered her unsuccessful search for a horse.

"How did you ever find a horse to buy in Newton?"

Garrett's eyes danced with amusement. "I take it you tried and failed?"

"Yes, as a matter of fact, but—" Maggie's words were lost in the rumble of thunder.

"I think we should get inside," Garrett suggested.

"I agree. I've been in one too many storms already," Maggie said, turning toward the dugout steps.

The storm roared across the prairie. The roof of the dugout leaked, and it swayed in the gusty winds. Maggie had to light the lamp twice because of the draft from the storm.

"We'll be lucky if there isn't hail," Garrett stated as he cracked open the door and looked out. "I'm glad Dottie went to town with Doc this morning."

"Do you think it will get much worse?" Maggie asked, paling at the thought.

"I don't know. The rain's letting up some, and the wind is dying down. Maybe the worst is past. I'm going to take a look," Garrett replied and opened the door. "You stay put."

Maggie watched Garrett's booted feet disappear up the stairs. Curious about what was happening, she followed him. He seemed intent on something to the south, and when Maggie made it to the top of the stairs, she found out why. She gasped as she caught sight of a large tornado heading toward them.

"I told you to stay down there!" Garrett yelled, pointing to the dugout.

"Dear God," Maggie breathed her prayer. "Deliver us."

The twister played out its energy on the open prairie, darting from side to side as if in some frenzied dance. Maggie could see bits of dirt and debris flying up in the air as the storm approached. The tornado was enormous, and its path still headed directly toward the dugout.

"Let's take cover," Garrett said.

"Where?" Maggie asked fearfully, running down the stairs in front of him. There were tears in her eyes.

Garrett took everything off the table and pushed it against the wall of the dugout.

"Here. Get under the table." He pulled the mattress and blankets off the bed.

"Take these," he said, thrusting the blankets at Maggie's huddled frame. He crawled under the table and pulled the mattress in with him, securing it around them to shield them from any debris.

"Give me those blankets," he instructed.

Maggie started to hand the blankets over when the roaring of the wind caught her attention. It had started as a dull, constant noise in the background. Now it sounded as if a train were nearly upon them. Maggie caught Garrett's expression and knew instinctively that it was the tornado.

Garrett grabbed the blankets and pulled them over their heads. He wrapped his arms around Maggie as the door to the dugout burst open, and the roof began to give way.

Above the roar of the Kansas twister, Garrett began to pray. "Dear Father, protect us from the destruction of this storm and give us shelter in Your watchful care. We pray this in Jesus' name, Amen."

"Amen," Maggie murmured in agreement. Warmth washed over her and her fears abated even though the storm continued to roar. Was this the peace of God that her grandmother had tried so often to explain?

Suddenly, Maggie found it difficult to breathe. It was as if all the air was being sucked out of the room. Her ears popped from the pressure of the storm. But more than anything else, she felt Garrett's strong arms around her.

Chapter Nine

The storm completely destroyed the roof of the dugout, but Maggie and Garrett escaped without a scratch. Maggie was amazed by the power of the storm, but even more, she wondered at the power of God to protect them from destruction.

When Doc and Dottie returned to the dugout, Garrett was already repairing the roof and Maggie was clearing debris.

"We were lucky," Doc said as he gave Garrett a hand with the long roof poles. "The twister didn't touch Newton."

"We were blessed here, too," an exhausted Garrett answered. "The twister only skirted the edge of the dugout. The barn and smokehouse had some shingles blown off, but the rest of the farm is undamaged."

Maggie and Dottie carried handfuls of sod outside and stopped to appraise the situation.

"Could'a been a lot worse," Dottie said, wiping sweat from her forehead.

"That's just what Garrett was saying, Dot," Doc replied as he secured his end of the support poles.

"I've been through some bad storms before, but usually it was from the comfort of a cellar," Maggie exclaimed, still amazed at the calm, unchanged land around them.

"Well these dugouts work very nearly as well," Doc exclaimed and took the sod and branches that Maggie still held. The four worked until nightfall. After a hearty supper of Dottie's fried potatoes and pork chops, everyone went to bed early.

Days later the dugout was back in order, and Dottie declared it better than ever. Maggie seemed to thrive on the physical work, and Doc declared her completely healed. With that announcement, Garrett determined that he and Maggie should move on to Newton and catch the earliest westbound train.

Maggie was sorry to leave Doc and Dottie, but more than that, she was scared to be traveling alone once again with Garrett. It wasn't that his company was unpleasant. It was the pleasure she found in his companionship that worried Maggie. Her fear was clearly reflected in her eyes, and she flinched when Garrett took hold of her arm after he'd finished packing their meager possessions in the buckboard.

"It's going to be all right, Maggie," Garrett whispered as he helped her into the wagon. "Trust me."

Maggie met Garrett's eyes. Excitement surged through her as she realized that this man would one day be her husband. *Trust him?* Maggie questioned her heart. *Was that possible?*

Maggie roused from her thoughts as Garrett and Doc sat down on either side of her. She waved a bittersweet goodbye to Dottie, promising to write. But once the farm was out of sight, Maggie fell back into silence. She thought about the future and wondered about God.

Maybe her grandmother had been right. Maybe Maggie never felt like she belonged because she didn't. She didn't belong to God.

Maggie lost herself in the memory of things her grandmother had told her about salvation. Over many Sunday dinners, the older woman had gently shared the need for Jesus Christ and eternal life.

"One can't outrun or outgrow one's need for Jesus, Maggie," Sophia had reminded her granddaughter. "Oh people try. They find ways to compensate for the loss of God in their life."

"Such as?" Maggie had questioned.

"Well, look at Lillie." Sophia had referred to Maggie's friend. "There is no need for God in Lillie's life, at least as far as she is concerned. Her money brings everything she thinks she needs."

"Don't be hard on Lillie. She's very precious to me," Maggie had argued with her grandmother.

"Exactly. If you knew Lillie was in danger—the kind of danger that could take her life—and you could show her how to be saved from that perilous end, would you save her?" Maggie remembered the question as if it had been yesterday.

"Of course, Grandmother, you know I'd give my life for Lillie," Maggie had replied, knowing where the conversation was leading.

"Well Maggie, Jesus has already given His life for Lillie and for you. You are both in risk of an eternal danger that I can never save you from. I can help you to see the need, but only God can deal with your heart, and only Jesus can save you from death."

Maggie chilled at the memory of her grandmother's words. She rubbed her temples. If only there weren't so many things to consider.

Garrett arranged for rooms at the Harvey House in Newton, and Maggie was grateful to find bathing accommodations that didn't require a metal wash pan. She lingered for a long time in the hot water.

"I do believe in God," Maggie reasoned with herself in the tub. "I just don't know about trusting Him with everything. Surely God expects me to take care of myself, especially when I get myself into trouble through carelessness." Just then a flash of pigtails, a bedroom window, and her mother's smile came to mind. Despite her best efforts, Maggie couldn't focus the memory. *What was haunting her?*

After warming the water in the tub twice, Maggie pulled a soft fluffy towel around her and prepared for dinner. She went to a small wardrobe and pulled out a pale blue silk gown, lavishly trimmed with Irish lace and satin ribbons.

Maggie pulled the dress over her head and gently smoothed it out. The Harvey House laundress had done a good job of removing most of the wrinkles. Maggie fastened the tiny buttons up the back of the gown, struggling to secure the last few.

She stood back to survey herself in the mirror, fluffing the slight fullness of the sleeves. Satisfied, Maggie sat down to the task of putting her hair in order. After another fifteen minutes, she was finished. She was just putting her hairbrush and mirror back, when a knock sounded at her door.

"Coming," Maggie called. She opened the door without thinking to ask who it was. She knew it would be Garrett.

Garrett studied her silently and smiled broadly. "I've seen the other women downstairs, and you'll outshine them all."

Maggie blushed, not knowing what to say. She was quite inexperienced at this type of flattery. Garrett seemed to understand and took her by the hand.

"Let's go to dinner. The train passengers have finished and the dining room will be serving supper to the public." Maggie pulled her door shut and allowed Garrett to lead her down the hall.

The dining room was no shoddy affair. People from town seemed to revel in the finery and quality of Fred Harvey's English taste and decorum. The crystal was spotless, the china without cracks or blemish, and even the fine linen tablecloths were immaculate.

Maggie ate lobster in a rich cream sauce, as well as baby carrots cooked with grated orange peel, greenbeans with red pimentos and almond slivers, and a variety of other things she couldn't even remember. After dinner, Garrett suggested a walk.

"Will you be sorry to meet him?" he asked.

"My father?" Maggie inquired, knowing very well the answer.

"Yes. Will you be sorry to meet him again?"

"Sorry? No, not really sorry. I was sorry that he had to go away and sorry that we both seemed to cause each other such heartache, but I can't honestly say that I'll be sorry to meet him again." Maggie went on to tell Garrett about the last time her father had come to Topeka.

"I stole out the back and ran to Lillie's house. Her parents weren't home, but she was. We went to her upstairs bedroom and spied on my father and grandmother as they looked for me. Part of me wanted to run back to him."

"Why didn't you?" Garrett questioned as he assisted Maggie over a missing portion of boardwalk.

"I don't know," she answered softly. Suddenly she didn't want to talk. They strolled in silence for the remainder of their walk.

When they returned to the hotel, Maggie reached into her purse for the key to her room. Without a word, Garrett took it from her and opened the door. "We'll be leaving quite early. I'll ask one of the Harvey girls to wake you in time for breakfast."

The silence fell between them once again, and Maggie felt the intensity of Garrett's stare. Sounds from the restaurant faded away, and even the commotion of hotel guests at the far end of the hall seemed to be in another world.

Garrett stepped forward, and Maggie knew he would kiss her. She wanted him to, and yet she remembered her grandmother's warning about being unequally yoked with unbelievers. Grandmother had spoken of men who might court Maggie, but the truth was that Maggie was the unbeliever.

Maggie backed into her room abruptly, leaving a surprised Garrett standing with his arms slightly outstretched.

"Goodnight, Garrett," Maggie whispered and closed the door.

Maggie leaned hard against the door after locking it. She wondered if Garrett was still on the other side. Her heart pounded and her mind was muddled with conflicting emotions. Maggie prepared for bed and hoped that sleep would come quickly.

The train ride to Trinidad, Colorado, passed uneventfully. Summer storms had cleared the air, making temperatures quite bearable. The air also became dryer the farther west they traveled. Maggie loved to study the changing landscape. They had passed from rolling prairie hills to parched lands of sagebrush and juniper.

Maggie knew her feelings for Garrett were growing, and Garrett had made it clear how he felt about her. The confusion came because of her own spiritual battle. Maggie didn't want to deal with God or her father, and on the last day of their train journey, she determined to put them both aside and concentrate on her feelings for Garrett.

When dark hues of purple lined the western horizon, Maggie grew curious. "Are those the mountains?" she asked Garrett in little girl excitement.

"Yes, but this distance doesn't do them justice. Wait until we're closer." Garrett shared Maggie's enthusiasm. The mountains meant they were almost home.

Several hours later, Maggie was rewarded with a pristine and glorious sight. The Rocky Mountains in their summer splendor towered majestically before them.

"I've never seen anything like it in all my life. Just look!" Maggie exclaimed as she lowered the train window. She quickly pulled her head back in, as cinders flew back from the smoke stack, stinging her eyes. She tried to fish her handkerchief out of her bag, but it eluded her.

"Here," Garrett offered. "Look at me and I'll get it." Eyes closed, Maggie obediently turned her face to Garrett and allowed him to work.

"There! Good as new," Garrett proclaimed.

When she opened her eyes, Maggie met Garrett's eyes only inches from her own.

"Thank you," she whispered. Desperate to regain her composure, she added, "Does it always look so grand?"

Garrett laughed softly. "Yes, it always does. I find it hard to believe you've never traveled to the mountains before. I'm surprised your grandmother never took you."

"Grandmother wasn't one for traveling. She liked to stay in Topeka, garden whenever possible, and go to church activities."

"I see," Garrett said thoughtfully. "What about you? What did you like to do?"

"Well, let's see. I liked to go to the picnics our church had down by the river. We'd have at least one a month during the summer. I also enjoyed reading and the parties Grandmother and I went to." Maggie poured out the words easily but continued to look out the window, refusing to miss a moment of the newness that passed by.

As the tracks began to climb the steep grade of Raton Pass, Maggie couldn't help but gasp at the scenery. The mountains rose imposingly on either side, and the evergreens reached for heaven. There was snow on the higher peaks, and wildflowers waved along the tracks.

"We certainly don't have anything like this in Kansas," Maggie said, turning briefly to meet Garrett's eyes.

"That's true," Garrett agreed.

"You must love it a lot," Maggie said thoughtfully.

"Indeed I do. I can only think of one other thing I care more about." Maggie knew Garrett was struggling with his feelings just as she was. They seemed to have an unspoken agreement to leave the subject alone, so Maggie attempted to steer the conversation to safer ground.

"Is my father's ranch this beautiful?"

"Every bit as much and more. It lies in a rich green valley on the other side of the mountains. It's protected on both sides by the Sangre de Cristo range."

"The what?" Maggie questioned, giving Garrett her undivided attention.

"Sangre de Cristo. It means the blood of Christ. Your father said it reminded him of what was important in life. His ranch sits in a deep valley. It's great land for cattle and horses. The Pueblos have a mission not far from the ranch house. Your father set it up for a missionary couple down there. The Pueblos raise fine crops and sheep, and they share portions with your father in exchange for beef," Garrett shared eagerly.

"The Pueblos? Who are they?" Maggie questioned.

"They're Indians. Perfectly harmless," Garrett added at the look of alarm on Maggie's face. "They have a way with irrigation and planting that would make your head spin, and they live in adobe houses like the ranch, only smaller."

"Adobe? I can see I'll have a great deal to learn," Maggie murmured thoughtfully. "We might as well put this time to good use. Tell me about adobe."

"Adobe is an orange clay brick." Garrett was more than happy to teach Maggie about her new life. "The bricks are formed from straw and clay," he continued, "and then allowed to dry in the sun. The adobe is used with a small amount of timber to create a house. Then the workers mud the entire house, filling in the cracks and smoothing over the surface of the walls. The bricks are quite thick and keep the houses well insulated."

"I see, and my father's house is made of such adobe?"

"That's right. It may not seem as refined as your house in Topeka, but it holds a charm all its own."

"And the interior?" Maggie asked, trying to get a mental picture.

"We don't waste much wood out here, and you won't find a lot of it used in the house. There are some hardwood floors and paneling is used on the walls in a couple rooms, but usually the stone walls are whitewashed. The interior of your father's house is as nice as any I've seen. I think you'll like it."

"I suppose so," Maggie said softly. She remembered her home in Potwin Place and how she'd helped her grandmother pick out the colors, wallpaper, and furnishings. "I know it will mean a great deal to my father if I do."

"You don't have put on a show for him, Maggie," Garrett replied. "Your father is a simple and very compassionate man. He only asks for honesty."

Maggie stared out the window. The train engine was straining to pull the cars through the tunnel at Raton Pass. They were barely moving.

"I think he expects a bit more than that," Maggie finally said.

"But he won't expect you to put on airs. Just be honest with him, Maggie. He'll want it that way."

The day grew quite warm, and in spite of her excitement, Maggie dozed off and on as they drew nearer her new home.

"Wake up Maggie," Garrett was shaking her shoulder. "We're in Springer."

Maggie jumped up quickly. "I must have fallen asleep."

"I'll say," Garrett drawled in mock sarcasm. "Pert near a three hour nap, little lady."

Maggie laughed. The sound warmed Garrett's heart. It was good to be at peace with Maggie, even though the peace was fragile.

"Will my father be here to greet us?" Maggie questioned, realizing that she didn't know.

"He'll be back at the ranch, waiting. He'll have sent the wagons for our gear and some other things we've ordered shipped here," Garrett answered as he pulled his black Stetson on. "Of course, most of the shipment was picked up a couple weeks ago due to our little delay to put you back in order."

Maggie felt a twinge of embarrassment for the detainment. She started to say something, but was stopped by Garrett's appearance. She'd never seen him in blue jeans before. His white cotton shirt was open at the neck, and his neatly trimmed beard gave him a mysterious air. Garrett had considered shaving his beard before they left the dugout, but Maggie had protested, telling him it gave him character. Not that Garrett Lucas didn't already have plenty of that, Maggie decided.

When they stepped off the train, Garrett was quickly surrounded by men. They laughed and slapped each other on the back, all talking at once for several minutes. Maggie was certain she'd overheard one of them say congratulations. She wondered if they'd betted on whether Garrett would make it back to New Mexico with her.

Garrett turned quickly to motion Maggie to join them. "Maggie, this is Bill. He's one of your father's right-hand men."

Maggie smiled shyly. "It's nice to meet you," she said softly. The man smiled from ear to ear, revealing several missing teeth. His hair, from what Maggie could see as it peeked out from under a grimy hat, was gray fading to white.

"Pleasure's mine, Miss Maggie!"

He seemed so pleased to meet Maggie that she almost didn't catch the name of the next cowboy as Garrett had her meet the entire crew.

"This is Mack, this tall, scraggly looking guy is Cactus Jack, and this old good-for-nothing is Pike." Garrett whirled Maggie around the circle. They all seemed happy to meet her and so genuine in their greetings and best wishes that Maggie felt warmly welcomed.

"Joe and Willy are waiting for us at Five Mile Junction," Bill announced to Garrett.

"Well, it's nearly noon, and I'd imagine if we're going to make Five Mile Junction by night, we'd better get a move on," Garrett announced. It was clear to Maggie from the response of the cowboys that Garrett was in charge.

Maggie tried to take everything in: the countryside, the town, the people. Springer was the county seat, but it was much smaller than Topeka.

She stood to one side watching a hired carriage pull away with a distinguished looking man and woman. The woman was fussing with her ill-fitting traveling clothes, and the bored man was studying the head of his cane. It appeared life was the same all over. Maggie couldn't help but smile to herself.

"Do you need to stop for anything before we get on the road?" Garrett was asking.

"No, I don't think so," Maggie replied, trying to think of anything she might need.

"There's a small trading post north of the ranch. We usually get supplies and anything else we need from there. If you think of something once you get home, let somebody know and we can add it to the list. Someone is always heading over to the post office every few weeks," Garrett explained.

"We'll be that far removed from civilization?" Maggie questioned, not realizing her look of astonishment.

"I never thought of it that way," Garrett answered thoughtfully. "I guess I never needed anything more, so it didn't seem that uncivilized."

"I didn't mean to insult the place," Maggie said apologetically. "I just presumed we'd live near town. I never thought much about my father's place."

Garrett helped Maggie into the wagon and easily jumped in to take a seat beside her.

"Well, you'll have a few days' ride to consider it." With that, Garrett gave the reins a flick and the horses took their place behind Mack's wagon.

The wagon wasn't nearly as comfortable as the train had been, and while the scenery was of intense interest, Maggie's backside was sorely abused from the rocky pathway they called a road.

Two hours later, they stopped to eat. The rest was quite brief, however, and Maggie soon found herself back on the dusty trail headed into the mountains of the Sangre de Cristo.

Maggie was disappointed with the countryside. From the train, the land had seemed greener and less sandy. Up close, it looked like the edge of a desert. Maggie hoped that her father's ranch would be different.

As the sun passed behind the mountain peaks and the sky took on a purple hue, Maggie grew quite chilly. As if reading her mind, Garrett halted the wagon long enough to take a blanket out from under the wagon seat.

"Here, this ought to help. We're almost to Five Mile Junction." Garrett helped Maggie pull the blanket around her shoulders.

Little more than a gathering of shacks and corrals, Five Mile Junction looked wonderful to Maggie. After a delicious supper of steak, potatoes, biscuits, and pie, Maggie was shown to a small room. She'd changed into her nightgown and was brushing out her waist-long hair when a knock sounded at the door.

"Yes?"

"It's me, Maggie," Garrett announced. "May I come in?"

"Of course, just one minute," she said as she pulled on her robe. "All right, come ahead."

Garrett sucked his breath in hard as he caught sight of Maggie illuminated by candle. She was so delicate, yet her strength astounded him. And if all went well, one day she'd be his.

"You're so beautiful," he said in a husky whisper.

Maggie lowered her gaze, refusing to meet his eyes. She could feel a blush coloring her cheeks.

Garrett closed the space between them in two strides. He stood directly in front of Maggie without touching her. Maggie lifted her eyes to meet his. Words seemed inadequate, yet both felt captive to a spell. A spell that needed to be broken.

Garrett took a step back. "This trip is getting rougher all the time." Maggie nodded. "Tomorrow, we've got a lot of ground to cover in a short time. Are you up to it?" Again Maggie nodded, finding it hard to speak.

"Good. I'll have the cook wake you at five."

Garrett took another step back. He wanted so much to hold Maggie in his arms. No one would have to know, no one but them—and God. That thought caused Garrett to remember that their future depended on more than physical attraction. He walked to the door and, with one last glance, pulled it shut behind him and breathed a sigh of relief.

Chapter Ten

Maggie couldn't remember a rougher ride or a more desolate land. Aside from sagebrush and scrawny trees, Maggie could see nothing to break the monotonous, dusty brown earth. How could her father love this country?

Garrett concentrated on steering the team through the narrow, rocky pass. He was growing painfully aware of Maggie's presence as she bounced back and forth in the wagon seat. He needed a way to distance himself from her long enough for Jason to have a chance to get to know his daughter.

"Is this all there is to it?" Maggie questioned disappointedly as she gazed from side to side.

"What do you mean?" Garrett asked.

"All of this," Maggie said motioning to the landscape. "I thought you said it was beautiful."

"Your home is beautiful. You'll see. This is just the way we get there," Garrett answered stiffly. The lead teams were slowing to a stop, and Garrett reined back on his team. "Whoa, whoa boys," he called softly.

"Why are we stopping?" Maggie inquired, forgetting the scenery.

"We'll water the horses here. They've had a long, hard haul," Garrett answered rather curtly.

"Garrett?" Maggie said his name, and Garrett swallowed hard. She was charming without being aware of it. Her cheeks were red from the wind, and her hair had come loose and hung in curled wisps around her face.

"Have I done something wrong?" Maggie questioned earnestly. "Is it because I don't like the land?"

Lifting Maggie from the wagon, Garrett looked deep into her sapphire eyes framed by long, sooty lashes. Why did he notice every detail about her? How could she be more beautiful out here than she'd been back in Kansas?

"Wrong? The land?" he whispered hoarsely. "I don't know what you're talking about," he lied and instantly regretted it. His hands lingered around her waist for a moment. Then he turned as if to leave.

"You've hardly said two words to me all day. If I've done something wrong, I have a right to know it." Maggie's words were a little harsher than she'd intended.

Garrett fought to control his emotions. How could he wait a year or more for Maggie to grow up and marry him? What if some other young man swept her heart away before he had a chance to insure that it belonged to him?

"I have to water the horses," Garrett said and walked away.

"Well!" Maggie huffed and turned to go for a walk. She climbed up the rocky ledge and became so winded that she had to sit down and catch her breath. Garrett had warned her about the altitude and how it would take time to get used to.

As she regained normal breathing, Maggie climbed the rock and marveled at the dainty wildflowers that sprinkled the ground around her. From the wagon, she'd been sure this land was devoid of any beauty.

She reached down and picked a frilly yellow flower that matched the gown she was wearing. After fingering the lacy edges of the flower, she tucked it in the lace lining the yoke of her bodice. She loved the feel of the mountain breeze through her hair and pulled loose the ribbon that tied back the bulk of her auburn hair. What a feeling! Perhaps this arid land had something to offer.

As she reached a small rocky ledge, Maggie was rewarded with a splendid view of the Sangre de Cristo. The snow-capped summit of the highest peak glistened and beckoned to her. She almost felt like she was coming home.

"Maggie!" Garrett's voice intruded on her thoughts.

What was bothering him? Maggie worked her way down the rocky path again. "I've done nothing to cause him grief," she muttered to herself as she checked her steps, remembering to walk from side to side as Garrett had taught her.

"Where have you been?" Garrett snapped. His eyes narrowed and grew darker. "I've been looking all over for you!"

"I just took a walk, that's all," Maggie answered calmly. She wasn't going to let Garrett Lucas cause her to lose her temper.

"You make sure somebody knows where you're going before you go heading off somewhere." Maggie bit her lower lip until she tasted blood. Garrett continued to scold her as if she were a child. "This isn't like Topeka. This country is wild and unpredictable."

"It's not alone," Maggie muttered.

"Just what's that supposed to mean?" Garrett questioned. He was already mad at himself for allowing his frustration to distance Maggie.

"It means you've never answered my question, and I don't understand why you're treating me so cruelly." Maggie stood against the sun, her jaw set. "Now are you going to give me an answer?"

Garrett reached out and took Maggie in his arms. He bent his lips to hers and had barely touched them when he pulled back and walked away. A few feet down the path, he turned on his heel, returned to Maggie, and kissed her soundly. Maggie could feel the dampness of his sweat-soaked shirt and the powerful muscles of his protective arms. Suddenly, Garrett pulled himself away and strode back to the team.

Maggie stared at his retreating back. *I guess that's the only answer I'll get,* she thought. *But what an answer.* After a few minutes, she joined Garrett at the wagon and allowed him to help her up.

"Mack's going to drive you," Garrett said and walked away.

Maggie was truly confused. If her company was so unpleasant, why had Garrett kissed her? And if it wasn't because of a distaste for her company, why had he sent Mack to drive the team?

Mack turned out to be a pleasant traveling companion. He was young and energetic like Garrett, but he wasn't Garrett. Mack told Maggie stories about cattle drives and growing up in Texas.

Maggie felt badly that she only half-listened. She was still consumed by questions about Garrett's attitude. She asked Mack why Garrett had requested him to trade wagons, but Mack only shrugged his shoulders and told her he was just following orders.

The day passed quickly, and when evening came, Maggie asked Mack, "Where will we stay the night?"

"Out here under the stars, Miss Maggie," he answered, surprised that she didn't already know.

"Oh, I see," she said, looking around her.

Moments later they stopped for the night. The men quickly unharnessed the horses, rubbing them down and giving them feed and water. Bill made a supper fire while Mack and Cactus Jack unloaded food and water.

Maggie felt totally useless. She didn't know the first thing about camping, and she couldn't find out where Garrett had gone. After about an hour, Bill announced that supper was as fit as it was going to get, and the party gathered around the fire to eat.

"Where is Garrett?" Maggie questioned, unable to contain her curiosity.

"He's on the ridge, Miss Maggie," Bill offered the words along with a tin plate of beans and warm spiced apples. "He'll keep the first watch of the night."

"Oh," Maggie whispered. She wondered what he was keeping watch over, but she was too fearful of the answer to ask. Was it animals or people? Perhaps it was the banditos Mack had told her of. Maggie shivered.

"You'd better sit here by the fire, Miss Maggie," Bill directed her to a blanket. "I'll bring you some biscuits and dried beef to go with that. How 'bout some coffee to wash it all down with?" The older man worried over her like a father.

"No, thank you. Water would be fine."

"Whatever you like, little lady," Bill said and was on the move to bring Maggie her water.

Supper passed quickly, and much to Maggie's surprise, the men went about cleaning up the dishes and leftovers without looking once in Maggie's direction for help. When she offered to dry the plates, Bill waved her off.

It was growing cold when Maggie realized that she'd left her shawl in the wagon. She remembered Garrett's earlier rebuke about not announcing her whereabouts and decided she'd better tell Bill where she was headed.

"Bill, I'm going to the wagon to get my shawl."

"Better take some light. There's hardly enough moon to see by tonight," Bill replied, looking up at the starry sky. Maggie nodded.

"Just grab ya some fire." Bill motioned to the campfire and went about his business.

In her seventeen years, Maggie had never had to pull a stick from a fire, and she wasn't sure how to go about it. She stood by the fire, wanting to ask one of the hands for help, but they were busy. She finally gave up and went to the wagon in the dark.

Maggie had just reached the wagon when she heard the lonely howl of a coyote. Maggie thought of her home in Topeka and wondered if her grandmother was lonely. She had Two Moons, but it wouldn't be the same. Grandmother loved conversation, and Two Moons rarely spoke.

There was also Lillie. Maggie missed her badly. It would be fun to share her adventures with Lillie when she got a chance to write.

Maggie carefully placed her foot on a wheel spoke and pulled herself to the top of the wagon. She climbed in back with little effort and was feeling rather proud of herself when she heard a low growling sound somewhere behind her.

She turned to see two greenish yellow eyes staring back at her. Maggie felt a scream in her throat, but it wouldn't release. Motionless, she watched and waited as the growling intensified. Her breath came in quick gasps, and her heart pounded.

"Garrett!" She managed to scream the name, causing the growling to stop for a moment. "Garrett!"

Maggie saw the eyes lunge at the wagon. She heard the impact of the animal as it hit the wooden side and the commotion of the men at the campfire.

Maggie had never been given to fainting, but she had never faced such fear. As she passed into unconsciousness, she heard a single gunshot ring out and then, nothing.

"Maggie? Maggie, are you all right?" Garrett called as he held her against his chest. Maggie felt herself floating. Finally, she opened her eyes. Someone had brought a lantern, and she heard Garrett assure the other men that she was okay.

"It's all right, Bill. She's not hurt," Garrett announced. Bill took the hint and motioned the rest of the ranch hands to follow him.

"Come on, boys. We've got a coyote to skin." Bill continued to talk to his companions as they walked back to camp, but Maggie was only aware of Garrett and the protection she felt.

"I'm beginning to wonder if I'm going to get you to your father alive," Garrett said as he held Maggie.

"I'm sorry. I told Bill where I was going. Honest, I did," Maggie said, struggling to met Garrett's eyes.

"I know, Bill told me. But he also told you to take a light."

"I didn't know how to get the stick out of the fire," Maggie admitted in a defeated voice. "I didn't want to be a bother."

Garrett threw back his head and laughed. "That coyote didn't mind the bother," he finally said. "The fire would've kept him at his distance."

"I didn't know," Maggie said feeling utterly dejected. How could she know what was expected of her in this new world?

"Oh mi quierda, you are a prize," Garrett whispered as he ran a finger along her jaw. "I wish I could go straight to Pastor David and have him marry us."

Maggie sat up rather abruptly. "But I thought you and Father planned for me, I mean us, to marry right away."

Garrett grinned. "I'd like that more than I can say, but that isn't the plan."

"What then?" Maggie questioned.

"You need to get to know your father, and—" He paused for a moment. "You need to do some growing up."

"Growing up? Well I never. I wouldn't be the first woman to get married at seventeen. Besides, on July 24th I'll be eighteen!" Maggie exclaimed, squaring her shoulders.

"Maggie, you need to learn about life, and you need to be a daughter before you become a wife." Garrett noticed the disappointment in Maggie's expression. "It's funny how just a few weeks ago, you were all spit and fire, hating me with your eyes if not your words. Now you can't understand why you can't be my wife. Maggie, have you ever thought of the responsibilities of a wife?"

Maggie blushed deeply. Garrett smiled as if reading her mind.

"I know how to cook, clean, sew, and most everything else a good wife would need to know," Maggie said, avoiding Garrett's eyes. "I hardly see what being a daughter has to do with being a good wife."

"It has a great deal to do with it, Maggie. Why wouldn't you have much to do with gentlemen callers?"

"How dare you delve into my personal life!" Maggie was indignant.

"Don't you think a husband should know such things?" Garrett inquired softly.

"But you aren't my husband, and it doesn't sound like you want to be," Maggie pouted. A spark of hope flared as she wondered if she could entice Garrett to marry her immediately. If she arrived on the ranch as Mrs. Garrett Lucas, perhaps she wouldn't have to deal so intensely with her father.

Garrett looked seriously at Maggie as he turned her to face him. "Magdelena Intissar, you'd better knock off the little girl theatrics and listen up. You will never be the woman you were meant to be as long as you don't reconcile your relationship with your Heavenly Father. You've never accepted Jesus as your Savior, and you'll never be happy without Him. But, just like with your pa, that relationship is a personal one. One that I can't interfere with or get for you. You'll have to take it one step at a time, on your own."

Maggie lowered her eyes. "I just don't know if I can, Garrett." Garrett pulled her tightly against him.

"I know you can," he breathed against her soft hair.

"Will you help me?"

Garrett was quiet for a moment. When he spoke, Maggie felt her heart nearly break. "No, I can't. I won't be there."

Maggie tore herself from his grasp. "You won't be there? Then where will you be?" she demanded.

"I'm going away. That way you'll have to deal with your father, and with God. I'll be nearby, but I won't be influencing your decisions and actions. You won't be so confused then."

"Just how do you know what I'll be and won't be? Garrett Lucas, I think you're a cruel man. How could you take me away from my home, thrust me into the presence of someone I don't know, and expect me to handle the situation alone?"

"But Maggie, you won't be alone. God will go with you."

"God doesn't appear to have come with me this far," Maggie said, immediately regretting the words.

"Maggie, you don't believe that. I know your words were spoken out of fear, but I'm telling you that you have nothing to fear. Your father adores you. He's missed you every day of your separation. You won't find it hard to span the years. I promise. And as for Jesus—well, He's been standing with open arms all your life."

"Words. Just words," Maggie said, pulling herself to her feet. "I'm in exactly the same position I was years ago: on my own, to stand alone. You probably won't come back." Her voice gave way to a sob.

Garrett was beside her in a flash. "I'll be back. Don't ever doubt it. I'm going to marry you one day, Maggie Intissar, and that is something you can most definitely count on."

Surprising herself and Garrett, Maggie jumped over the side of the wagon and headed toward the campfire light.

"I mean it Maggie. Don't ever doubt me," Garrett called after her. Maggie kept going.

Taking a blanket that Bill offered, she rested on the makeshift bed that Bill had prepared from pine needles and blankets. She refused to let the men see her cry, but long after the sounds of heavy breathing and snoring filled the air, another sound joined the night. It was the sound of Maggie's intense, muffled sobs—cries that did not escape Garrett Lucas.

Chapter Eleven

The next day, Maggie was riding with Bill when they paused at the opening to the valley her father ranched. Maggie stared in awe.

Piñon Canyon, as the ranch was called, stretched for miles. The burnt orange, adobe ranch house contrasted sharply with the sturdy green piñon pines that grew in abundance in the valley. Other, smaller buildings dotted the landscape, and several huge corrals stood in direct angles from the house. Beyond the inner circle of the ranch threaded a wide, silvery stream.

"I can hardly believe it," Maggie said in wonder. "I never would've guessed that something so heavenly could be hidden in the middle of the desolation we've been riding through. It's beautiful!"

"That it is, Miss Maggie. I've called it home for nearly twelve years now, and it's always a welcome sight," Bill said enthusiastically.

"Twelve years? But my father has only been in the territory for eight years."

"That's so, but I worked this ranch for the former owner. Course it weren't nothing like what your pa has made of it. It was just a little stomping ground then. I was one of only three hands. Your father keeps over fifty." Bill urged the horses forward with a flick of the reins.

"Fifty? Why does my father need so many people?" Maggie questioned, suddenly wanting to know everything.

"There's enough work for fifty people, so he hired fifty," Bill said in his joking manner. "See, there's a lot more to a ranch than meets the eye. Somebody's got to keep up with the herd's feeding, watering, herding, branding, medicating, and such. Then there's those that keep up the land and the property. Those fences didn't just put themselves up, and they don't stay up without help. That's not to mention the house help."

"I get the picture, Bill," Maggie laughed. Then, more seriously, she asked, "What's my father like?"

"I think pretty highly of your pa. He's an honest man, pays a fair wage, and see's to it that no one goes without. He even keeps a mission on the property. It's over that ridge, 'bout twelve miles. He supports the minister and his wife who keep it up for the Pueblos."

"Oh yes, the Indians," Maggie tried to sound intelligent.

"That's right. Your pa looks after everybody."

"But why? Why does he care so much?" Maggie wondered aloud.

"I 'spect it has to do with what your pa is always saying. God was good to him, so he'll just pass it on and be good to others." Bill fell silent, and Maggie didn't ask anything else.

The day passed quickly, and after several stops to rest and water the horses, the travelers were in the valley, making their way down the well-worn path that led to Piñon Canyon.

As they approached the first corral, several brown-skinned cowboys came riding up on horseback. They rode alongside Garrett talking in Spanish and laughing. Some fell back to greet the others and cast glances at Maggie. While she couldn't understand what they said, their smiles and excitement led her to believe she'd passed inspection.

Maggie suddenly grew self-conscious about her appearance. She was wearing the same yellow dress that she'd had on for days. She was freckled and sunburned, and her hair hung in a lifeless braid down her back. What would her father think?

Once again, Maggie began to fear her reunion with her father. What if Jason Intissar had love and kindness for everyone except his daughter? What if she still stirred painful memories of her mother? Maggie had been told by her grandmother that she resembled her mother more than ever. What if her father couldn't deal with the haunting image?

In less than a heartbeat, the group halted at the huge stone walkway leading to the double doors of the ranch house. Maggie wanted to run. Her eyes darted around, and she gripped the side of the wagon. The muscles in her chest tightened, making normal breathing impossible.

Just then, Maggie caught Garrett's sympathetic look. He winked at her as Bill helped her from the wagon. The ranch house doors opened, and Jason Intissar burst through.

"Magdelena! You're really here! Oh, my Maggie, my daughter!" Maggie's father embraced her tightly. She could feel his bony thinness.

Jason stepped back to eye his daughter. Maggie said nothing. The feelings she'd buried so long ago, feelings of an eight-year-old girl watching her father walk away, threatened to overwhelm her. She wanted to say something, but her mouth refused to form the words.

"Oh, Maggie. It's really me," Jason laughed, hoping the assurance would help Maggie put aside her worried expression. "I've missed you so much! I can't believe you're finally here." Jason took her hand and twirled her in a circle before him. Maggie felt her body mechanically respond, but her heart was too overwhelmed to allow rational thought.

"You're more beautiful than your painting. Your mama would be proud. You look just like her. My, but how I miss her, mi quierda."

"That phrase—what does it mean?" Maggie questioned.

Jason smiled and took hold of her hand, "Desired one, my daughter. Just as you are to me."

Maggie raised an eyebrow, remembering Garrett's use of the phrase, but said nothing, noting the sadness in Jason's eyes.

Garrett Lucas broke the spell. "Well, Jason, here she is. I knew it would be worth the effort, didn't you?" Garrett's words were both sincere and mocking. Maggie flashed fiery eyes at him, but Garrett's lazy grin and laughing eyes were too much. She looked away.

"It was worth the effort and the wait. How do I thank you, my dear friend?" Jason exclaimed, turning to grab Garrett's hand with his free one.

"You've already rewarded me by promising me your daughter in marriage," Garrett said casually. He stared intently at Maggie, until she could feel herself blush from head to toe.

"Garrett!" Jason cried. Garrett waved his concern away.

"She knows all about it. She's even happy about it. She just doesn't like the waiting," Garrett said, pushing back the brim of his hat. Maggie fumed at the nonchalant way in which Garrett treated their betrothal.

"Is this true, Maggie?" Jason questioned. Maggie was touched by the deep concern in her father's voice. She allowed her eyes to meet his. He was grayer than she'd remembered, and his shoulders seemed more stooped. He wasn't an old man, but the sickness had taken its toll. And, try as she might, Maggie couldn't find a reason to hate her father any longer.

"Maggie, is it true that you're willing to marry Garrett?" her father asked pleadingly.

Maggie squared her shoulders and looked first to Garrett. He was actually enjoying this moment. He raised a mocking eyebrow as if to mimic her father's question. Maggie let go of her father's hand. She thought of denying it all, but when she saw the anguish in her father's eyes, she couldn't.

"Yes," she whispered and turned her eyes to the smooth stone beneath her feet.

"Praise God!" her father exclaimed. "I had only hoped to dare that this marriage might take place. Oh, what happy news the two of you have brought me."

Maggie felt defeated and tired. She wanted to get even with Garrett, but she didn't have the energy to fight back.

The warmth of the noon sun was bearing down on them, and Jason motioned them to the house. "Come on. We need to get you out of this heat. I'll bet you'd like a bath," Jason said, taking hold of Maggie's arm and leading her into the house.

Garrett had been right, as usual. She loved the interior of the ranch as much as she'd loved the outside. Her father had made it warm and cheery with vast amounts of Indian pottery and fresh flowers. Indian blankets woven from coarse wool in intricate and colorful patterns were hanging from the walls.

Jason began showing Maggie first one thing and then another. The dining room was richly warm with wooden floors and dark cherry furniture. Heavy brocade draperies at the large windows blocked out the hot afternoon sun.

Maggie barely heard her father's words as he explained the meaning behind different pieces of furniture. It was all she could do to comprehend that she was in her father's house and that Garrett was going to leave.

Finally Maggie spoke. "Please, could I see it all later? I'm so tired."

"Forgive me, of course. I'm just so anxious for you to feel at home here," Jason said as he paused to embrace Maggie once again. "I love you, my little Maggie. Welcome home."

Maggie felt strange going to bed in the middle of the day, but her father had explained that everyone took a siesta during the heat of the day. She found a bath drawn for her and, once she'd bathed and donned a soft cotton nightgown, she was shown to her bed by Carmalita, the young woman who was to be her maid.

Carmalita was young, perhaps twenty or so, Maggie judged. She was plump and very pretty. Maggie immediately liked her.

"We've looked forward to your arrival, Miss Magdelena." Carmalita spoke perfect English, although her accent betrayed her Mexican heritage.

"Please just call me Maggie and don't be so formal. I find myself in need of new friends and hope to start with you," Maggie said sincerely.

"I would be most honored to call you friend, Miss—Maggie." Carmalita replied softly. There weren't many women on the ranch, and Maggie was a welcomed change.

"Good. I will rely on you to teach me everything, but first I want to sleep," Maggie yawned and laid back against the softness of down pillows.

"I will wake you for afternoon refreshments," Carmalita replied gently as she closed the door behind her.

Maggie surveyed the room. It looked out of place with the rest of the house. This room was clearly designed with a woman's tastes in mind. The walls were papered in a lavender rose print. Lavender shutters were closed tightly over a window. French doors with lavender ruffled curtains were set in an archway. Maggie wondered where the doors led, but weariness kept her from exploring.

Suddenly she began to think of Garrett. Did he really mean to leave? And what of Jason's contentment as he'd bid her pleasant dreams? He seemed so genuinely happy to have her home.

Home. Strange that one word should stir so many different feelings. Home had always meant Topeka, yet Maggie felt torn. Coming to this mountainous paradise had been like coming home. How did one explain such feelings?

Maggie shook off the worries of the past few weeks and closed her eyes. She fervently wished she could put Garrett's smiling face from her mind, but it refused to leave. Exhausted, she gave up and slept, oblivious to the conversation taking place in her father's study.

"Garrett, it's so good to have you back," a wearied Jason was exclaiming as he weakly lowered himself to a chair.

"Good to be back, although I wondered at times if we'd make it."

"She was pretty ornery, was she?" Jason laughingly asked.

"She was everything you warned me of, and more. Did you know I had to pull her off a two-story trellis?" Garrett smiled as he remembered the scene and quickly joined Jason's hearty laugh.

"I'm not kidding. Sophia had warned me that Maggie would make a run for it. I figured somebody looking as prim and proper as your daughter would sneak down the back stairs or hide in another room until she could slip out the front, but not Maggie. She hiked up her skirts, all those petticoats and such, and stepped as pretty as you please out her bedroom window and onto the trellis."

Jason alternated between laughing and coughing.

"Maybe I should stop," Garrett said, concerned about Jason's condition. The older man's health had rapidly deteriorated during Garrett's absence.

"No, please. I want to know. I need to hear it all," Jason said, the smile never leaving his face. " 'A merry heart doeth good like a medicine,' the Scripture says. Now continue so that my heart can have a good dosing."

Garrett chuckled in spite of his concern. "Well, there she was, picking her way through the roses and lattice work, all the while yelling about the injustice of life. I wouldn't have seen her up there, if I hadn't heard her first. Quite a set of lungs on your daughter, sir."

Jason fairly howled at this. "Got it from her mother," he gasped.

"I'm sure." Garrett winked and continued. "Anyway, when she got close enough, I reached up and grabbed her."

"She didn't see you?" Jason coughed the words. He hadn't enjoyed himself this much for years.

"No, sir," Garrett managed while holding his side and laughing. "She doesn't see as much when her mouth is open."

"At any rate," Jason said, trying to compose himself. "You're here. Through all the trials and Maggie's stubbornness, you've managed to bring my daughter back to me. Thank you so much."

"You know how I feel about it, Jason. I love your daughter more than ever." Garrett's declaration nearly moved Jason to tears.

"Strange how quickly a body can pass from hilarity into sober reflection," Jason murmured thoughtfully. "I think I'll follow my advice to Maggie and take a nap. This has taken a lot out of me." Jason struggled to get to his feet, and Garrett offered his a steady hand.

"Sounds like an excellent idea," Garrett agreed. "First though, I'll see to you."

Garrett helped Jason into bed and walked toward the bedroom door. That's when it caught his eye. The life-sized portrait of Maggie hung in regal splendor across from Jason's bed. Garrett paused to study the teasing smile and passionate blue eyes. He wanted to grow old with that smile. Turning to leave, Garrett couldn't resist smiling back.

Chapter Twelve

Maggie woke several hours later to Carmalita's gentle nudge. She stretched leisurely thinking that she hadn't slept so well in weeks.

"You will find that Señor, your father, has thoughtfully purchased all the things you will need," Carmalita remarked, opening the doors of a huge mahogany wardrobe.

Maggie gasped. "There are so many clothes!" she said. There were gowns for every occasion possible, as well as some native-style skirts and peasant blouses. Maggie found these particularly interesting.

"Señor thought you might like them," Carmalita offered. "It gets quite warm here, and they are most comfortable."

"I can't imagine that it gets much hotter than Kansas. There were days when you scarcely could move from the heat," Maggie said. Could it have only been weeks since she'd been safe in her own room in Topeka?

Maggie found riding outfits with long split skirts, petticoats, and lightweight camisoles. Just when Maggie thought she'd seen everything, Carmalita would open a drawer or pull Maggie along to another chest. Maggie was amazed. She found boots, slippers, gloves, shawls, and things that she'd never thought about owning.

"Carmalita, how in the world did my father arrange for these things? How did he know they would fit?"

"Señor had your former dressmaker send your measurements. Then he ordered materials, and I made them into clothing. Of course, I had help and some things we ordered from the catalog."

"I see," Maggie said.

"Come, you must select something. Your father will expect you to join him and Señor Garrett for tea."

"Oh, he will? Perhaps I should decline and show them both that they can't anticipate my actions." Carmalita looked puzzled, and Maggie put aside the notion of causing a disturbance at Carmalita's expense.

"I'll wear this," Maggie said, taking a white cotton peasant blouse and colorful skirt. Carmalita smiled broadly at this sign of acceptance.

"Come. I'll show you how to wear them."

Several minutes later, Maggie surveyed her image in the dressing table mirror. "I look so different, almost wild." she observed. Her hair hung down to her waist in auburn waves.

"How would you like to wear your hair?" Carmalita questioned. "I am quite good at dressing hair."

"I think I prefer to leave it down for now. I might as well go completely casual," Maggie murmured.

Carmalita left and returned with Mexican sandals. "These will make your outfit complete," she said, handing the sandals to Maggie.

"They are beautiful. I've never seen anything like them." Maggie sat down while Carmalita showed her how to put them on.

"Oh, they're so comfortable. I love them, Carmalita."

Carmalita smiled more broadly than ever, but mindful of the time, she motioned Maggie to follow. "Come. Your father is waiting."

"And Señor Garrett?" Maggie questioned sarcastically.

"Si. Your novio is waiting," Carmalita answered as she guided Maggie down a long hallway.

"My what?" Maggie asked Carmalita in a hushed whisper.

"Your fiancé. Your sweetheart. You are to marry Señor Garrett, is it not so?" Carmalita questioned.

Maggie rolled her eyes and pushed back a long strand of hair. "I suppose everyone knows about this arrangement." It was more a statement than a question, and Carmalita said nothing as she led Maggie down the long corridor.

"Finally!" Jason Intissar exclaimed loudly as Maggie stepped into the room. Garrett turned from the fireplace and swallowed hard. The look on his face told

Maggie that her appearance had taken its planned toll. *Good,* Maggie thought. *I hope he realizes what he's throwing away. I am not to be put aside like a child's toy.*

"Child, you're positively radiant. The climate agrees with you. Did Carmalita show you everything?" Maggie's father questioned eagerly. He hugged Maggie warmly.

Maggie wanted to respond to her father's embrace, but caution flooded her heart and she stood perfectly still. If the reaction pained Jason, he said nothing.

"Garrett and I were discussing your trip. I'm so glad you gave up your plans to run away. You could have been killed, Maggie." Jason's words were full of concern. He didn't sound condemning as Maggie had expected.

"I did what I felt I had to do," Maggie said, taking a seat in the woven cane chair that Jason offered her. An uncomfortable stillness blanketed the room.

Jason broke the silence. "Well, you're here now, and I pray that you'll be happy. I've done everything I could think of to welcome you and make you comfortable. I know Carmalita showed you the clothes, but there is more than that. I had special furniture made for your room, I've had several geldings made available for your choice of mount, and I've tried to prepare an abundance of reading materials in the library."

"That was quite thoughtful of you, Father. However, it wasn't necessary. While I've never had to live without the things I needed, I am not like most well-to-do women. I can live quite simply if I need to." Maggie lifted her chin in a defiant move that her grandmother would have recognized as a warning.

"Maggie, we need to talk. We three," Jason said, motioning toward Garrett. Maggie stared icily in Garrett's direction. "Pray continue, Father," she said with slight sarcasm.

"Stop it, Maggie. Your father deserves better than one of your temper tantrums," an angry Garrett stated. "He's only trying to make it easy on you. Now stop acting like a spoiled child."

"You seem rather intent on making an issue of my age. As I've told you before, I will be eighteen in less than three weeks. Most of my friends are married, and some even have children. I am not a child, nor do I act childish. I am, however, running out of patience with this game.

"I am here, Father. Not by my wishes, but by Garrett Lucas's and yours. I am not happy that I had to leave Grandmother. She's an old woman, and her health is failing. Now she will live out her days alone, and I resent that." Maggie paused briefly to note the expression of surprise on her father's face.

Maggie didn't want to hurt her father, but overpowering fear was gripping her heart. She didn't want to remember thoughts and feelings that were threatening to surface. Anger seemed the only way to hold them at bay.

"Does my ability to speak for myself surprise you? Did you think I'd come running back for the happy reunion? I don't hate you as I once did." Maggie heard her father gasp and regretted her words. But it was too late.

"Yes, that's right. I did hate you," Maggie said the words to her father, but it was Garrett she was thinking of. Garrett and his plans to desert her just as her father had, just as God had.

"You left me. I had just lost my mother and the baby brother I had yearned for, and then you turned and walked away. I was ridiculed as an orphan. The few friends I had pitied my loss and my life. My only hope was in Grandmother. She stood by me and held me when I was afraid. She kept me on the narrow path when I felt sure I would stray." Tears threatened to spill from Maggie's eyes. She could see that her father, too, had tears. Garrett, however, remained strangely still.

Maggie softened her voice. "I don't hate you anymore. Garrett told me why you left, and while I suppose Grandmother tried to explain it to me many times, Garrett finally accomplished getting through to me. I won't pretend that I'm not fearful of this entire arrangement, and while it's true that I have come to accept the idea of marriage to your choice of a husband," she said waving her hand toward Garrett, "I don't believe the man in question has the same desire."

Garrett's lips curled into a smile. Jason looked first to Garrett and then back to Maggie before both he and Garrett burst into laughter. "Oh, Maggie, you have no idea." Jason's words stung.

"Then why don't you fill me in? Or don't I have a right to know what is to become of me?" Maggie's words were devoid of emotion. Everything inside her went numb.

Jason started to speak, but Garrett raised his hand. "I told you before, Maggie. I fully intend to marry you, but it will be in my own good time and after you've made peace with your father and God."

Jason said nothing, and Maggie noticed that he strained to breathe. She didn't want to fight the sick, frail man her father had become.

Maggie turned to face Garrett. "I have spent a lifetime distancing myself from painful relationships. If what you said to me last night was true, then I am about to begin that task once again."

"But, Maggie," Jason interjected. "Garrett loves you. If you can't see that, you're blind. He's trying to tell you that we need to break down the wall between us. It hurts me so much to see you like this, Maggie."

"I can't pretend to be what I'm not. Nor can I conjure feelings that aren't there," Maggie spoke slowly. "I can't forget what happened, and I don't think you can either."

"What are you talking about?" Jason questioned earnestly.

Maggie wasn't sure. More than a feeling, a vague memory filled her mind. It had to be quite terrible, Maggie decided, or her mind would let her remember.

"Never mind," Maggie replied firmly. Something kept her from continuing. "As for you, Garrett Lucas, either you want to marry me or you don't. You have no right to put me off."

Garrett toyed with an Indian pitcher. He smiled slightly as he traced the pattern etched on the pitcher's side. "You mean like you're putting off your father and God?"

Maggie jumped to her feet. "Stop it! I won't tolerate any more of this!" She walked quickly from the room, nearly running by the time she approached the long hallway. She suddenly realized she had no idea where she was going. Tears blinded her, causing her to stumble. Strong hands steadied her, and in a heartbeat, Maggie felt herself held firmly in Garrett Lucas's arms.

"Leave me alone!" she exclaimed in a half sob. She jerked wildly, trying to escape.

"When are you going to give this up? Trust me, I know what I'm doing," Garrett whispered in Maggie's ear.

Maggie went limp against Garrett's chest. "You can't leave me here. I don't know him. I don't know how to live here," Maggie sobbed.

"You'll learn, and do so much faster and more thoroughly without me here. Remember, until a few weeks ago, you didn't know me either. Now you're ready to commit your life to me."

"I don't believe you! I don't believe that you will come back. You'll be just like him. You'll walk away and keep going." Maggie's words tore at Garrett's heart.

"Hush," he said softly, as he stroked Maggie's hair. "I'm sorry, mi quierda. I never thought about it that way." Gently he lifted her tear-stained face to meet his searching gaze. "I promise, Maggie. I promise you that we'll be man and wife one day. I won't leave without returning to claim what is mine. But," he paused, losing himself in the liquid blue of her eyes. "I don't believe you can ever be mine until you resolve your feelings toward Jason. I know, too, that we can't be anything to each other until you come to salvation in Jesus."

Maggie pushed away from Garrett's embrace. She squared her shoulders and wiped her eyes. There was a new composure about her, and Garrett showed his surprise.

"When will you leave?" Maggie calmly questioned.

Garrett said nothing for a moment, as if considering her question. Finally, he spoke the word Maggie dreaded. "Tomorrow."

Maggie smoothed the front of her skirt and lifted a stony face. "As you wish. Garrett Lucas, I release you from any commitment you think we might have between us. I'm on my own from this moment. I don't believe in you or my father, and I am beginning to question what possible reason a merciful God could have for all this. " She began to walk down the hall when Garrett pulled her back.

"Sorry. It doesn't work that way. I don't release you, Maggie. I don't release you to run away from me and hide in your bedroom. I don't release you to run away from dealing with your father and the pain that is firmly planted between you. And most of all," he spoke with determination, "I don't release you from a reconciliation with God." With that, Garrett turned and walked away.

Maggie stood open mouthed, looking after him. She was still standing there when Carmalita found her. Maggie waved her away. She needed to be alone.

What if Garrett was right? How could she learn to deal with all that stood between her and her father? Maggie suddenly remembered the Bible verse she'd found while on the train: "And he shall turn the heart of the fathers to the children, and the heart of the children to their fathers, lest I come and smite the earth with a curse."

Was God cursing her by taking Garrett Lucas away? What if something happened to Garrett and he died before being able to return to her? Would God curse her because she had been unwilling to put the past behind and open her heart to her father's love?

Chapter Thirteen

July and August passed in a blur. Maggie's birthday came and went, and even though her father thoughtfully surprised her with gifts, Maggie barely acknowledged the day. Her heart ached. Garrett was gone.

Day after day, Jason approached his daughter, only to be waved off. Occasionally, Maggie had asked her father about Garrett's whereabouts, but Jason had promised not to tell her. His reward was his daughter's stubborn refusal to have anything to do with him. Jason refused to give up, however, and continued to find some small place in his daughter's life.

As September approached, Maggie's emotional state had not improved. She'd taken to riding Thunder every day. The huge Morgan crossbreed was aptly named. He was as black as midnight and stood fifteen hands high.

Everyone on the ranch murmured about the Señor's sad-eyed daughter. Maggie spoke only to Carmalita and her father, and then, only when she had to.

As autumn flooded Piñon Canyon with golds and oranges, Jason began to worry. He wanted to make things right with Maggie before he died, but he couldn't reach through her pain and depression. Daily, he prayed for insight. His health was failing fast, and Jason feared that if a reconciliation didn't take place soon, it might not take place at all.

On one particularly hot day, Maggie entered the courtyard where Jason was taking breakfast. She had grown extremely thin, and despite her golden tan from day after day in the sun, she didn't look well. Dark circles around her eyes gave her face a gaunt, inhuman look.

"Maggie, sit here with me," Jason commanded gently.

"I'm not hungry," Maggie said, pulling on her riding gloves. "I'm going to ride Thunder up on the ridge today."

"Maggie, I need you to sit for a moment with me. Surely you can give me. . . ." Jason's words gave way to a fit of coughing. Maggie was painfully aware that the frequency of her father's coughing spells was increasing. The doctor had explained that Jason's lungs were filling with fluid, and his heart couldn't work hard enough.

Maggie looked at her father's reddened face. As the coughing began to subside, she took the chair beside her father.

"Thank you, Maggie," Jason whispered. "Thank you for hearing me out."

Maggie said nothing. She allowed Carmalita to pour her some orange juice but waved away her offer of eggs and toast.

"Maggie, you need to take better care of yourself. You must eat. It isn't right." Maggie knew she had a problem. Carmalita had already taken in Maggie's clothes twice.

"Please don't worry," Maggie said. She didn't intend to grieve Jason. She was only trying to forget the pain of losing Garrett.

"Maggie, I want you to listen to me. I know we can work this out, and I know you can come to love me again." Jason's voice broke, and Maggie ached at the thought of his pain.

She thought for a moment, then offered, "But I do love you, Papa. I don't want you to worry. I do love you, and I know you love me." The words came mechanically and without feeling. It seemed a small price to offer the dying man.

"Maggie, love is so much more than words. I want to spend time with you. I want to know your heart, and I want you to know mine. I have much to teach you about the ranch, and above everything else, I want you to come to know Jesus."

Maggie stiffened. God seemed to hammer her from every direction. Even when she rode Thunder and struggled to forget the image of Garrett's handsome, bearded face, God's words filled her mind. Maggie lowered her face, fearful of facing her father's eyes.

"I know you miss Garrett; I miss him too. He was my right hand, especially after I got sick," Jason continued. "I feel his absence daily, especially with winter coming on and the problems with the banditos in the hills." Jason hadn't intended to mention that to Maggie. He saw her eyes widen slightly.

"Bandits here?" Maggie questioned.

"It's possible. We've found some butchered cows, and several head are missing. It's unlikely that it's the Pueblos. I give them whatever they need through the mission." Maggie nodded.

"Maggie, I can't take back the past. God knows I would if it were possible. We both know, however, that it's not." Jason struggled for air.

Maggie felt herself straining with every breath. For the first time she noticed the purplish red color of her father's skin—skin that barely stretched over the bones of his face. Tears formed against Maggie's will.

"I don't know what to think anymore," she whispered. "I don't want to remember the pain of the past, and I don't understand why Garrett doesn't write. Why doesn't he let us know that he's okay?" The words came out as whimpers, the fearful whimpers of a small child.

"I don't know, Maggie. I know we'd both feel better if he did, but I do know that Garrett Lucas rides with God. Wherever he might be, God is by his side," Jason remarked confidently.

"If God rides with Garrett, maybe that's why He doesn't seem to be here," Maggie replied.

"God not here?" Jason exclaimed. "How can you say such a thing? God is all around us. He's urging your heart to listen. He is calling you to forgive and accept His forgiveness."

"Forgive?" Maggie questioned.

"Yes, forgive. I want you to forgive me for leaving you, Maggie. I want you to forgive me for shutting you out. Do you think that's possible?" Jason asked sincerely.

"I don't think it's a matter of forgiveness, Papa," Maggie began slowly. "I can't forget what happened. It changed so many things about me. It made me stronger, more independent, and I suppose more distant.

"I didn't make many friends. I feared that they, too, would leave me. When Garrett told me he was going, it was like watching it happen all over. I don't think it's a matter of forgiveness," Maggie said, lifting her eyes to face her father's surprised expression.

"But it is. Maggie, you haven't let go of the past. If you had forgiven me, you could have let Garrett go with his promise of return and believed him. You wouldn't be questioning your Heavenly Father, either."

Maggie thought over her father's words. Could they be true?

"I don't understand," Maggie finally said. "What does this have to do with God?"

"Maggie, your Heavenly Father is more reliable than your earthly one. You can count on God to be there every time, all the time, whenever you call out to Him. Don't harden your heart toward God. He isn't punishing you."

Jason's words seemed so clear, so truthful, yet Maggie hated to allow old feelings to surface. She hated to touch the emotions of that little girl from long ago, and she resented the fact that she had to.

"If God loves me so much, why is He allowing me to hurt so badly?" Maggie couldn't hold back the tears. She put her face in her gloved hands and cried. "If God loves me, why did He take my mother and brother away?"

Jason was beside her in a moment, holding her and stroking her hair. There were tears in his eyes as well.

Eight years of pain and anguish poured from Maggie's heart. "He can't possibly love me. It isn't possible. I just know God hates me." Maggie's sobs tore at Jason's heart.

"Oh, Maggie, God does love you. As much as I love you, God loves you much more. We are like the silver and gold ore that runs through the rocks of the mountains. Precious and brilliant, but useless without refining. We are being refined for God's purposes. I learned after your mother died that I had to accept God's will for my life and forgive."

Maggie lifted her face. "Forgive me?"

"No, Maggie," Jason whispered. "Forgive myself."

"What do you mean? You hadn't done anything wrong. I was the one who caught the fever, and all because I went to Lillie's house without permission." Maggie's sudden confession brought back her buried memories.

"Lillie's house!" Maggie whispered the words. Lillie's family had had the fever. Maggie remembered the red quarantine flag that had hung on the fence gate and front door of the Johnston house.

"I went to Lillie's house. Remember before Potwin Place, when we lived side by side in town?" Maggie questioned, painfully remembering details that she'd successfully repressed for years.

"I remember," Jason murmured.

"Mother was too busy to play with me. I was willful and spiteful, and I wanted to show her that I could take care of myself. Mother told me to stay home. She explained the quarantine, but I didn't care.

"When she went to her room to rest, I went to Lillie's. I slipped in the back door, past their cook, and up the backstairs. Lillie wasn't as sick as her sisters, and I played with her. When I got sick the next day, I knew God hated me. Mother died because of me. She really did! Now I know why God is punishing me!" Maggie's body racked with uncontrollable sobs. "I killed my mother and brother!"

"No, Maggie! Listen to me," Jason said, pulling Maggie to her feet.

"It was all my fault, all my fault!" Maggie wailed hysterically.

It took all the strength Jason had to shake Maggie. "Stop it. Stop it, now! You did not kill your mother, but that mistaken idea has always stood between us, Maggie. Because of it, you thought I blamed you for her death." Maggie regained a bit of her composure, but tears still poured down her face.

"Well, didn't you? Even a little bit?"

"No, because I knew the truth," Jason said sadly.

"What truth?"

"We shared water from the same well as the Johnstons. Our well had caved in nearly three weeks earlier because of the flood. Remember? We had to stay with my mother because the Kaw River had flooded its banks. After the water receded and we returned home, I found that the well was beyond repair."

Maggie wiped her eyes. "I remember the flood. I remember all the mud we had to clean out of the house."

Jason smiled sadly. "You couldn't have caught typhoid overnight from a simple visit to Lillie. You were already exposed through the water we shared. Your mother was sick when you came down with the fever. It wasn't because of the baby that she couldn't continue to care for you through your illness. It was because she was sick herself. Don't you see, Maggie? She didn't get typhoid from you. She was already sick."

A tremendous weight lifted from Maggie's shoulders. "Then God didn't punish me for being disobedient by taking my mother and brother, and . . ." Maggie paused to study her father's face. "You!" she whispered softly.

"No, Maggie. God didn't punish you then, and He's not punishing you now. He's standing with open arms, just as I am."

"Oh, Papa. I'm so sorry. Please forgive me!" Maggie threw her arms around her father's neck.

"Maggie, my Maggie, it is I who seek your forgiveness. Can you forgive me?"

"Oh, yes. A hundred times, yes!" They stood for several minutes holding each other. Jason's heart was filled with pure joy. His Maggie was home!

The remainder of the day passed much too quickly. Maggie listened to Jason talk of his early days in New Mexico, trips to Colorado in search of gold and silver, and the ranch he'd created.

Maggie, in turn, tried to explain a lifetime of feelings and dreams. She was sharing a memory from her school days when Jason suggested a short walk in the rose garden.

Maggie linked her arms through Jason's and allowed his slow, faltering lead. "Please finish what you were saying," Jason encouraged.

Maggie started to speak, but just then Jason brought her to the garden. "It's beautiful!" she exclaimed. Jason had created a paradise. The rich, sweet fragrance of roses filled the air.

"How could I have lived here all this time and not known about this?" Maggie wondered aloud.

"Often we have precious things at our fingertips and fail to see them," Jason answered thoughtfully.

Maggie nodded and reached down to touch the velvet softness of a delicate yellow rose. "These are my favorites," she proclaimed, looking at the other roses as if to make certain.

Jason smiled proudly. "I've been experimenting with mixing varieties. This is one of my newer plants."

"What do you call it?"

"God's Hope."

Maggie stiffened slightly. "Papa?"

"Yes?" Jason gave his daughter full attention.

"How can I be sure? About God, I mean. How can I be sure I'm saved? Grandmother told me on many, many occasions, but it all seems so distant now."

Jason's heart soared. "It's very simple, Maggie. You ask God to forgive you, and He does. You have to trust Him, Maggie. I know your trust doesn't come easily, but that's what faith is all about. Just repent and believe on the name of Jesus. He'll do the rest."

Later that night, Maggie knelt beside her bed for the first time in years.

"Heavenly Father, I know I am a willful and childish young woman. I know, too, that I am the one who's put walls between us. Thank you for letting me see this before it was too late. Please forgive me and help me to seek Your will in my life. I want Jesus to be my Savior, and I want to trust you all the days of my life. In Jesus' name I pray, Amen."

As she got up, Maggie wondered, *Am I really saved?* She didn't feel different. Could she do as her father had suggested and trust God?

"If the Bible is true," Maggie said aloud, "and I believe it is, then I must trust. I need faith in God's ability to save me and to bring me new life through His Son. He's offered me a place to belong, but it's up to me to accept."

Maggie walked to the open French doors and looked out into the starlit sky. Garrett was out there somewhere. Would she ever see him again? He'd promised he'd be back for her, but could she believe him?

In the distance, coyotes yipped and howled at the moon. The echo of their mournful cries chilled Maggie.

"Please God," Maggie prayed aloud. "Please bring Garrett back to me."

Chapter *Fourteen*

Garrett's mood was black and stormy. He stood beside his horse, Alder, using firm brush strokes to rid the animal's coat of clay and mud that had accumulated during their ride. It was the last day of September, and instead of giving routine orders to ready Piñon Canyon for the winter, Garrett was trapped twelve miles away at the mission Jenny and David Monroe had established for the Pueblos.

Alder sensed his master's mood and stood still as stone. Garrett finished currying his horse, and after knocking most of the mud from his boots, he made his way to David and Jenny's house. The sky started to pour rain as Garrett entered the kitchen. Warmth hit his face in a welcome wave. The smell of tortillas and meat made him recognize how hungry he was.

"Garrett Lucas, you get in here and change those clothes!" Jenny Monroe demanded. Garrett smiled. Jenny was Garrett's junior by at least two or three years, but at times she seemed years older.

"Yes, ma'am," Garrett drawled lazily and tipped his Stetson.

"Hurry up. Supper will be on shortly." That was all the encouragement Garrett needed.

An hour later, Garrett pushed away from the crude wood table and patted his stomach. "Good grub, Jenny!" he declared, and several little voices mimicked him.

"Good grub!"

Jenny Monroe looked down the twelve-foot table into the grateful brown eyes of the orphans she cared for.

"Go on with all of you," she said and stood to clear the table. She turned loving eyes to her husband of five years.

"David, why don't you and Garrett take yourselves to the sitting room, and I'll have Mary and Anna get these kids to bed." Seven little moans echoed down the length of the table, but the children who were old enough to take care of themselves got up from the table and raced upstairs. The older girls, Mary and Anna, tenderly cared for the youngest three.

"Come along, Garrett," David Monroe called. Garrett rose slowly from the table. He was tired and stiff from bringing down strays from the upper ranges.

The sitting room was warm and inviting. Garrett sat down in front of the fire, appreciating its warmth. He watched David Monroe put more wood on the fire. Garrett longed to hear of news from Piñon Canyon, but he waited patiently for David to sit.

"I suppose you'd like to hear the latest," David said, joining Garrett in a chair by the fire.

"You know I would. It was all I could do to wait through dinner. How's Maggie?" Garrett asked anxiously.

"I have a letter. Would you like to read it?" David asked, pulling the envelope from his pocket. Garrett nearly leaped from the chair to take the precious paper from his friend. He scanned the pages with intense interest. At one point David thought he saw tears in Garrett's eyes, but just as quickly his eyes dried.

"She's accepted the past. That's good," Garrett said absently. "And she's accepted Jesus as her Savior. That's even better!" Joy surged through Garrett's heart. Maggie was working through the past with her father, and soon, very soon, he could return to the ranch and marry her.

"David, this is wonderful news! Why didn't you tell me sooner?"

David Monroe chuckled. "Easy, Garrett. There's still a long way to go."

"I know all that, but it's a huge step forward. I mean, if you'd seen her these last few months. She's skin and bones, and the dangerous way she rode that gelding made me want to give up at least a thousand times."

"I told you it wasn't wise to spy on her," David reminded.

"I know, but I couldn't help it. I just had to feel close to her. I've loved her for so long."

David nodded. "I know what you mean. It was a good thing Jenny lived in the same town as the Bible college I attended. I would have gone mad without her."

"Then you understand," Garrett whispered. "David, sometimes, I'm not sure what to make of it. At first I thought it was a silly infatuation. But as I listened to the letters from her grandmother, I drank in every word about Maggie and couldn't wait to meet her," Garrett paused, remembering his anticipation of their first meeting.

"When I finally stood outside her house in Potwin, I wasn't sure I could play my part. I'd already told Jason how I felt, and he couldn't have been happier. But I knew that I'd need to convince Maggie, and I wasn't sure I could. Boy, the prayer that went into that one!"

David smiled. "I always believed God was setting you up for something special, Garrett."

"He sure was. When I realized that Maggie was falling for me, I started to panic. There was the matter of her pa, and I was even more troubled by the wall she'd built to shut out God. She couldn't see God's love for her. That's why this letter offers the best possible news. Maggie has learned that she can count on God."

The two men barely heard the rustling of Jenny's skirts as she brought coffee into the sitting room.

"Here we are," she said in her soft, gentle voice. Garrett had heard that voice comfort heartbroken children and soothe the worried heart of her husband. Jenny Monroe's every action reflected her Savior.

"Thank you, Jenny," Garrett said as he took the offered cup. "David just showed me the letter. Isn't it great news?"

"It certainly is, Garrett. Just what we've prayed for. We must continue to pray, however. You know how hard this time will be." Jenny spoke with authority. Garrett wondered if something in her past gave her special insight.

"I reckon it will be at that," Garrett replied. Truth was, he hadn't considered anything past the contents of the letter.

"I think it would be a good time to drop a note of encouragement, Garrett," David interjected.

"Oh, yes," Jenny agreed, sitting next to her husband. They exchanged a look of tenderness that made Garrett's heart ache.

"You think so?" Garrett asked hopefully. He'd wanted to write Maggie every day, but at the advice of Jenny and David, he'd given Maggie the opportunity to make the right choices on her own.

"Definitely," David began. "She'll need to know you still care, and she'll need to know that you've been praying for her—that you're still praying for her. Maybe," David added, remembering something Garrett had said earlier, "maybe you should let her know you've never been far away, that you've been watching over her."

"I think that'd be nice, Garrett," Jenny said. "I know a woman's heart likes to hear things like that. Share some encouraging Scripture, too. She'll need the Word as she learns to walk in faith."

Garrett got to his feet, nearly spilling his coffee. "I'll do it right now. Do you suppose Lupe could deliver it tomorrow?"

"I'm sure he'd be happy to," David said enthusiastically. "I've got some papers to send to Jason anyway, so the trip will be necessary for both of us."

Jenny placed her hand upon her husband's cheek. "Why don't we leave Garrett to his letter? I would love an evening stroll." The love shone clear in her eyes, and David wrapped an arm around her and pulled her close.

"I'd like that too," he agreed. "If you'll excuse us," David said, rising to his feet. "We have a walk to take."

Garrett watched as they left the room. Jenny and David Monroe shared a deep, abiding love. Garrett dreamed of a love like that with Maggie, and the news he'd just received finally made it possible.

Later that night, after pouring his heart onto three pages of David's personal stationery, Garrett lay in bed staring up at the ceiling. "How much longer, Lord?" he wondered aloud. "How much longer until I can go home?"

He thought about the words he'd written. He'd wanted to explain everything he felt. He kept remembering how Maggie had told him she wouldn't wait for him. How would she feel now that she'd made peace with God and her father?

Long into the night, Garrett tossed and turned. His sleep was fitful, and more than once he woke up drenched in sweat. Morning couldn't come too soon.

Back at Piñon Canyon, Maggie awoke to a warmth of fall sunshine. She stretched slowly and purposefully like a sleek mountain puma.

For a moment, Maggie listened to the morning sounds of the ranch. She smiled at the smell of hot coffee and bacon. Maria was preparing breakfast. After months of near starvation, Maggie felt like making up for lost time.

Quickly, she threw back the covers and went to her vanity. She poured cool water from the pitcher and washed the sleep from her face. Carmalita hadn't arrived to help her dress, but Maggie didn't mind. She went to the wardrobe and pulled out a dusty rose day dress. Just as Maggie was securing the last few buttons, Carmalita knocked and entered the room.

"Señorita Maggie, you should have called for me," Carmalita said, rushing to help Maggie.

"Nonsense. I'm not an invalid, even if I've acted like a sick cow for the last few months." Carmalita looked shocked, and Maggie gave a little laugh. "I'm sorry, Carmalita. I'm really not loco, as Maria would call it. I've finally found peace."

Carmalita began to brush Maggie's thick, auburn hair as Maggie continued to explain. "These past months, I died a little each day, wondering if my harsh words had driven away the man I hoped to marry. I hated myself for hurting my father and for being so ungrateful. But you know, Carmalita," Maggie said, pausing to put her thoughts in just the right words. "The worst part was my alienation from God."

"What do you mean?" Carmalita questioned.

Maggie took hold of Carmalita's hands. "Carmalita, two days ago I gave my heart to Jesus. I'm at peace with God, and now I can truly begin to live."

Carmalita smiled shyly, but with understanding. "That is good, Señorita Maggie. I, too, am a Christian."

"You are!" Maggie exclaimed with positive delight. "How wonderful. We can help each other."

Carmalita seemed happy with the change in her mistress. She finished Maggie's hair quickly and went to tidy up the room.

Maggie whirled in front of the mirror, suddenly very interested in how she looked. The rose colored dress hugged her slim figure, and the gored skirt swept out from her hips and flowed to the floor. The wine trim on the bodice and sleeves made her hair look a deeper, coppery color. Satisfied with her appearance, Maggie joined her father for breakfast.

"My, you're up early, aren't you?" Jason said as Maggie took her place at the table. "And don't you look pretty."

"Thank you, Papa."

Maria placed platters of fried potatoes, scrambled eggs, and ham on the table. Maggie helped herself to generous portions of everything.

"What would you like to do today?" Maggie asked her father between bites.

"I'm afraid that I'm not up to a great deal." Jason gave a series of hoarse coughs which left him breathless.

"What if we enjoy each other's company here in the house? You can tell me more stories about the years we've missed, and I can tell you some of mine."

Maggie tried to hide her concern for her father, but it was evident by the furrow of her brow.

"You mustn't worry, Maggie. I don't fear death. I have found peace with God and with my beloved daughter. I can go home to heaven with a peace I'd only dreamed possible."

"I wish you wouldn't talk about dying, Papa. It seems like asking for trouble." Maggie sounded tense and curt. She hated her father referring to his death. She wasn't ready to let go of him.

"Maggie, you can't pretend something isn't going to happen just because you don't like the idea," Jason sighed. "I wish I could stay to see you married and with children of your own. I'd like to watch you and Garrett take over the running of this ranch. But I only asked God to let me live long enough for us to put our differences aside. He's given me that and more. I'd say anything else is added blessings."

"But, Papa." Maggie started to protest, but Jason waved his hand.

"Don't blame God or resent his timing. Promise me, Maggie. Promise me that you won't allow my death to cause bitterness in your heart."

Maggie looked at her father for a moment. His faded blue eyes were sunk deep into his face. There was a grayish pallor to his skin and frailty to his movements.

"How can I promise a thing like that? I don't want to lose you. It seems like I just found you, and now you'll be taken from me." Maggie said thoughtfully.

"You must trust God, Maggie. In His infinite wisdom, He will work all things together for good. Would you have me stay and suffer like this?"

"No, Papa. Never! I didn't mean—"

"I know you never meant it that way," Jason said, taking hold of Maggie's hand. "But you must consider my viewpoint. I'm tired of the weakness, the lack of air, the coughing. It pains me to remember the man I used to be and to see the man I've become."

Her father was right, Maggie realized. It was pure selfishness to want her father to continue living. And for what? Her pleasure? Her need?

"Forgive me, Papa. I want the very best for you, and I promise that I won't hate God for whatever that best may be. If it means losing you soon, and I pray that it doesn't, then I will accept His will. In the meantime, I want to enjoy every moment." Maggie gave her father's hand a squeeze.

"Good. You have no way of knowing the contentment that gives me."

Maggie smiled and felt at peace. She finally had the father she'd longed for, and with him came the security of belonging.

Chapter Fifteen

Before Garrett's letter could be delivered by Lupe, another letter arrived at Piñon Canyon. With it came the news that Sophia Intissar had passed away.

Devastated, Maggie sat in front of the fireplace, watching the dying embers of a late morning fire. Her heart ached and her throat felt painfully tight. She wanted to cry, but the tears wouldn't come.

Maggie couldn't forget the anguished look on her father's face when he'd read the news. Jason had collapsed on the nearest chair and cried bitter, pain-filled tears. When her father's emotions had sent him into paroxysms of coughing, Maggie had called for Miguel to help Jason to bed. Medication had finally brought her father the relief of sleep.

Several hours had passed, and Maggie couldn't believe how quiet the house had grown. Usually the muffled sounds of Maria singing in the kitchen or Carmalita talking excitedly about her upcoming wedding to Miguel filled the house.

Maggie lifted the letter again. It had been penned more than a week earlier by Lillie Johnston Phillips. Lillie had always loved Sophia as her own grandmother. She told Maggie that Sophia had died peacefully in her sleep. Lillie, nearly four months a bride, had helped her parents arrange for the burial services, despite the fact that she had discovered she was in a family way.

Maggie smiled at Lillie's reference to the new life she carried. One life ended and another began. And in her father's bedroom, still another life hung in the balance.

Maggie noted that her grandmother had been buried the same day she and her father had resolved their differences. Perhaps her grandmother had sensed an end to the painful past and knew she could go to heaven unhampered by regrets and worries. Maggie smiled at the thought of her grandmother walking the streets of heaven and enjoying the company of many old friends.

"Heavenly Father," Maggie prayed. "I thank You for the years I shared with Grandmother. I'll miss her very much, but I know she's safe and happy, and for now, that seems enough. Please be with Papa. He isn't strong enough to bear much more, and I'm not ready to let go of him. Help me to prepare for his passing, and please don't let him suffer. In Jesus' name, Amen." When she finished praying, Maggie felt a great peace that gave her the strength to go on.

Later that afternoon, another letter was placed in Maggie's hands. Even though she had never seen Garrett's handwriting before, she knew the letter was from him. Retreating to the privacy of her bedroom, she tore open the envelope. Her heart beat faster as she read his greeting.

My beloved Maggie,

A tremendous burden has been lifted. I was just told of your reconciliation with Jason, and your acceptance of Jesus as Savior. I want to shout for joy. I know how you have struggled with God over the years. I know that it was never easy to see God as the loving Father that He is. Now, however, I desire more than ever to share my life with you and grow together in the love that He has given us.

The letter continued, and Maggie drank in each word. Every sentence was exactly what she'd longed to hear. She read Garrett's words of love and pledges of lifelong devotion. How it thrilled her to see each cherished promise and know without doubt that he loved her. Maggie's one disappointment was that Garrett didn't give a specific time when he would return. She folded the letter and tucked it into her skirt pocket to read again later.

Even though it was the beginning of October and the afternoons no longer held the intense heat of summer, Maggie had grown accustomed to siesta. After checking on her father, she decided to stretch out and take a nap.

Nearly two hours later, Carmalita urgently woke Maggie.

"Maggie, Maggie! Come quickly. Your father is very ill." The fear in Carmalita's voice left Maggie shaken. She ran after Carmalita to where Jason Intissar lay vomiting blood.

"Carmalita, what are we going to do?" Maggie cried. She held her father's bony shoulders steady as another spell of coughing began.

"We can send Miguel for the doctor," Carmalita offered.

"Then do it, and tell him to go quickly!" Maggie exclaimed. "And Carmalita . . ."

"Si?" Carmalita answered, pausing in the doorway.

"You'd better get a couple ranch hands—men my father is fond of. I'm going to need help until Miguel and the doctor get here."

"Right away," Carmalita replied and quickly left the room.

Maggie turned her attention back to her father. "Papa, is the cough passing?"

"I think so. Let me lay back on the pillows." Jason's voice was barely audible.

Maggie eased her father back. Her father seemed oblivious to any comfort the new position offered. He strained for each breath, and Maggie fought the urge to run from the room.

To get her mind off her father's ragged breathing, Maggie began cleaning up the area around his bed. Carmalita returned and took over the cleaning, urging Maggie to care for her father.

Maggie sat stroking her father's balding head. She dipped a cloth in cool water and began to wipe away blood stains from his face.

"We came as quick as we could, ma'am."

Maggie looked up to find the compassionate eyes of Bill, her father's trusted foreman. Behind him stood a young man she'd never met.

"This here is Mack's little brother, Rob," Bill explained. Maggie offered a brief smile to the shy, sandy-haired young man.

"Thank you both for coming. Father's been taken by quite a bad spell this time. I sent Miguel for the doctor, but I know I'll need help with him before they return," she whispered. Her father's labored breathing became even louder, and Maggie could barely concentrate on what she was saying.

"No problem, ma'am. I'd give my life for Mr. Jason. He's been a right good boss and friend," Bill said, lowering his eyes to the dusty hem of his jeans. Rob remained silent.

"Bill, I think Father would rest better if we could prop him up. I can't lift him, but if you and Rob could help me, we might get the job done."

"Sure thing, Miss Maggie." Bill's voice held the devoted enthusiasm that Maggie needed to hear. Together, the three worked to ease Jason into a more comfortable position.

The hours wore on, and Maggie felt encouraged as her father's breathing became less ragged. She dozed in a chair, and only when the clock chimed midnight did she agree to turn in.

Maggie started to slip into bed fully clothed. There seemed little sense in undressing. What if her father grew suddenly worse? Carmalita would hear nothing of it.

"No one will care if you appear at your father's bedside in your robe. But you need your rest," Carmalita said, taking charge of Maggie as if she were a child.

"But," Maggie started to protest.

"You'll sleep much better in your nightgown, and you'll need all your strength." Carmalita finished pulling Maggie's blood-stained dress over her head and replaced it with a fresh cotton nightgown.

"I'll have Bill wake me if your father wakes up or gets any worse." Carmalita said, blowing out the candle. Maggie wanted to argue, but her mind wouldn't make sense of the situation. Reluctantly, she fell back against her pillow and slept.

The first crimson rays of the late fall sun were peeking over the mountaintops when Maggie woke with a start. Remembering her father, she threw back the covers, pulled on her robe, and raced down the hallway.

When she opened the door, Maggie was surprised to find Dr. Avery leaning over her father. He looked up as Maggie entered the room.

"Good morning, Miss Intissar," he said in his deep, rumbling voice. "I've been here for about an hour."

"I wanted to check . . . I mean, how is he?" Maggie asked in a nervous whisper.

"He's sleeping. I've given him morphine," Dr. Avery informed her.

"Morphine? What's that?" Maggie asked. Finding her courage, she drew closer to her father's bed.

"It's a drug that will take your father's pain away and help him to sleep. You father is a very sick man, Miss Intissar, but of course you know this."

"Yes, I do. I want the truth, though. Is he going to die? I mean right away, today?" Maggie's voice betrayed the pain of her heart.

"I can't be certain, but I don't look for him to leave this bed again," Dr. Avery said with finality. Maggie's knees weakened. Her face turned ashen as the meaning of the doctor's words sunk in.

"I'm sorry, Miss Intissar," the doctor said, helping Maggie to a chair. "You must be strong. You'll not be any good to him this way."

"I know," Maggie whispered. "But it seems so unfair. I just found him, and now I will lose him once more." Dr. Avery turned back to his medical bag.

"I am going to leave enough morphine powder so you can give it to him regularly. He won't be in his right mind while on the medicine, but he won't hurt either," the doctor explained matter-of-factly. "Should I instruct Maria about the dosing?"

"Please, that would be best," Maggie said, recognizing that she herself wouldn't remember any instructions.

"I'll be leaving, then. There's nothing more I can do. I've been with your father through the thick and thin of this illness. We both knew it would come to this. I must tell you, Miss Intissar, that your father has faced his illness bravely, always insisting on the truth no matter how bad the news. He's been a good friend, and I will miss him sorely when he's gone." Dr. Avery's rock solid voice broke.

Tears fell unbidden down Maggie's cheeks. What a beautiful memorial to the man who lay dying. "Thank you, Dr. Avery. Thank you for being his friend, and thank you for coming to care for him once more. I'll let you know when it's over." Maggie got to her feet. "Forgive me for not walking with you to the kitchen, but I want to stay with my father."

"I understand, Miss Intissar," Dr. Avery said, turning to leave. "If it's any comfort," he added. "Your father won't know what's happening. He won't feel the pain, and he won't strain to breathe."

Maggie gently stroked her father's icy hand. "Thank you. Thank you so much."

Chapter Sixteen

A few days later, Maggie was presented with a problem she'd not anticipated. Bill informed her that the regular supply trip hadn't been made to finish stocking up for the winter.

"I know it's late notice, ma'am. We should've thought of it a lot sooner, but what with your pa so sick and all, it just slipped my mind," Bill offered apologetically.

"I understand, Bill. I'm just not sure what we should do about it. I don't know anything about running this ranch. Papa wanted me to learn and we had great plans, but now it's apparently not to be," Maggie said sadly.

"We've been lucky so far. The snows have stayed put, and we've enjoyed mild weather. But I think that's about to end. My joints have been bothering me somethin' fierce, and that always means a change in the weather," Bill said, rubbing his elbow.

"What should we do?" Maggie asked earnestly. Just then, Carmalita entered the room with hot mugs of coffee.

"Maria thought you'd enjoy this Mexican coffee."

"Mexican coffee?" Maggie questioned, sniffing the contents of her mug.

"Si, it has cinnamon in it," Carmalita said with a smile. Carmalita smiled a great deal these days because she planned to marry Miguel shortly before Christmas.

"How interesting," Maggie murmured and sipped the coffee. "It's delicious." She cast a bittersweet smile at the dark-eyed servant. Maggie longed for a wedding of her own.

"Maria's Mexican coffee warms a fellow's bones and treats the tongue to a feast," Bill said with enthusiasm.

"Well, I'm afraid despite the good coffee, we still have a big problem. Bill, do you know anything about the book running of the ranch?" Maggie asked the bewildered foreman.

"Not a thing, Miss Maggie. Never had to. Your Pa always left that to Garrett, that is, when he didn't take care of it himself."

Maggie sighed. "I wish we had Garrett with us now. I'd gladly let him take over everything."

"I could have Miguel ride out after him," Carmalita suggested.

"What?" Maggie's voice clearly showed her surprise. "You know where Garrett is?"

"Si," Carmalita answered matter-of-factly. "Your father has kept in touch with him at the Pueblo mission."

"That's our answer, Miss Maggie. If we can get Garrett here, we'll be fixed fine. He'll be knowin' just what to do and when," Bill remarked, handing his mug back to Carmalita. "Now if you'll excuse me, I've got some ranch hands to see to."

"Thank you, Bill. I'll have Miguel go after Garrett immediately," Maggie called out to the retreating figure. She turned to Carmalita. "Send Miguel right away. Have him tell Garrett everything."

"Si," Carmalita replied and rushed off to locate Miguel.

Maggie went to check on her father. She could hardly contain her excitement. Garrett would be coming home. She smiled to herself. It had been over three months since Garrett had walked out of her life. Even so, Maggie remembered his promise to make her his wife. A shiver ran through her. *Garrett's wife!*

Jason Intissar slept peacefully. The morphine had made him oblivious to everything, but at least he didn't hurt. For that Maggie was grateful.

Absentmindedly, she picked up some knitting she'd left beside her father's bed. It was to be a blanket for Lillie's baby. The thought of her young friend newly married and expecting her first child brought a tear to Maggie's eye. She remembered leaving the note for Lillie before she left Topeka and promising to return in time for the wedding.

Maggie smiled at the memory of the smug, spoiled girl she had been. Spoiled. That was what Garrett had called her, and he'd been quite accurate.

Maggie worked on the blanket and thought of what their meeting would be like. Would she be sitting down to dinner when Garrett came rushing through the door? Perhaps he wouldn't make it until morning. Maggie's mind raced with thoughts. Would he see the change in her, or would he still believe her to be a spoiled child?

Carmalita came in to tend the fire. The late autumn days had grown chilly, and while the adobe ranch house was well insulated with its thick walls, there was an undeniable hint of winter in the air. Bill's joints must have been right about the change in weather.

"Did you send Miguel?" Maggie asked anxiously.

"Si, he was happy to go. He has missed Señor Lucas, but more I think he wanted to talk to Pastor Monroe. He will marry us," Carmalita replied as she stoked the fire. The wood she added to the cherry red coals ignited immediately, warming the room.

"Are you finished with your wedding dress yet?" Maggie inquired, caught up in Carmalita's excitement.

"Not quite," the girl answered. She went around the room, tidying up anything that seemed out of place.

"Do you need anything else to complete it?" Maggie questioned, thinking she could go with Garrett to get supplies.

"No, I have everything. It's just the waiting that's hard." Maggie nodded in heartfelt agreement with Carmalita's words.

The day stretched into evening, and when Maggie found her legs cramped from hours of sitting, she decided to take a walk. The liquid gold sun dripped lazily between two snow-covered peaks. Golds, pinks, purples, and oranges swirled delicate fingers against the cold gray-blue of the evening sky. It was breathtaking!

Maggie wandered to the corral where Thunder stood stomping at the dirt. He wanted to run as much as Maggie wished to ride. As she approached, he whinnied softly and came to greet her. His nudging muzzle was disappointed to find that Maggie's cupped hand held no surprise of sugar or carrots.

"Sorry, boy. Not this time." Maggie watched the sleek gelding move away to seek out food. She loved him. She loved almost everything about Piñon Canyon Ranch. Strange that she had fought coming here. It was somewhat like coming home. No, it was more. She had come home.

As Maggie walked slowly back to the house, her thoughts again drifted to Garrett. She looked up to the mountains and wondered if he could see her now. But the mountains surrounding Piñon Canyon refused to give up any secrets.

Supper was quiet and lonely. Maggie's slim frame was only starting to fill out again. Carmalita was always trying to get her to eat. Many times, Maria sent tempting treats from the kitchen for "Señor's skinny daughter," as Maria teasingly called Maggie.

Maggie picked at her meal. It wasn't a lack of hunger that kept her pushing the food from one side of the plate to the other. It was the memory of Garrett. Everywhere she looked, she saw laughing blue eyes, and when she was least expecting it, the wind carried the sweet musky scent of his cologne.

Maggie finally gave up on the roasted chicken and went to the library. Carmalita had thoughtfully started a fire in the library's wood stove, and the room beckoned to Maggie. She loved the library.

Maggie picked up a book that she'd been trying to read since her father had fallen ill. The book still held little interest, however, and Maggie placed it back on the shelf.

She went to the huge walnut desk that commanded the attention of anyone who enter the room. Jason had ordered this desk made to fit his specifications. Solid walnut, it had been varnished slightly to bring out the dark lines of the wood's natural grain. It was trimmed with brass handles for the four drawers that lined either side and with brass corner plates at the top edges of the desk.

Maggie sat down in the black leather chair that she'd seen her father work from. It swallowed her up. Lovingly, Maggie touched the desktop and its contents. These were the papers her father had been working on before becoming ill. How she wished she understood the running of the ranch books. She'd see to it that Garrett taught her all about them. It seemed very important to know every detail of the ranch—how it was run, when they performed certain duties, and why.

Maggie reluctantly made the familiar walk down the long hall to her father's bedroom. Bill was preparing to bed down on the small cot at the foot of the bed. Maggie glanced at the clock on the fireplace mantel, surprised to see that it was nearly ten o'clock.

Confident that her father was sleeping soundly, Maggie found Carmalita and informed her that she was going to bed. Bill would notify them if anything needed their attention.

Maggie smiled when she discovered that Carmalita had already prepared a fire in Maggie's bedroom. Maggie warmed herself for a moment, and then slipped into a nightgown. She was about to get into bed when she heard a knock at the door. It was Carmalita.

"Come quickly, Maggie. Señor is not good."

Maggie threw on her robe and raced down the hall after Carmalita. Nothing could have prepared Maggie for the sight of her father writhing and crying out in agony. How could this be? Moments ago, he'd rested comfortably.

"What happened, Bill?" Maggie cried as she rushed to her father's side.

"I don't rightly know, Miss Maggie," Bill began. "I was just getting to sleep when he started a thrashin' and moanin'. I'm afeared the medicine ain't doin' its job."

"That doesn't make any sense. We gave him the regular dosage. It's always worked before," Maggie stated in utter confusion. How could she stop her father's intense pain?

"Papa, it's Maggie. Papa?"

For a moment, the older man's eyes opened. They seemed to flash recognition, but then they rolled back, their heavy lids closed. Maggie's tears burned hot on her cheeks. *Dear God, how much more can he stand? Why is he allowed to suffer like this?*

Maria arrived with a larger dose of medication, and after Bill, Maggie, and Carmalita were able to hold Jason's thrashing body still, Maria forced the medicine down his throat.

Maggie sat for the next two hours, waiting as her father's pain faded into peaceful sleep. She dozed off and on, and when Bill suggested that she make her way back to bed, she didn't argue.

Gratefully, Maggie climbed once again into the warmth and comfort of her own bed. Her eyes refused to stay open, and her mind was clouded with sleep. Her last clear thought was to wonder what was keeping Garrett and Miguel.

Chapter Seventeen

When Garrett and Miguel hadn't shown up by the end of the second day, both Carmalita and Maggie began to worry.

"They should have been here by now," Maggie said, pulling back the curtain and searching for any sign of the two men.

"Si," Carmalita said softly as she cleared the breakfast dishes.

As the day warmed to an unseasonable temperature, Maggie determined to ride out on Thunder in hopes of meeting the men as they returned. Even Carmalita agreed that it was a good plan.

Maggie checked in on her father first. He slept soundly, and Maria was keeping careful watch for any signs of discomfort. There was little need to worry about the addictive effects of the medication. It was clear to everyone that Jason Intissar would soon join his wife in heaven.

Maggie slipped into a dark blue riding skirt. She pulled on her long boots. They almost felt foreign to her. It had been over a week since she'd ridden. She finished dressing and tied her auburn hair at the nape of her neck with a ribbon.

Making her way to the corral, Maggie located Bill and coaxed him into saddling Thunder for her. Bill had been an absolute lifesaver, and Maggie intended to thank him properly when things settled down.

Although Maggie had never been to the mission, she'd paid careful attention to Bill's directions and landmarks. She didn't intend to go very far, but by midday, she'd covered quite a bit of ground. The sun was blazing overhead.

Maggie paused to take a drink from her canteen, grateful that Bill had insisted on her taking it. Thunder whinnied softly.

"It's okay, boy," Maggie said, recognizing her mount's thirst. "If Bill's directions are right, a water hole lies just ahead."

As Maggie neared the water hole, a hideous odor filled the air. The stench grew unbearable as Maggie approached the water. She could see strange mounds of dirt on the far side of the hole, but as she drew near, Maggie realized they weren't mounds of dirt at all. The ground was littered with partially butchered cattle carcasses.

Maggie felt nauseated, and Thunder whinnied nervously at the sight. The bloated carcasses were not only beside the water hole, but in the water itself, hopelessly fouling the contents for human or animal use.

Maggie's mind whirled. What could it mean? She'd heard the hands speak of rustlers in the area and there was the ever-present worry of banditos. The renegade band of Mexicans, Indians, and mixed breeds were a constant worry to the outlying ranches. Banditos had families hidden high in the rocky hills, and they were considered a brotherhood of the utmost secrecy.

Maggie knew that Maria had family among the banditos, although she never spoke of it to Maggie. Carmalita had whispered the secret to Maggie, telling her it was one reason Piñon Canyon suffered no more loss than an occasional steer.

Surveying the carnage and waste, Maggie grew cold. She pulled Thunder's reins hard and put him into a full gallop. She wanted to get back home, and she pressed Thunder to the limit of his endurance, fully aware of the white foam that spotted the gelding's coat.

After covering half the distance to the ranch, Maggie remembered Thunder's need for water. She reined the huge gelding to a stop and dismounted. Pouring the contents of her canteen into her hat, she placed it under Thunder's nuzzle. Thunder greedily lapped up the water. It seemed such an inadequate offering, but Maggie had no other choice.

Silently, she surveyed the land around her. It was rocky and dry. Climbing back into her well-worn saddle, Maggie felt uncomfortable. Once again she looked around her. The mountains rose majestically, and their snow-capped peaks shown as brilliant halos against the intense blue of the sky. Nothing here should make her uneasy, but remembering the water hole, Maggie decided things weren't as innocent as they appeared. Cautiously, she made her way back to the ranch.

The sun was starting down when Maggie rode into the corral yard. Bill was frantic.

"Where've ya been? I've been worried sick, feared that maybe those banditos got hold of ya. I should'a never let ya go," Bill ranted as he helped Maggie dismount.

"I'm fine, Bill. Really," Maggie said.

"Then what's that tone of voice about?" Bill questioned as he handed Thunder's reins to one of Maria's sons.

"Bill," Maggie began as soon as the boy was out of ear shot. "I found some dead steers at the first water hole."

"What'd ya say?" Bill asked, uncertain that his ears had heard right. Maggie started walking toward the house, and Bill realized that she meant for him to follow.

"I don't want anyone to overhear me," Maggie offered as a brief explanation. She paused as they neared the house. "I found seven or eight partially butchered steers. They are all around the water hole and some were even dumped in the water itself."

"Banditos!" Bill exclaimed.

"Do you think so?" Maggie asked, feeling sick again as she remembered the sight at the water hole.

"Has to be. Rustler wouldn't butcher 'em. They'd drive 'em off and sell them. Banditos can't drive the steers up into their hideouts, so they take what they want or need and leave the carcasses."

"If it is banditos, what will they do next?" Maggie wondered aloud.

"Probably nothing right now," Bill answered deep in thought.

"Bill, we've got to get to Garrett and Miguel. Is there someone else we can send to the mission?" Maggie questioned. "I, we need him so much right now," she added, desperation mounting.

"I'll get Mack. If I send him in the morning, they should be back by night-fall." Bill's words offered little comfort, but when the older man's large, weather-worn hand came down on Maggie's, warmth and closeness briefly stilled her fears.

The following morning, Maggie and Bill stood in the yard watching Mack ride away. Maggie offered a silent prayer for Mack's safety and speed. As she turned to go to the house, she noticed Bill's hesitant steps.

"Maybe we should'a sent someone with him," Bill muttered, and Maggie wondered if he was right. Neither one said another word. Maggie nodded slightly and Bill touched the brim of his dirty white hat as they parted for their respective duties.

The day moved in slow motion. The only positive bit of excitement was Jason. Maggie entered the sickroom to find Maria talking in low whispers to her father.

"Papa, but how? Oh, Maria. I thought I'd never be able to talk to him again," Maggie cried as she knelt beside the bed of her father. Jason's slightly drugged eyes fell on his daughter.

"Your papa is doing much better," Maria explained, "so I lessened his med-ication."

"You aren't hurting?" Maggie questioned, taking hold of her father's hand and holding it to her cheek.

"No, not as much." Jason barely whispered the words.

Maggie breathed a sigh of relief. "Papa, there is so much I need to talk to you about. I need you so much." Maggie let her tears fall unashamed against her father's hand.

"Don't cry," Jason murmured and, using all his strength, he gave Maggie's hand a slight squeeze.

"Papa, I can't lose you now. Please get well," Maggie begged.

Jason shook his head. His eyes were nearly lifeless. Maggie could see the pal-lor had not changed, and every breath her father drew brought a hideous rattling sound. A death rattle, Maria had called it.

Maggie straightened her shoulders. It was enough that she could share a few more words of endearment. It was enough that she could tell her father of her love one more time. Peace settled over her, and Maggie decided against telling her father about the ranch's needs and Miguel's absence.

"I love you, Papa," Maggie said, smoothing his forehead.

"I love you too," Jason breathed weakly.

"I'm glad you made me come here. I'm thankful to God that you sent Garrett for me. I know that it was right for me to put the past behind and to accept your forgiveness and God's." Jason said nothing, but the slight upturning of his mouth told Maggie that he was pleased.

Maggie continued to talk even as Jason dozed and the shadows of afternoon fell across the room. The room chilled. Maggie placed a few pieces of kindling in the fireplace and watched with satisfaction as the wood ignited. The room grew comfortable again, and Maggie was just settling down beside Jason's bed when Carmalita came in to light the lamps. The worried look on her face reflected the torture she felt at Miguel's absence.

"Don't worry, Carmalita. They'll all be back soon." Maggie tried to offer the words as an encouragement, but Carmalita rushed out of the room sobbing. Maggie started to go after her, but Jason's weak voice stopped her.

"Who'll be back, Maggie?"

"Oh Papa, don't worry about it. Everything is fine, really it is," Maggie said soothingly. She didn't want Jason to worry.

"Where's Garrett? I'd like to see him, Maggie." Jason said, seeming to forget his concern.

"I've sent for him, Papa. He'll be here soon."

"You do love him, don't you? I wouldn't force you to marry him. You know that, don't you?" His words required great effort.

"I know, Papa. I know," Maggie assured her father.

"You didn't answer me," Jason whispered and coughed. Maggie feared that the cough would return and sought to quiet her father.

"Hush now, Papa. Please relax or you'll spend all your energy." Maggie gently stroked her father's hand, hoping to quiet him.

"Maggie," Jason struggled to speak. "I . . . have to . . . know." He was gasping for breath and Maggie wondered if she should find Maria. She stood as if to go, but Jason refused to release her hand. "I have to know," he said more firmly.

"Know what, Papa?" Maggie asked, confused by her father's sudden strength.

"I have to know if you love him. Do you love Garrett Lucas, as a woman should love a man who'll be her husband?" Jason's eyes were suddenly clear, and Maggie knew that he was studying her intently. Perhaps he couldn't die in peace without knowing that she'd be happy.

Maggie fell to her knees beside the bed. "Yes, Papa. I love Garrett very much. I think I've loved him since I first laid eyes on him in our parlor back in Potwin. If not then, I'm sure I fell in love with him when he caught me in his arms as I was trying to escape down the trellis." It was the first time Maggie had admitted to herself when her love for Garrett had taken root.

Carmalita reentered the room, but Maggie continued to talk unashamedly of her love for Garrett. "Papa, you were so wise in choosing such a man for me. I'm sorry that I was such a willful and spoiled child. Garrett called me that, you know? Willful and spoiled," Maggie remembered with a laugh. "I was, too." A sudden thought caused Maggie to worry, and her concern was reflected on her face.

"What is it, Maggie? There's something more you aren't telling me." Jason's look of alarm caused Maggie to share her fears aloud.

"It's only that I told Garrett to stay away. I told him I wouldn't wait for him. I wasn't very nice, Papa."

"Is that all?" Her father sounded relieved. The sudden smile on his face confused Maggie all the more.

"Is that all? Isn't that enough? I love him," Maggie said, lowering her eyes. "What if he doesn't love me anymore?"

Maggie felt firm hands on her shoulders, and Garrett's deep voice stilled all her fears. "There's no chance of that, Maggie Intissar. I will always love you."

"Garrett!" Maggie jumped to her feet and lost herself in his laughing blue eyes. Regardless of what others would think, Maggie threw her arms around Garrett's neck.

Garrett exchanged a smile over Maggie's back with Jason. Both men silently acknowledged the transfer of Maggie's care from Jason to Garrett.

Garrett held Maggie tightly and could hardly contain his happiness. His Maggie loved him.

Maggie pulled herself away, becoming aware for the first time of the man standing behind Garrett. She lowered her eyes and blushed at the thought of this man overhearing her words of endearment.

Garrett's soft chuckle told Maggie he understood her sudden silence. "This is David Monroe, our local preacher."

Maggie raised her eyes and took the hand that David offered her.

"I'm pleased to meet you, Miss Intissar."

"Please call me Maggie. I'm pleased to meet you, too. My father has nothing but the highest praise for you," Maggie said and turned to her father. "Look who's here, Papa. It's Garrett and Pastor Monroe."

Jason nodded ever so slightly.

"I'll agree to call you Maggie, but you must drop the formalities and call me David," the blond man said, smiling broadly at her. Maggie liked him immediately and soon forgot her discomfort.

"Agreed," she declared.

"Maggie, I'd like to speak to you," Garrett said, taking her arm. "In private." Maggie looked first to David and then to her father.

"Papa, I need to speak with Garrett. Will you be all right?" she questioned, fearing that if she left her father for even a moment, something might go wrong.

"I'll be fine. I want to talk to David anyway," Jason assured her. Maggie nodded, wondering if David would offer her father comforting images of eternity in heaven. As she walked into the hallway with Garrett, she strained to hear their words.

"Did you hear me, Maggie?" Garrett questioned in a whispered hush.

"What?" Maggie asked, turning to see a concerned Garrett.

"There's no easy way to tell you this, but Miguel is dead."

Chapter Eighteen

"How? Where?" Maggie asked, her mind flooding with questions.

"Banditos," Garrett replied. Maggie shivered uncontrollably. She felt cold and dizzy. Concerned, Garrett put an arm gently around her and said, "Come with me to the library and we'll talk."

Maggie tried to make her feet work, but her brain refused to function. She sat where Garrett directed her to sit, not knowing what to say.

Garrett sat across from Maggie and told the story. "Miguel never made it to the mission. When Mack showed up and told me about the butchered steers, I figured there wouldn't be good news about Miguel. We looked for signs of him on the trail, but there was nothing. Then we decided to take a look at the water hole where you found the carcasses. We found Miguel at the bottom of the pond."

"Dear Lord." Maggie breathed the words, and Garrett knew they were a prayer all their own.

"We buried him. We couldn't bring him back here in the shape he was in."

Maggie nodded dumbly. She suddenly realized that she had been at the site of Miguel's murder. While she had sat on Thunder, Miguel had lain dead at the bottom of the water hole. The room began to spin.

"I'm so sorry, Maggie," Garrett offered softly. "I know this is difficult. There was no easy way to tell you." Again Maggie nodded and said nothing. Garrett continued talking, but Maggie's mind went to Carmalita.

"Oh, Garrett," she interrupted. "What about Carmalita? Does she know?"

"I told Maria. She said she'd break the news to her," Garrett replied, rubbing the back of his neck.

Garrett was dusty and sweat soaked, but Maggie had never known a more welcome sight. God had sent him back safely to her. She offered a silent prayer of thanksgiving for Garrett's safety, but she couldn't forget Carmalita's sorrow.

Slowly she got to her feet. "I'll have Maria prepare you a bath. I must go to Carmalita." With that Maggie turned and went in search of the two women.

Garrett stared after Maggie for several minutes. He was amazed at the change in her. Where once had been a childish young girl, now stood a woman. A woman who compassionately put her pain aside to tend to the hurts of others. Garrett smiled. His Maggie had grown up.

Maria went to draw a bath for Garrett, but she could offer Maggie little help in locating Carmalita. Maggie looked throughout the ranch house but found no sign of the missing girl. She searched the quiet courtyard without success.

Maggie finally made her way to Carmalita's room. When there was no response to her knock, she quietly opened the bedroom door. A single lantern burned on the night stand, but Carmalita was gone.

Maggie returned to her father's room and found him listening to David Monroe read from the Psalms. Knowing what comfort her father found from the Bible, she decided against disturbing them and went to seek out Garrett.

Garrett sat refreshed and clean behind Jason's large walnut desk. He was dividing his attention between a cup of black coffee and a ledger book when Maggie arrived.

"I can't find Carmalita!" Maggie's voice betrayed the worry she felt. Garrett looked up from the papers.

"Have you looked everywhere?"

Maggie nodded. "I checked the entire house. Oh, Garrett. I'm worried. Miguel was everything to Carmalita. Where could she be?"

Garrett pushed the papers aside and grabbed his coat. "I'll check the barn and the corrals. You stay put. I'll be back shortly."

Maggie paced the room until she was certain she'd worn a hole in the heavy Indian rug. She tried to sit, but her mind was consumed with worry and grief. Just then, Garrett came rushing into the room.

"She took a horse. I've a feeling she's gone to find where we buried Miguel," Garrett announced.

Maggie rushed to where Garrett stood. "But it's dark and growing colder by the minute."

"I've sent a couple hands after her. I felt it was important for me to stay. I hope that's okay with you."

"Oh yes, Garrett. Please don't leave me again." For once, Maggie didn't try to hide her tears. Garrett took her into his strong arms.

"Hush, now. I'm here and I'm not going anywhere—at least not without you," he added softly.

"Señor, Señorita." Maria burst into the room, panting from her hard running.

"What is it, Maria? Have you found Carmalita?" Maggie asked as she rushed to Maria's side.

"I found this," Maria said, holding up a piece of paper.

Garrett took the note from Maria. His eyes narrowed slightly as he read it.

"What is it, Garrett?" Maggie questioned anxiously.

"It says that Carmalita knows who killed Miguel. She's gone to avenge Miguel's death," Garrett spoke gravely. "I'll have to go, Maggie. Maria, go find Bill for me, and hurry."

"Si." Maria was still breathless, but she sped from the room.

"Garrett, you can't go! What if it's a plot? What if they want to kill you?" Maggie cried.

Garrett unlocked the gun cabinet. "I can't expect Carmalita to face banditos on her own. She's probably unarmed, and a lone woman approaching a rowdy bunch like that? Well, I'd rather not say what I'm thinking."

Garrett opened the cabinet and took out a rifle and some cartridges. Maggie crossed the room to his side.

"Please don't go. Send someone else." She was crying. Garrett placed the rifle and cartridges on the table and took Maggie in his arms.

"Shh, don't cry. It's going to be all right. We might even catch up to her before she gets very far." Garrett stroked Maggie's damp cheek, knowing that the tears she cried were from love for him.

Maggie lifted her face to Garrett's and looked deep into his eyes. She saw his resolve. "I love you, Garrett," she whispered.

"Maggie, you can't know how I've dreamed of hearing you say that. I've waited a lifetime for you. I love you, and I'm not going to do anything foolish to risk the happiness that I know we'll share." With those words, Garrett leaned down and kissed her. It was a long and loving kiss. A kiss that left Maggie flushed and breathless.

"Garrett," Maggie's voice still held the urgency that she felt. "Let's pray together before you go."

Garrett smiled. "I can't think of anything more necessary," he answered. Taking down a well-worn Bible from the fireplace mantel, Garrett turned to Psalm 91. " 'He that dwelleth in the secret place of the most High,' " Garrett read, " 'shall abide under the shadow of the Almighty. I will say of the Lord, He is my refuge and my fortress: my God; in Him will I trust. Surely He shall deliver thee from the snare of the fowler, and from the noisome pestilence. He shall cover thee with His feathers, and under His wings shalt though trust: His truth shall be thy shield and buckler.' "

Garrett replaced the Bible and knelt with Maggie. "Father, we seek Your guidance. You know the situation and our need better than we do. We ask that You cover us in Your protection. Protect Carmalita too, Father. She's out there somewhere. We don't know where—but You do. Place a shield of protection around her. In Jesus' name—"

"Wait," Maggie interrupted. "Father, please watch over Garrett. I know I've been a stubborn child in the past, but Garrett has sought Your will for a long, long time. I know he places his trust in You. Sometimes it's hard for me to trust, but I know You love him even more than I do. Please bring him safely back to me. In Jesus' name, Amen."

"Amen," Garrett added and squeezed Maggie's hand. "And to think," he smiled. "I get to share this with you for a lifetime."

Maggie smiled too. "I feel better. Now I can let you go without fearing the worst." Getting to her feet with Garrett's help, Maggie laughed nervously.

"What?" Garrett asked.

"I wish I had a piano."

"A piano?" Garrett responded. "What does that have to do with anything?"

"Back in Topeka, whenever things got bad or I felt lonely, I would pound out my frustrations on the piano. It helped to pass the time, and it soothed my nerves." Maggie smiled and looked around the room. "Papa bought me a wardrobe full of clothes, but there isn't a single piano on the ranch." She feigned utter misery.

Garrett laughed and whirled Maggie in a circle. "You shall have the best and finest piano money can buy for a wedding gift from me," he said as he finally let Maggie's feet touch the ground. "Though I haven't the slightest idea how we'll get it here." At this they both laughed.

Bill came rushing into the room, knowing the gravity of the situation from Maria's brief explanation. He was somewhat confused to find Garrett and Maggie laughing. He cleared his throat to gain their attention.

Garrett was the first to sober. "Bill, we've got to go after Carmalita." Maggie grew solemn.

Bill nodded his head. "Maria told me. I've got ten men who'll ride with us."

"Good. Then let's be at it," Garrett replied.

"There's somethin' else you ought to know, Boss."

"What?" Garrett questioned.

"The boys finished a head count on the stock. We're short nearly a hundred steers."

"A hundred? Are you sure?"

Maggie didn't like the tone of Garrett's voice. Something in Bill's statement had signaled more danger, of this she was certain.

"They're sure all right. Herd's been down from the hills for over a week. Them that we didn't sell, we turned loose on the ridge. Since I saw signs of snow, I had the boys bring 'em on down. After we got 'em all corralled, we counted about ninety-eight missing."

"What does this mean, Garrett?" Maggie asked.

"Most likely rustlers," he replied and went to the desk to retrieve the rifle and ammunition.

"Rustlers and banditos? And poor Carmalita out there? Please be careful, Garrett." Maggie's voice quivered as she placed her hand on his arm.

"I will. Keep praying." Then he kissed her and was gone.

Chapter Nineteen

Maggie went silently to her father's room. David was reading the Bible in a gentle, even tone. Silently, Maggie took up her knitting and sat in a chair across the room. The words David recited offered her comfort as no others could.

David sensed something was wrong, but he knew better than to disturb Jason's rest by asking questions.

After an hour, Maggie could no longer sit still. "Excuse me, David. I think we should let Papa sleep now." David nodded, sensing the urgency in Maggie's voice.

"Jason," David said. "I'll be in the kitchen trying to talk Maria out of her spectacular custard. If you need me, just give a holler."

"Thank you, David. You've been a comfort, but Maggie's right. Sleep will do me good." Jason's words were hoarse whispers.

"Papa, do you need more medication?" Maggie knew it had been several hours since his last dose of morphine.

"No, no. I feel surprisingly better. You run along and fix David up with something to eat. I'm fine, child. Really." Jason raised his hand weakly to flag them on their way. Maggie took hold of it.

"I love you, Papa. I'll be close by. You just rest."

Maggie led David to the kitchen, but Maria sent them off to the dining room, promising to serve them her best custard.

"Things aren't as they should be," Maggie began as David helped her with her chair.

"I thought as much, but I didn't want to worry your father. He's perceptive for a sick man."

"A dying man," Maggie murmured.

"Yes, that's true. Hard to believe though," David declared. "I've never met a man who lived life to the degree your father has." David paused as he studied Maggie. It was easy to see why Garrett was drawn to her. "Has your father told you about the mission?"

"A bit here and there. Until a short time ago, we weren't on speaking terms.

And I wasn't on listening terms, either. I missed a great deal of time with him because of my stubbornness."

"You can't live your life under a rock of regrets. We all have things we wished we'd done differently. Some things we wish we hadn't done at all, but what's done is done. We seek God's forgiveness, change our ways, and make amends. You're doing a fine job, Maggie. It's clear you've brought him happiness."

Maria entered the room and placed two warm bowls of custard on the table. Moments later, she returned with David's favorite caramel sauce.

"You spoil me, Maria. But I love it." David laughed and ran a hand through his straight blond hair.

"Thank you, Maria. It looks wonderful," Maggie added.

"Don't tell me you've never had Maria's caramel custard?" David asked, a look of disbelief on his face.

"I might have and not remembered. Not much of the past few months registered. I was so angry. I could have eaten about anything and never known."

"Mostly, Señorita didn't eat at all," Maria stated matter-of-factly.

"That's true," Maggie laughed. "Twice, Carmalita had to alter my clothes. Poor Carmalita," Maggie's voice sobered.

"What is it?" David questioned.

"Carmalita took off after the people who killed Miguel. She left a note saying she knew who was responsible. Garrett rounded up some men and took off after her."

"It's awfully cold and dark out there," David began. "But Garrett knows every inch of this land. If anyone can find her, he can. But I'm sure glad I didn't ask about this while we were with your father."

"Yes," Maggie said, tasting the custard. "Maria, this is wonderful!"

"Gracias, I'm glad you like it. I'll be in the kitchen if you need me."

Maggie nodded and continued explaining to David. "On top of everything else, some cattle are missing. It seems that the rustlers and banditos are plotting to destroy us."

Just then, Maria came rushing into the room. "Señorita, Señorita! You must come quickly."

"What is it, Maria?" Maggie said as she followed Maria to the kitchen door. David was close behind the women.

Maria opened the door to admit a young Mexican boy. He looked twelve or thirteen, and Maria introduced him as her grandson. "He lives in the mountains," Maria added, admitting to his life with the banditos.

Maggie looked back and forth from Maria to the young boy. "Well? What is it?" Maggie asked, no longer able to contain her concern.

The boy rattled off in Spanish, and while David nodded his understanding,

Maggie didn't know what was being said. When the boy finished delivering his message, David interpreted it for Maggie.

"He says his people didn't butcher your cattle. He's been sent here by his parents because they knew his grandmother would protect him," David explained. Then he turned and questioned the boy.

The boy answered hesitantly, but his response satisfied David. "He says the banditos would never harm Señor Jason's hacienda. He's been very good to them, and that is why they've sent word to you. They don't want to be blamed for this."

"How did they find out about it?" Maggie questioned.

"They found the mess at the water hole. They knew someone had made it look like banditos were to blame." David answered. "They wanted to vindicate themselves."

Suddenly Maggie grew cold. If Carmalita knew the person who had killed Miguel and it wasn't done by banditos, then the murderer had to be someone on the ranch. As if reading Maggie's mind, David instructed Maria to have her grandson stay the night and to lock all the doors and windows.

"David, the killer could be riding with Garrett right now," Maggie sobbed. "I can't lose him." She started for the door, but David held her fast.

"I can't let you go, Maggie. You know that, and you know why. Now come with me, and we'll sit with your father," David said firmly.

"But what of your wife?" Maggie asked. "Will she be safe at the mission?"

David's jaw tightened. "Let's go sit with Jason."

The hours passed, and Maggie struggled to appear at ease in front of her father. David had started reading the Bible once more, and Maggie wondered if he were doing so in part to answer his fear for Jenny.

Jason had fallen into a deep sleep, so David put aside the Bible and stretched his long legs by walking to the bedroom window.

"If you like, I could show you to the guest room," Maggie offered. Her own body was suffering from the tension. She had considered retiring to her room, but she hated to leave David alone.

"No. I think we should stay together," David said, turning to meet Maggie's worried expression.

"Don't worry, Maggie. I've always been overly cautious. It's one of my faults."

Maggie smiled. She knew David was trying to put her at ease. The wind picked up, and a light mist started to fall. Maggie listened to the rain grow heavy and then lighten again. She remembered times in Topeka when she'd sat in her room listening to the rain. She'd loved to snuggle down under the covers of her bed as the rain beat against the window panes. It had always made her feel safe. What she wouldn't give to feel safe now!

Uneasy, Maggie joined the others in fitful sleep. As the first light of dawn crept over the eastern mountains, Maggie and David were jerked awake by thundering horse hooves. Maggie glanced at Jason, but he still slept soundly.

David went first to the window and then to the bedroom door. "Stay here," he ordered, and Maggie nodded. For once, she had no thought of disobeying orders.

She went to the window, anxious to see if she could catch sight of the riders. The scene revealed nothing. Maggie twisted her hands together. She paced back and forth at the end of her father's bed.

"Dear God, Garrett has to be all right. You have to keep him safe for me." Suddenly, her prayers sounded selfish. Maggie reconsidered her words. "Father, I know You have a plan for each of us. I can't imagine a plan for me without Garrett by my side, but I trust You. I believe You'll care for Garrett and for me in the best way. I give it over to Your will, Lord." Before Maggie could finish her prayer, voices in the hallway interrupted.

Maggie rushed to the door just as it opened. Garrett stood before her. Seeing that Jason was asleep, Garrett pulled Maggie into the hall and closed the door.

Maggie sobbed as she fell against Garrett's chest. "You're all right!" she whispered between her tears.

"Come with me, Maggie," Garrett said, refusing to let her go. They joined David in the living room. Garrett led Maggie to the high-backed sofa and had her sit beside him.

"Is it—did they?" Maggie couldn't bring herself to ask the questions on her mind. She was shaking from head to toe.

"It's over. At least for now," Garrett said softly, putting his arm around her in support.

"Carmalita?" Maggie dared to ask.

"She'll be staying at the mission while she recovers from all this," Garrett said. Noticing David's anxious expression, he added, "Everything is fine there." David sighed in relief.

"We can talk about this later if you like," Garrett offered.

Maggie nodded, relieved that she wouldn't have to hear the details of what had taken place.

"I think I'll bid Jason goodbye and go home," David announced. "Jenny's bound to be beside herself."

Garrett nodded and added, "I had a couple men stay on until you get there."

A relieved look passed over David's face. "Thanks, friend."

"I think I owe you thanks as well," Garrett replied. They shared a nod, each acknowledging the other's actions.

For a long time after David had left the living room, Maggie did nothing but allow Garrett to hold her. Silently she thanked God over and over for bringing

Garrett home safely. She praised Him for keeping Jenny and Carmalita safe, too.

Just then, David returned. "Maggie," he said. "Your father is asking for you." Maggie dried her tears with her apron and followed David to her father's room.

"I'm here, Papa. What can I do for you?" Maggie tried to smile as she knelt beside her father's bed.

Jason Intissar turned his weary blue eyes to the daughter he'd spent a lifetime loving. Behind her stood Garrett, arms folded across his chest, feet planted slightly apart.

"Papa?" Maggie's small voice drew Jason's attention. "Is everything all right? Are you in pain?"

"No, child. I called you here for something else." Jason paused to take a deep breath. "Maggie, I know I'm not going to live much longer. I thank God for these few moments with you, but I'm not a selfish man in respect to life. I've had a good one, and I'm ready to meet my God and your ma."

Jason stopped to draw another ragged breath. His body was seized by a fit of coughing, but to Maggie's surprise the spell lasted only a few moments.

"Papa, you need to rest. We can come back later," Maggie said, getting to her feet.

Jason held out his thin hand. "Please wait."

"What is it, Papa?"

"I have only one request, Maggie. Just one thing before I die," Jason said in uneven words. "I've already told David about it."

Maggie turned to meet David Monroe's tender eyes. She turned back to her father.

"I know a girl wants things a certain way on her wedding day and you're deserving of that, but I want to see you married, Maggie. I don't have the time for a fancy wedding, and I'm asking a favor of you." Jason's words died off into a barely audible whisper. "I want you to marry Garrett here, today."

Maggie's heart lurched. She worried about hurting Carmalita by marrying so soon after Miguel's death. She also had no idea what Garrett had just been through. Perhaps he wouldn't want to get married right away. But her father's request was appropriate, and Maggie knew that he didn't have much time.

Almost fearing the intensity of Garrett's eyes, Maggie turned to find him smiling. She blushed and lowered her eyes. Marriage to Garrett was what she'd dreamed of. It was hard to imagine that in a few moments that dream would become reality.

Maggie turned back to her father. "I'd be happy to marry Garrett, right this minute, Papa. Dresses, parties, and rooms full of people aren't as important as sharing this moment with you. If it meets with Garrett's approval, David can marry us this very minute."

Jason's face lit up with a huge smile.

"Well, what do you say, Mr. Lucas?" Maggie turned boldly toward Garrett. "Will you marry me?"

Forgetting the terror of the night and his deep concern for Maggie's safety, Garrett relaxed and even managed to laugh. "Are you proposing, Miss Intissar?"

Maggie joined his laughter, "Yes, I believe I am."

"In that case, I accept. But don't go getting any ideas about bossing me around in the future. This here is just a favor to Jason," he drawled, and everyone broke into laughter.

Chapter Twenty

While Maria was summoned to get Bill and Mack and anyone else who wanted to witness the event, David prepared for the wedding service. Garrett conferred with Jason in hushed whispers, and Maggie was suddenly alone.

She stood at the window, watching the rain. Rain was a bad omen on a wedding day. Maggie tried to remember the old saying. Something about the number of raindrops that fell would be the number of tears the bride would cry.

But, Maggie reminded herself, she didn't believe in bad luck. She believed in God's guidance. The rain was just rain.

"Scared?" Garrett's question was barely audible as he came up behind Maggie.

"A little—I guess," Maggie said. She looked up, slowly meeting Garrett's eyes—eyes so blue and powerful that she felt herself grow weak.

"You haven't changed your mind, have you?" Garrett asked seriously.

Maggie's face shot up and her eyes flashed. "Never!"

"Then there's nothing to fear. We look to God for our future. I love you, Magdelena Intissar. I love you with all that I am." A tear slid down Maggie's cheek.

"I love you, Garrett Lucas. I can only pray that I will be the wife you need." Maggie murmured. Garrett took her in his arms and held her tightly.

"Whoa, now. We haven't gotten to that part yet," David Monroe called from beside the fireplace. Everyone laughed and the tension broke.

Maggie joined hands with Garrett and stood at the foot of her father's bed. She glanced around the room at the ranch workers who'd become her friends. She only wished that her mother and grandmother could have lived to see her wedding.

Maggie looked down at her attire and smiled, thinking how appalled her friend Lillie would have been at the blue calico dress. But Maggie knew Lillie would have liked Garrett.

Once or twice, Maggie gazed over her shoulder to find her father looking on, contentment beaming from his face. This moment was for him.

A few minutes later, David told Garrett that he could kiss his bride. Garrett pulled Maggie close. His arms wrapped around her like a warm blanket. Their eyes met, and the promise of new life flashed before them. Then Garrett kissed Maggie deeply while the wedding guests cheered.

Jason held his hands up to Maggie and Garrett. "I've waited a long time for this day. I'm proud to call you son," Jason said, his eyes planted firmly on Garrett. "I'm trusting you to care for my daughter and to keep your family in line with the plans the good Lord has for you. This ranch and all that I have is yours. Yours to share with Maggie." Garrett nodded and squeezed his father-in-law's hand.

"And my Maggie," Jason sighed. "How beautiful you are today. I want you to be happy. I want you to enjoy what I've made here, but most of all I want you to keep your heart close to God. I'm so glad that I was here when you accepted Jesus as your Savior. I can go on now—knowing you're in God's care and Garrett's."

"Surprise!" Maria exclaimed as she reentered the room. Maggie turned to see that Maria had brought refreshments.

"How wonderful!" Maggie cried, rushing to Maria. "Our own reception."

Garrett joined his wife with a smile. "She's more interested in food than her new husband." Maggie blushed, suddenly aware that she'd rushed from Garrett and Jason to a tray of pastries.

Garrett laughed all the more at the sight of Maggie's embarrassment. "Well, I just thought it was kind of Maria," Maggie added, giving up at the roar of laughter from everyone.

The ranch hands didn't need second invitations to enjoy the treats. Maria poured steaming cups of Mexican coffee while the hands helped themselves to the tray of goodies.

David joined in the revelry. He had downed his third pastry by the time Maria offered him a cup of coffee. "These are some good eats, Maria. I wish Jenny had the recipe."

"I could write it down for her," Maria offered. David nodded in appreciation. "You do that, Maria. I'd be much obliged."

Maggie had glanced over at her father once or twice. He was beaming. She was about to ask him if he wanted something to eat when Garrett asked her something.

"I'm sorry. I wasn't listening," Maggie said apologetically.

"I was wondering if you thought this might be too much for your pa. Maybe we should herd everybody out of here," Garrett whispered.

Maggie glanced around Garrett to where her father rested. Suddenly, her heart stopped. Color drained from her face, and she pushed past Garrett and ran to her father's bedside.

Jason still bore the smile that Maggie had seen earlier, but his lifeless eyes betrayed the secret that he'd passed from one world to the next. Maggie placed his hand against her cheek, patting it gently.

"Papa? Papa, wake up," she cried, but in her heart she knew her father was dead.

Garrett and David were the only ones who noticed what was taking place. Garrett stood behind Maggie. He gently placed his hands on her shoulders. David moved to the opposite side of the bed and felt for a pulse. There was none.

"He's gone," David murmured softly.

It was only when David closed Jason's eyes that Maggie felt the impact of his words. Maria noticed what David was doing and quickly crossed herself and whispered a prayer. This caught the attention of the three ranch hands.

"He's past the pain now," Bill offered softly. "Mighty sorry to lose him, though. Mighty sorry." Maggie saw tears in Bill's eyes and heard his voice quiver. Bill had cared deeply for her father. Mack and Rob were silent, though Maggie noticed Mack turn to wipe his eyes with his sleeve.

Maggie moved away from Garrett and the bed, watching David tend to her father's body. Everything was moving in slow motion. Bill said something to Garrett, but Maggie couldn't make out the words. She couldn't hear anything over the pounding of her heart. The room began to swim, and desperately, Maggie reached out to steady herself. She saw Garrett look at her, and then she collapsed at the foot of her father's bed.

Garrett rushed to lift Maggie in his arms. "Maria, get me a cold cloth."

"Si, Señor," Maria said as she hastened from the bedroom.

"David, I've got to get her out of here," Garrett called over his shoulder.

"Don't worry about it. Take care of your wife," David answered. *My wife*, Garrett thought. After months of separation, they were finally married.

Garrett was moving toward the west wing of the house when he came across Maria.

"Come with me, Maria. We'll put her in my room."

Maria nodded and brought the basin of water and washcloth that she'd gone for. She managed to balance the basin while opening the door for Garrett. He moved across the study that adjoined his bedroom, grateful that he'd left the bedroom door open. Maria followed, watching the tender way Garrett placed Maggie on the bed.

"Give me the cloth," Garrett requested. He placed the cloth across Maggie's forehead and began to pat her hand.

"Maggie, mi quierda, wake up."

Maria moved forward to loosen the buttons at the neck of Maggie's gown. Maggie stirred slightly, and Garrett gently wiped her face with the damp cloth, hoping the coolness would bring her back to consciousness.

"Papa," Maggie moaned softly. With a jerk, her eyes flew open. "No-o-o!" she cried. She struggled to sit up, but Garrett's firm hands held her back.

"Just rest a minute," insisted Garrett.

"Oh, Garrett," Maggie sobbed into her hands. Her body shook uncontrollably, and Garrett held her long after her tears had soaked the front of his shirt. "He can't be dead, Garrett! He can't be."

Maggie pulled back and turned her red, swollen eyes toward Maria. "Maria, please tell me he isn't dead."

But Maria found it hard to speak. She lowered her eyes, her own tears falling freely, and quickly left the room.

Maggie looked back to Garrett whose eyes were also wet with tears. "We'll all miss him," Garrett whispered.

It was then that Maggie became aware of Garrett's pain. She steadied herself, studying the weary face of the man who was now her husband. The strain was as great on him as it was on her.

"Oh, Garrett, I'm so sorry. I know how you loved him," Maggie said, her heart filled with aching for the sadness she saw in Garrett's eyes. When tears began to roll down Garrett's cheeks, Maggie held him tightly. Together they shared their sorrow. It was not the wedding day either one would have planned, but their shared pain brought deeper intimacy to their marriage.

Two days later, Maggie joined Garrett beside the grave of her father. In torrential rain, Bill and Mack had taken turns digging the final resting place of their boss and friend. Maria had prepared Jason's body with David Monroe's help.

Garrett had finalized arrangements for the last of the winter supplies to be brought in. He'd also handed the rustlers who had murdered Miguel over to the law.

Maggie had been horrified to learn that the rustlers' leader was Cactus Jack, her father's own ranch hand. Knowing that Jason was growing sicker and that Garrett was nowhere around, Cactus Jack had figured they'd have a good chance of stealing lots of cattle.

The plan might have worked, but Carmalita had overheard pieces of a conversation between Cactus Jack and Miguel. Cactus Jack had wanted Miguel to join his operation, and when he'd refused, Cactus Jack had threatened his life.

With God's help, Garrett had been able to locate Carmalita before she'd found Cactus Jack and his men. Garrett had seen her safely to the mission and then turned his sights on collecting both his cattle and the rustlers responsible for their disappearance.

"It's time, Maggie," she heard Garrett saying. Maggie nodded somberly. She was grateful so many people were taking care of her. Everyone had pitched in. Maggie hadn't needed to lift a finger to help with the funeral or the ranch.

As she stood in the rain, watching little rivers run down the side of the dirt mound that would soon cover her father's casket, Maggie shivered. Garrett quickly placed his coat around Maggie's shoulders. Maggie turned her eyes briefly to meet those of her husband.

Suddenly she felt out of place. Garrett had his duties. Bill, Mack, and Maria all had their jobs. But Maggie's days of caring for her father were over, and she had nothing to do. Now that Carmalita was staying at the mission, Maggie didn't even have her to talk to.

Maggie glanced at the western ridge. She'd given up hope of Carmalita coming to the funeral. In this wet weather, the twelve mile ride to the ranch would be miserable for the heartiest ranch hand. Silently, Maggie chided herself for expecting Carmalita to put aside her grief over Miguel to attend the funeral.

Just as Maggie tried to concentrate on David's words, Carmalita came into view. Motionless, she looked down from the crest of a ridge and then nudged her horse to the valley and across to the ranch. She sat proudly, almost regally, in the saddle. David's words fell silent as all eyes turned to watch the stately procession. When Carmalita approached the graveside, Maggie left Garrett's side and went to her.

Pain and sorrow clouded Carmalita's face. "This," Carmalita said as she revealed a small pin wreath, "is for Señor."

Maggie reached up and took the gift. Dark green branches were intricately woven with red braided calico. Maggie appreciated the honor being paid to her father.

"Gracias, Carmalita," Maggie whispered, knowing further conversation would be meaningless. Maggie walked to the grave and lovingly placed the wreath upon her father's casket. Then she glanced back toward Carmalita. Carmalita nodded and started her horse back toward the mission.

"I'll miss her," Maggie whispered.

"We all will," Garrett said as he put his arm around his wife.

Maggie tried to focus on the words David had chosen to comfort those gathered for her father's funeral. " 'I am the resurrection, and the life: he that believeth in me, though he were dead, yet shall he live: And whosoever liveth and believeth in me shall never die,' " David quoted with love and assurance.

Maggie knew the words were true. Her father's death wasn't disturbing her as much as the feeling of being displaced. When David finished speaking, Maggie excused herself and moved to the house. Maria followed closely behind.

"Would you like some coffee or tea, Señora?" she asked in her thick accent.

"Thank you, Maria. I think I would like some coffee. I didn't sleep well last night," Maggie replied gratefully.

"Where will you take it?" questioned Maria as she shook the rain from her coat.

"Bring it to my room," Maggie began and then thought better of returning to her old bedroom. "No, please bring it to my father's room. I'd like some time alone." Maria nodded and left for the kitchen.

Maggie shook the rain from her coat and hung it to dry. She went to a small chest of drawers in the pantry and pulled out a fresh apron. During her father's illness, she had needed an apron's large, roomy pockets to carry a variety of things, but as Maggie tied the strings into a bow, she questioned her action.

I don't know why I'm putting on an apron, Maggie thought. *There's no one to nurse and nothing to do. I'm not needed.* Maggie walked to her father's room and sat in the rocking chair.

Maria had thoughtfully started a crackling fire that was warming the cool, damp air. Sitting opposite her portrait, Maggie studied the youthful image of herself. She remembered with sadness the hours she'd spent sitting for the portrait so that her father would let her stay in Topeka.

Maria arrived with the coffee, but knowing Maggie wanted solitude, she did nothing more than pour a cup and leave.

Maggie sipped the dark liquid, enjoying the warmth that spread through her body. So many relationships had come to an end, but what of the gains? She had a new husband, but she wasn't sure what she was supposed to do with him.

Dear God, please help me to know my place and to find contentment in it. I feel so confused right now, Maggie prayed. *I want to belong, but with so many people I loved now gone, I don't know where to start. Please guide me, Lord. Teach me how to be a good wife.*

Garrett entered the room.

"Mind if I join you?" he drawled. Maggie could tell he was trying to be light-hearted.

"No, not really. At first I wanted to be alone, but not now," Maggie replied. Calm was beginning to spread through her soul, and Maggie knew her Heavenly Father was giving her peace.

"I'm glad," Garrett said, sounding old. "I need you." Maggie's eyes widened.

"You need me? Whatever for?" she questioned curiously.

"How can you ask?" Garrett inquired as he took a chair.

"Well, I have to confess I was feeling unnecessary. I don't know anything about the running of this ranch, and you have it all under control anyway. I'm not needed in the house—Maria manages nicely by herself. Winter is here, so there's little I can do outdoors. Even if I could go outside, what would I do?" Maggie asked.

She paused, studying the details of her father's now-familiar room. "When Papa was alive, when he needed me to care for him, I knew I had a place to belong. I had a purpose."

"You think you have no purpose now?" Garrett questioned, contemplating Maggie's words.

"Yes," she admitted. "I suppose that sounds foolish, but there it is. I'm eighteen years old, and I feel so stupid. I don't know the first thing about being a rancher's wife. For that matter, I don't know much about anything."

"Come here, Maggie," Garrett ordered and motioned her with his finger. "Right now. Come here."

Maggie tilted her head and studied her husband. Setting her coffee aside, she walked slowly to where Garrett sat. When she stood beside him, Maggie could see tears in his eyes.

Garrett reached up and pulled Maggie to his lap. "I want you to listen, and listen good. Do you understand?" he questioned in a stern voice.

Maggie nodded. She could feel the warmth of his arms around her. It felt good to be held.

"A long time ago, I asked God to send me a wife. A helpmate, just like Eve was intended for Adam. I knew I wouldn't enjoy going through life without a companion. I never cared enough for my own company, I guess," he said with a little grin. Maggie smiled slightly.

"Fact is, I always saw myself with a woman by my side and children of my own. Family is mighty important to me, Maggie, especially because I lost mine at such an early age." Again Maggie nodded, but said nothing.

"God answered my prayer by sending you, and I praise Him daily for such a blessing. But I know nothing about being a husband except what the Bible tells me. By watching my own pa and yours, I saw what a father's heart was like. I learned to have the mind of a businessman and rancher. But I didn't learn anything about the heart of a husband. I'm starting from scratch, just like you."

Maggie's heart swelled at the deep love Garrett felt for her. She did belong. She belonged to God as His eternal child, and God had also blessed her with a husband—a husband who prayed for her. Maggie thanked God that she belonged to Garrett.

"I understand," Maggie said with wonder. "It doesn't matter that I don't know the first thing about ranching or being a wife. What matters is that I belong—that we belong to God and to each other."

Garrett held Maggie tightly and gazed steadily into her eyes. "That's all that matters, Maggie," he said with certainty.

"I love you, Garrett Lucas," Maggie whispered softly.

"And I love you, Maggie Lucas."

Outside, the rain poured harder than ever. Thunder echoed in the distance. But inside, two hearts had found shelter in the shadow of the Most High, a place to belong.

About the Authors

Colleen L. Reece is one of the most popular authors of inspirational romance. With over ninety books in print, including fourteen *Heartsong Presents* titles, Colleen's army of fans continues to grow. She loves to travel and at the same time do research for her historical romances. Colleen resides in Washington state.

Norene Morris was born, as she says, "with a pencil in my hand." Morris makes her home in north-eastern Ohio and spends much of her time enjoying her grandchildren, as well as her great-grandchildren.

Maryn Langer is a popular writer of romance fiction. Her works include *Moon for A Candle, Wait for the Sun, Divide the Joy,* and *Eyes of the Heart.* Langer resides with her husband in Albion, Idaho.

Tracie J. Peterson is a popular inspirational writer and a regular columnist for a Christian newspaper in Topeka, Kansas. Tracie has also written eight successful *Heartsong Presents* titles under the name of Janelle Jamison. One of those books, *Iditarod Dream,* was voted 1994's "Best Inspirational" by *Affaire de Coeur* magazine in their annual reader's poll.